KATHLEEN GROS

ANNE

AN ADAPTATION OF
ANNE OF GREEN GABLES
(SORT OF)

Quill Tree Books
Imprints of HarperCollinsPublishers

HARPER
alley

FOR MONTY
(OBVIOUSLY)

Quill Tree Books is an imprint of HarperCollins Publishers.
HarperAlley is an imprint of HarperCollins Publishers.

Anne: An Adaptation of Anne of Green Gables (Sort Of)
Copyright © 2022 by Kathleen Gros
All rights reserved. Manufactured in Bosnia and Herzegovina.
No part of this book may be used or reproduced in any manner
whatsoever without written permission except in the case of brief
quotations embodied in critical articles and reviews. For information
address HarperCollins Children's Books, a division of HarperCollins
Publishers, 195 Broadway, New York, NY 10007.
www.harperalley.com

Library of Congress Control Number: 2022930815
ISBN 978-0-06-305766-1 — ISBN 978-0-06-305765-4 (pbk.)

The artist used Photoshop to create the digital illustrations for this book.
Typography by Kathleen Gros and Laura Mock
22 23 24 25 26   GPS   10 9 8 7 6 5 4 3 2 1
❖
First Edition

CHAPTER 1

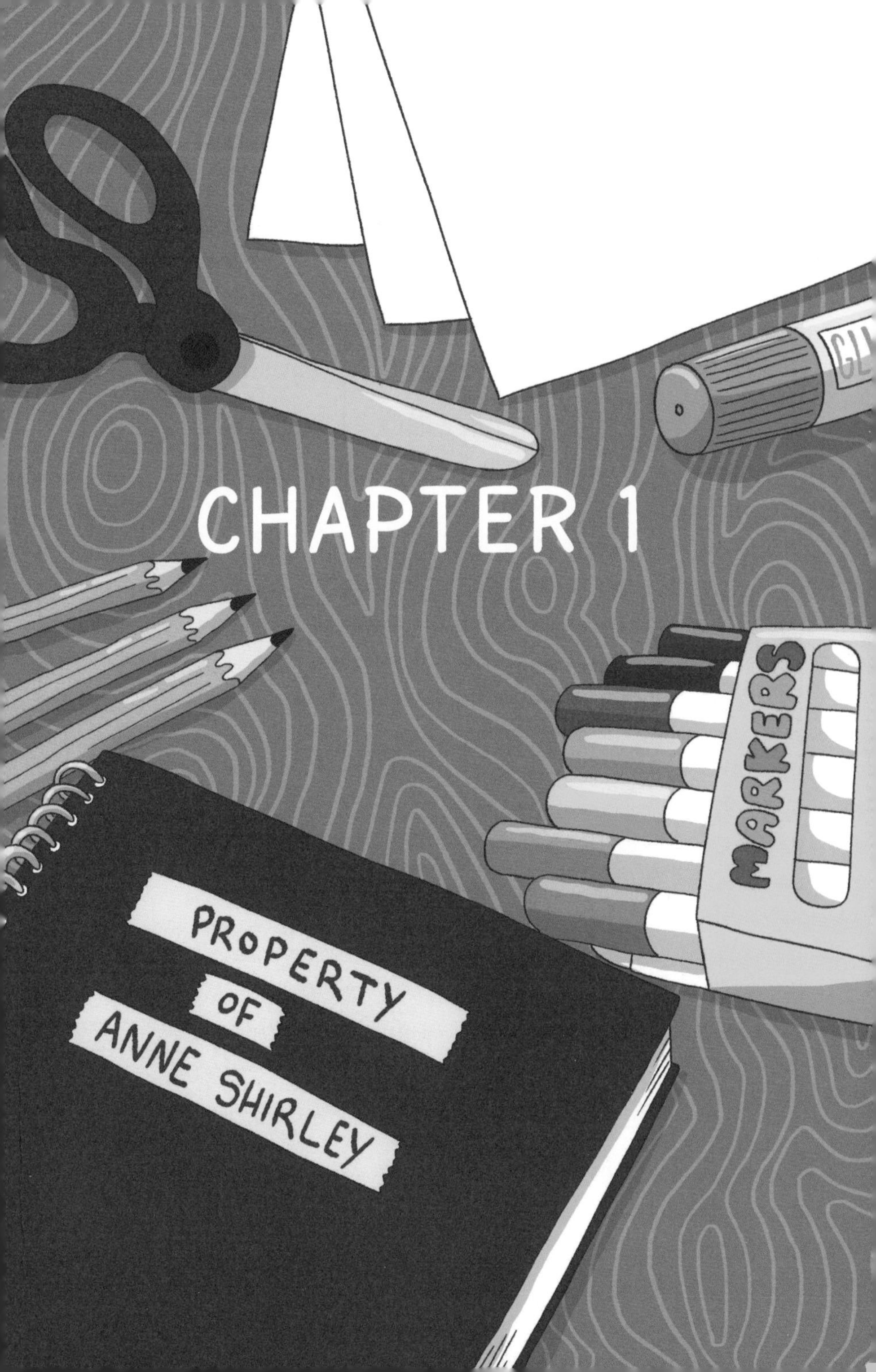
MARKERS
PROPERTY
OF
ANNE SHIRLEY

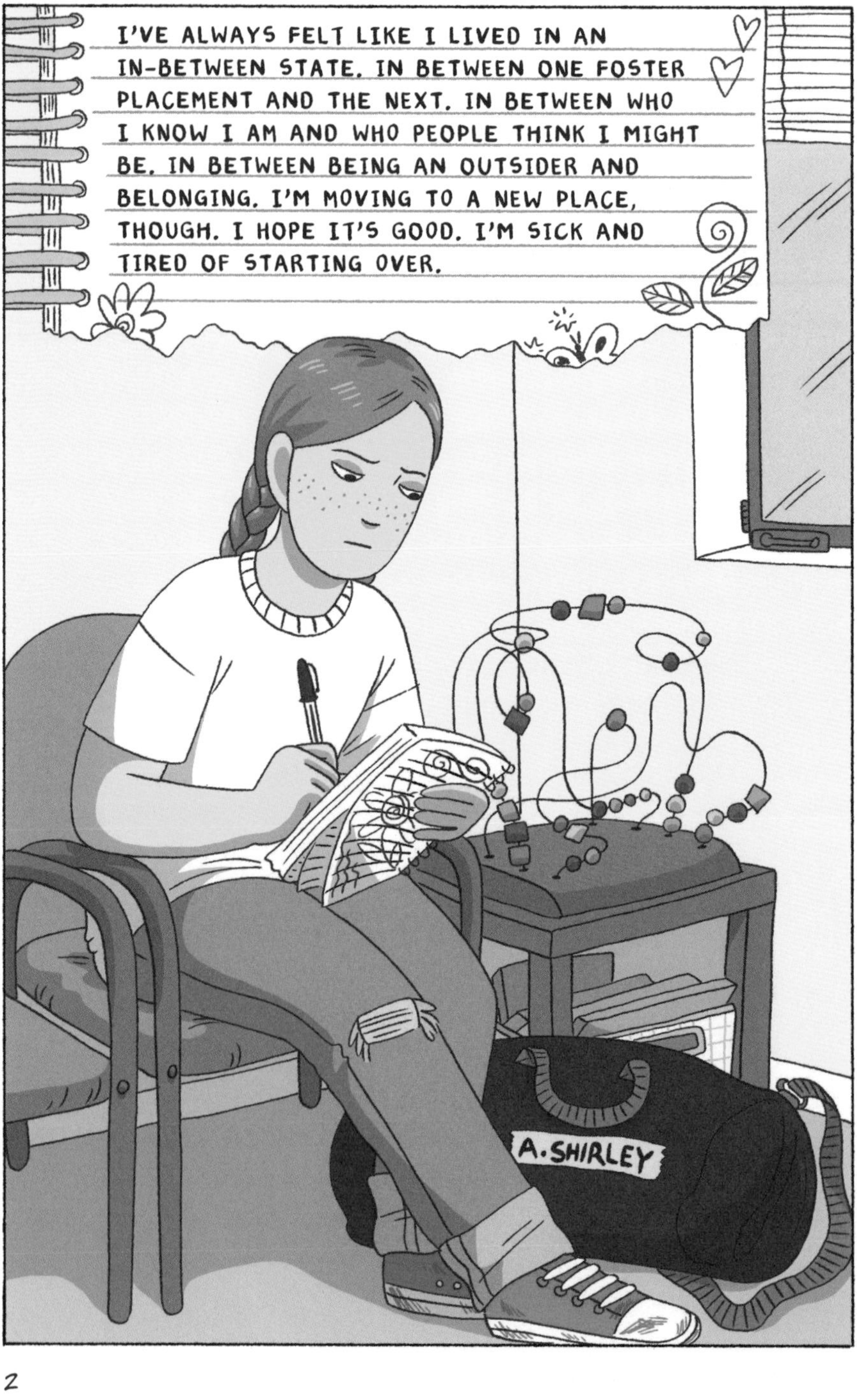
I'VE ALWAYS FELT LIKE I LIVED IN AN IN-BETWEEN STATE. IN BETWEEN ONE FOSTER PLACEMENT AND THE NEXT. IN BETWEEN WHO I KNOW I AM AND WHO PEOPLE THINK I MIGHT BE. IN BETWEEN BEING AN OUTSIDER AND BELONGING. I'M MOVING TO A NEW PLACE, THOUGH. I HOPE IT'S GOOD. I'M SICK AND TIRED OF STARTING OVER.
A. SHIRLEY

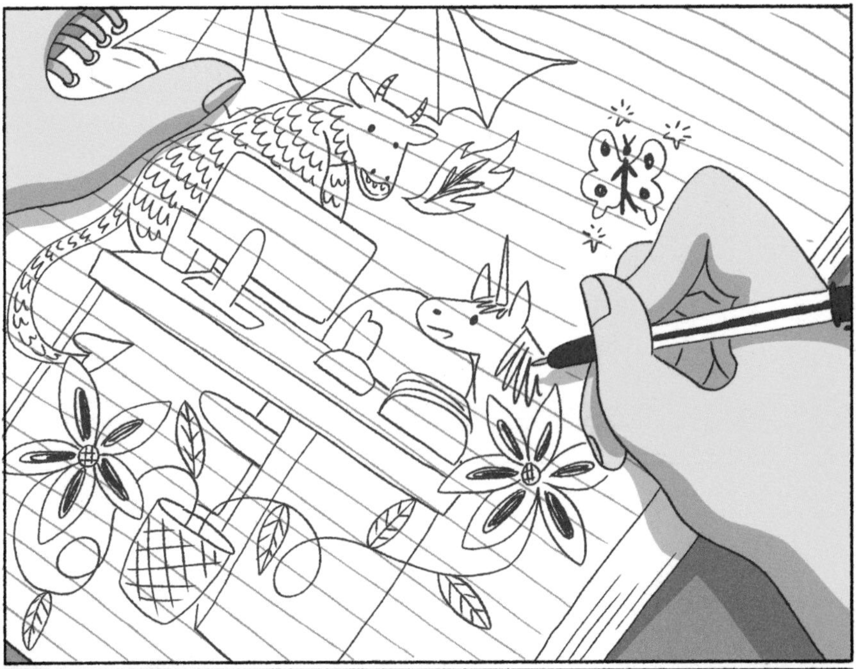

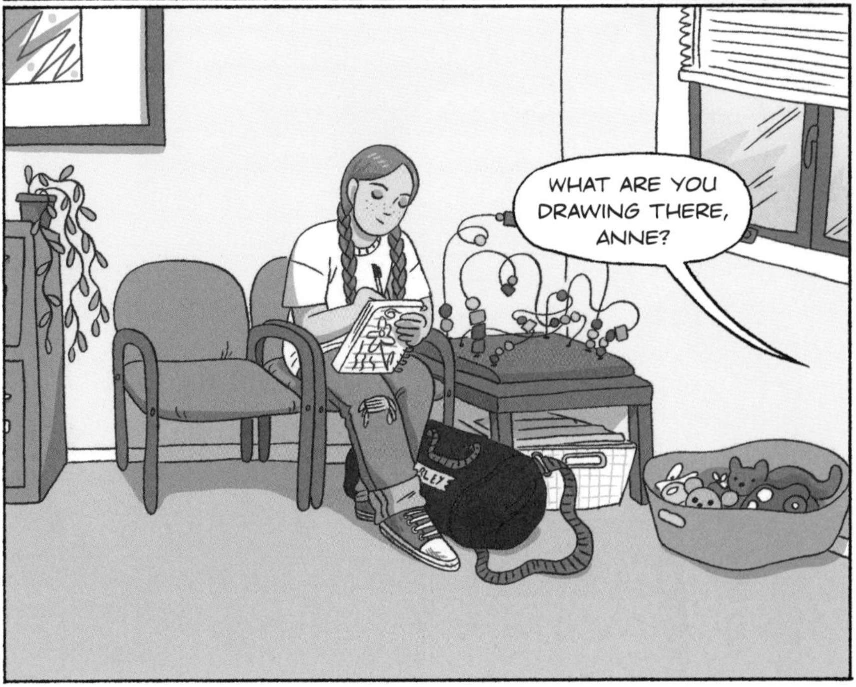
WHAT ARE YOU DRAWING THERE, ANNE?

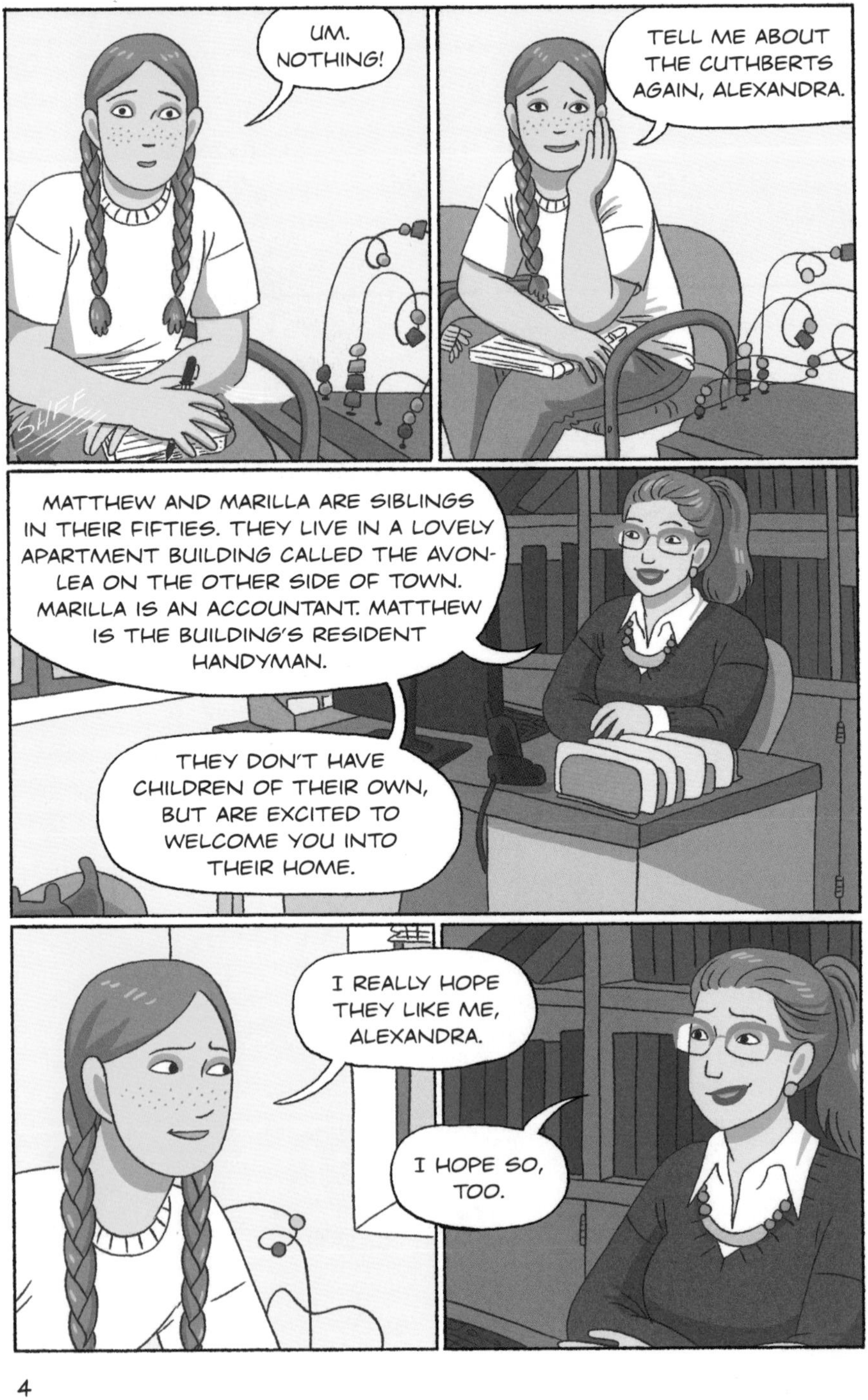
UM. NOTHING!
SHIFF
TELL ME ABOUT THE CUTHBERTS AGAIN, ALEXANDRA.
MATTHEW AND MARILLA ARE SIBLINGS IN THEIR FIFTIES. THEY LIVE IN A LOVELY APARTMENT BUILDING CALLED THE AVON-LEA ON THE OTHER SIDE OF TOWN. MARILLA IS AN ACCOUNTANT. MATTHEW IS THE BUILDING'S RESIDENT HANDYMAN.
THEY DON'T HAVE CHILDREN OF THEIR OWN, BUT ARE EXCITED TO WELCOME YOU INTO THEIR HOME.
I REALLY HOPE THEY LIKE ME, ALEXANDRA.
I HOPE SO, TOO.

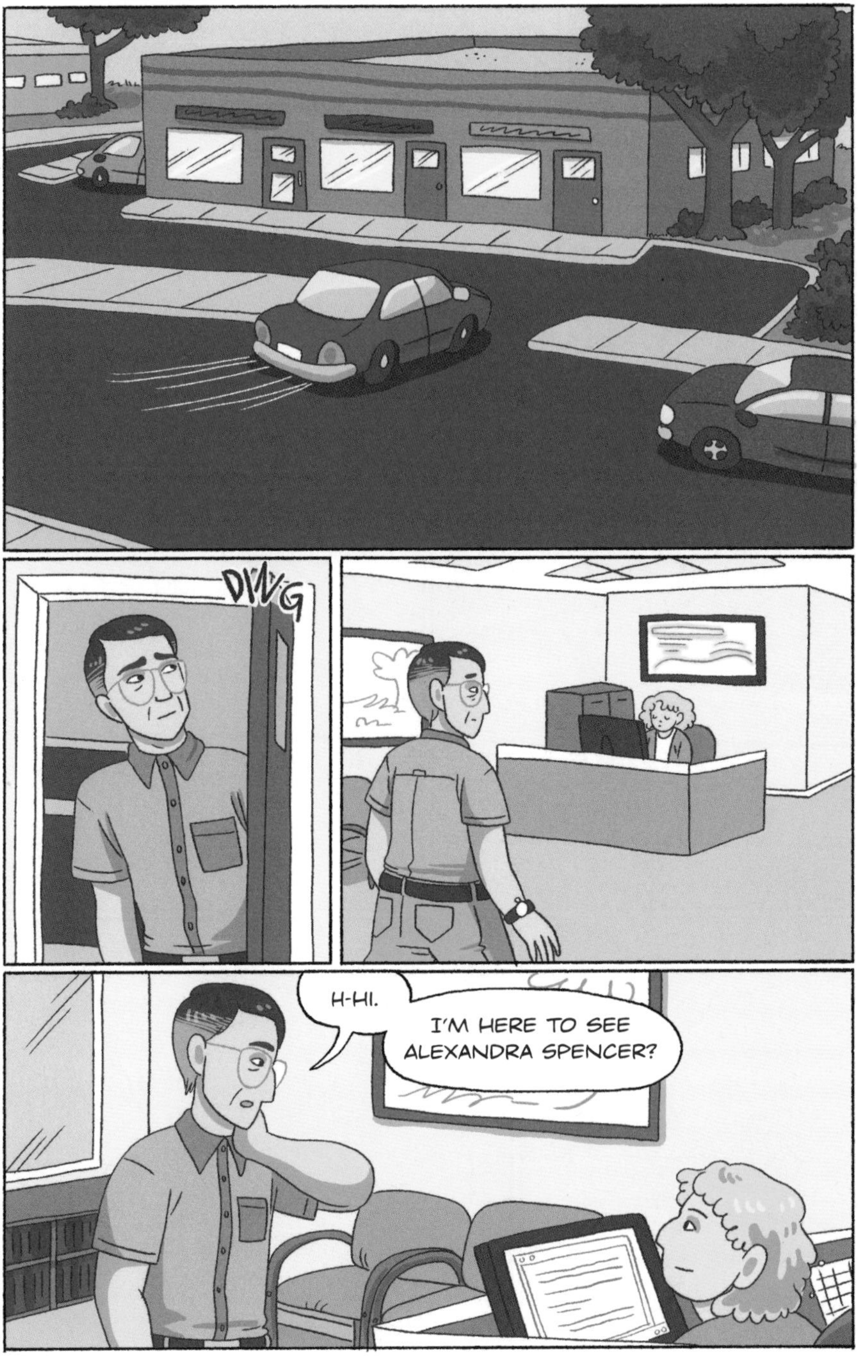
DING
H-HI.
I'M HERE TO SEE ALEXANDRA SPENCER?

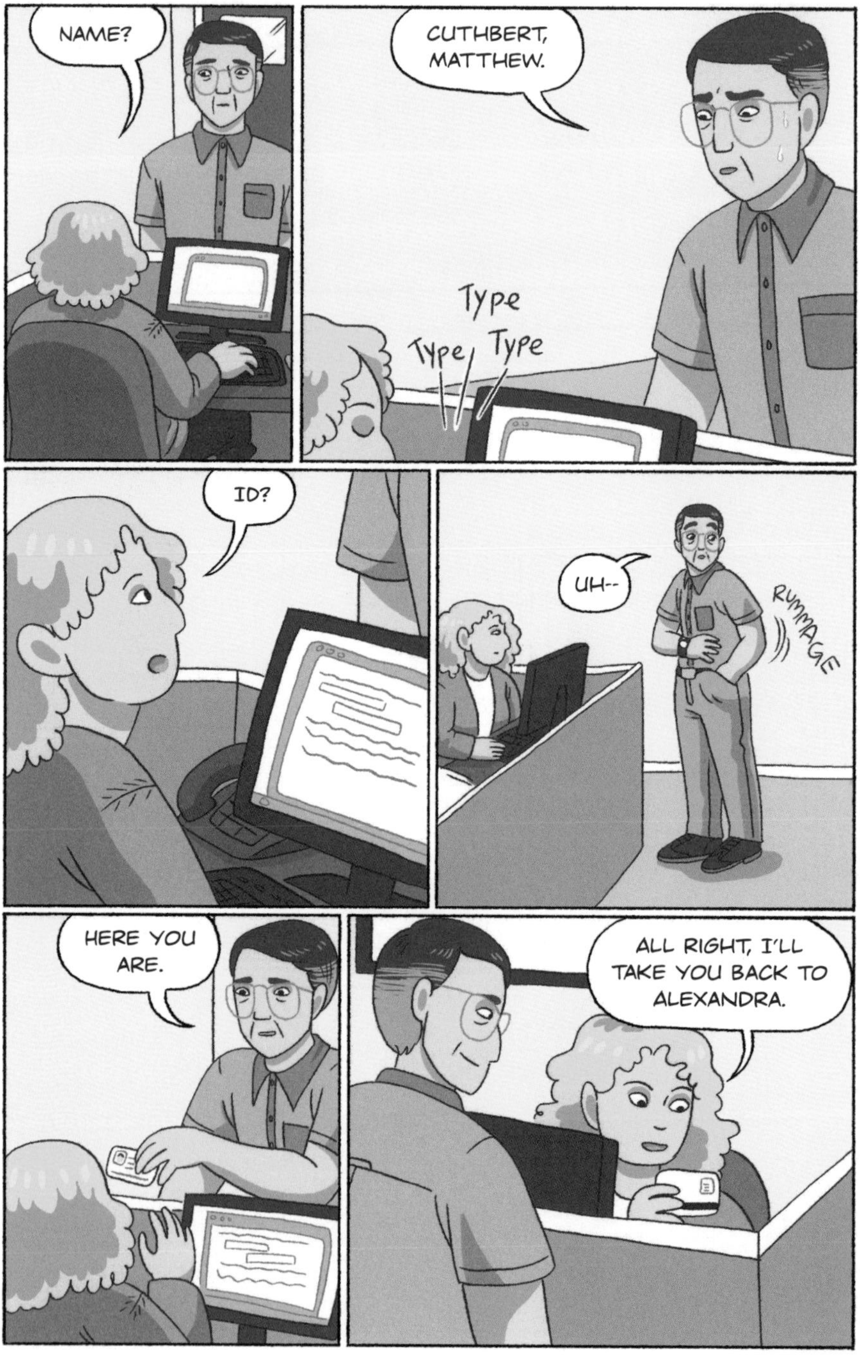
NAME?
CUTHBERT, MATTHEW.
Type
Type
Type
ID?
UH--
RUMMAGE
HERE YOU ARE.
ALL RIGHT, I'LL TAKE YOU BACK TO ALEXANDRA.

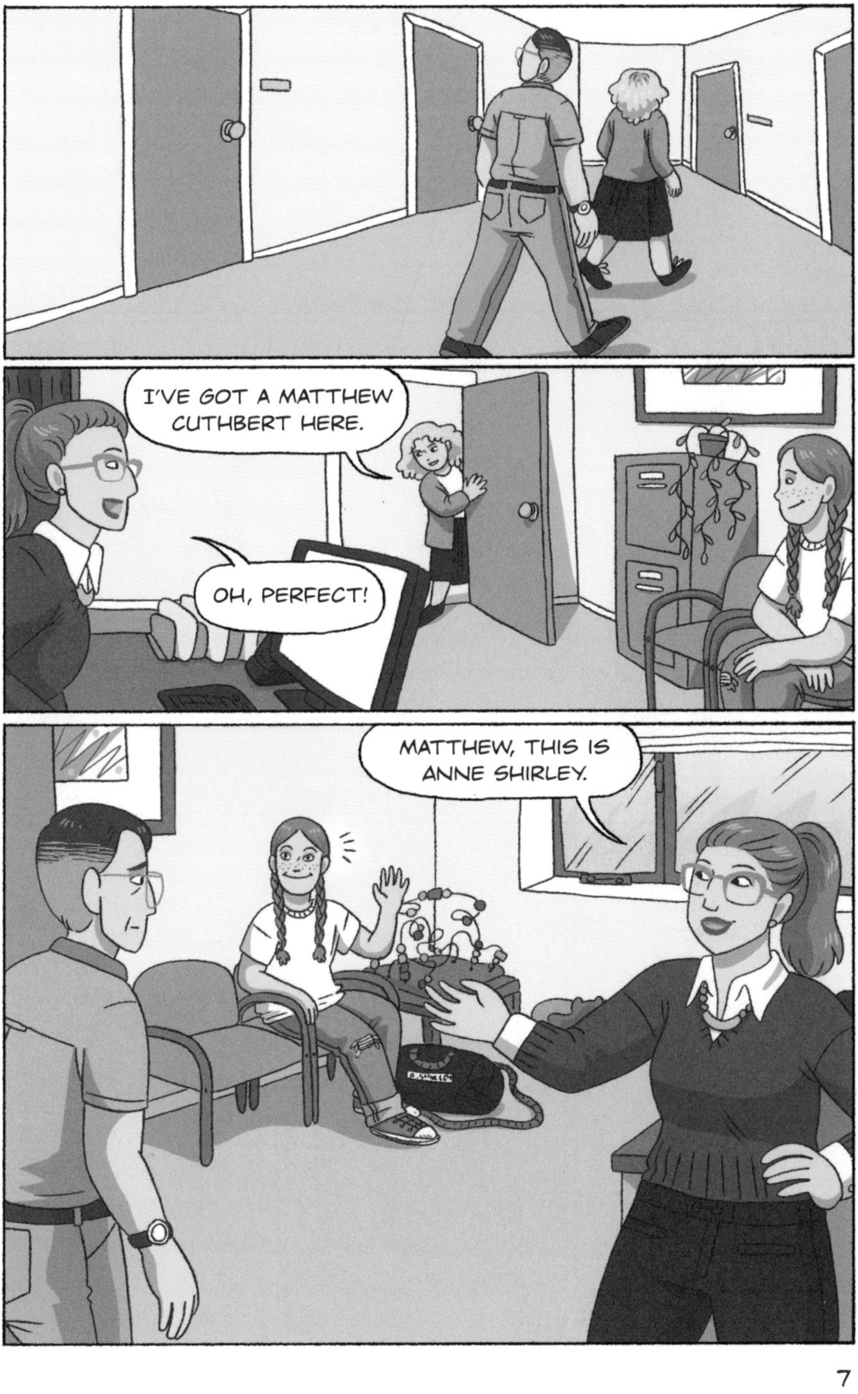
I'VE GOT A MATTHEW CUTHBERT HERE.
OH, PERFECT!
MATTHEW, THIS IS ANNE SHIRLEY.

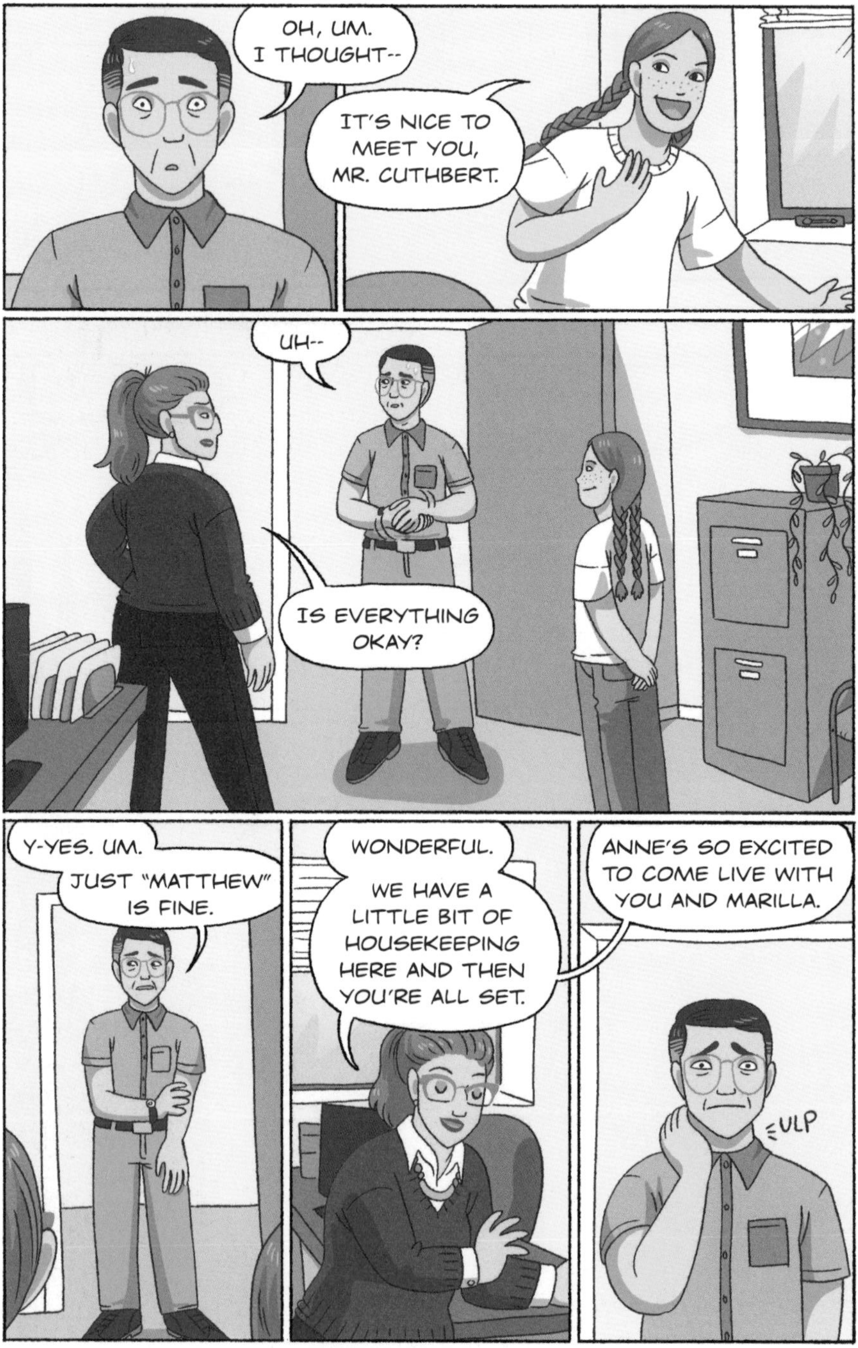
OH, UM.
I THOUGHT--
IT'S NICE TO MEET YOU, MR. CUTHBERT.
UH--
IS EVERYTHING OKAY?
Y-YES. UM.
JUST "MATTHEW" IS FINE.
WONDERFUL.
WE HAVE A LITTLE BIT OF HOUSEKEEPING HERE AND THEN YOU'RE ALL SET.
ANNE'S SO EXCITED TO COME LIVE WITH YOU AND MARILLA.
ULP

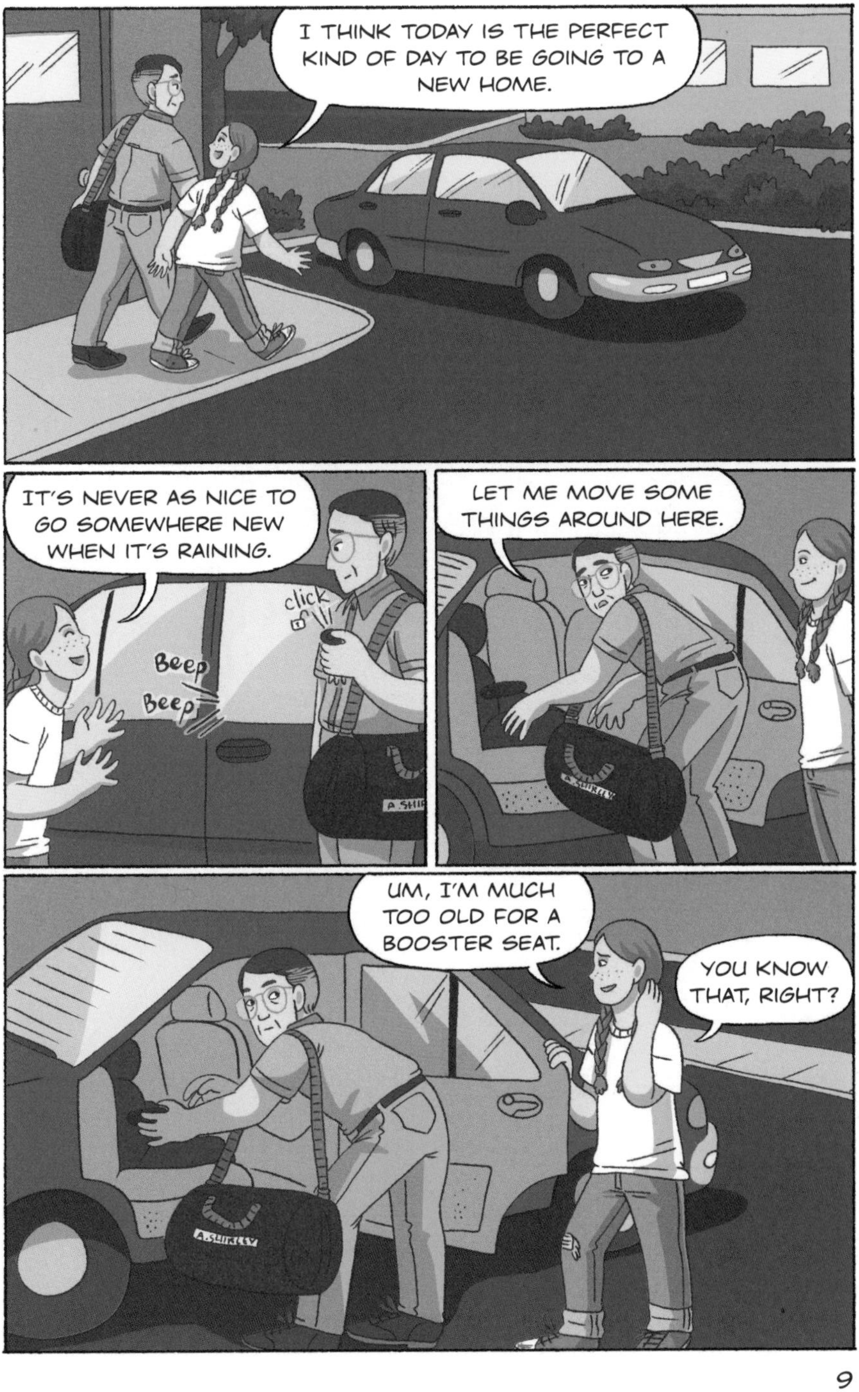
I THINK TODAY IS THE PERFECT KIND OF DAY TO BE GOING TO A NEW HOME.
IT'S NEVER AS NICE TO GO SOMEWHERE NEW WHEN IT'S RAINING.
click
Beep
Beep
A. SHIR
LET ME MOVE SOME THINGS AROUND HERE.
A. SHIRLEY
UM, I'M MUCH TOO OLD FOR A BOOSTER SEAT.
YOU KNOW THAT, RIGHT?
A. SHIRLEY

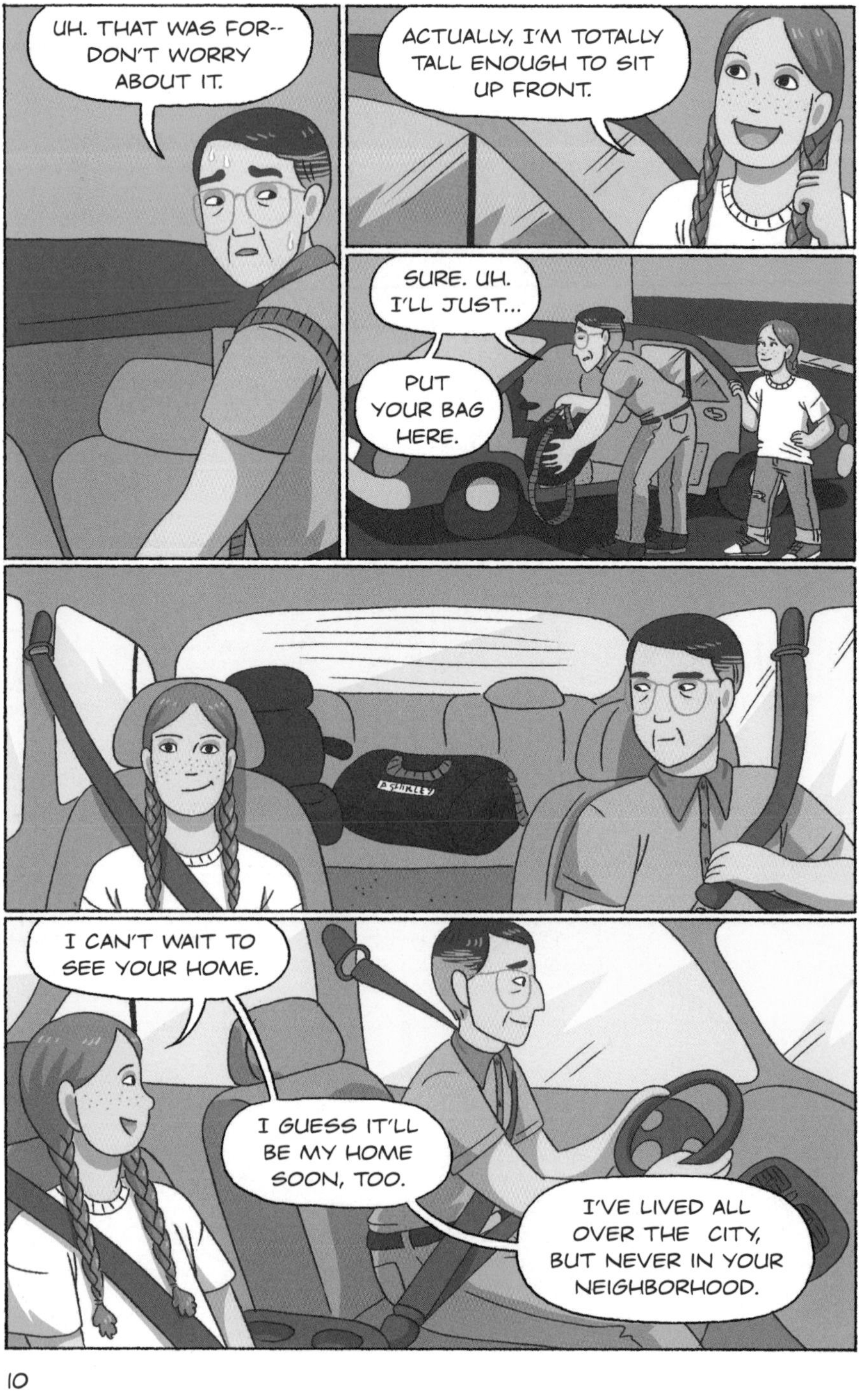
UH. THAT WAS FOR-- DON'T WORRY ABOUT IT.
ACTUALLY, I'M TOTALLY TALL ENOUGH TO SIT UP FRONT.
SURE. UH. I'LL JUST...
PUT YOUR BAG HERE.
I CAN'T WAIT TO SEE YOUR HOME.
I GUESS IT'LL BE MY HOME SOON, TOO.
I'VE LIVED ALL OVER THE CITY, BUT NEVER IN YOUR NEIGHBORHOOD.

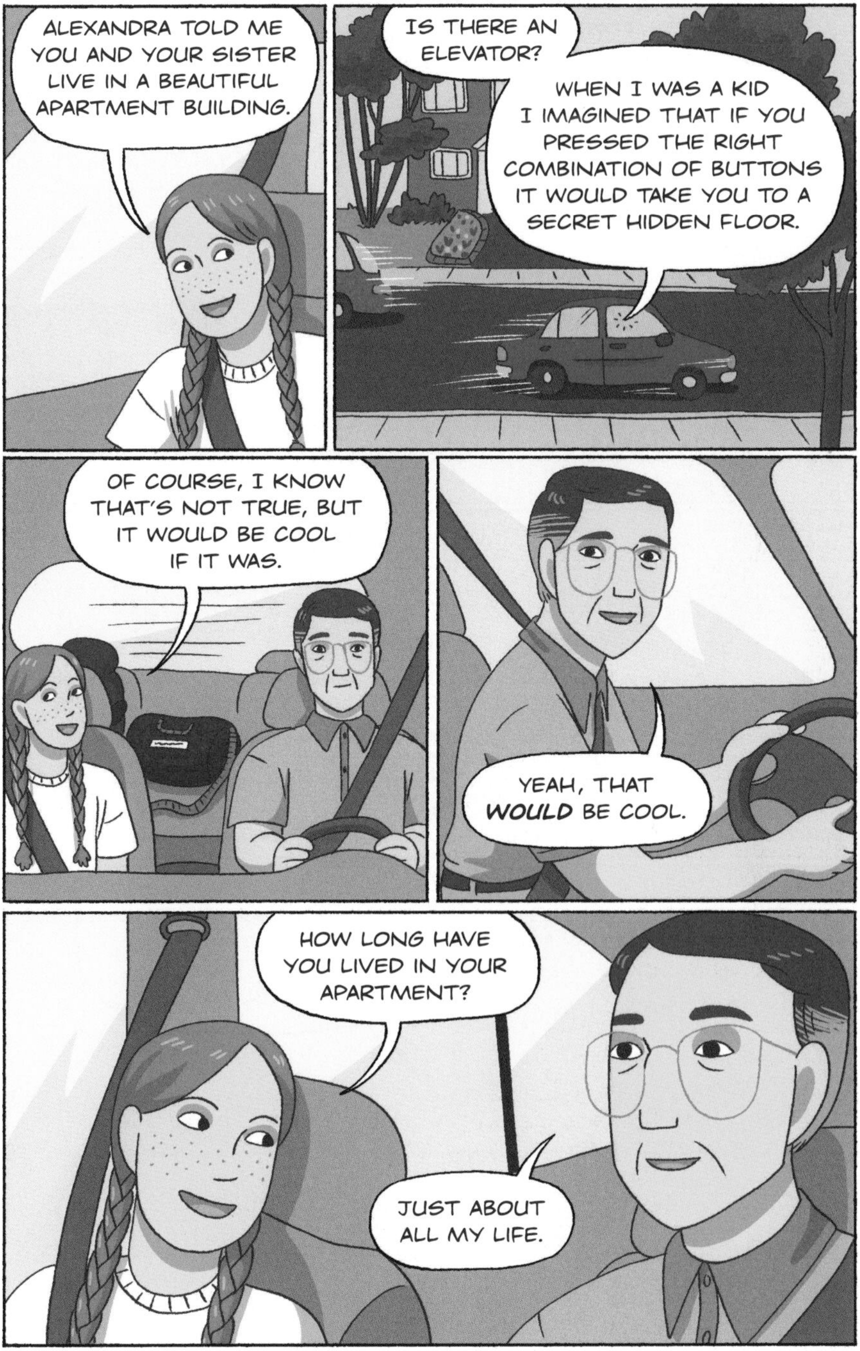
ALEXANDRA TOLD ME YOU AND YOUR SISTER LIVE IN A BEAUTIFUL APARTMENT BUILDING.
IS THERE AN ELEVATOR?
WHEN I WAS A KID I IMAGINED THAT IF YOU PRESSED THE RIGHT COMBINATION OF BUTTONS IT WOULD TAKE YOU TO A SECRET HIDDEN FLOOR.
OF COURSE, I KNOW THAT'S NOT TRUE, BUT IT WOULD BE COOL IF IT WAS.
YEAH, THAT **WOULD** BE COOL.
HOW LONG HAVE YOU LIVED IN YOUR APARTMENT?
JUST ABOUT ALL MY LIFE.

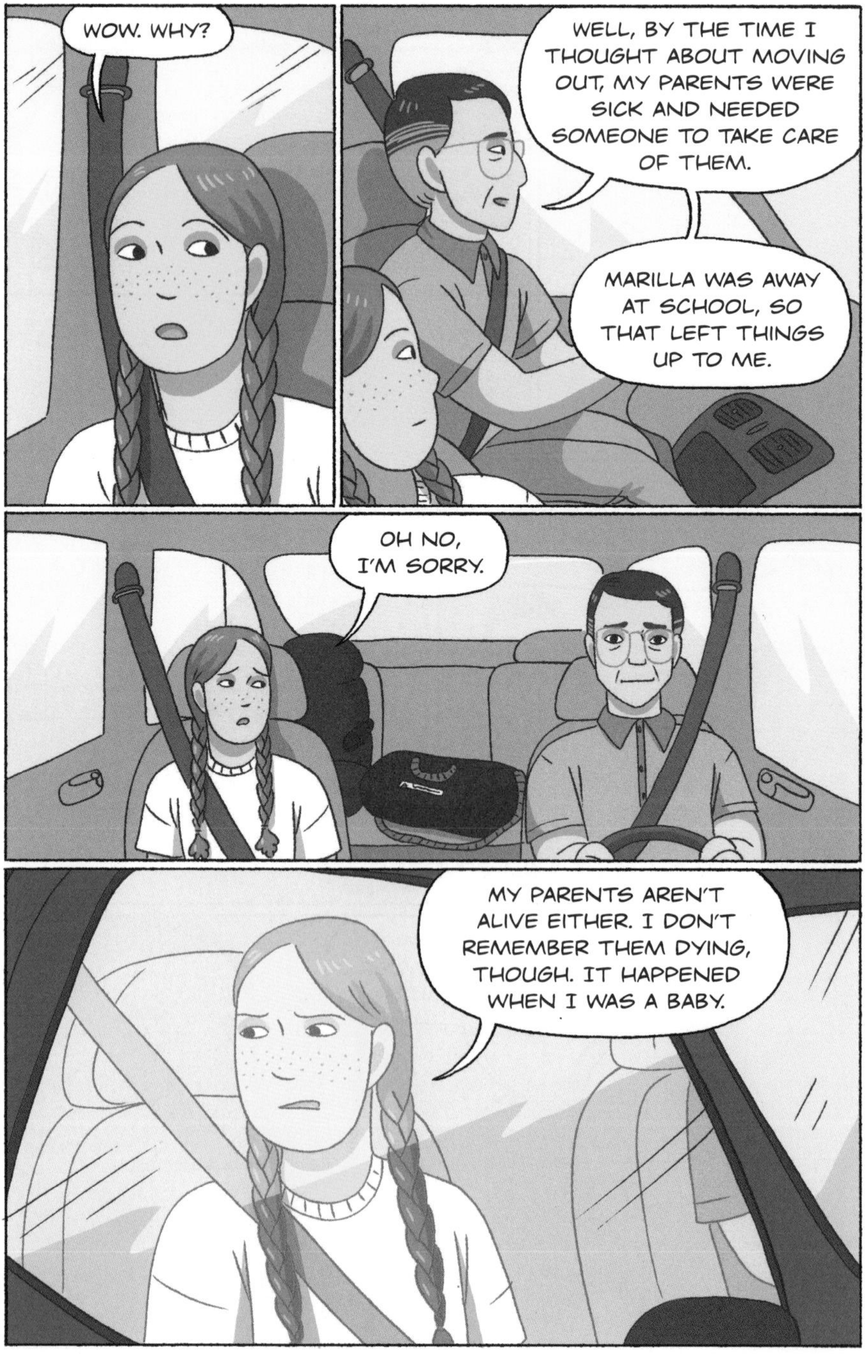
WOW. WHY?
WELL, BY THE TIME I THOUGHT ABOUT MOVING OUT, MY PARENTS WERE SICK AND NEEDED SOMEONE TO TAKE CARE OF THEM.
MARILLA WAS AWAY AT SCHOOL, SO THAT LEFT THINGS UP TO ME.
OH NO, I'M SORRY.
MY PARENTS AREN'T ALIVE EITHER. I DON'T REMEMBER THEM DYING, THOUGH. IT HAPPENED WHEN I WAS A BABY.

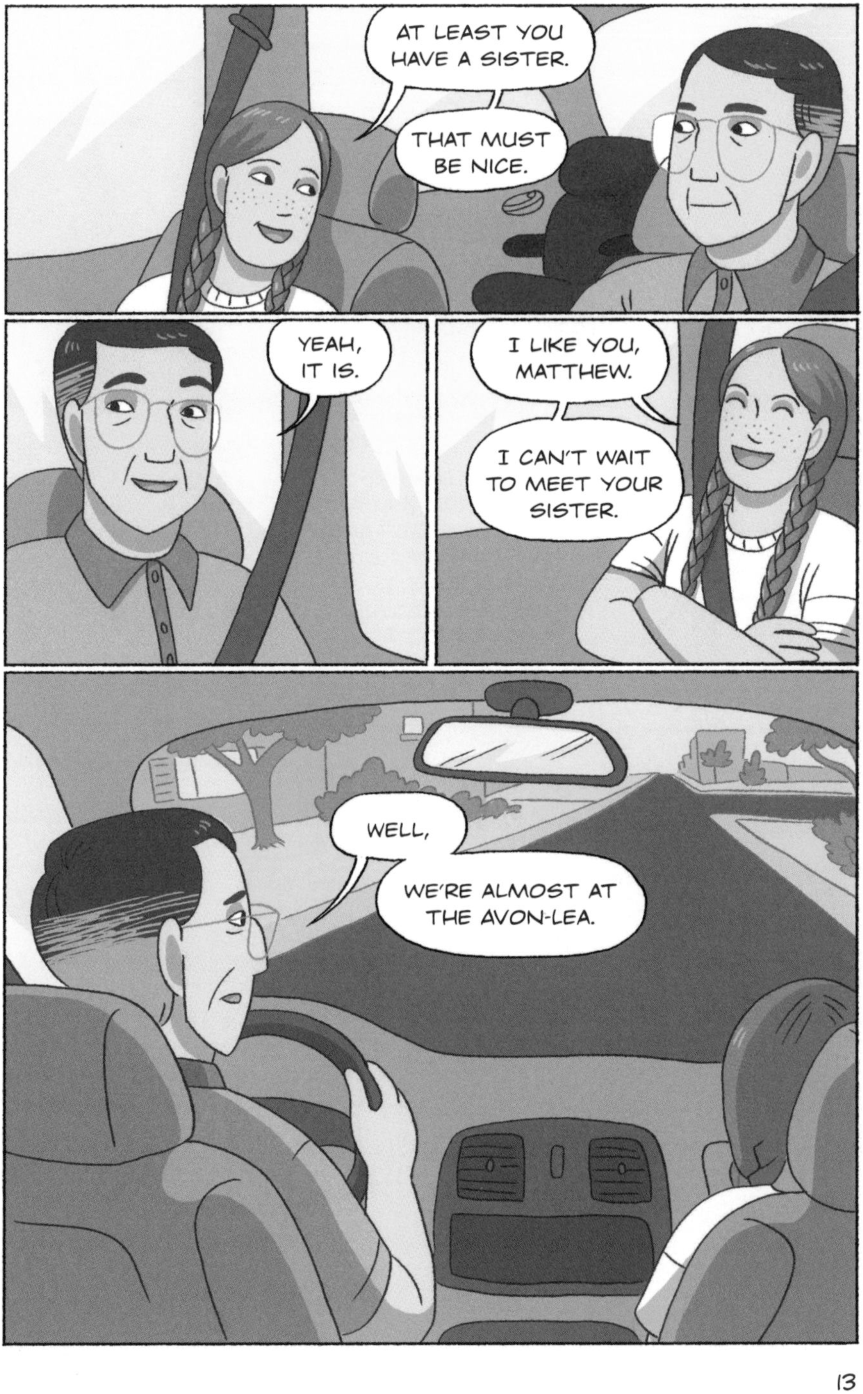
AT LEAST YOU HAVE A SISTER.
THAT MUST BE NICE.
YEAH, IT IS.
I LIKE YOU, MATTHEW.
I CAN'T WAIT TO MEET YOUR SISTER.
WELL,
WE'RE ALMOST AT THE AVON-LEA.

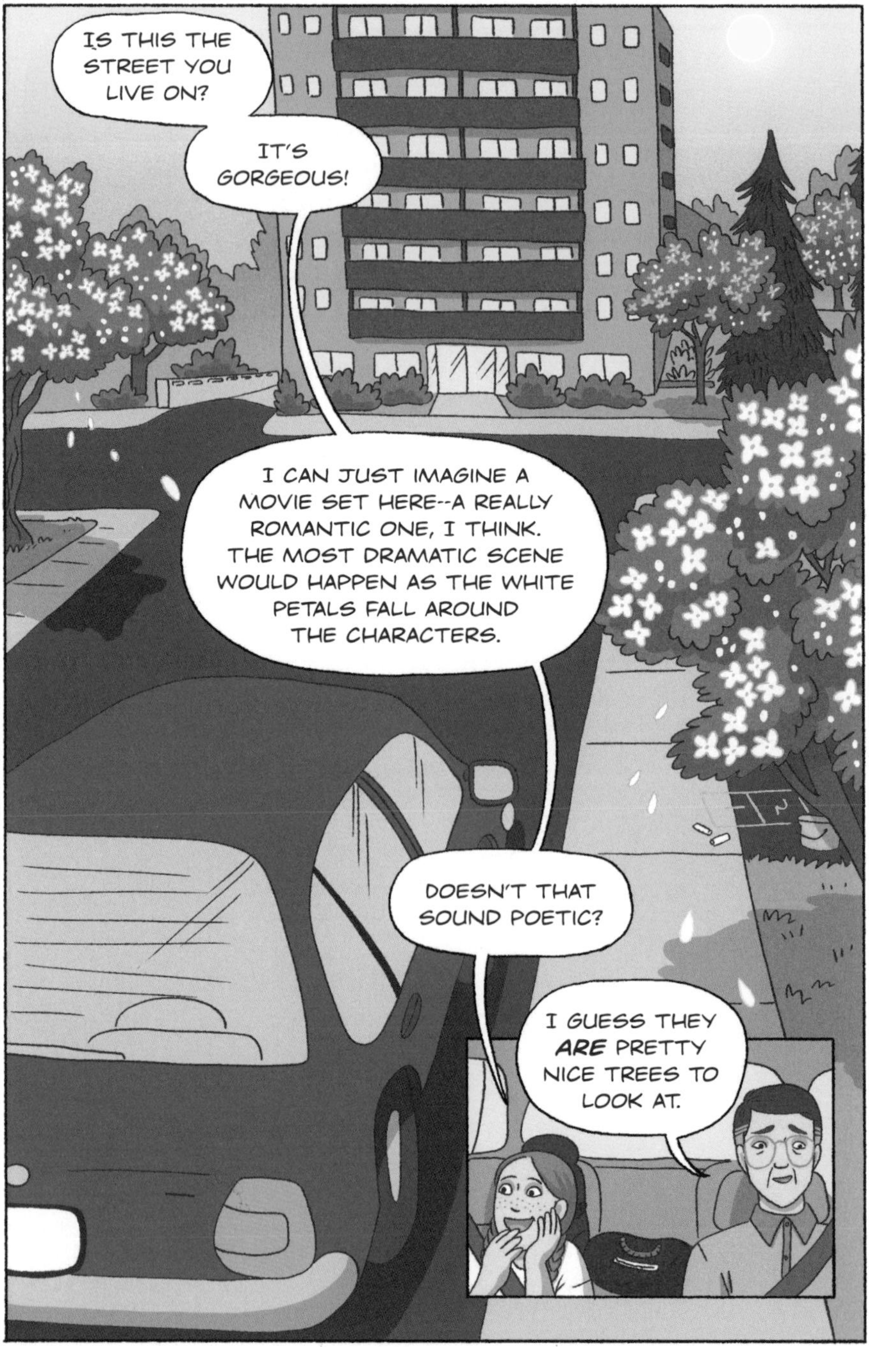
IS THIS THE STREET YOU LIVE ON?
IT'S GORGEOUS!
I CAN JUST IMAGINE A MOVIE SET HERE--A REALLY ROMANTIC ONE, I THINK. THE MOST DRAMATIC SCENE WOULD HAPPEN AS THE WHITE PETALS FALL AROUND THE CHARACTERS.
DOESN'T THAT SOUND POETIC?
I GUESS THEY *ARE* PRETTY NICE TREES TO LOOK AT.

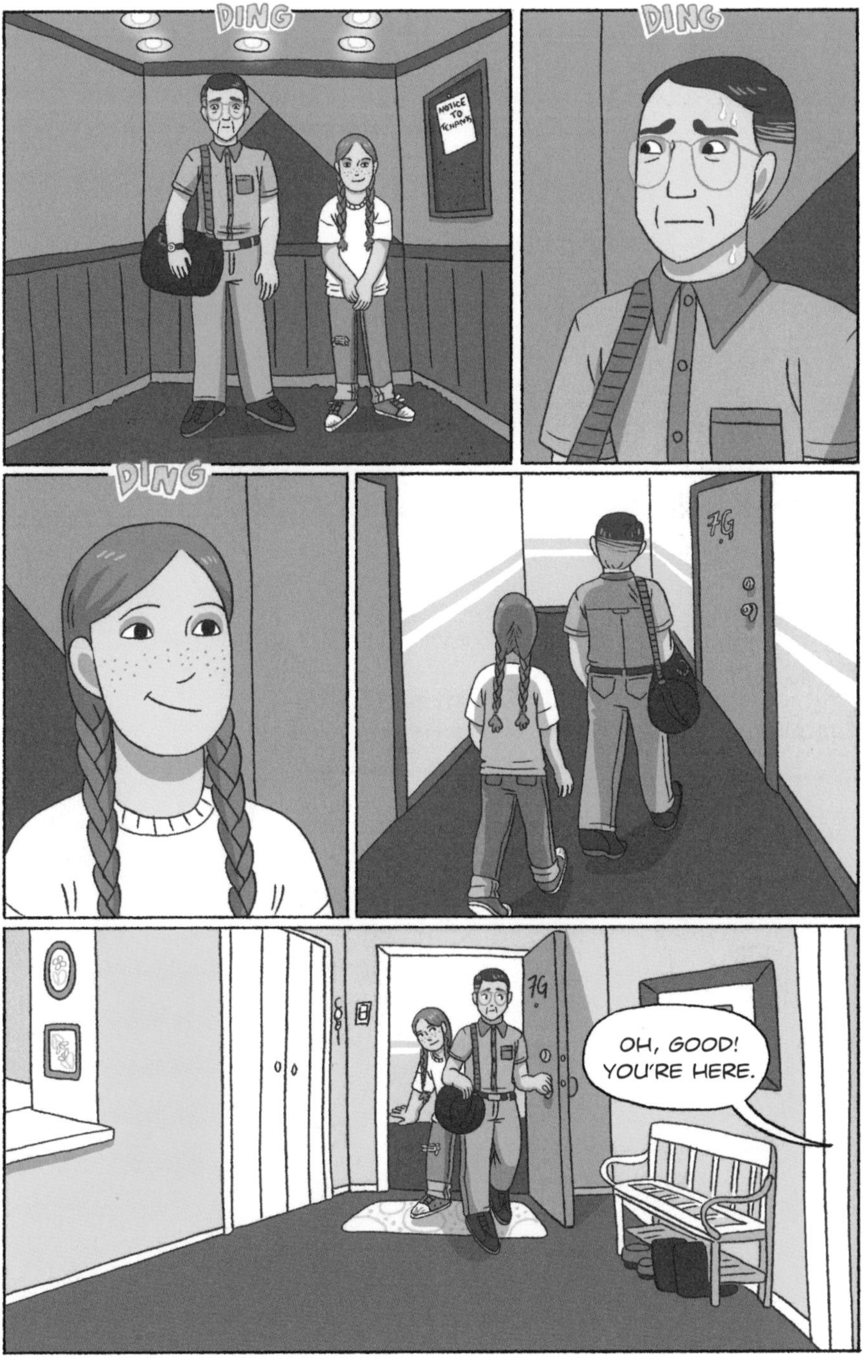
DING
NOTICE TO TENANTS
DING
DING
7G
7G
OH, GOOD! YOU'RE HERE.

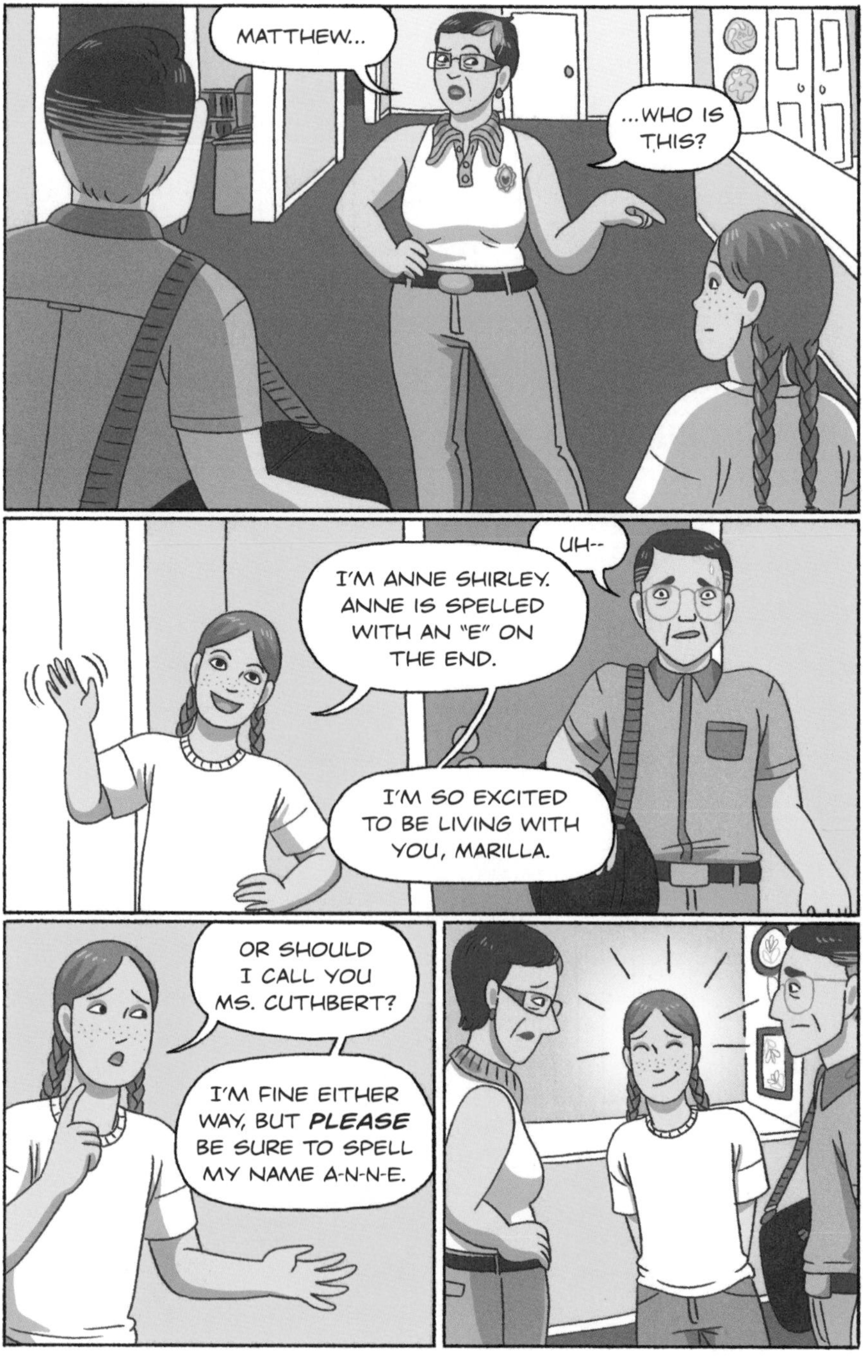
MATTHEW...
...WHO IS THIS?
UH--
I'M ANNE SHIRLEY. ANNE IS SPELLED WITH AN "E" ON THE END.
I'M SO EXCITED TO BE LIVING WITH YOU, MARILLA.
OR SHOULD I CALL YOU MS. CUTHBERT?
I'M FINE EITHER WAY, BUT ***PLEASE*** BE SURE TO SPELL MY NAME A-N-N-E.

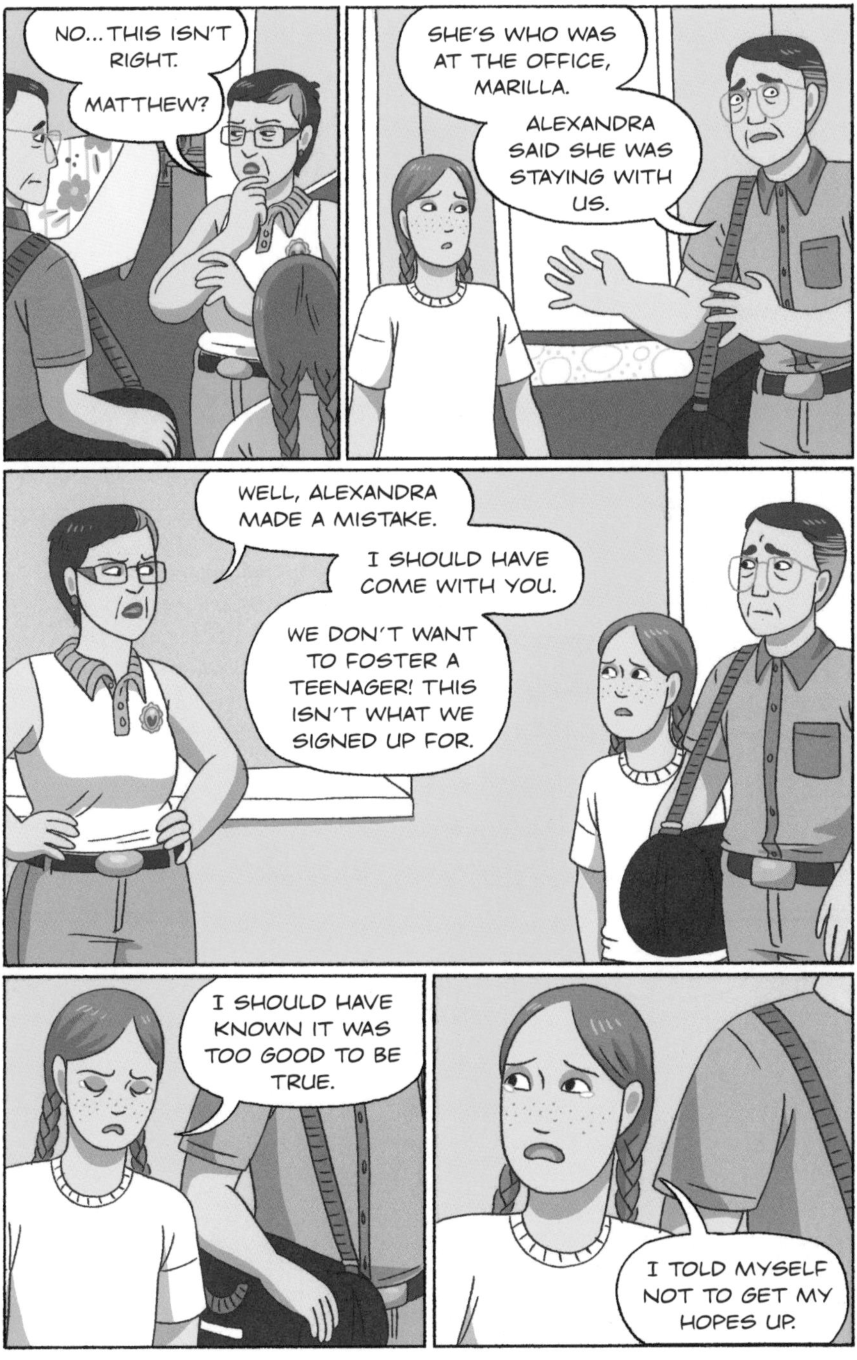
NO... THIS ISN'T RIGHT.
MATTHEW?
SHE'S WHO WAS AT THE OFFICE, MARILLA.
ALEXANDRA SAID SHE WAS STAYING WITH US.
WELL, ALEXANDRA MADE A MISTAKE.
I SHOULD HAVE COME WITH YOU.
WE DON'T WANT TO FOSTER A TEENAGER! THIS ISN'T WHAT WE SIGNED UP FOR.
I SHOULD HAVE KNOWN IT WAS TOO GOOD TO BE TRUE.
I TOLD MYSELF NOT TO GET MY HOPES UP.

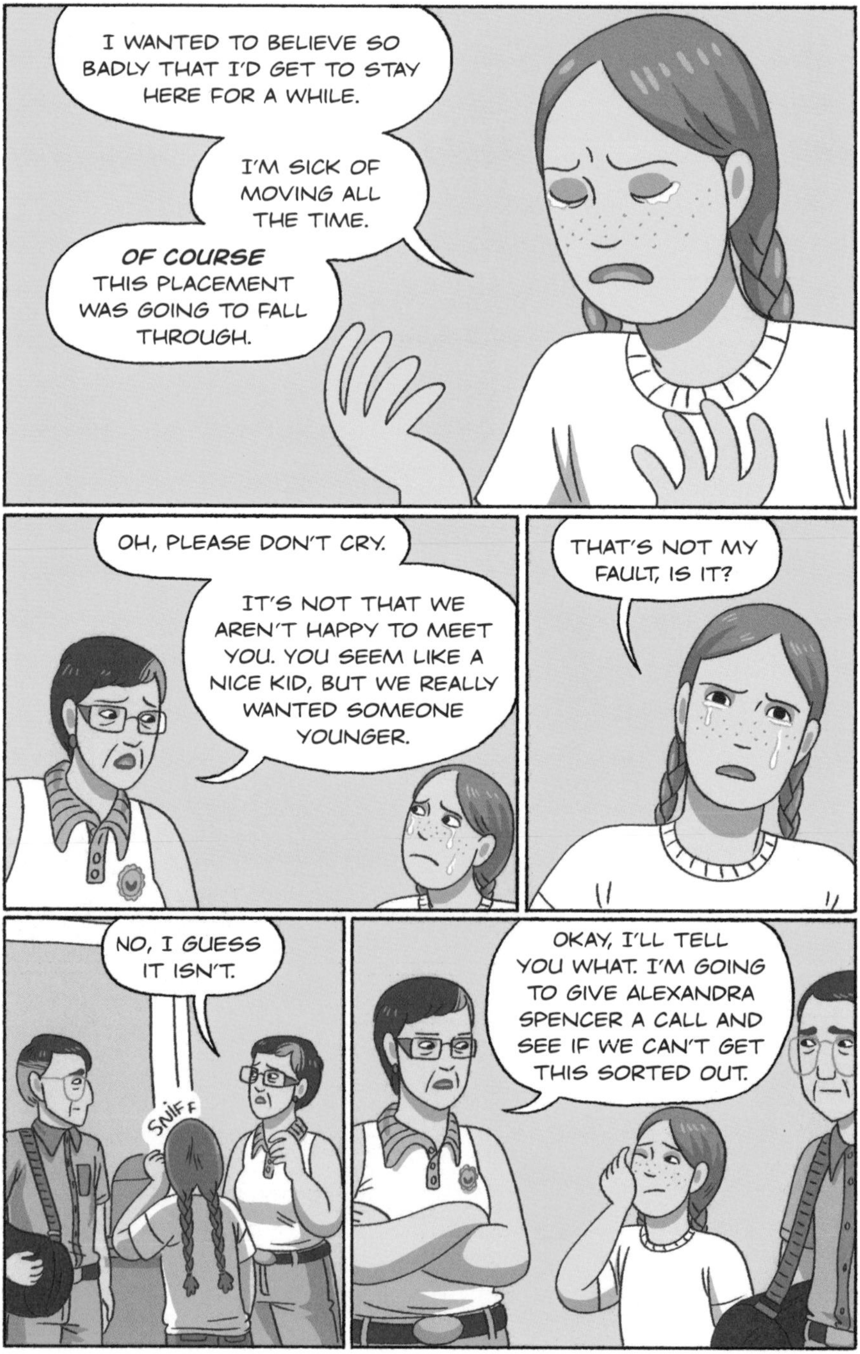
I WANTED TO BELIEVE SO BADLY THAT I'D GET TO STAY HERE FOR A WHILE.
I'M SICK OF MOVING ALL THE TIME.
OF COURSE THIS PLACEMENT WAS GOING TO FALL THROUGH.
OH, PLEASE DON'T CRY.
IT'S NOT THAT WE AREN'T HAPPY TO MEET YOU. YOU SEEM LIKE A NICE KID, BUT WE REALLY WANTED SOMEONE YOUNGER.
THAT'S NOT MY FAULT, IS IT?
NO, I GUESS IT ISN'T.
SNIFF
OKAY, I'LL TELL YOU WHAT. I'M GOING TO GIVE ALEXANDRA SPENCER A CALL AND SEE IF WE CAN'T GET THIS SORTED OUT.

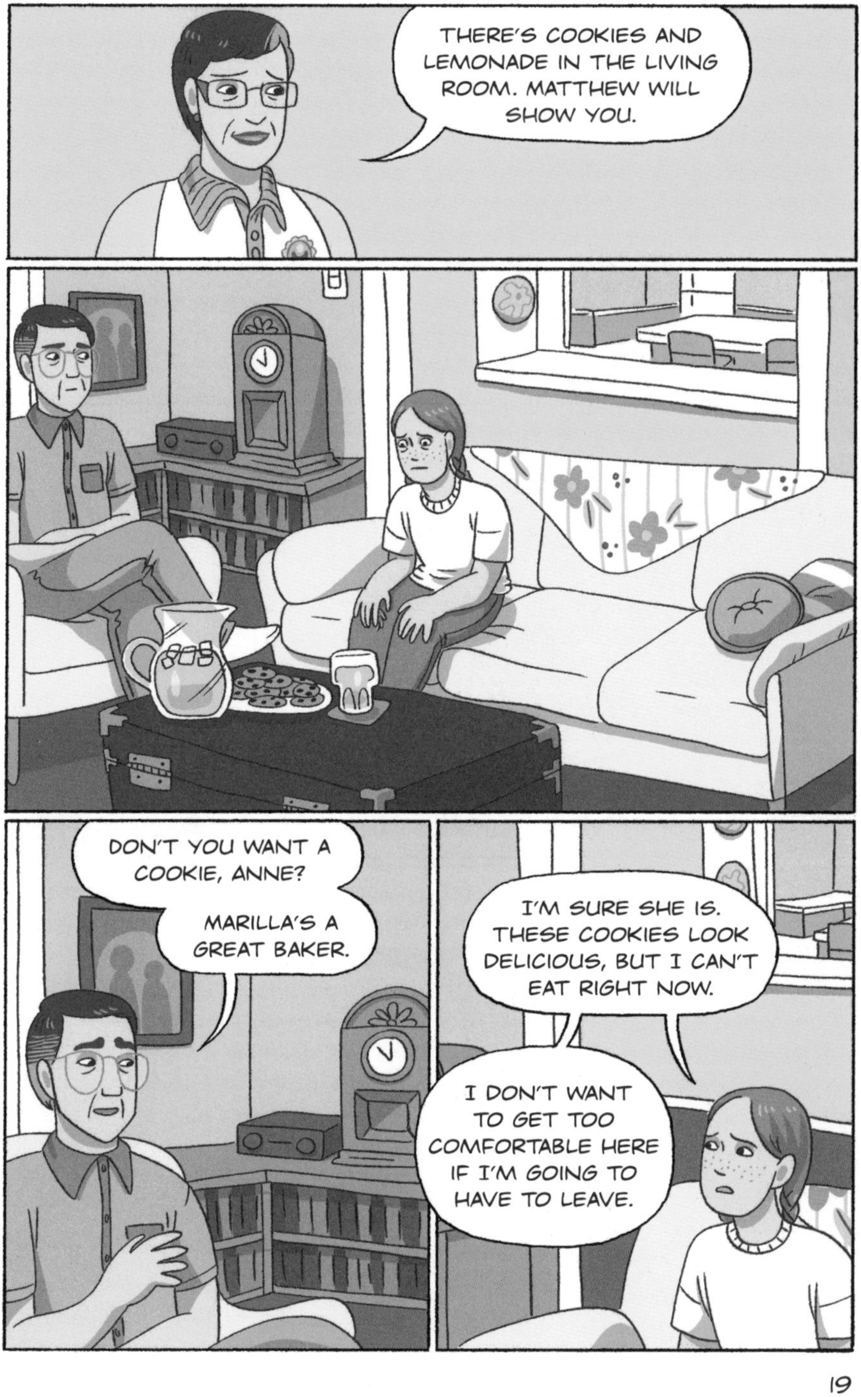
THERE'S COOKIES AND LEMONADE IN THE LIVING ROOM. MATTHEW WILL SHOW YOU.
DON'T YOU WANT A COOKIE, ANNE?
MARILLA'S A GREAT BAKER.
I'M SURE SHE IS. THESE COOKIES LOOK DELICIOUS, BUT I CAN'T EAT RIGHT NOW.
I DON'T WANT TO GET TOO COMFORTABLE HERE IF I'M GOING TO HAVE TO LEAVE.

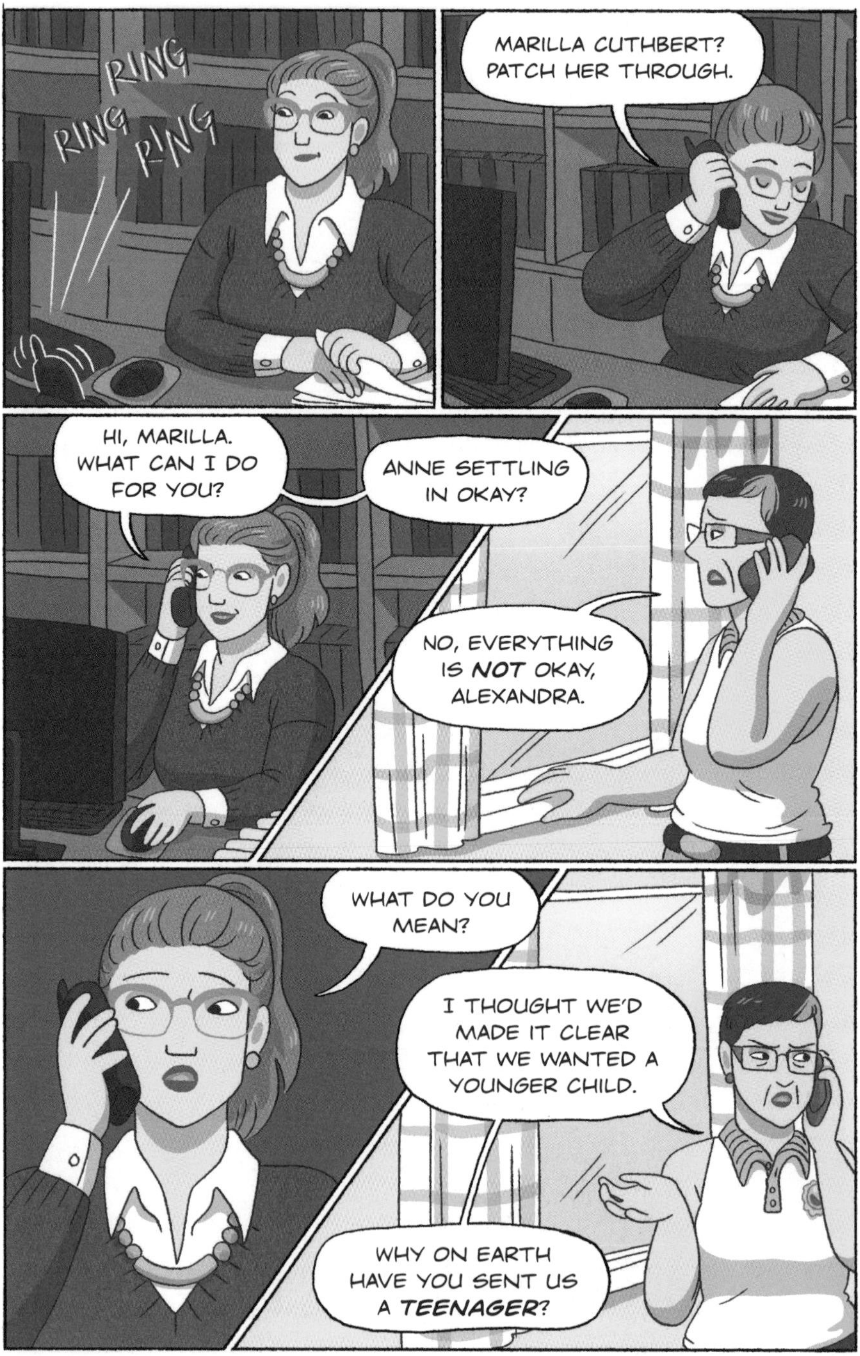
RING
RING
RING
MARILLA CUTHBERT? PATCH HER THROUGH.
HI, MARILLA. WHAT CAN I DO FOR YOU?
ANNE SETTLING IN OKAY?
NO, EVERYTHING IS **NOT** OKAY, ALEXANDRA.
WHAT DO YOU MEAN?
I THOUGHT WE'D MADE IT CLEAR THAT WE WANTED A YOUNGER CHILD.
WHY ON EARTH HAVE YOU SENT US A ***TEENAGER***?

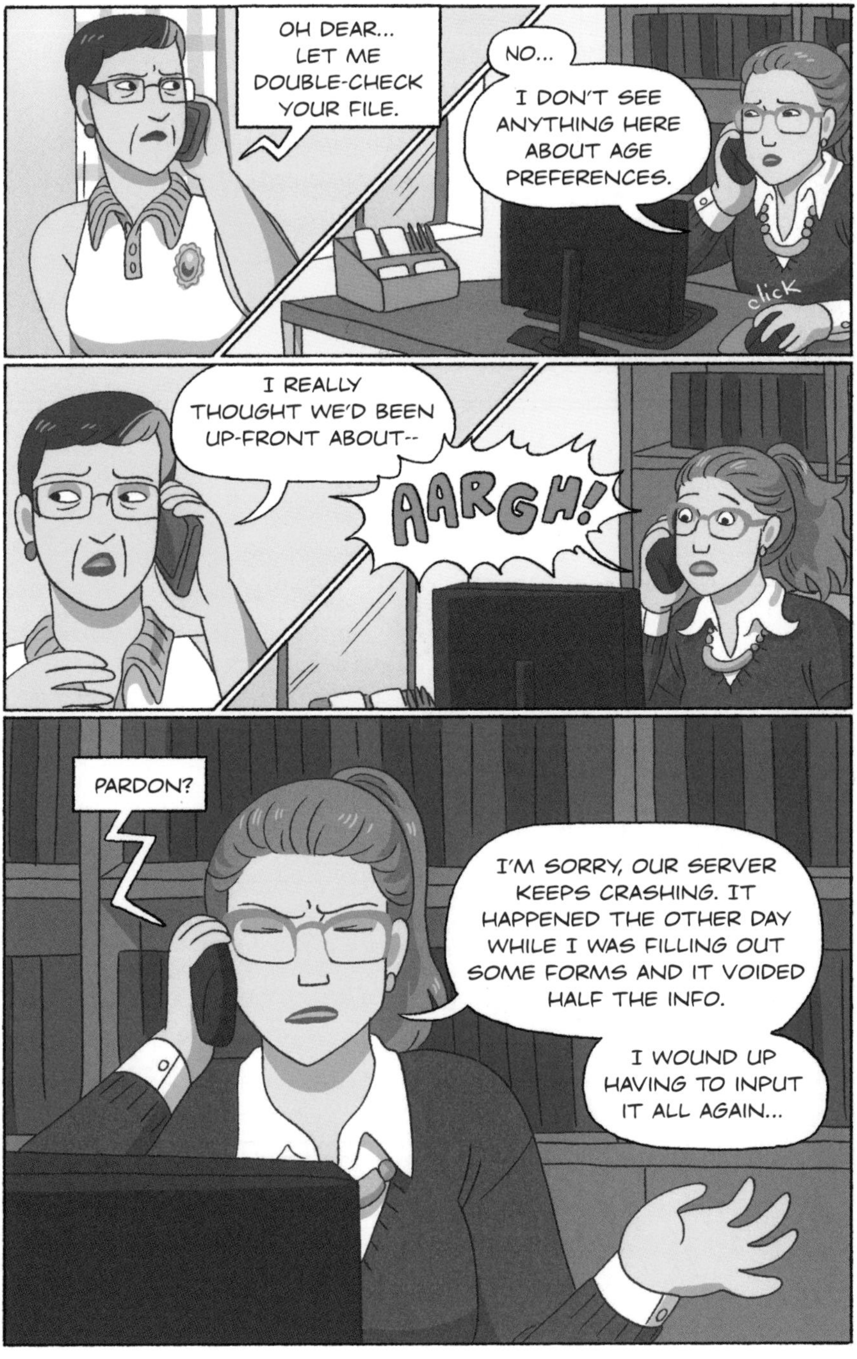
OH DEAR... LET ME DOUBLE-CHECK YOUR FILE.
NO...
I DON'T SEE ANYTHING HERE ABOUT AGE PREFERENCES.
click
I REALLY THOUGHT WE'D BEEN UP-FRONT ABOUT--
AARGH!
PARDON?
I'M SORRY, OUR SERVER KEEPS CRASHING. IT HAPPENED THE OTHER DAY WHILE I WAS FILLING OUT SOME FORMS AND IT VOIDED HALF THE INFO.
I WOUND UP HAVING TO INPUT IT ALL AGAIN...

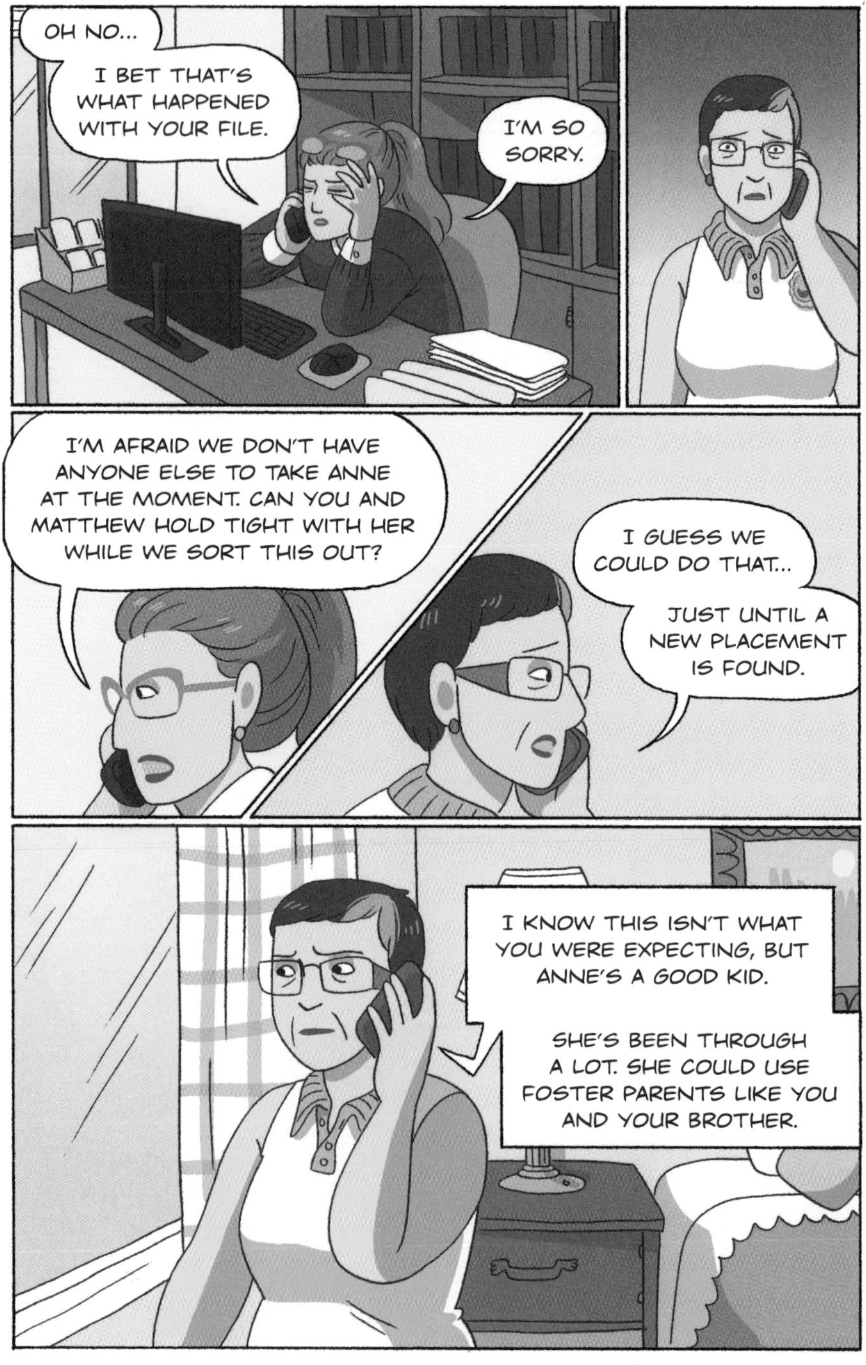
OH NO...
I BET THAT'S WHAT HAPPENED WITH YOUR FILE.
I'M SO SORRY.
I'M AFRAID WE DON'T HAVE ANYONE ELSE TO TAKE ANNE AT THE MOMENT. CAN YOU AND MATTHEW HOLD TIGHT WITH HER WHILE WE SORT THIS OUT?
I GUESS WE COULD DO THAT...
JUST UNTIL A NEW PLACEMENT IS FOUND.
I KNOW THIS ISN'T WHAT YOU WERE EXPECTING, BUT ANNE'S A GOOD KID.
SHE'S BEEN THROUGH A LOT. SHE COULD USE FOSTER PARENTS LIKE YOU AND YOUR BROTHER.

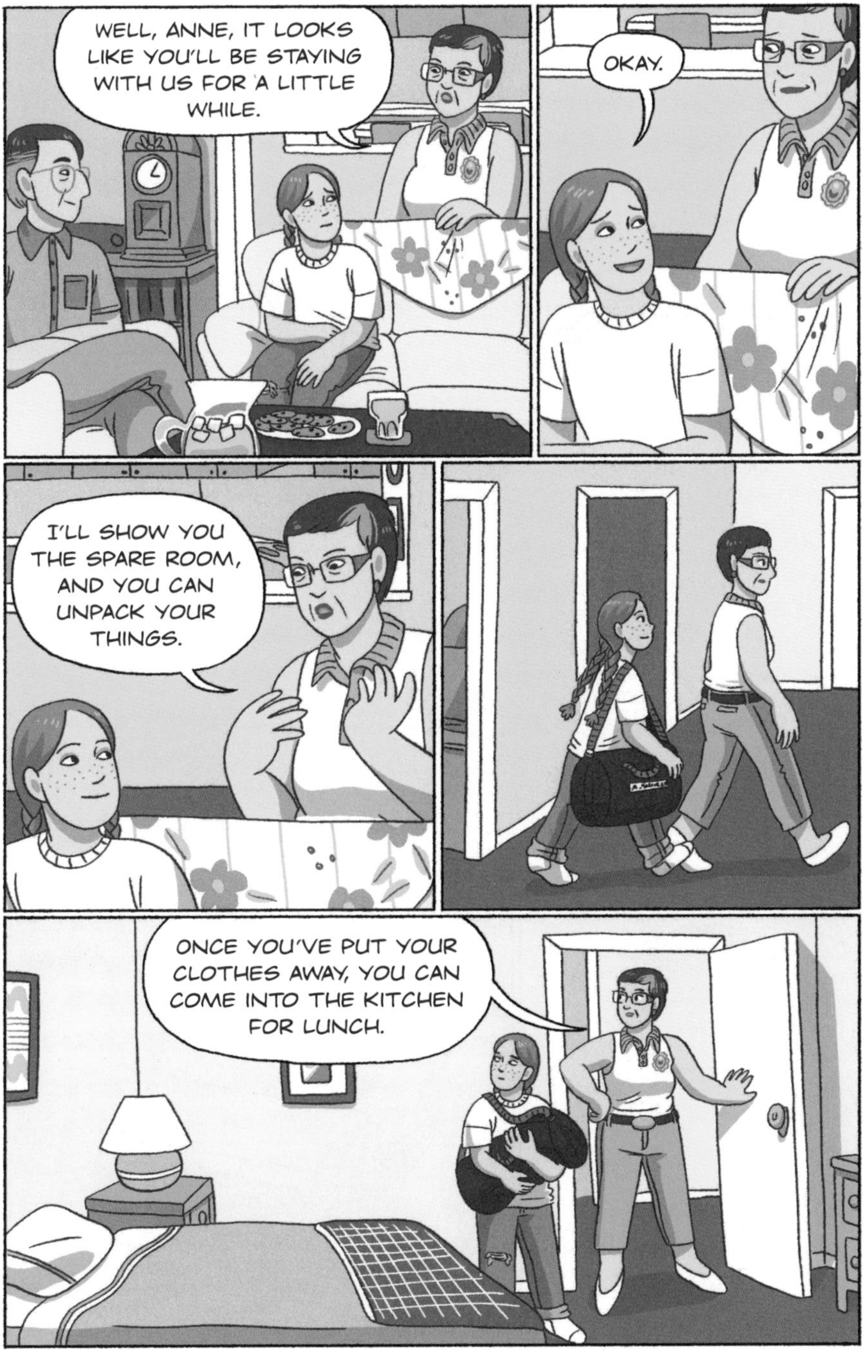
WELL, ANNE, IT LOOKS LIKE YOU'LL BE STAYING WITH US FOR A LITTLE WHILE.
OKAY.
I'LL SHOW YOU THE SPARE ROOM, AND YOU CAN UNPACK YOUR THINGS.
ONCE YOU'VE PUT YOUR CLOTHES AWAY, YOU CAN COME INTO THE KITCHEN FOR LUNCH.

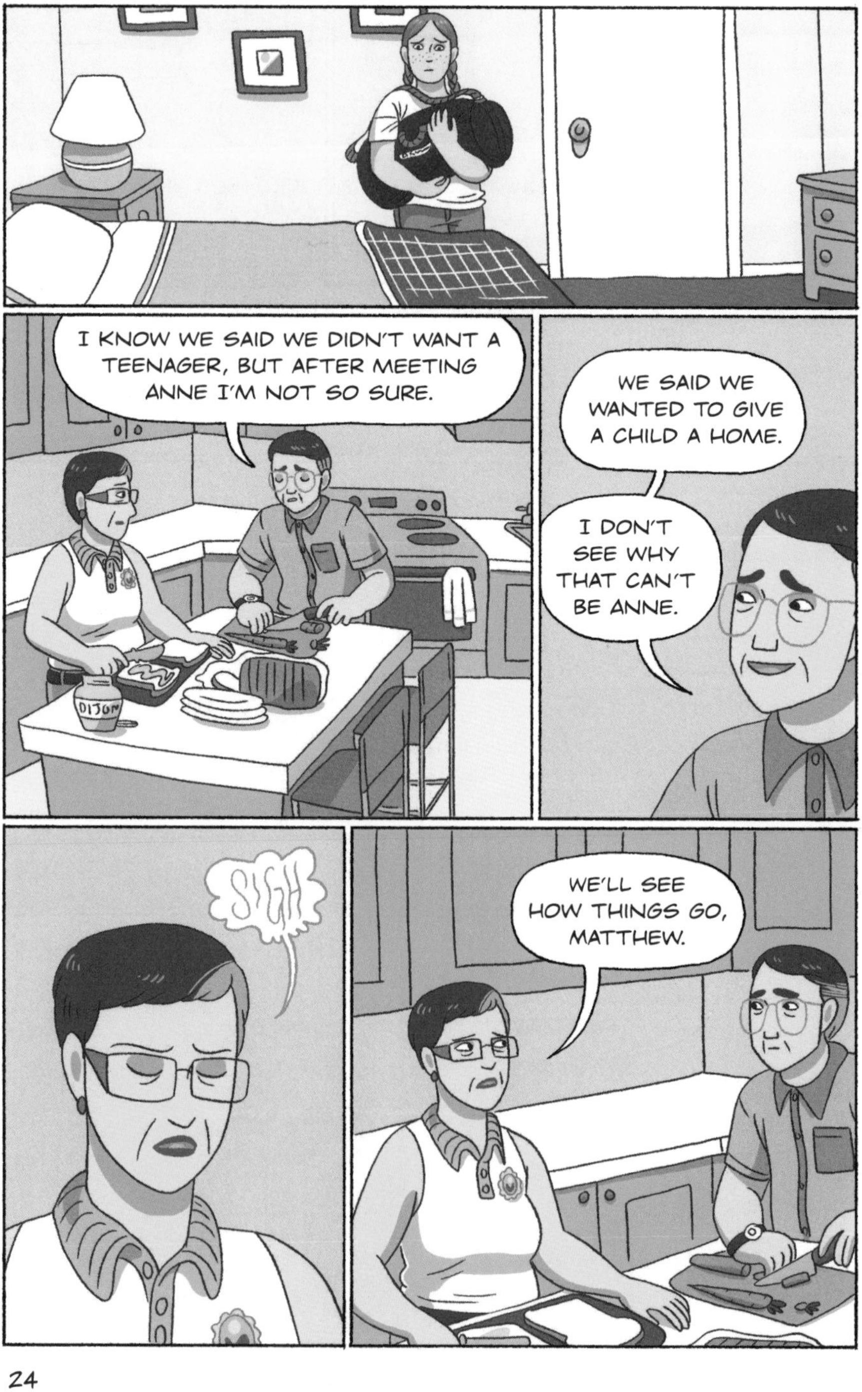
I KNOW WE SAID WE DIDN'T WANT A TEENAGER, BUT AFTER MEETING ANNE I'M NOT SO SURE.
DIJON
WE SAID WE WANTED TO GIVE A CHILD A HOME.
I DON'T SEE WHY THAT CAN'T BE ANNE.
SIGH
WE'LL SEE HOW THINGS GO, MATTHEW.

WHY DOES NOTHING WORK OUT FOR ME?

MATTHEW SEEMS NICE, THE APARTMENT IS NICE, AND MARILLA SEEMS LIKE SHE'D BE NICE IF SHE RELAXED FOR A SECOND.

MAYBE I WAS BORN UNDER AN UNLUCKY STAR. THAT WOULD EXPLAIN MY RED HAIR, MY TOO MANY FRECKLES, AND EVERYTHING ELSE THAT SEEMS TO GO WRONG.

IT'S NOT FAIR!

UNLUCKY

CHAPTER 2

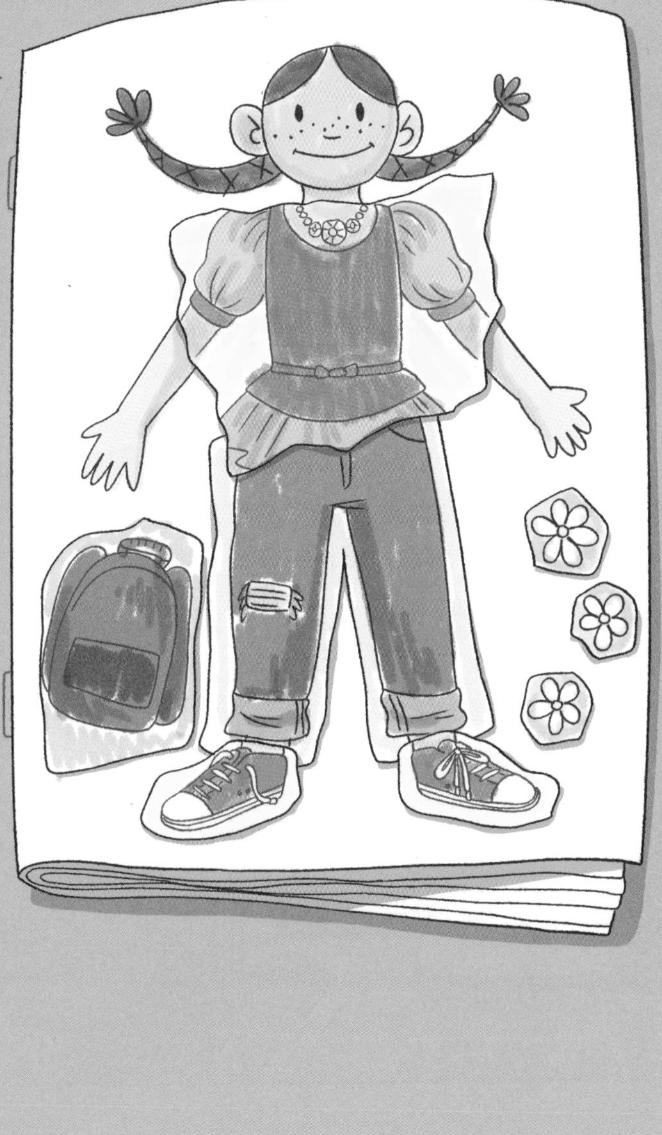

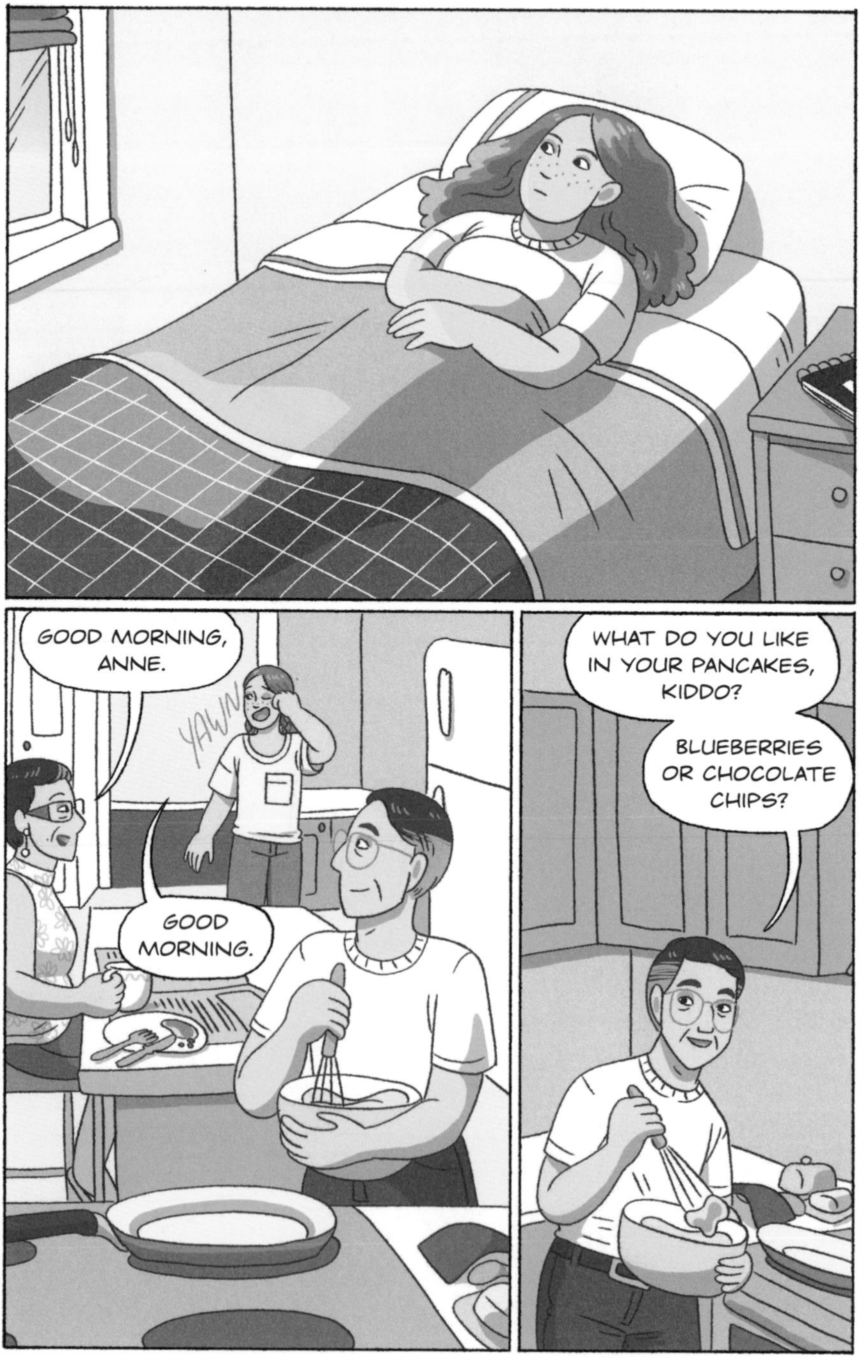
GOOD MORNING, ANNE.
YAWN
GOOD MORNING.
WHAT DO YOU LIKE IN YOUR PANCAKES, KIDDO?
BLUEBERRIES OR CHOCOLATE CHIPS?

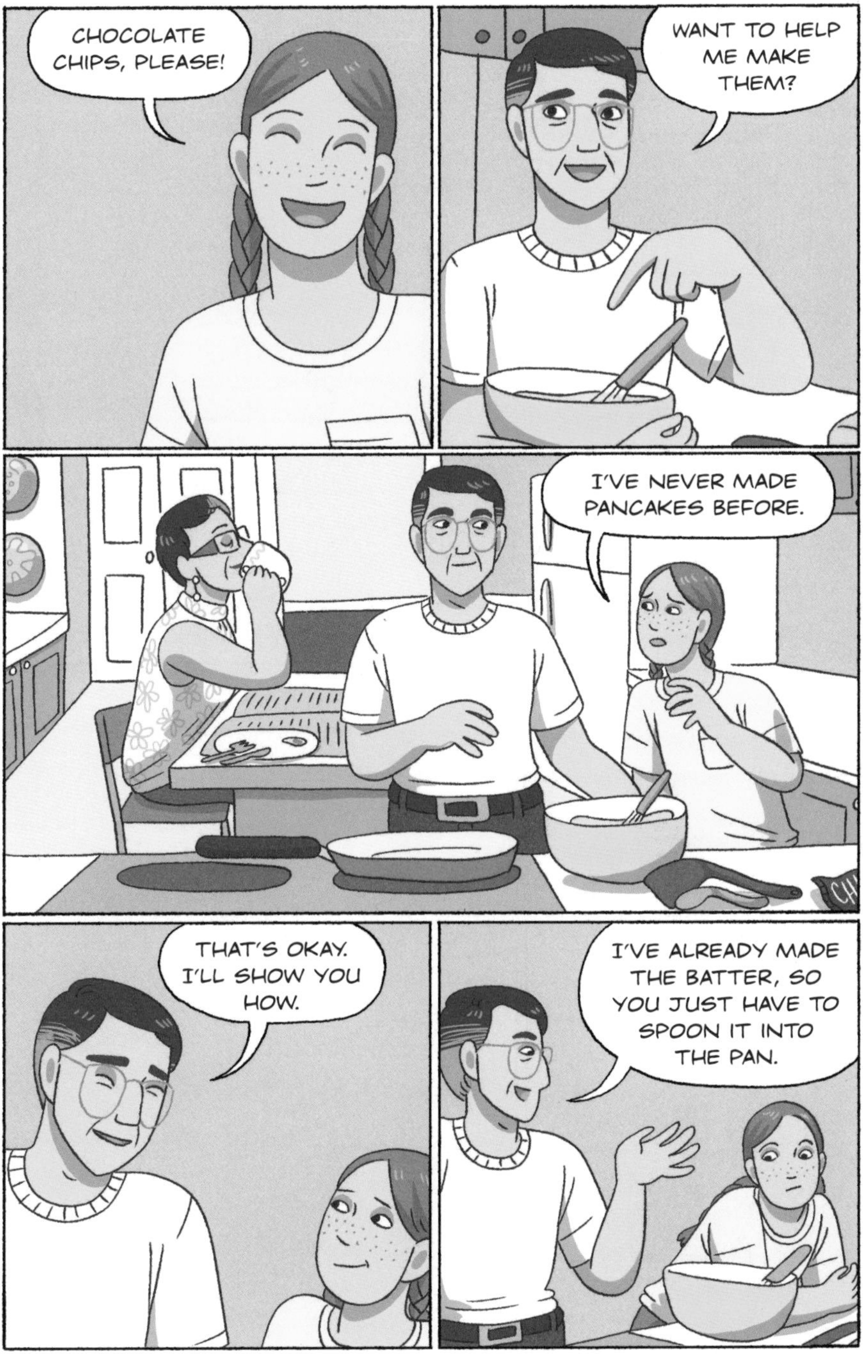
CHOCOLATE CHIPS, PLEASE!
WANT TO HELP ME MAKE THEM?
I'VE NEVER MADE PANCAKES BEFORE.
THAT'S OKAY. I'LL SHOW YOU HOW.
I'VE ALREADY MADE THE BATTER, SO YOU JUST HAVE TO SPOON IT INTO THE PAN.

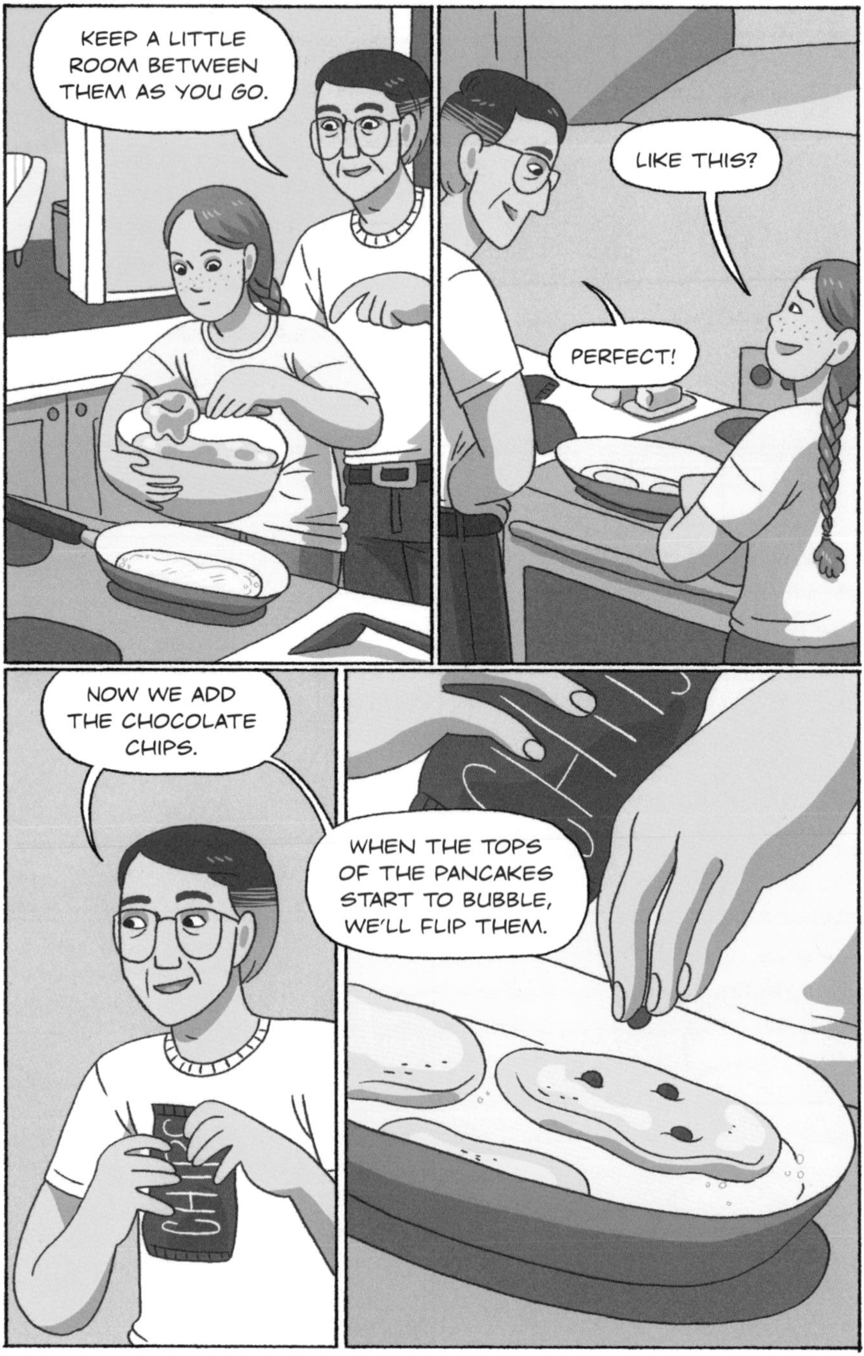
KEEP A LITTLE ROOM BETWEEN THEM AS YOU GO.
LIKE THIS?
PERFECT!
NOW WE ADD THE CHOCOLATE CHIPS.
CHIPS
WHEN THE TOPS OF THE PANCAKES START TO BUBBLE, WE'LL FLIP THEM.
CHIPS

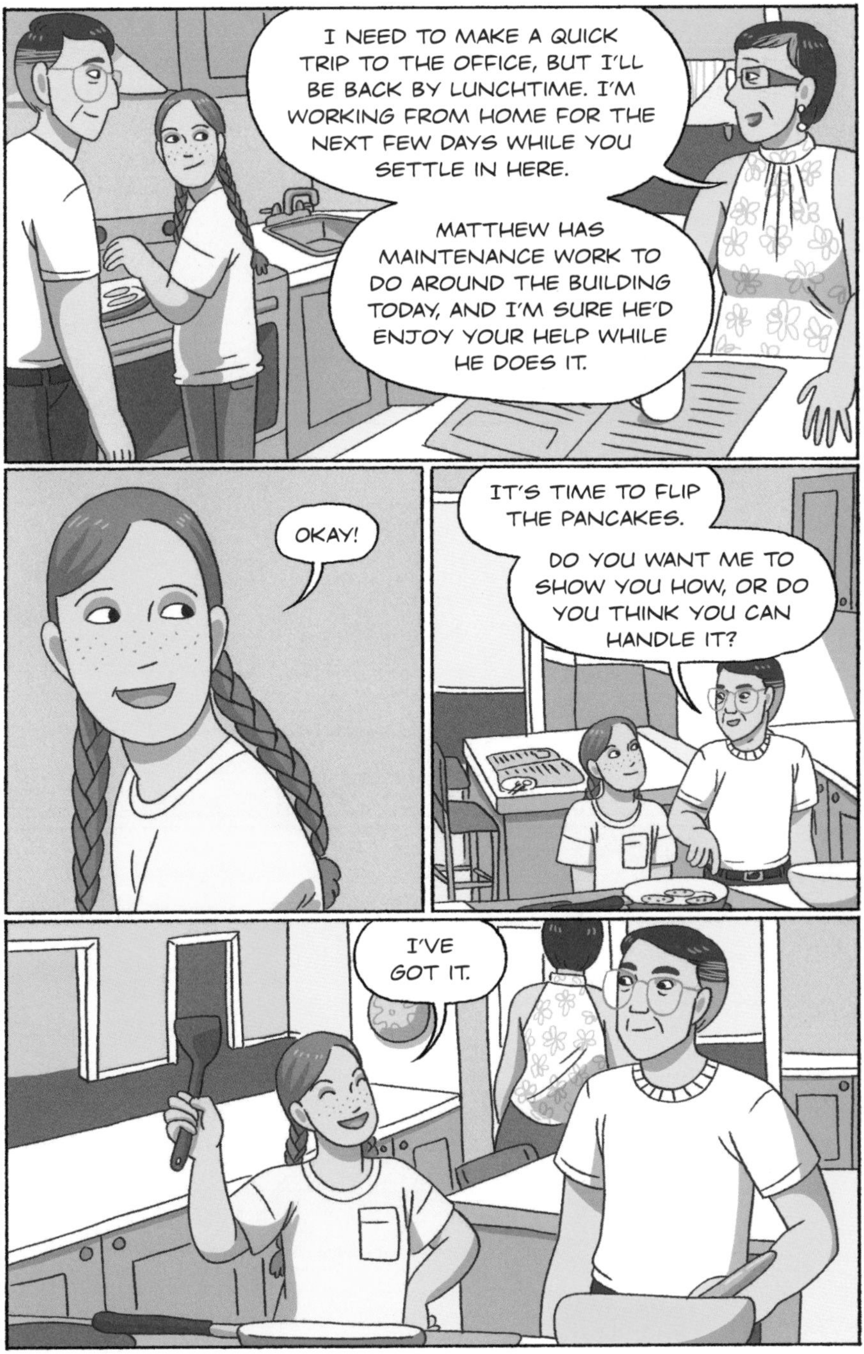
I NEED TO MAKE A QUICK TRIP TO THE OFFICE, BUT I'LL BE BACK BY LUNCHTIME. I'M WORKING FROM HOME FOR THE NEXT FEW DAYS WHILE YOU SETTLE IN HERE.
MATTHEW HAS MAINTENANCE WORK TO DO AROUND THE BUILDING TODAY, AND I'M SURE HE'D ENJOY YOUR HELP WHILE HE DOES IT.
OKAY!
IT'S TIME TO FLIP THE PANCAKES.
DO YOU WANT ME TO SHOW YOU HOW, OR DO YOU THINK YOU CAN HANDLE IT?
I'VE GOT IT.

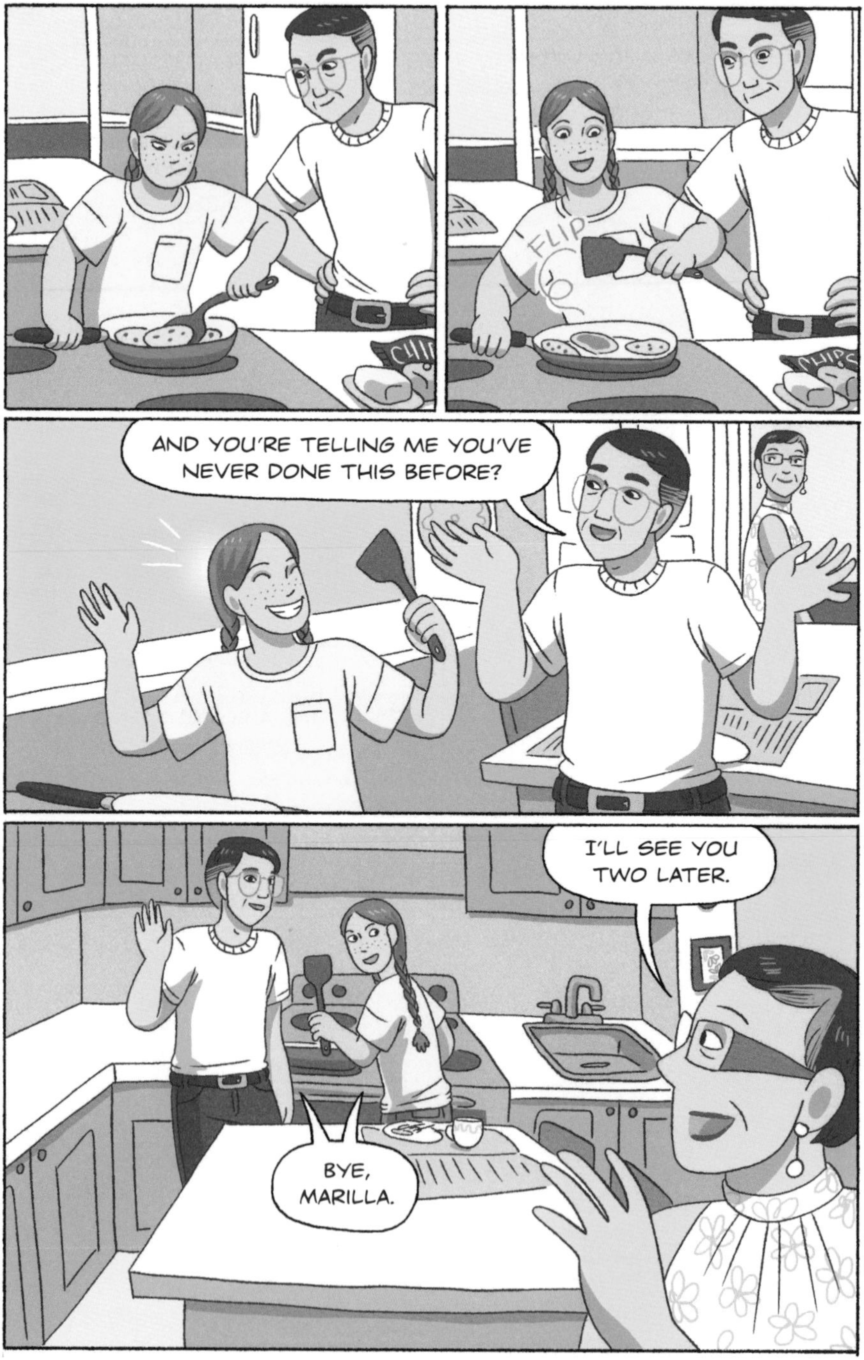
FLIP
CHIPS
AND YOU'RE TELLING ME YOU'VE NEVER DONE THIS BEFORE?
I'LL SEE YOU TWO LATER.
BYE, MARILLA.

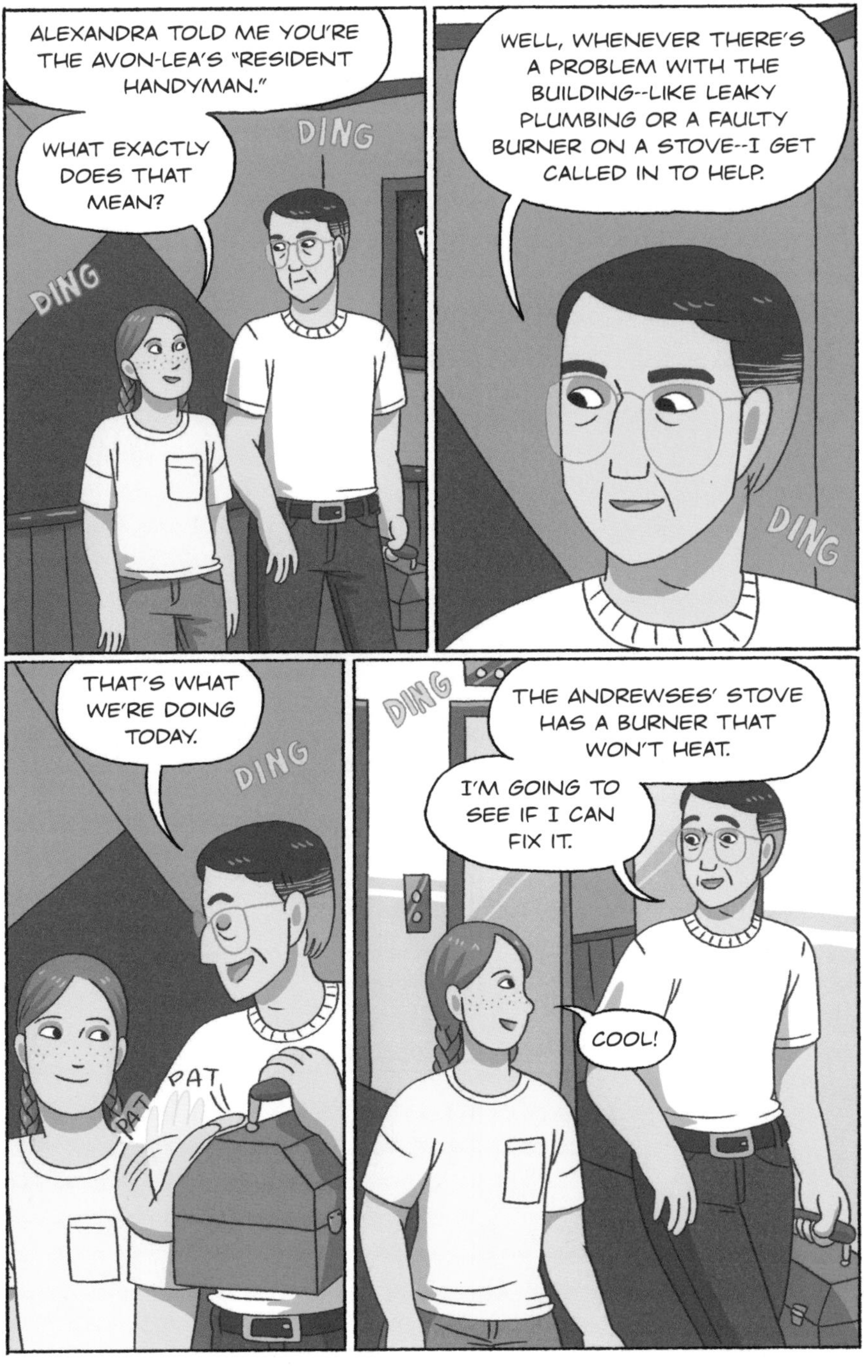
ALEXANDRA TOLD ME YOU'RE THE AVON-LEA'S "RESIDENT HANDYMAN."
WHAT EXACTLY DOES THAT MEAN?
DING
DING
WELL, WHENEVER THERE'S A PROBLEM WITH THE BUILDING--LIKE LEAKY PLUMBING OR A FAULTY BURNER ON A STOVE--I GET CALLED IN TO HELP.
DING
THAT'S WHAT WE'RE DOING TODAY.
DING
PAT
PAT
DING
THE ANDREWSES' STOVE HAS A BURNER THAT WON'T HEAT.
I'M GOING TO SEE IF I CAN FIX IT.
COOL!

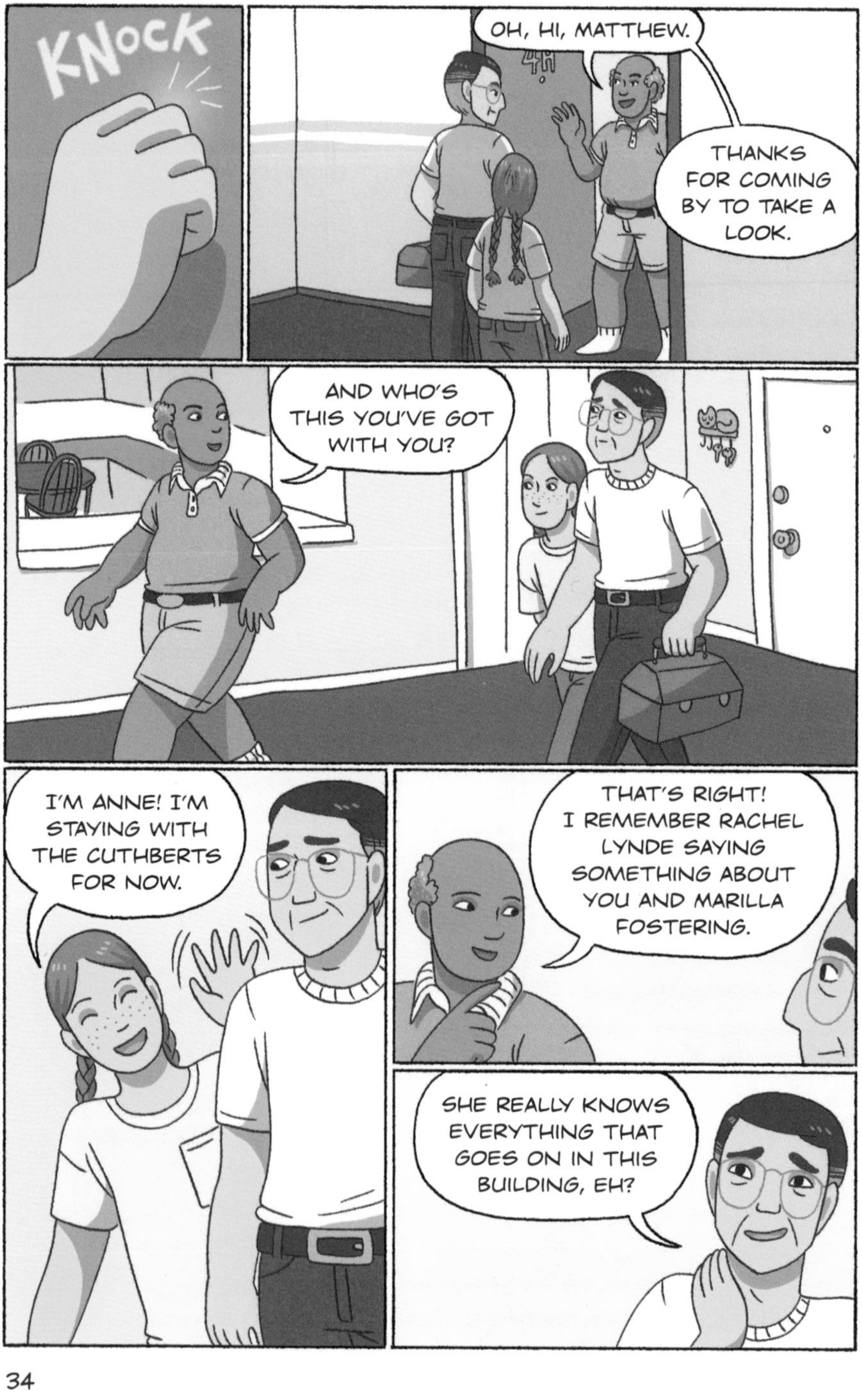
KNOCK
OH, HI, MATTHEW.
THANKS FOR COMING BY TO TAKE A LOOK.
AND WHO'S THIS YOU'VE GOT WITH YOU?
I'M ANNE! I'M STAYING WITH THE CUTHBERTS FOR NOW.
THAT'S RIGHT! I REMEMBER RACHEL LYNDE SAYING SOMETHING ABOUT YOU AND MARILLA FOSTERING.
SHE REALLY KNOWS EVERYTHING THAT GOES ON IN THIS BUILDING, EH?

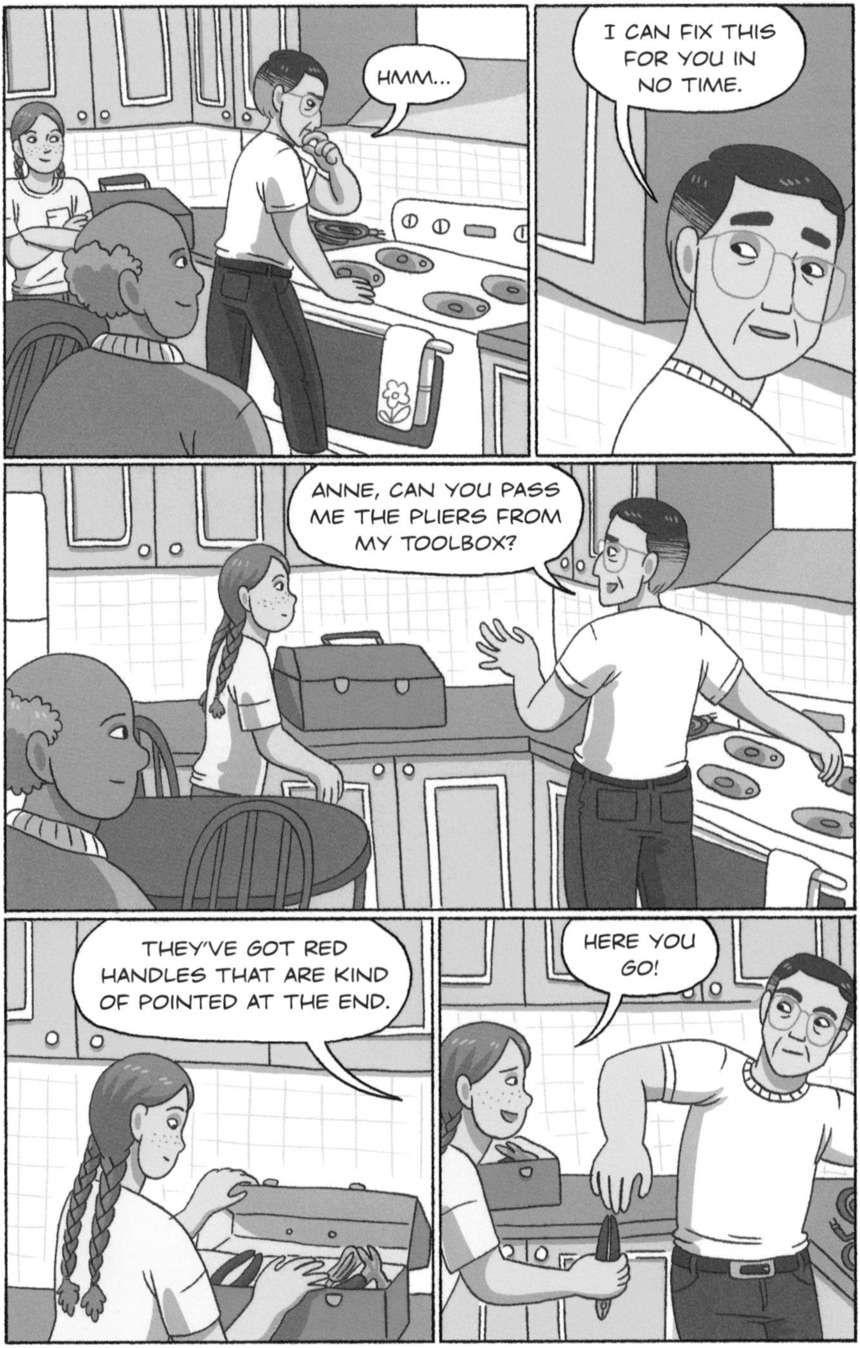
HMM...
I CAN FIX THIS FOR YOU IN NO TIME.
ANNE, CAN YOU PASS ME THE PLIERS FROM MY TOOLBOX?
THEY'VE GOT RED HANDLES THAT ARE KIND OF POINTED AT THE END.
HERE YOU GO!

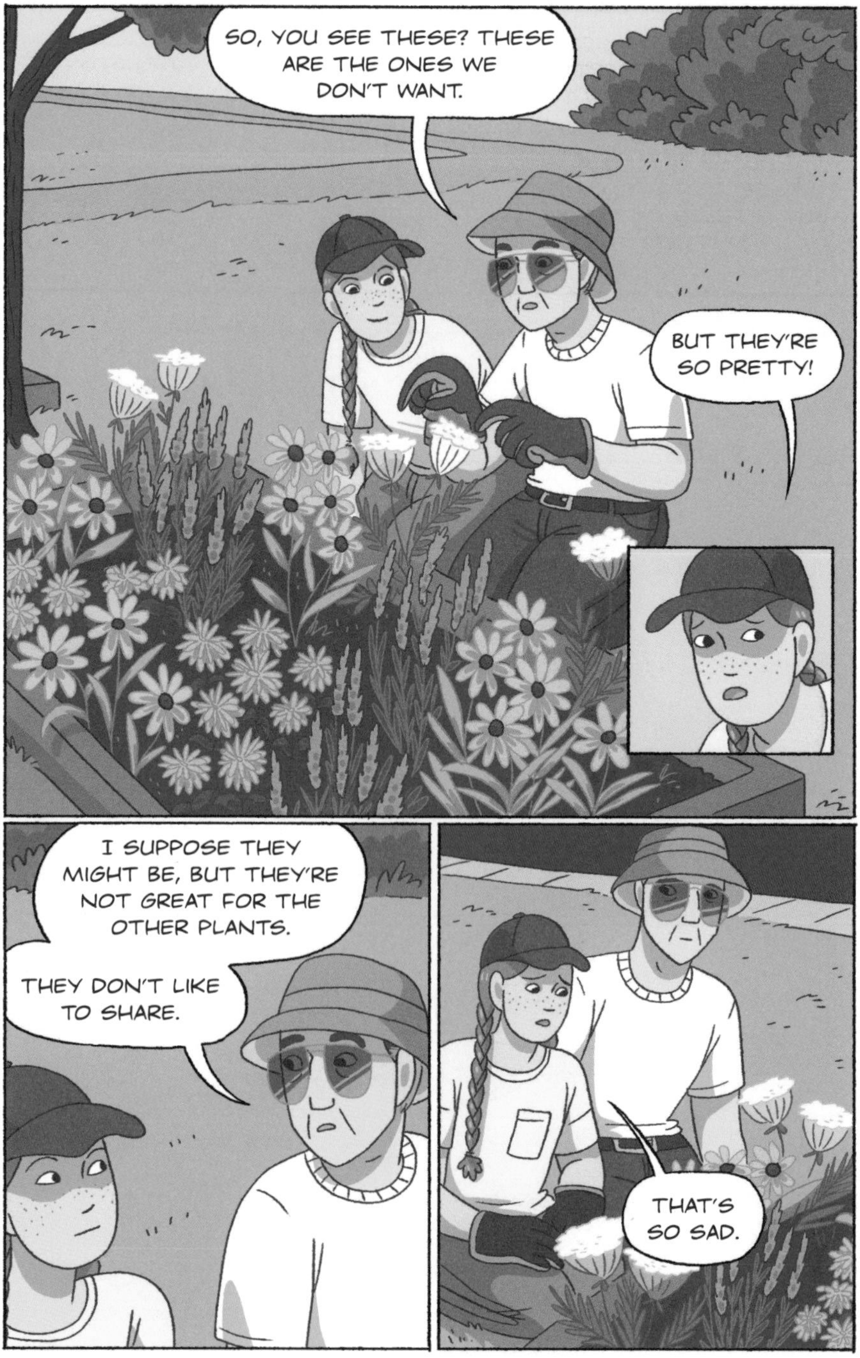
SO, YOU SEE THESE? THESE ARE THE ONES WE DON'T WANT.
BUT THEY'RE SO PRETTY!
I SUPPOSE THEY MIGHT BE, BUT THEY'RE NOT GREAT FOR THE OTHER PLANTS.
THEY DON'T LIKE TO SHARE.
THAT'S SO SAD.

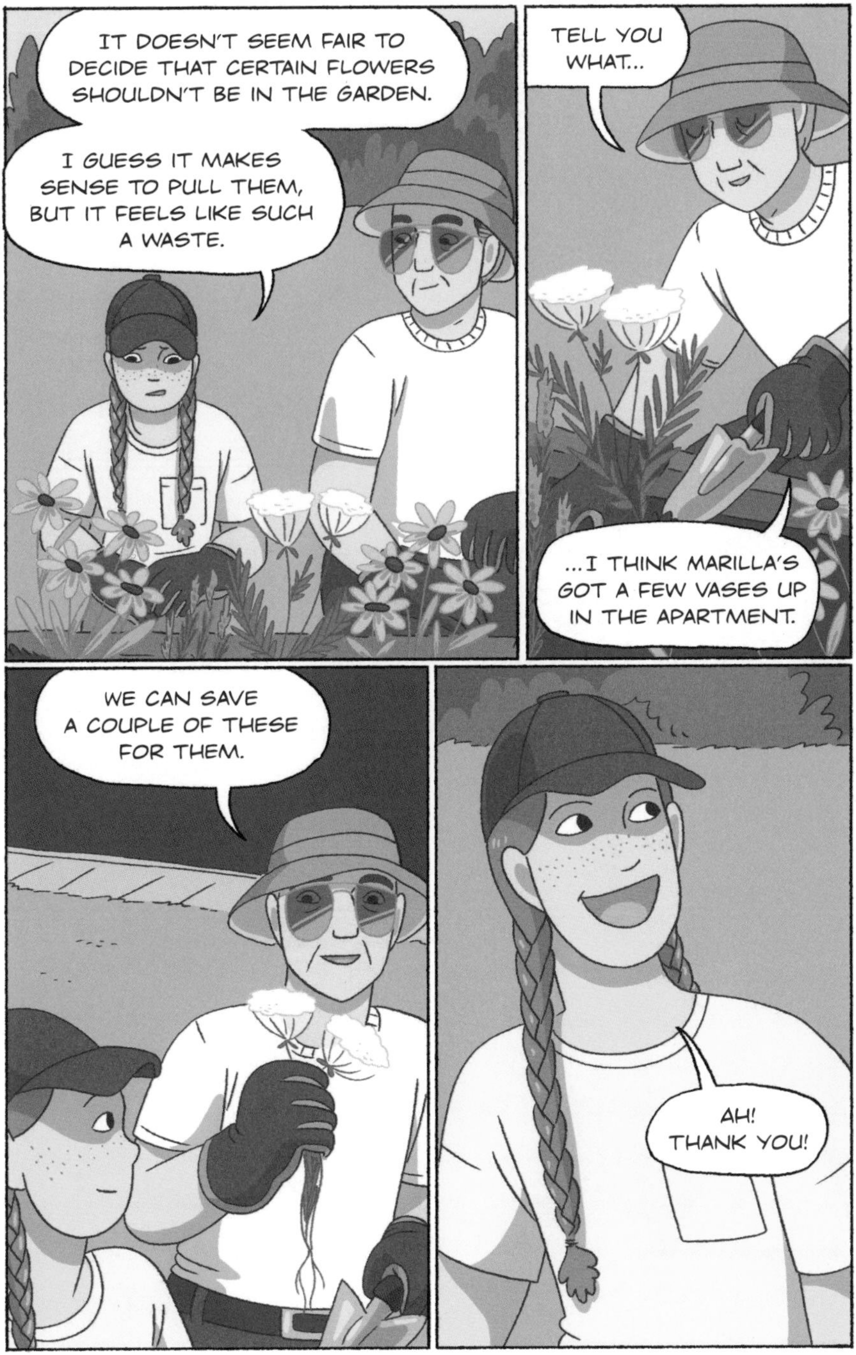
IT DOESN'T SEEM FAIR TO DECIDE THAT CERTAIN FLOWERS SHOULDN'T BE IN THE GARDEN.
I GUESS IT MAKES SENSE TO PULL THEM, BUT IT FEELS LIKE SUCH A WASTE.
TELL YOU WHAT...
...I THINK MARILLA'S GOT A FEW VASES UP IN THE APARTMENT.
WE CAN SAVE A COUPLE OF THESE FOR THEM.
AH! THANK YOU!

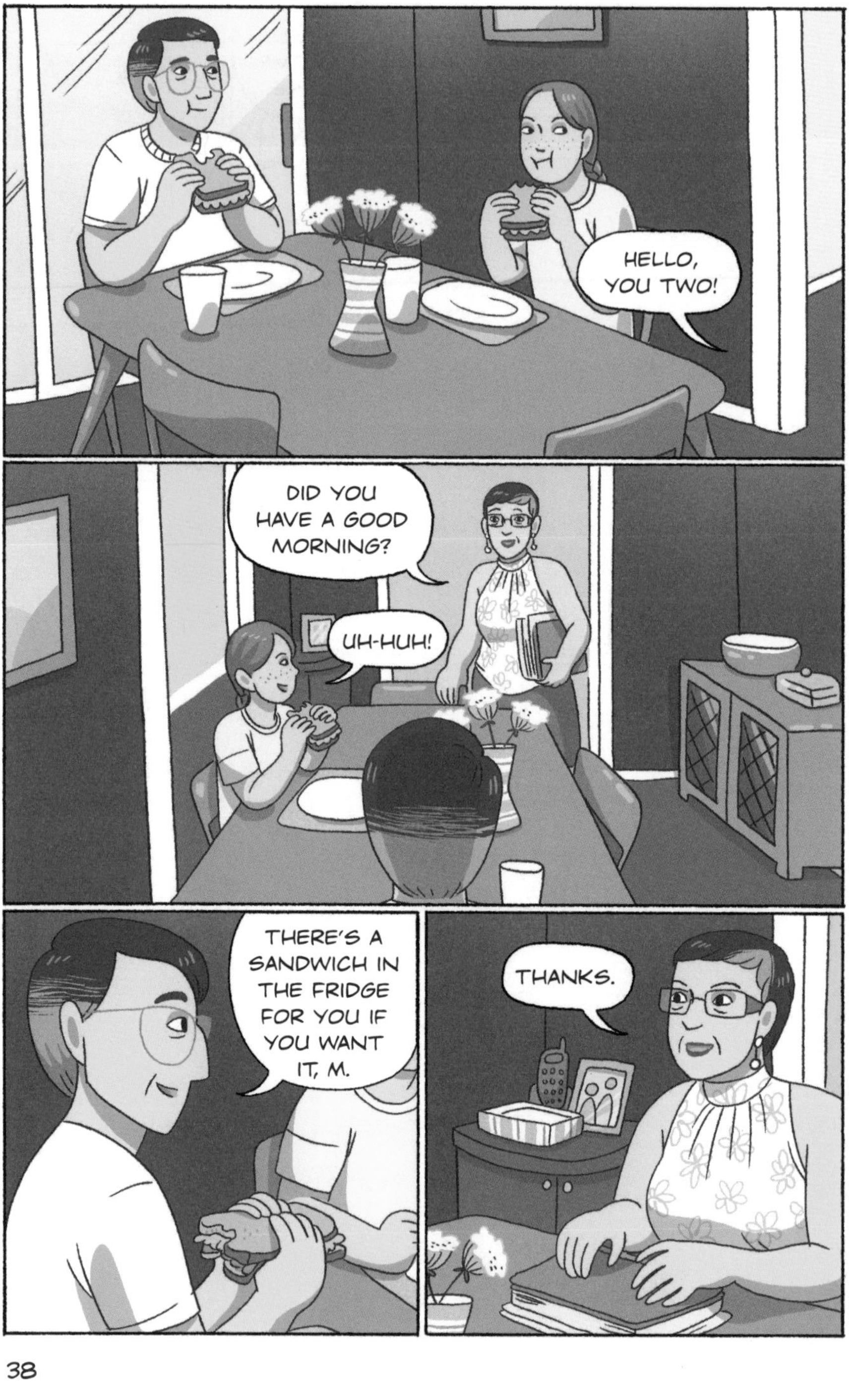
HELLO, YOU TWO!
DID YOU HAVE A GOOD MORNING?
UH-HUH!
THERE'S A SANDWICH IN THE FRIDGE FOR YOU IF YOU WANT IT, M.
THANKS.

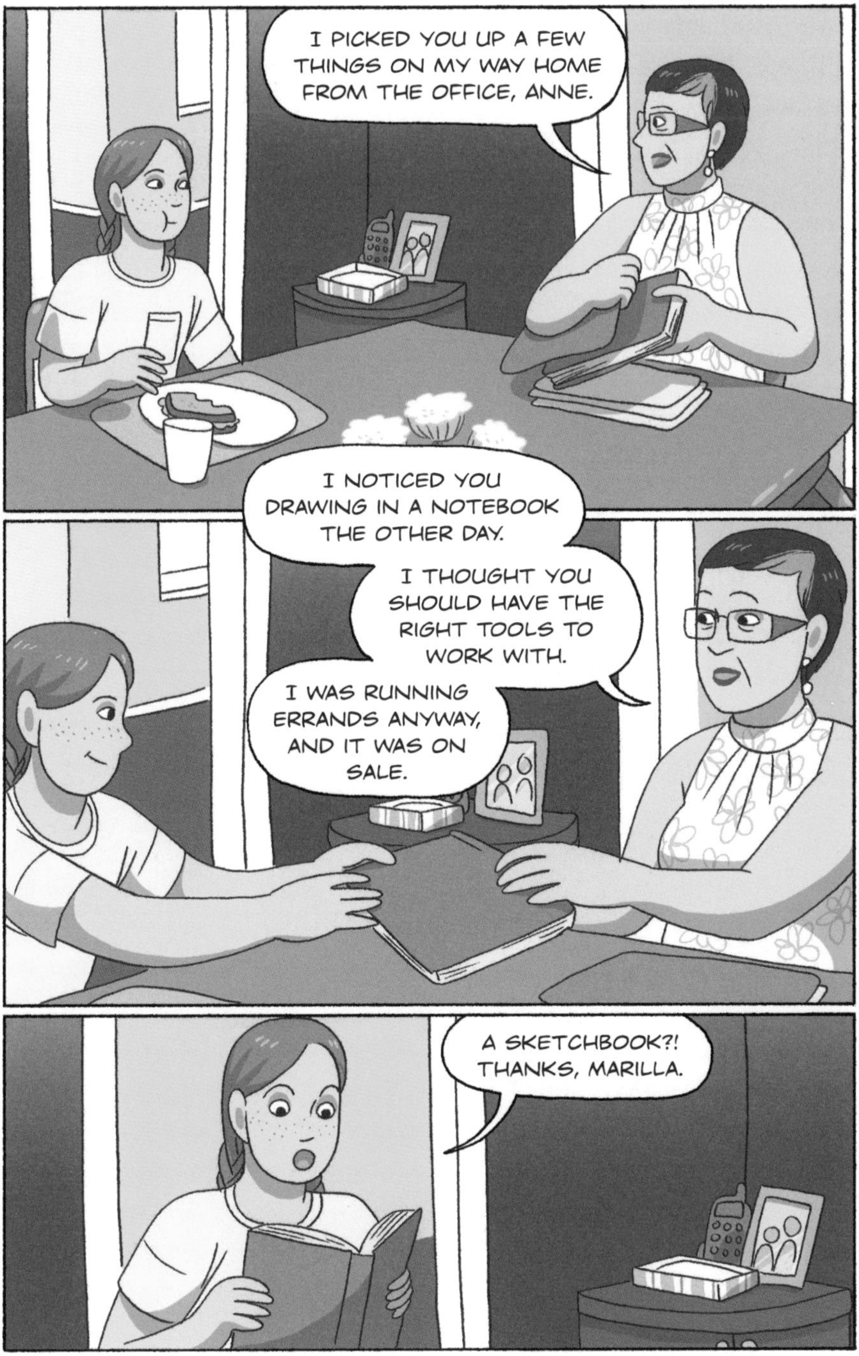
I PICKED YOU UP A FEW THINGS ON MY WAY HOME FROM THE OFFICE, ANNE.
I NOTICED YOU DRAWING IN A NOTEBOOK THE OTHER DAY.
I THOUGHT YOU SHOULD HAVE THE RIGHT TOOLS TO WORK WITH.
I WAS RUNNING ERRANDS ANYWAY, AND IT WAS ON SALE.
A SKETCHBOOK?! THANKS, MARILLA.

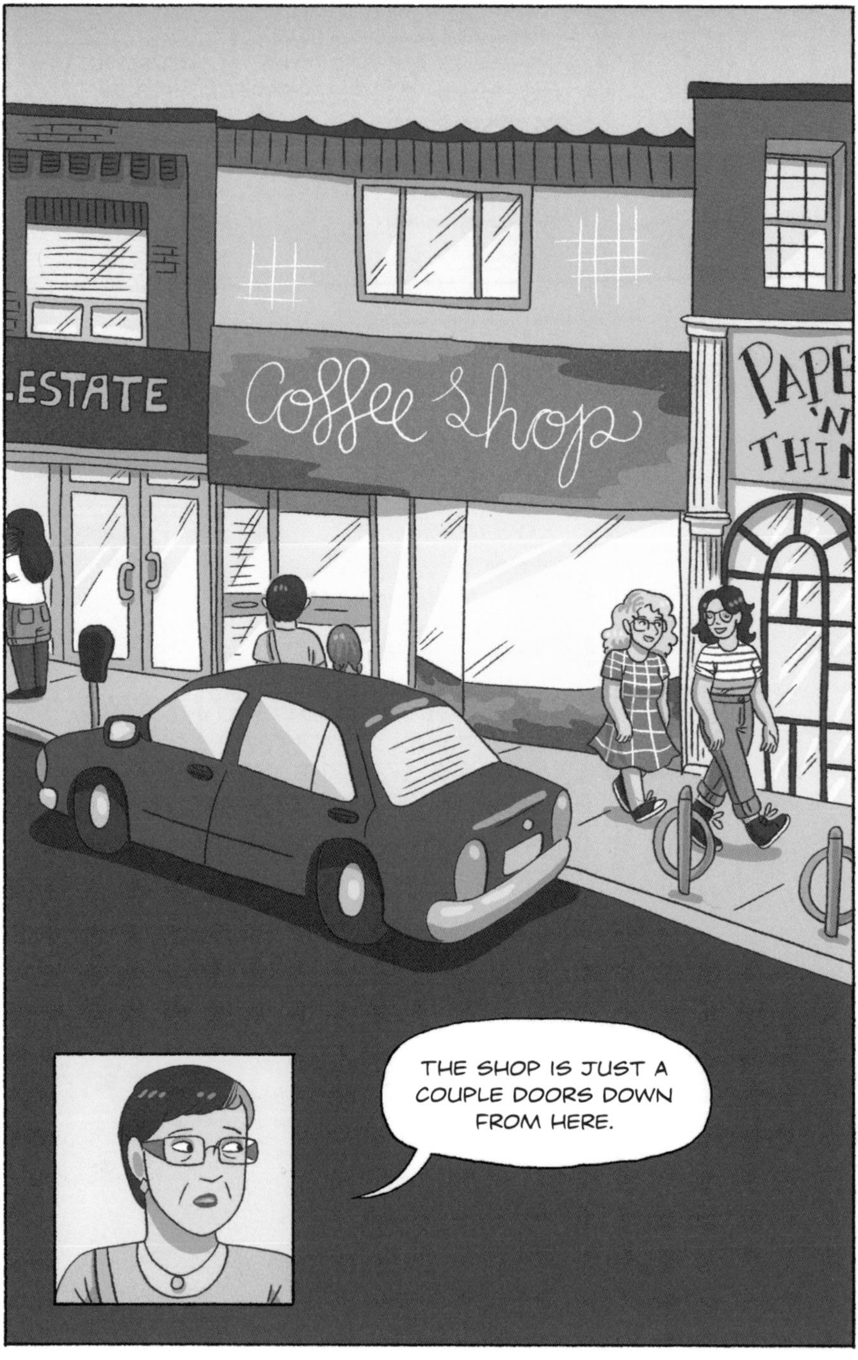
ESTATE
Coffee Shop
PAPE 'N THIN
THE SHOP IS JUST A COUPLE DOORS DOWN FROM HERE.

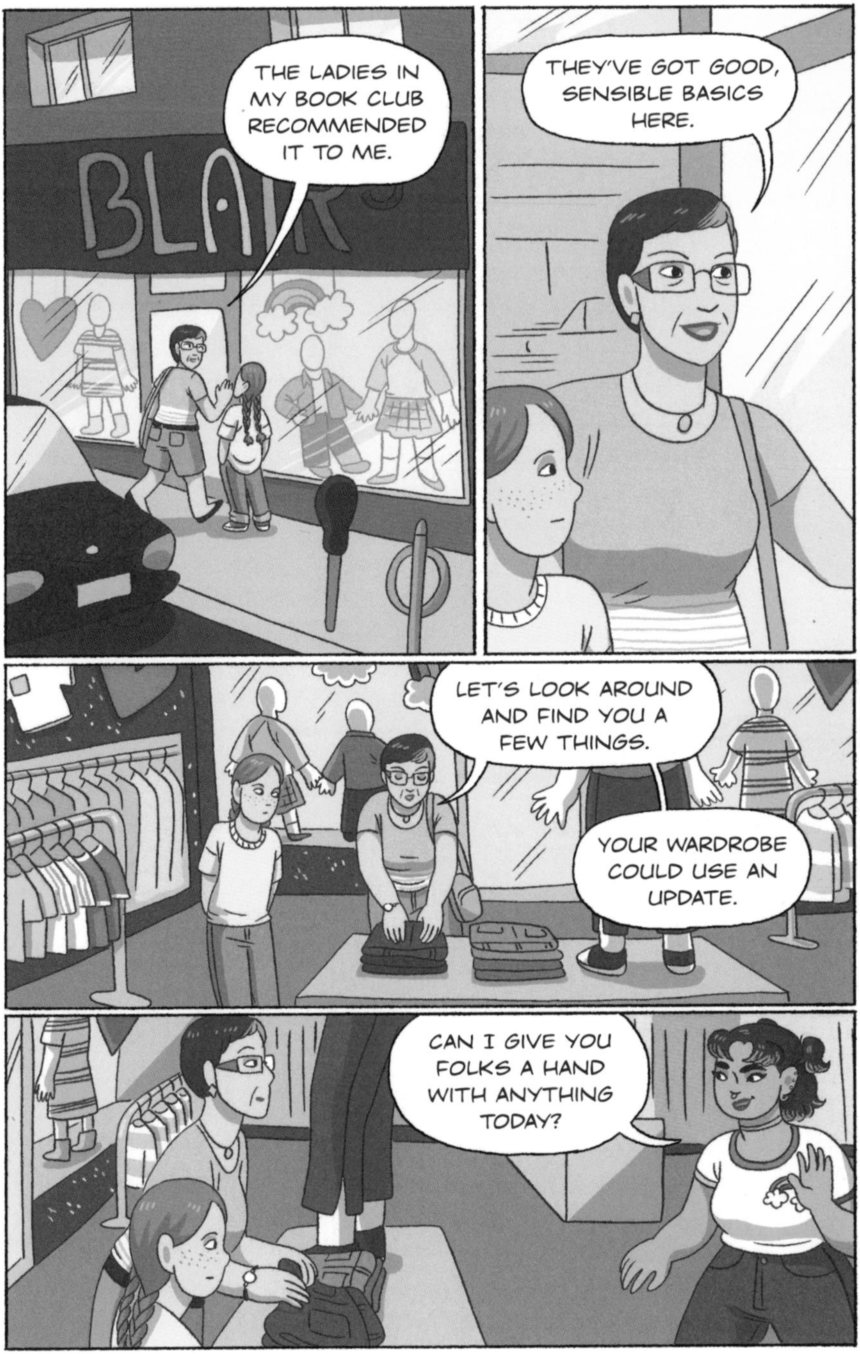
THE LADIES IN MY BOOK CLUB RECOMMENDED IT TO ME.
BLAIR'S
THEY'VE GOT GOOD, SENSIBLE BASICS HERE.
LET'S LOOK AROUND AND FIND YOU A FEW THINGS.
YOUR WARDROBE COULD USE AN UPDATE.
CAN I GIVE YOU FOLKS A HAND WITH ANYTHING TODAY?

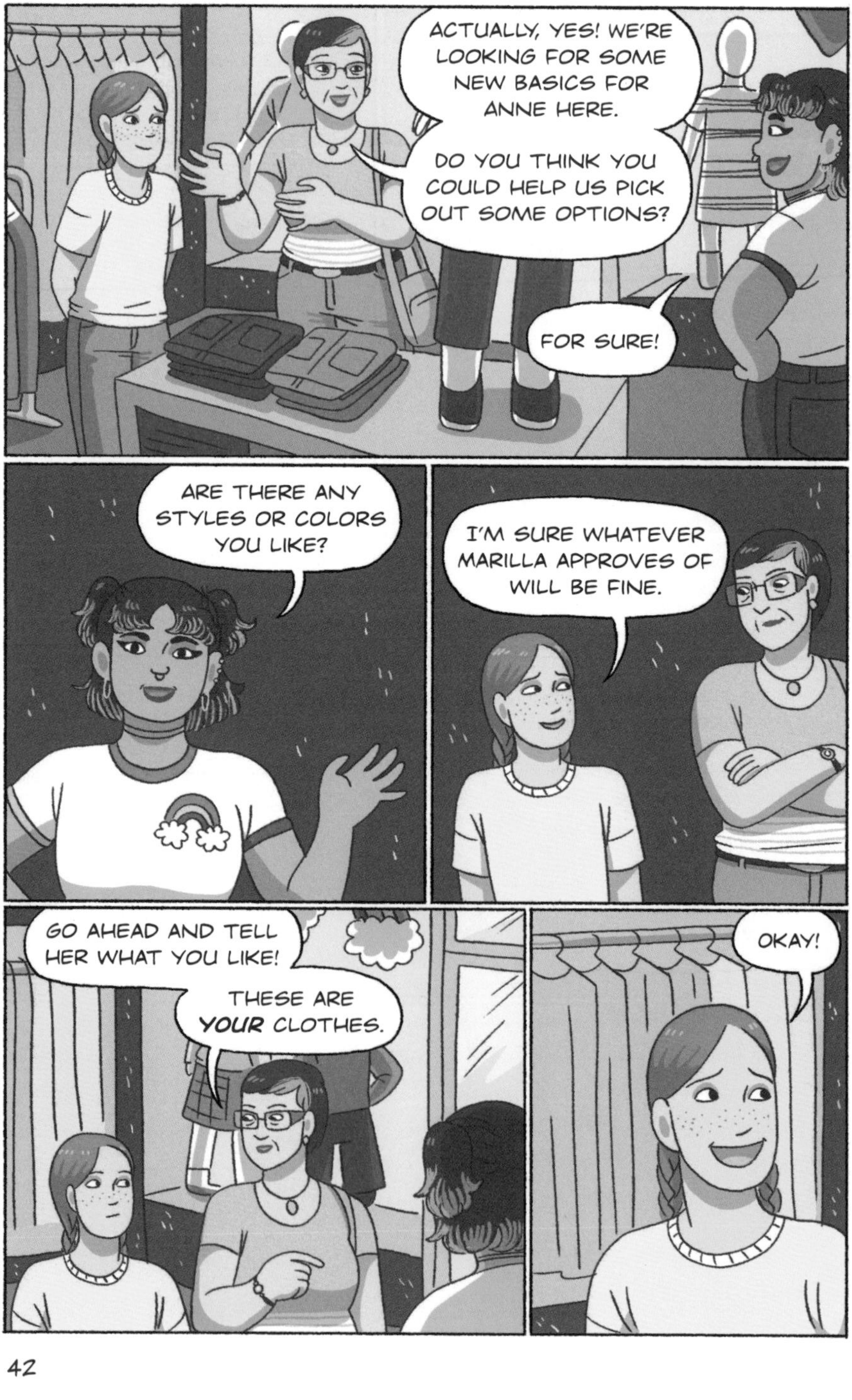
ACTUALLY, YES! WE'RE LOOKING FOR SOME NEW BASICS FOR ANNE HERE.
DO YOU THINK YOU COULD HELP US PICK OUT SOME OPTIONS?
FOR SURE!
ARE THERE ANY STYLES OR COLORS YOU LIKE?
I'M SURE WHATEVER MARILLA APPROVES OF WILL BE FINE.
GO AHEAD AND TELL HER WHAT YOU LIKE!
THESE ARE YOUR CLOTHES.
OKAY!

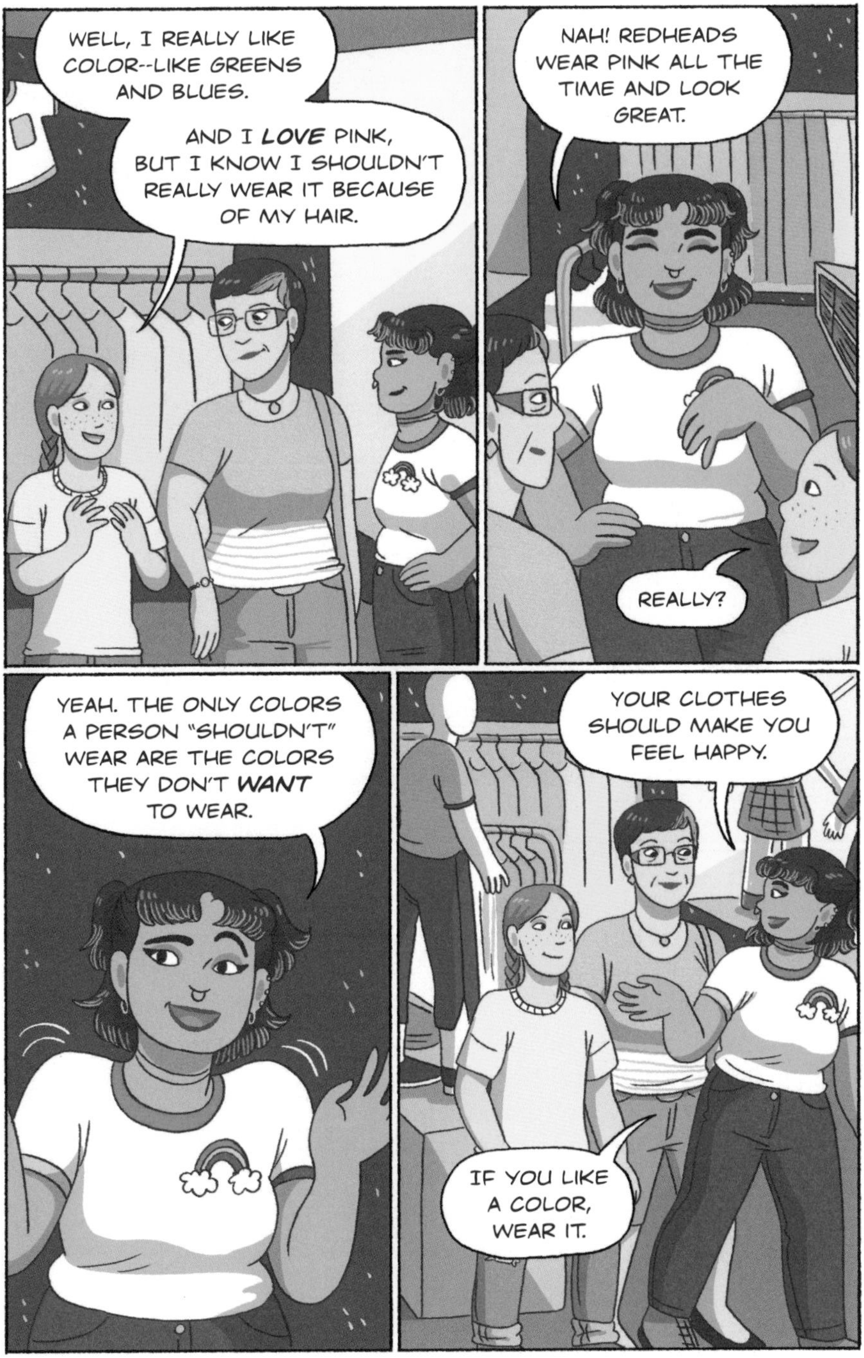
WELL, I REALLY LIKE COLOR--LIKE GREENS AND BLUES.
AND I LOVE PINK, BUT I KNOW I SHOULDN'T REALLY WEAR IT BECAUSE OF MY HAIR.
NAH! REDHEADS WEAR PINK ALL THE TIME AND LOOK GREAT.
REALLY?
YEAH. THE ONLY COLORS A PERSON "SHOULDN'T" WEAR ARE THE COLORS THEY DON'T WANT TO WEAR.
YOUR CLOTHES SHOULD MAKE YOU FEEL HAPPY.
IF YOU LIKE A COLOR, WEAR IT.

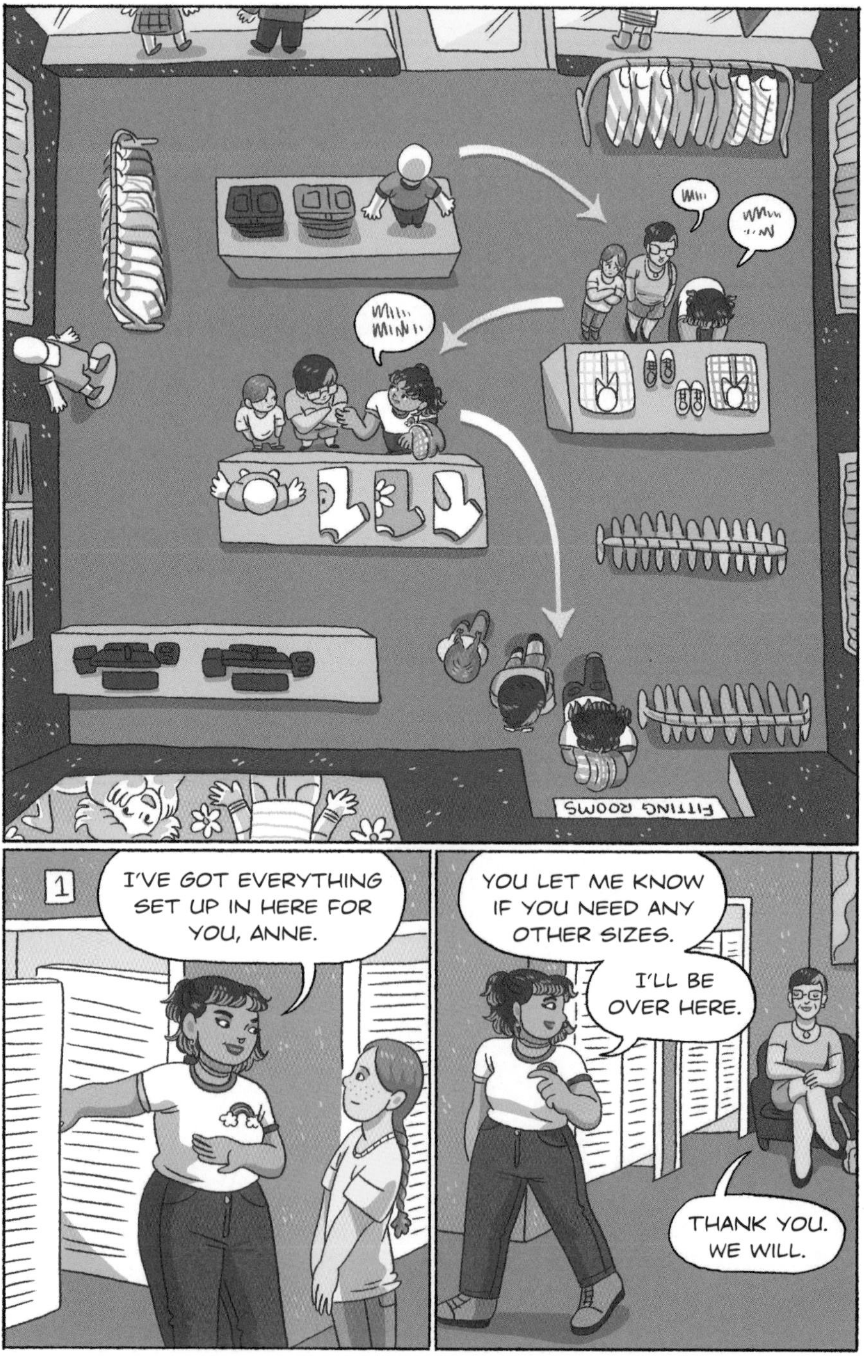
FITTING ROOMS
1
I'VE GOT EVERYTHING SET UP IN HERE FOR YOU, ANNE.
YOU LET ME KNOW IF YOU NEED ANY OTHER SIZES.
I'LL BE OVER HERE.
THANK YOU. WE WILL.

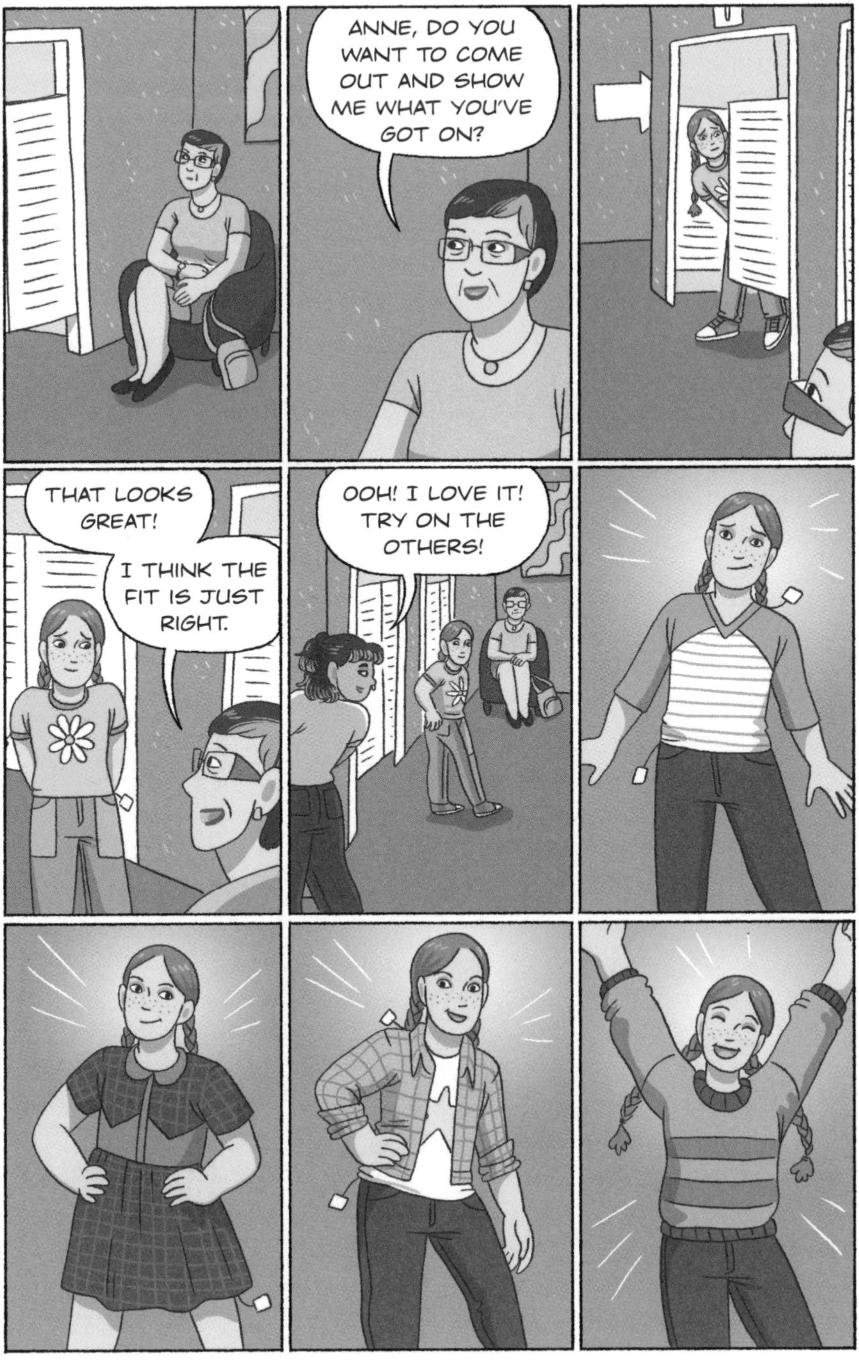
ANNE, DO YOU WANT TO COME OUT AND SHOW ME WHAT YOU'VE GOT ON?
THAT LOOKS GREAT!
I THINK THE FIT IS JUST RIGHT.
OOH! I LOVE IT! TRY ON THE OTHERS!

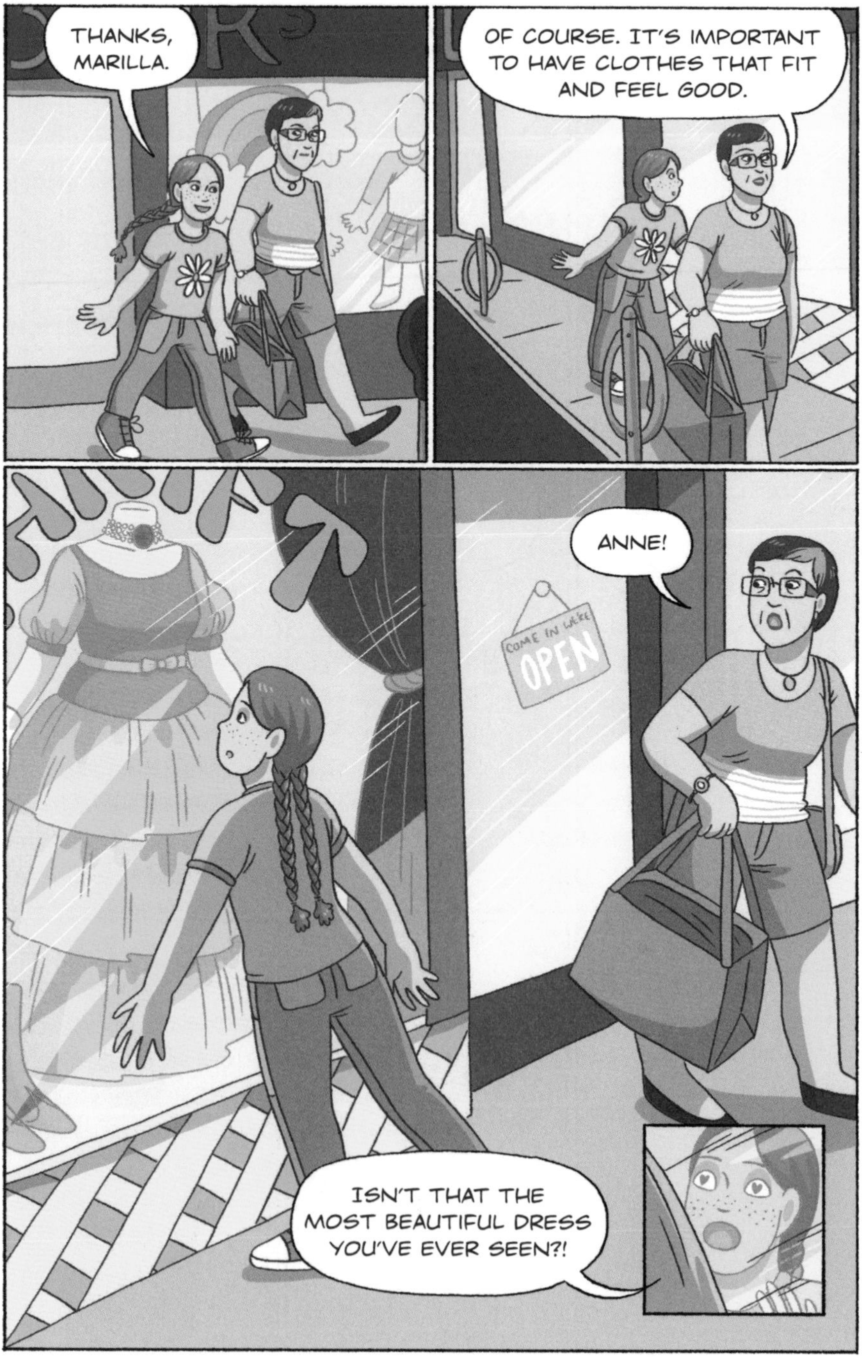
THANKS, MARILLA.
OF COURSE. IT'S IMPORTANT TO HAVE CLOTHES THAT FIT AND FEEL GOOD.
ANNE!
COME IN WE'RE OPEN
ISN'T THAT THE MOST BEAUTIFUL DRESS YOU'VE EVER SEEN?!

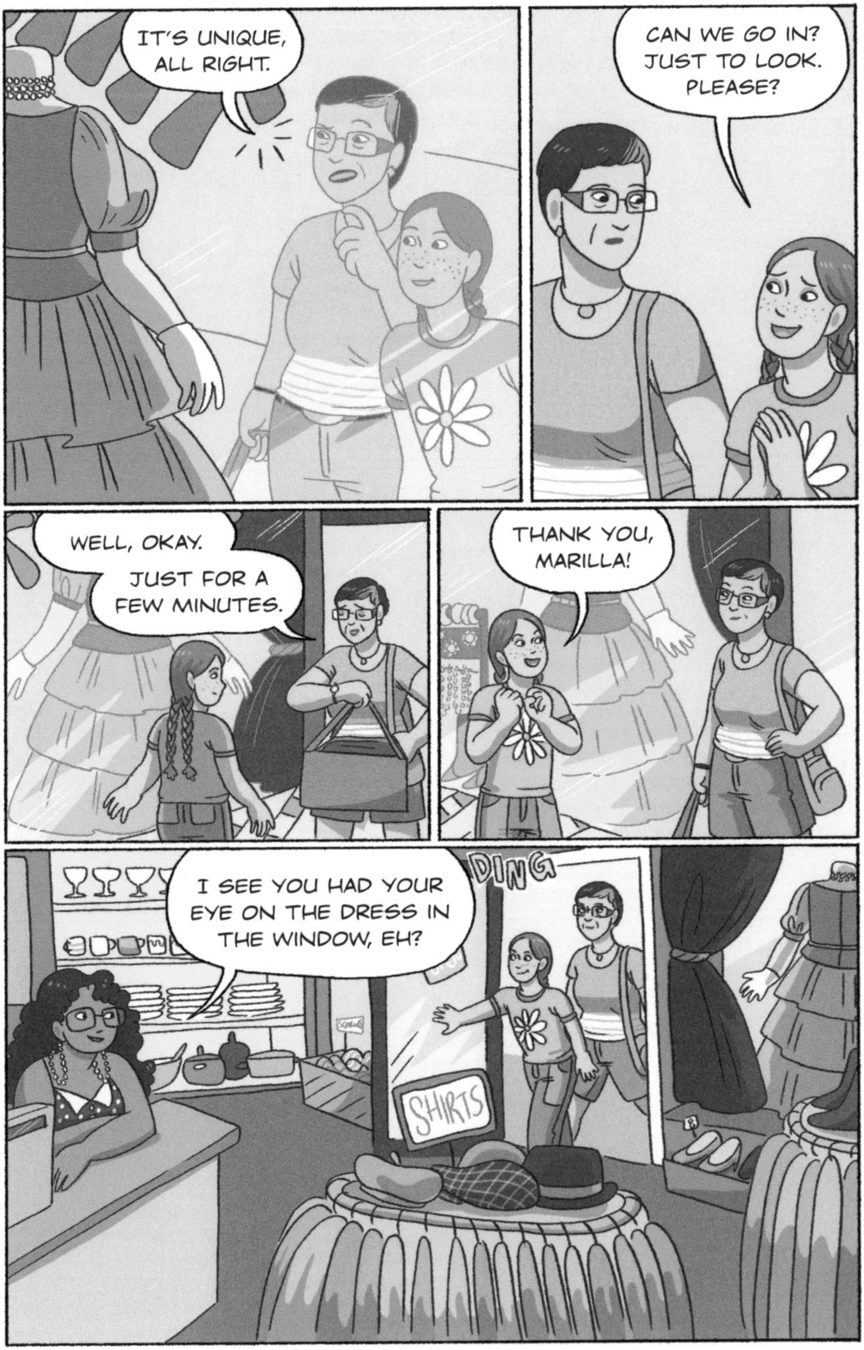
IT'S UNIQUE, ALL RIGHT.
CAN WE GO IN? JUST TO LOOK. PLEASE?
WELL, OKAY.
JUST FOR A FEW MINUTES.
THANK YOU, MARILLA!
I SEE YOU HAD YOUR EYE ON THE DRESS IN THE WINDOW, EH?
DING
SHIRTS

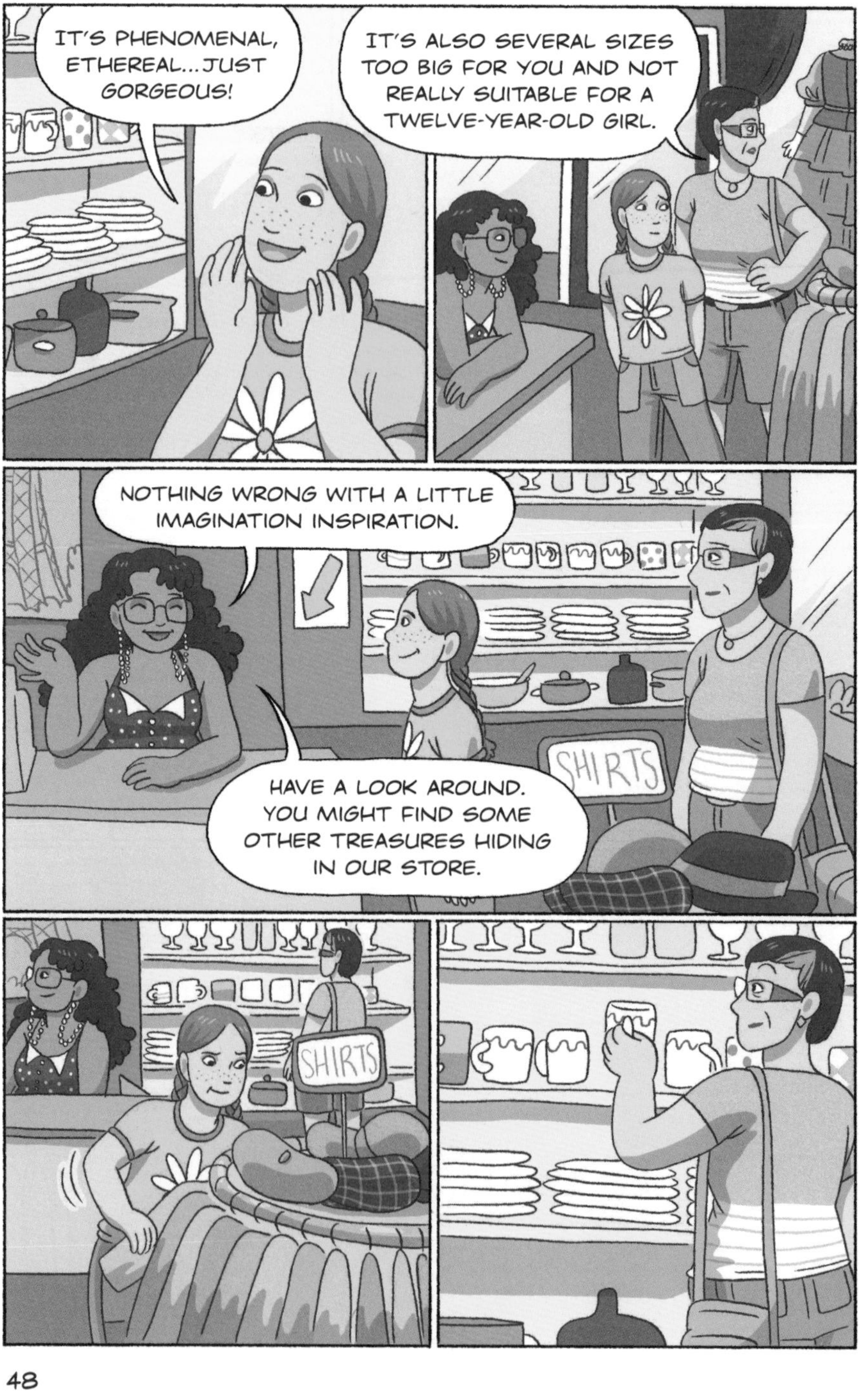
IT'S PHENOMENAL, ETHEREAL...JUST GORGEOUS!
IT'S ALSO SEVERAL SIZES TOO BIG FOR YOU AND NOT REALLY SUITABLE FOR A TWELVE-YEAR-OLD GIRL.
NOTHING WRONG WITH A LITTLE IMAGINATION INSPIRATION.
HAVE A LOOK AROUND. YOU MIGHT FIND SOME OTHER TREASURES HIDING IN OUR STORE.
SHIRTS
SHIRTS

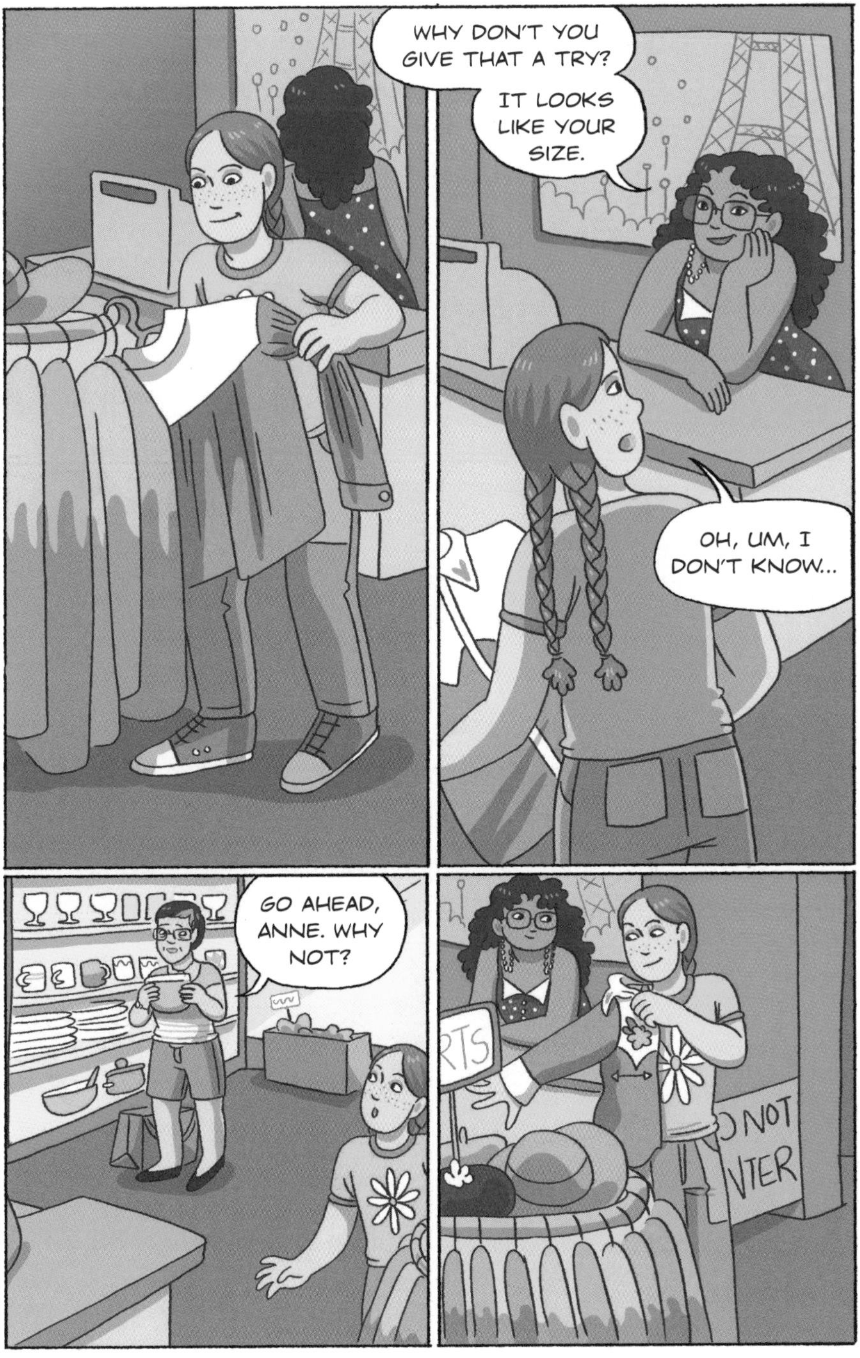
WHY DON'T YOU GIVE THAT A TRY?
IT LOOKS LIKE YOUR SIZE.
OH, UM, I DON'T KNOW...
GO AHEAD, ANNE. WHY NOT?

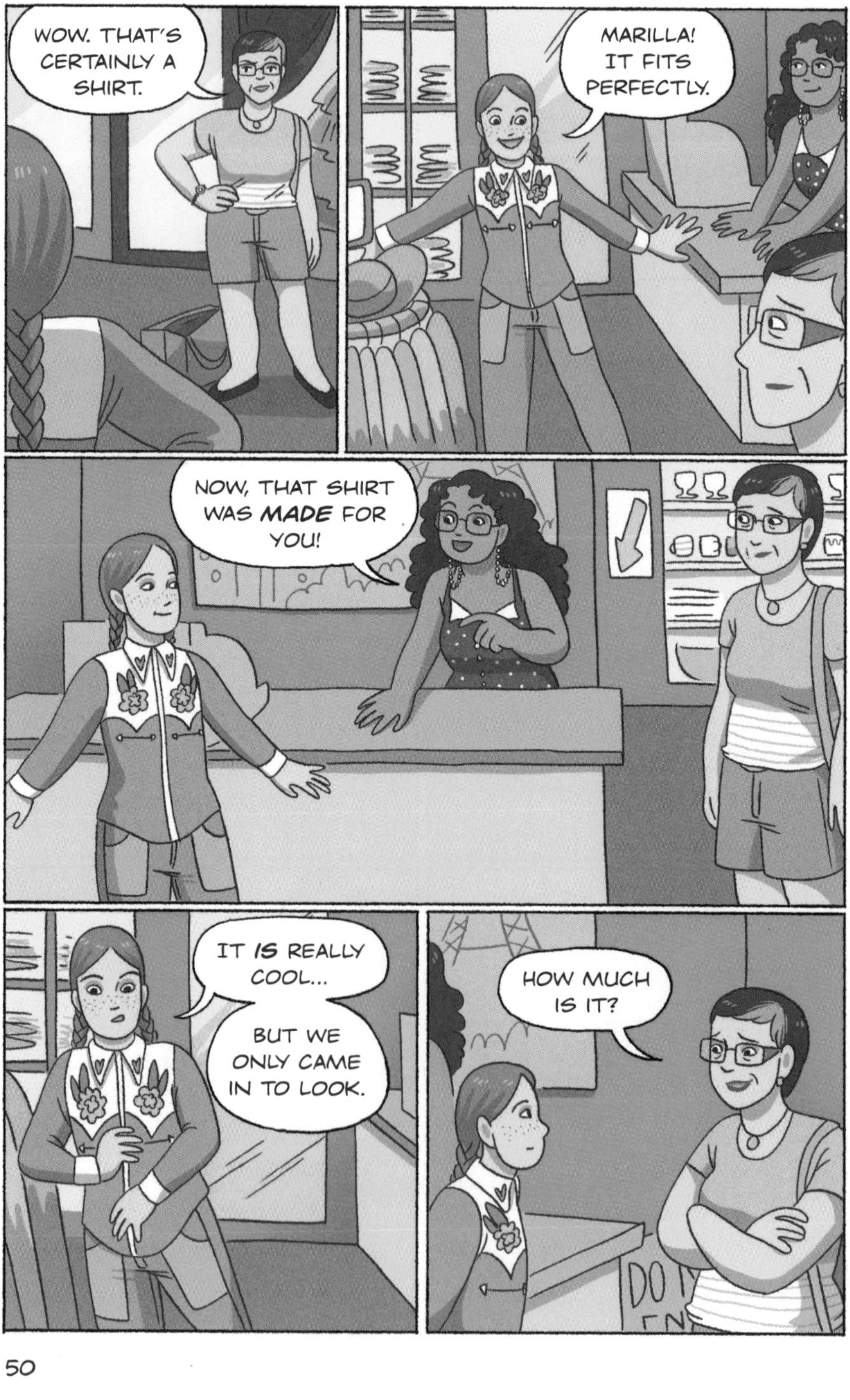
WOW. THAT'S CERTAINLY A SHIRT.
MARILLA! IT FITS PERFECTLY.
NOW, THAT SHIRT WAS **MADE** FOR YOU!
IT **IS** REALLY COOL...
BUT WE ONLY CAME IN TO LOOK.
HOW MUCH IS IT?

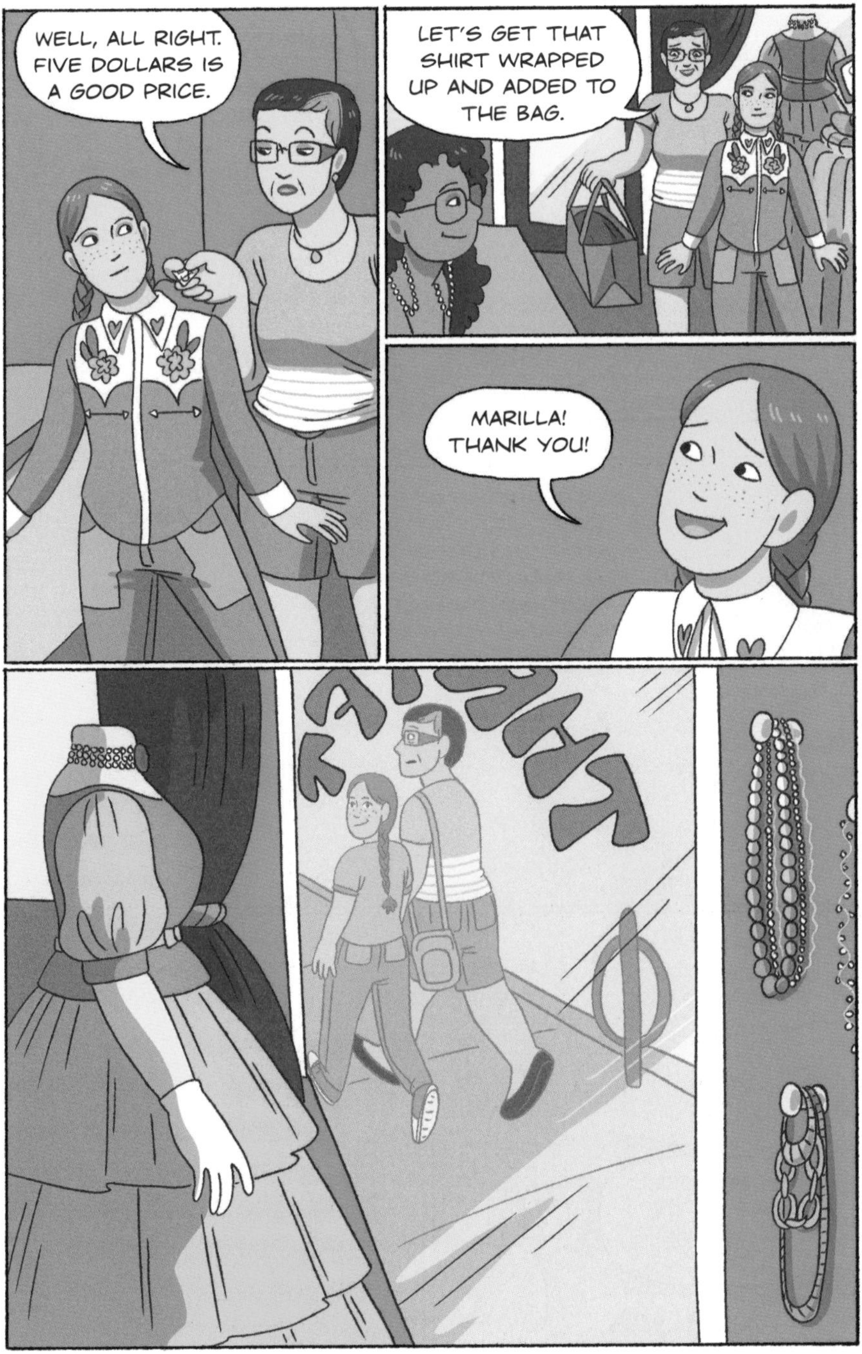
WELL, ALL RIGHT. FIVE DOLLARS IS A GOOD PRICE.
LET'S GET THAT SHIRT WRAPPED UP AND ADDED TO THE BAG.
MARILLA! THANK YOU!

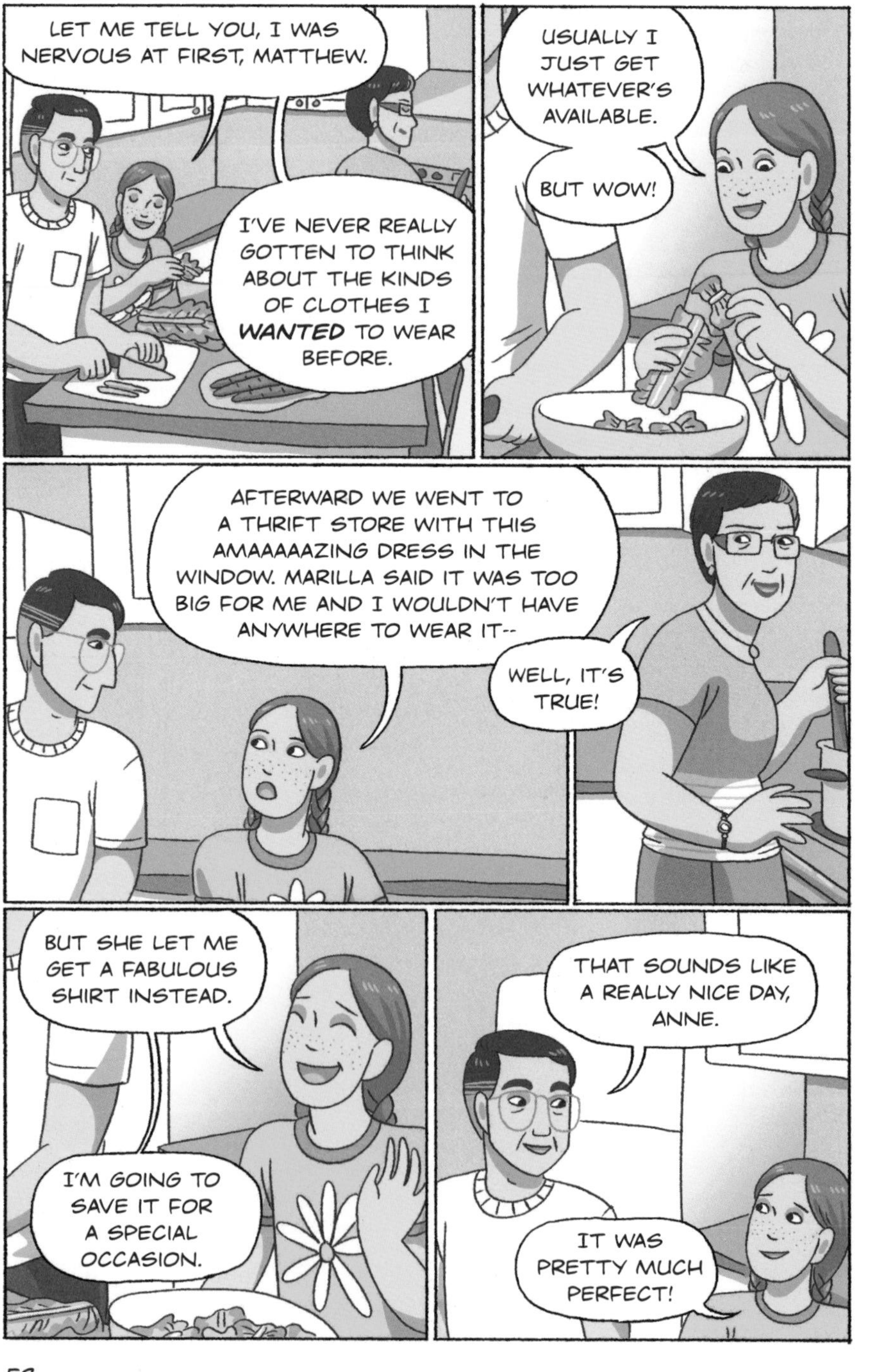
LET ME TELL YOU, I WAS NERVOUS AT FIRST, MATTHEW.
I'VE NEVER REALLY GOTTEN TO THINK ABOUT THE KINDS OF CLOTHES I *WANTED* TO WEAR BEFORE.
USUALLY I JUST GET WHATEVER'S AVAILABLE.
BUT WOW!
AFTERWARD WE WENT TO A THRIFT STORE WITH THIS AMAAAAAZING DRESS IN THE WINDOW. MARILLA SAID IT WAS TOO BIG FOR ME AND I WOULDN'T HAVE ANYWHERE TO WEAR IT--
WELL, IT'S TRUE!
BUT SHE LET ME GET A FABULOUS SHIRT INSTEAD.
I'M GOING TO SAVE IT FOR A SPECIAL OCCASION.
THAT SOUNDS LIKE A REALLY NICE DAY, ANNE.
IT WAS PRETTY MUCH PERFECT!

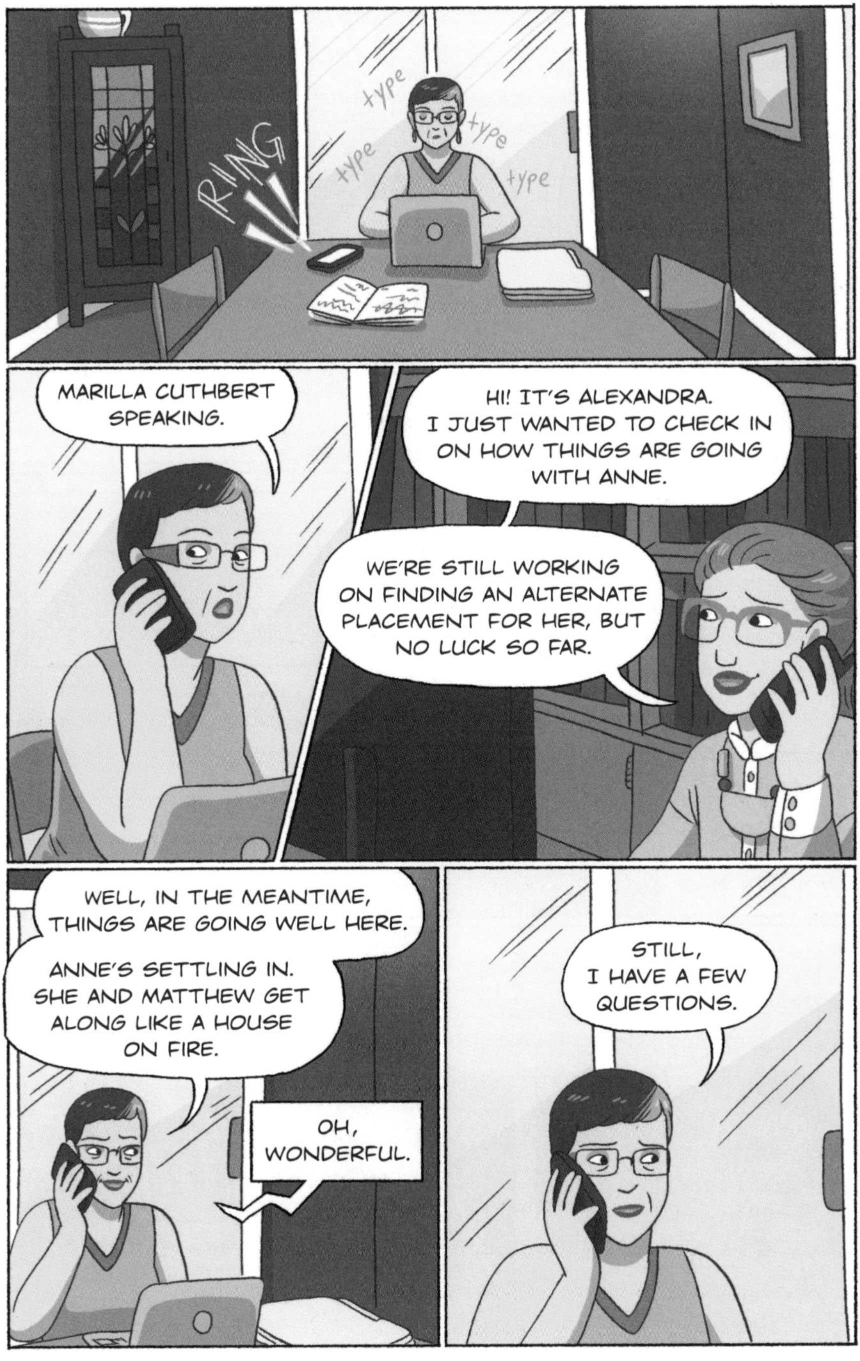
type
type
type
type
RING
MARILLA CUTHBERT SPEAKING.
HI! IT'S ALEXANDRA. I JUST WANTED TO CHECK IN ON HOW THINGS ARE GOING WITH ANNE.
WE'RE STILL WORKING ON FINDING AN ALTERNATE PLACEMENT FOR HER, BUT NO LUCK SO FAR.
WELL, IN THE MEANTIME, THINGS ARE GOING WELL HERE.
ANNE'S SETTLING IN. SHE AND MATTHEW GET ALONG LIKE A HOUSE ON FIRE.
OH, WONDERFUL.
STILL, I HAVE A FEW QUESTIONS.

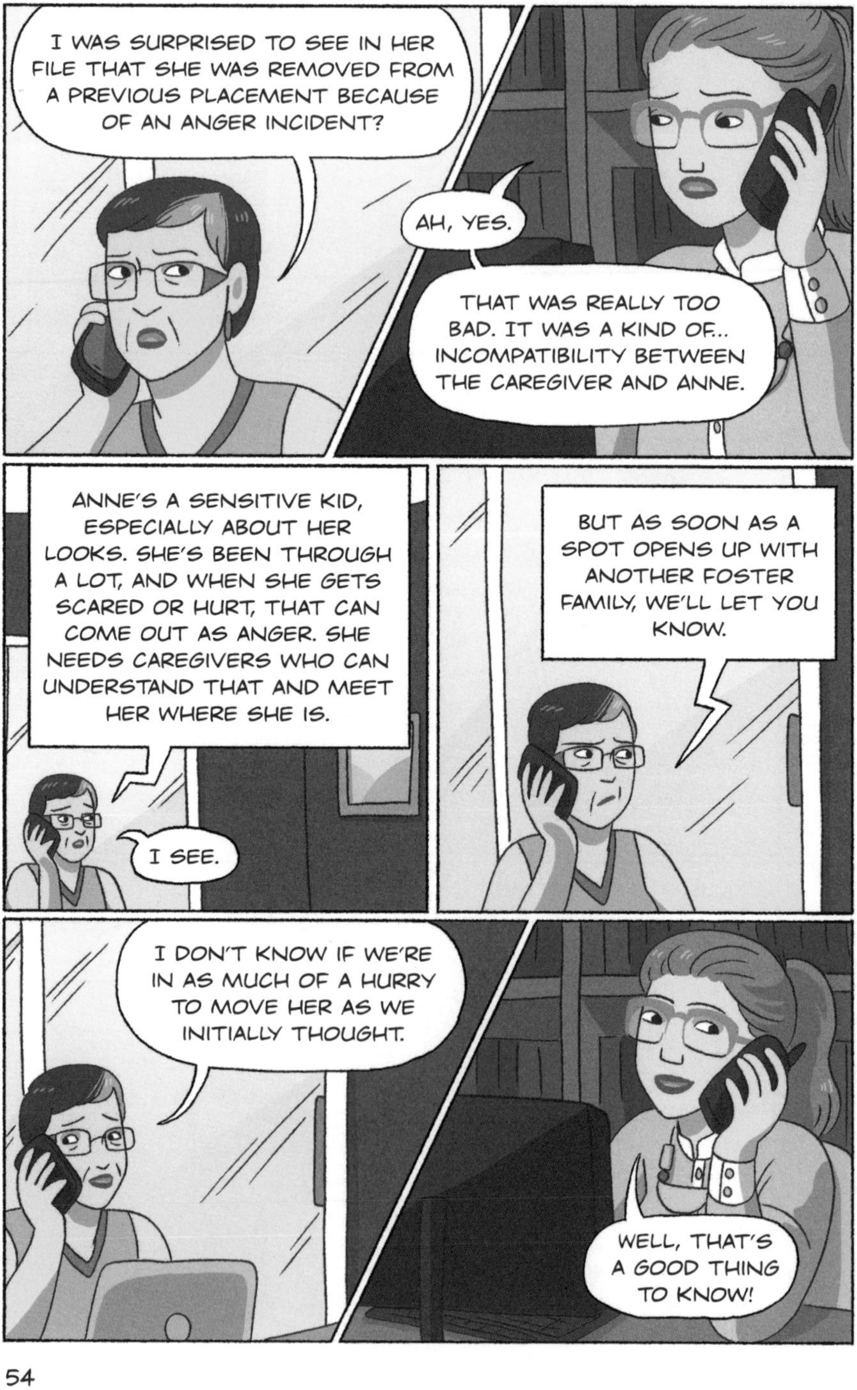
I WAS SURPRISED TO SEE IN HER FILE THAT SHE WAS REMOVED FROM A PREVIOUS PLACEMENT BECAUSE OF AN ANGER INCIDENT?
AH, YES.
THAT WAS REALLY TOO BAD. IT WAS A KIND OF... INCOMPATIBILITY BETWEEN THE CAREGIVER AND ANNE.
ANNE'S A SENSITIVE KID, ESPECIALLY ABOUT HER LOOKS. SHE'S BEEN THROUGH A LOT, AND WHEN SHE GETS SCARED OR HURT, THAT CAN COME OUT AS ANGER. SHE NEEDS CAREGIVERS WHO CAN UNDERSTAND THAT AND MEET HER WHERE SHE IS.
I SEE.
BUT AS SOON AS A SPOT OPENS UP WITH ANOTHER FOSTER FAMILY, WE'LL LET YOU KNOW.
I DON'T KNOW IF WE'RE IN AS MUCH OF A HURRY TO MOVE HER AS WE INITIALLY THOUGHT.
WELL, THAT'S A GOOD THING TO KNOW!

CHAPTER 3

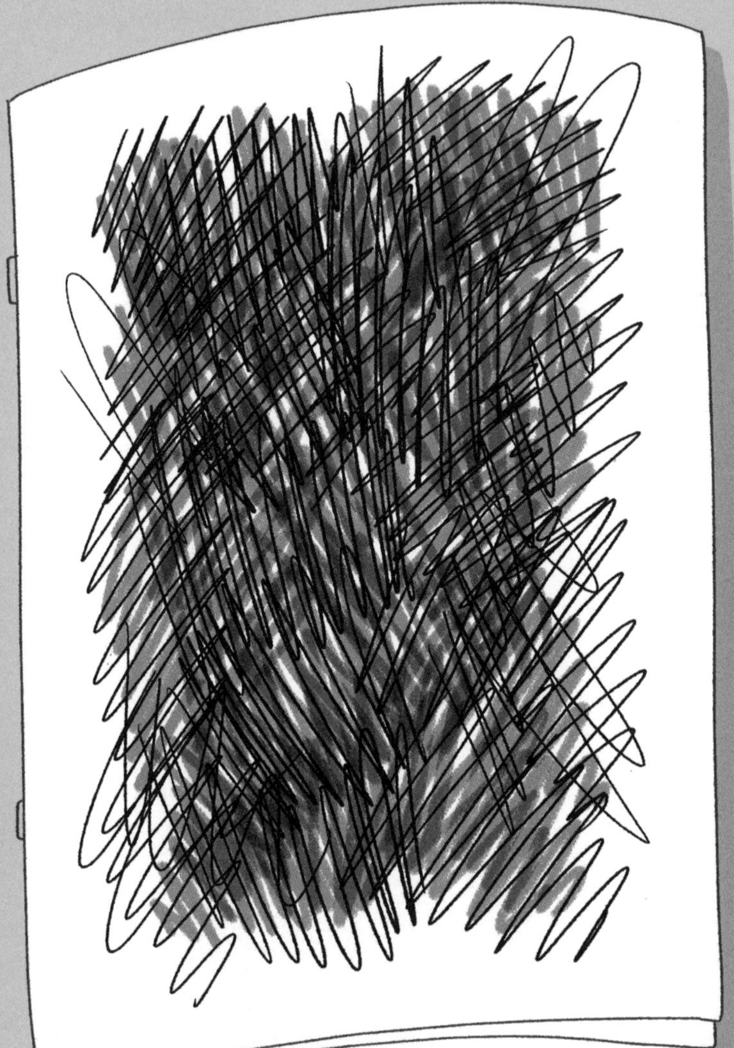

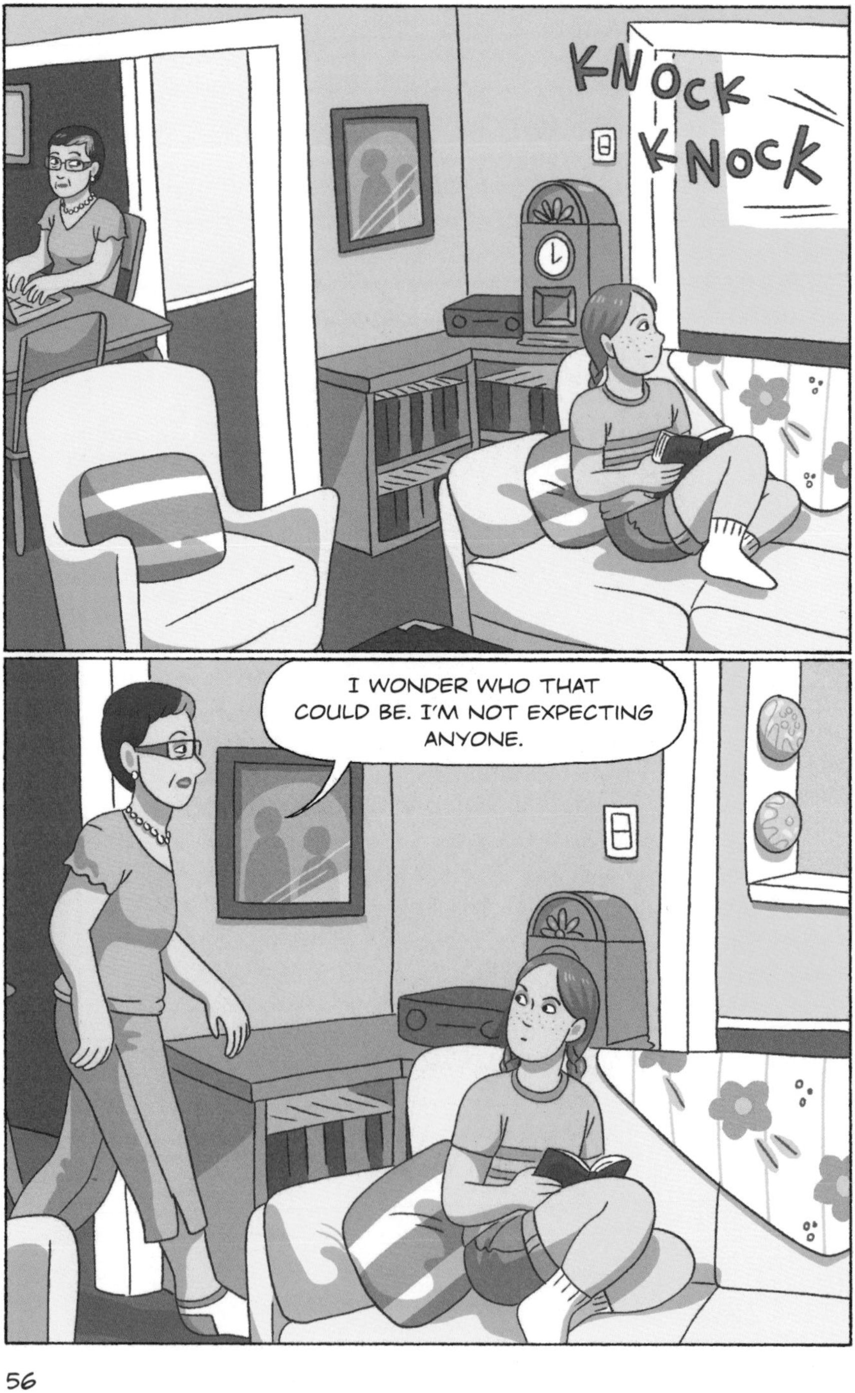
KNOCK KNOCK
I WONDER WHO THAT COULD BE. I'M NOT EXPECTING ANYONE.

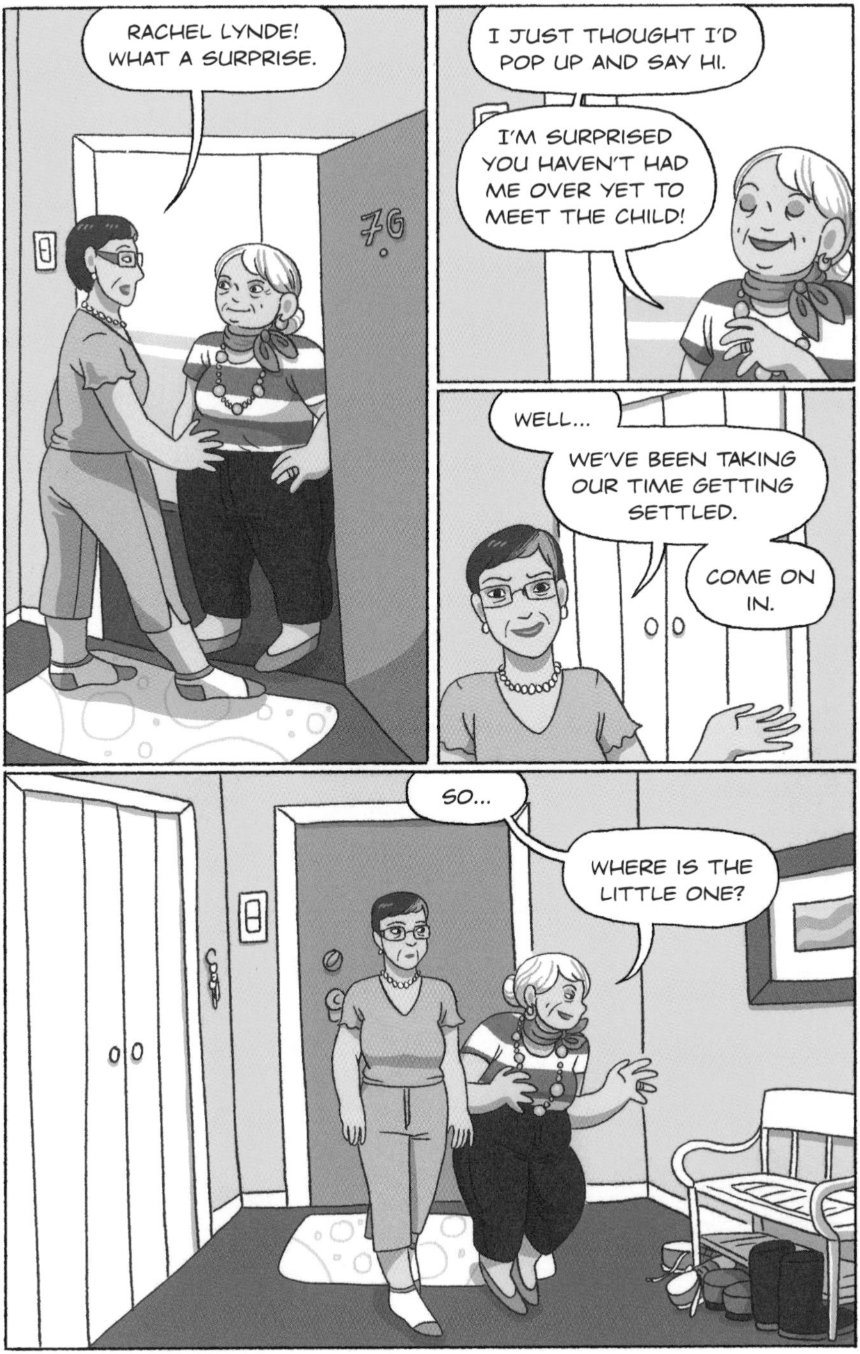
RACHEL LYNDE! WHAT A SURPRISE.
7G
I JUST THOUGHT I'D POP UP AND SAY HI.
I'M SURPRISED YOU HAVEN'T HAD ME OVER YET TO MEET THE CHILD!
WELL...
WE'VE BEEN TAKING OUR TIME GETTING SETTLED.
COME ON IN.
SO...
WHERE IS THE LITTLE ONE?

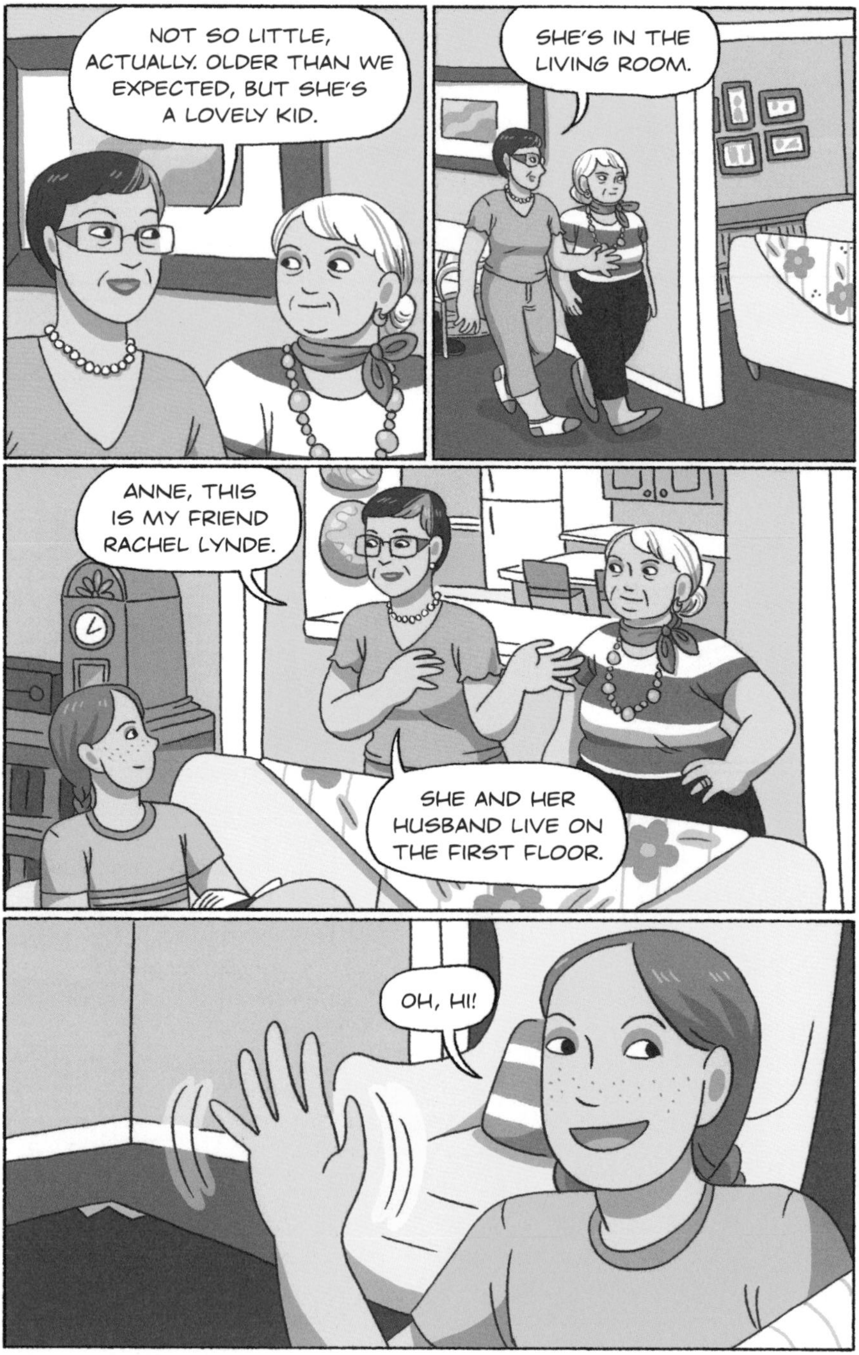
NOT SO LITTLE, ACTUALLY. OLDER THAN WE EXPECTED, BUT SHE'S A LOVELY KID.
SHE'S IN THE LIVING ROOM.
ANNE, THIS IS MY FRIEND RACHEL LYNDE.
SHE AND HER HUSBAND LIVE ON THE FIRST FLOOR.
OH, HI!

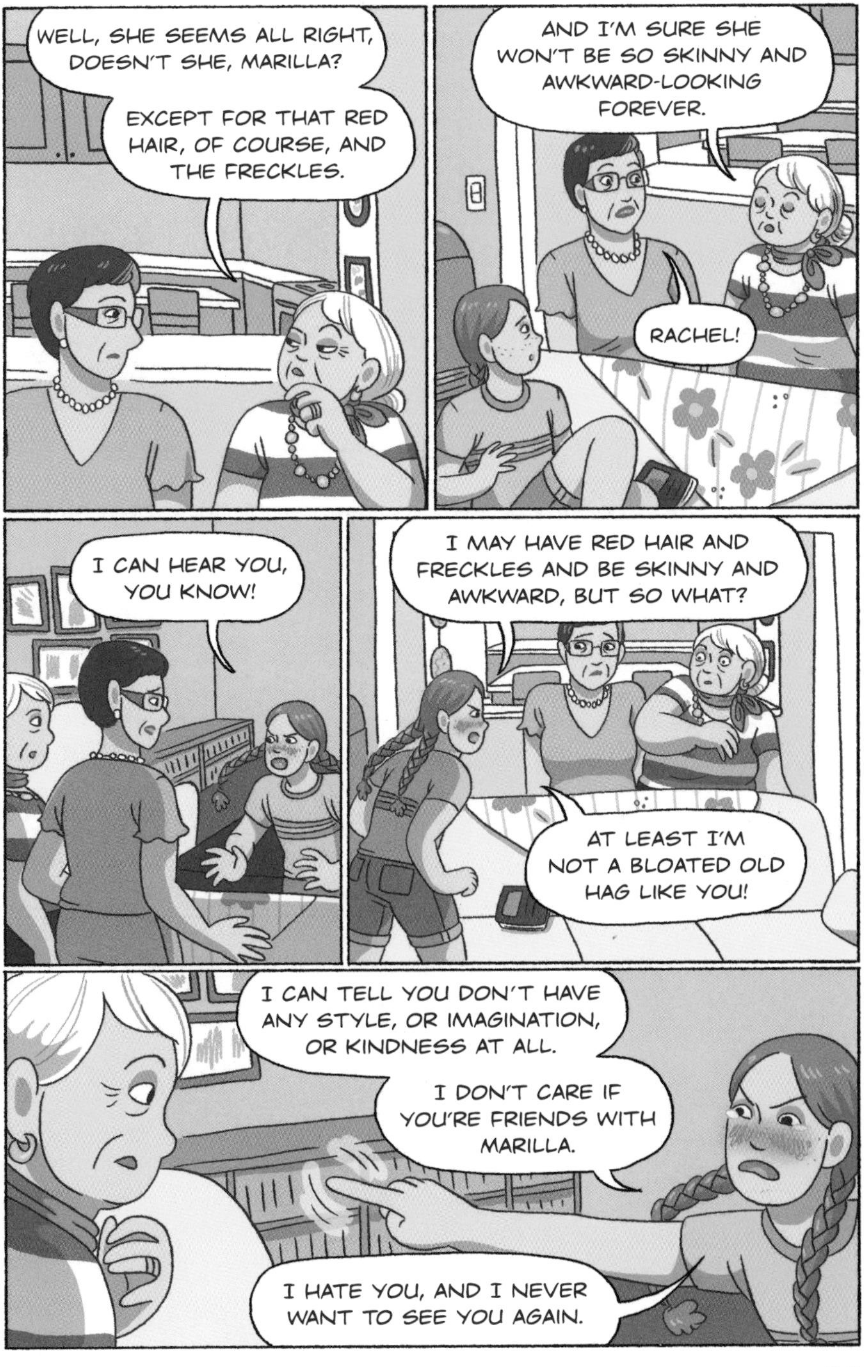
WELL, SHE SEEMS ALL RIGHT, DOESN'T SHE, MARILLA?
EXCEPT FOR THAT RED HAIR, OF COURSE, AND THE FRECKLES.
AND I'M SURE SHE WON'T BE SO SKINNY AND AWKWARD-LOOKING FOREVER.
RACHEL!
I CAN HEAR YOU, YOU KNOW!
I MAY HAVE RED HAIR AND FRECKLES AND BE SKINNY AND AWKWARD, BUT SO WHAT?
AT LEAST I'M NOT A BLOATED OLD HAG LIKE YOU!
I CAN TELL YOU DON'T HAVE ANY STYLE, OR IMAGINATION, OR KINDNESS AT ALL.
I DON'T CARE IF YOU'RE FRIENDS WITH MARILLA.
I HATE YOU, AND I NEVER WANT TO SEE YOU AGAIN.

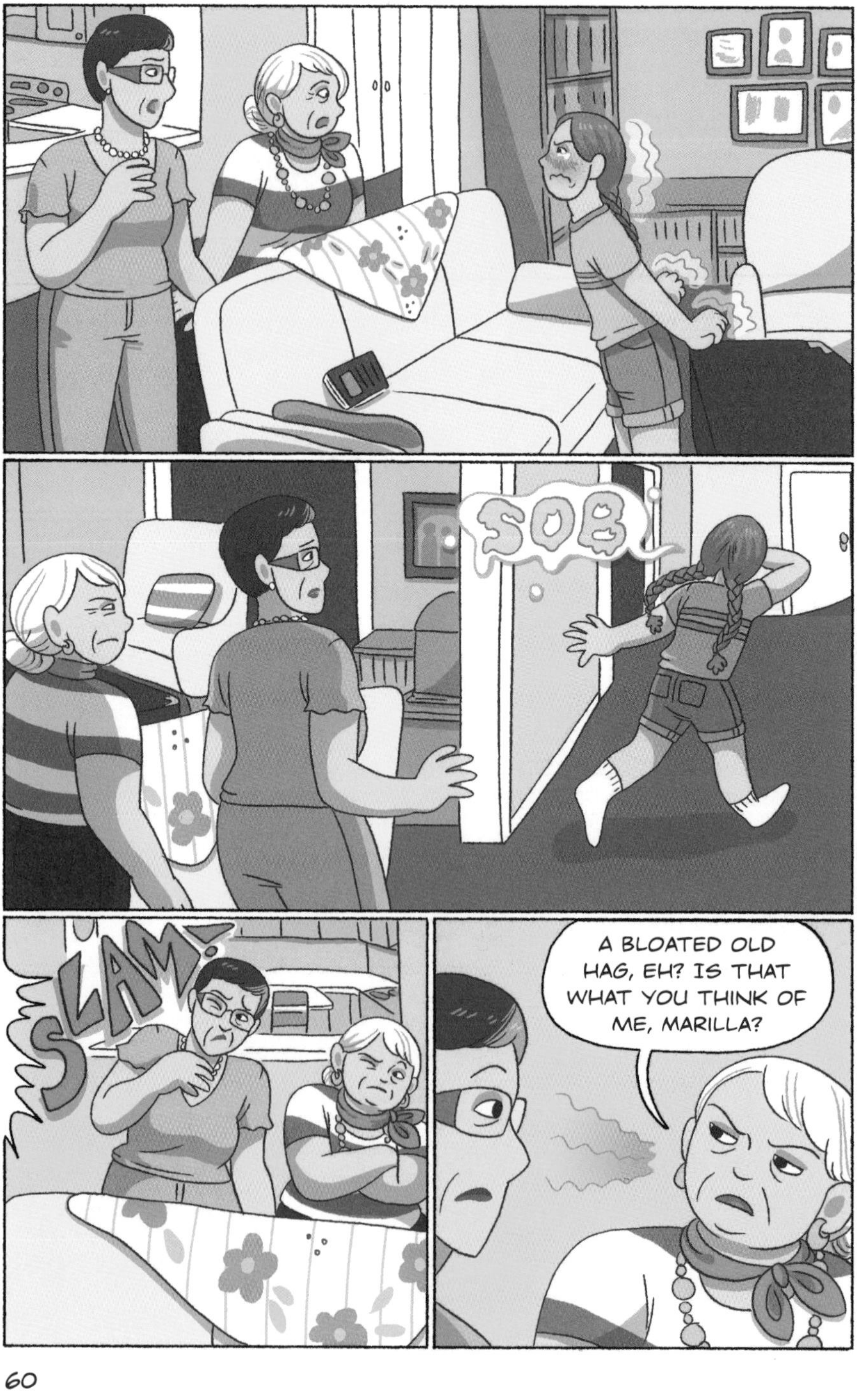
SOB
SLAM!
A BLOATED OLD HAG, EH? IS THAT WHAT YOU THINK OF ME, MARILLA?

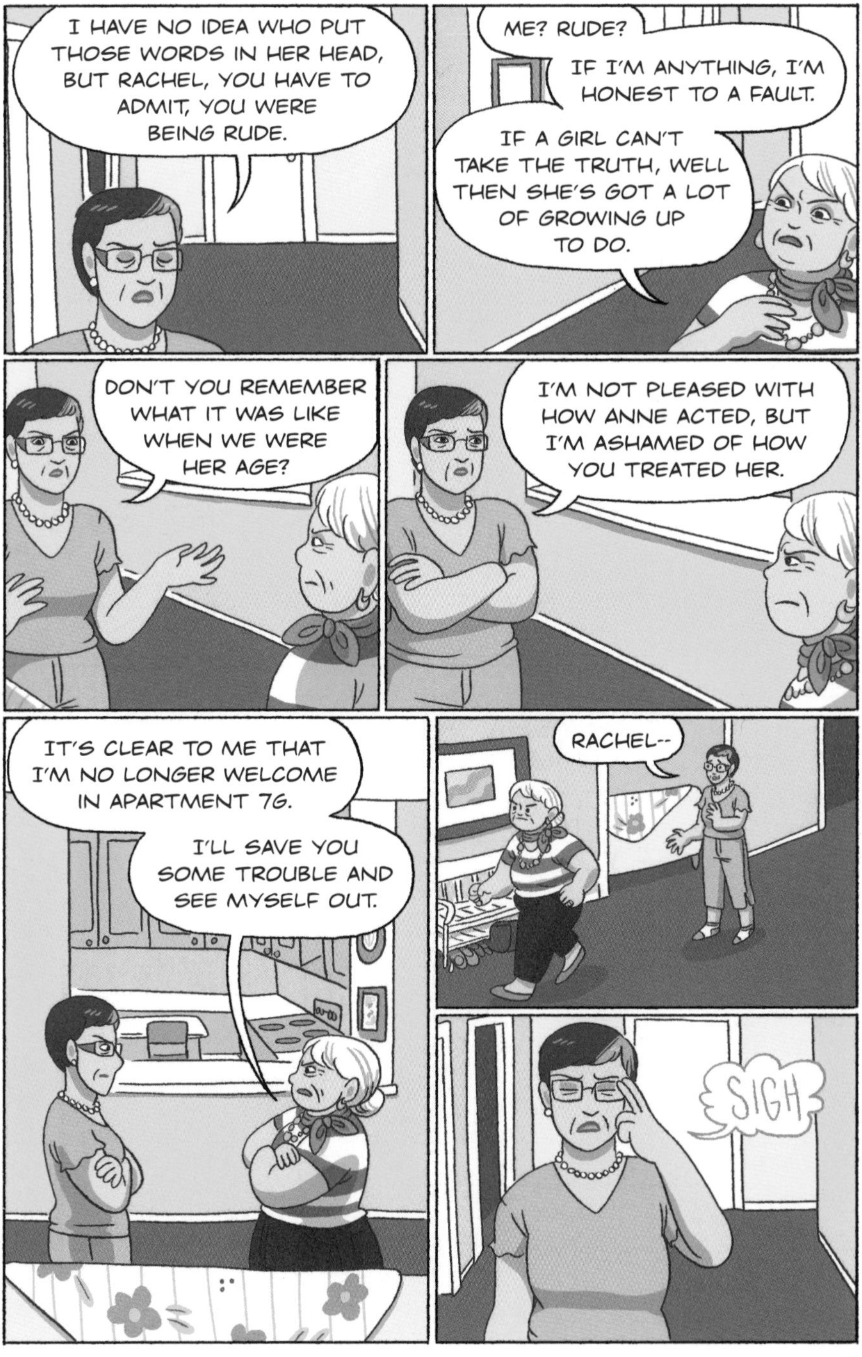
I HAVE NO IDEA WHO PUT THOSE WORDS IN HER HEAD, BUT RACHEL, YOU HAVE TO ADMIT, YOU WERE BEING RUDE.
ME? RUDE?
IF I'M ANYTHING, I'M HONEST TO A FAULT.
IF A GIRL CAN'T TAKE THE TRUTH, WELL THEN SHE'S GOT A LOT OF GROWING UP TO DO.
DON'T YOU REMEMBER WHAT IT WAS LIKE WHEN WE WERE HER AGE?
I'M NOT PLEASED WITH HOW ANNE ACTED, BUT I'M ASHAMED OF HOW YOU TREATED HER.
IT'S CLEAR TO ME THAT I'M NO LONGER WELCOME IN APARTMENT 7G.
I'LL SAVE YOU SOME TROUBLE AND SEE MYSELF OUT.
RACHEL--
SIGH

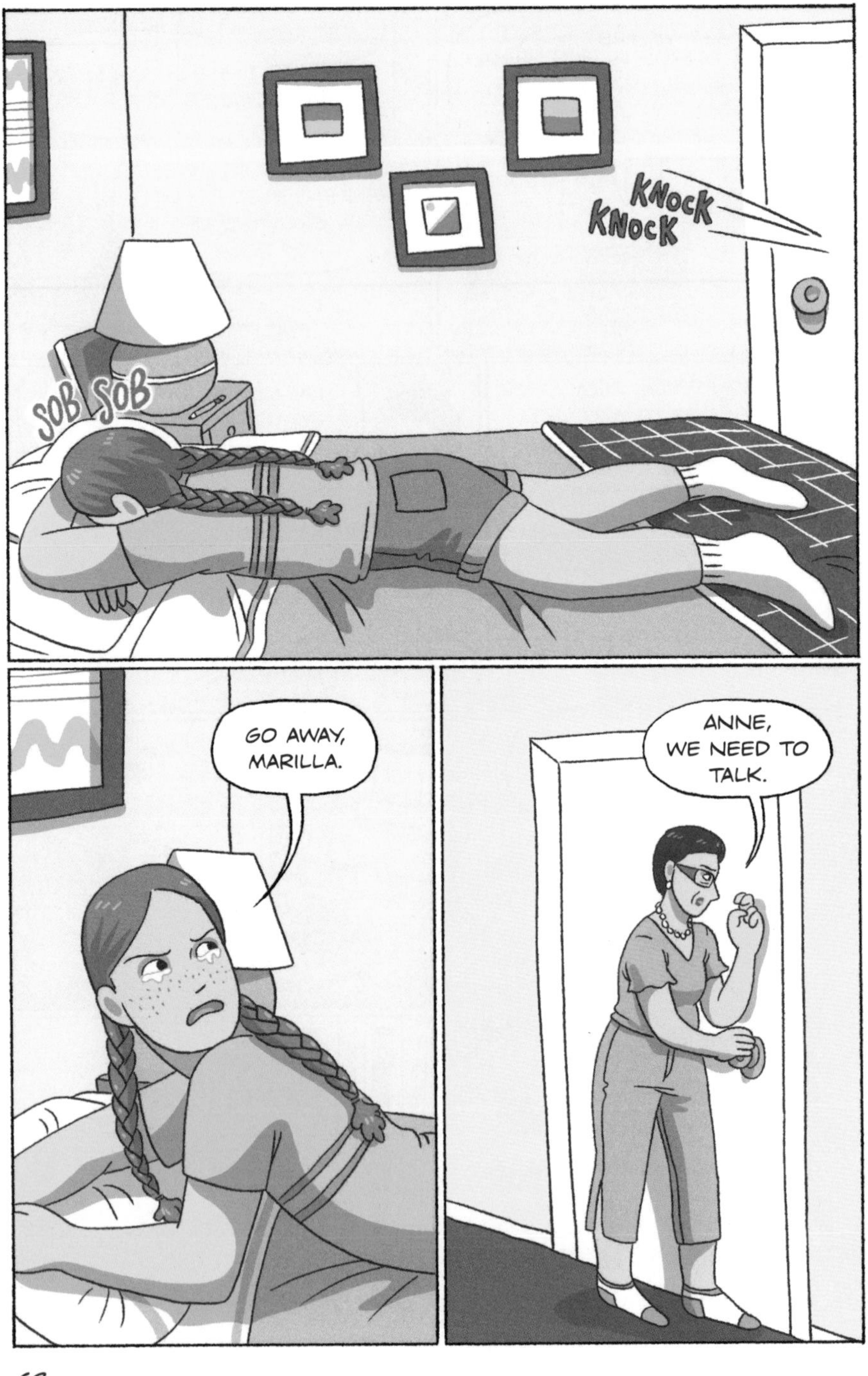
SOB SOB
KNOCK
KNOCK
GO AWAY, MARILLA.
ANNE, WE NEED TO TALK.

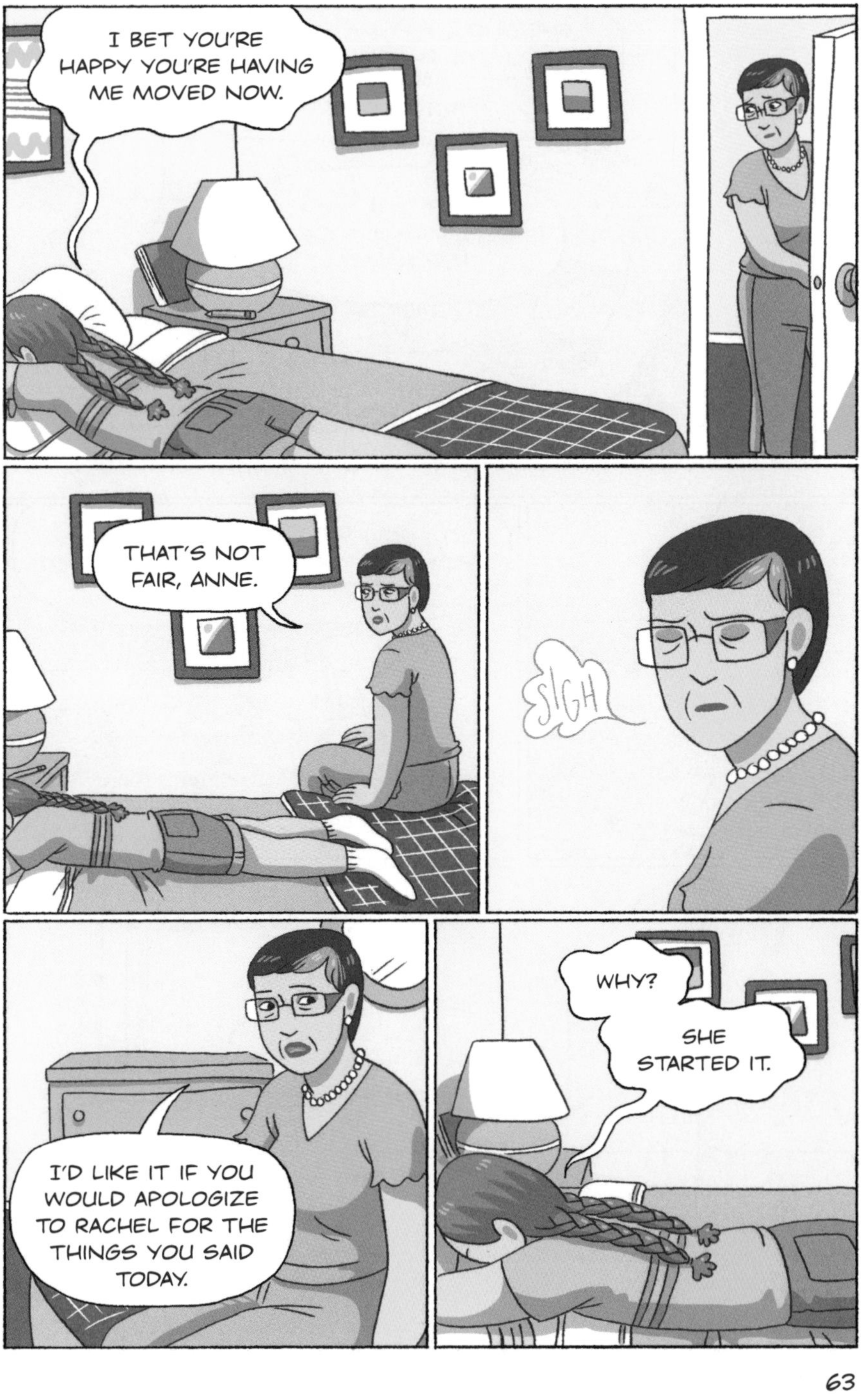
I BET YOU'RE HAPPY YOU'RE HAVING ME MOVED NOW.
THAT'S NOT FAIR, ANNE.
SIGH
I'D LIKE IT IF YOU WOULD APOLOGIZE TO RACHEL FOR THE THINGS YOU SAID TODAY.
WHY?
SHE STARTED IT.

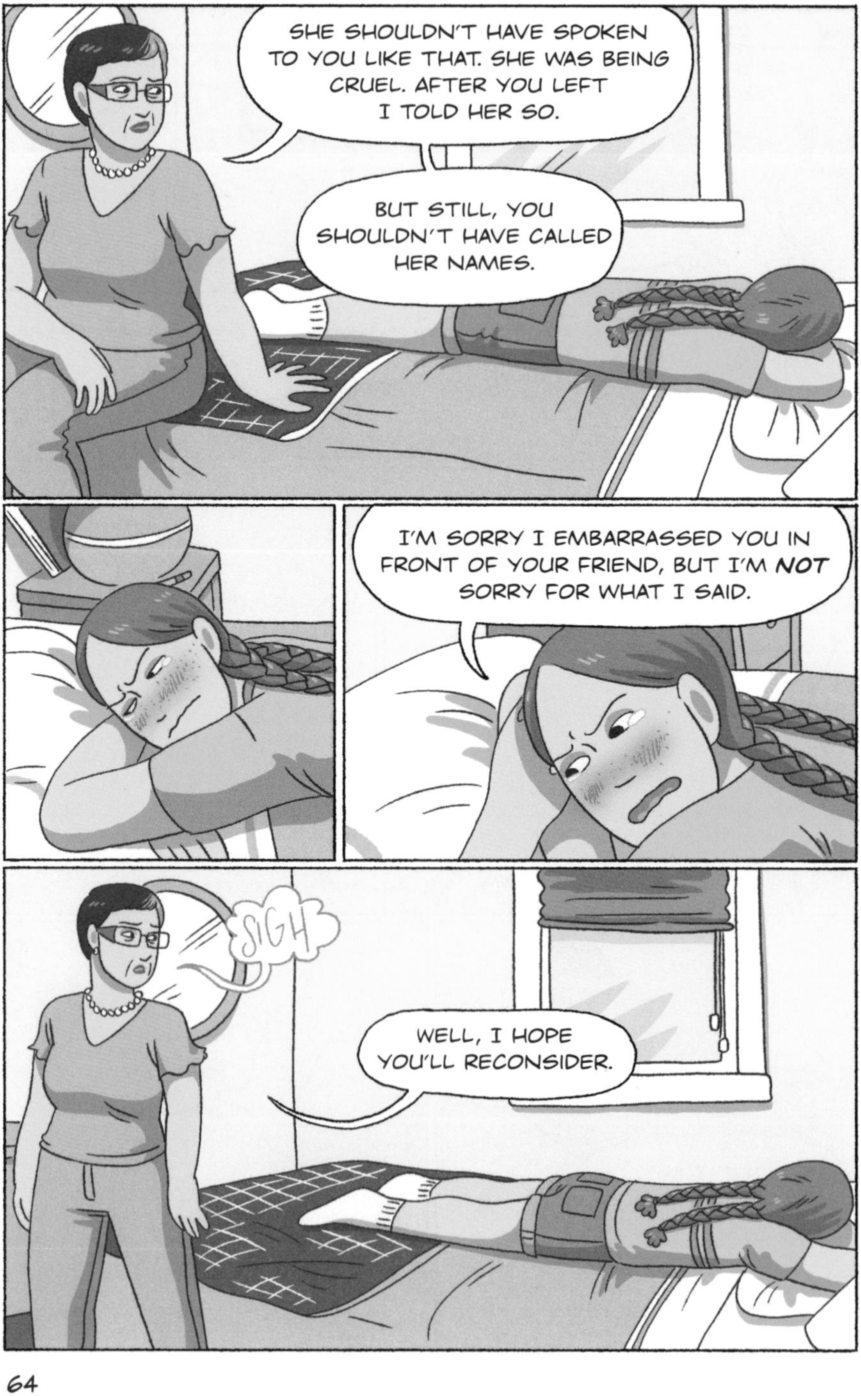
SHE SHOULDN'T HAVE SPOKEN TO YOU LIKE THAT. SHE WAS BEING CRUEL. AFTER YOU LEFT I TOLD HER SO.
BUT STILL, YOU SHOULDN'T HAVE CALLED HER NAMES.
I'M SORRY I EMBARRASSED YOU IN FRONT OF YOUR FRIEND, BUT I'M **NOT** SORRY FOR WHAT I SAID.
SIGH
WELL, I HOPE YOU'LL RECONSIDER.

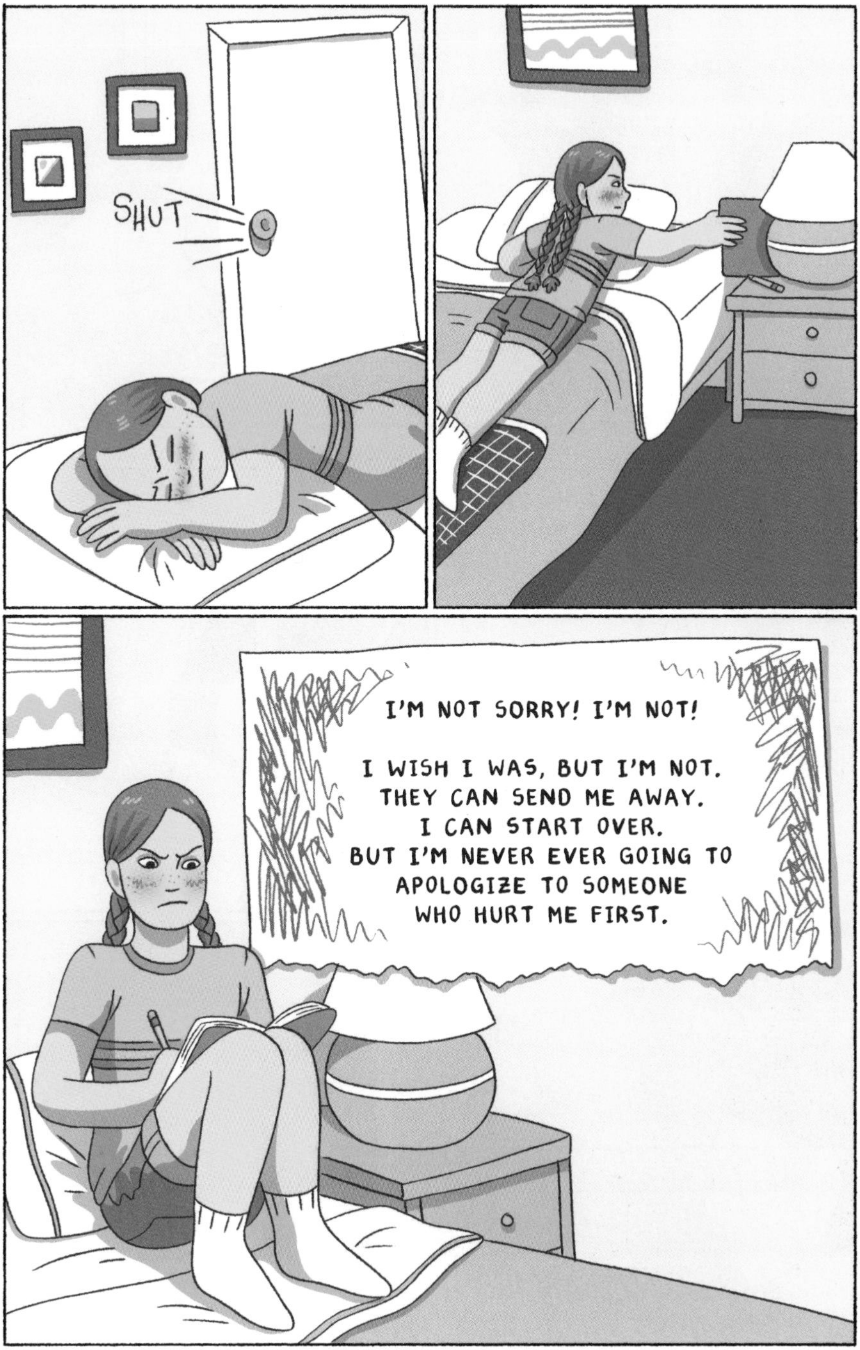
SHUT
I'M NOT SORRY! I'M NOT!
I WISH I WAS, BUT I'M NOT.
THEY CAN SEND ME AWAY.
I CAN START OVER.
BUT I'M NEVER EVER GOING TO
APOLOGIZE TO SOMEONE
WHO HURT ME FIRST.

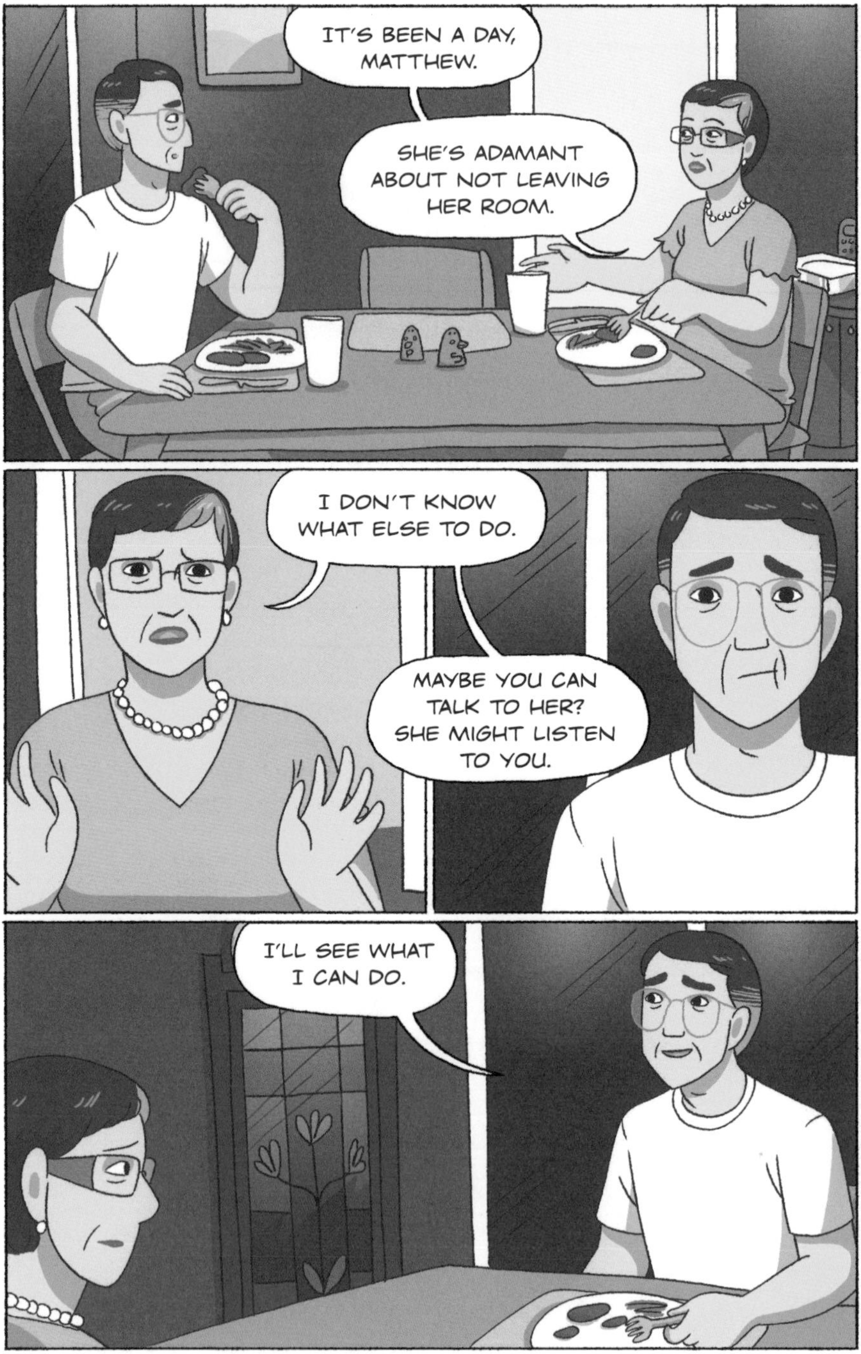
IT'S BEEN A DAY, MATTHEW.
SHE'S ADAMANT ABOUT NOT LEAVING HER ROOM.
I DON'T KNOW WHAT ELSE TO DO.
MAYBE YOU CAN TALK TO HER? SHE MIGHT LISTEN TO YOU.
I'LL SEE WHAT I CAN DO.

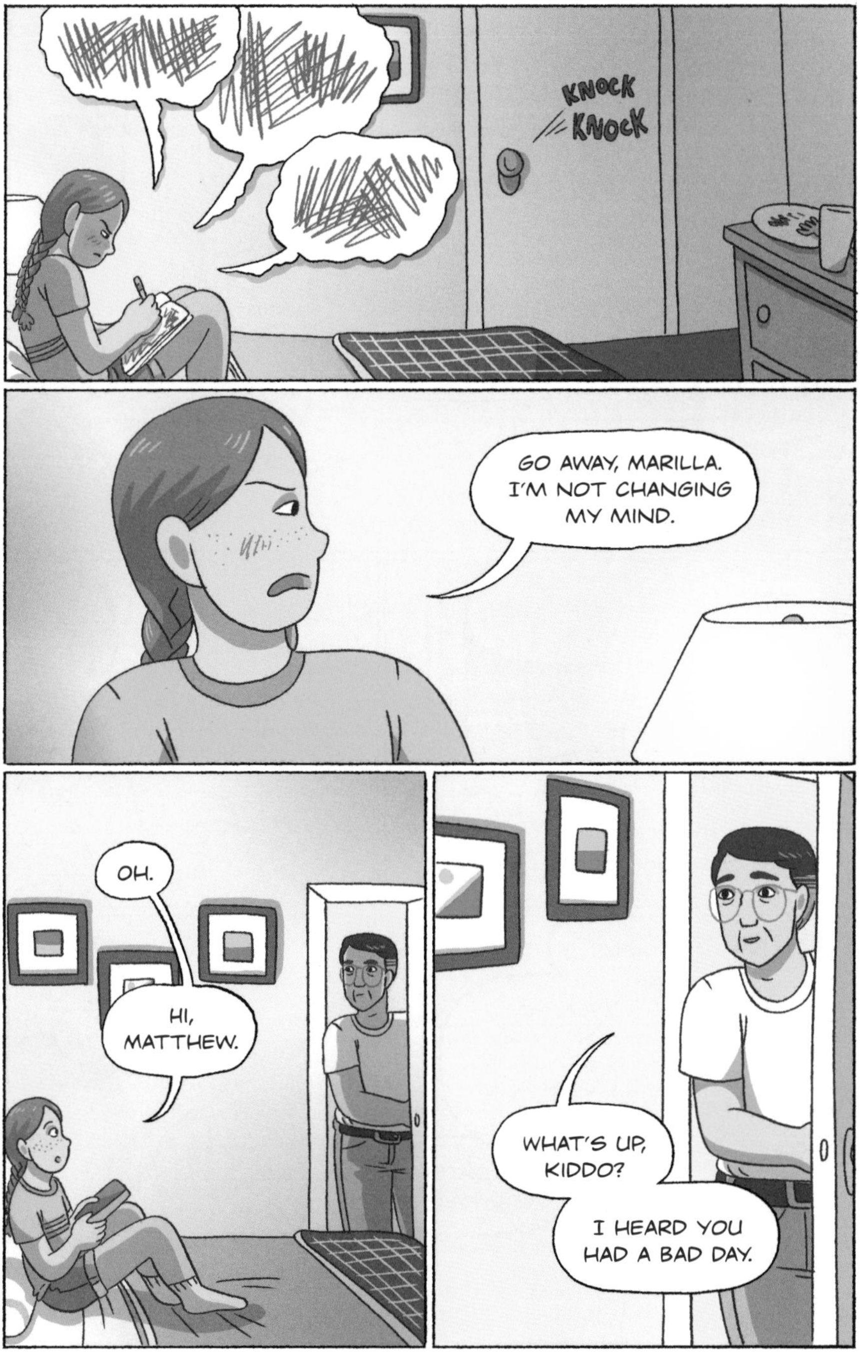
KNOCK
KNOCK
GO AWAY, MARILLA. I'M NOT CHANGING MY MIND.
OH.
HI, MATTHEW.
WHAT'S UP, KIDDO?
I HEARD YOU HAD A BAD DAY.

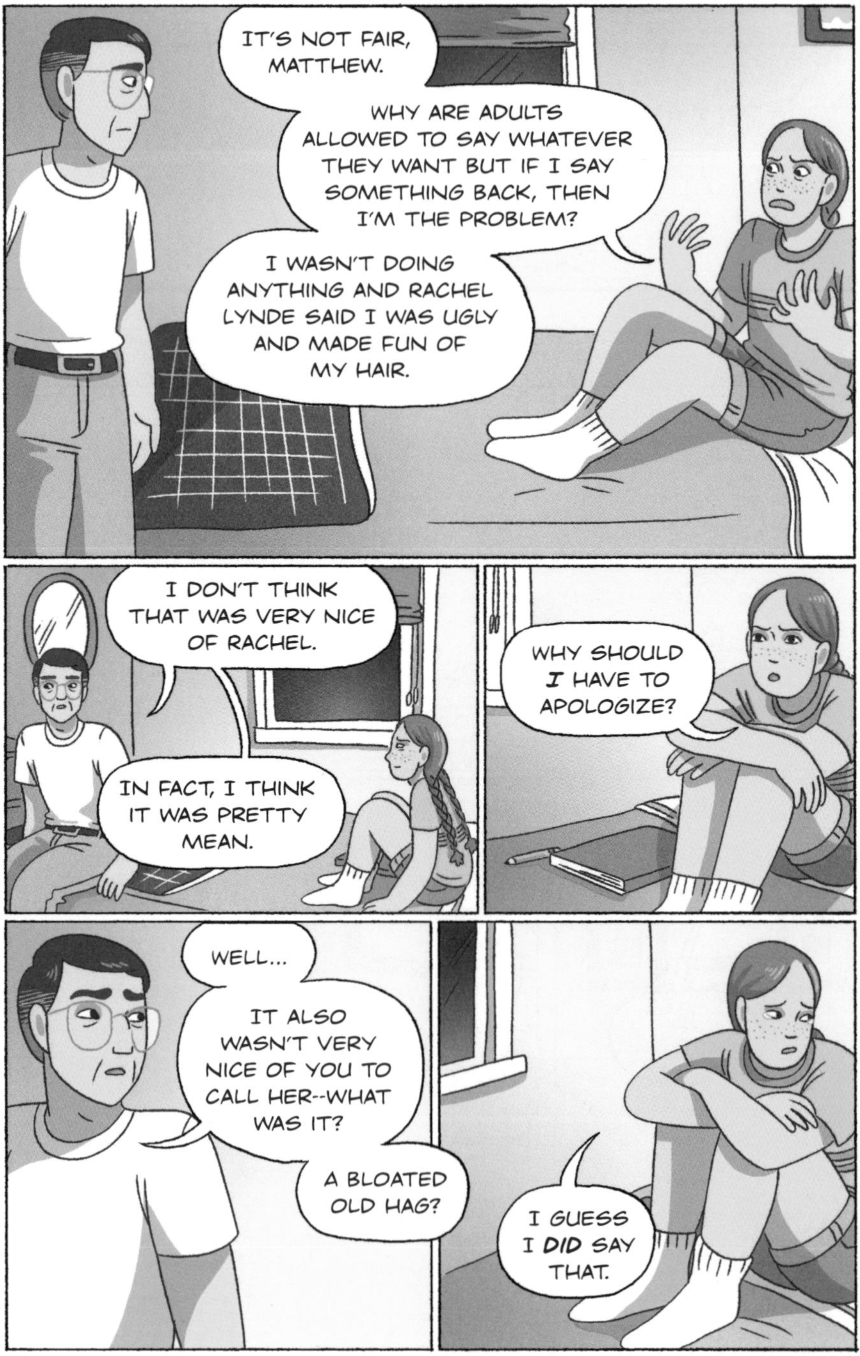
IT'S NOT FAIR, MATTHEW.
WHY ARE ADULTS ALLOWED TO SAY WHATEVER THEY WANT BUT IF I SAY SOMETHING BACK, THEN I'M THE PROBLEM?
I WASN'T DOING ANYTHING AND RACHEL LYNDE SAID I WAS UGLY AND MADE FUN OF MY HAIR.
I DON'T THINK THAT WAS VERY NICE OF RACHEL.
IN FACT, I THINK IT WAS PRETTY MEAN.
WHY SHOULD *I* HAVE TO APOLOGIZE?
WELL...
IT ALSO WASN'T VERY NICE OF YOU TO CALL HER--WHAT WAS IT?
A BLOATED OLD HAG?
I GUESS I **DID** SAY THAT.

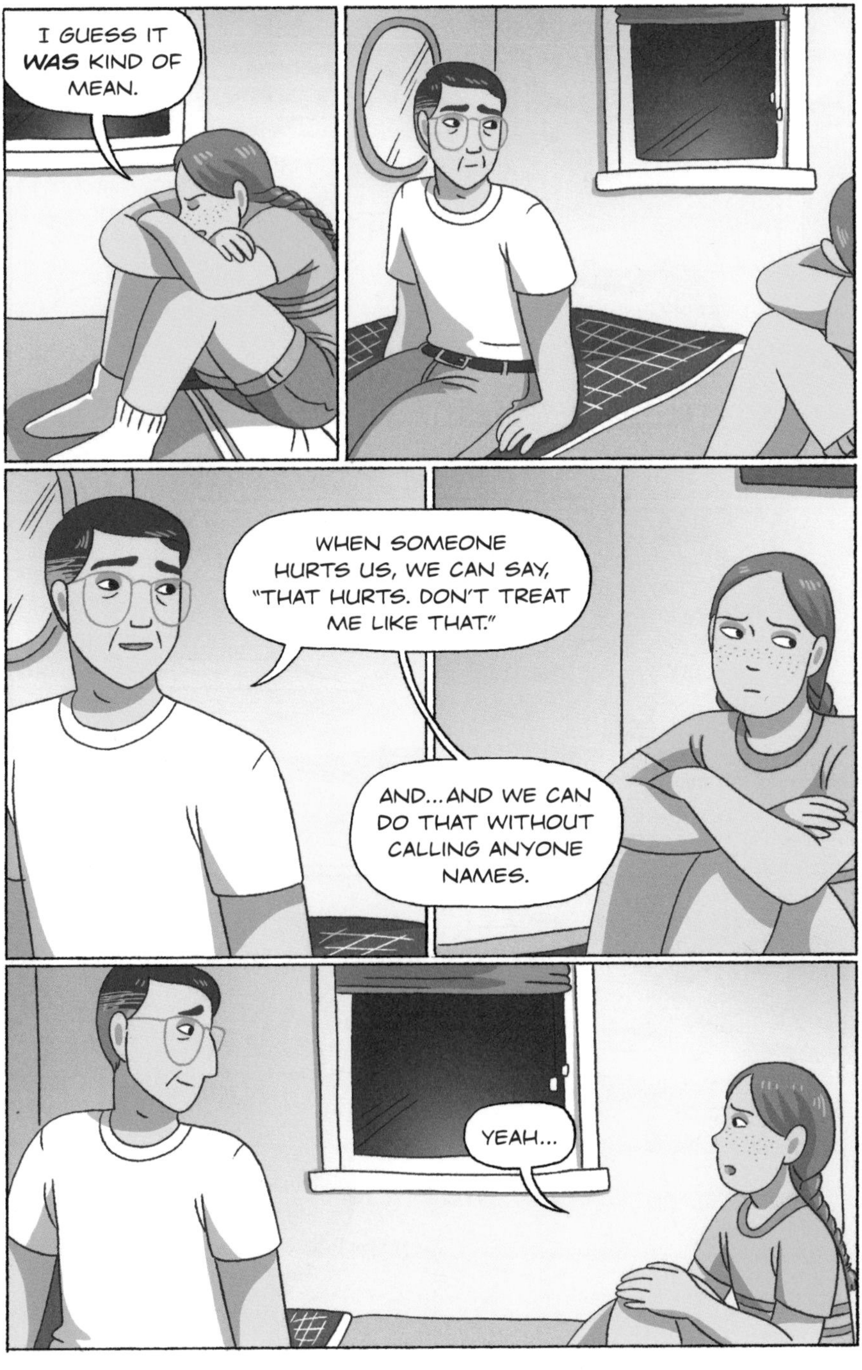
I GUESS IT **WAS** KIND OF MEAN.
WHEN SOMEONE HURTS US, WE CAN SAY, "THAT HURTS. DON'T TREAT ME LIKE THAT."
AND...AND WE CAN DO THAT WITHOUT CALLING ANYONE NAMES.
YEAH...

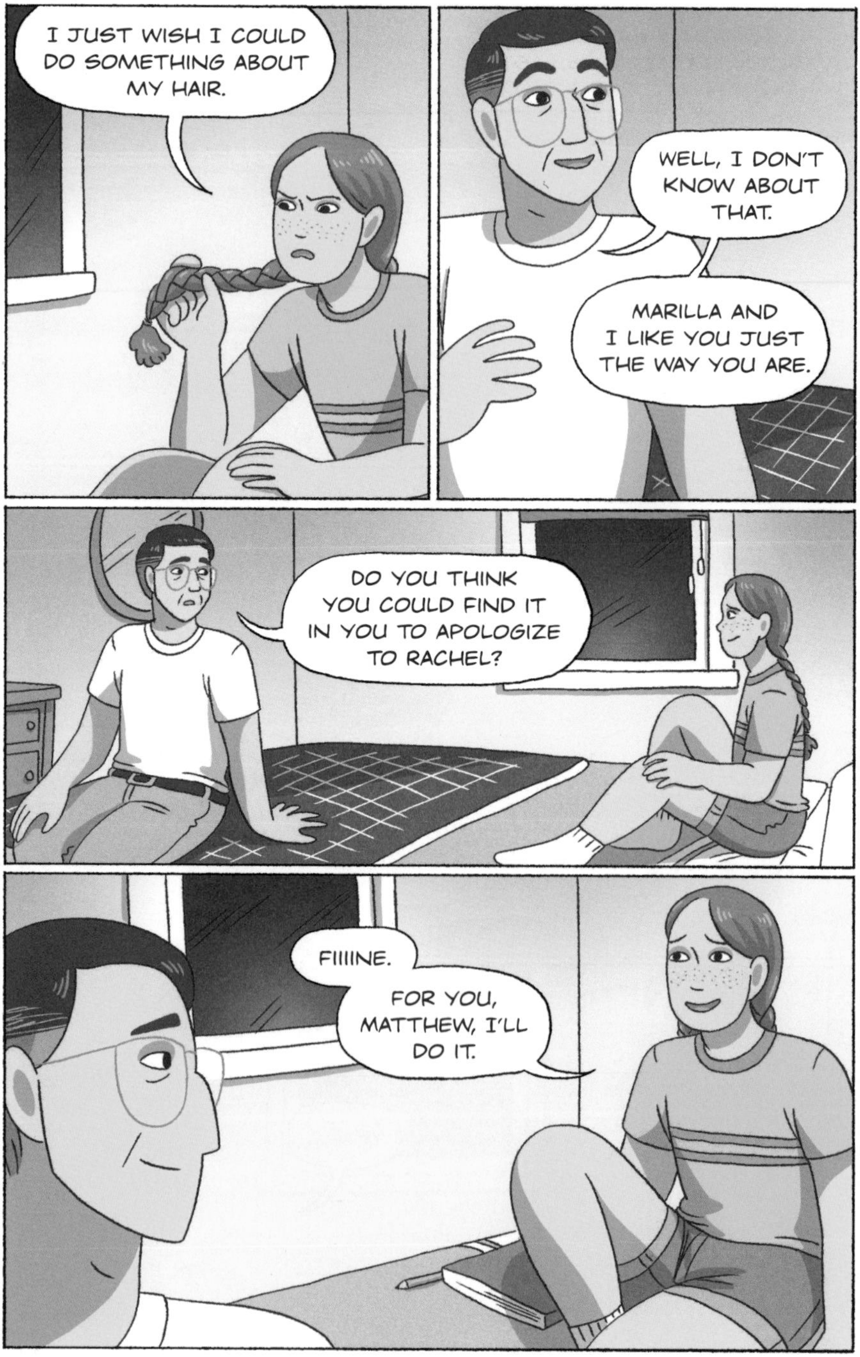
I JUST WISH I COULD DO SOMETHING ABOUT MY HAIR.
WELL, I DON'T KNOW ABOUT THAT.
MARILLA AND I LIKE YOU JUST THE WAY YOU ARE.
DO YOU THINK YOU COULD FIND IT IN YOU TO APOLOGIZE TO RACHEL?
FIIIINE.
FOR YOU, MATTHEW, I'LL DO IT.

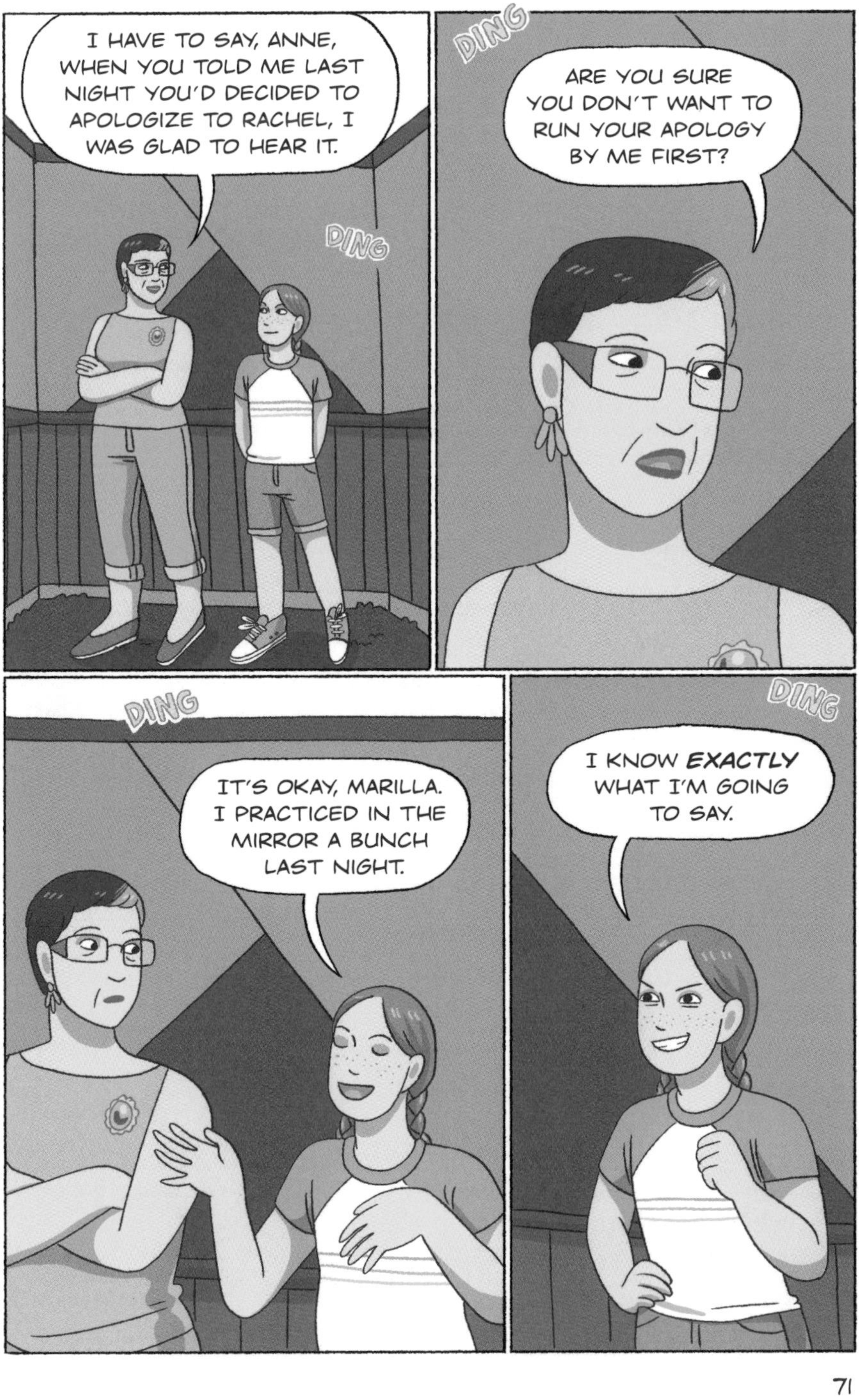
I HAVE TO SAY, ANNE, WHEN YOU TOLD ME LAST NIGHT YOU'D DECIDED TO APOLOGIZE TO RACHEL, I WAS GLAD TO HEAR IT.
DING
DING
ARE YOU SURE YOU DON'T WANT TO RUN YOUR APOLOGY BY ME FIRST?
DING
IT'S OKAY, MARILLA. I PRACTICED IN THE MIRROR A BUNCH LAST NIGHT.
DING
I KNOW **EXACTLY** WHAT I'M GOING TO SAY.

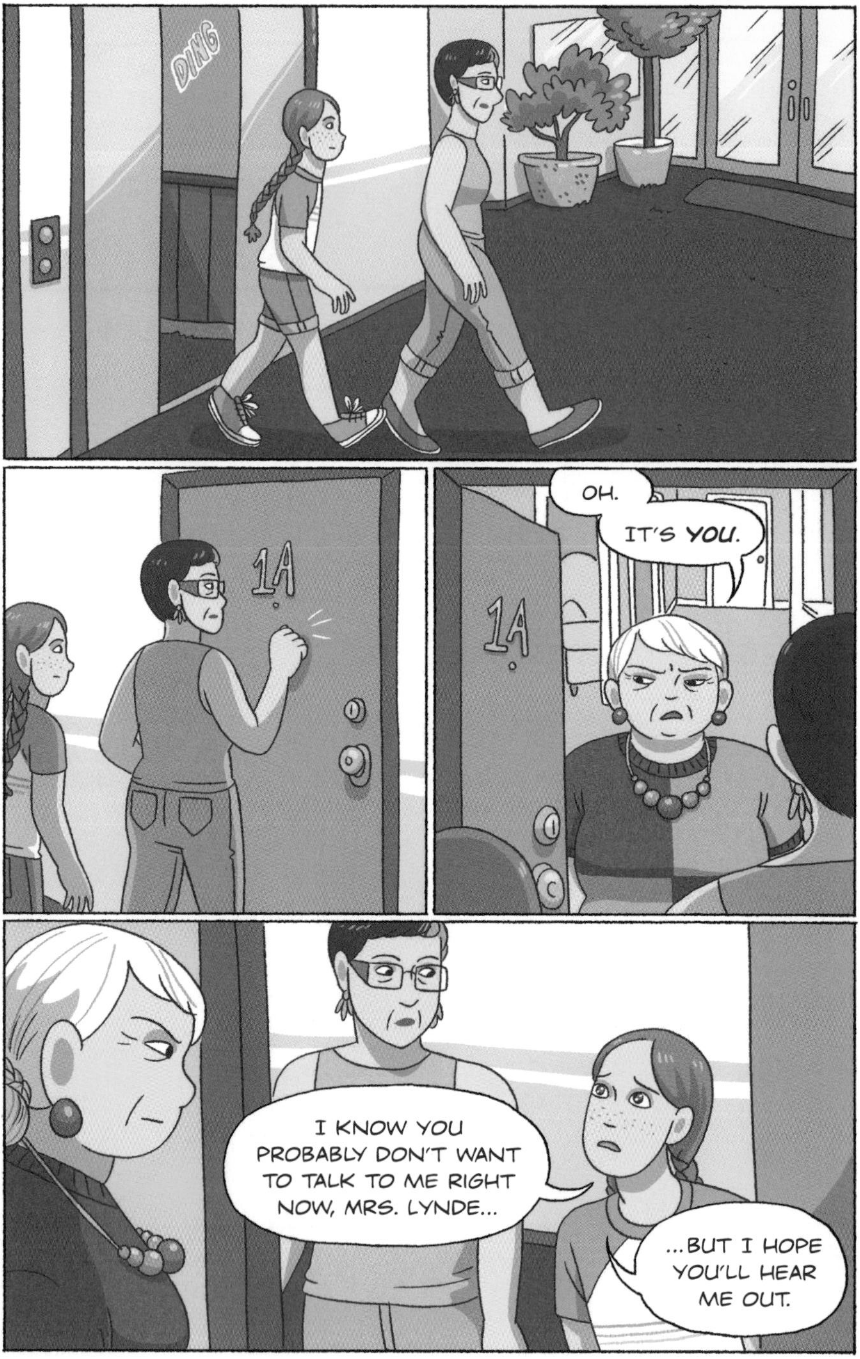
DING
1A
1A
OH.
IT'S **YOU**.
I KNOW YOU PROBABLY DON'T WANT TO TALK TO ME RIGHT NOW, MRS. LYNDE...
...BUT I HOPE YOU'LL HEAR ME OUT.

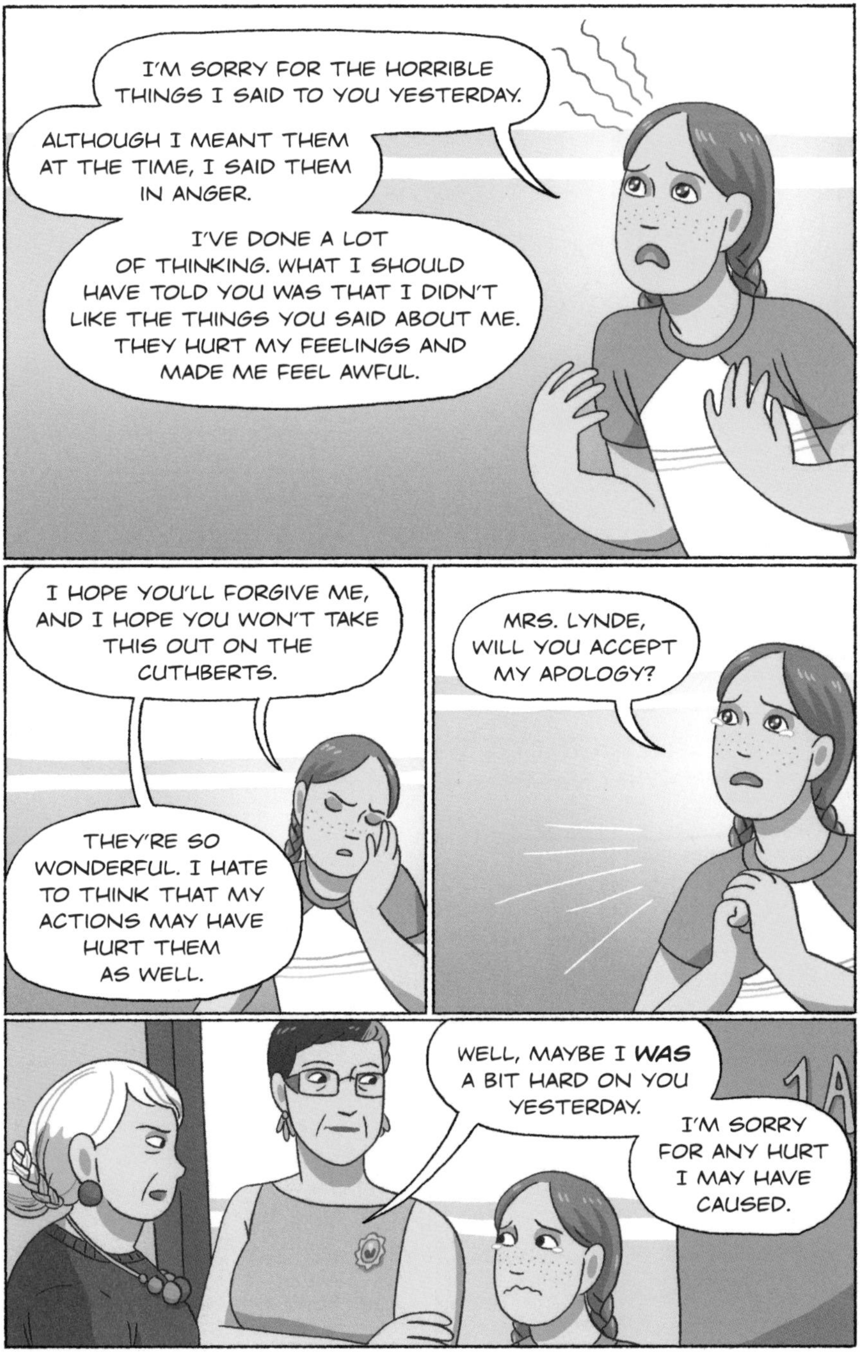
I'M SORRY FOR THE HORRIBLE THINGS I SAID TO YOU YESTERDAY.
ALTHOUGH I MEANT THEM AT THE TIME, I SAID THEM IN ANGER.
I'VE DONE A LOT OF THINKING. WHAT I SHOULD HAVE TOLD YOU WAS THAT I DIDN'T LIKE THE THINGS YOU SAID ABOUT ME. THEY HURT MY FEELINGS AND MADE ME FEEL AWFUL.
I HOPE YOU'LL FORGIVE ME, AND I HOPE YOU WON'T TAKE THIS OUT ON THE CUTHBERTS.
THEY'RE SO WONDERFUL. I HATE TO THINK THAT MY ACTIONS MAY HAVE HURT THEM AS WELL.
MRS. LYNDE, WILL YOU ACCEPT MY APOLOGY?
WELL, MAYBE I **WAS** A BIT HARD ON YOU YESTERDAY.
I'M SORRY FOR ANY HURT I MAY HAVE CAUSED.
1A

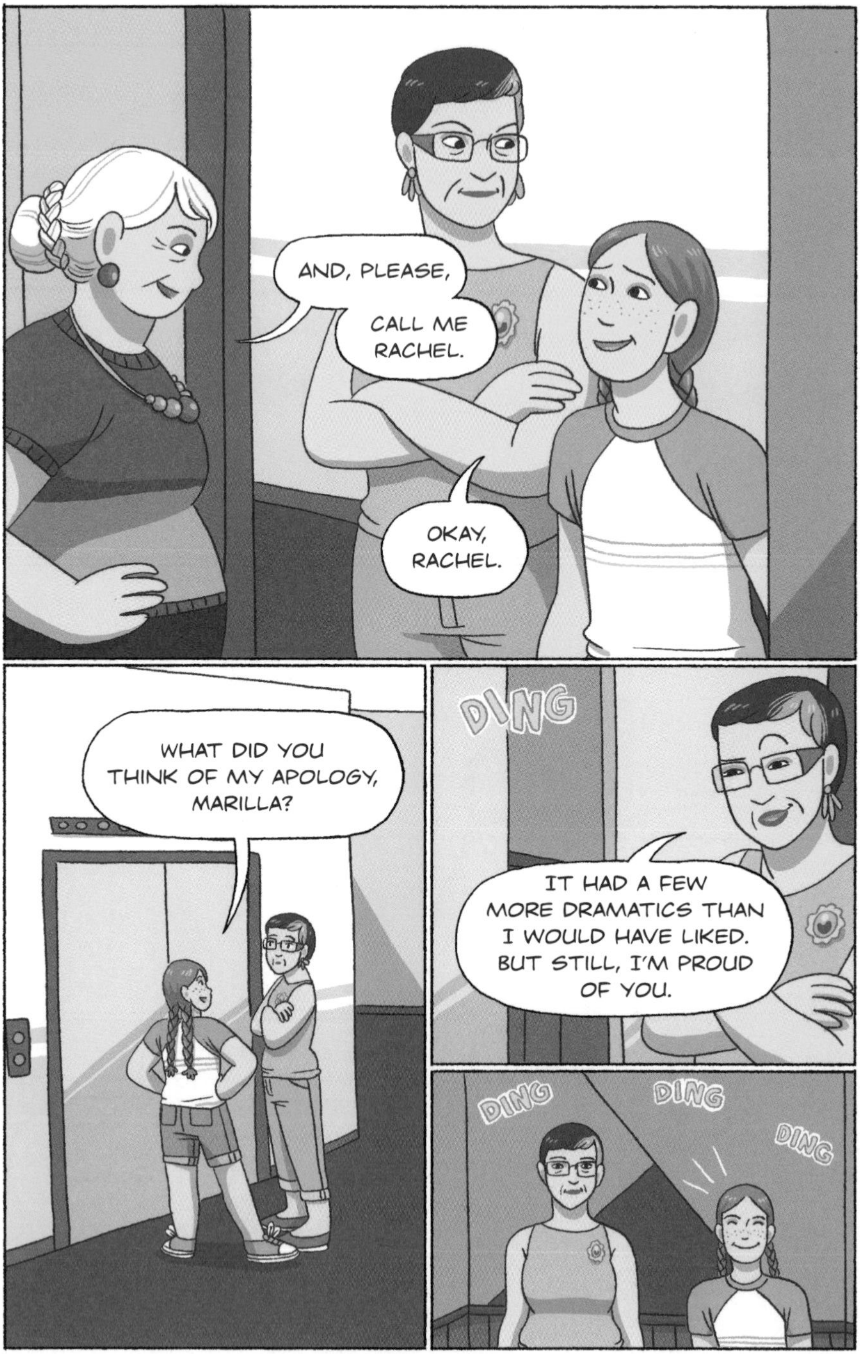
AND, PLEASE,
CALL ME RACHEL.
OKAY, RACHEL.
WHAT DID YOU THINK OF MY APOLOGY, MARILLA?
DING
IT HAD A FEW MORE DRAMATICS THAN I WOULD HAVE LIKED. BUT STILL, I'M PROUD OF YOU.
DING
DING
DING

CHAPTER 4

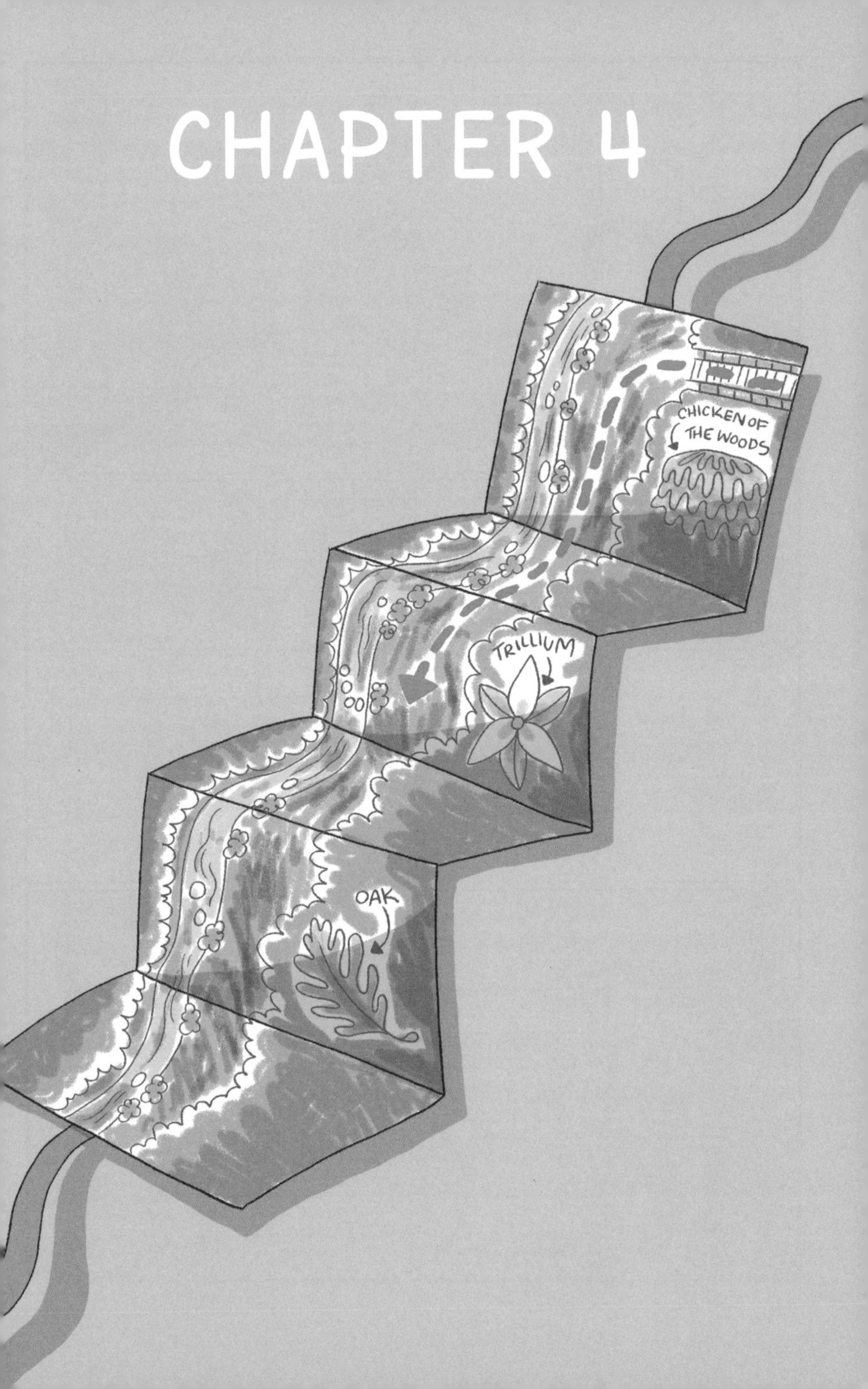
CHICKEN OF THE WOODS
TRILLIUM
OAK

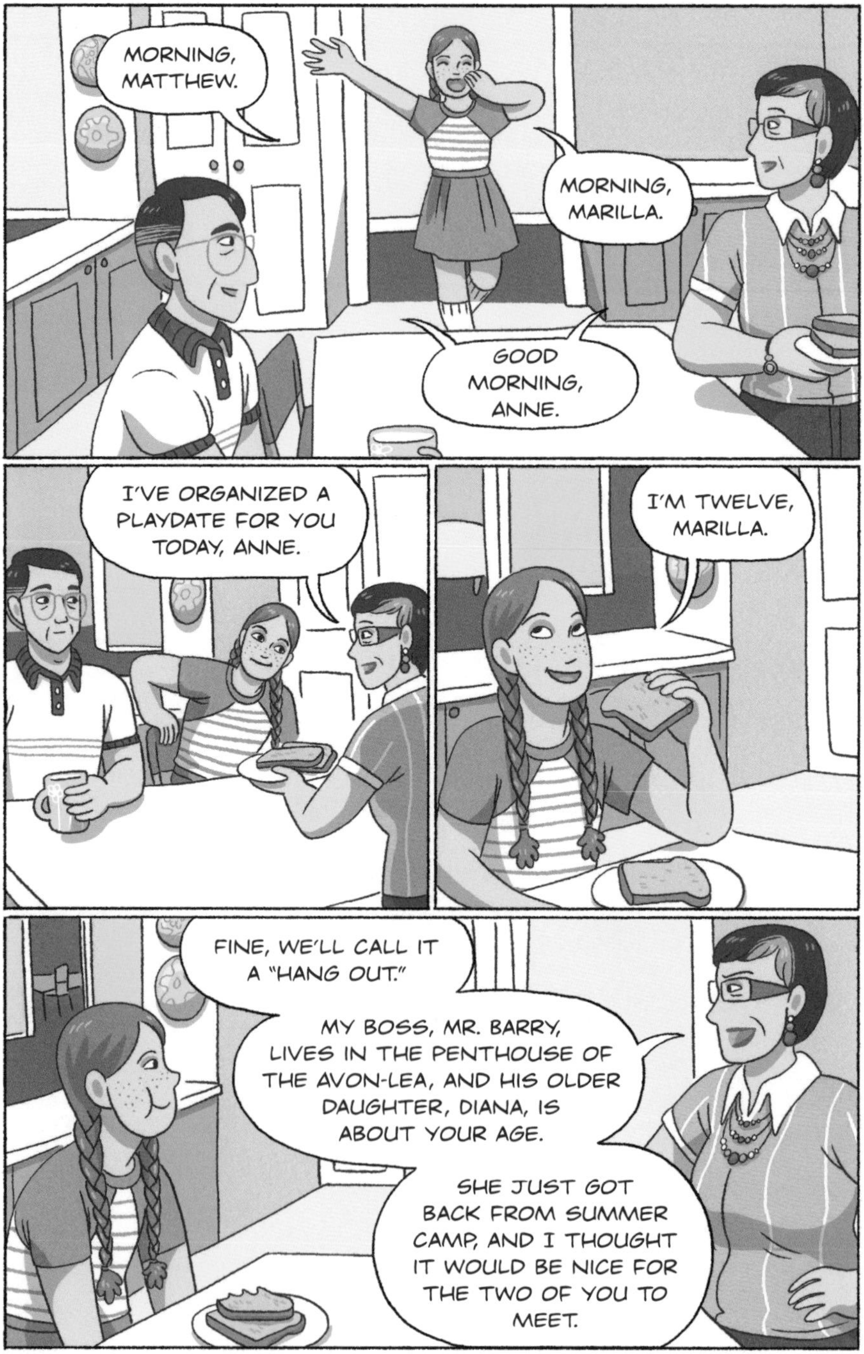
MORNING, MATTHEW.
MORNING, MARILLA.
GOOD MORNING, ANNE.
I'VE ORGANIZED A PLAYDATE FOR YOU TODAY, ANNE.
I'M TWELVE, MARILLA.
FINE, WE'LL CALL IT A "HANG OUT."
MY BOSS, MR. BARRY, LIVES IN THE PENTHOUSE OF THE AVON-LEA, AND HIS OLDER DAUGHTER, DIANA, IS ABOUT YOUR AGE.
SHE JUST GOT BACK FROM SUMMER CAMP, AND I THOUGHT IT WOULD BE NICE FOR THE TWO OF YOU TO MEET.

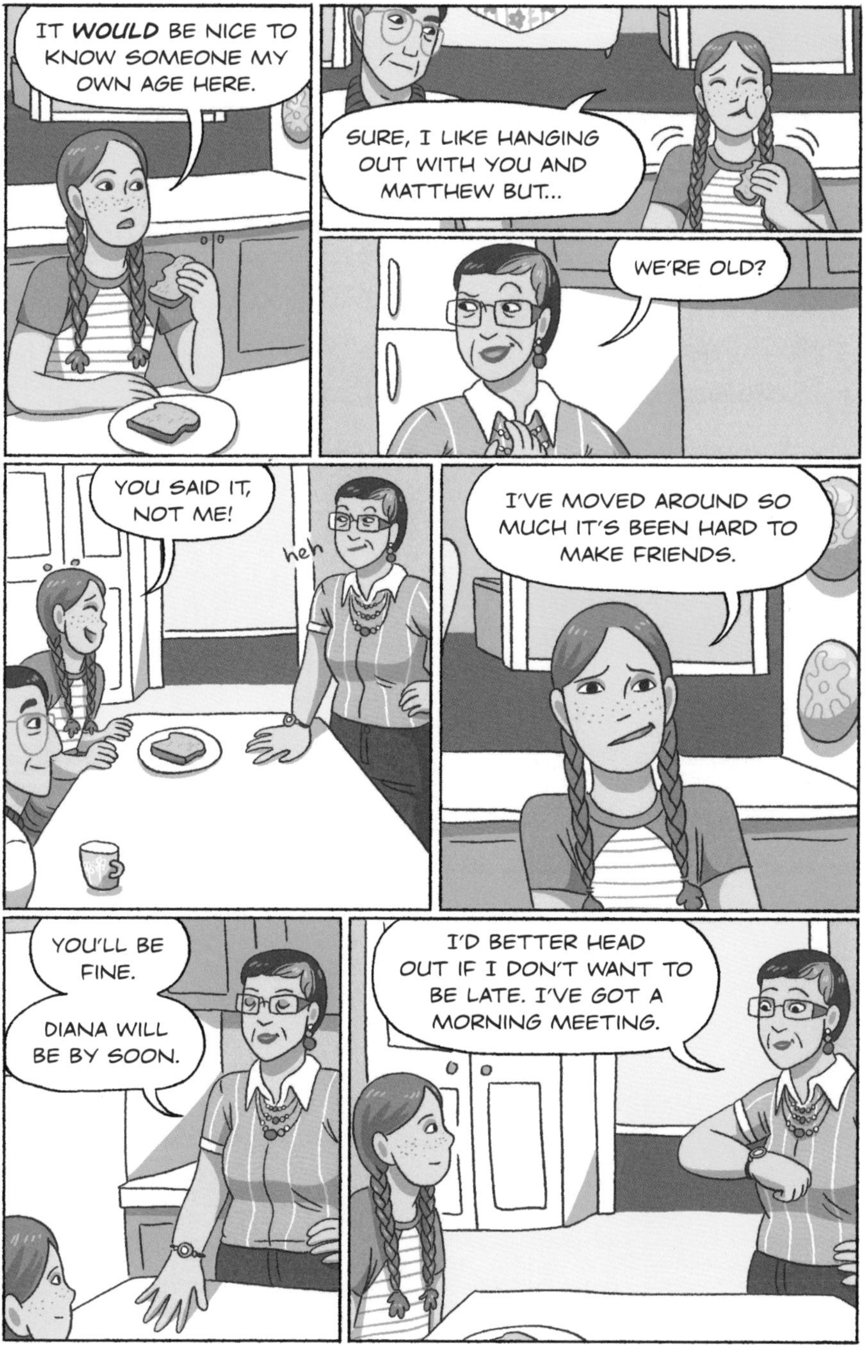
IT *WOULD* BE NICE TO KNOW SOMEONE MY OWN AGE HERE.
SURE, I LIKE HANGING OUT WITH YOU AND MATTHEW BUT...
WE'RE OLD?
YOU SAID IT, NOT ME!
heh
I'VE MOVED AROUND SO MUCH IT'S BEEN HARD TO MAKE FRIENDS.
YOU'LL BE FINE.
DIANA WILL BE BY SOON.
I'D BETTER HEAD OUT IF I DON'T WANT TO BE LATE. I'VE GOT A MORNING MEETING.

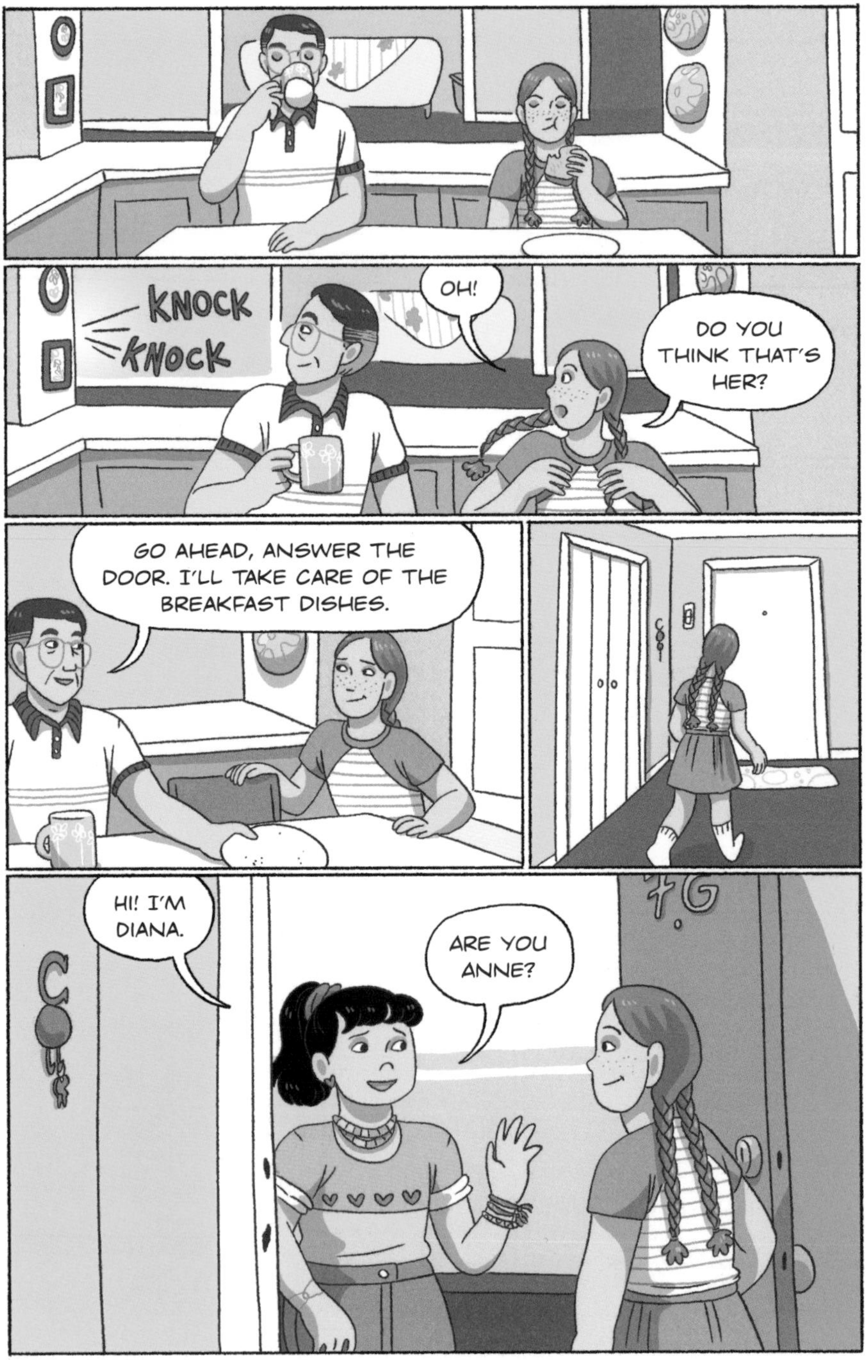

KNOCK
KNOCK
OH!
DO YOU THINK THAT'S HER?
GO AHEAD, ANSWER THE DOOR. I'LL TAKE CARE OF THE BREAKFAST DISHES.
HI! I'M DIANA.
ARE YOU ANNE?

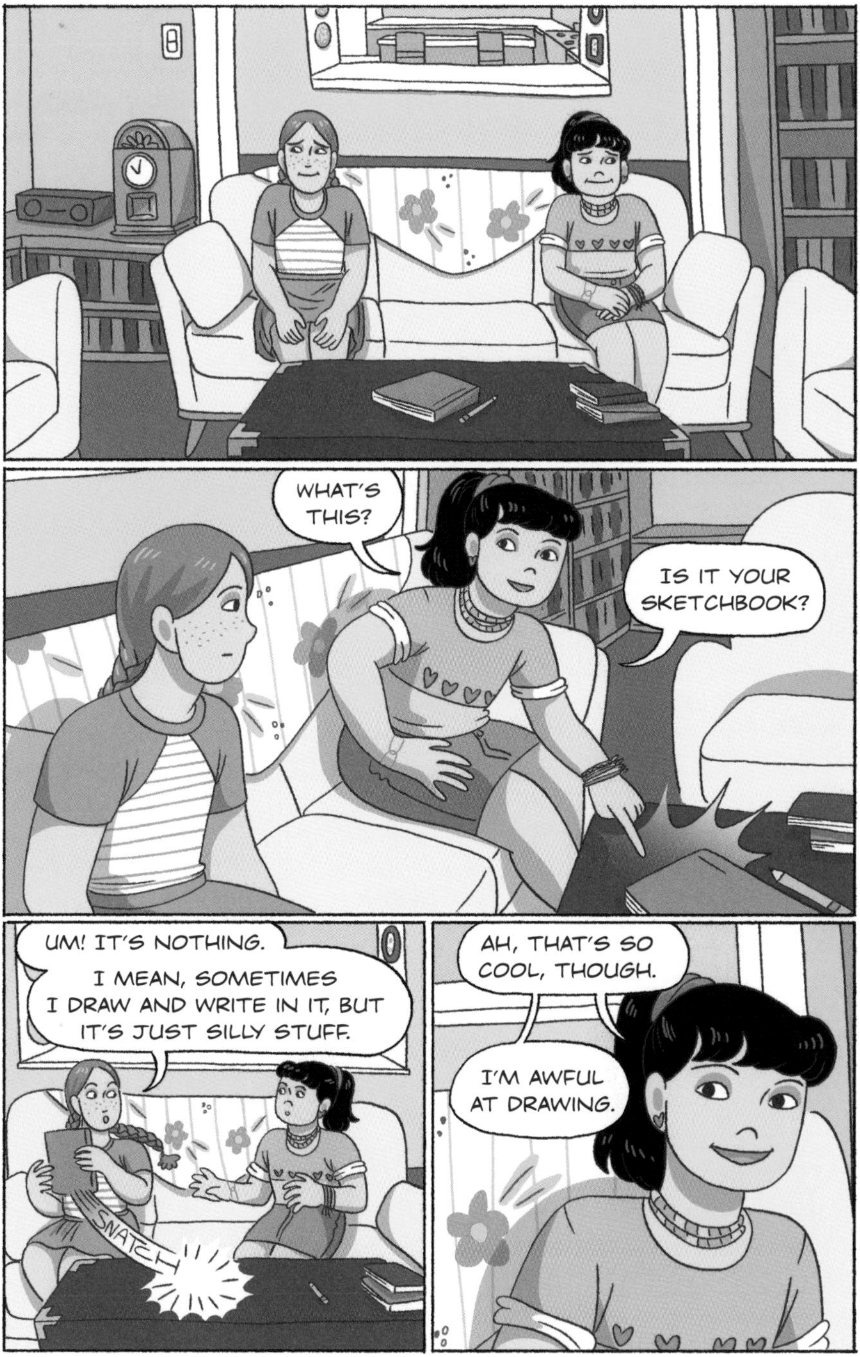
WHAT'S THIS?
IS IT YOUR SKETCHBOOK?
UM! IT'S NOTHING.
I MEAN, SOMETIMES I DRAW AND WRITE IN IT, BUT IT'S JUST SILLY STUFF.
SNATCH
AH, THAT'S SO COOL, THOUGH.
I'M AWFUL AT DRAWING.

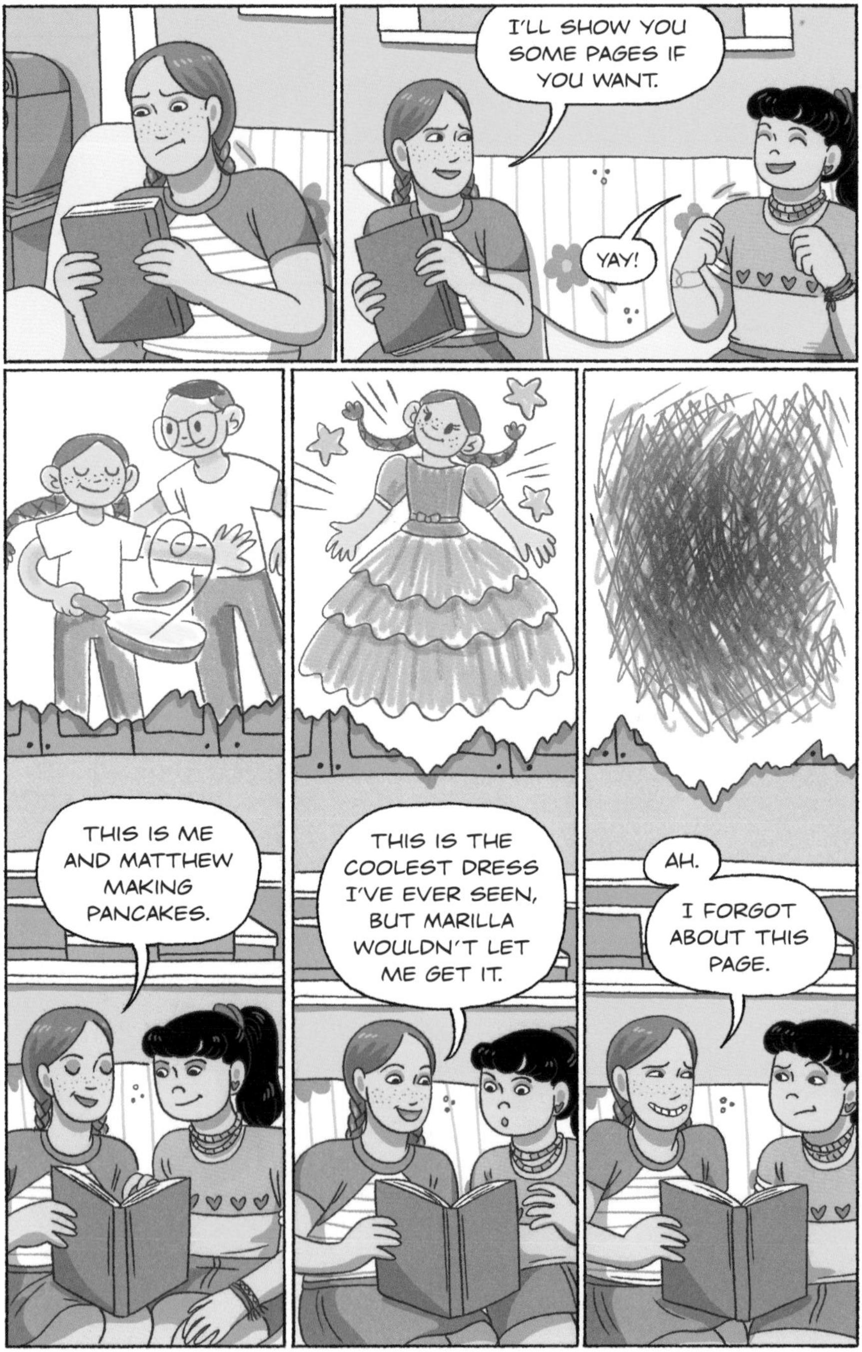
I'LL SHOW YOU SOME PAGES IF YOU WANT.
YAY!
THIS IS ME AND MATTHEW MAKING PANCAKES.
THIS IS THE COOLEST DRESS I'VE EVER SEEN, BUT MARILLA WOULDN'T LET ME GET IT.
AH.
I FORGOT ABOUT THIS PAGE.

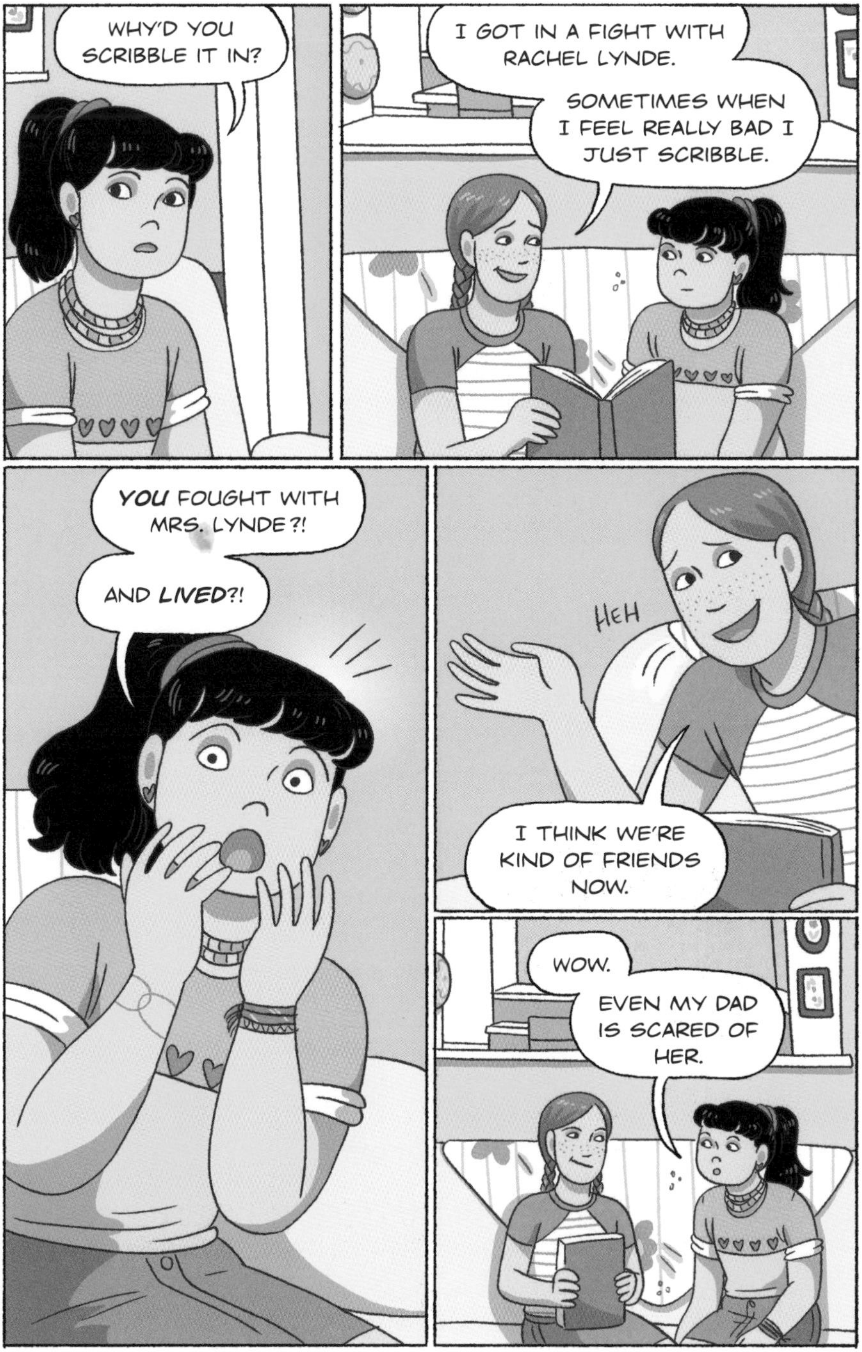
WHY'D YOU SCRIBBLE IT IN?
I GOT IN A FIGHT WITH RACHEL LYNDE.
SOMETIMES WHEN I FEEL REALLY BAD I JUST SCRIBBLE.
YOU FOUGHT WITH MRS. LYNDE?!
AND LIVED?!
HEH
I THINK WE'RE KIND OF FRIENDS NOW.
WOW.
EVEN MY DAD IS SCARED OF HER.

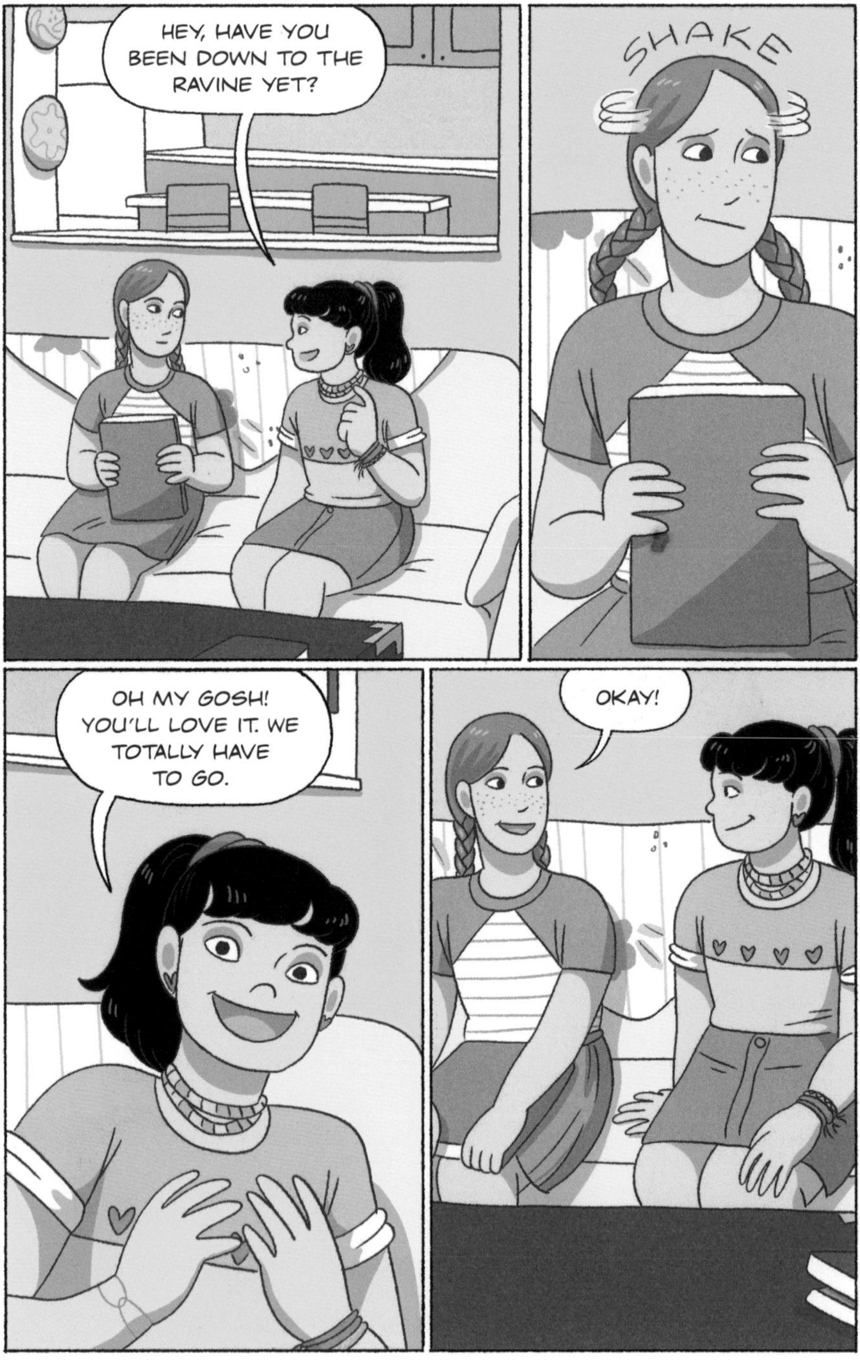
HEY, HAVE YOU BEEN DOWN TO THE RAVINE YET?
SHAKE
OH MY GOSH! YOU'LL LOVE IT. WE TOTALLY HAVE TO GO.
OKAY!

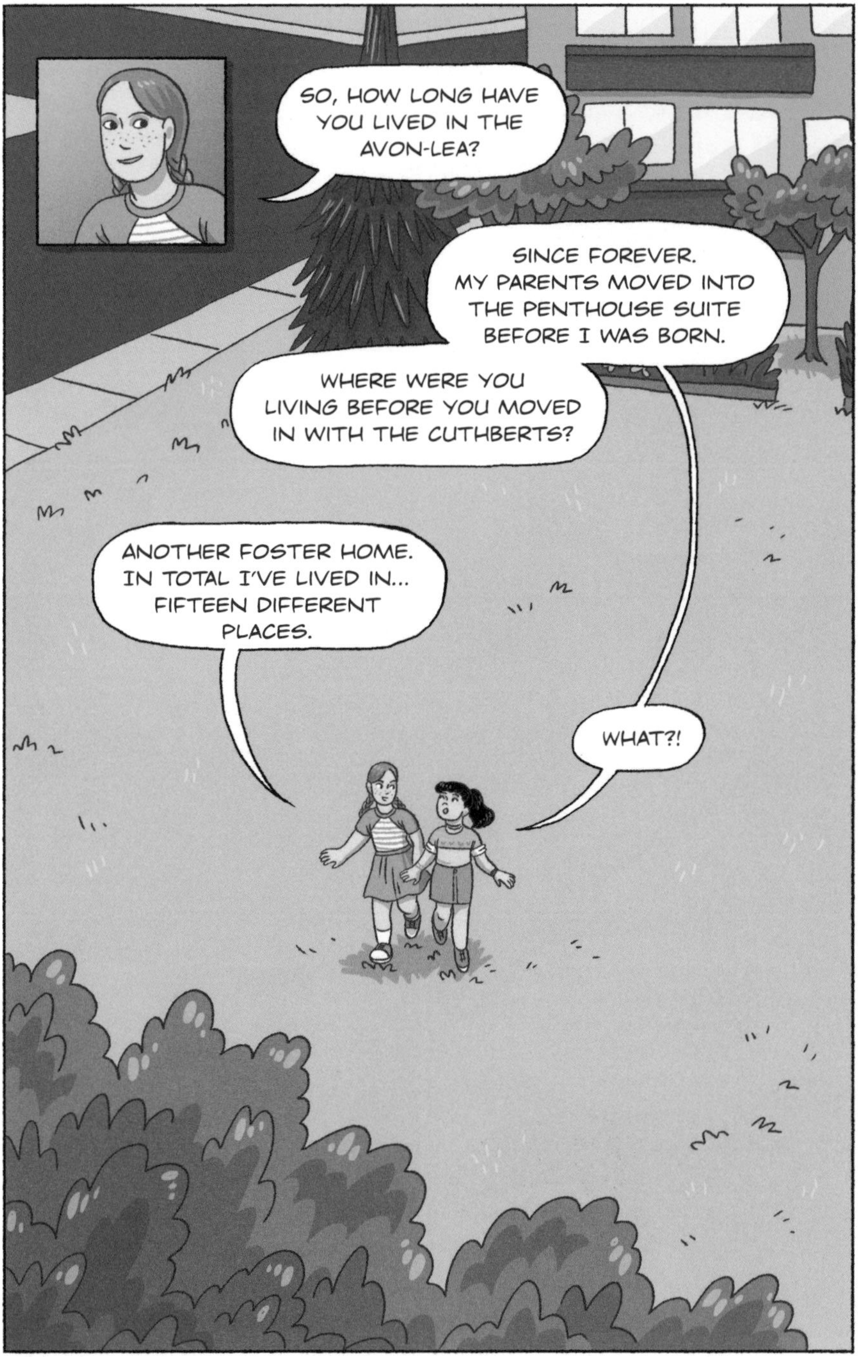
SO, HOW LONG HAVE YOU LIVED IN THE AVON-LEA?
SINCE FOREVER. MY PARENTS MOVED INTO THE PENTHOUSE SUITE BEFORE I WAS BORN.
WHERE WERE YOU LIVING BEFORE YOU MOVED IN WITH THE CUTHBERTS?
ANOTHER FOSTER HOME. IN TOTAL I'VE LIVED IN... FIFTEEN DIFFERENT PLACES.
WHAT?!

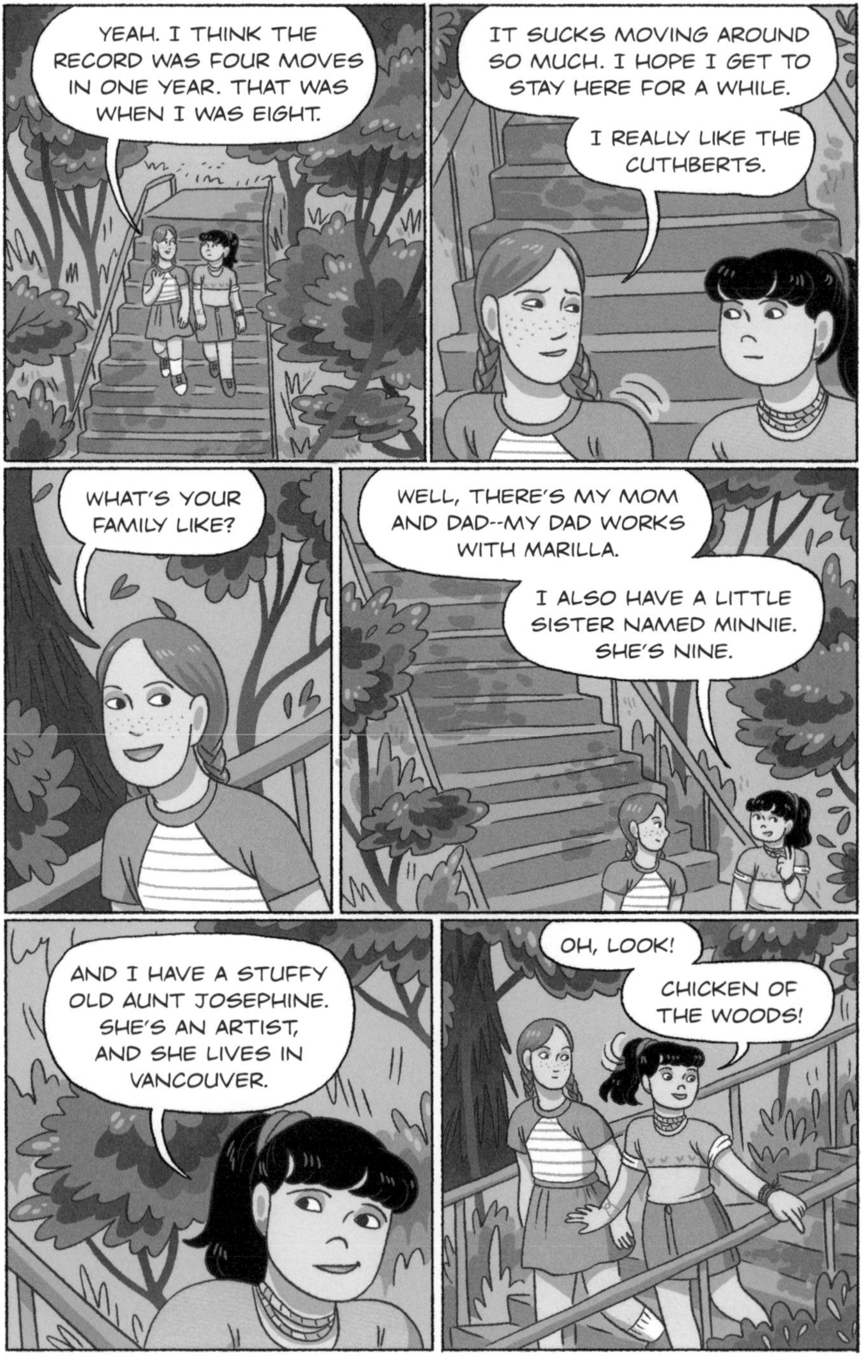
YEAH. I THINK THE RECORD WAS FOUR MOVES IN ONE YEAR. THAT WAS WHEN I WAS EIGHT.
IT SUCKS MOVING AROUND SO MUCH. I HOPE I GET TO STAY HERE FOR A WHILE.
I REALLY LIKE THE CUTHBERTS.
WHAT'S YOUR FAMILY LIKE?
WELL, THERE'S MY MOM AND DAD--MY DAD WORKS WITH MARILLA.
I ALSO HAVE A LITTLE SISTER NAMED MINNIE. SHE'S NINE.
AND I HAVE A STUFFY OLD AUNT JOSEPHINE. SHE'S AN ARTIST, AND SHE LIVES IN VANCOUVER.
OH, LOOK!
CHICKEN OF THE WOODS!

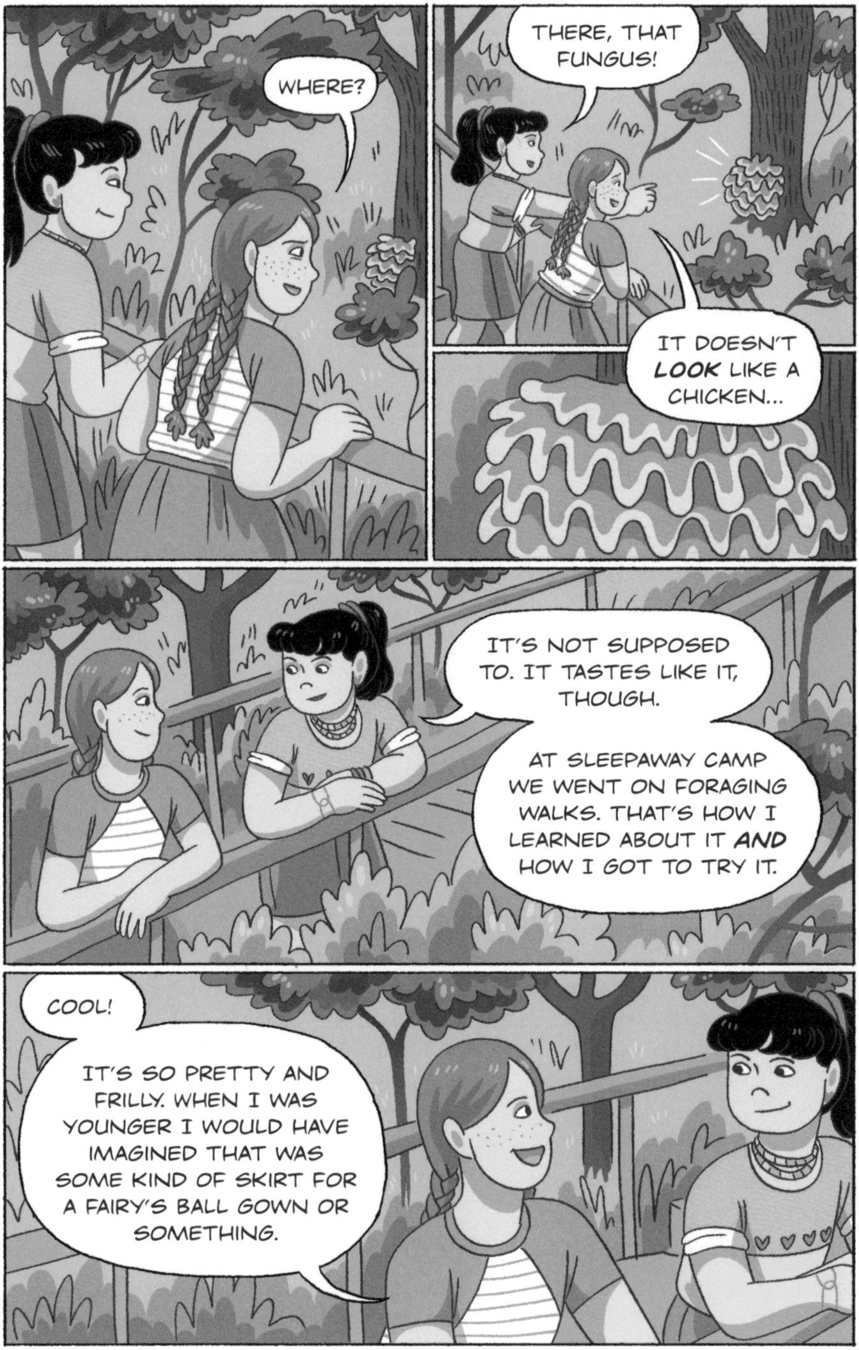
WHERE?
THERE, THAT FUNGUS!
IT DOESN'T **LOOK** LIKE A CHICKEN...
IT'S NOT SUPPOSED TO. IT TASTES LIKE IT, THOUGH.
AT SLEEPAWAY CAMP WE WENT ON FORAGING WALKS. THAT'S HOW I LEARNED ABOUT IT **AND** HOW I GOT TO TRY IT.
COOL!
IT'S SO PRETTY AND FRILLY. WHEN I WAS YOUNGER I WOULD HAVE IMAGINED THAT WAS SOME KIND OF SKIRT FOR A FAIRY'S BALL GOWN OR SOMETHING.

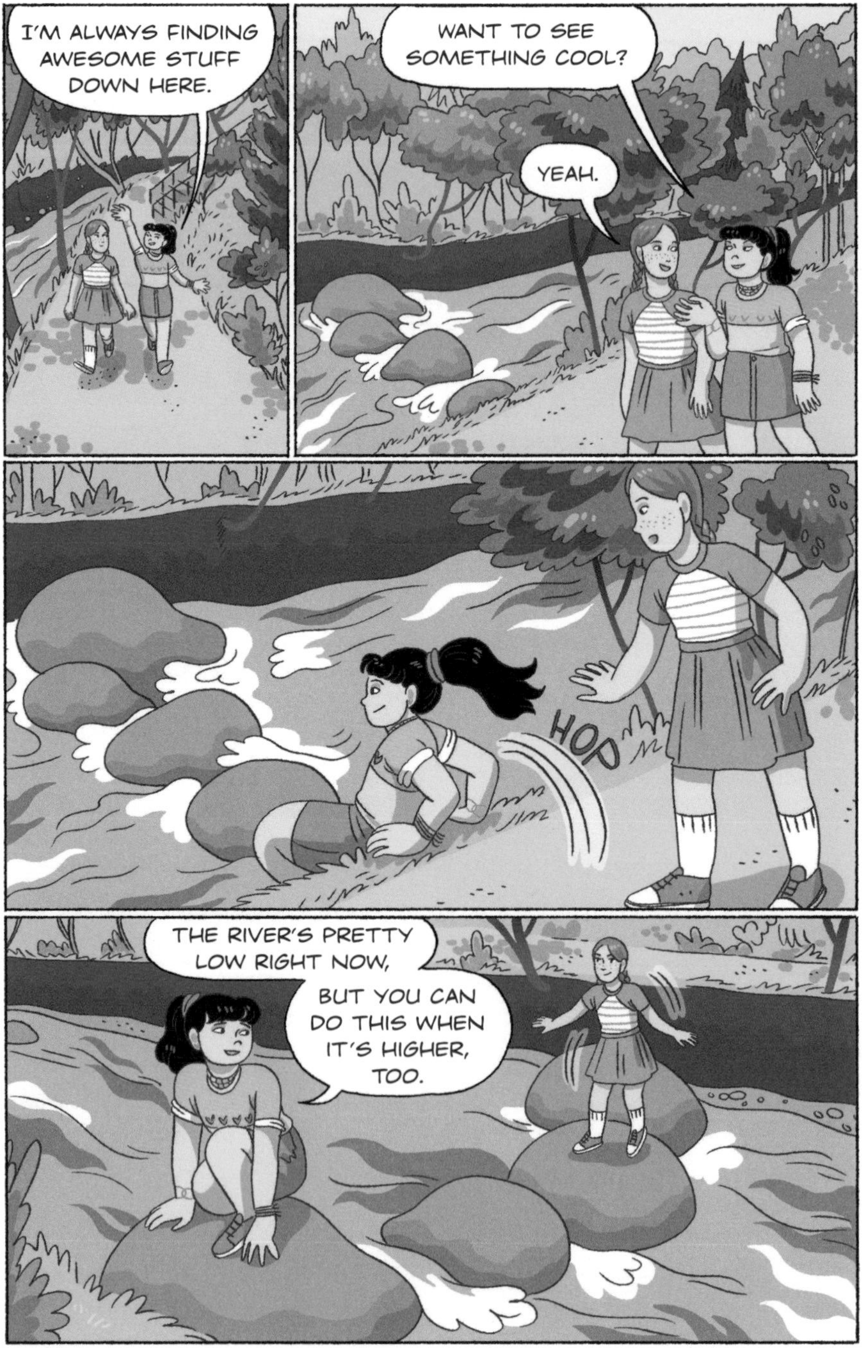
I'M ALWAYS FINDING AWESOME STUFF DOWN HERE.
WANT TO SEE SOMETHING COOL?
YEAH.
HOP
THE RIVER'S PRETTY LOW RIGHT NOW,
BUT YOU CAN DO THIS WHEN IT'S HIGHER, TOO.

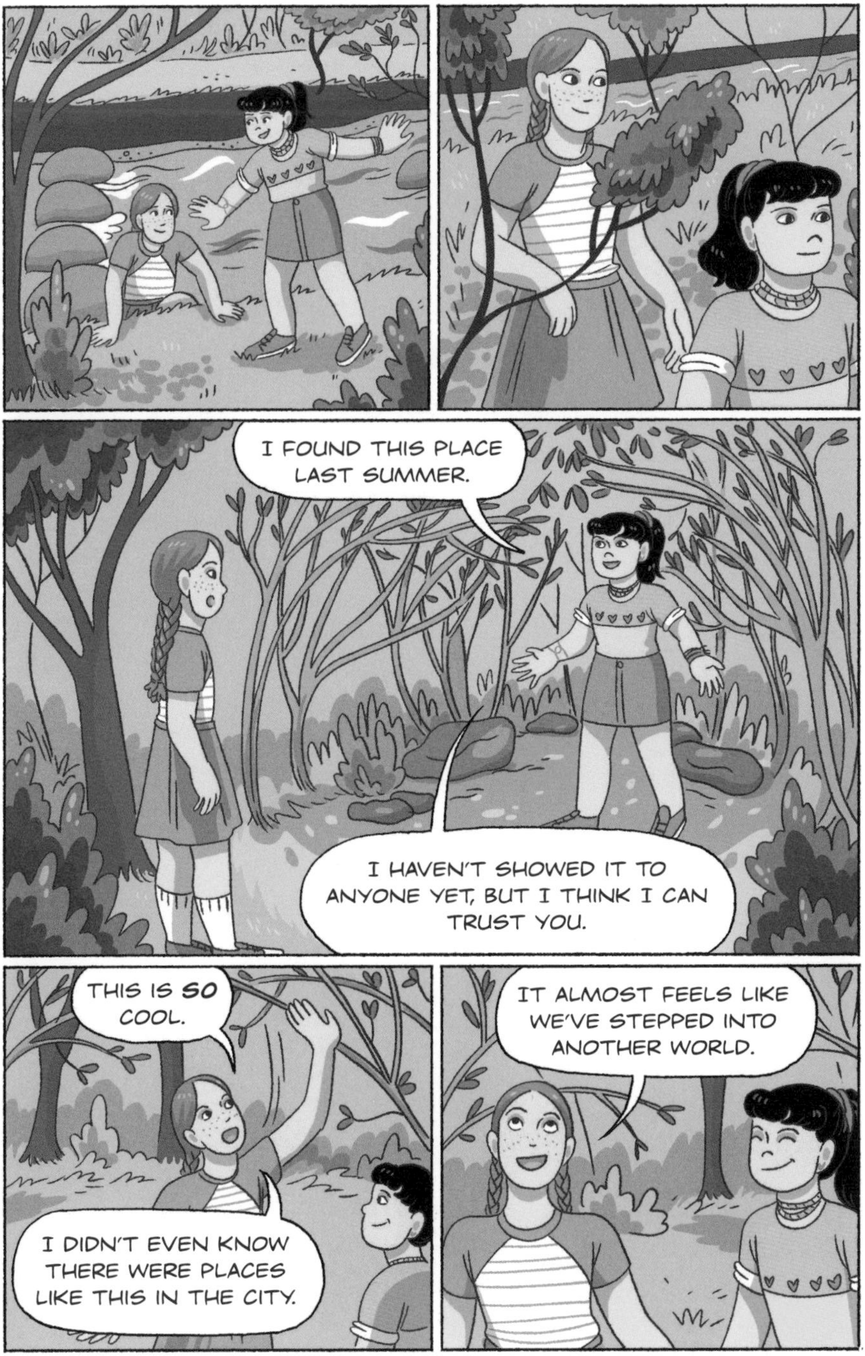
I FOUND THIS PLACE LAST SUMMER.
I HAVEN'T SHOWED IT TO ANYONE YET, BUT I THINK I CAN TRUST YOU.
THIS IS **SO** COOL.
I DIDN'T EVEN KNOW THERE WERE PLACES LIKE THIS IN THE CITY.
IT ALMOST FEELS LIKE WE'VE STEPPED INTO ANOTHER WORLD.

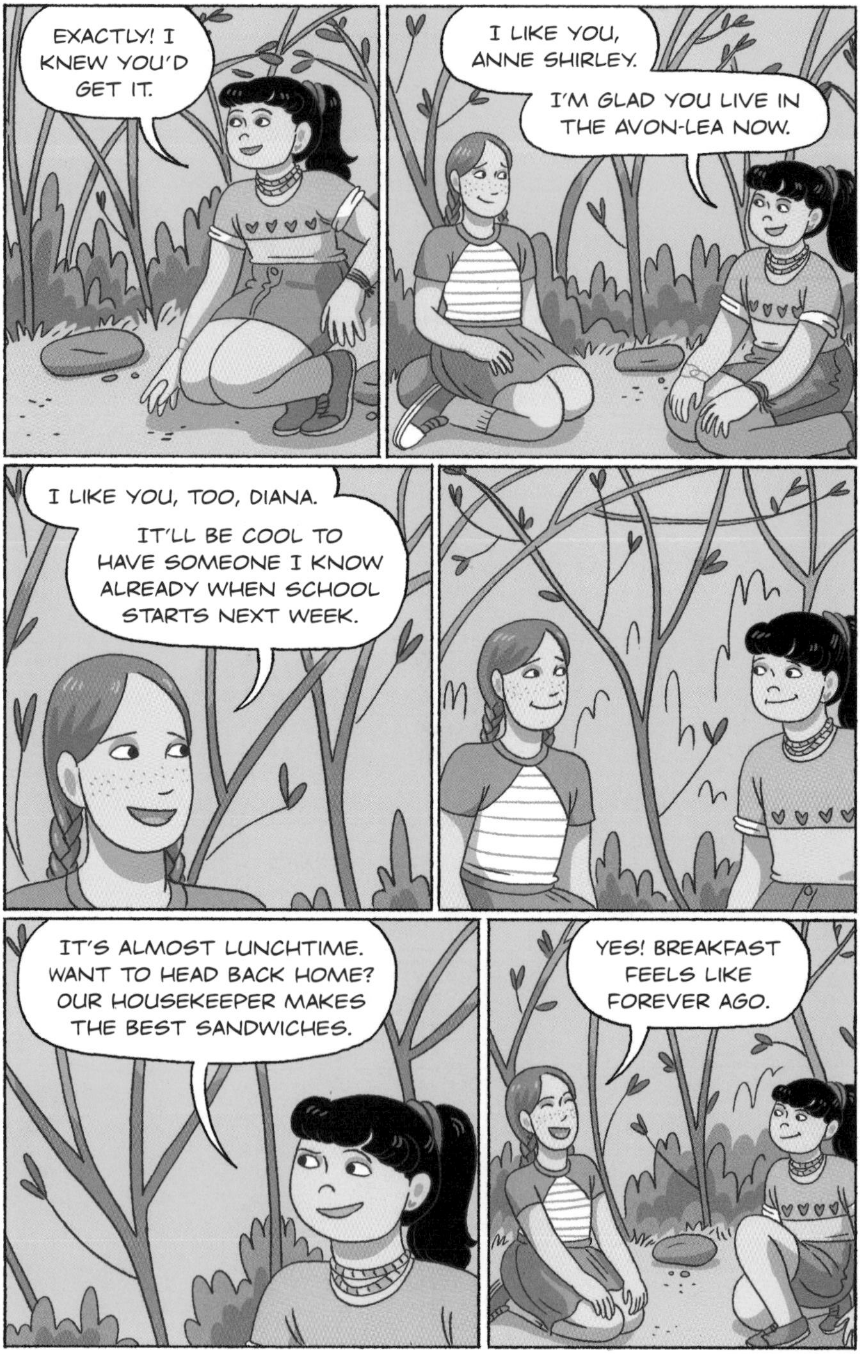
EXACTLY! I KNEW YOU'D GET IT.
I LIKE YOU, ANNE SHIRLEY.
I'M GLAD YOU LIVE IN THE AVON-LEA NOW.
I LIKE YOU, TOO, DIANA.
IT'LL BE COOL TO HAVE SOMEONE I KNOW ALREADY WHEN SCHOOL STARTS NEXT WEEK.
IT'S ALMOST LUNCHTIME. WANT TO HEAD BACK HOME? OUR HOUSEKEEPER MAKES THE BEST SANDWICHES.
YES! BREAKFAST FEELS LIKE FOREVER AGO.

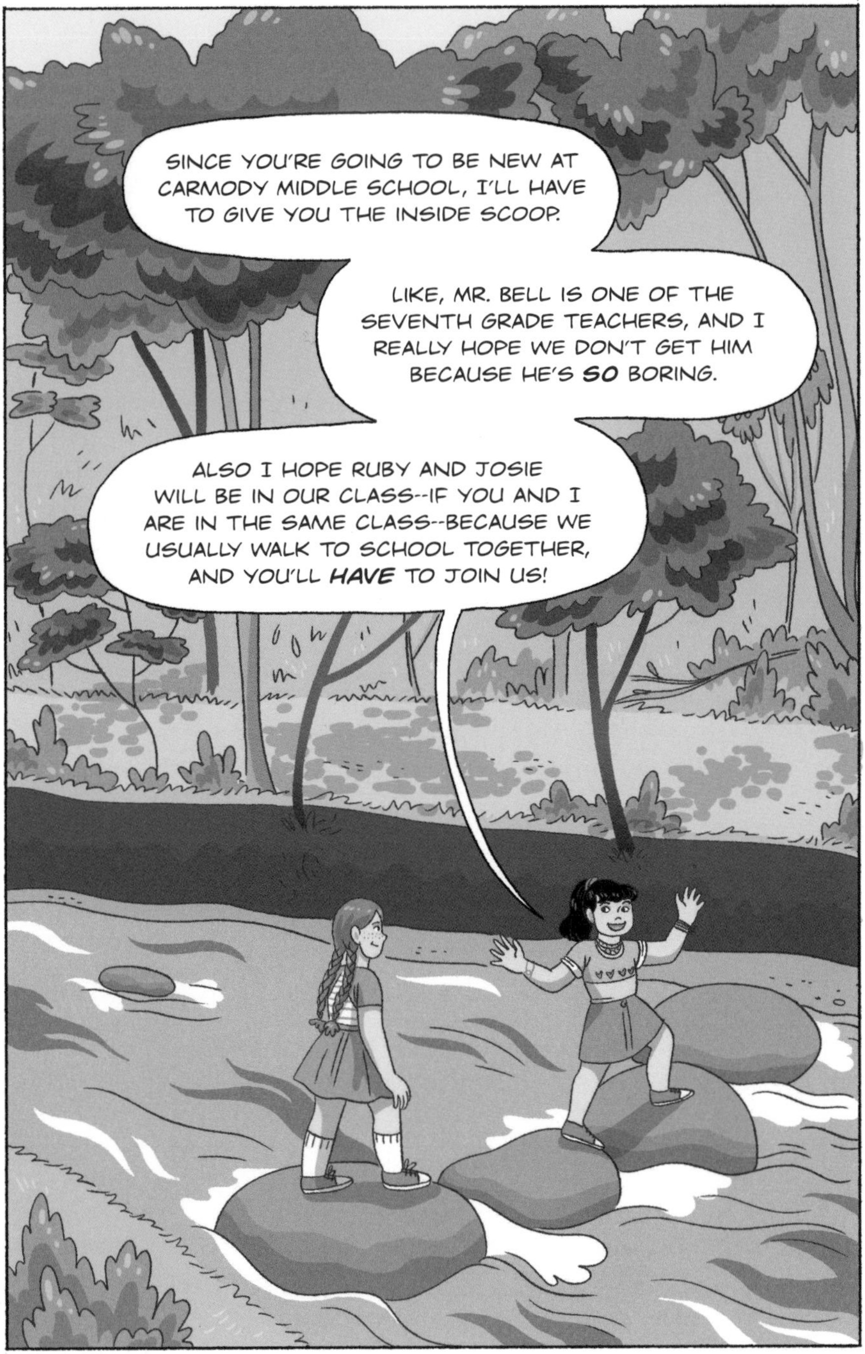
SINCE YOU'RE GOING TO BE NEW AT CARMODY MIDDLE SCHOOL, I'LL HAVE TO GIVE YOU THE INSIDE SCOOP.
LIKE, MR. BELL IS ONE OF THE SEVENTH GRADE TEACHERS, AND I REALLY HOPE WE DON'T GET HIM BECAUSE HE'S **SO** BORING.
ALSO I HOPE RUBY AND JOSIE WILL BE IN OUR CLASS--IF YOU AND I ARE IN THE SAME CLASS--BECAUSE WE USUALLY WALK TO SCHOOL TOGETHER, AND YOU'LL ***HAVE*** TO JOIN US!

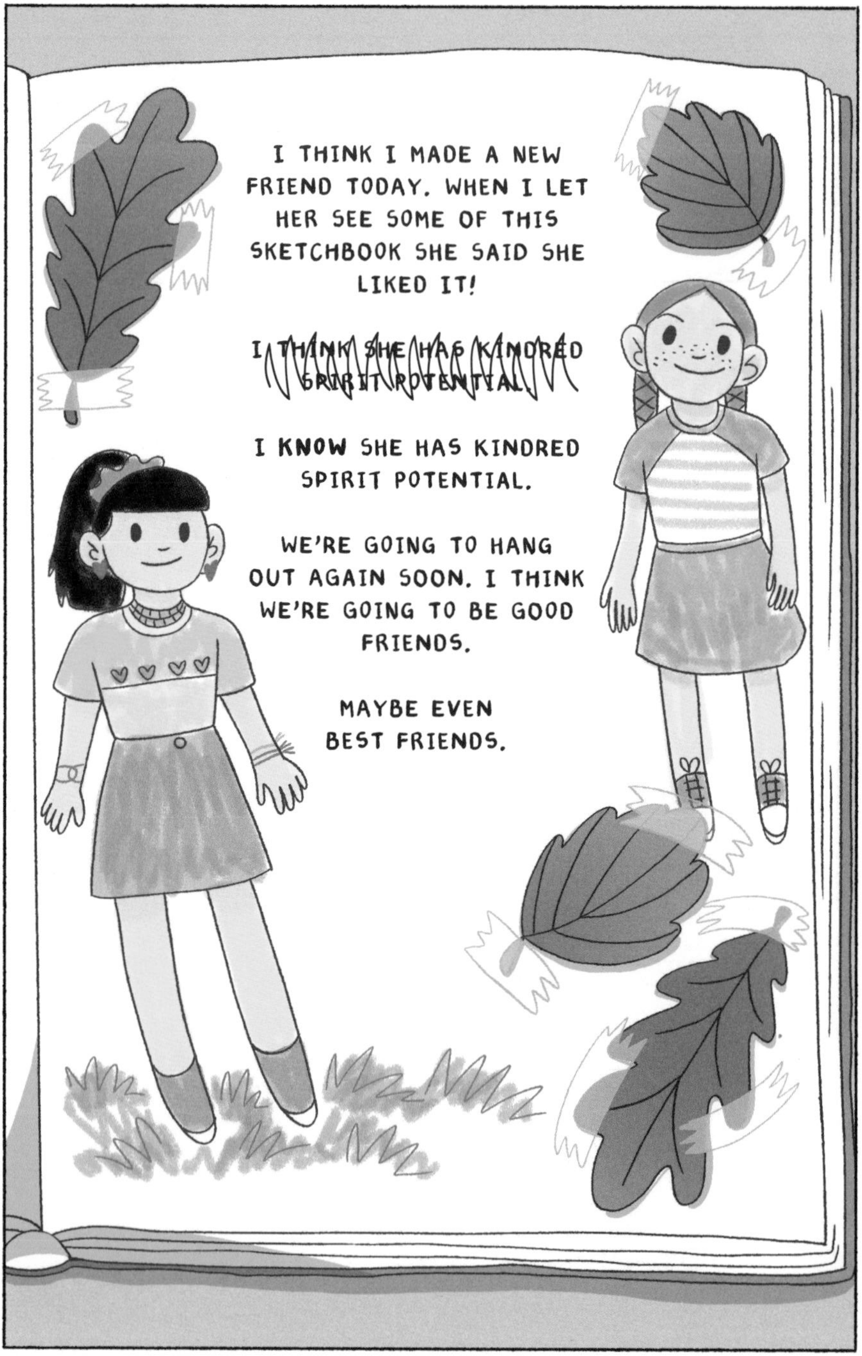
I THINK I MADE A NEW FRIEND TODAY. WHEN I LET HER SEE SOME OF THIS SKETCHBOOK SHE SAID SHE LIKED IT!
~~I THINK SHE HAS KINDRED SPIRIT POTENTIAL.~~
I **KNOW** SHE HAS KINDRED SPIRIT POTENTIAL.
WE'RE GOING TO HANG OUT AGAIN SOON. I THINK WE'RE GOING TO BE GOOD FRIENDS.
MAYBE EVEN BEST FRIENDS.

CHAPTER 5

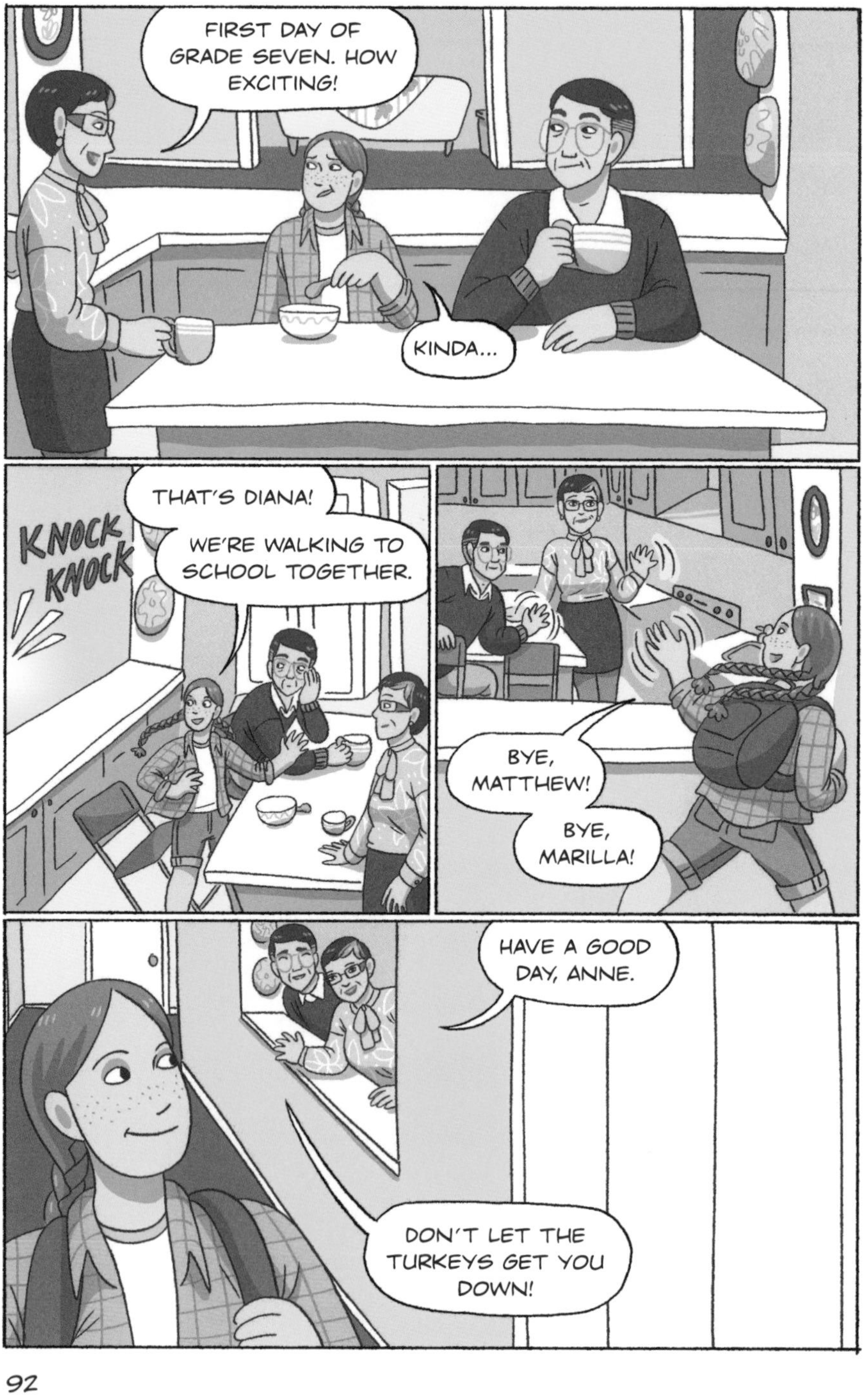
FIRST DAY OF GRADE SEVEN. HOW EXCITING!
KINDA...
KNOCK KNOCK
THAT'S DIANA!
WE'RE WALKING TO SCHOOL TOGETHER.
BYE, MATTHEW!
BYE, MARILLA!
HAVE A GOOD DAY, ANNE.
DON'T LET THE TURKEYS GET YOU DOWN!

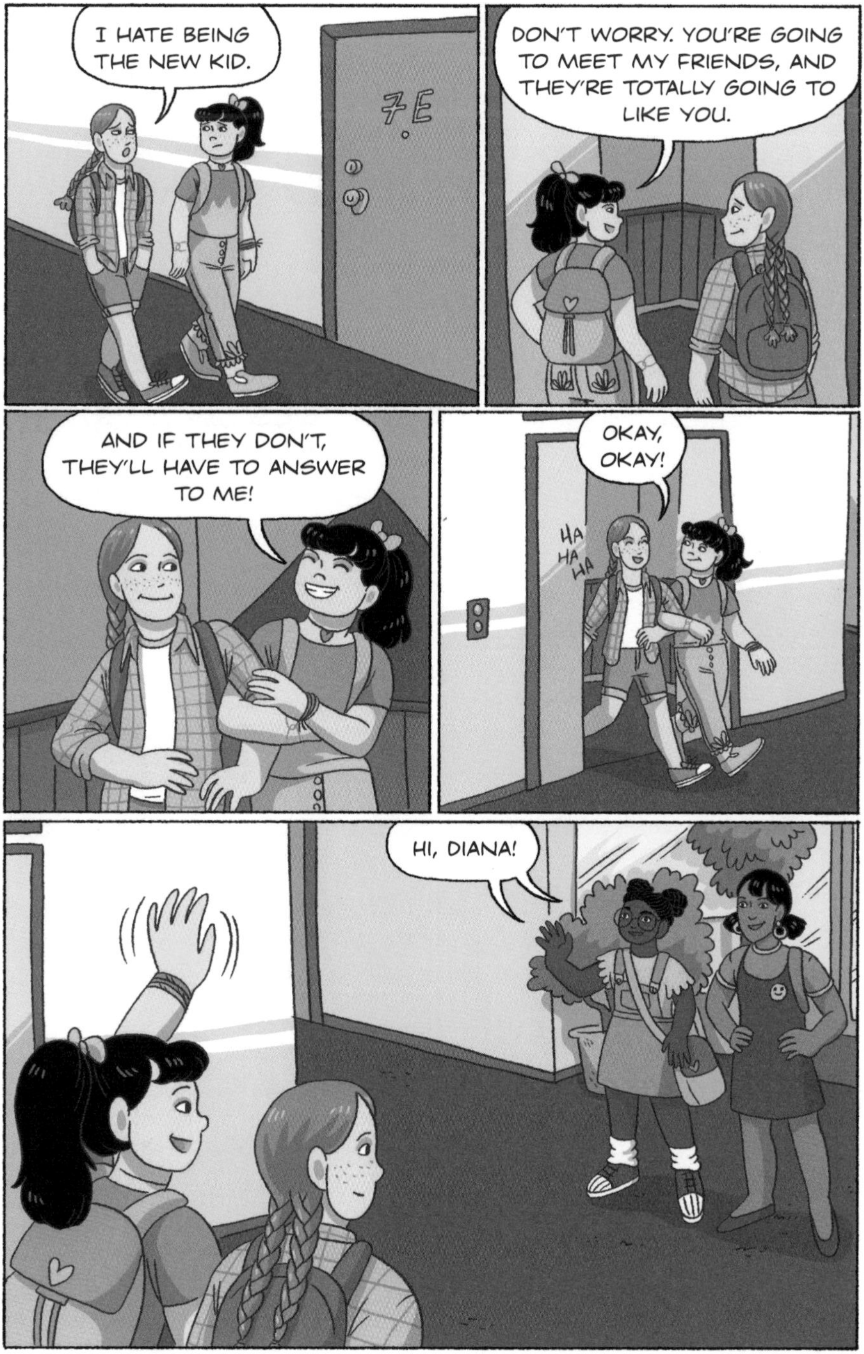

I HATE BEING THE NEW KID.
7E
DON'T WORRY. YOU'RE GOING TO MEET MY FRIENDS, AND THEY'RE TOTALLY GOING TO LIKE YOU.
AND IF THEY DON'T, THEY'LL HAVE TO ANSWER TO ME!
OKAY, OKAY!
HA HA HA
HI, DIANA!

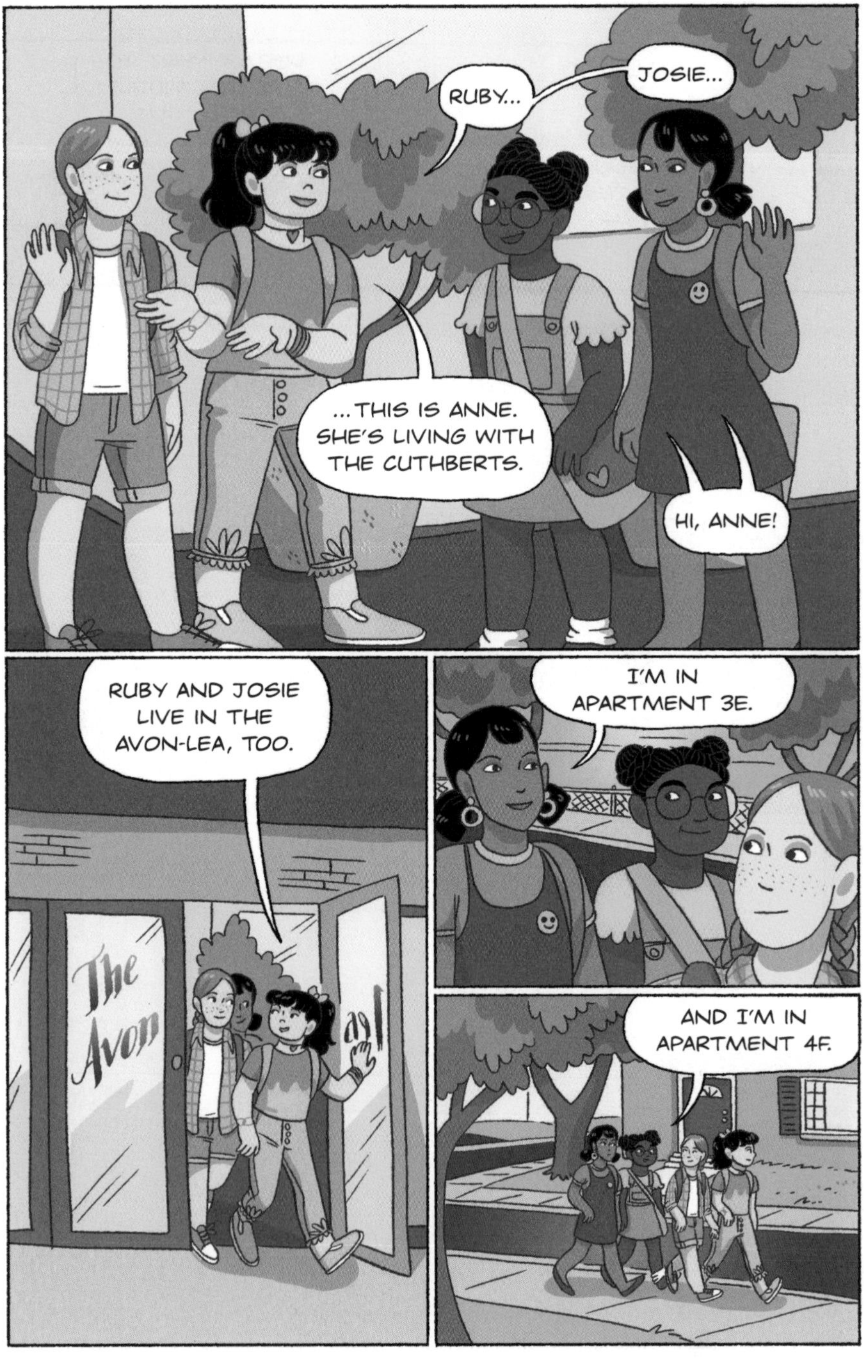
RUBY...
JOSIE...
...THIS IS ANNE. SHE'S LIVING WITH THE CUTHBERTS.
HI, ANNE!
RUBY AND JOSIE LIVE IN THE AVON-LEA, TOO.
The Avon lea
I'M IN APARTMENT 3E.
AND I'M IN APARTMENT 4F.

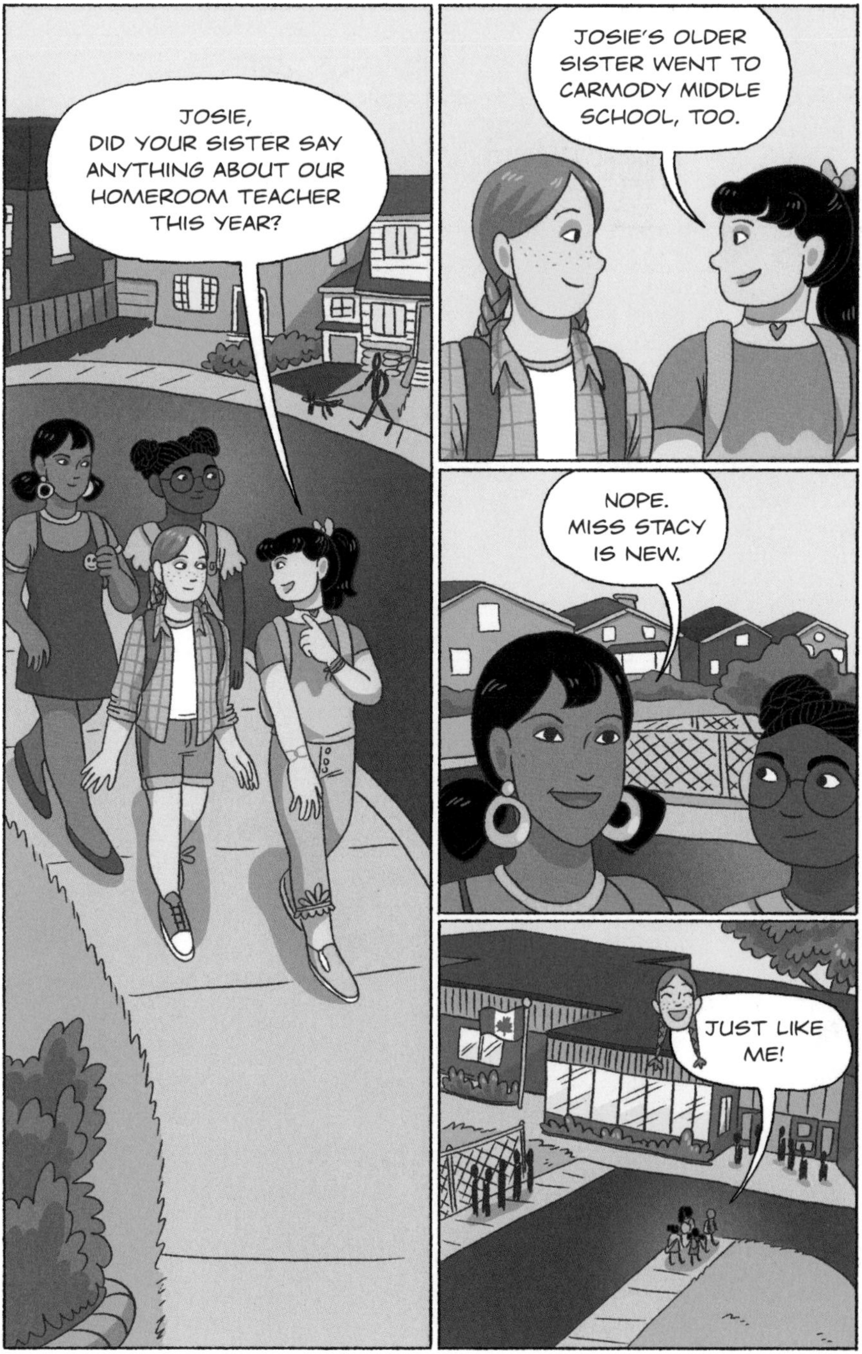
JOSIE, DID YOUR SISTER SAY ANYTHING ABOUT OUR HOMEROOM TEACHER THIS YEAR?
JOSIE'S OLDER SISTER WENT TO CARMODY MIDDLE SCHOOL, TOO.
NOPE. MISS STACY IS NEW.
JUST LIKE ME!

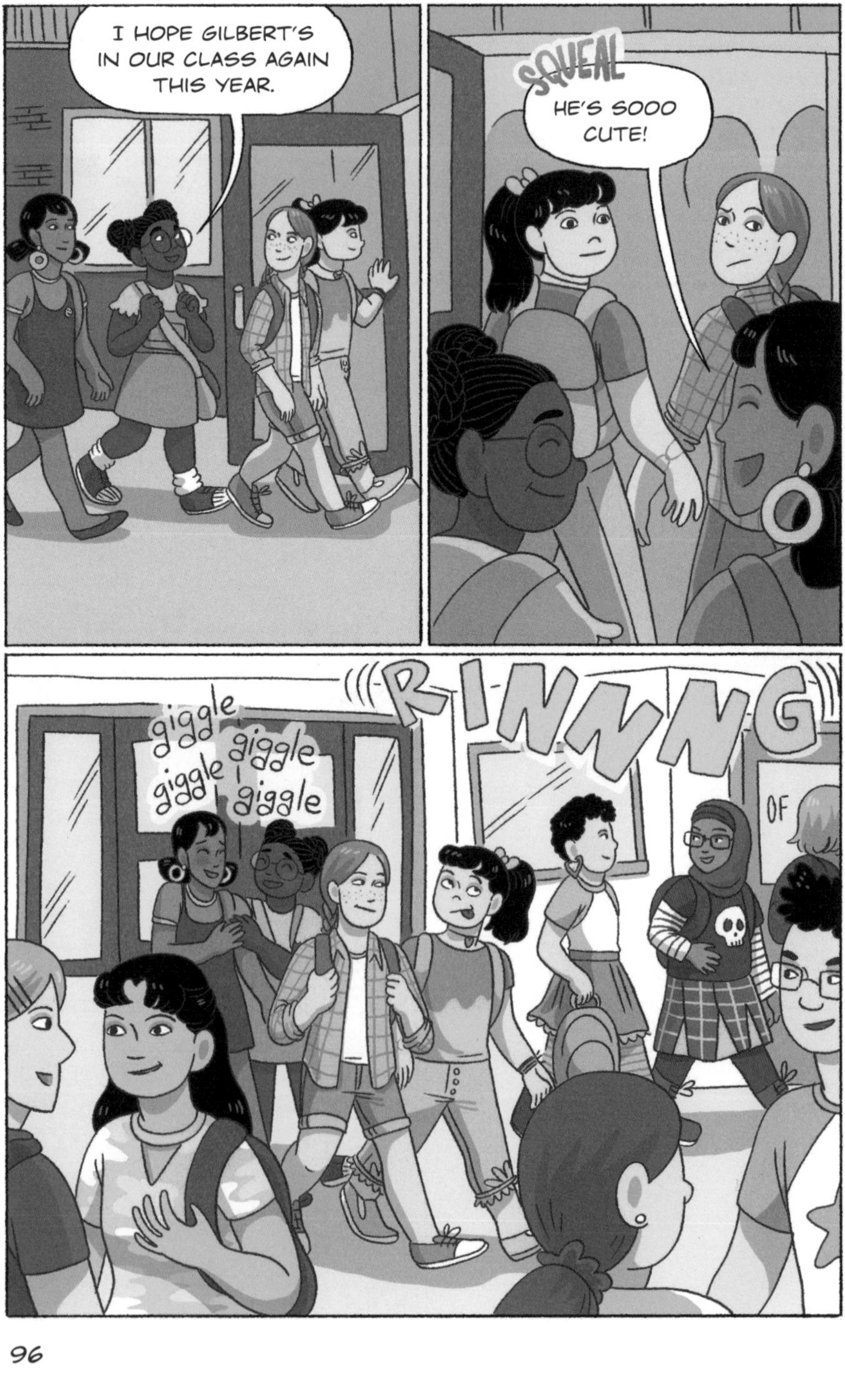
I HOPE GILBERT'S IN OUR CLASS AGAIN THIS YEAR.
SQUEAL
HE'S SOOO CUTE!
RINNNG
giggle
giggle
giggle
giggle
giggle
OF

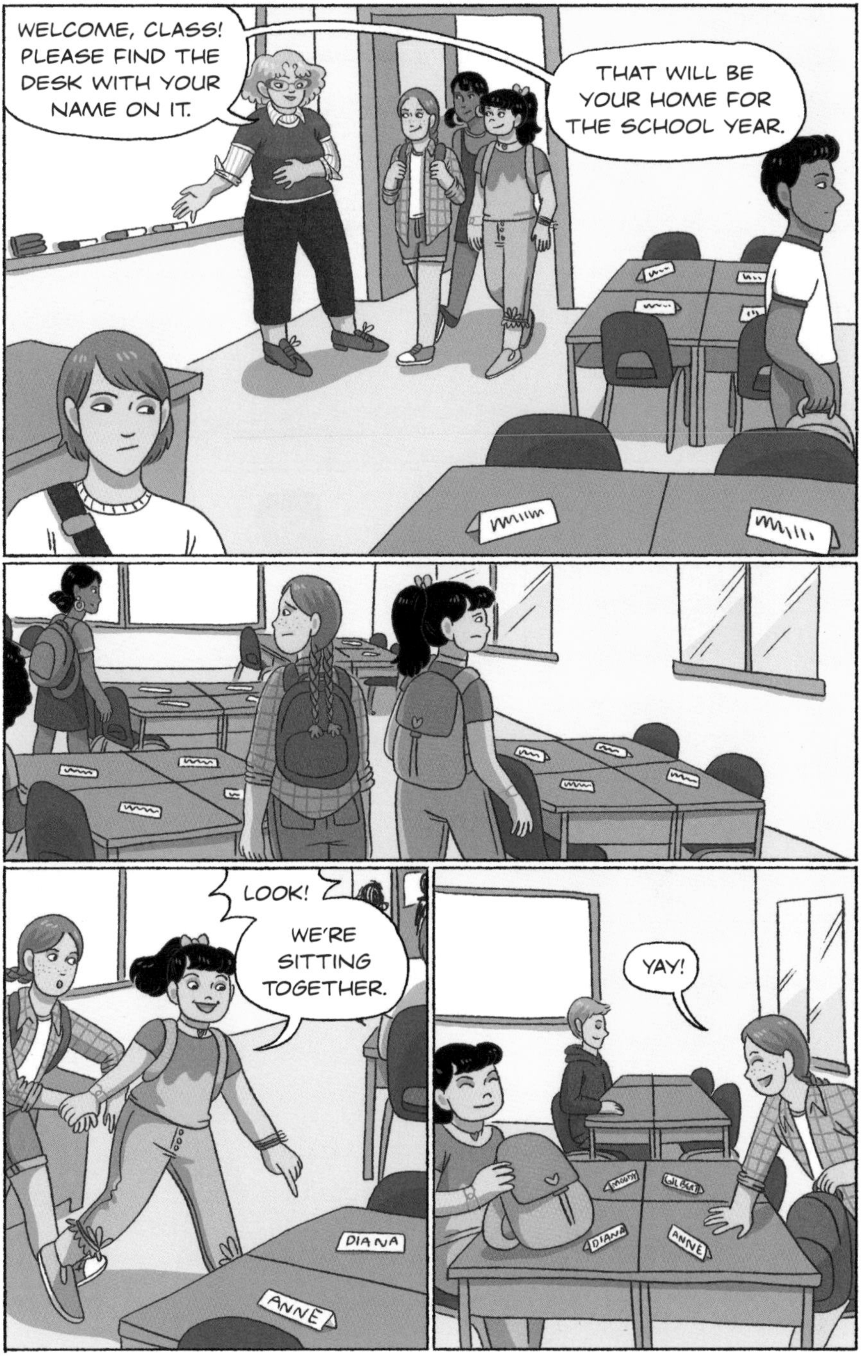
WELCOME, CLASS! PLEASE FIND THE DESK WITH YOUR NAME ON IT.
THAT WILL BE YOUR HOME FOR THE SCHOOL YEAR.
LOOK!
WE'RE SITTING TOGETHER.
DIANA
ANNE
YAY!
DIANA
ANNE

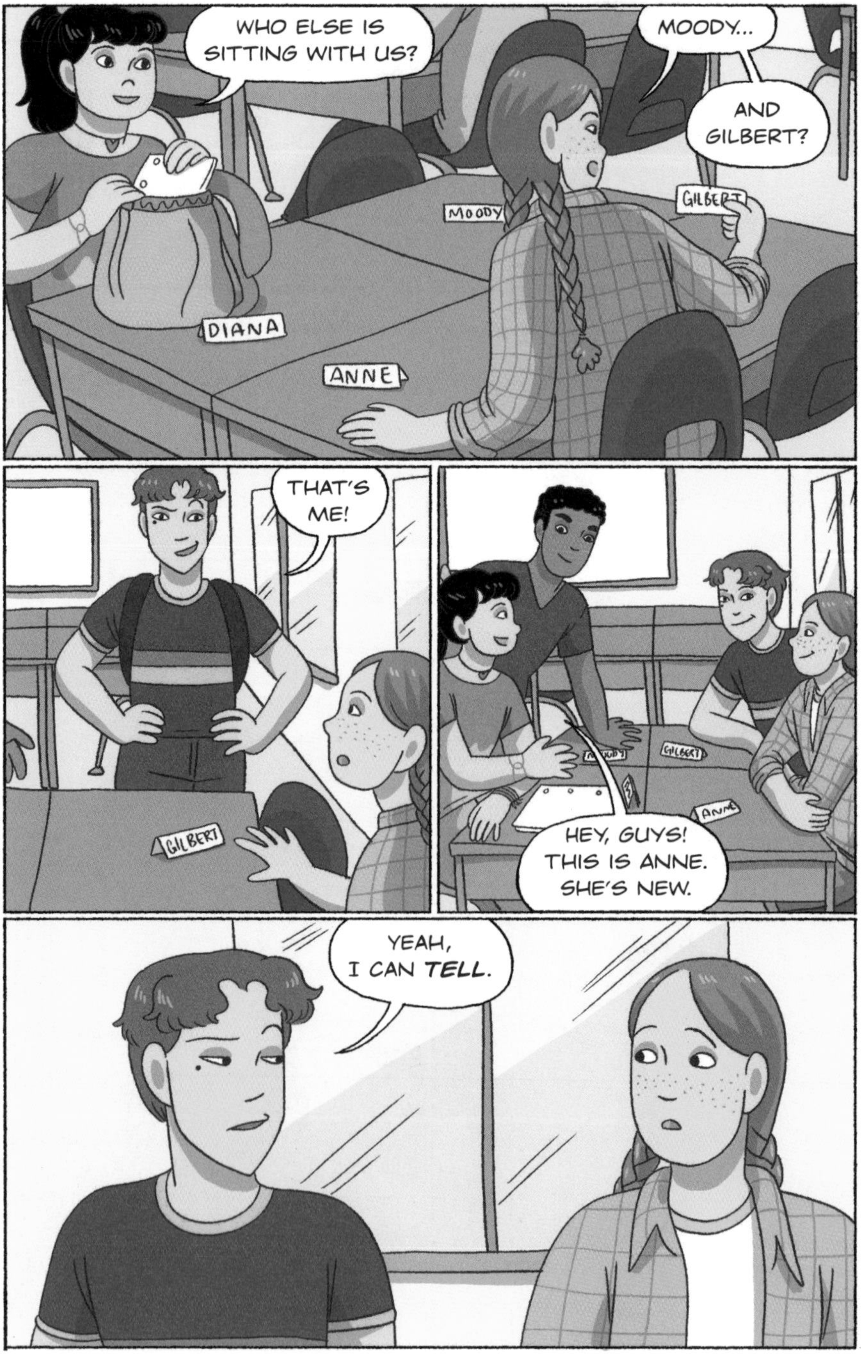
WHO ELSE IS SITTING WITH US?
MOODY...
AND GILBERT?
GILBERT
MOODY
DIANA
ANNE
THAT'S ME!
GILBERT
GILBERT
ANNE
HEY, GUYS! THIS IS ANNE. SHE'S NEW.
YEAH, I CAN **TELL**.

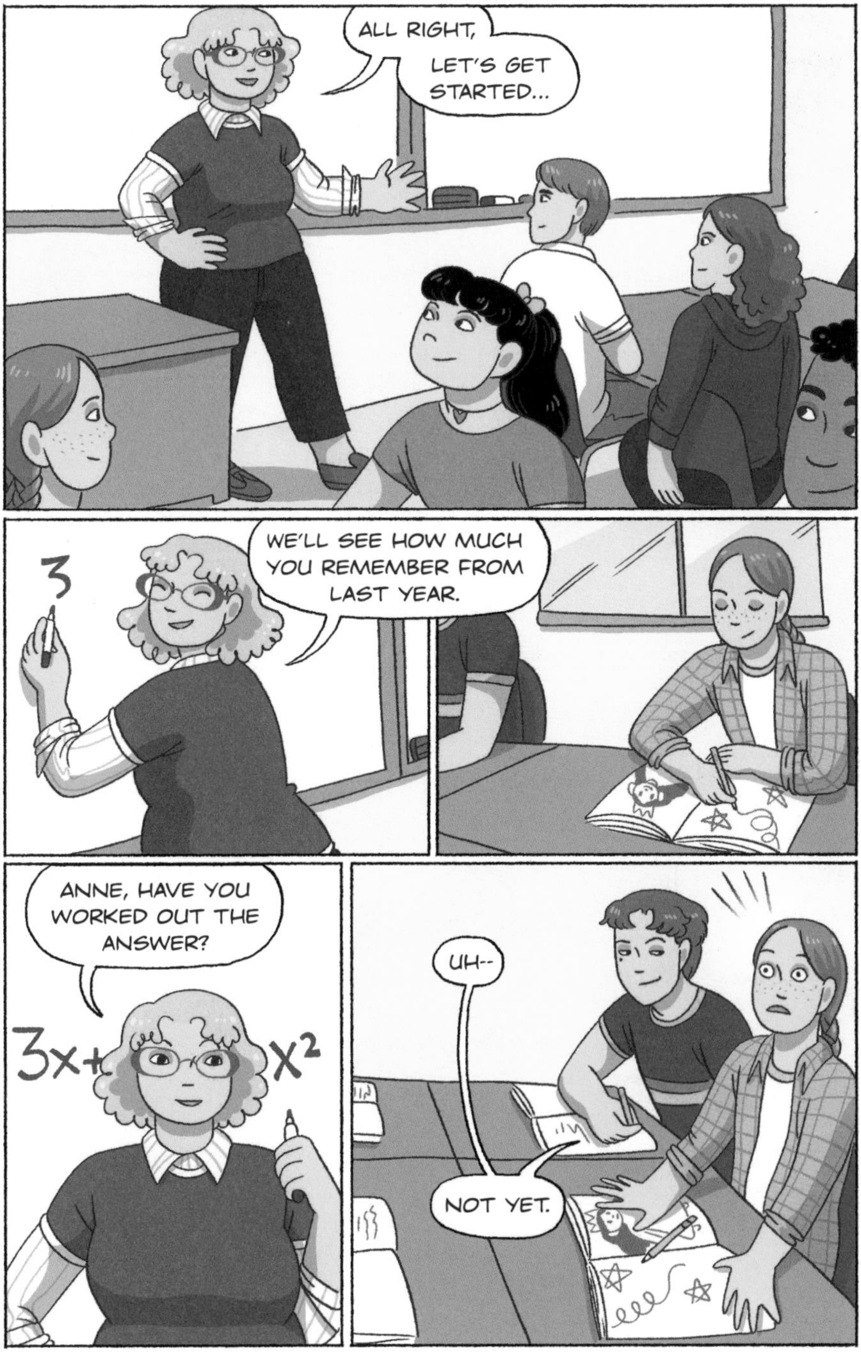
ALL RIGHT,
LET'S GET STARTED...
3
WE'LL SEE HOW MUCH YOU REMEMBER FROM LAST YEAR.
ANNE, HAVE YOU WORKED OUT THE ANSWER?
3x+ x²
UH--
NOT YET.

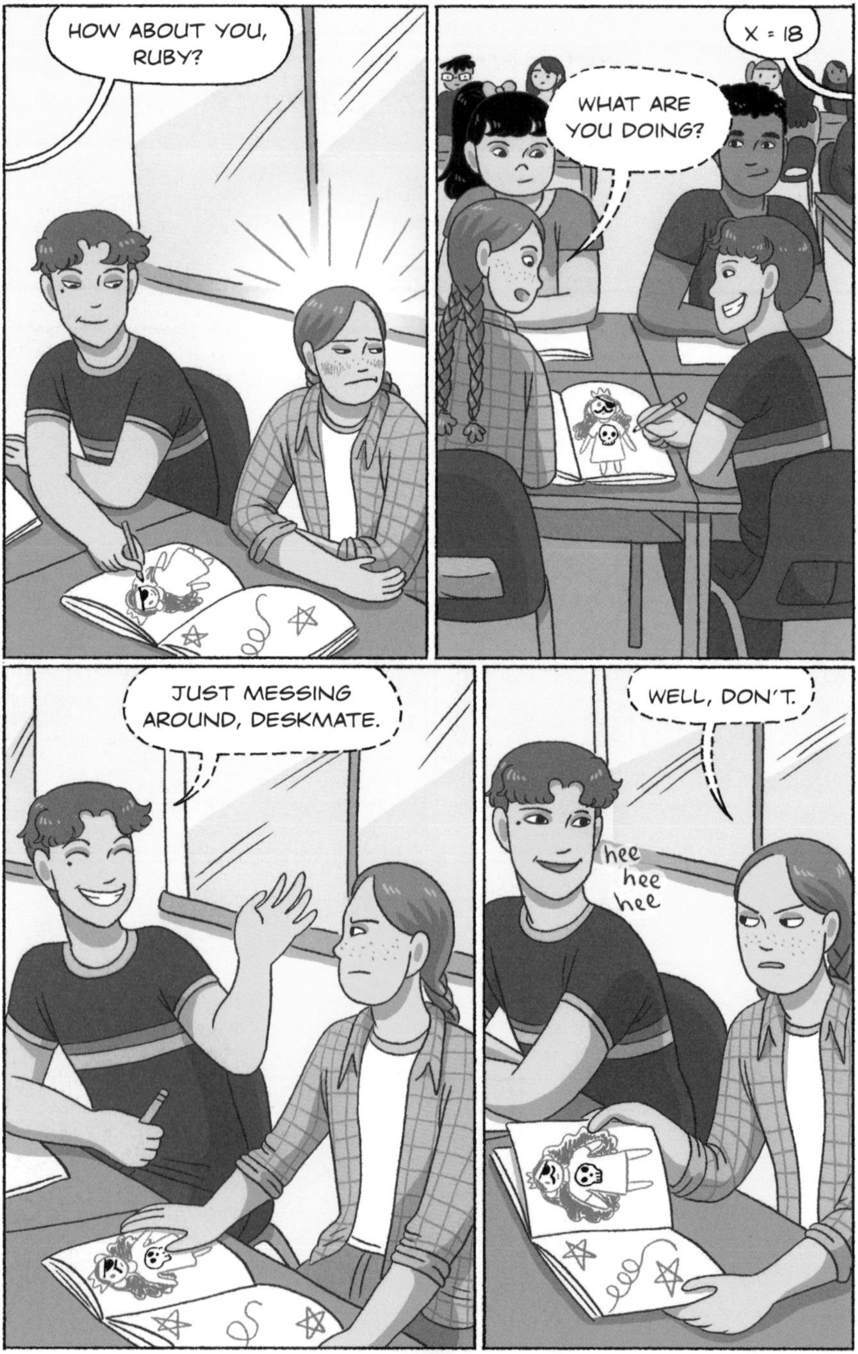
HOW ABOUT YOU, RUBY?
X = 18
WHAT ARE YOU DOING?
JUST MESSING AROUND, DESKMATE.
WELL, DON'T.
hee hee hee

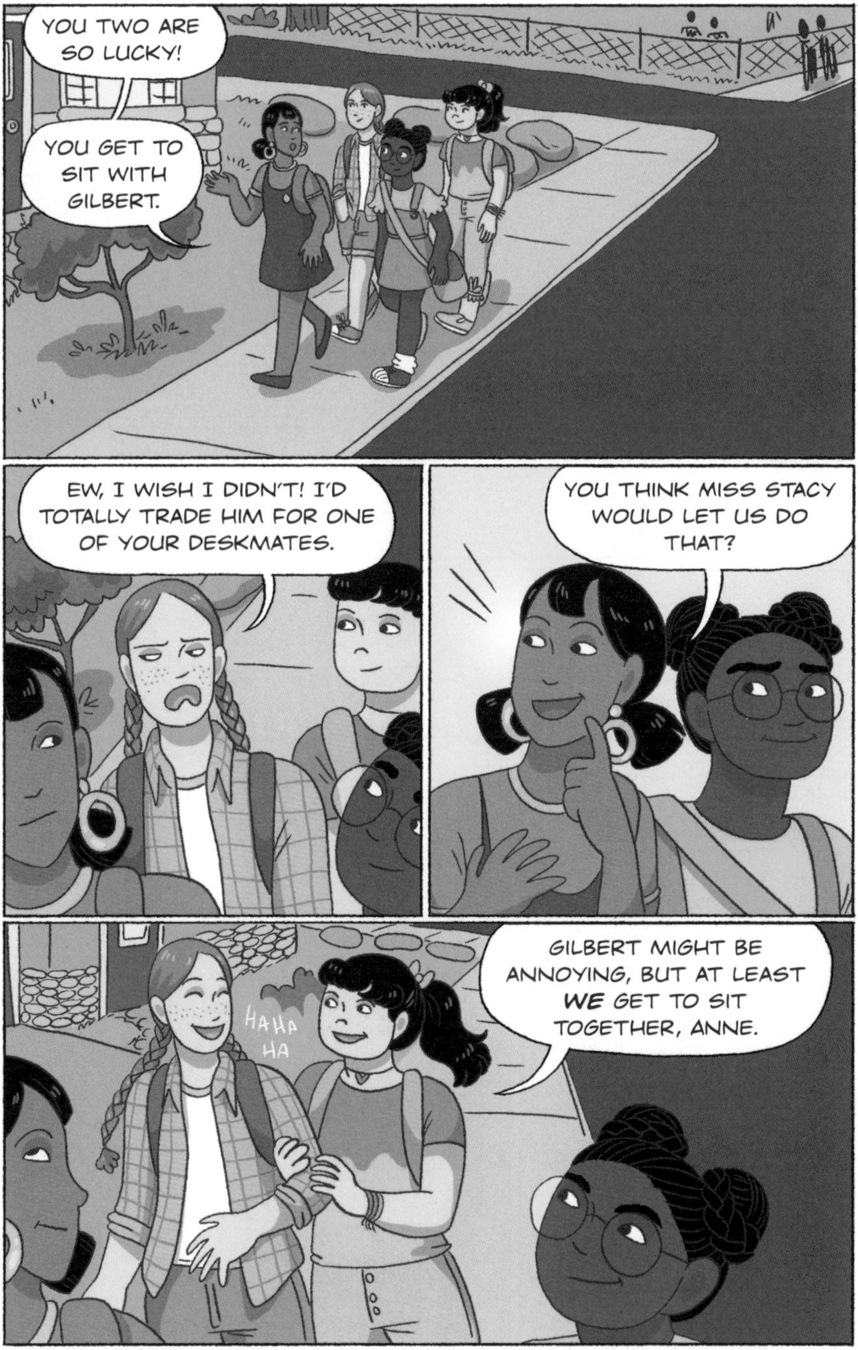
YOU TWO ARE SO LUCKY!
YOU GET TO SIT WITH GILBERT.
EW, I WISH I DIDN'T! I'D TOTALLY TRADE HIM FOR ONE OF YOUR DESKMATES.
YOU THINK MISS STACY WOULD LET US DO THAT?
HAHA HA
GILBERT MIGHT BE ANNOYING, BUT AT LEAST **WE** GET TO SIT TOGETHER, ANNE.

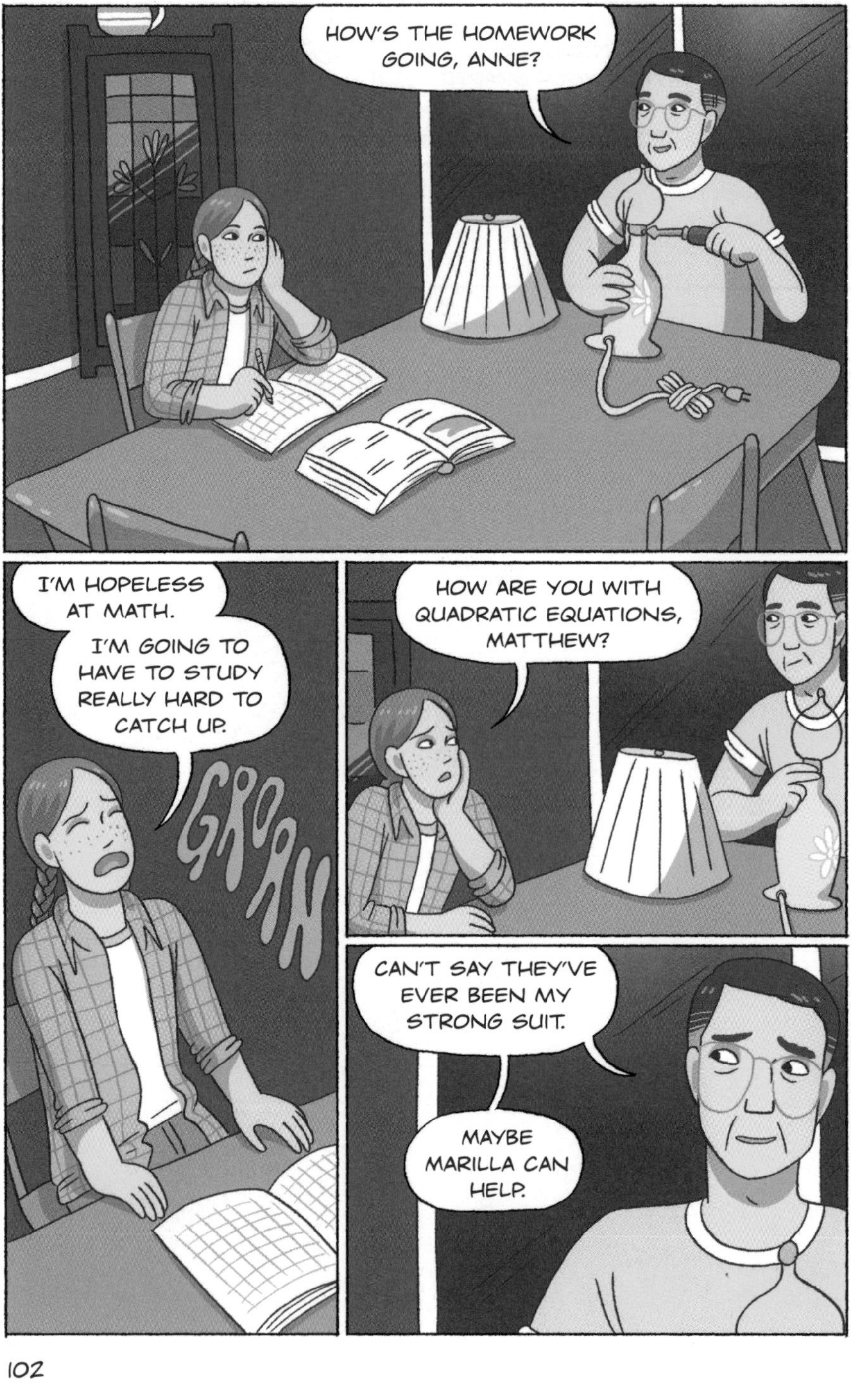
HOW'S THE HOMEWORK GOING, ANNE?
I'M HOPELESS AT MATH.
I'M GOING TO HAVE TO STUDY REALLY HARD TO CATCH UP.
GROAN
HOW ARE YOU WITH QUADRATIC EQUATIONS, MATTHEW?
CAN'T SAY THEY'VE EVER BEEN MY STRONG SUIT.
MAYBE MARILLA CAN HELP.

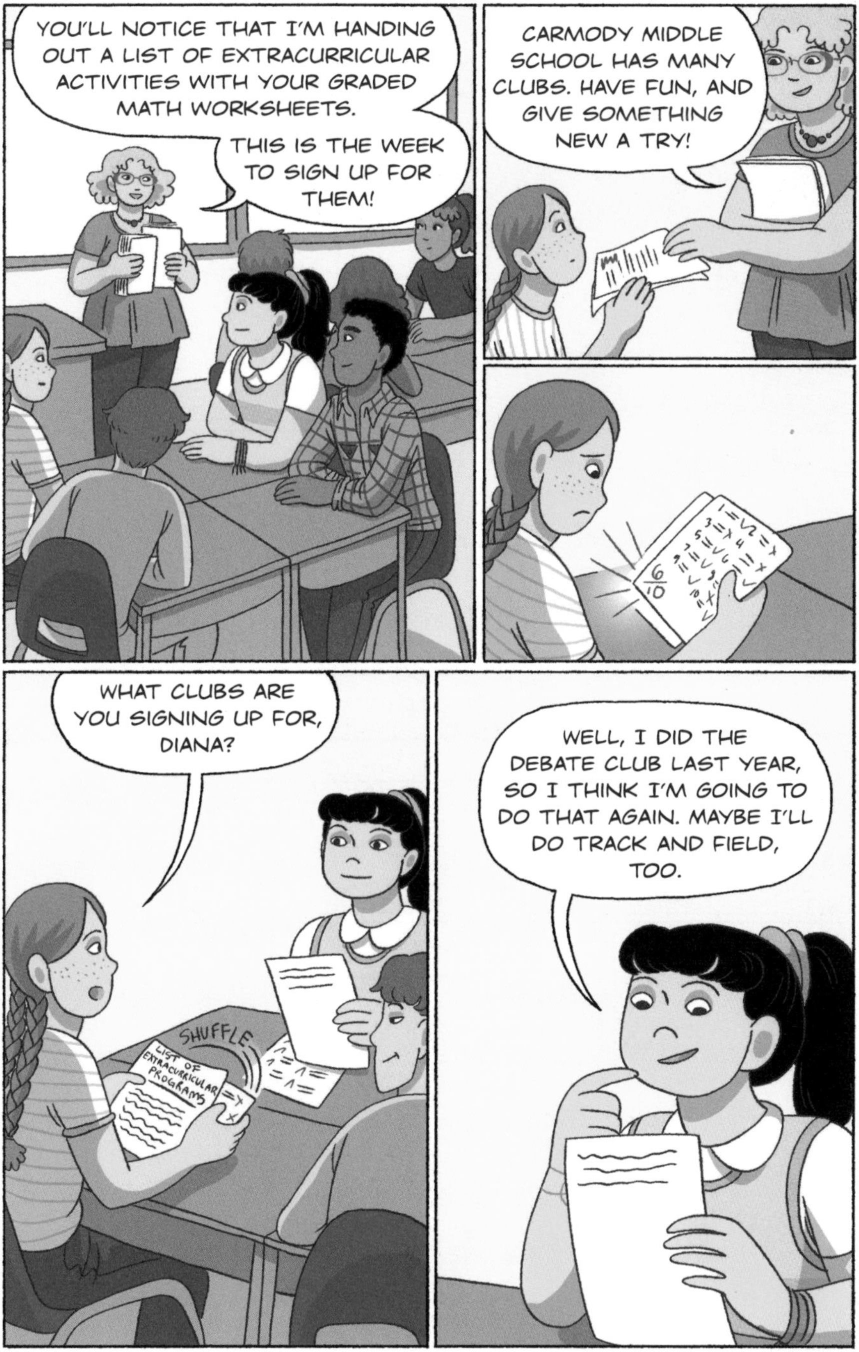
YOU'LL NOTICE THAT I'M HANDING OUT A LIST OF EXTRACURRICULAR ACTIVITIES WITH YOUR GRADED MATH WORKSHEETS.
THIS IS THE WEEK TO SIGN UP FOR THEM!
CARMODY MIDDLE SCHOOL HAS MANY CLUBS. HAVE FUN, AND GIVE SOMETHING NEW A TRY!
6/10
WHAT CLUBS ARE YOU SIGNING UP FOR, DIANA?
SHUFFLE
LIST OF EXTRACURRICULAR PROGRAMS
WELL, I DID THE DEBATE CLUB LAST YEAR, SO I THINK I'M GOING TO DO THAT AGAIN. MAYBE I'LL DO TRACK AND FIELD, TOO.

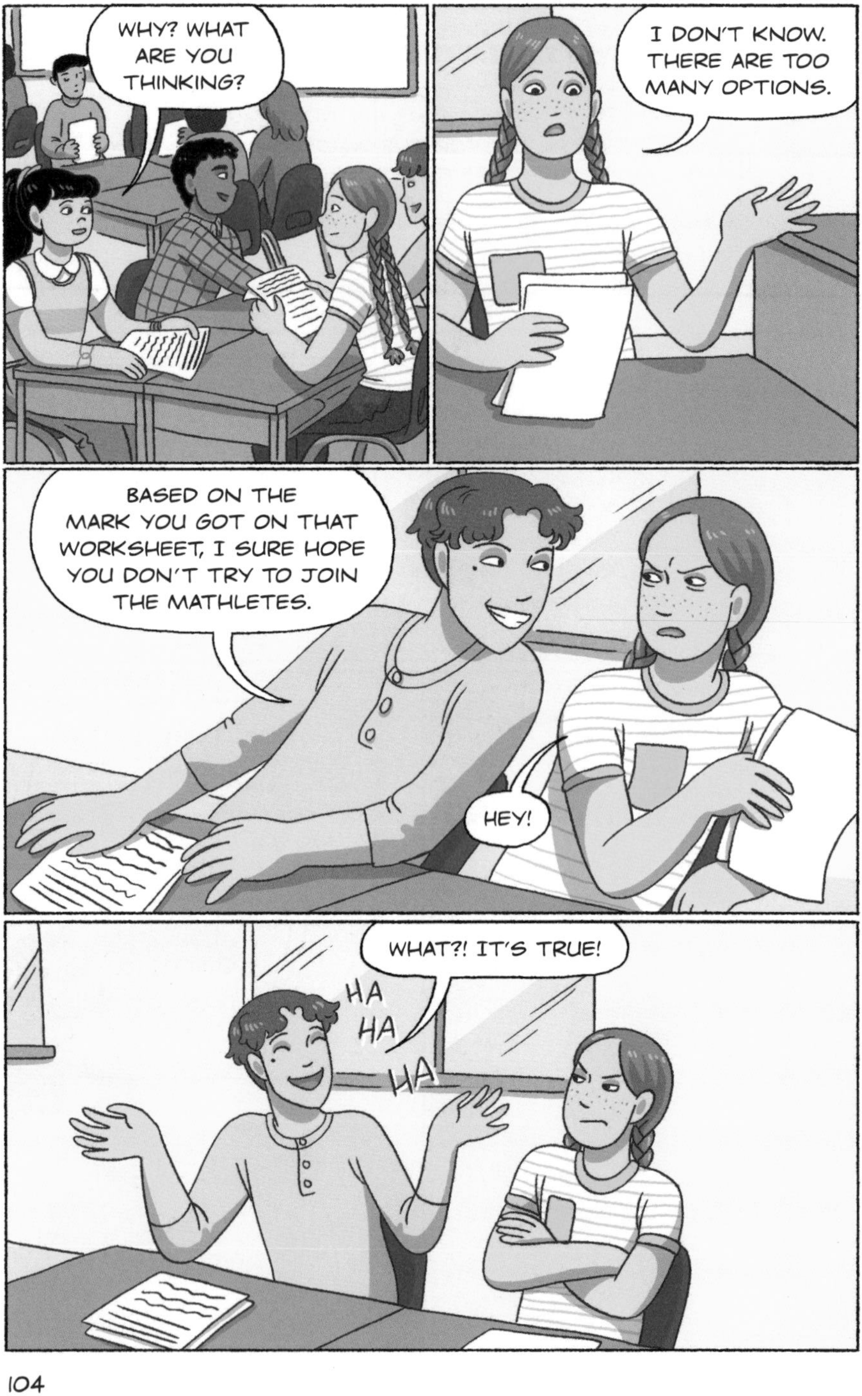
WHY? WHAT ARE YOU THINKING?
I DON'T KNOW. THERE ARE TOO MANY OPTIONS.
BASED ON THE MARK YOU GOT ON THAT WORKSHEET, I SURE HOPE YOU DON'T TRY TO JOIN THE MATHLETES.
HEY!
WHAT?! IT'S TRUE!
HA HA HA

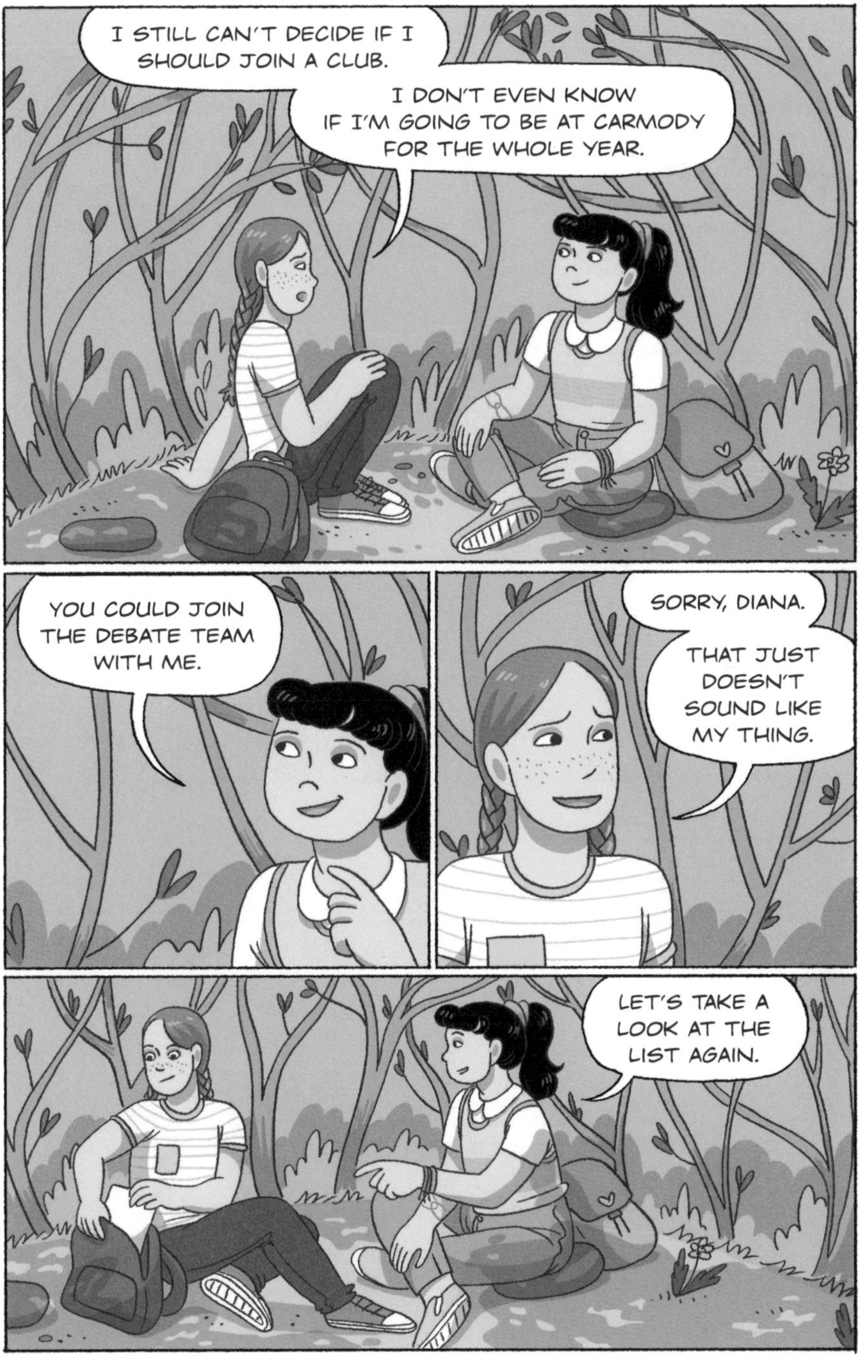
I STILL CAN'T DECIDE IF I SHOULD JOIN A CLUB.
I DON'T EVEN KNOW IF I'M GOING TO BE AT CARMODY FOR THE WHOLE YEAR.
YOU COULD JOIN THE DEBATE TEAM WITH ME.
SORRY, DIANA.
THAT JUST DOESN'T SOUND LIKE MY THING.
LET'S TAKE A LOOK AT THE LIST AGAIN.

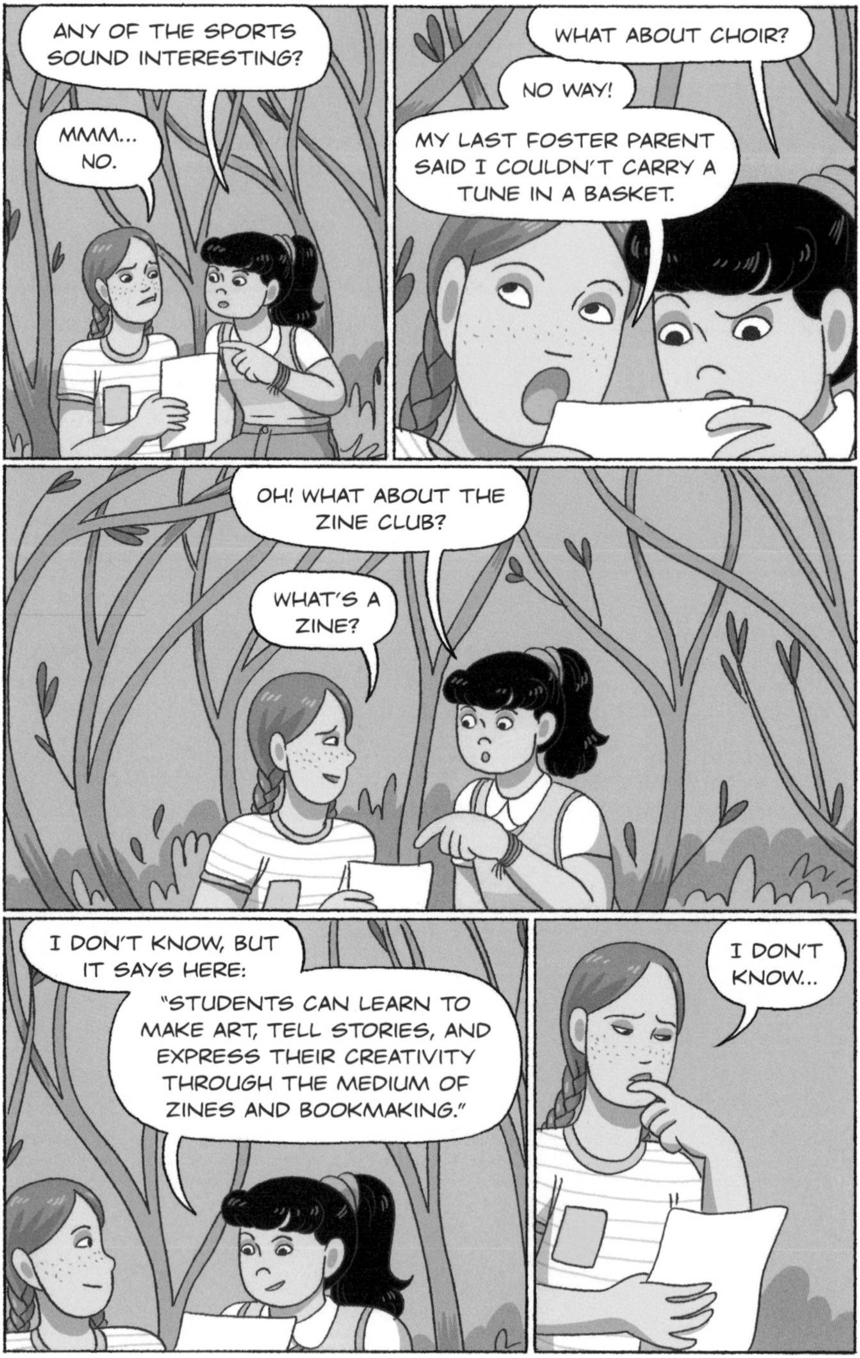
ANY OF THE SPORTS SOUND INTERESTING?
MMM... NO.
WHAT ABOUT CHOIR?
NO WAY!
MY LAST FOSTER PARENT SAID I COULDN'T CARRY A TUNE IN A BASKET.
OH! WHAT ABOUT THE ZINE CLUB?
WHAT'S A ZINE?
I DON'T KNOW, BUT IT SAYS HERE:
"STUDENTS CAN LEARN TO MAKE ART, TELL STORIES, AND EXPRESS THEIR CREATIVITY THROUGH THE MEDIUM OF ZINES AND BOOKMAKING."
I DON'T KNOW...

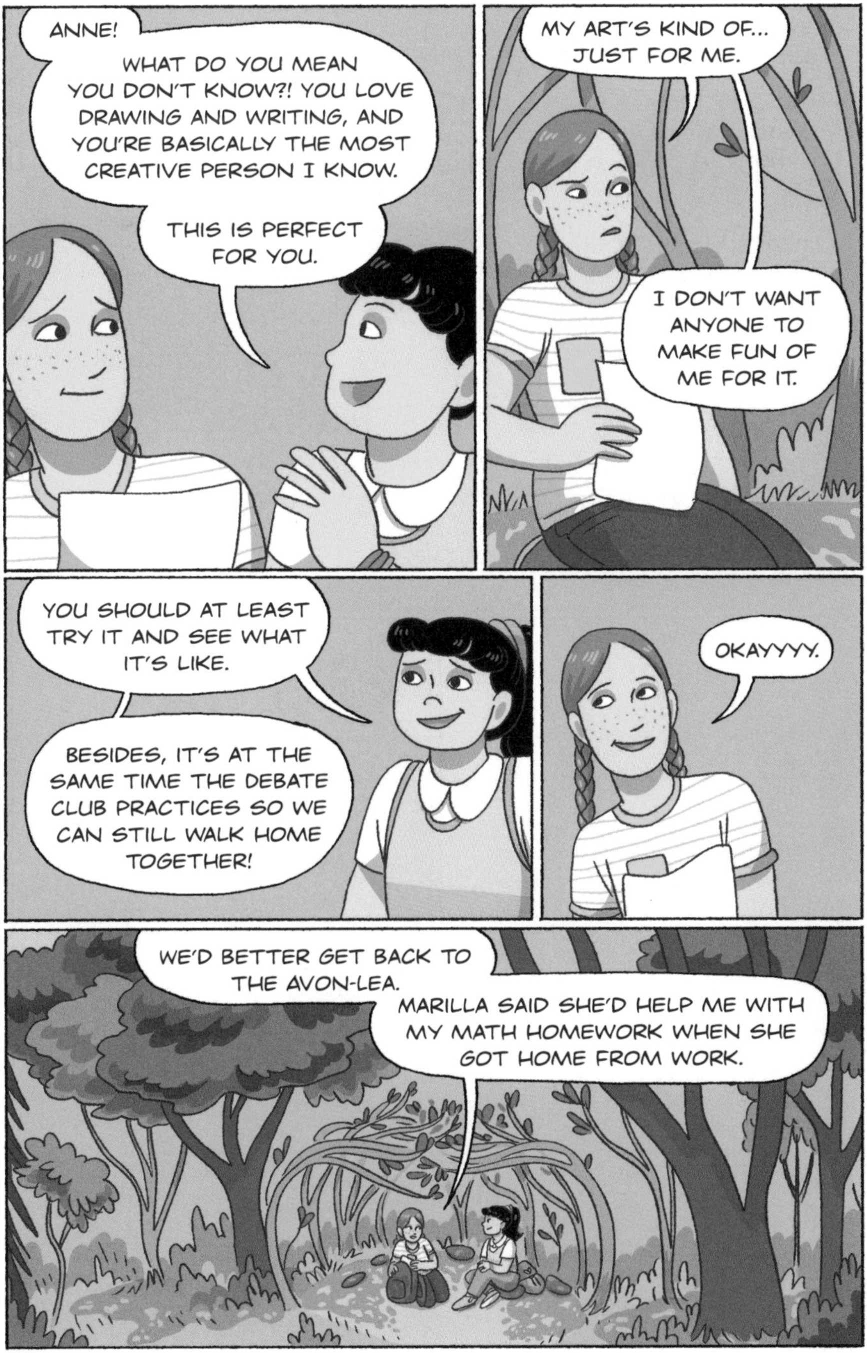
ANNE!
WHAT DO YOU MEAN YOU DON'T KNOW?! YOU LOVE DRAWING AND WRITING, AND YOU'RE BASICALLY THE MOST CREATIVE PERSON I KNOW.
THIS IS PERFECT FOR YOU.
MY ART'S KIND OF... JUST FOR ME.
I DON'T WANT ANYONE TO MAKE FUN OF ME FOR IT.
YOU SHOULD AT LEAST TRY IT AND SEE WHAT IT'S LIKE.
BESIDES, IT'S AT THE SAME TIME THE DEBATE CLUB PRACTICES SO WE CAN STILL WALK HOME TOGETHER!
OKAYYYY.
WE'D BETTER GET BACK TO THE AVON-LEA.
MARILLA SAID SHE'D HELP ME WITH MY MATH HOMEWORK WHEN SHE GOT HOME FROM WORK.

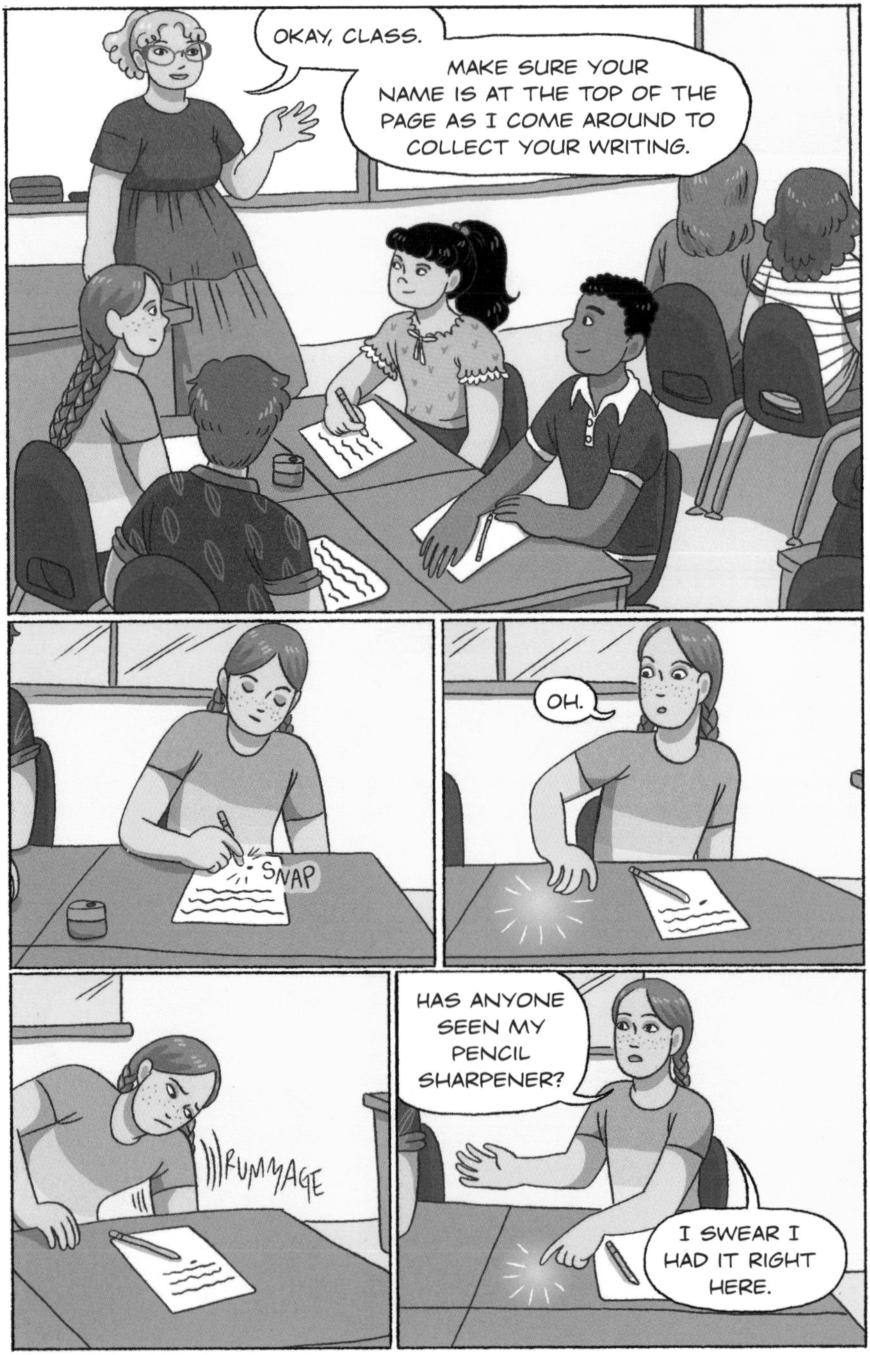
OKAY, CLASS.
MAKE SURE YOUR NAME IS AT THE TOP OF THE PAGE AS I COME AROUND TO COLLECT YOUR WRITING.
SNAP
OH.
RUMMAGE
HAS ANYONE SEEN MY PENCIL SHARPENER?
I SWEAR I HAD IT RIGHT HERE.

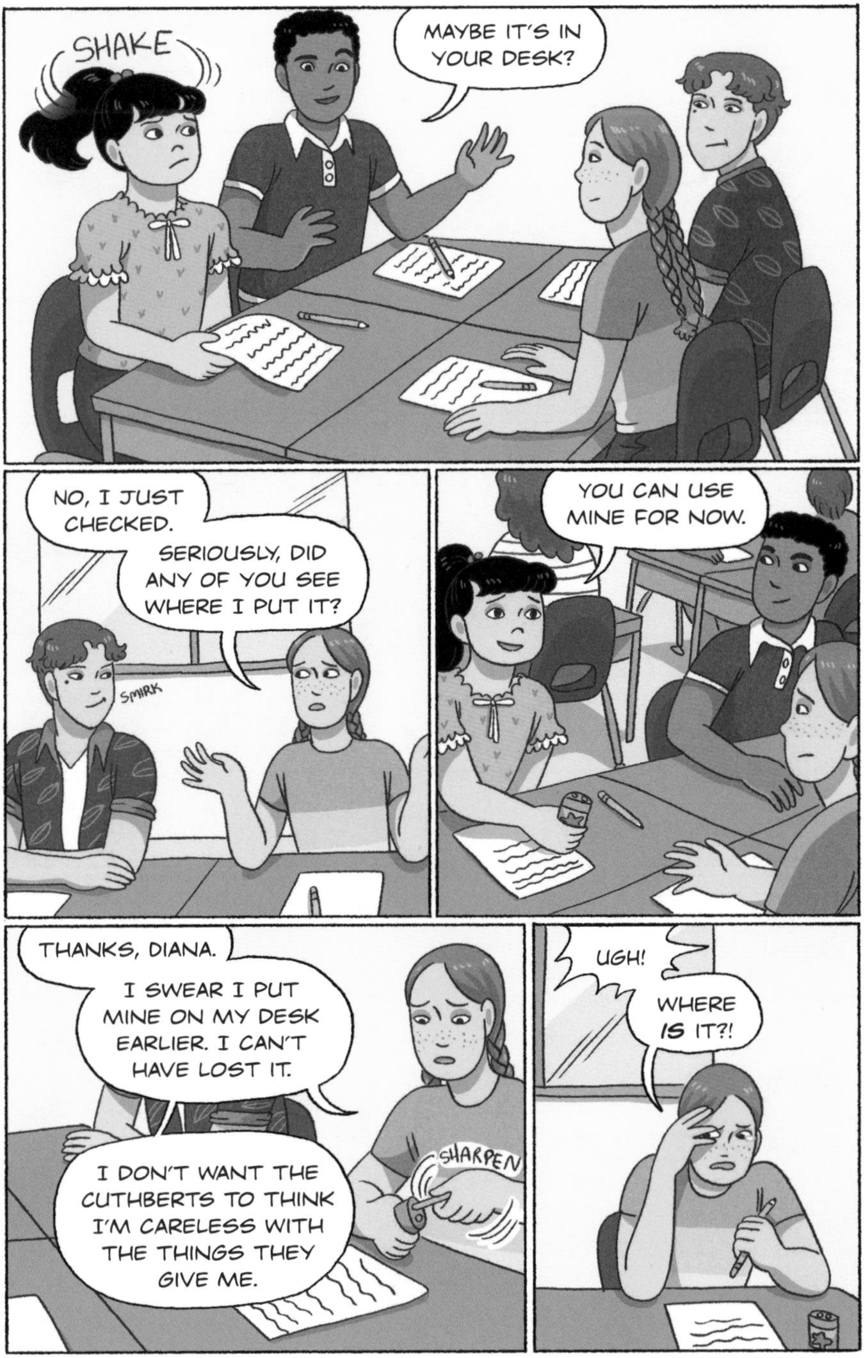
SHAKE
MAYBE IT'S IN YOUR DESK?
NO, I JUST CHECKED.
SERIOUSLY, DID ANY OF YOU SEE WHERE I PUT IT?
SMIRK
YOU CAN USE MINE FOR NOW.
THANKS, DIANA.
I SWEAR I PUT MINE ON MY DESK EARLIER. I CAN'T HAVE LOST IT.
I DON'T WANT THE CUTHBERTS TO THINK I'M CARELESS WITH THE THINGS THEY GIVE ME.
SHARPEN
UGH!
WHERE **IS** IT?!

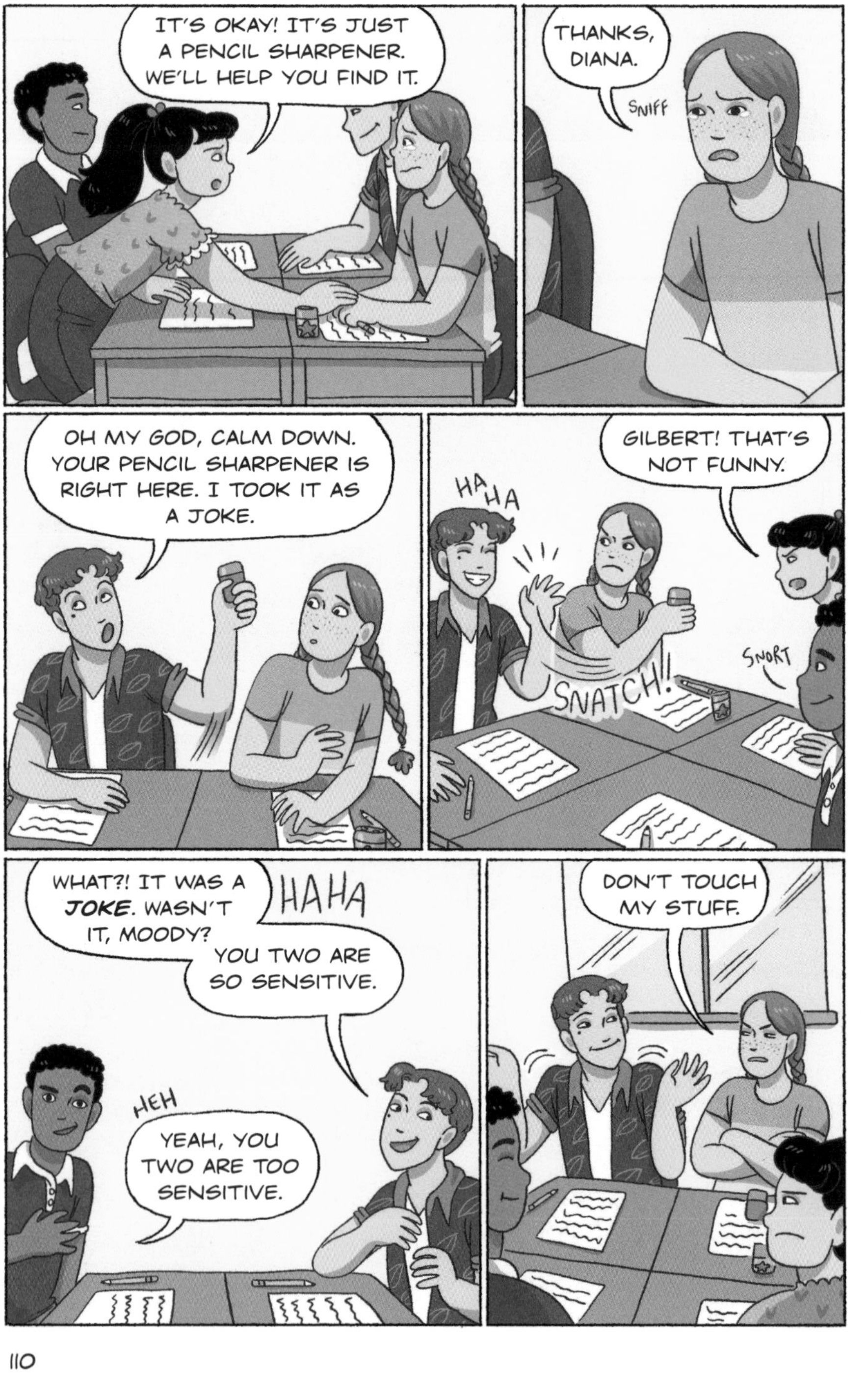
IT'S OKAY! IT'S JUST A PENCIL SHARPENER. WE'LL HELP YOU FIND IT.
THANKS, DIANA.
SNIFF
OH MY GOD, CALM DOWN. YOUR PENCIL SHARPENER IS RIGHT HERE. I TOOK IT AS A JOKE.
HA HA
GILBERT! THAT'S NOT FUNNY.
SNATCH!
SNORT
WHAT?! IT WAS A **JOKE**. WASN'T IT, MOODY?
HAHA
YOU TWO ARE SO SENSITIVE.
HEH
YEAH, YOU TWO ARE TOO SENSITIVE.
DON'T TOUCH MY STUFF.

DOES GILBERT EVER... LIKE...BOTHER YOU GUYS?

WHAT DO YOU MEAN?

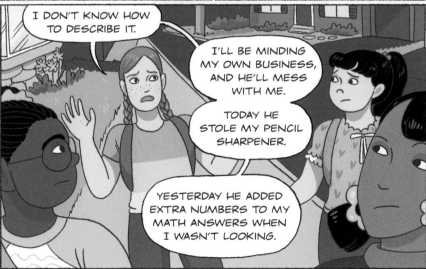

I DON'T KNOW HOW TO DESCRIBE IT.

I'LL BE MINDING MY OWN BUSINESS, AND HE'LL MESS WITH ME.

TODAY HE STOLE MY PENCIL SHARPENER.

YESTERDAY HE ADDED EXTRA NUMBERS TO MY MATH ANSWERS WHEN I WASN'T LOOKING.

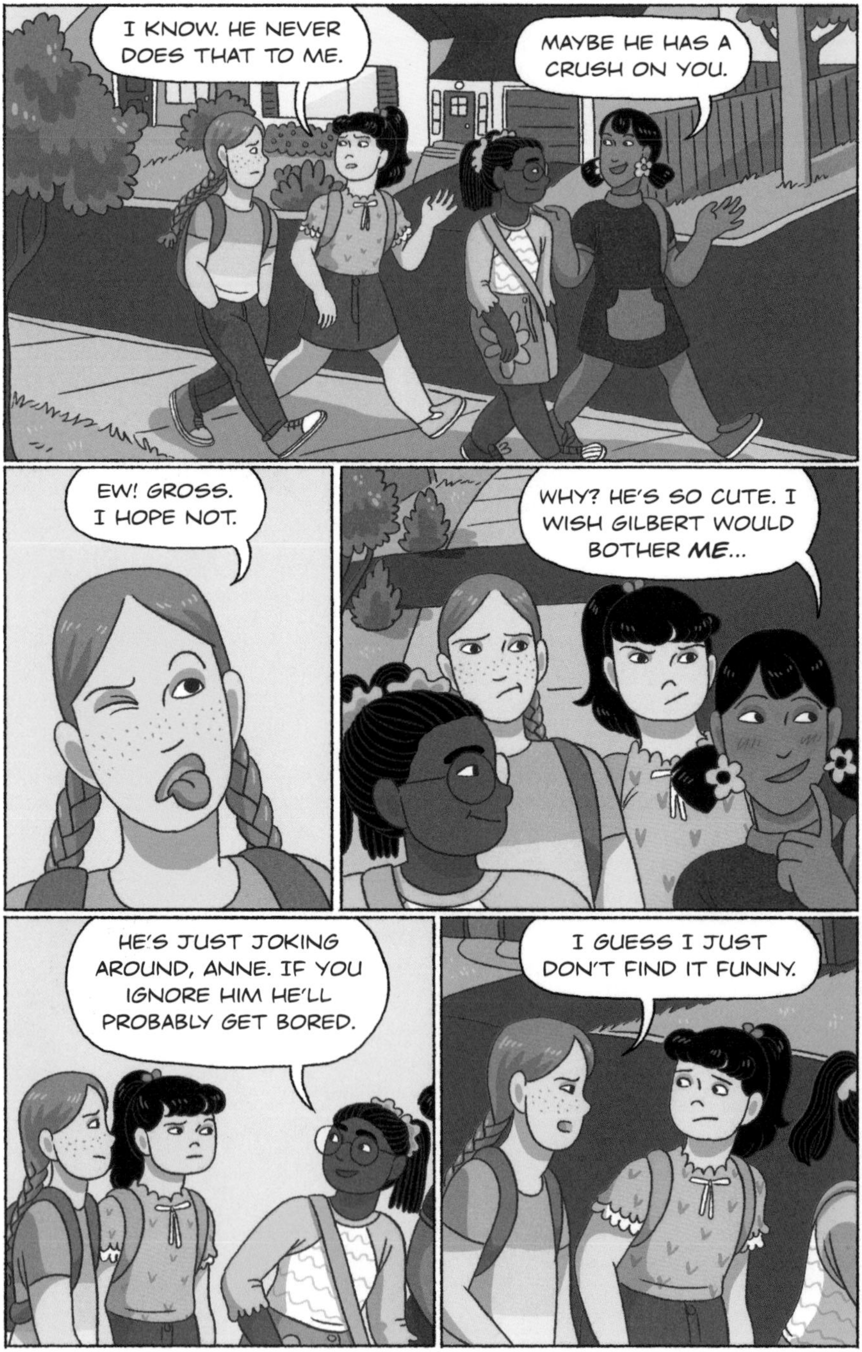
I KNOW. HE NEVER DOES THAT TO ME.
MAYBE HE HAS A CRUSH ON YOU.
EW! GROSS. I HOPE NOT.
WHY? HE'S SO CUTE. I WISH GILBERT WOULD BOTHER **ME**...
HE'S JUST JOKING AROUND, ANNE. IF YOU IGNORE HIM HE'LL PROBABLY GET BORED.
I GUESS I JUST DON'T FIND IT FUNNY.

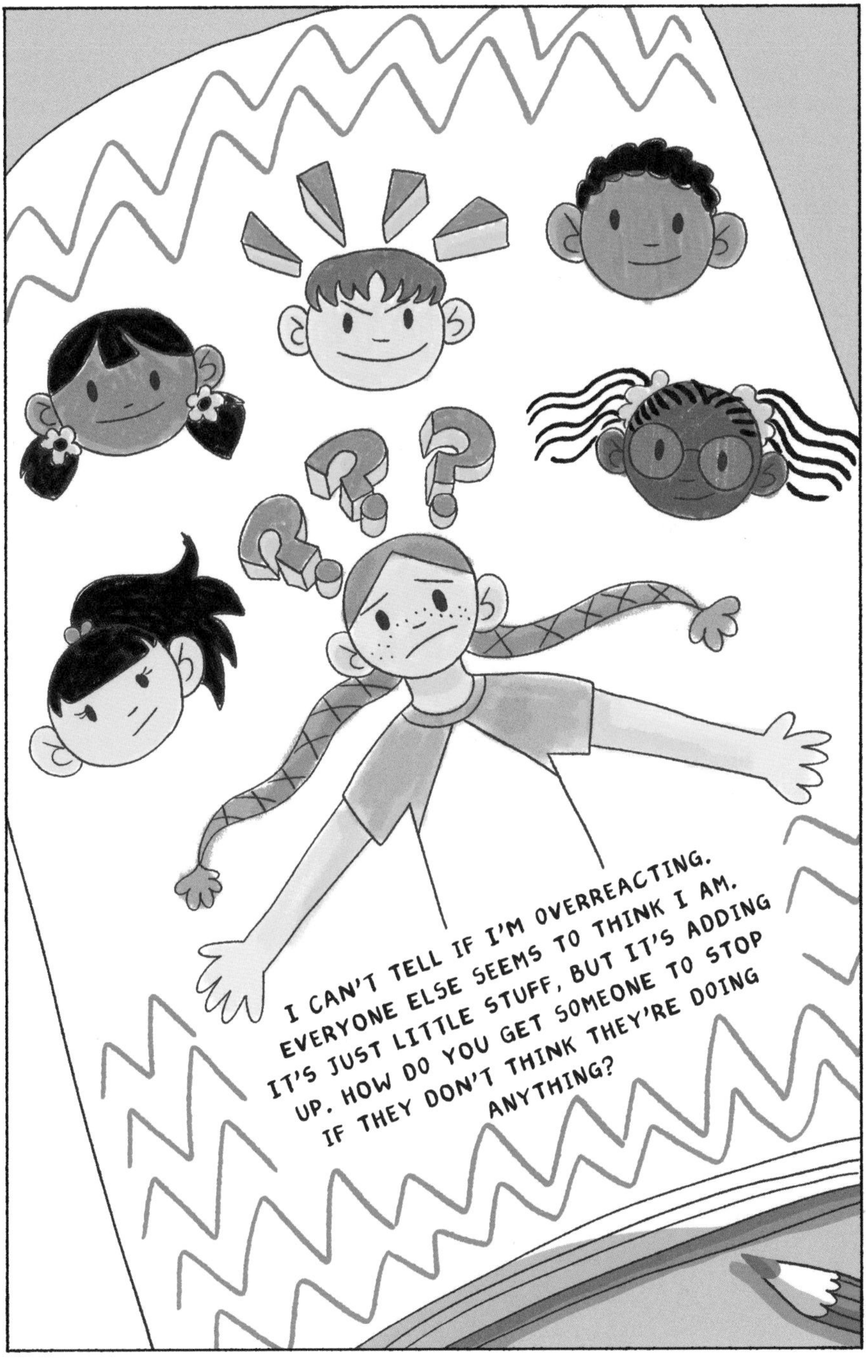
I CAN'T TELL IF I'M OVERREACTING. EVERYONE ELSE SEEMS TO THINK I AM. IT'S JUST LITTLE STUFF, BUT IT'S ADDING UP. HOW DO YOU GET SOMEONE TO STOP IF THEY DON'T THINK THEY'RE DOING ANYTHING?

CHAPTER 6

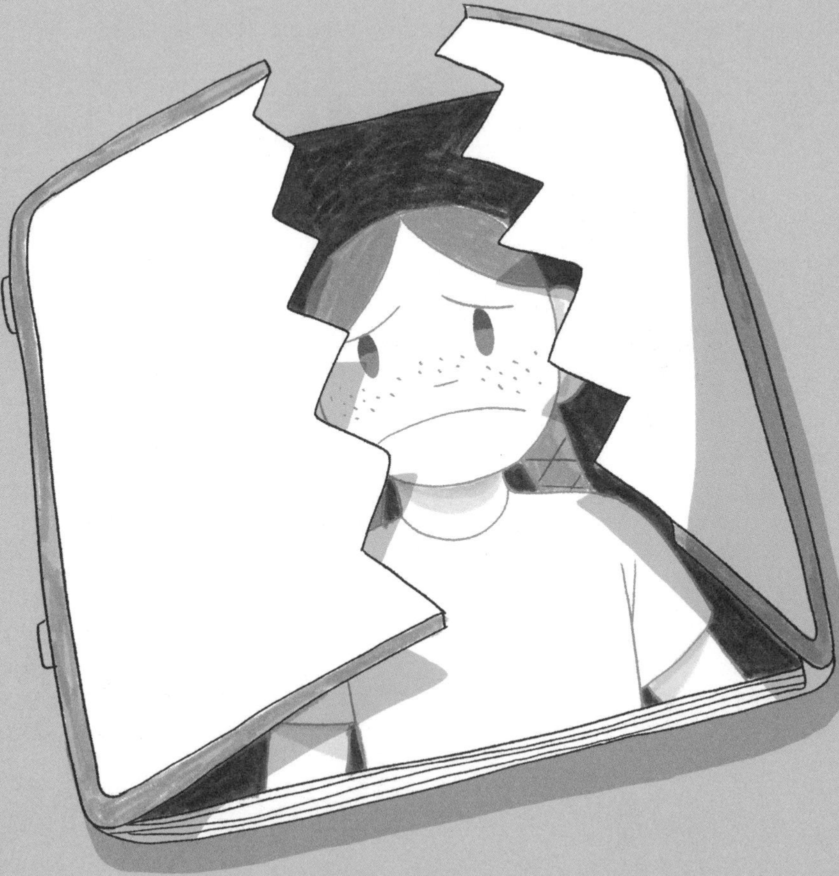

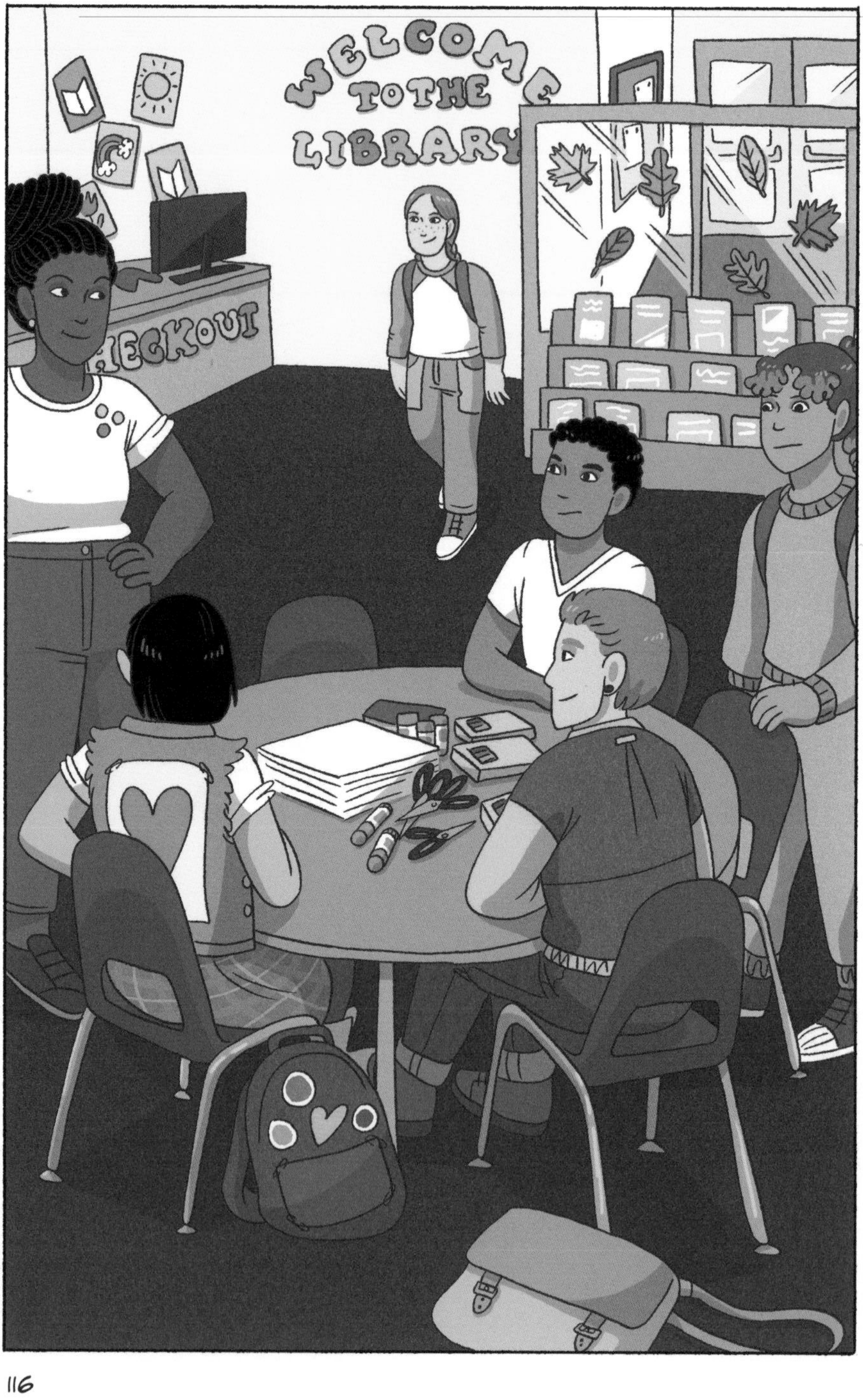
WELCOME
TO THE
LIBRARY
CHECKOUT

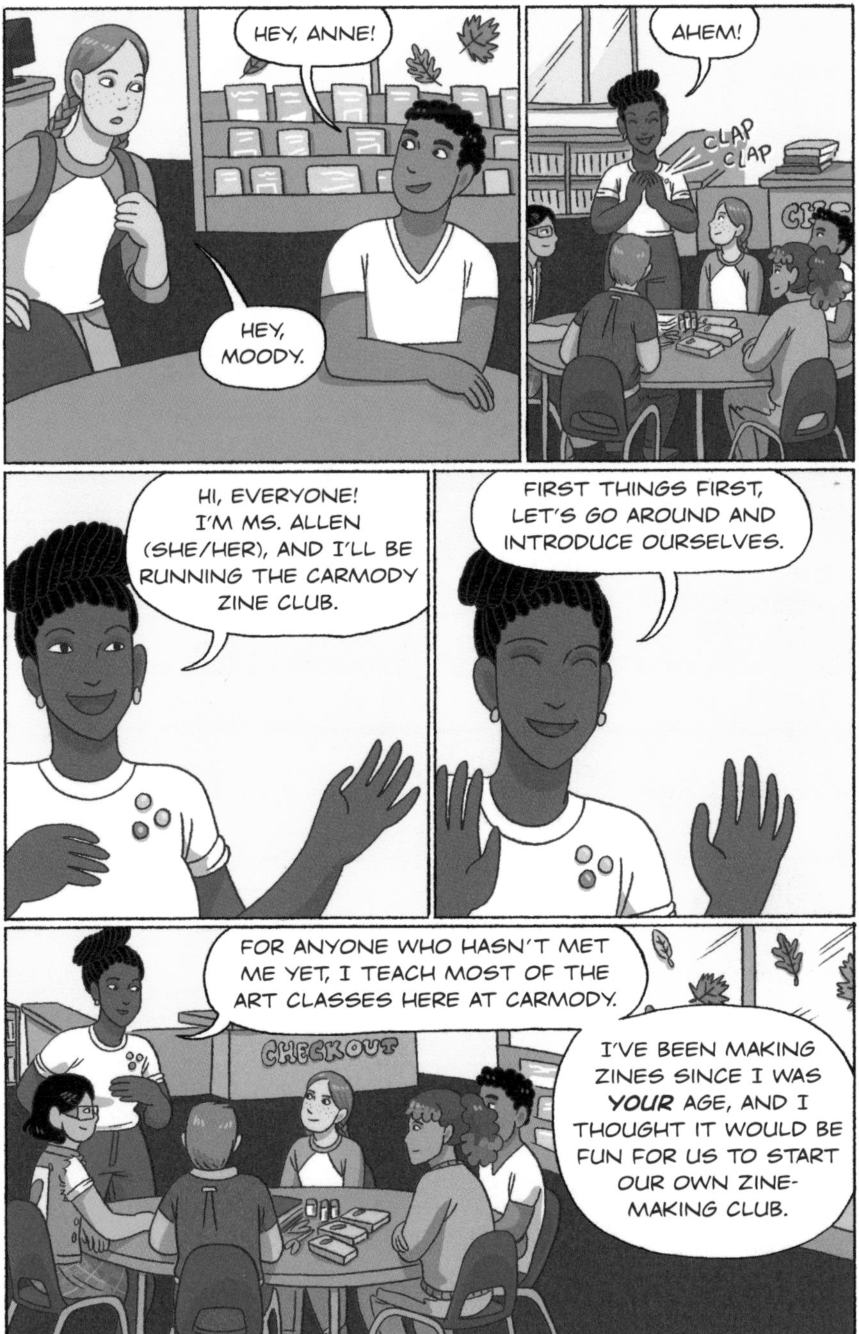
HEY, ANNE!
HEY, MOODY.
AHEM!
CLAP CLAP
HI, EVERYONE! I'M MS. ALLEN (SHE/HER), AND I'LL BE RUNNING THE CARMODY ZINE CLUB.
FIRST THINGS FIRST, LET'S GO AROUND AND INTRODUCE OURSELVES.
FOR ANYONE WHO HASN'T MET ME YET, I TEACH MOST OF THE ART CLASSES HERE AT CARMODY.
CHECKOUT
I'VE BEEN MAKING ZINES SINCE I WAS **YOUR** AGE, AND I THOUGHT IT WOULD BE FUN FOR US TO START OUR OWN ZINE-MAKING CLUB.

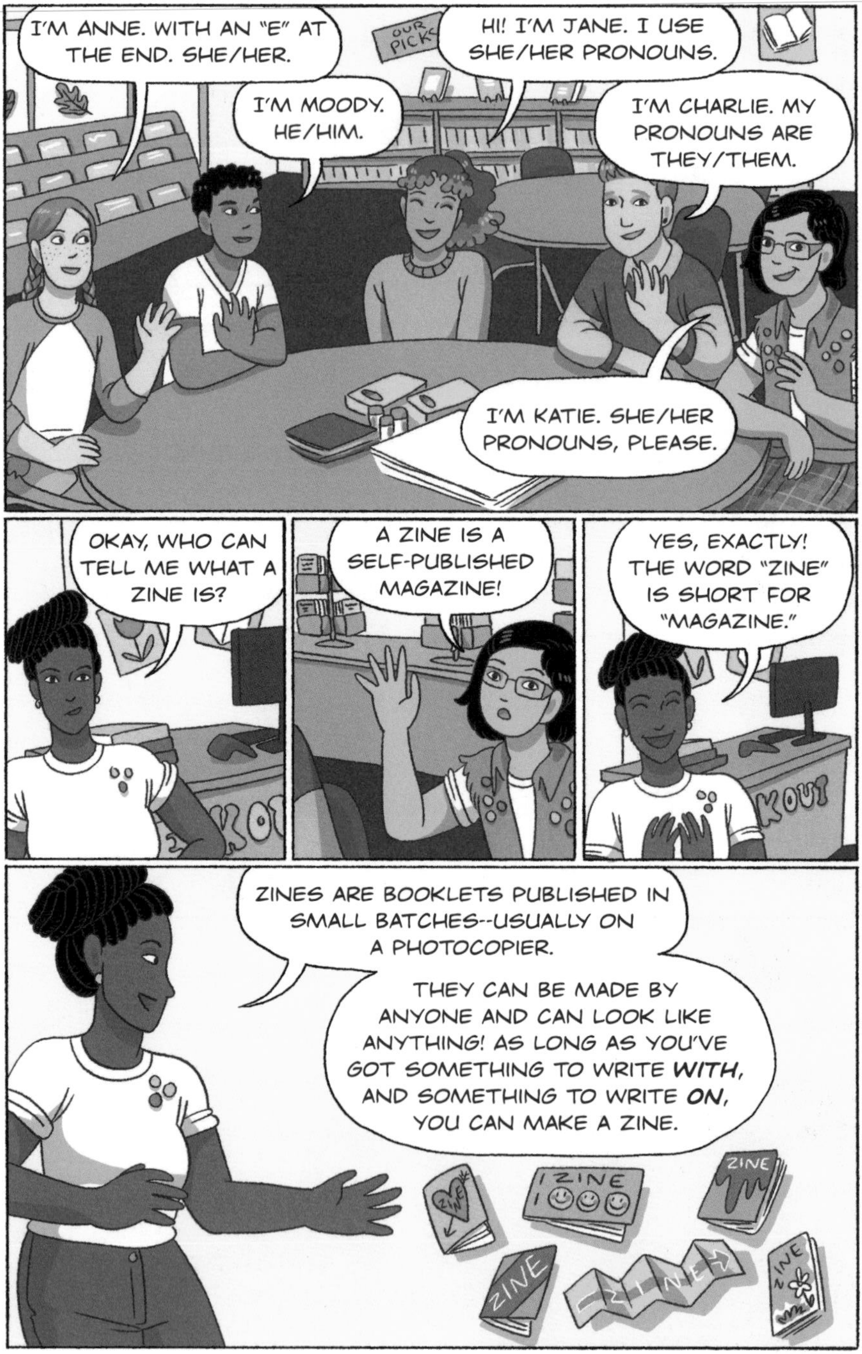
I'M ANNE. WITH AN "E" AT THE END. SHE/HER.
I'M MOODY. HE/HIM.
HI! I'M JANE. I USE SHE/HER PRONOUNS.
I'M CHARLIE. MY PRONOUNS ARE THEY/THEM.
I'M KATIE. SHE/HER PRONOUNS, PLEASE.
OKAY, WHO CAN TELL ME WHAT A ZINE IS?
A ZINE IS A SELF-PUBLISHED MAGAZINE!
YES, EXACTLY! THE WORD "ZINE" IS SHORT FOR "MAGAZINE."
ZINES ARE BOOKLETS PUBLISHED IN SMALL BATCHES--USUALLY ON A PHOTOCOPIER.
THEY CAN BE MADE BY ANYONE AND CAN LOOK LIKE ANYTHING! AS LONG AS YOU'VE GOT SOMETHING TO WRITE **WITH**, AND SOMETHING TO WRITE **ON**, YOU CAN MAKE A ZINE.

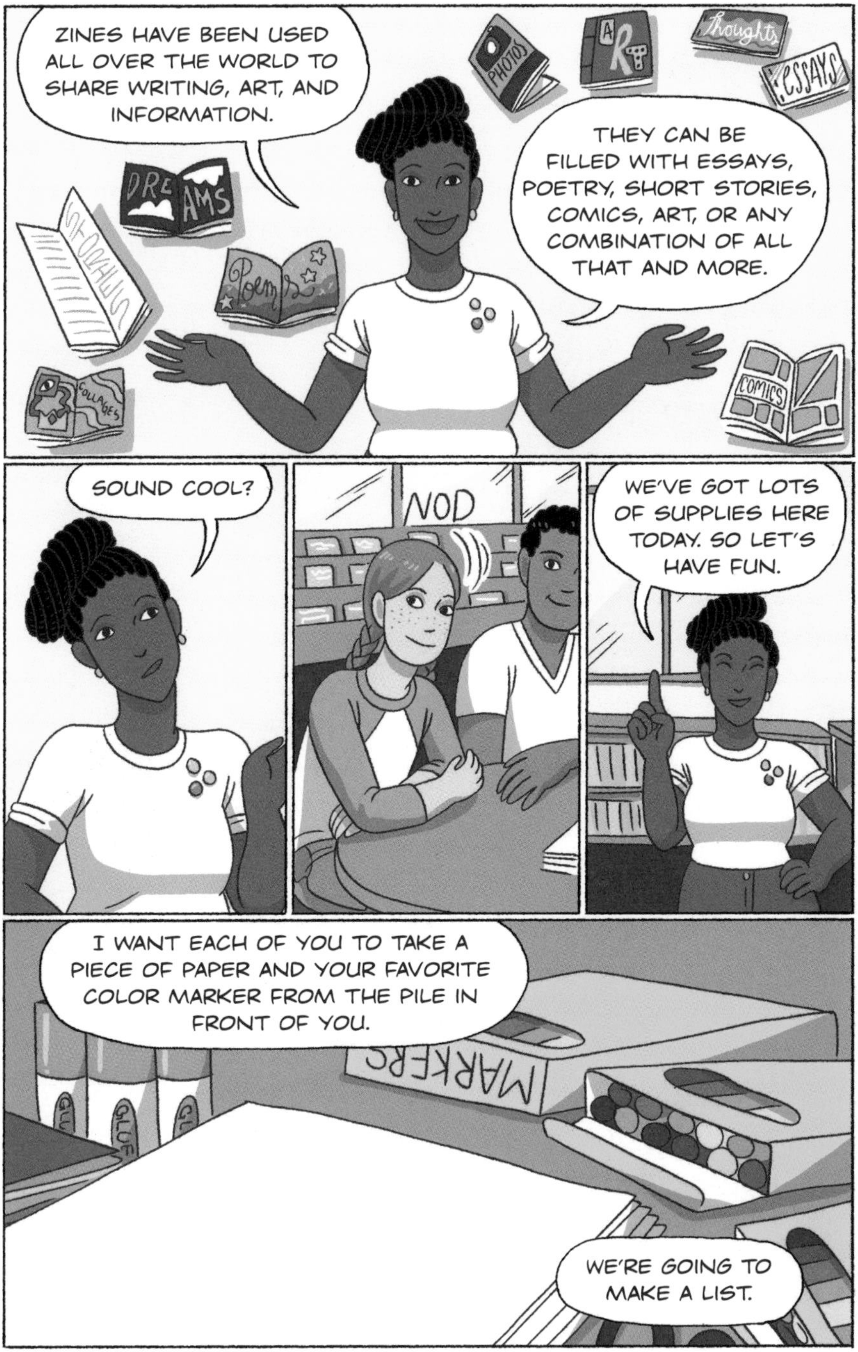
ZINES HAVE BEEN USED ALL OVER THE WORLD TO SHARE WRITING, ART, AND INFORMATION.
THEY CAN BE FILLED WITH ESSAYS, POETRY, SHORT STORIES, COMICS, ART, OR ANY COMBINATION OF ALL THAT AND MORE.
PHOTOS
ART
Thoughts
ESSAYS
DREAMS
STORIES
Poems
COLLAGES
COMICS
SOUND COOL?
NOD
WE'VE GOT LOTS OF SUPPLIES HERE TODAY. SO LET'S HAVE FUN.
I WANT EACH OF YOU TO TAKE A PIECE OF PAPER AND YOUR FAVORITE COLOR MARKER FROM THE PILE IN FRONT OF YOU.
MARKERS
GLUE
WE'RE GOING TO MAKE A LIST.

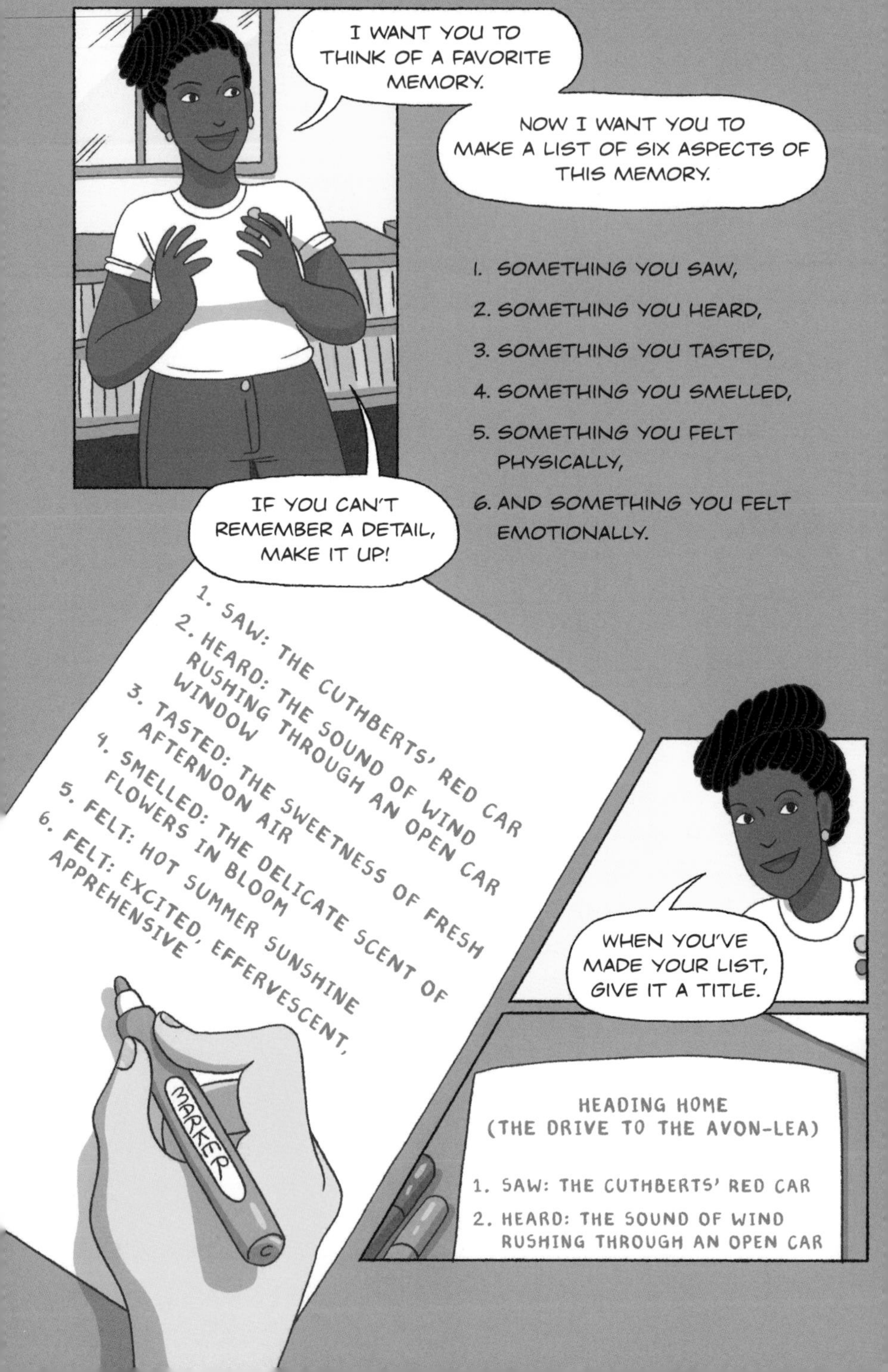

I WANT YOU TO THINK OF A FAVORITE MEMORY.
NOW I WANT YOU TO MAKE A LIST OF SIX ASPECTS OF THIS MEMORY.
1. SOMETHING YOU SAW,
2. SOMETHING YOU HEARD,
3. SOMETHING YOU TASTED,
4. SOMETHING YOU SMELLED,
5. SOMETHING YOU FELT PHYSICALLY,
6. AND SOMETHING YOU FELT EMOTIONALLY.
IF YOU CAN'T REMEMBER A DETAIL, MAKE IT UP!
1. SAW: THE CUTHBERTS' RED CAR
2. HEARD: THE SOUND OF WIND RUSHING THROUGH AN OPEN CAR WINDOW
3. TASTED: THE SWEETNESS OF FRESH AFTERNOON AIR
4. SMELLED: THE DELICATE SCENT OF FLOWERS IN BLOOM
5. FELT: HOT SUMMER SUNSHINE
6. FELT: EXCITED, EFFERVESCENT, APPREHENSIVE
MARKER
WHEN YOU'VE MADE YOUR LIST, GIVE IT A TITLE.
HEADING HOME
(THE DRIVE TO THE AVON-LEA)
1. SAW: THE CUTHBERTS' RED CAR
2. HEARD: THE SOUND OF WIND RUSHING THROUGH AN OPEN CAR

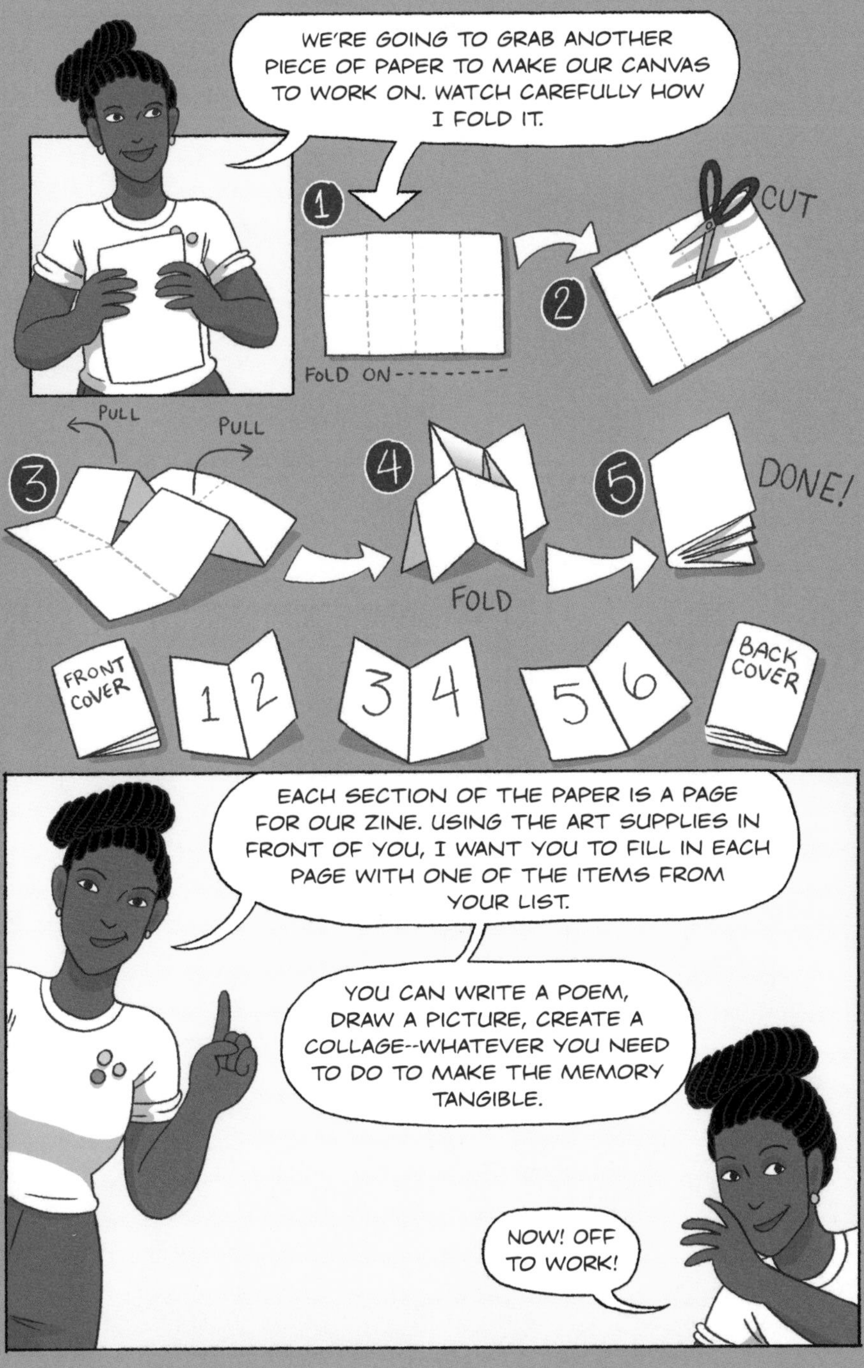
WE'RE GOING TO GRAB ANOTHER PIECE OF PAPER TO MAKE OUR CANVAS TO WORK ON. WATCH CAREFULLY HOW I FOLD IT.
1
FOLD ON---------
2
CUT
3
PULL
PULL
4
FOLD
5
DONE!
FRONT COVER
1 2
3 4
5 6
BACK COVER
EACH SECTION OF THE PAPER IS A PAGE FOR OUR ZINE. USING THE ART SUPPLIES IN FRONT OF YOU, I WANT YOU TO FILL IN EACH PAGE WITH ONE OF THE ITEMS FROM YOUR LIST.
YOU CAN WRITE A POEM, DRAW A PICTURE, CREATE A COLLAGE--WHATEVER YOU NEED TO DO TO MAKE THE MEMORY TANGIBLE.
NOW! OFF TO WORK!

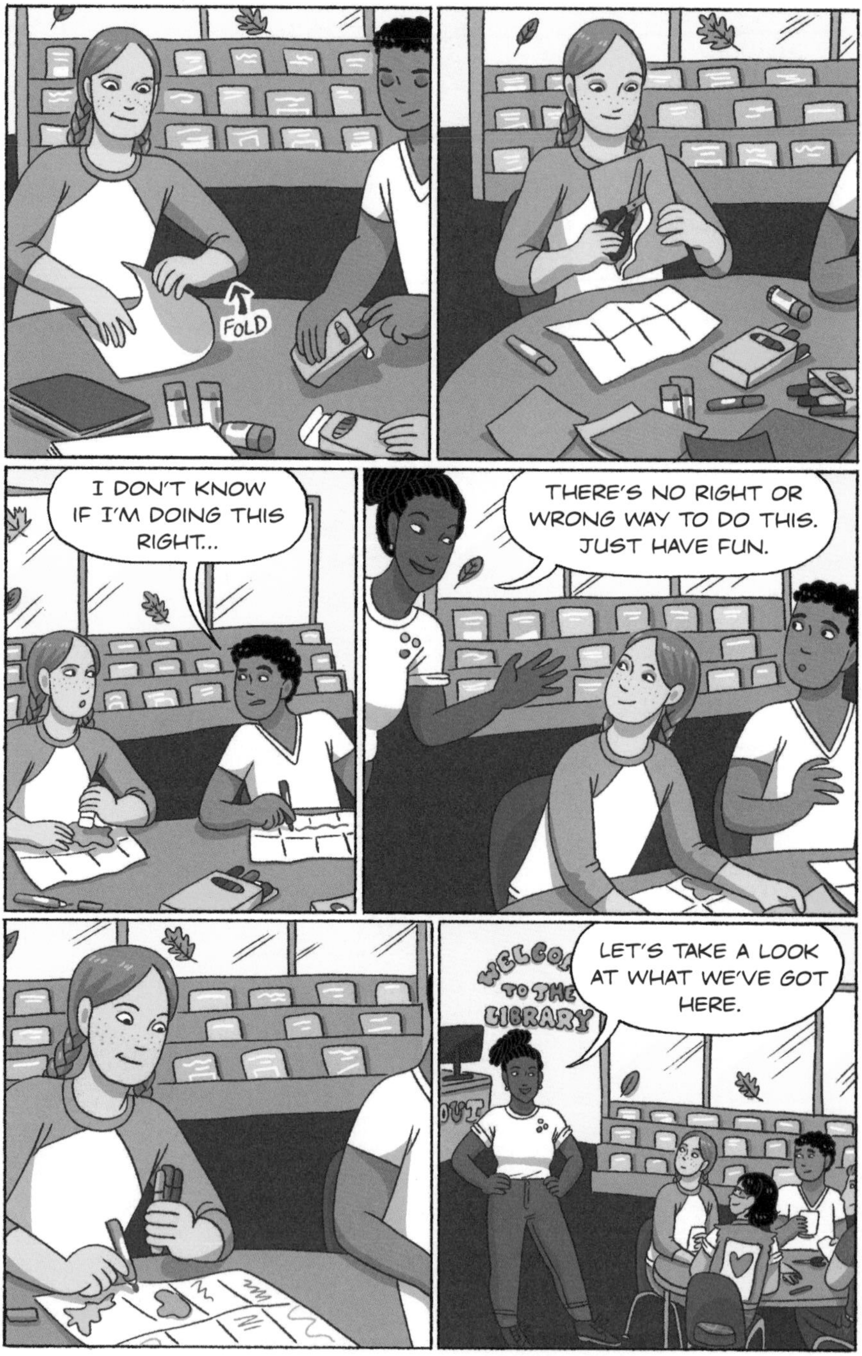
FOLD
I DON'T KNOW IF I'M DOING THIS RIGHT...
THERE'S NO RIGHT OR WRONG WAY TO DO THIS. JUST HAVE FUN.
WELCOME TO THE LIBRARY
LET'S TAKE A LOOK AT WHAT WE'VE GOT HERE.

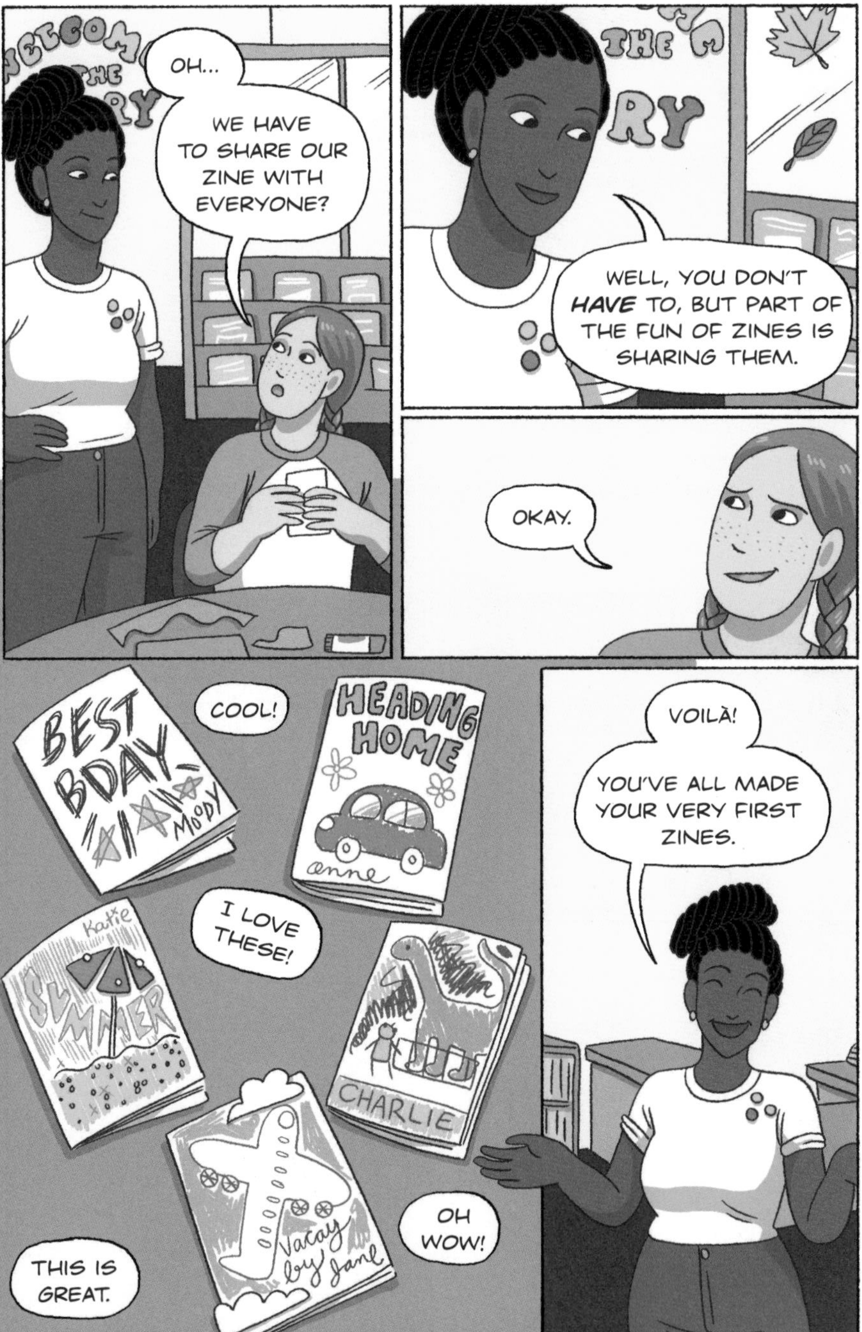
OH...
WE HAVE TO SHARE OUR ZINE WITH EVERYONE?
WELL, YOU DON'T HAVE TO, BUT PART OF THE FUN OF ZINES IS SHARING THEM.
OKAY.
BEST BDAY MOODY
COOL!
HEADING HOME
anne
I LOVE THESE!
Katie
SUMMER
CHARLIE
Vacay by Jane
OH WOW!
THIS IS GREAT.
VOILÀ!
YOU'VE ALL MADE YOUR VERY FIRST ZINES.

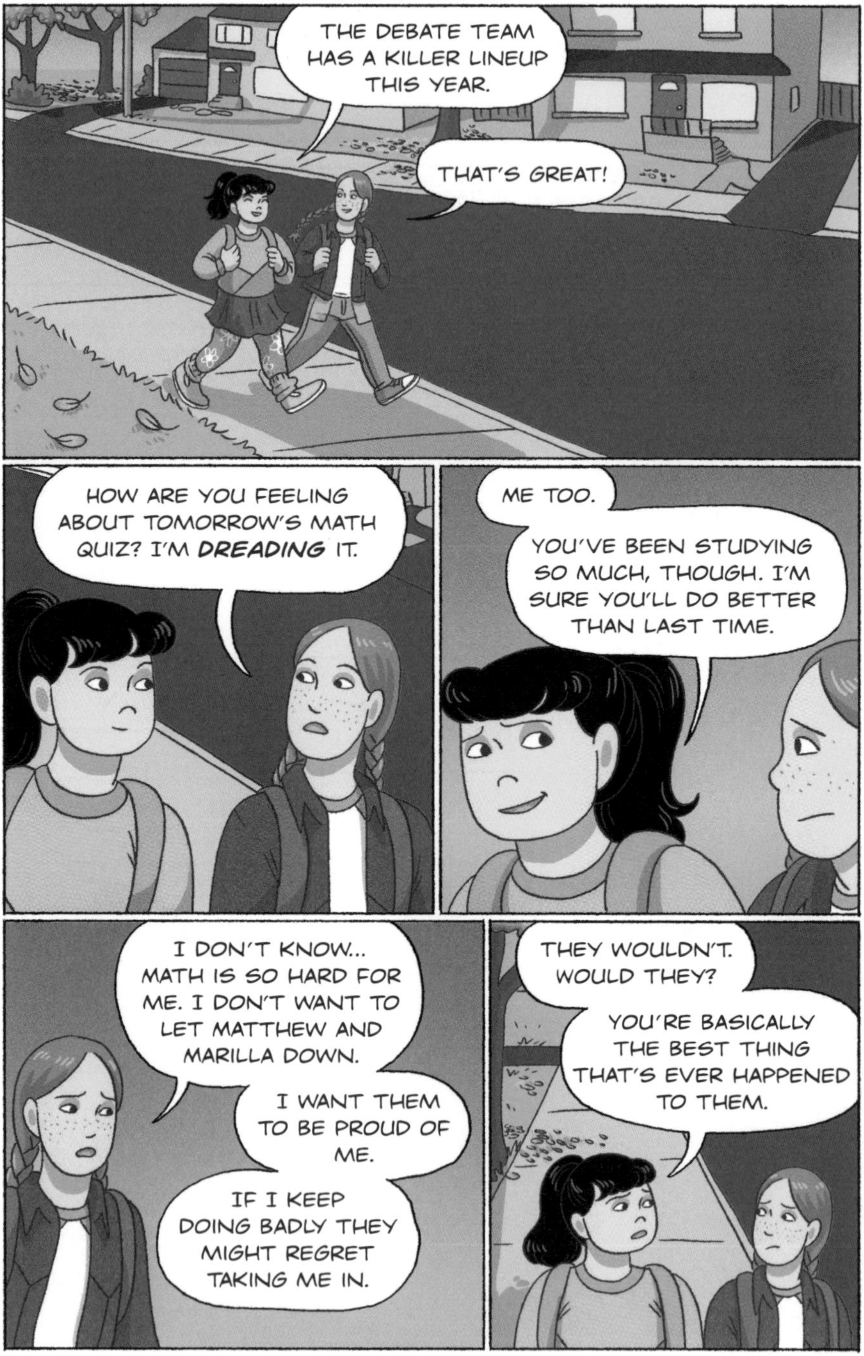
THE DEBATE TEAM HAS A KILLER LINEUP THIS YEAR.
THAT'S GREAT!
HOW ARE YOU FEELING ABOUT TOMORROW'S MATH QUIZ? I'M **DREADING** IT.
ME TOO.
YOU'VE BEEN STUDYING SO MUCH, THOUGH. I'M SURE YOU'LL DO BETTER THAN LAST TIME.
I DON'T KNOW... MATH IS SO HARD FOR ME. I DON'T WANT TO LET MATTHEW AND MARILLA DOWN.
I WANT THEM TO BE PROUD OF ME.
IF I KEEP DOING BADLY THEY MIGHT REGRET TAKING ME IN.
THEY WOULDN'T. WOULD THEY?
YOU'RE BASICALLY THE BEST THING THAT'S EVER HAPPENED TO THEM.

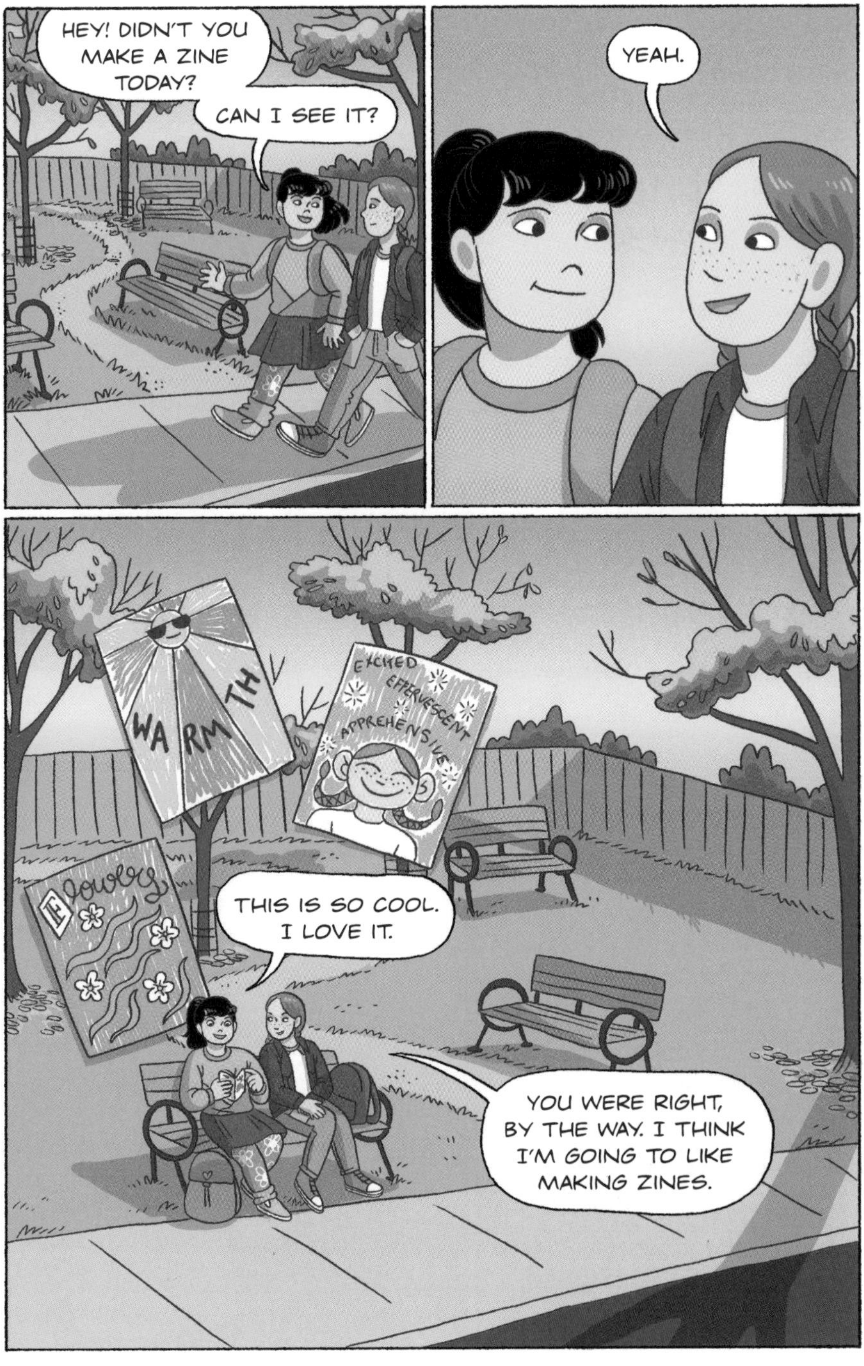
HEY! DIDN'T YOU MAKE A ZINE TODAY?
CAN I SEE IT?
YEAH.
WARMTH
EXCITED
EFFERVESCENT
APPREHENSIVE
Flowery
THIS IS SO COOL. I LOVE IT.
YOU WERE RIGHT, BY THE WAY. I THINK I'M GOING TO LIKE MAKING ZINES.

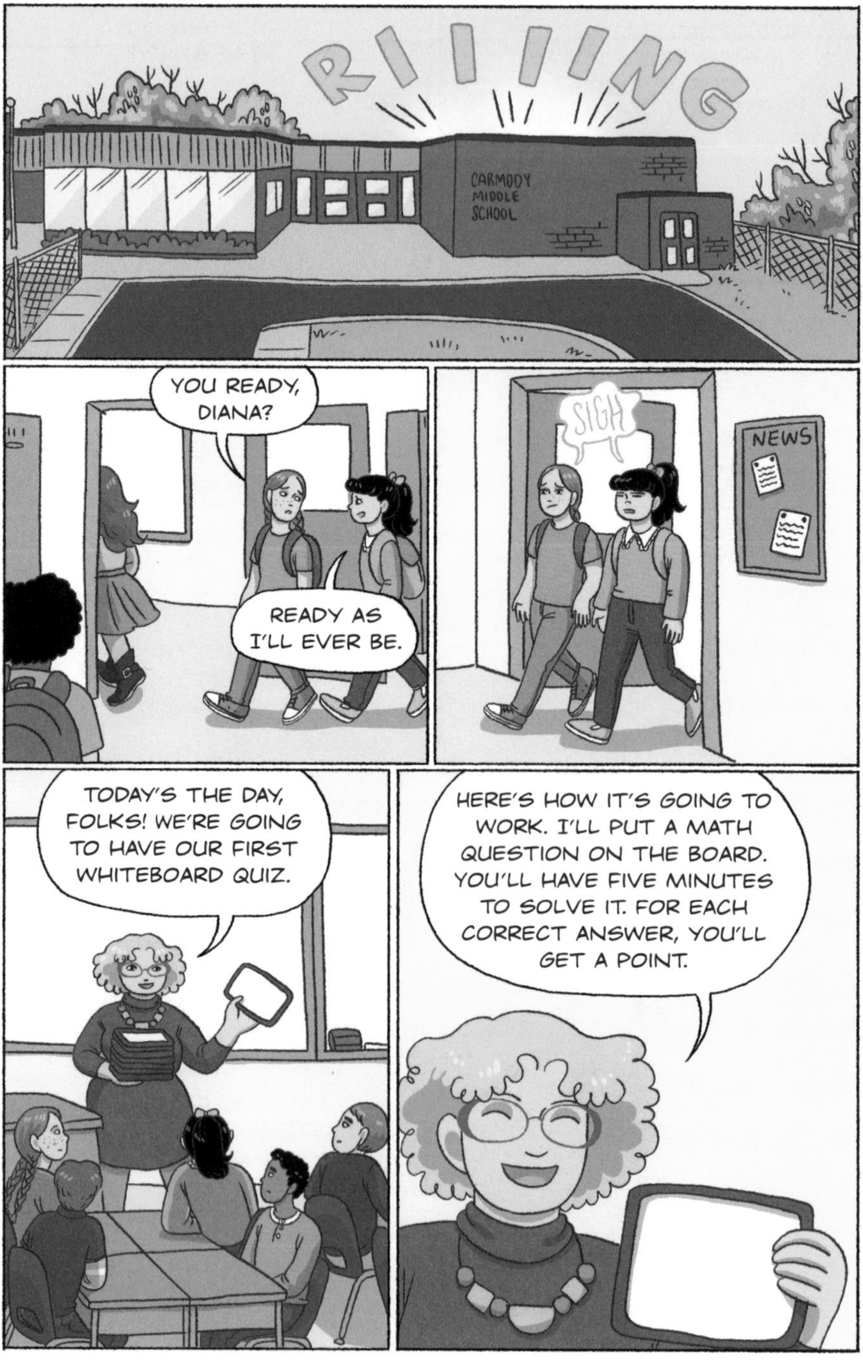
RIIIING
CARMODY MIDDLE SCHOOL
YOU READY, DIANA?
READY AS I'LL EVER BE.
SIGH
NEWS
TODAY'S THE DAY, FOLKS! WE'RE GOING TO HAVE OUR FIRST WHITEBOARD QUIZ.
HERE'S HOW IT'S GOING TO WORK. I'LL PUT A MATH QUESTION ON THE BOARD. YOU'LL HAVE FIVE MINUTES TO SOLVE IT. FOR EACH CORRECT ANSWER, YOU'LL GET A POINT.

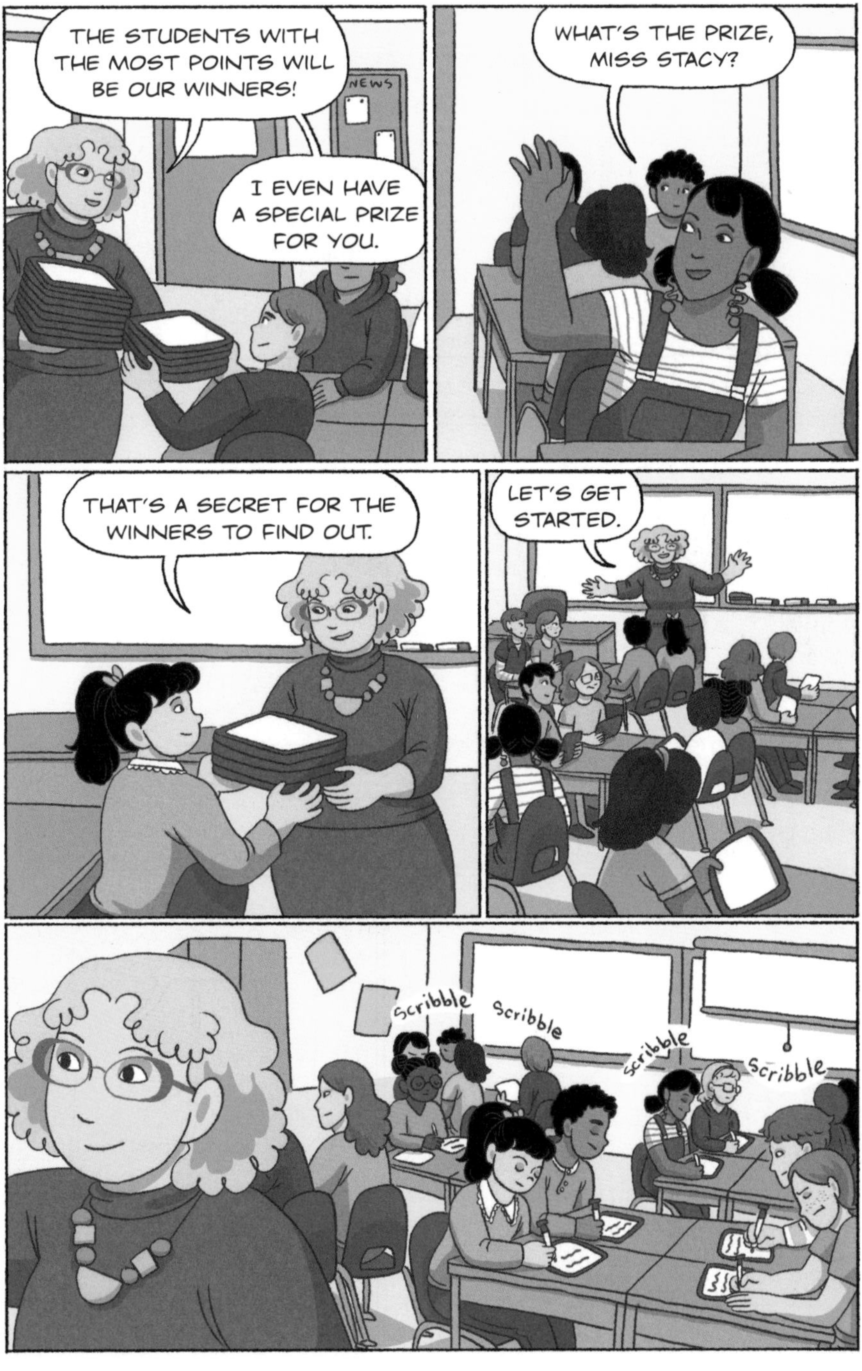
THE STUDENTS WITH THE MOST POINTS WILL BE OUR WINNERS!
NEWS
I EVEN HAVE A SPECIAL PRIZE FOR YOU.
WHAT'S THE PRIZE, MISS STACY?
THAT'S A SECRET FOR THE WINNERS TO FIND OUT.
LET'S GET STARTED.
scribble
scribble
scribble
scribble

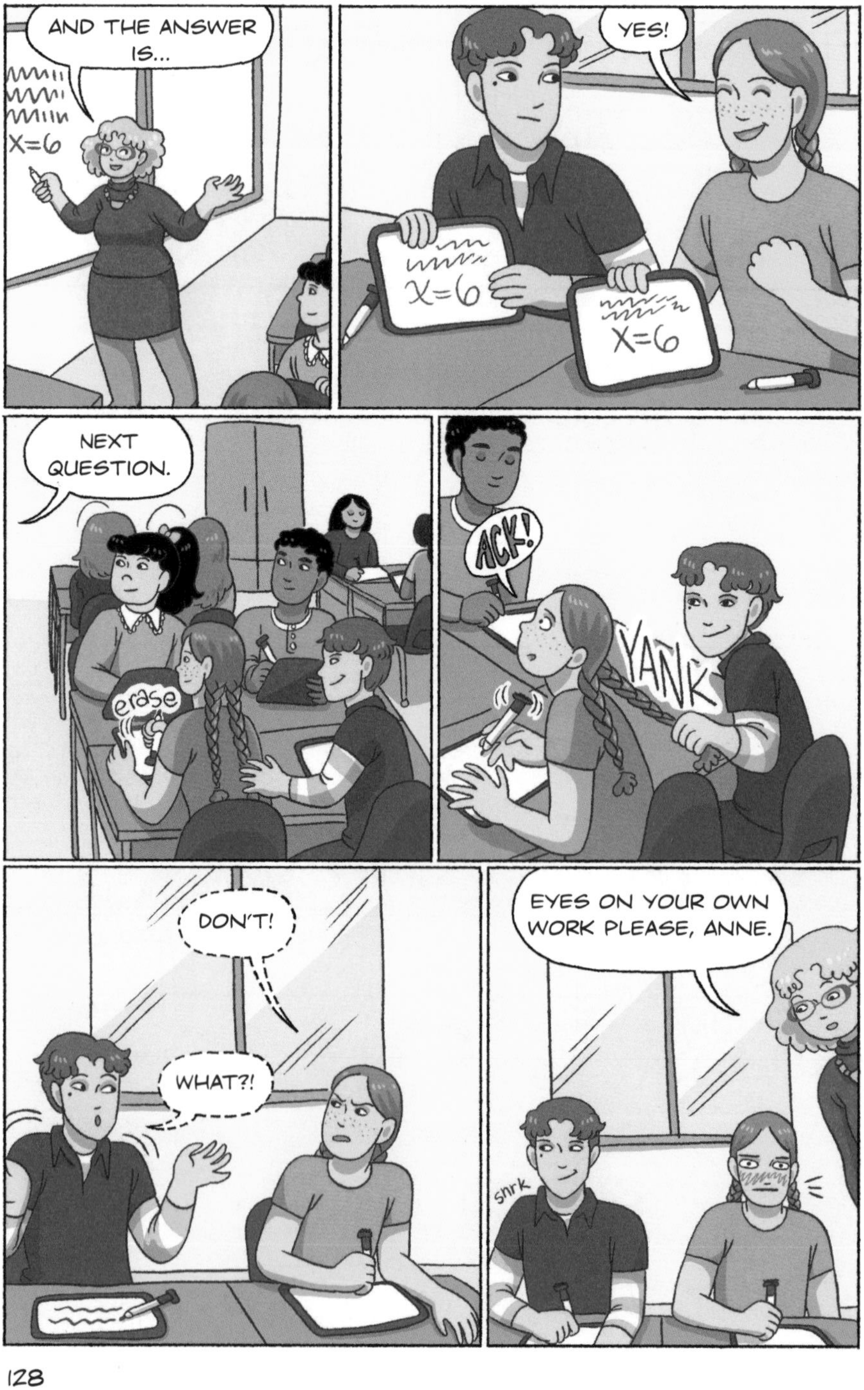
AND THE ANSWER IS...
X=6
YES!
X=6
X=6
NEXT QUESTION.
erase
ACK!
YANK
DON'T!
WHAT?!
EYES ON YOUR OWN WORK PLEASE, ANNE.
shrk

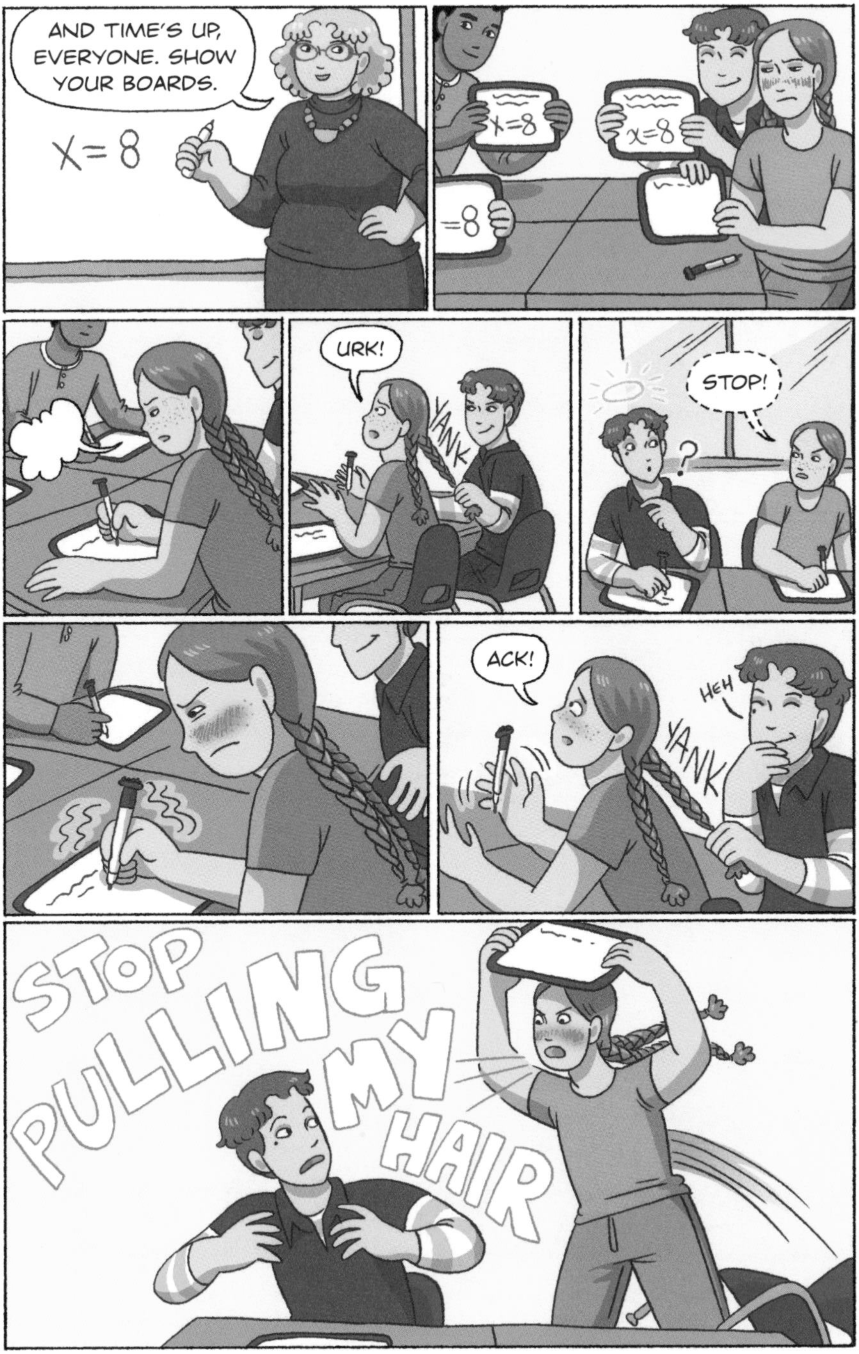
AND TIME'S UP, EVERYONE. SHOW YOUR BOARDS.
X=8
x=8
x=8
=8
URK!
YANK
STOP!
?
ACK!
HEH
YANK
STOP PULLING MY HAIR

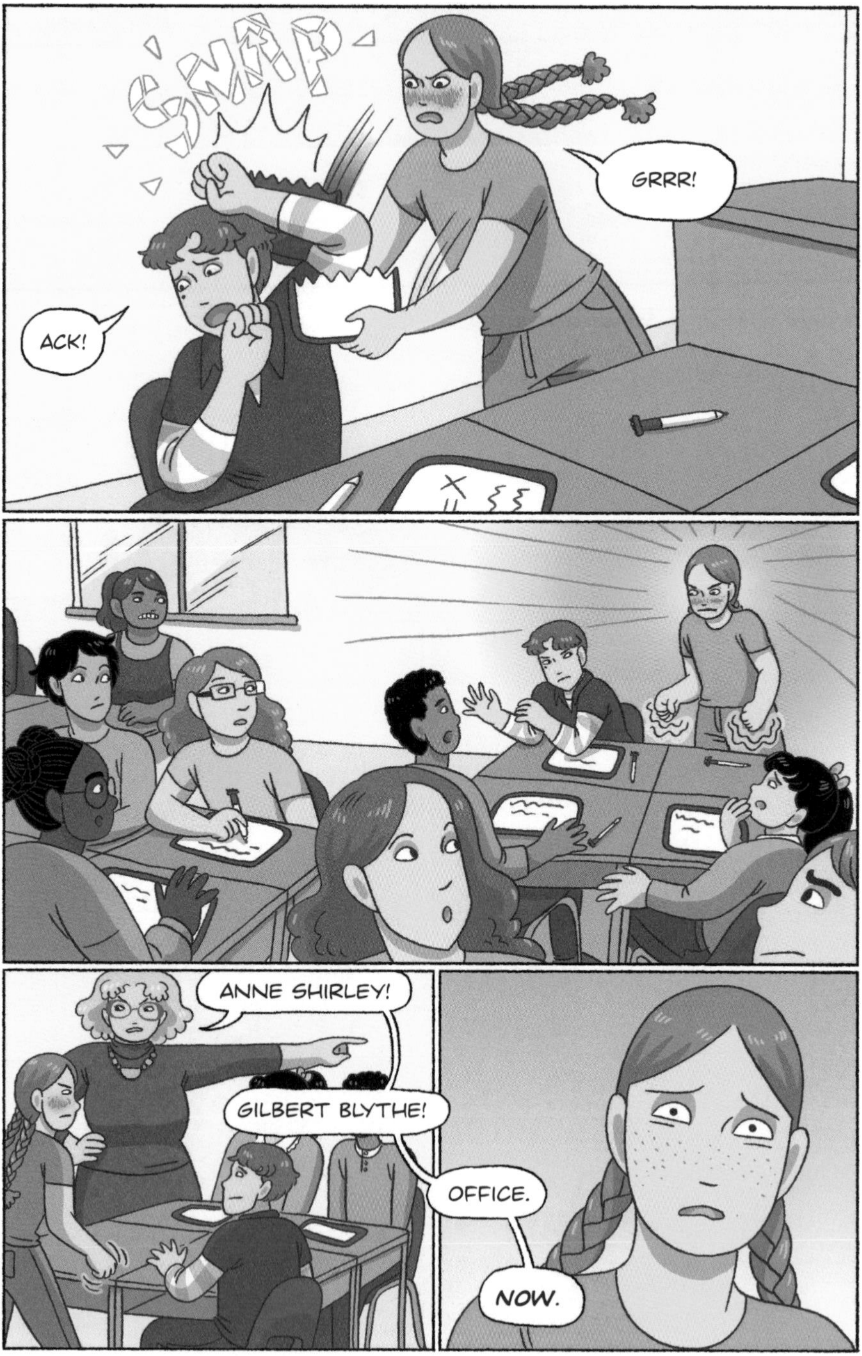
SNAP
GRRR!
ACK!
ANNE SHIRLEY!
GILBERT BLYTHE!
OFFICE.
NOW.

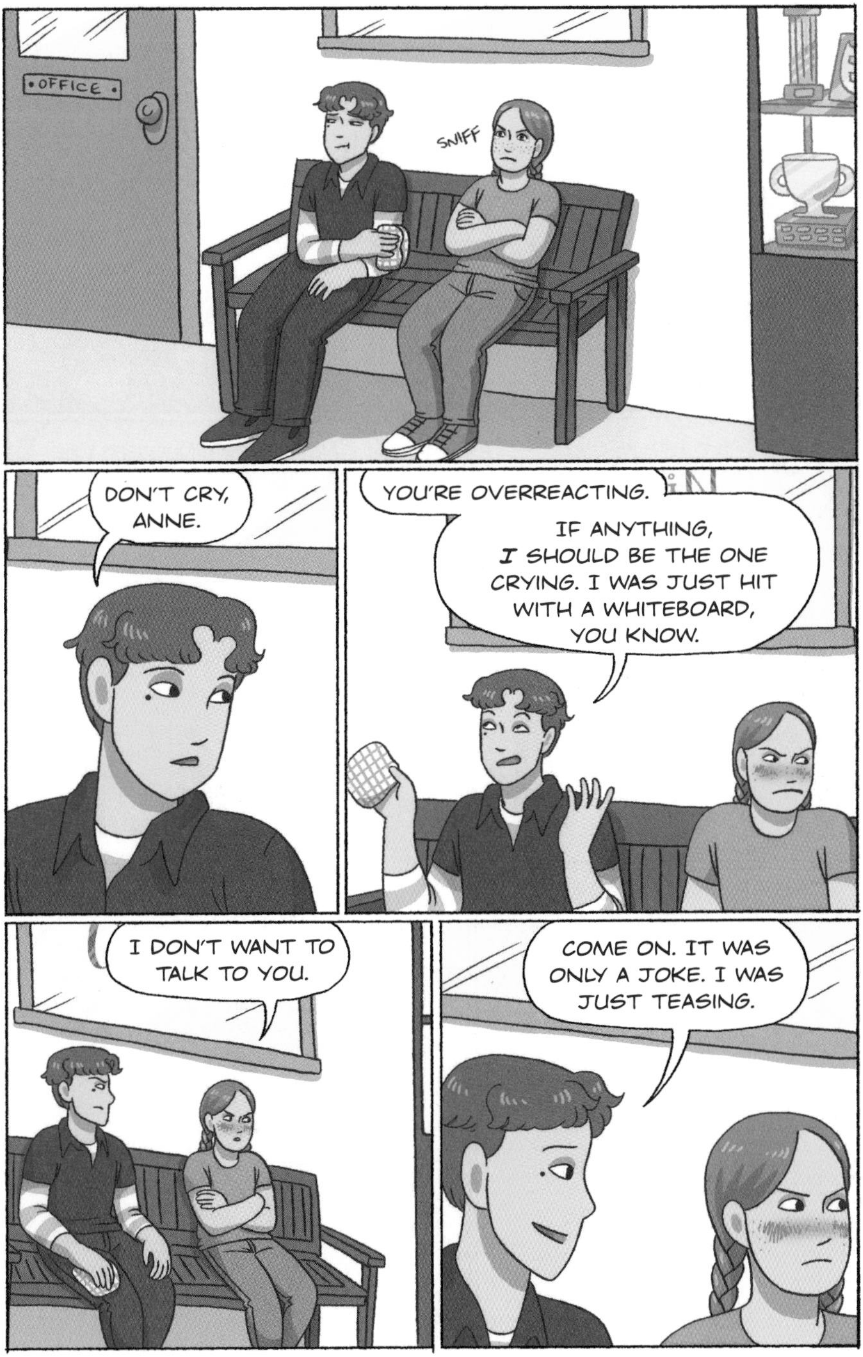
OFFICE
SNIFF
DON'T CRY, ANNE.
YOU'RE OVERREACTING.
IF ANYTHING, I SHOULD BE THE ONE CRYING. I WAS JUST HIT WITH A WHITEBOARD, YOU KNOW.
I DON'T WANT TO TALK TO YOU.
COME ON. IT WAS ONLY A JOKE. I WAS JUST TEASING.

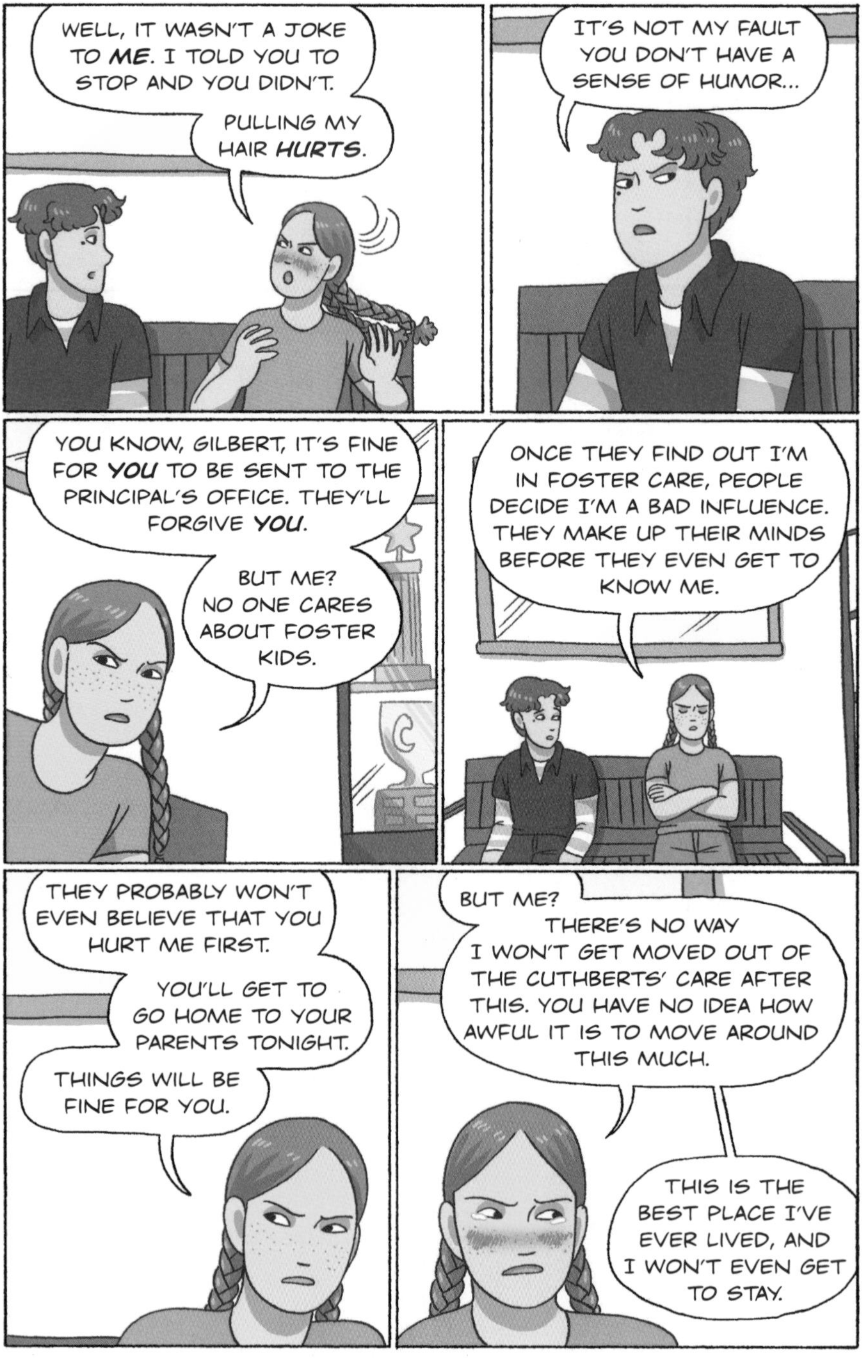
WELL, IT WASN'T A JOKE TO **ME**. I TOLD YOU TO STOP AND YOU DIDN'T.
PULLING MY HAIR **HURTS**.
IT'S NOT MY FAULT YOU DON'T HAVE A SENSE OF HUMOR...
YOU KNOW, GILBERT, IT'S FINE FOR **YOU** TO BE SENT TO THE PRINCIPAL'S OFFICE. THEY'LL FORGIVE **YOU**.
BUT ME? NO ONE CARES ABOUT FOSTER KIDS.
ONCE THEY FIND OUT I'M IN FOSTER CARE, PEOPLE DECIDE I'M A BAD INFLUENCE. THEY MAKE UP THEIR MINDS BEFORE THEY EVEN GET TO KNOW ME.
THEY PROBABLY WON'T EVEN BELIEVE THAT YOU HURT ME FIRST.
YOU'LL GET TO GO HOME TO YOUR PARENTS TONIGHT.
THINGS WILL BE FINE FOR YOU.
BUT ME?
THERE'S NO WAY I WON'T GET MOVED OUT OF THE CUTHBERTS' CARE AFTER THIS. YOU HAVE NO IDEA HOW AWFUL IT IS TO MOVE AROUND THIS MUCH.
THIS IS THE BEST PLACE I'VE EVER LIVED, AND I WON'T EVEN GET TO STAY.

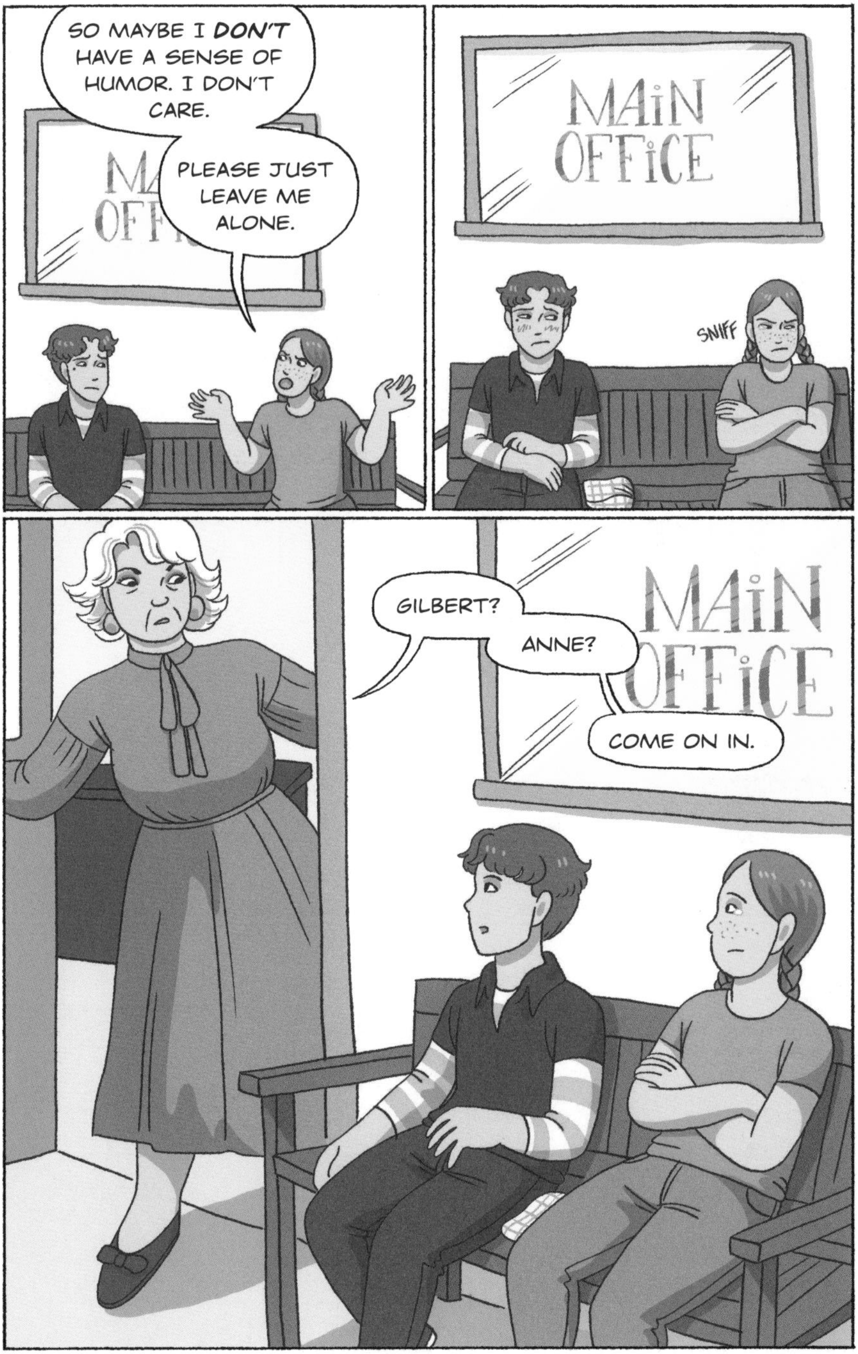
SO MAYBE I **DON'T** HAVE A SENSE OF HUMOR. I DON'T CARE.
PLEASE JUST LEAVE ME ALONE.
MAIN OFFICE
MAIN OFFICE
SNIFF
MAIN OFFICE
GILBERT?
ANNE?
COME ON IN.

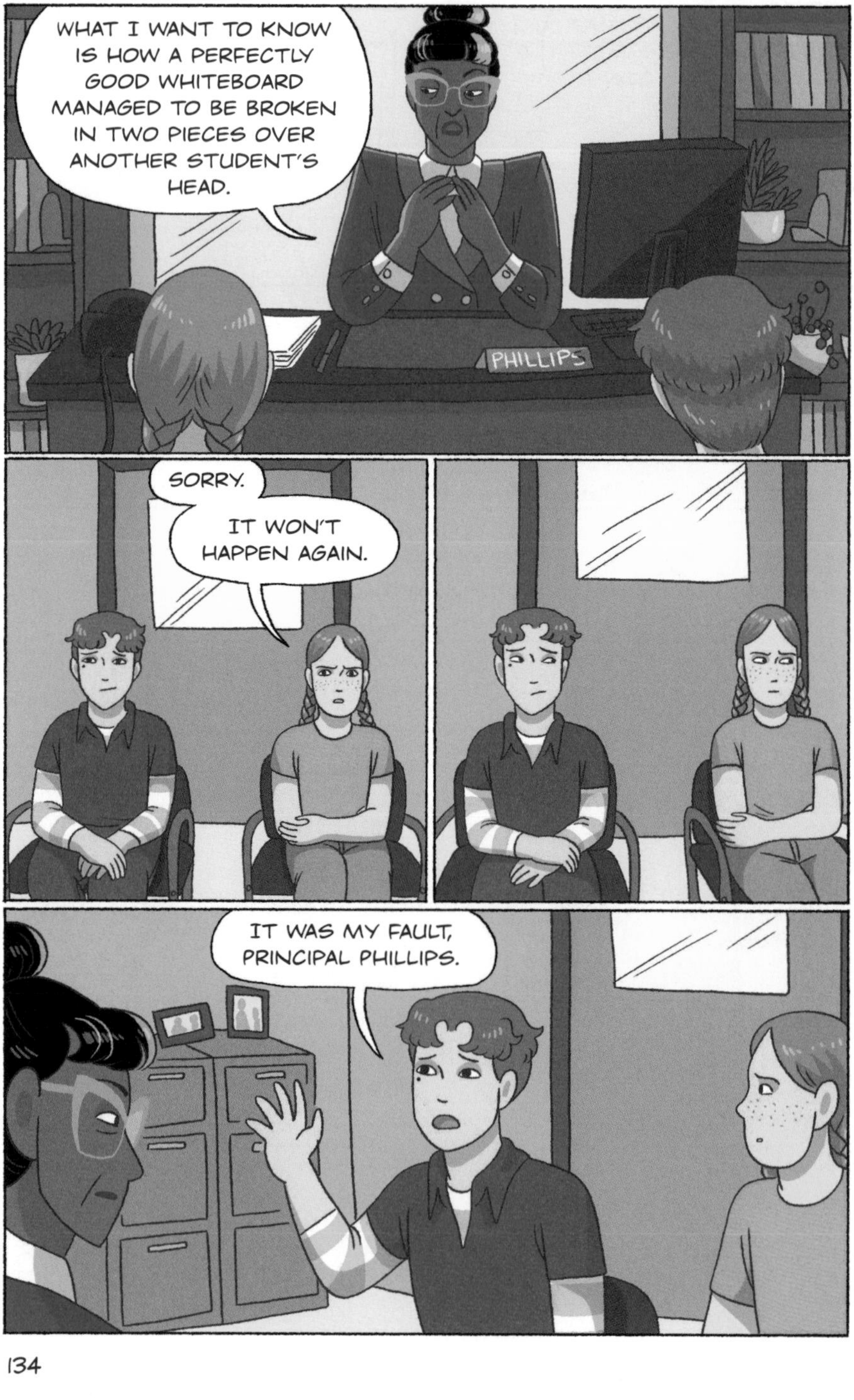
WHAT I WANT TO KNOW IS HOW A PERFECTLY GOOD WHITEBOARD MANAGED TO BE BROKEN IN TWO PIECES OVER ANOTHER STUDENT'S HEAD.
PHILLIPS
SORRY.
IT WON'T HAPPEN AGAIN.
IT WAS MY FAULT, PRINCIPAL PHILLIPS.

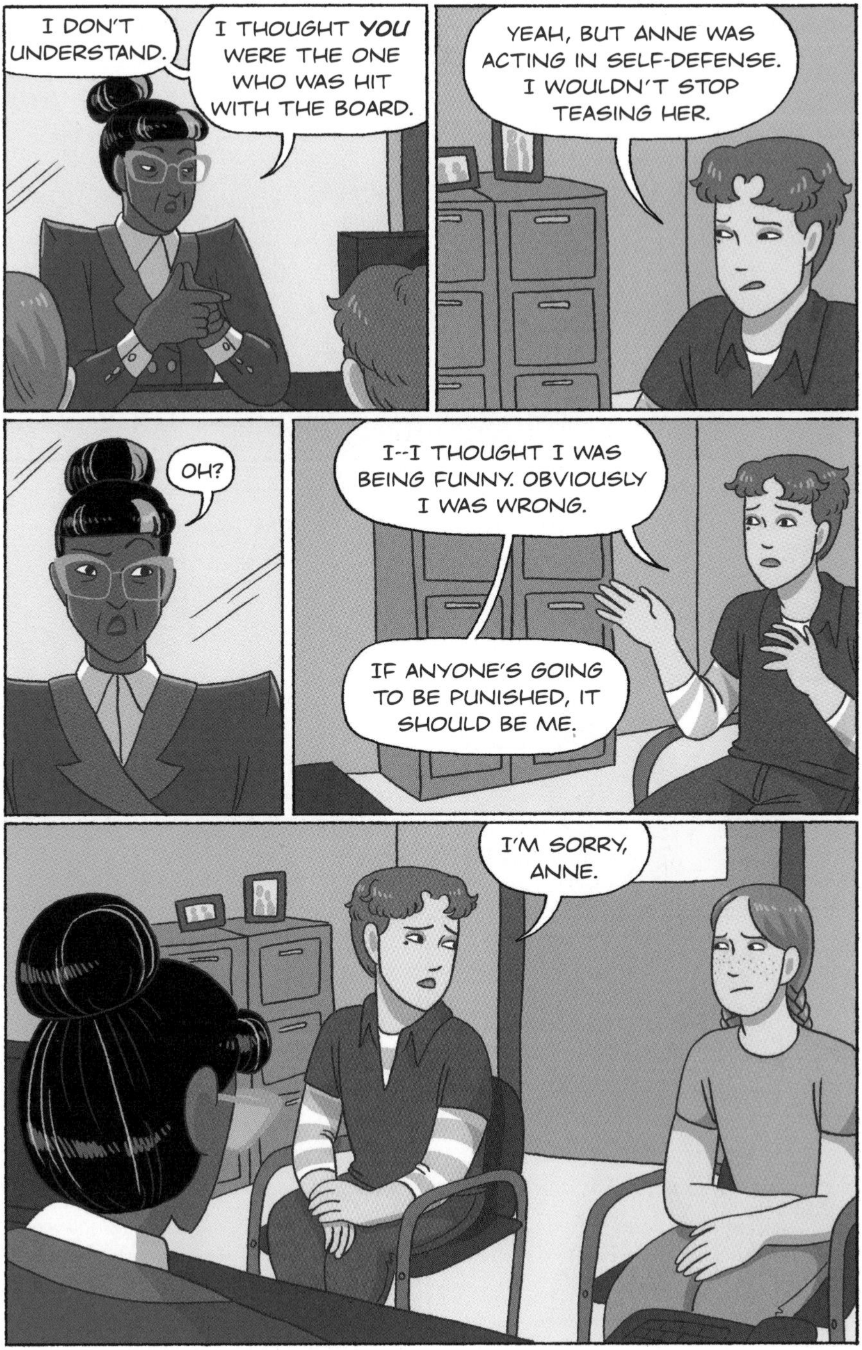
I DON'T UNDERSTAND.
I THOUGHT *YOU* WERE THE ONE WHO WAS HIT WITH THE BOARD.
YEAH, BUT ANNE WAS ACTING IN SELF-DEFENSE. I WOULDN'T STOP TEASING HER.
OH?
I--I THOUGHT I WAS BEING FUNNY. OBVIOUSLY I WAS WRONG.
IF ANYONE'S GOING TO BE PUNISHED, IT SHOULD BE ME.
I'M SORRY, ANNE.

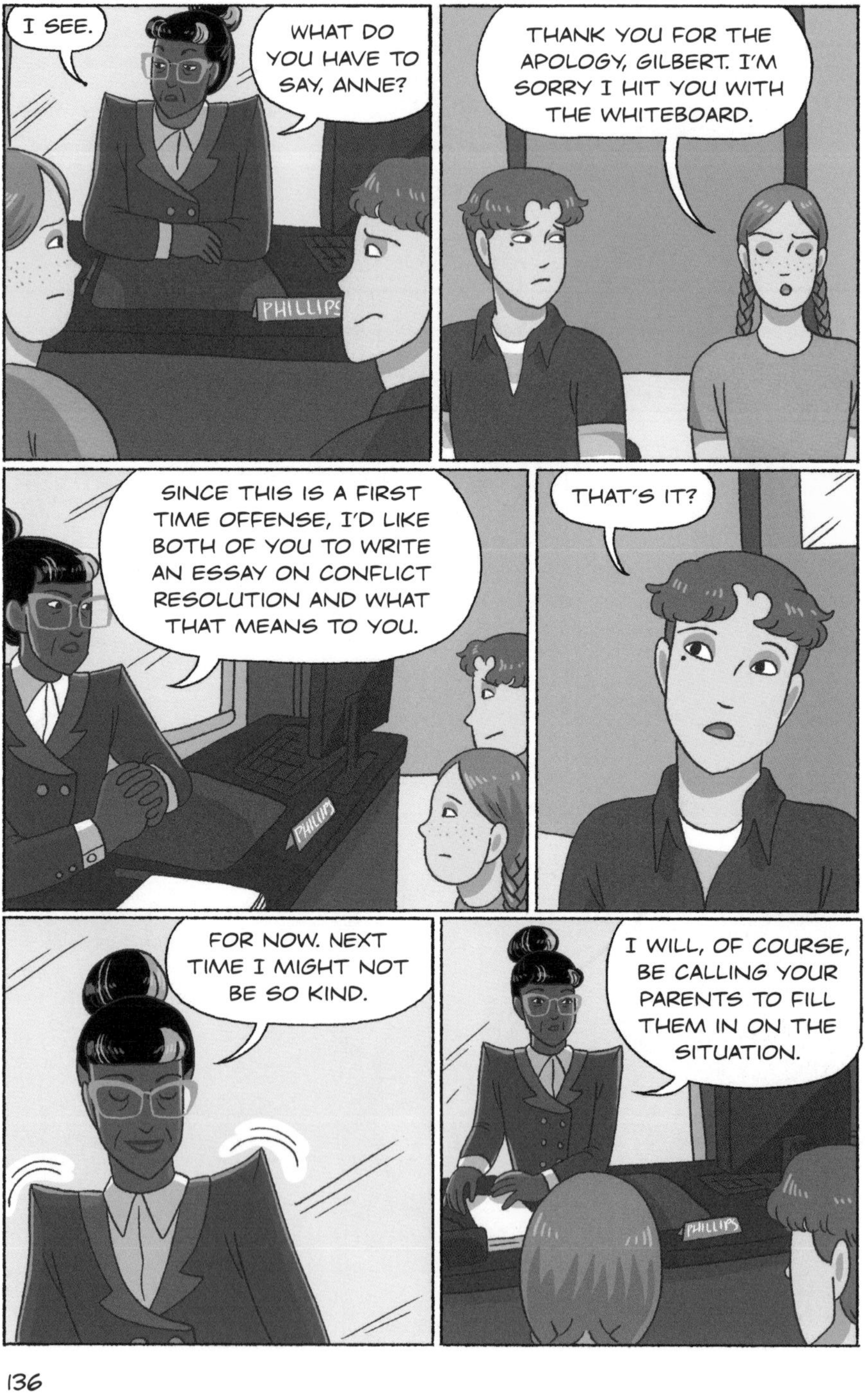
I SEE.
WHAT DO YOU HAVE TO SAY, ANNE?
PHILLIPS
THANK YOU FOR THE APOLOGY, GILBERT. I'M SORRY I HIT YOU WITH THE WHITEBOARD.
SINCE THIS IS A FIRST TIME OFFENSE, I'D LIKE BOTH OF YOU TO WRITE AN ESSAY ON CONFLICT RESOLUTION AND WHAT THAT MEANS TO YOU.
PHILLIPS
THAT'S IT?
FOR NOW. NEXT TIME I MIGHT NOT BE SO KIND.
I WILL, OF COURSE, BE CALLING YOUR PARENTS TO FILL THEM IN ON THE SITUATION.
PHILLIPS

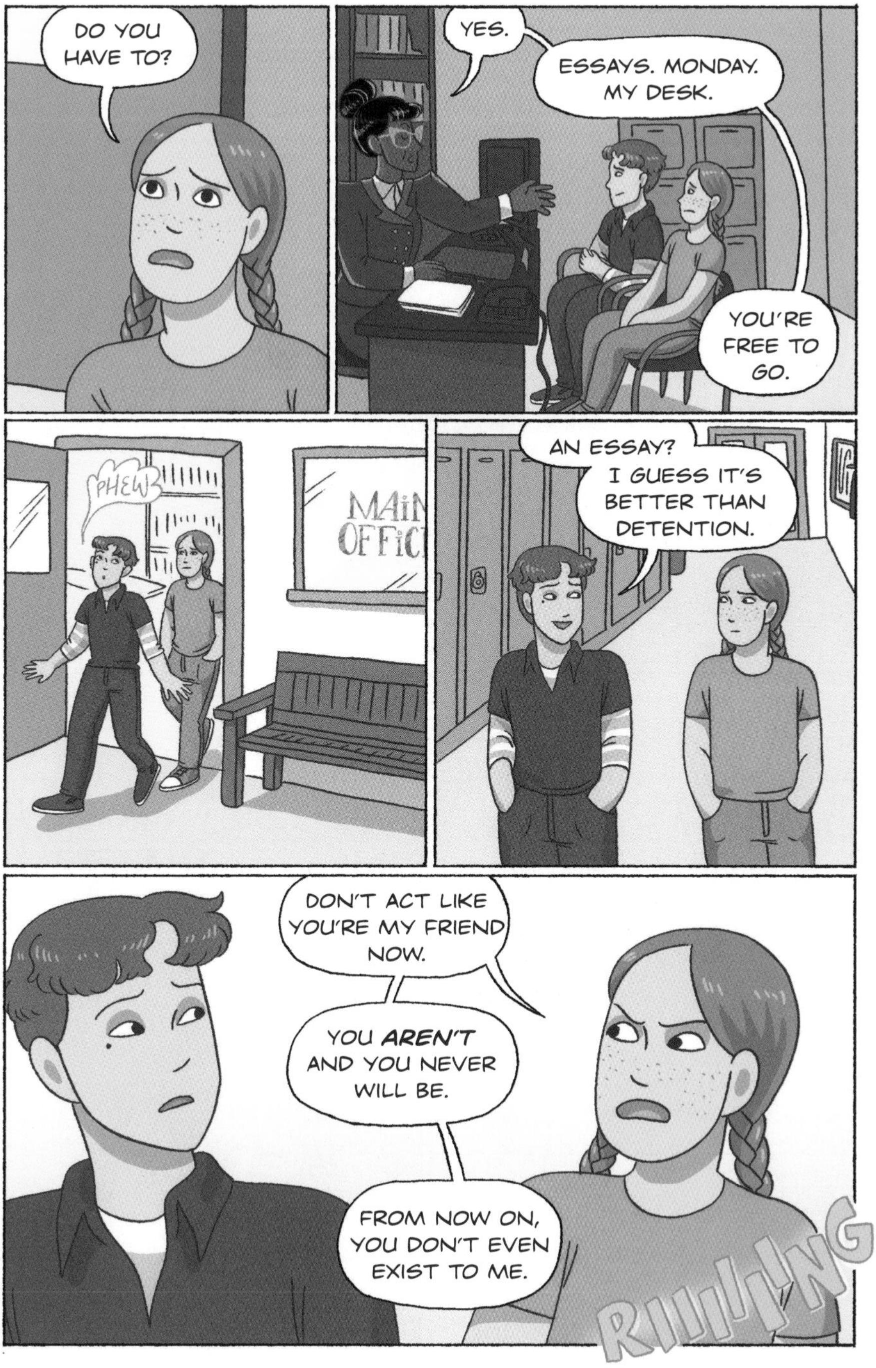
DO YOU HAVE TO?
YES.
ESSAYS. MONDAY. MY DESK.
YOU'RE FREE TO GO.
PHEW
MAIN OFFICE
AN ESSAY?
I GUESS IT'S BETTER THAN DETENTION.
DON'T ACT LIKE YOU'RE MY FRIEND NOW.
YOU **AREN'T** AND YOU NEVER WILL BE.
FROM NOW ON, YOU DON'T EVEN EXIST TO ME.
RIIIIING

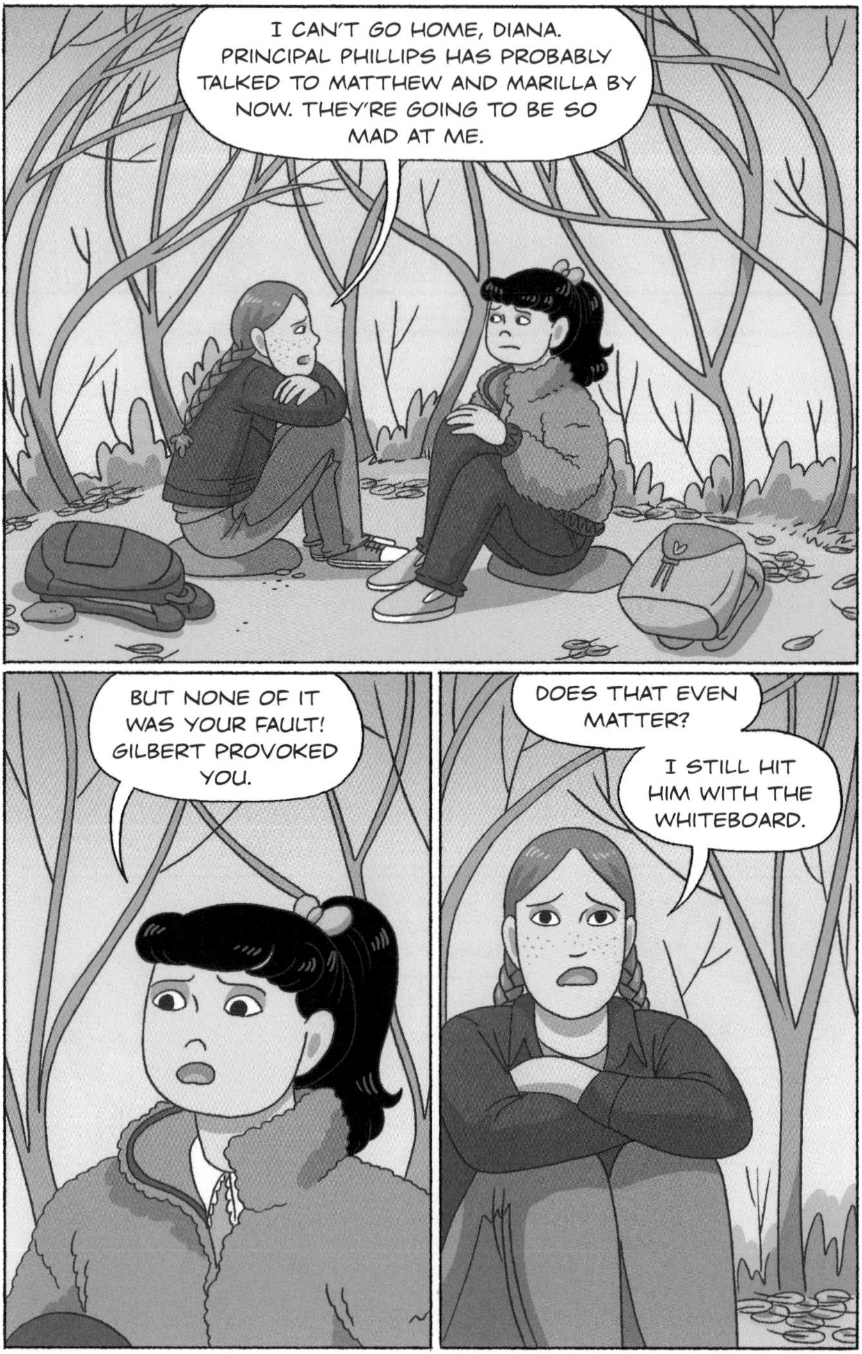
I CAN'T GO HOME, DIANA. PRINCIPAL PHILLIPS HAS PROBABLY TALKED TO MATTHEW AND MARILLA BY NOW. THEY'RE GOING TO BE SO MAD AT ME.
BUT NONE OF IT WAS YOUR FAULT! GILBERT PROVOKED YOU.
DOES THAT EVEN MATTER?
I STILL HIT HIM WITH THE WHITEBOARD.

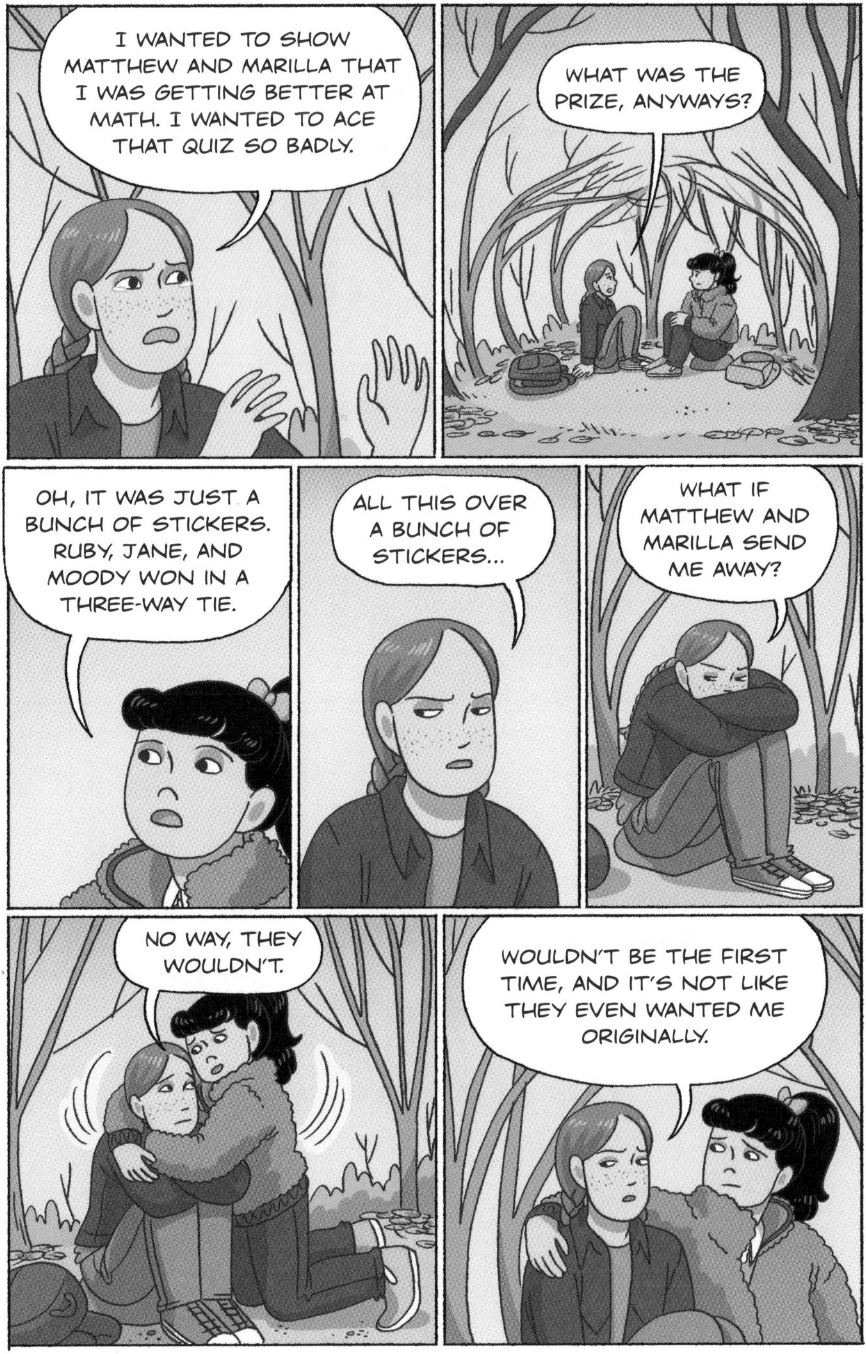
I WANTED TO SHOW MATTHEW AND MARILLA THAT I WAS GETTING BETTER AT MATH. I WANTED TO ACE THAT QUIZ SO BADLY.
WHAT WAS THE PRIZE, ANYWAYS?
OH, IT WAS JUST A BUNCH OF STICKERS. RUBY, JANE, AND MOODY WON IN A THREE-WAY TIE.
ALL THIS OVER A BUNCH OF STICKERS...
WHAT IF MATTHEW AND MARILLA SEND ME AWAY?
NO WAY, THEY WOULDN'T.
WOULDN'T BE THE FIRST TIME, AND IT'S NOT LIKE THEY EVEN WANTED ME ORIGINALLY.

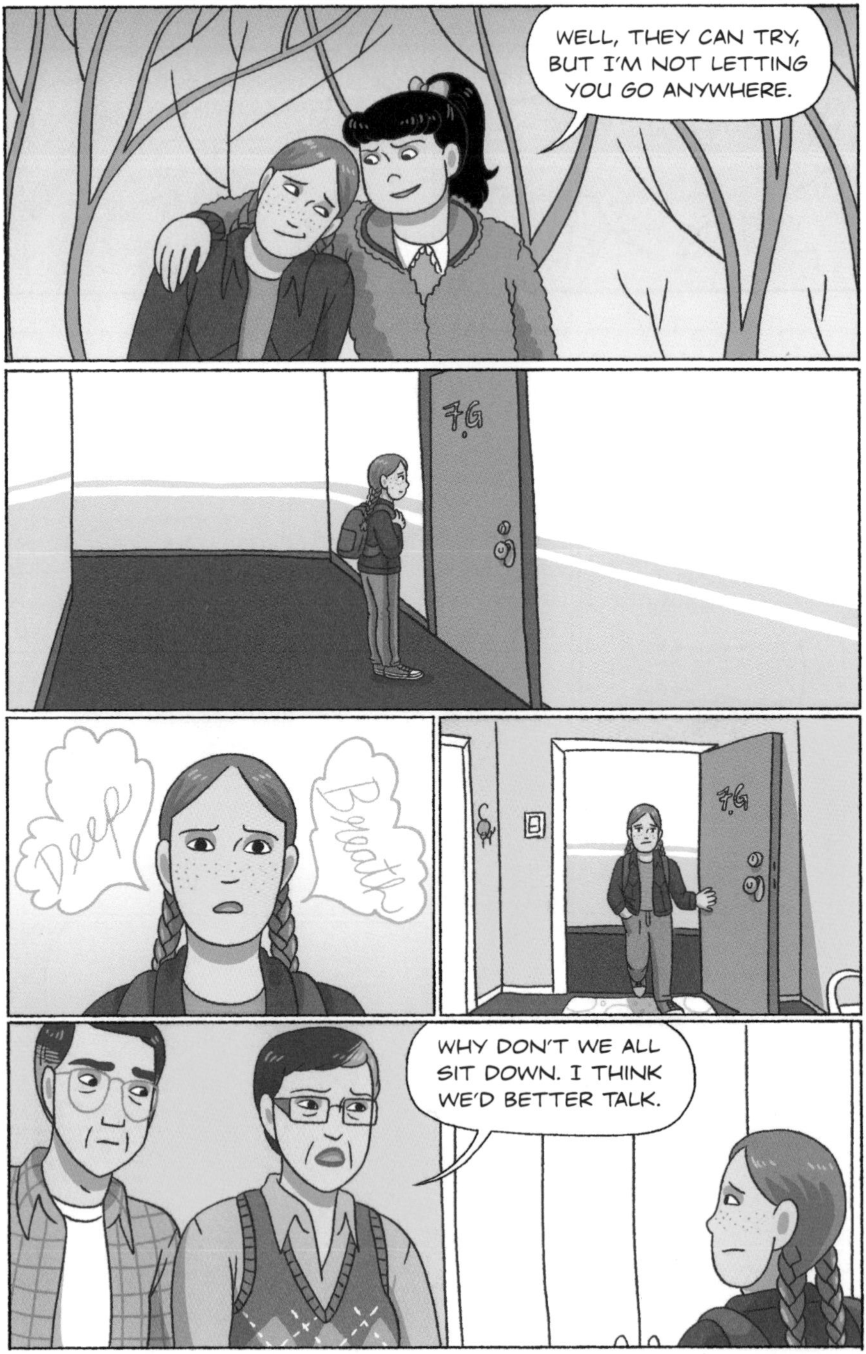
WELL, THEY CAN TRY, BUT I'M NOT LETTING YOU GO ANYWHERE.
7G
Deep
Breath
7G
WHY DON'T WE ALL SIT DOWN. I THINK WE'D BETTER TALK.

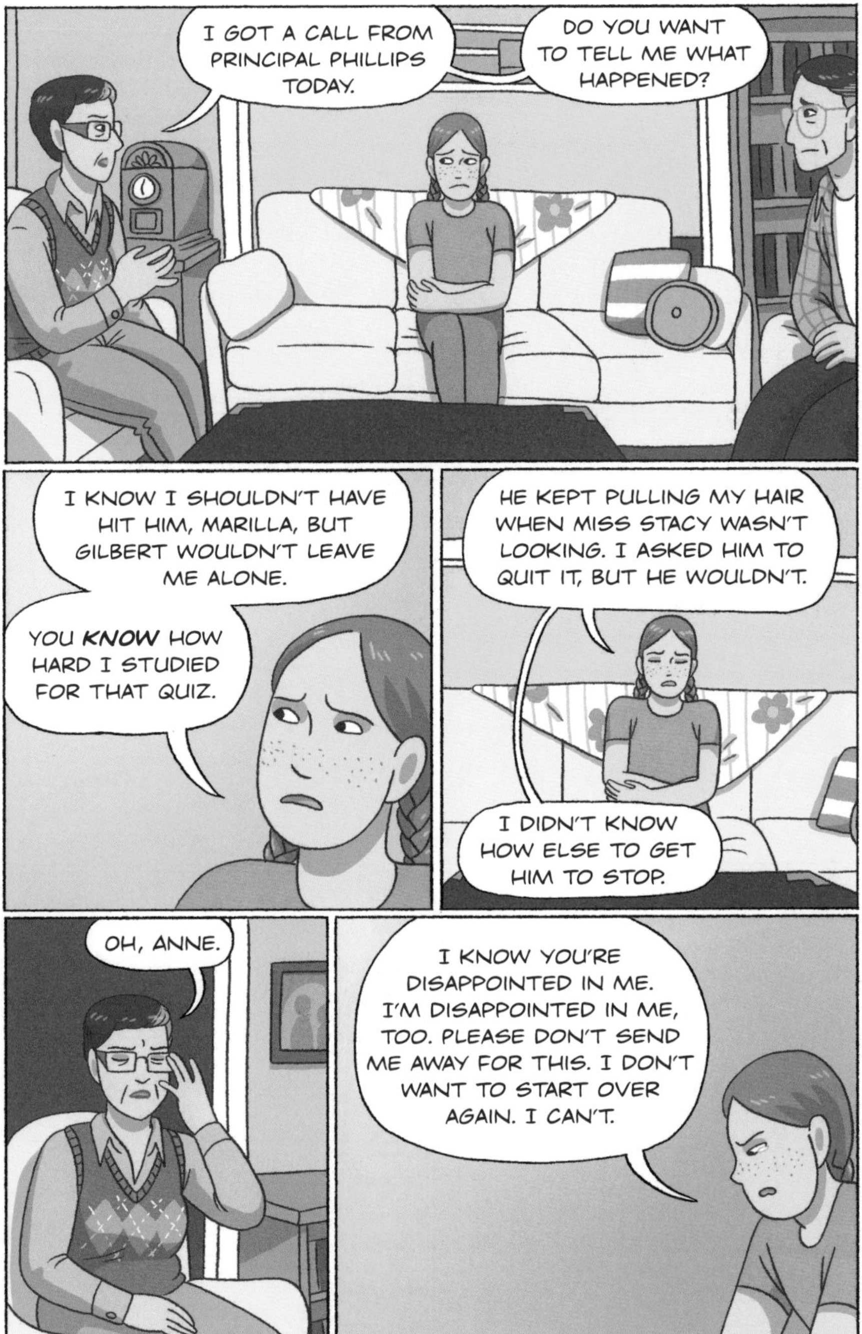
I GOT A CALL FROM PRINCIPAL PHILLIPS TODAY.
DO YOU WANT TO TELL ME WHAT HAPPENED?
I KNOW I SHOULDN'T HAVE HIT HIM, MARILLA, BUT GILBERT WOULDN'T LEAVE ME ALONE.
YOU **KNOW** HOW HARD I STUDIED FOR THAT QUIZ.
HE KEPT PULLING MY HAIR WHEN MISS STACY WASN'T LOOKING. I ASKED HIM TO QUIT IT, BUT HE WOULDN'T.
I DIDN'T KNOW HOW ELSE TO GET HIM TO STOP.
OH, ANNE.
I KNOW YOU'RE DISAPPOINTED IN ME. I'M DISAPPOINTED IN ME, TOO. PLEASE DON'T SEND ME AWAY FOR THIS. I DON'T WANT TO START OVER AGAIN. I CAN'T.

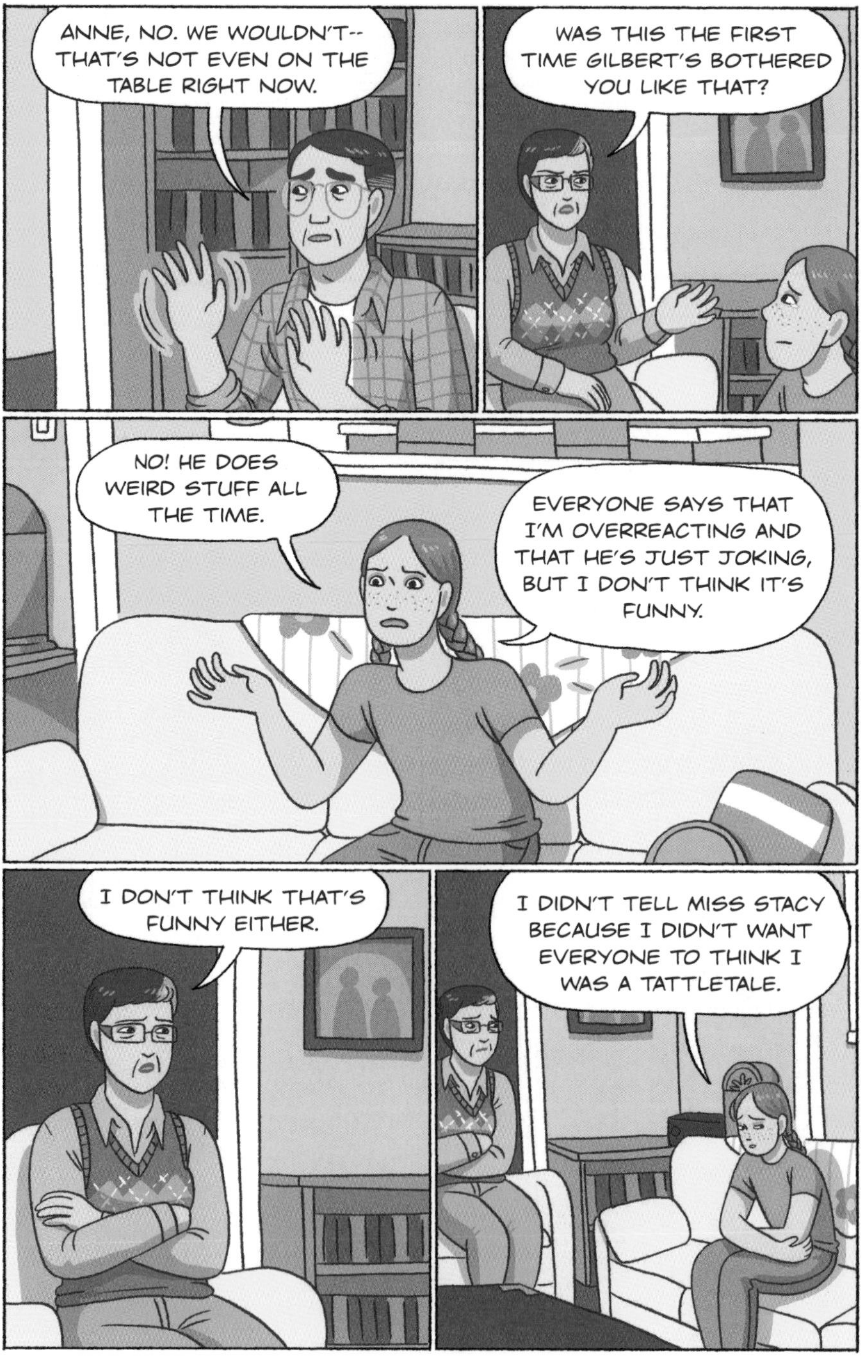
ANNE, NO. WE WOULDN'T--THAT'S NOT EVEN ON THE TABLE RIGHT NOW.
WAS THIS THE FIRST TIME GILBERT'S BOTHERED YOU LIKE THAT?
NO! HE DOES WEIRD STUFF ALL THE TIME.
EVERYONE SAYS THAT I'M OVERREACTING AND THAT HE'S JUST JOKING, BUT I DON'T THINK IT'S FUNNY.
I DON'T THINK THAT'S FUNNY EITHER.
I DIDN'T TELL MISS STACY BECAUSE I DIDN'T WANT EVERYONE TO THINK I WAS A TATTLETALE.

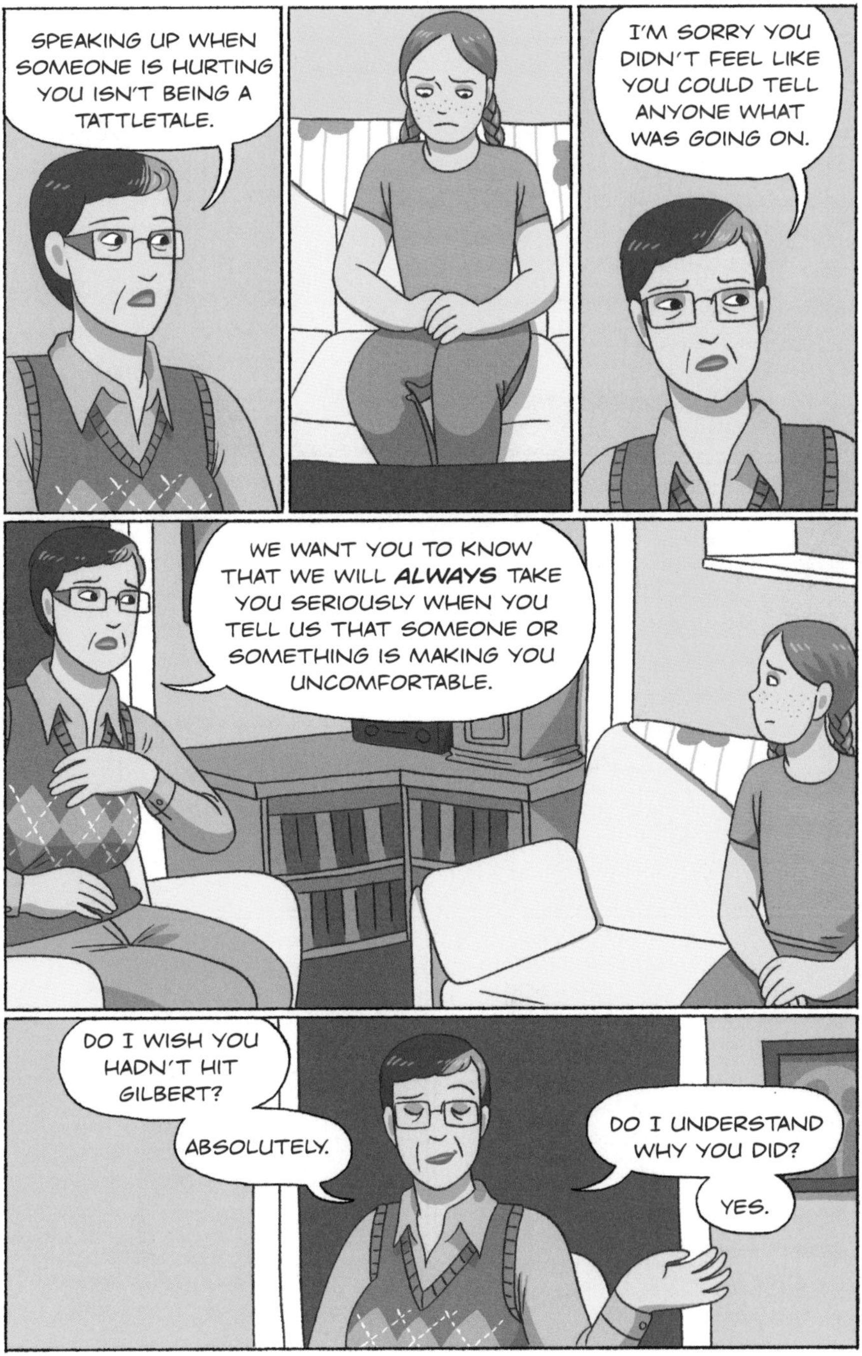

SPEAKING UP WHEN SOMEONE IS HURTING YOU ISN'T BEING A TATTLETALE.
I'M SORRY YOU DIDN'T FEEL LIKE YOU COULD TELL ANYONE WHAT WAS GOING ON.
WE WANT YOU TO KNOW THAT WE WILL **ALWAYS** TAKE YOU SERIOUSLY WHEN YOU TELL US THAT SOMEONE OR SOMETHING IS MAKING YOU UNCOMFORTABLE.
DO I WISH YOU HADN'T HIT GILBERT?
ABSOLUTELY.
DO I UNDERSTAND WHY YOU DID?
YES.

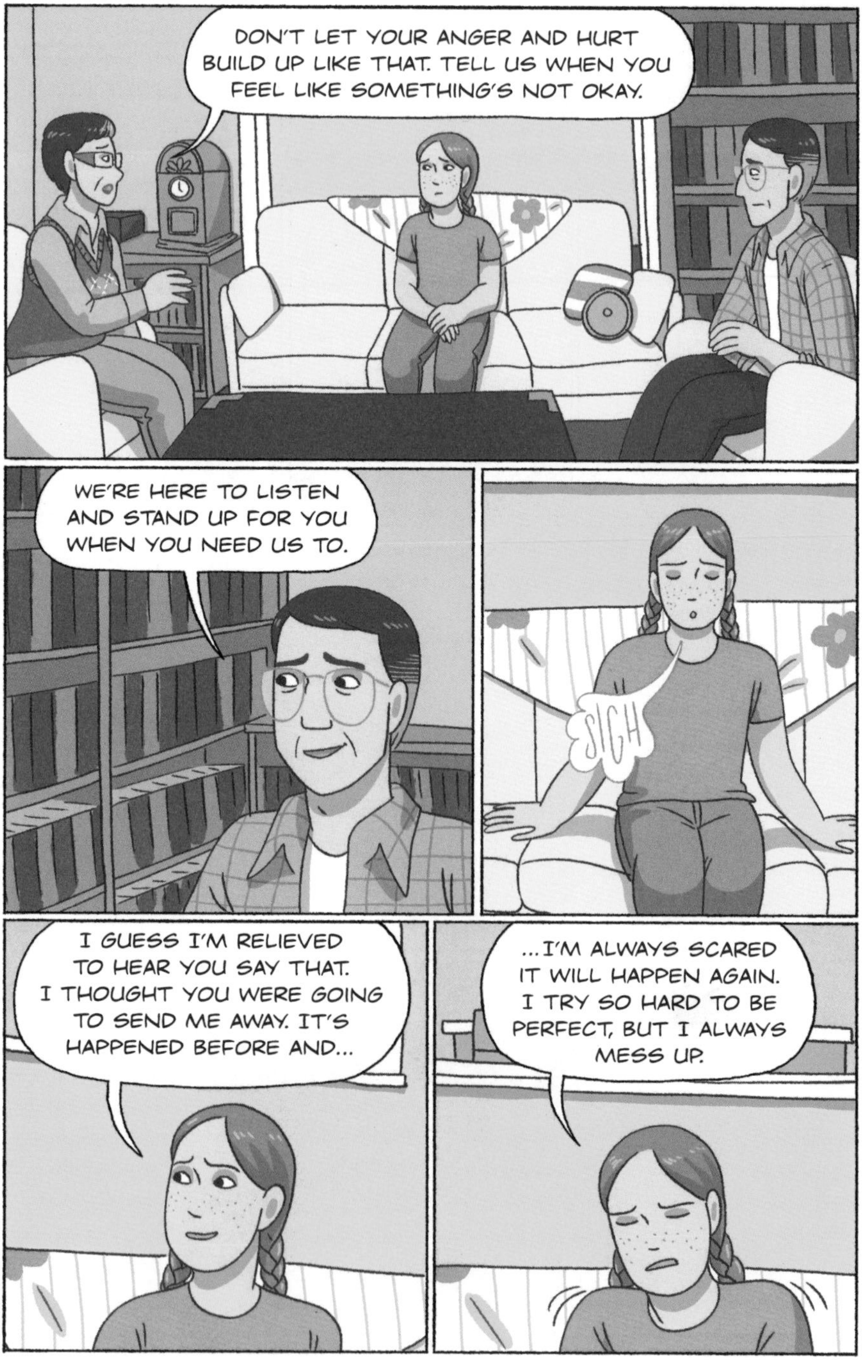
DON'T LET YOUR ANGER AND HURT BUILD UP LIKE THAT. TELL US WHEN YOU FEEL LIKE SOMETHING'S NOT OKAY.
WE'RE HERE TO LISTEN AND STAND UP FOR YOU WHEN YOU NEED US TO.
SIGH
I GUESS I'M RELIEVED TO HEAR YOU SAY THAT. I THOUGHT YOU WERE GOING TO SEND ME AWAY. IT'S HAPPENED BEFORE AND...
...I'M ALWAYS SCARED IT WILL HAPPEN AGAIN. I TRY SO HARD TO BE PERFECT, BUT I ALWAYS MESS UP.

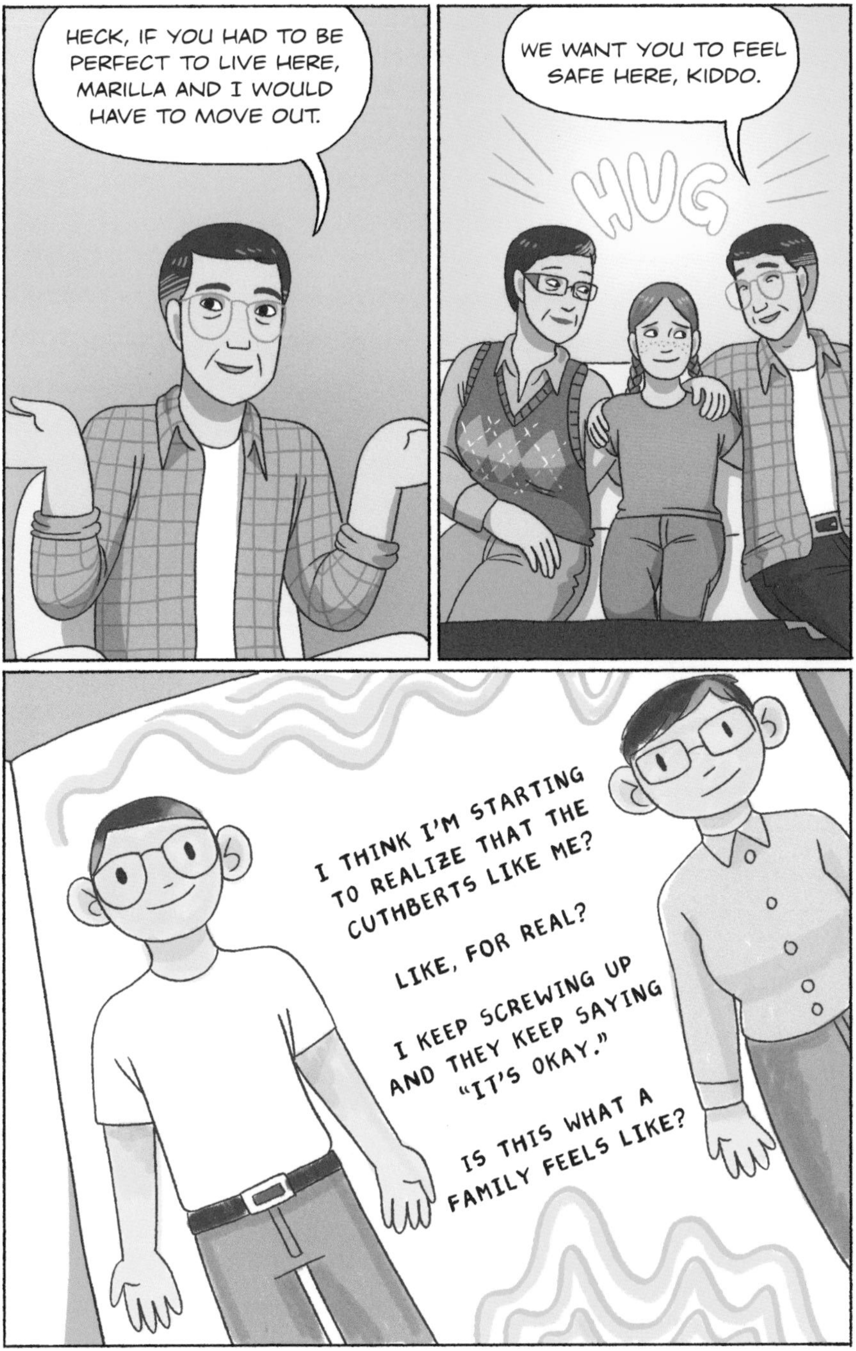
HECK, IF YOU HAD TO BE PERFECT TO LIVE HERE, MARILLA AND I WOULD HAVE TO MOVE OUT.
WE WANT YOU TO FEEL SAFE HERE, KIDDO.
HUG
I THINK I'M STARTING TO REALIZE THAT THE CUTHBERTS LIKE ME?
LIKE, FOR REAL?
I KEEP SCREWING UP AND THEY KEEP SAYING "IT'S OKAY."
IS THIS WHAT A FAMILY FEELS LIKE?

CHAPTER 7

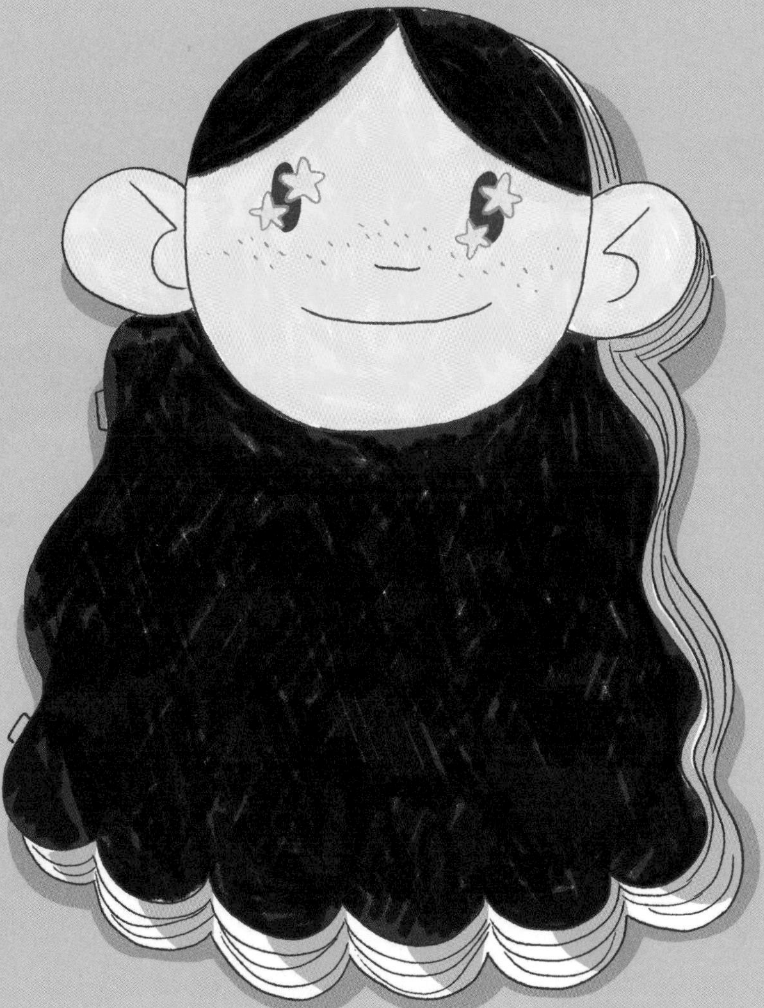

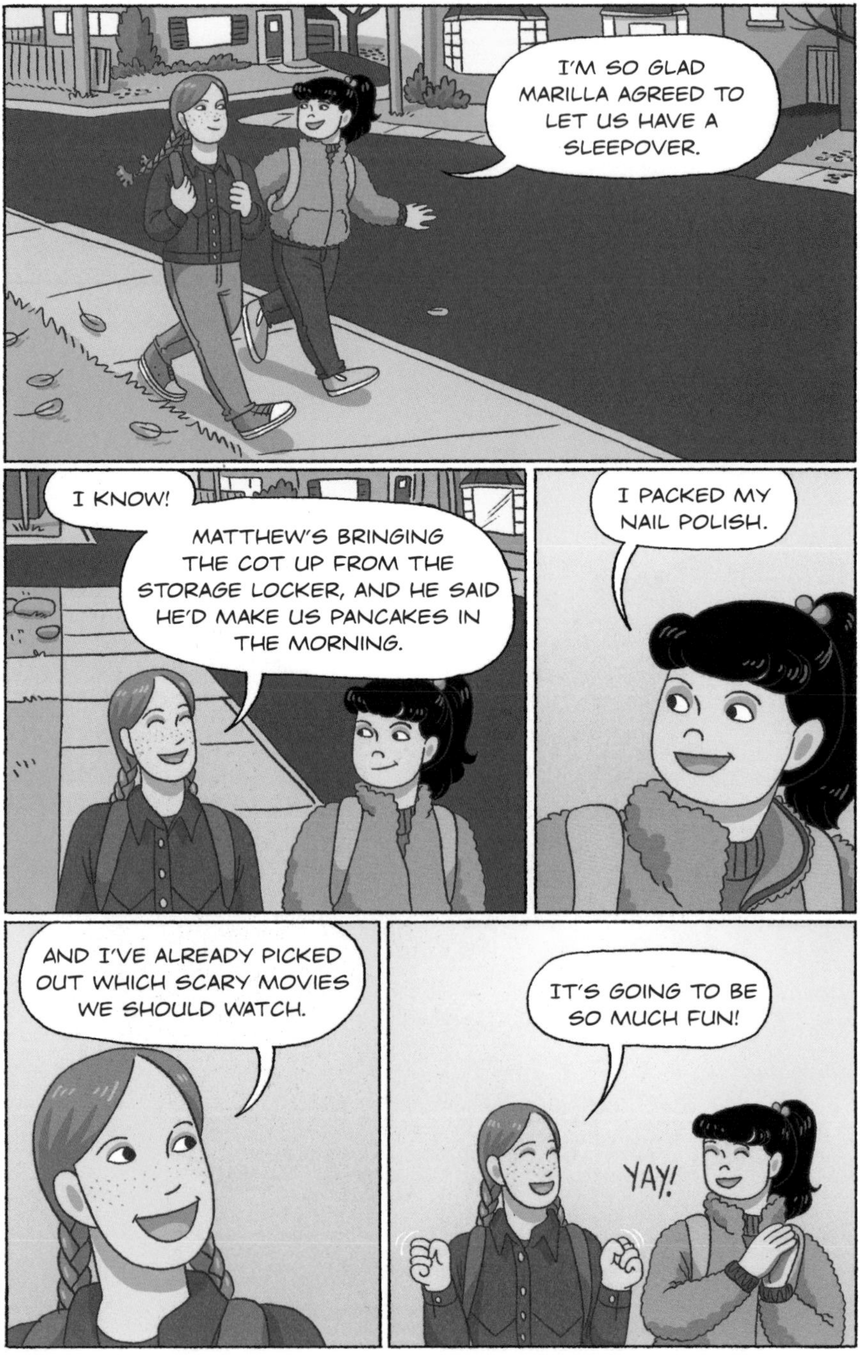
I'M SO GLAD MARILLA AGREED TO LET US HAVE A SLEEPOVER.
I KNOW!
MATTHEW'S BRINGING THE COT UP FROM THE STORAGE LOCKER, AND HE SAID HE'D MAKE US PANCAKES IN THE MORNING.
I PACKED MY NAIL POLISH.
AND I'VE ALREADY PICKED OUT WHICH SCARY MOVIES WE SHOULD WATCH.
IT'S GOING TO BE SO MUCH FUN!
YAY!

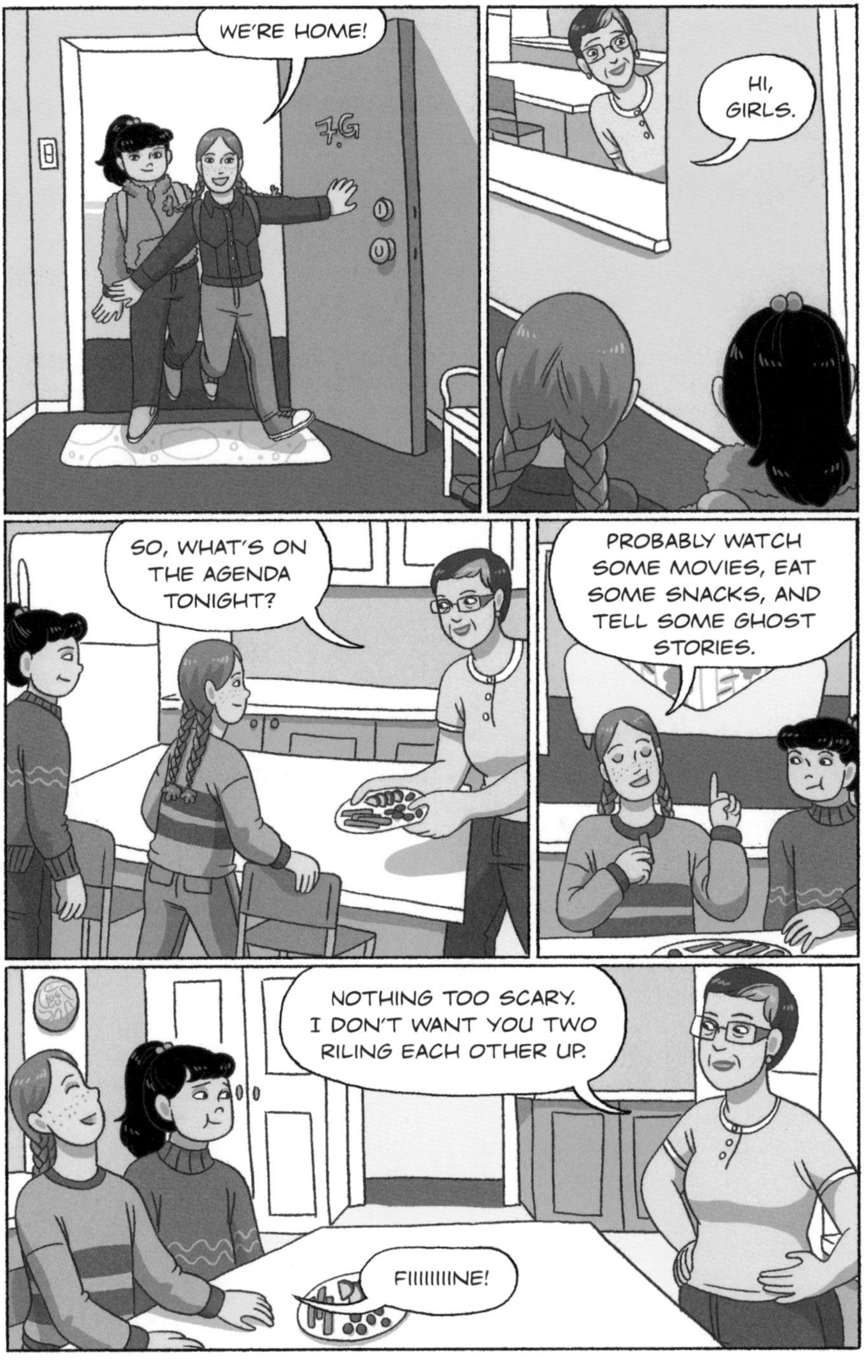
WE'RE HOME!
HI, GIRLS.
SO, WHAT'S ON THE AGENDA TONIGHT?
PROBABLY WATCH SOME MOVIES, EAT SOME SNACKS, AND TELL SOME GHOST STORIES.
NOTHING TOO SCARY. I DON'T WANT YOU TWO RILING EACH OTHER UP.
FIIIIIIIINE!

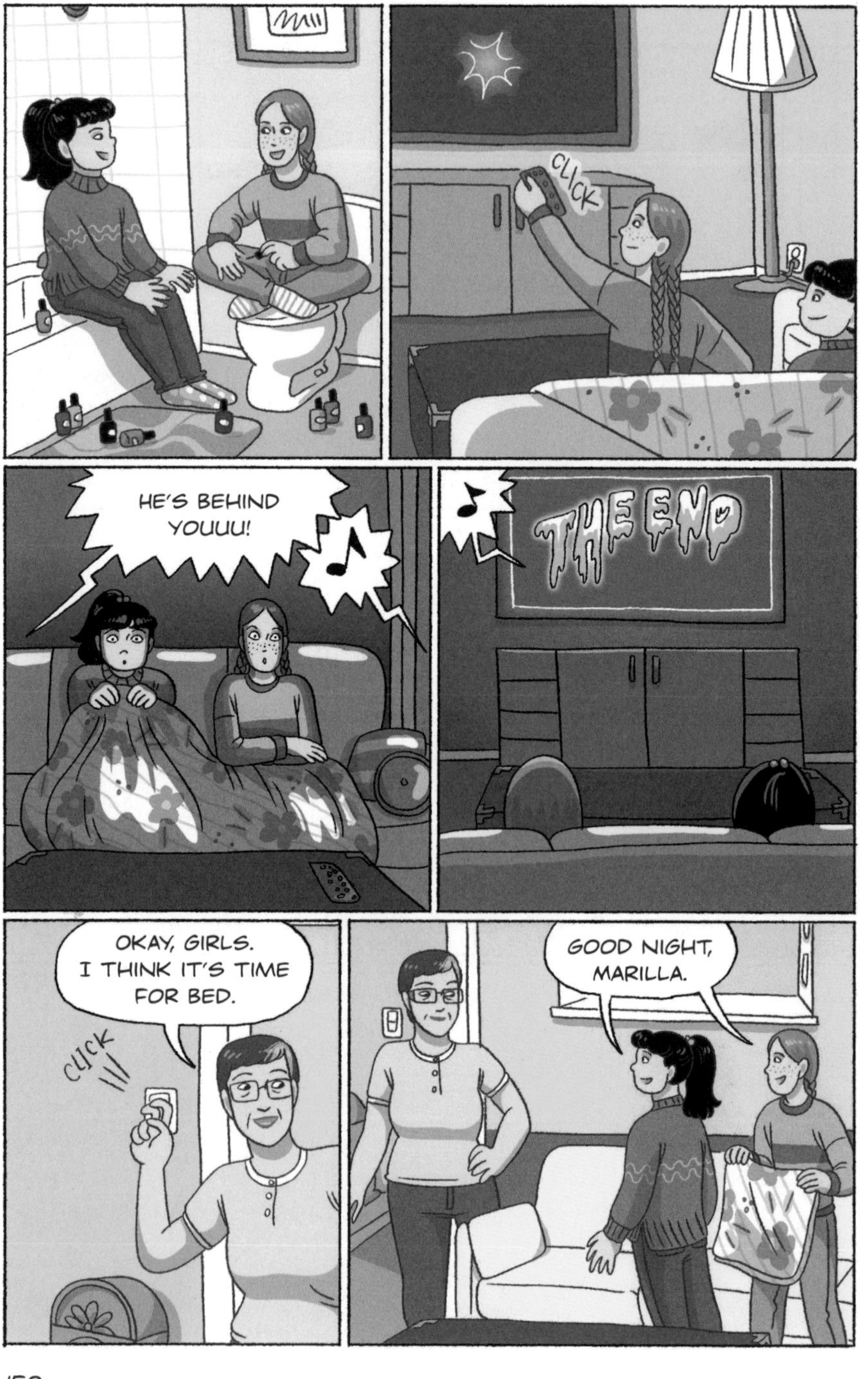
CLICK
HE'S BEHIND YOUUU!
THE END
OKAY, GIRLS. I THINK IT'S TIME FOR BED.
CLICK
GOOD NIGHT, MARILLA.

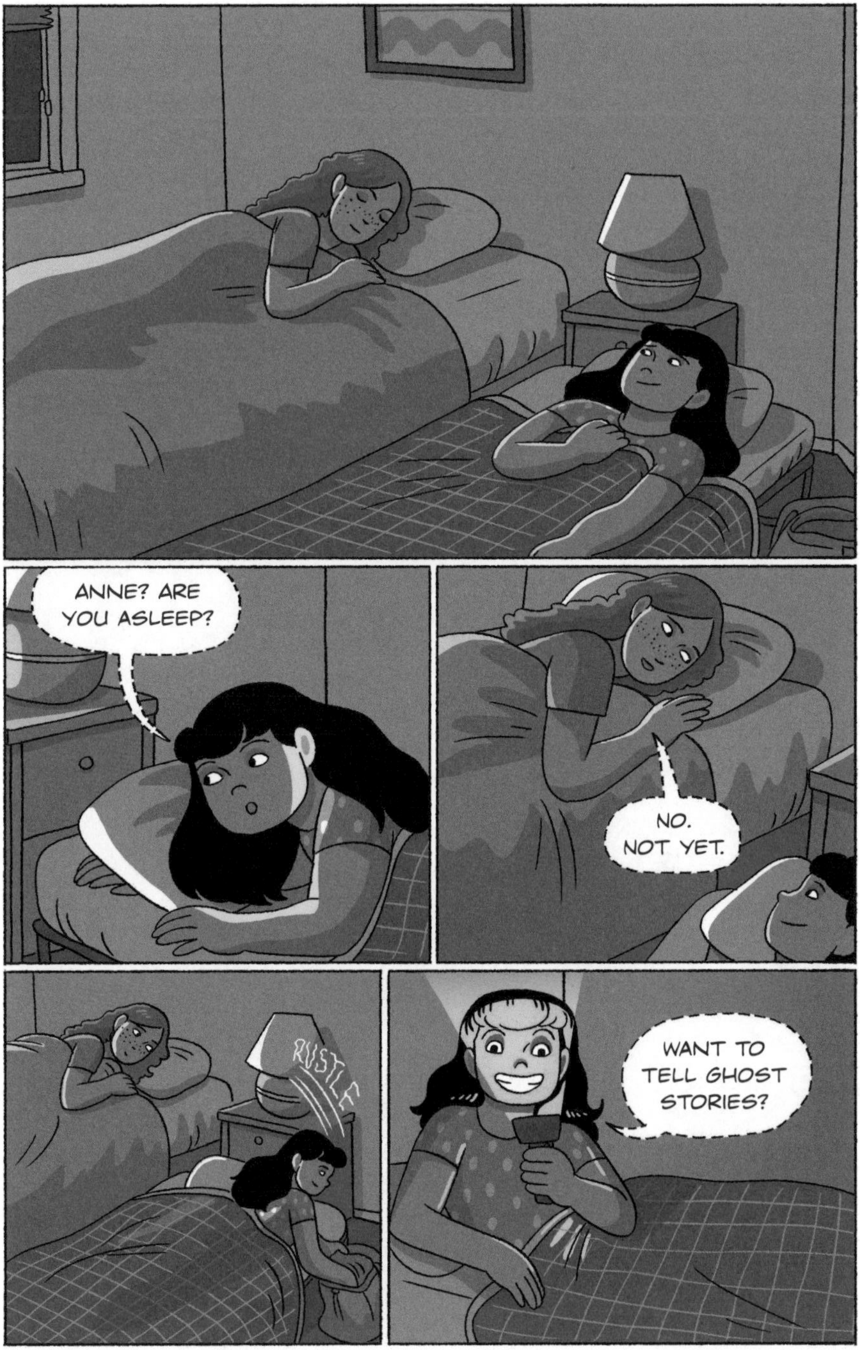
ANNE? ARE YOU ASLEEP?
NO. NOT YET.
RUSTLE
WANT TO TELL GHOST STORIES?

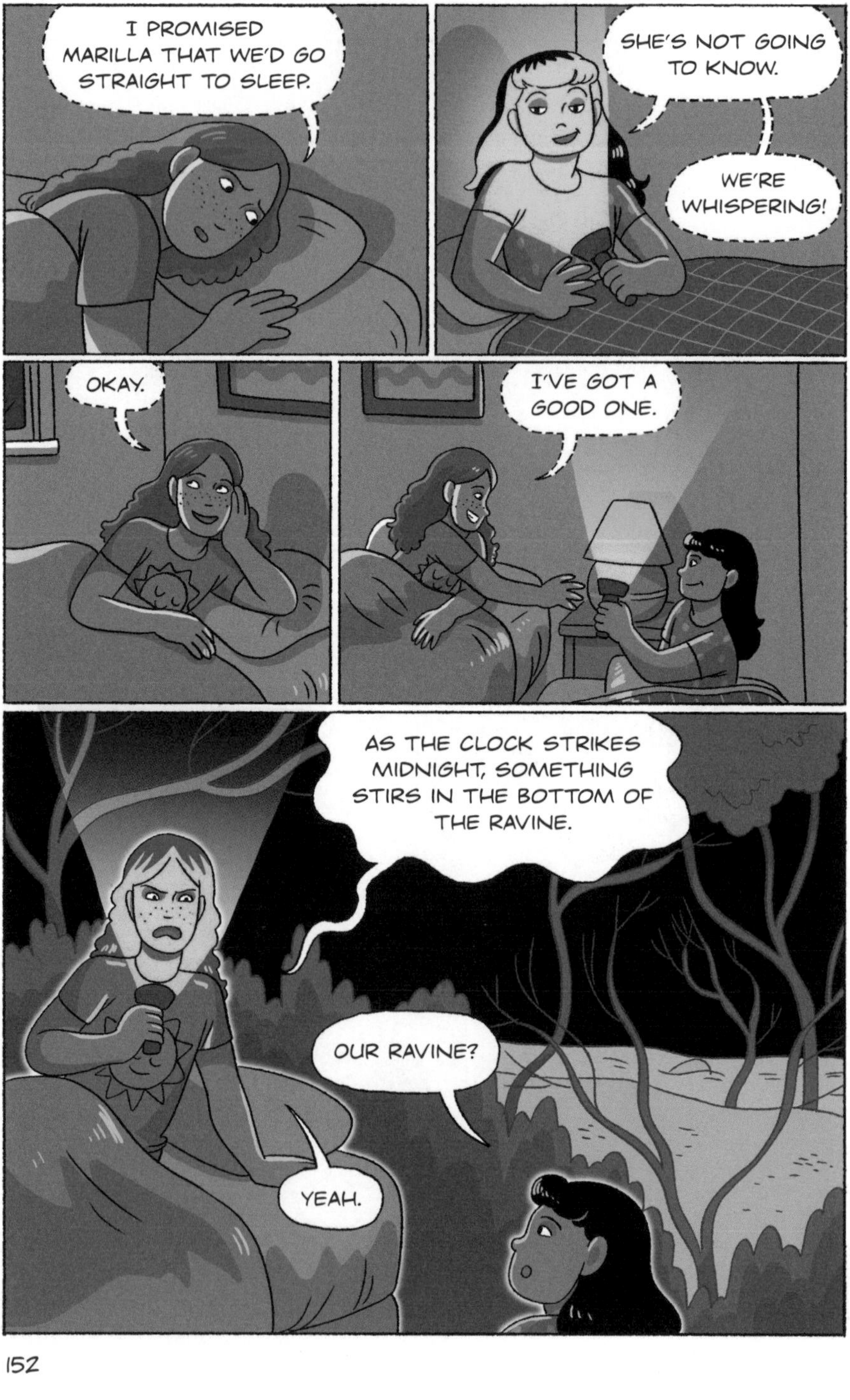
I PROMISED MARILLA THAT WE'D GO STRAIGHT TO SLEEP.
SHE'S NOT GOING TO KNOW.
WE'RE WHISPERING!
OKAY.
I'VE GOT A GOOD ONE.
AS THE CLOCK STRIKES MIDNIGHT, SOMETHING STIRS IN THE BOTTOM OF THE RAVINE.
OUR RAVINE?
YEAH.

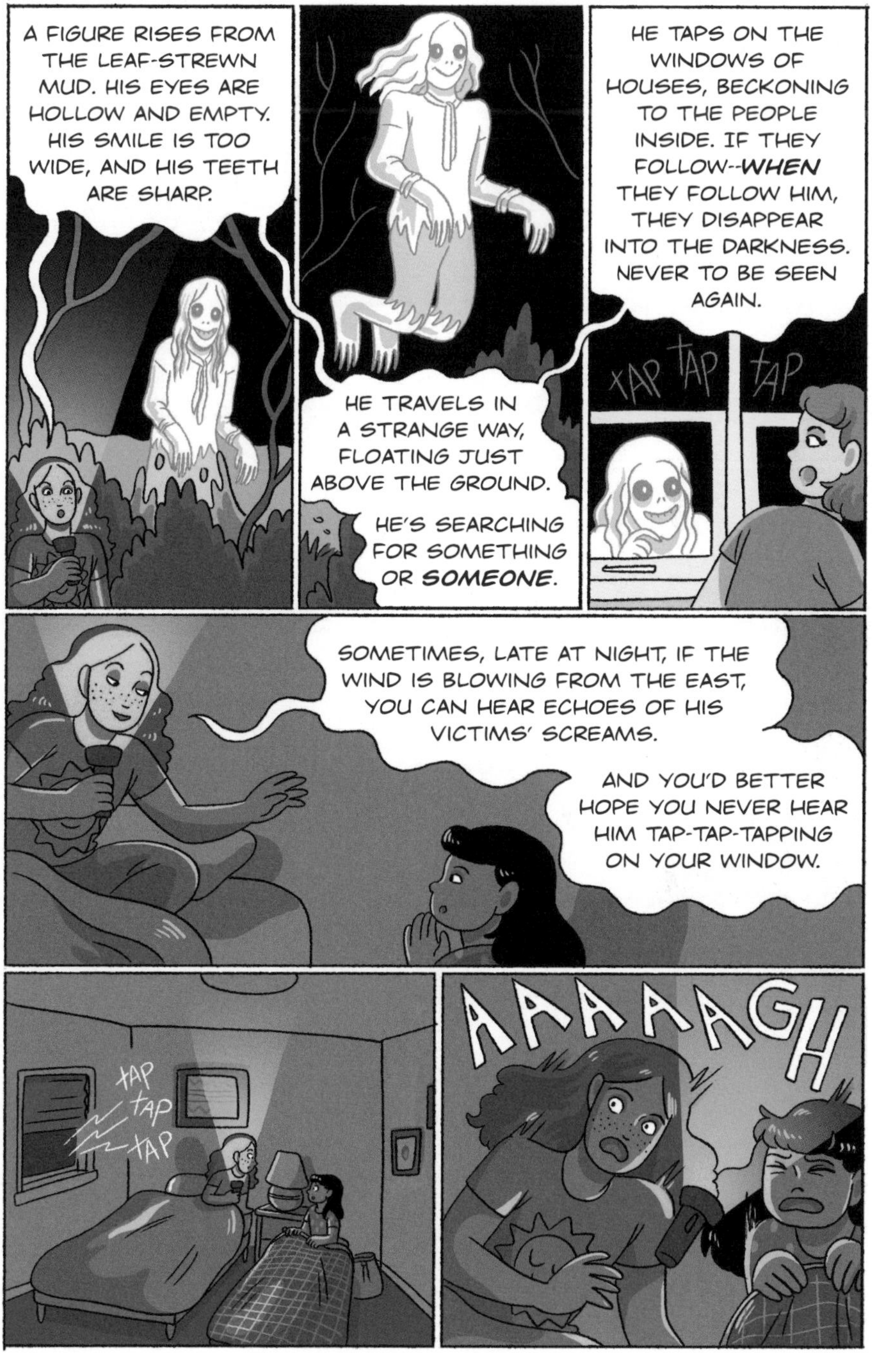
A FIGURE RISES FROM THE LEAF-STREWN MUD. HIS EYES ARE HOLLOW AND EMPTY. HIS SMILE IS TOO WIDE, AND HIS TEETH ARE SHARP.
HE TRAVELS IN A STRANGE WAY, FLOATING JUST ABOVE THE GROUND.
HE'S SEARCHING FOR SOMETHING OR **SOMEONE**.
HE TAPS ON THE WINDOWS OF HOUSES, BECKONING TO THE PEOPLE INSIDE. IF THEY FOLLOW--***WHEN*** THEY FOLLOW HIM, THEY DISAPPEAR INTO THE DARKNESS. NEVER TO BE SEEN AGAIN.
TAP TAP TAP
SOMETIMES, LATE AT NIGHT, IF THE WIND IS BLOWING FROM THE EAST, YOU CAN HEAR ECHOES OF HIS VICTIMS' SCREAMS.
AND YOU'D BETTER HOPE YOU NEVER HEAR HIM TAP-TAP-TAPPING ON YOUR WINDOW.
TAP TAP TAP
AAAAAGH

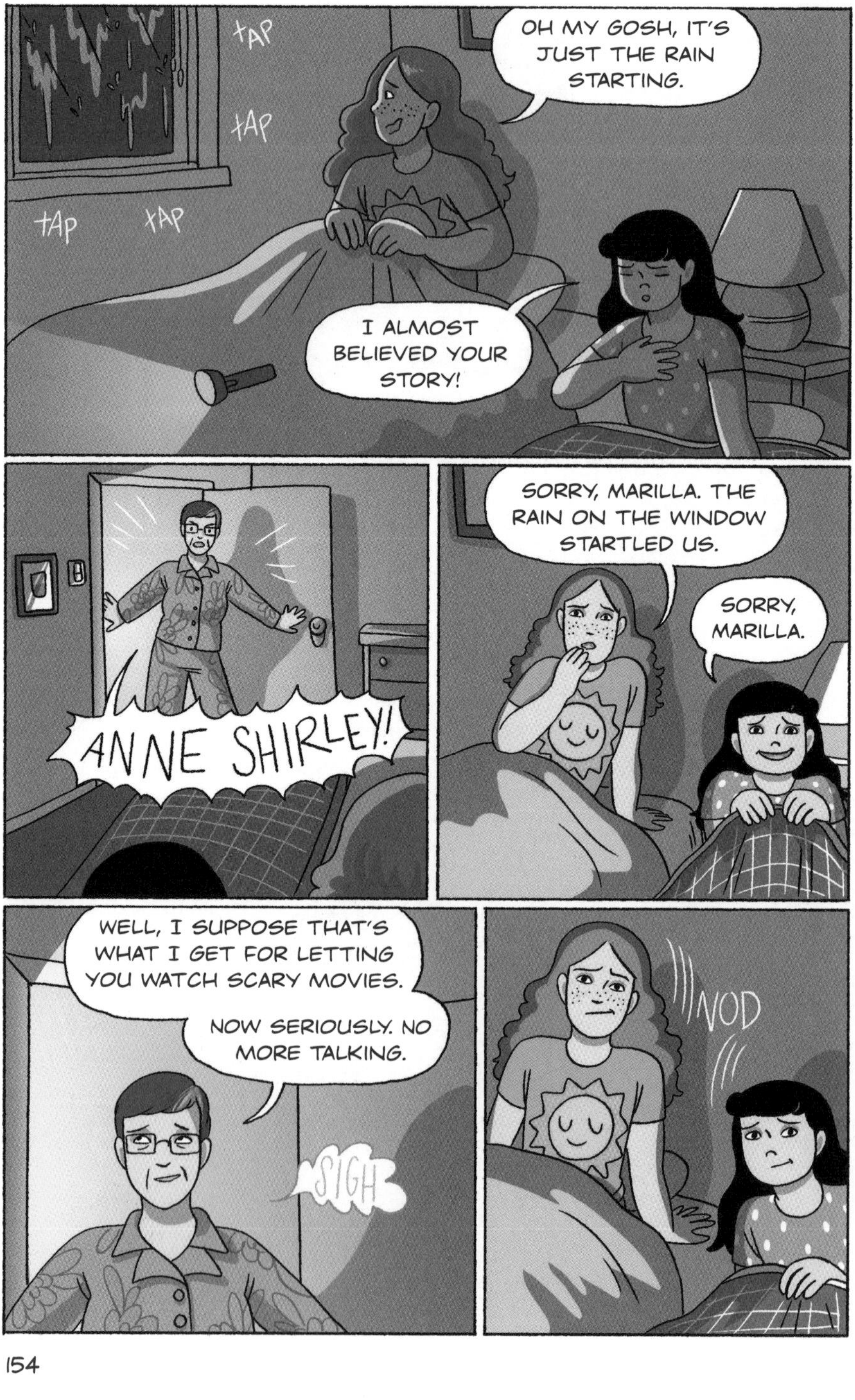
tAP
tAP
tAP
tAP
OH MY GOSH, IT'S JUST THE RAIN STARTING.
I ALMOST BELIEVED YOUR STORY!
ANNE SHIRLEY!
SORRY, MARILLA. THE RAIN ON THE WINDOW STARTLED US.
SORRY, MARILLA.
WELL, I SUPPOSE THAT'S WHAT I GET FOR LETTING YOU WATCH SCARY MOVIES.
NOW SERIOUSLY. NO MORE TALKING.
SIGH
NOD

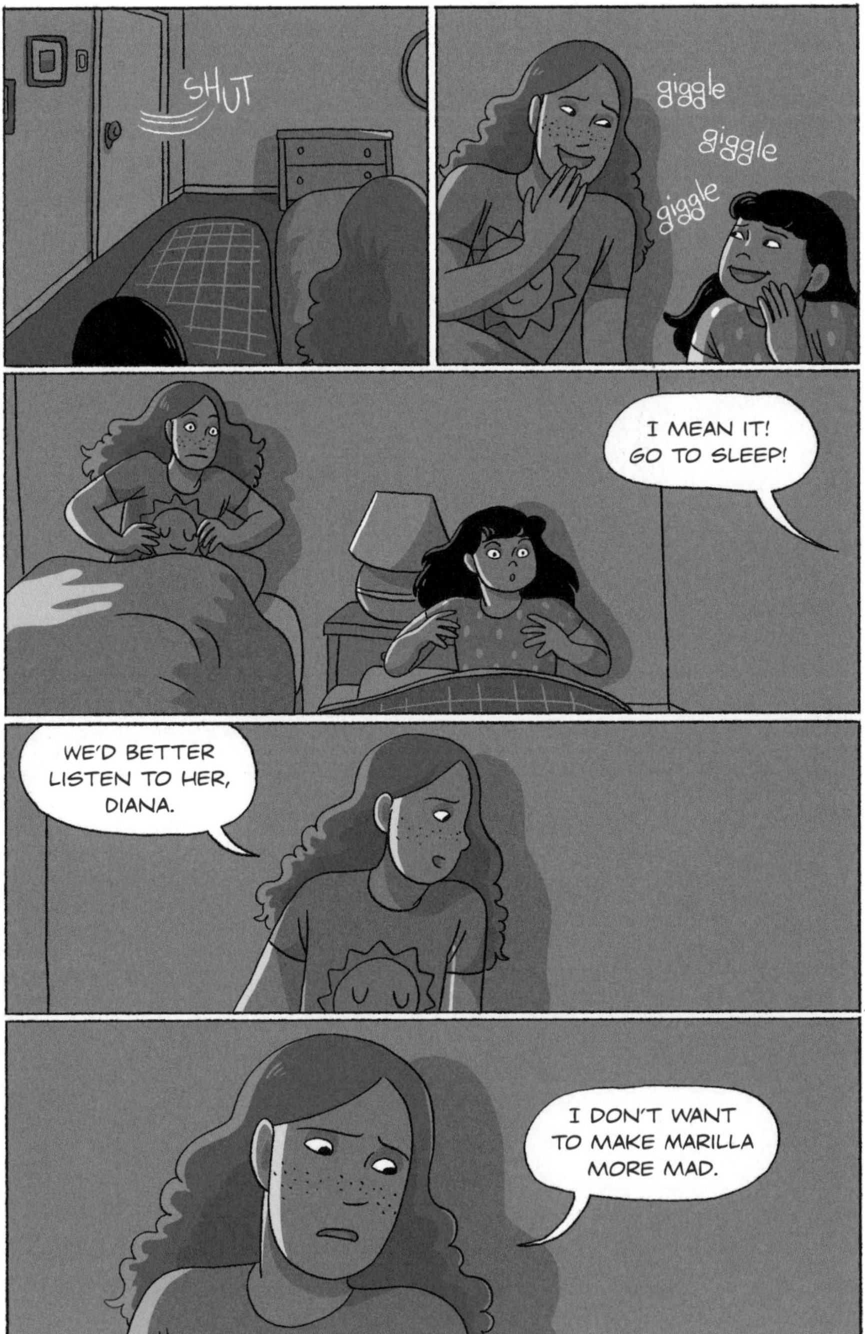
SHUT
giggle
giggle
giggle
I MEAN IT! GO TO SLEEP!
WE'D BETTER LISTEN TO HER, DIANA.
I DON'T WANT TO MAKE MARILLA MORE MAD.

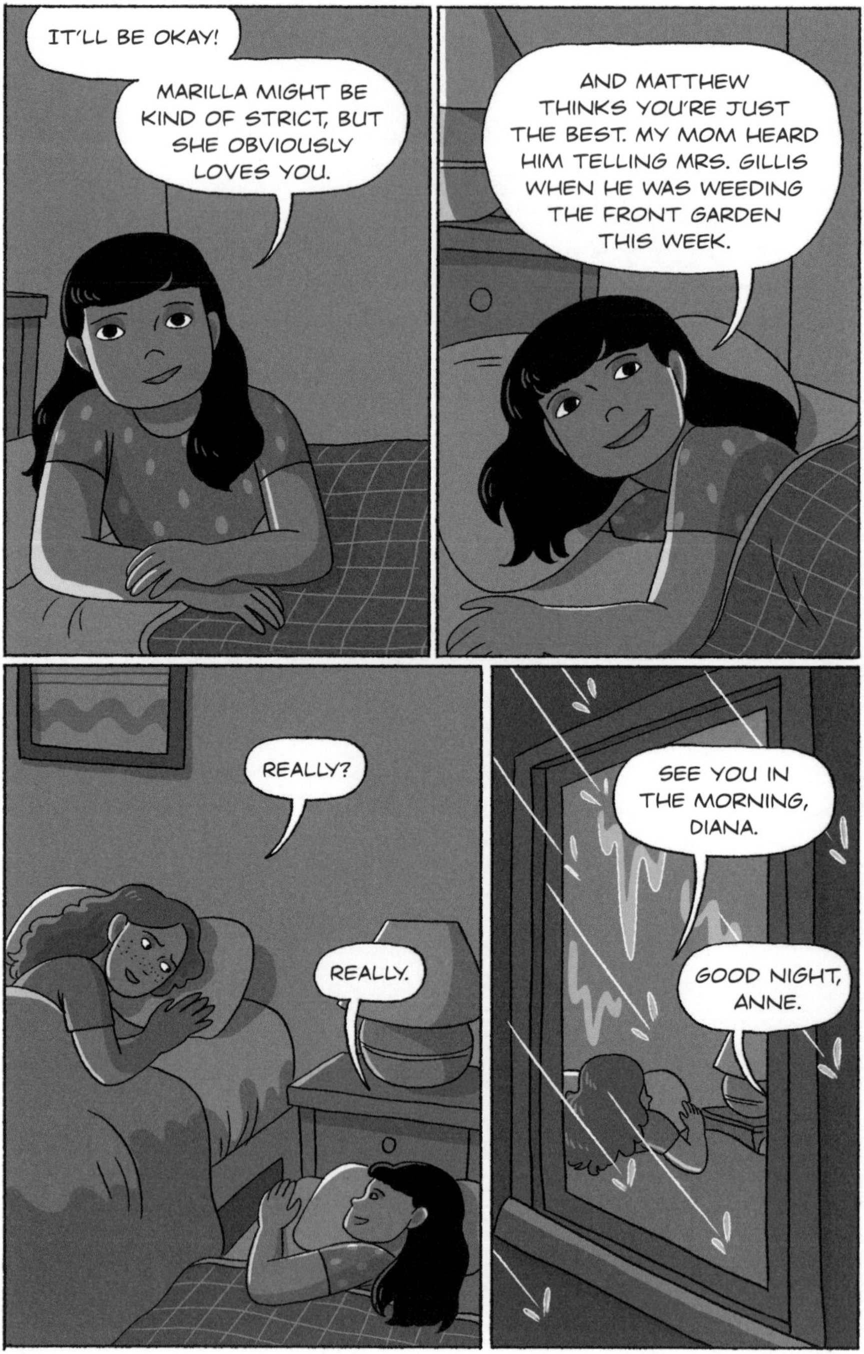
IT'LL BE OKAY!
MARILLA MIGHT BE KIND OF STRICT, BUT SHE OBVIOUSLY LOVES YOU.
AND MATTHEW THINKS YOU'RE JUST THE BEST. MY MOM HEARD HIM TELLING MRS. GILLIS WHEN HE WAS WEEDING THE FRONT GARDEN THIS WEEK.
REALLY?
REALLY.
SEE YOU IN THE MORNING, DIANA.
GOOD NIGHT, ANNE.

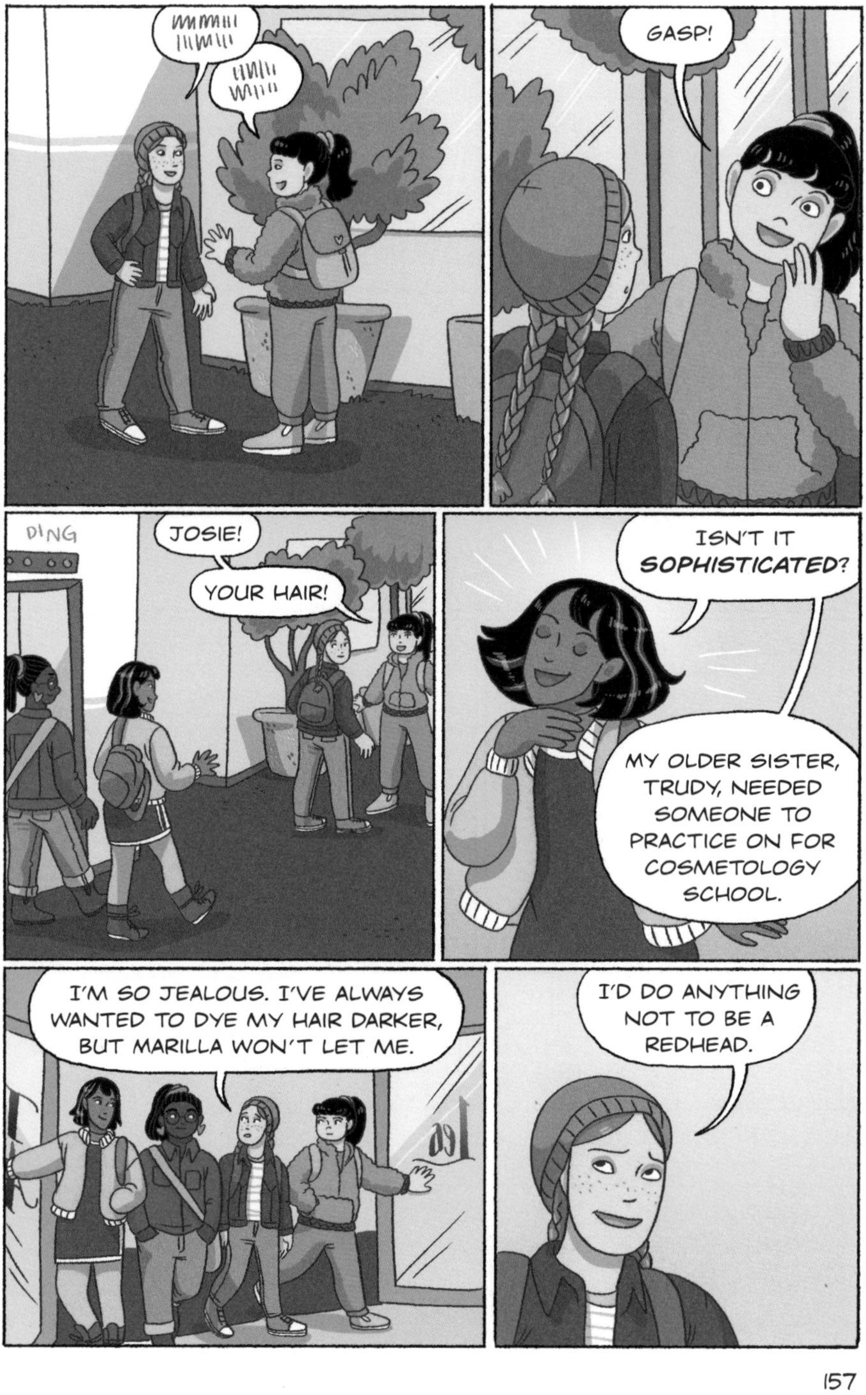
GASP!
DING
JOSIE!
YOUR HAIR!
ISN'T IT *SOPHISTICATED*?
MY OLDER SISTER, TRUDY, NEEDED SOMEONE TO PRACTICE ON FOR COSMETOLOGY SCHOOL.
I'M SO JEALOUS. I'VE ALWAYS WANTED TO DYE MY HAIR DARKER, BUT MARILLA WON'T LET ME.
I'D DO ANYTHING NOT TO BE A REDHEAD.

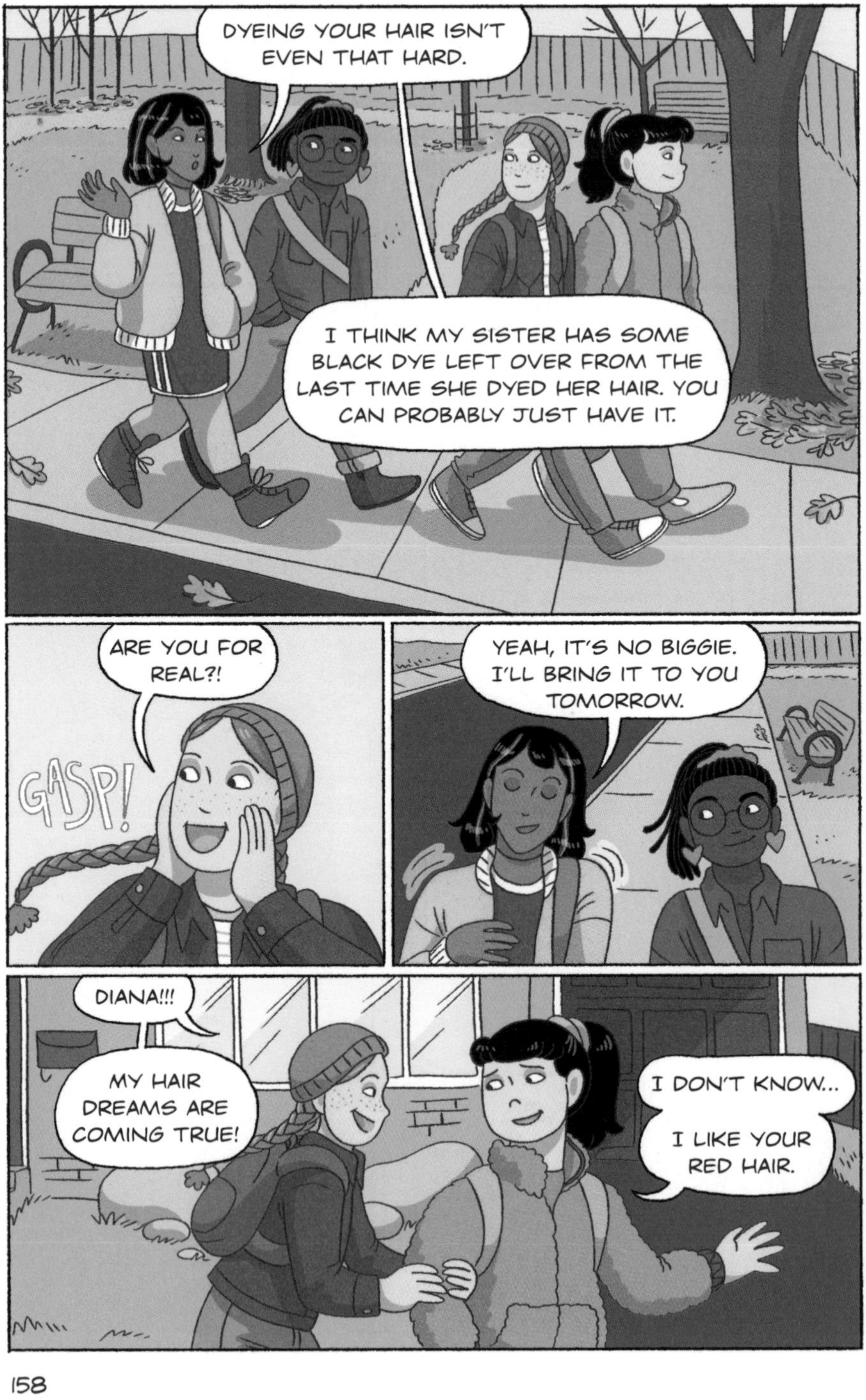
DYEING YOUR HAIR ISN'T EVEN THAT HARD.
I THINK MY SISTER HAS SOME BLACK DYE LEFT OVER FROM THE LAST TIME SHE DYED HER HAIR. YOU CAN PROBABLY JUST HAVE IT.
ARE YOU FOR REAL?!
GASP!
YEAH, IT'S NO BIGGIE. I'LL BRING IT TO YOU TOMORROW.
DIANA!!!
MY HAIR DREAMS ARE COMING TRUE!
I DON'T KNOW...
I LIKE YOUR RED HAIR.

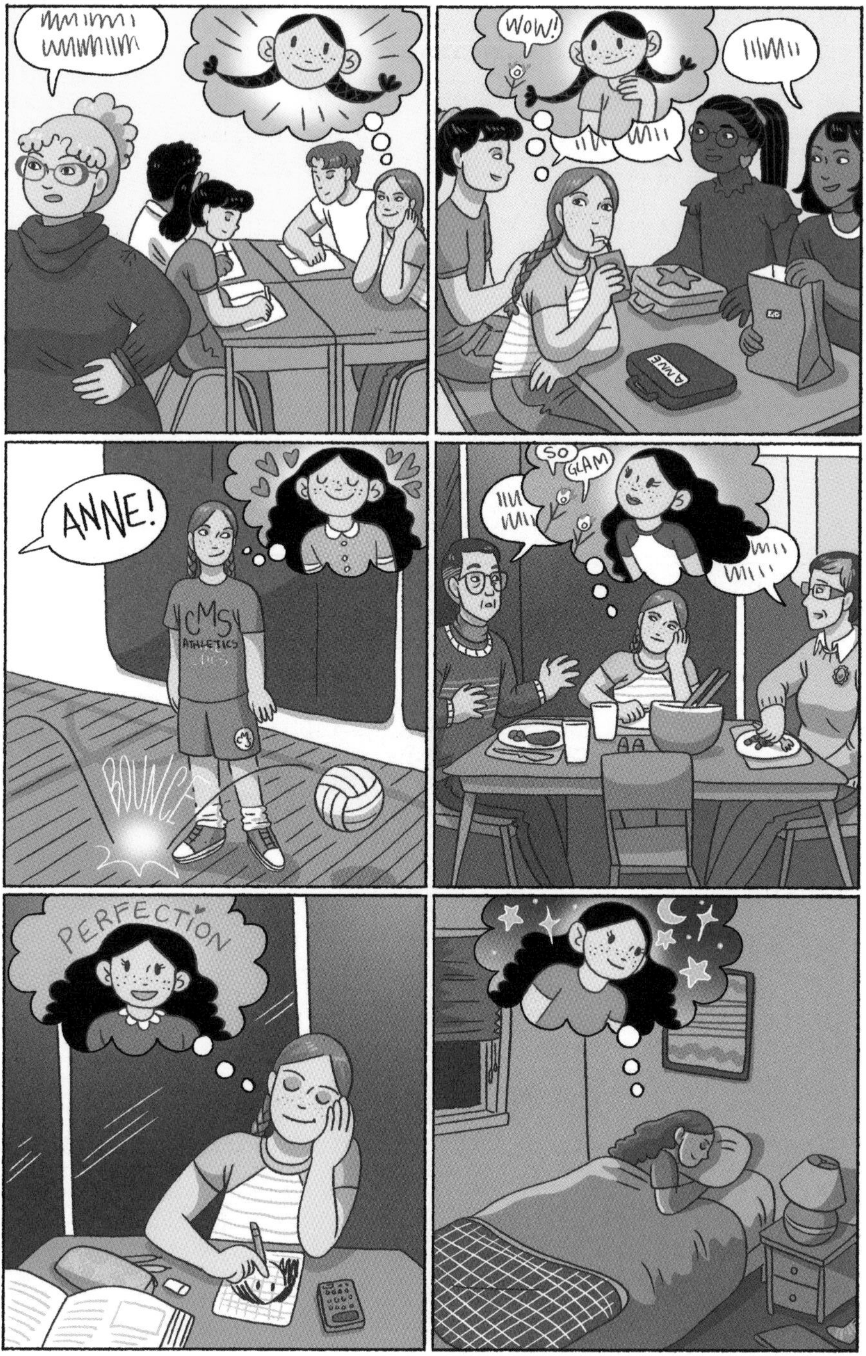
WOW!
ANNE
ANNE!
CMS
ATHLETICS
BOUNCE
SO
GLAM
PERFECTION

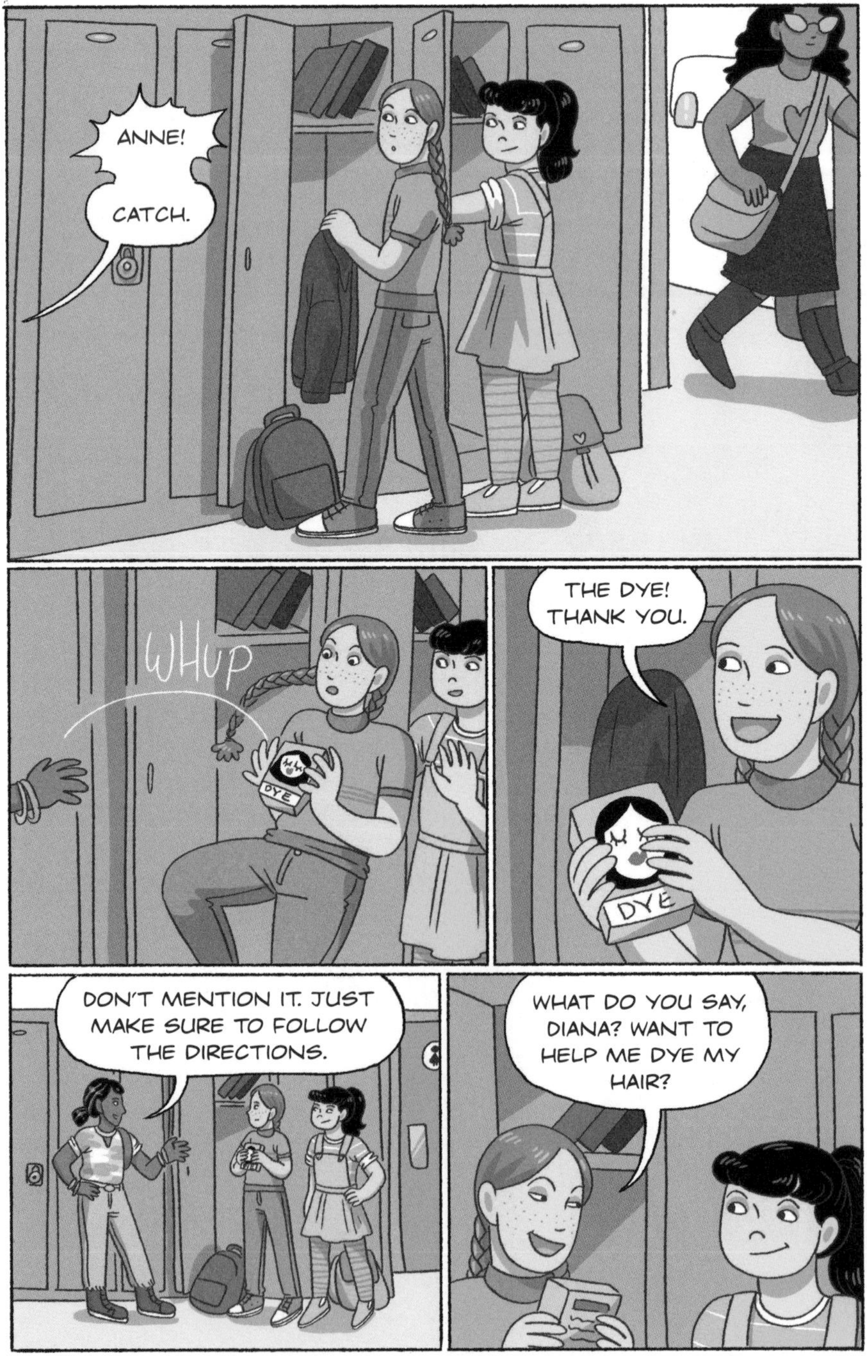
ANNE!
CATCH.
WHUP
DYE
THE DYE! THANK YOU.
DYE
DON'T MENTION IT. JUST MAKE SURE TO FOLLOW THE DIRECTIONS.
WHAT DO YOU SAY, DIANA? WANT TO HELP ME DYE MY HAIR?

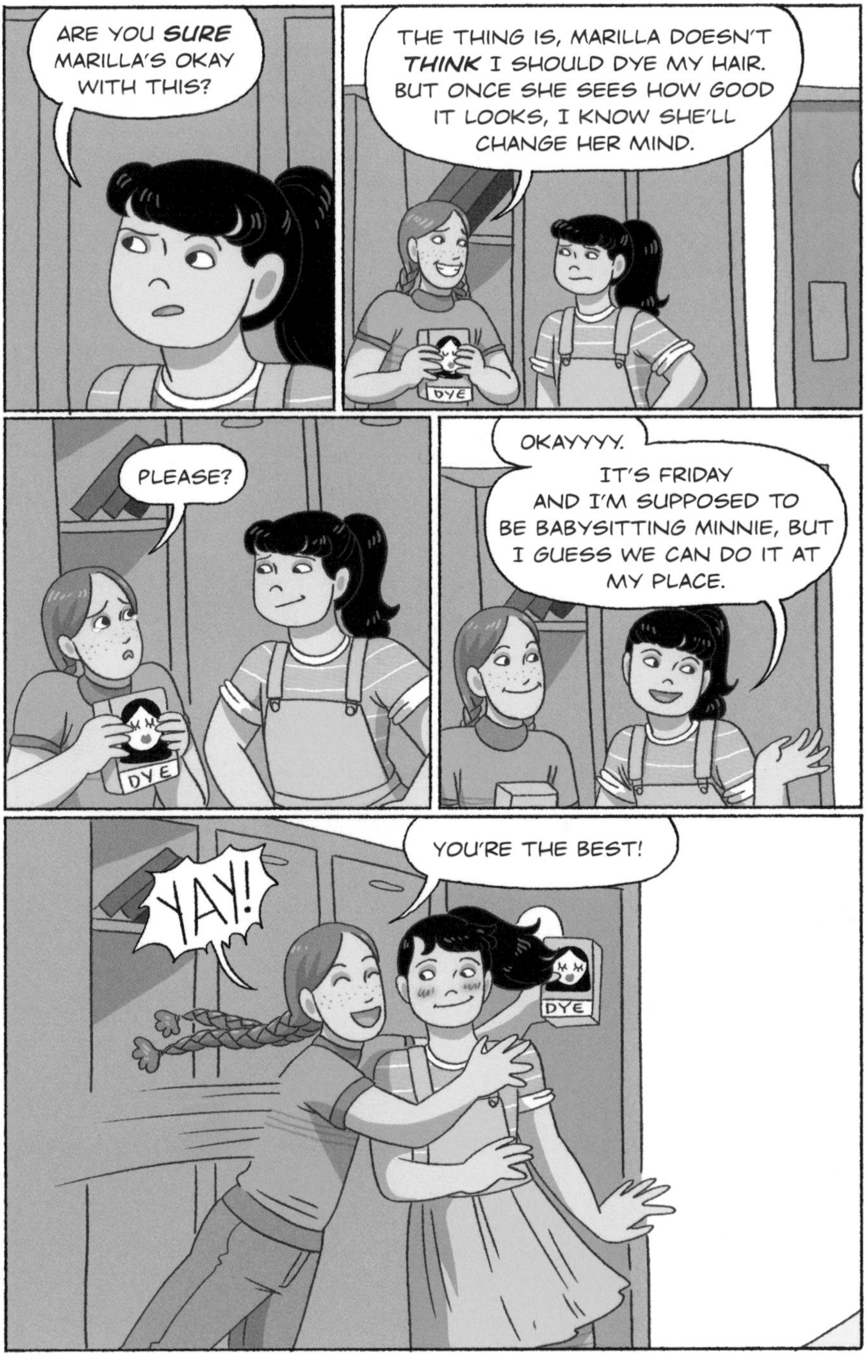
ARE YOU **SURE** MARILLA'S OKAY WITH THIS?
THE THING IS, MARILLA DOESN'T **THINK** I SHOULD DYE MY HAIR. BUT ONCE SHE SEES HOW GOOD IT LOOKS, I KNOW SHE'LL CHANGE HER MIND.
DYE
PLEASE?
DYE
OKAYYYY.
IT'S FRIDAY AND I'M SUPPOSED TO BE BABYSITTING MINNIE, BUT I GUESS WE CAN DO IT AT MY PLACE.
YAY!
YOU'RE THE BEST!
DYE

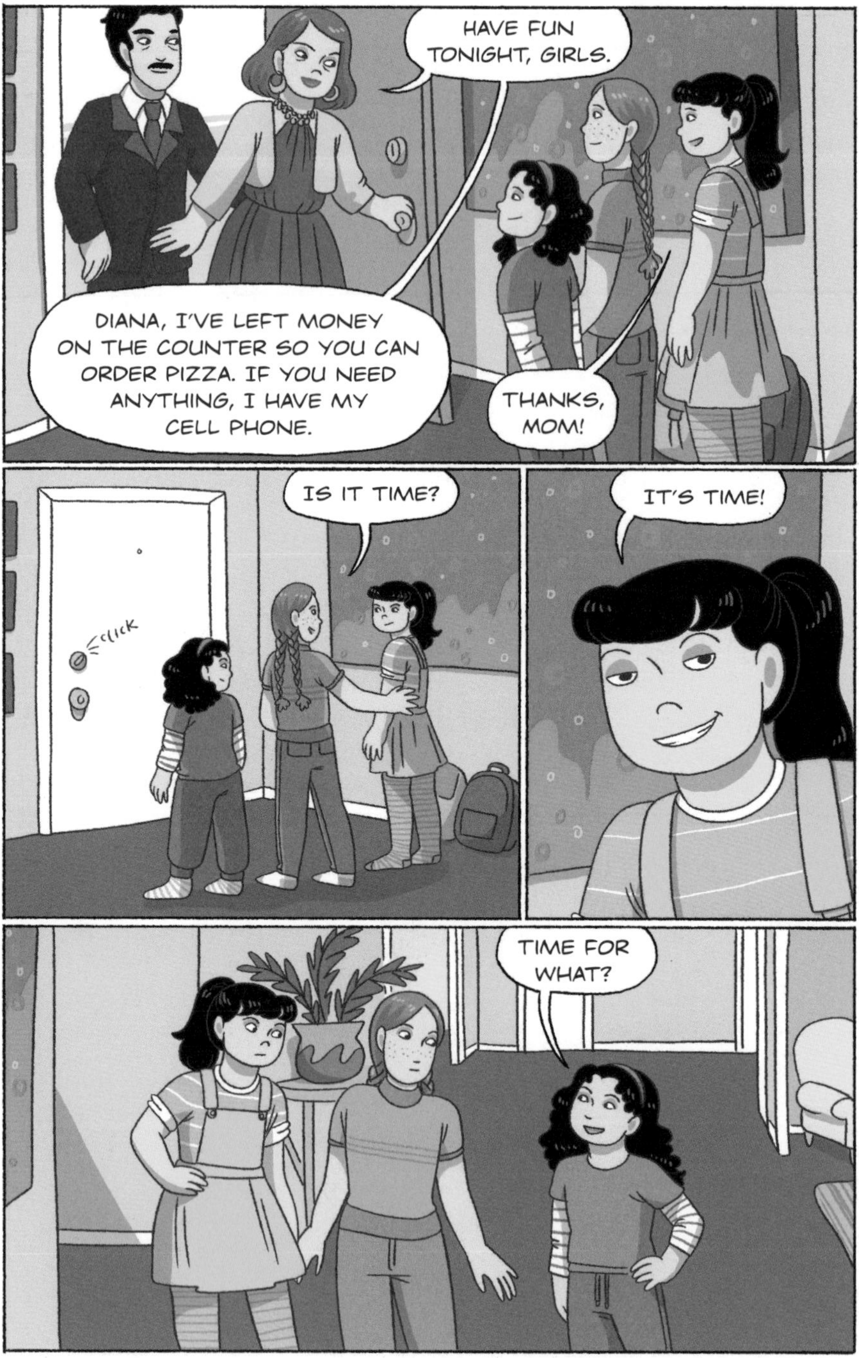
HAVE FUN TONIGHT, GIRLS.
DIANA, I'VE LEFT MONEY ON THE COUNTER SO YOU CAN ORDER PIZZA. IF YOU NEED ANYTHING, I HAVE MY CELL PHONE.
THANKS, MOM!
CLICK
IS IT TIME?
IT'S TIME!
TIME FOR WHAT?

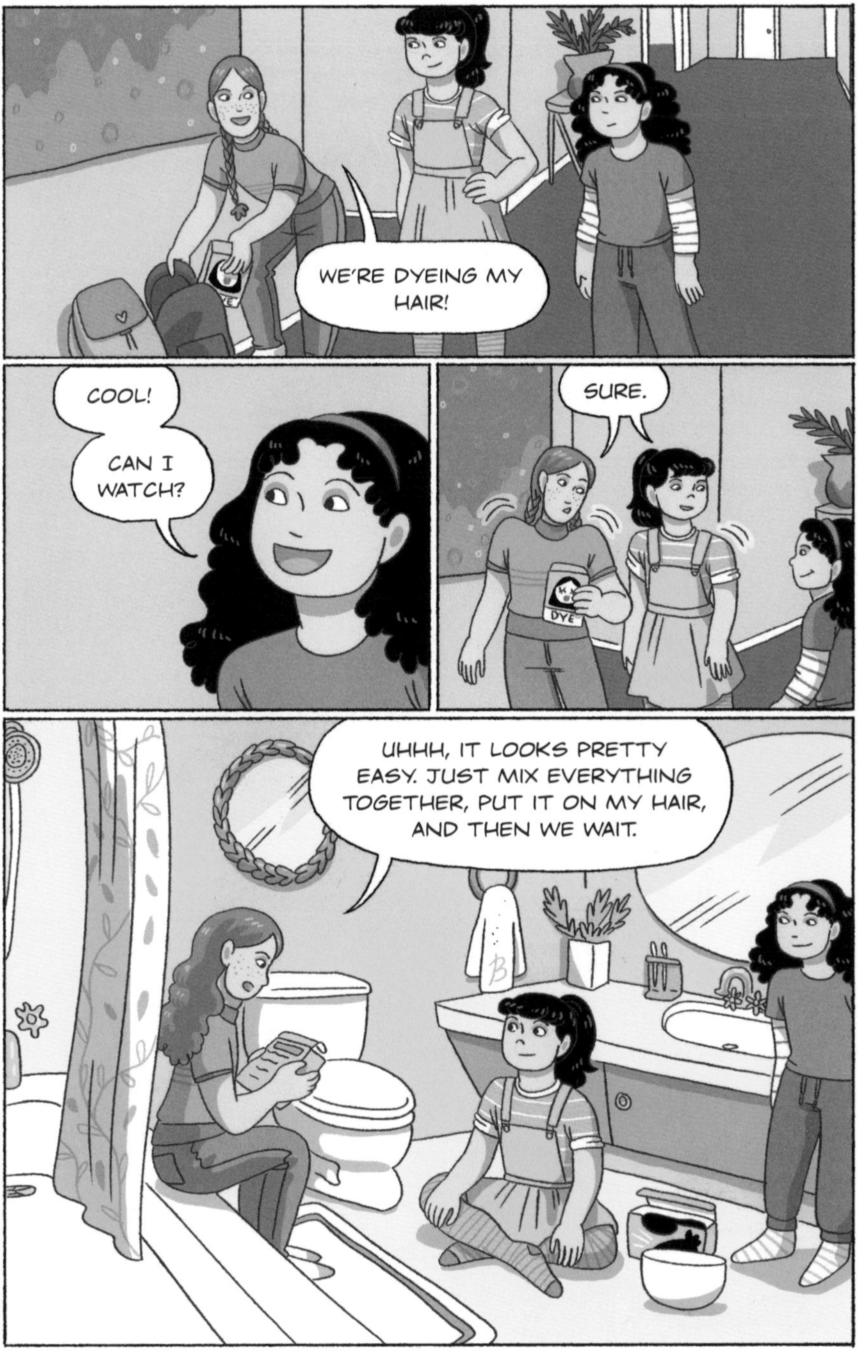
WE'RE DYEING MY HAIR!
DYE
COOL!
CAN I WATCH?
SURE.
DYE
UHHH, IT LOOKS PRETTY EASY. JUST MIX EVERYTHING TOGETHER, PUT IT ON MY HAIR, AND THEN WE WAIT.

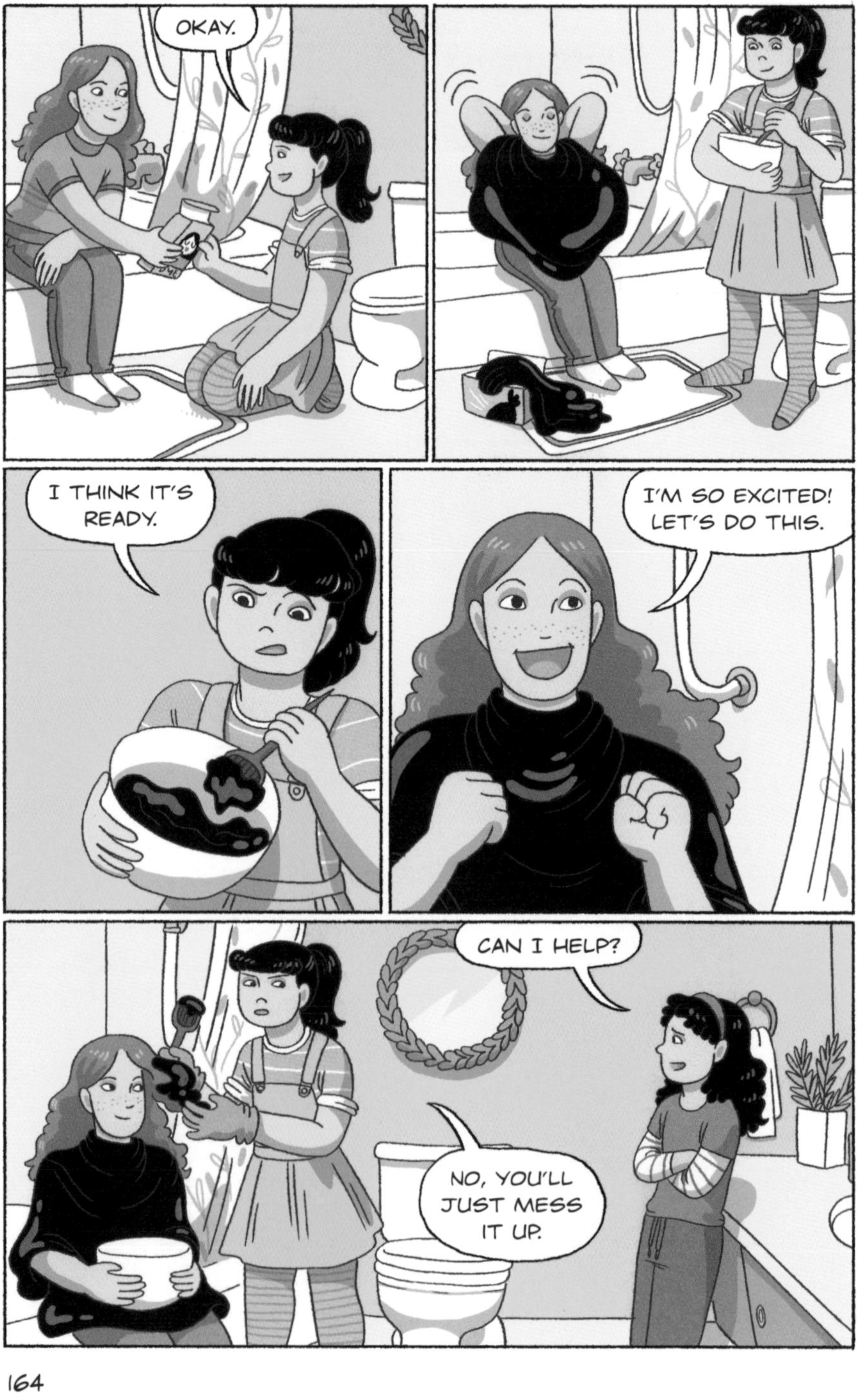
OKAY.
I THINK IT'S READY.
I'M SO EXCITED! LET'S DO THIS.
CAN I HELP?
NO, YOU'LL JUST MESS IT UP.

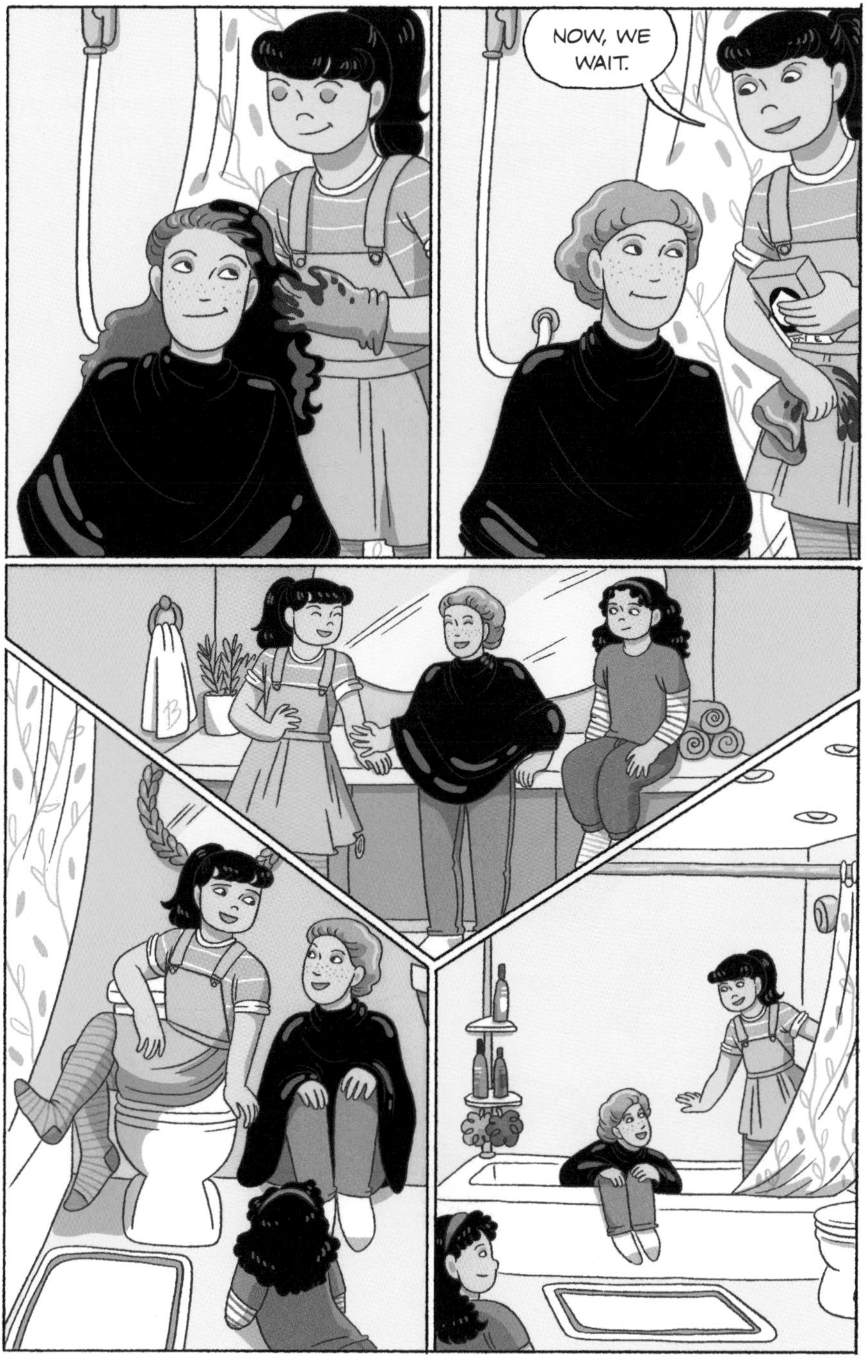
NOW, WE WAIT.

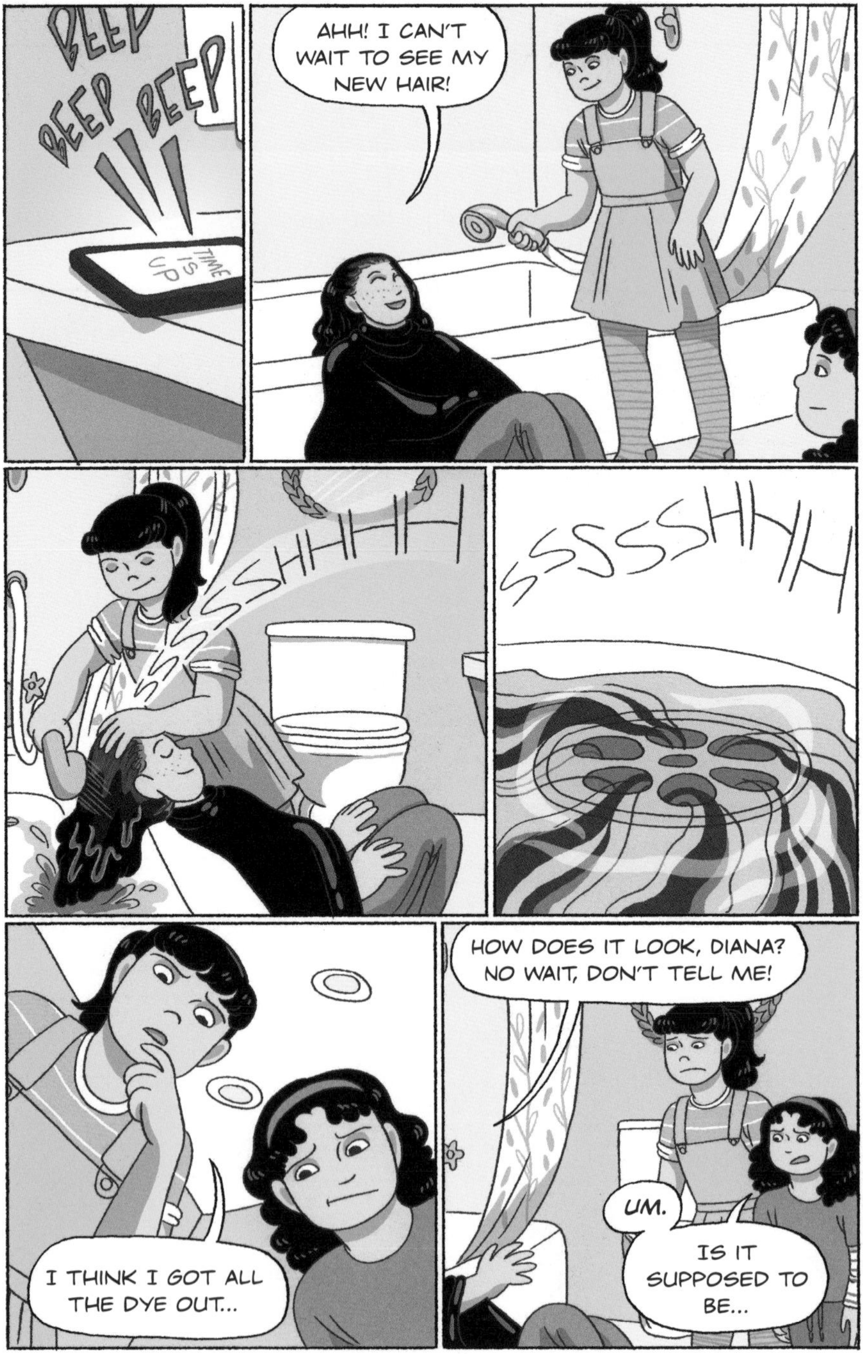
BEEP
BEEP BEEP BEEP
TIME IS UP
AHH! I CAN'T WAIT TO SEE MY NEW HAIR!
SSHHHHH
SSSSSHHHH
I THINK I GOT ALL THE DYE OUT...
HOW DOES IT LOOK, DIANA? NO WAIT, DON'T TELL ME!
UM.
IS IT SUPPOSED TO BE...

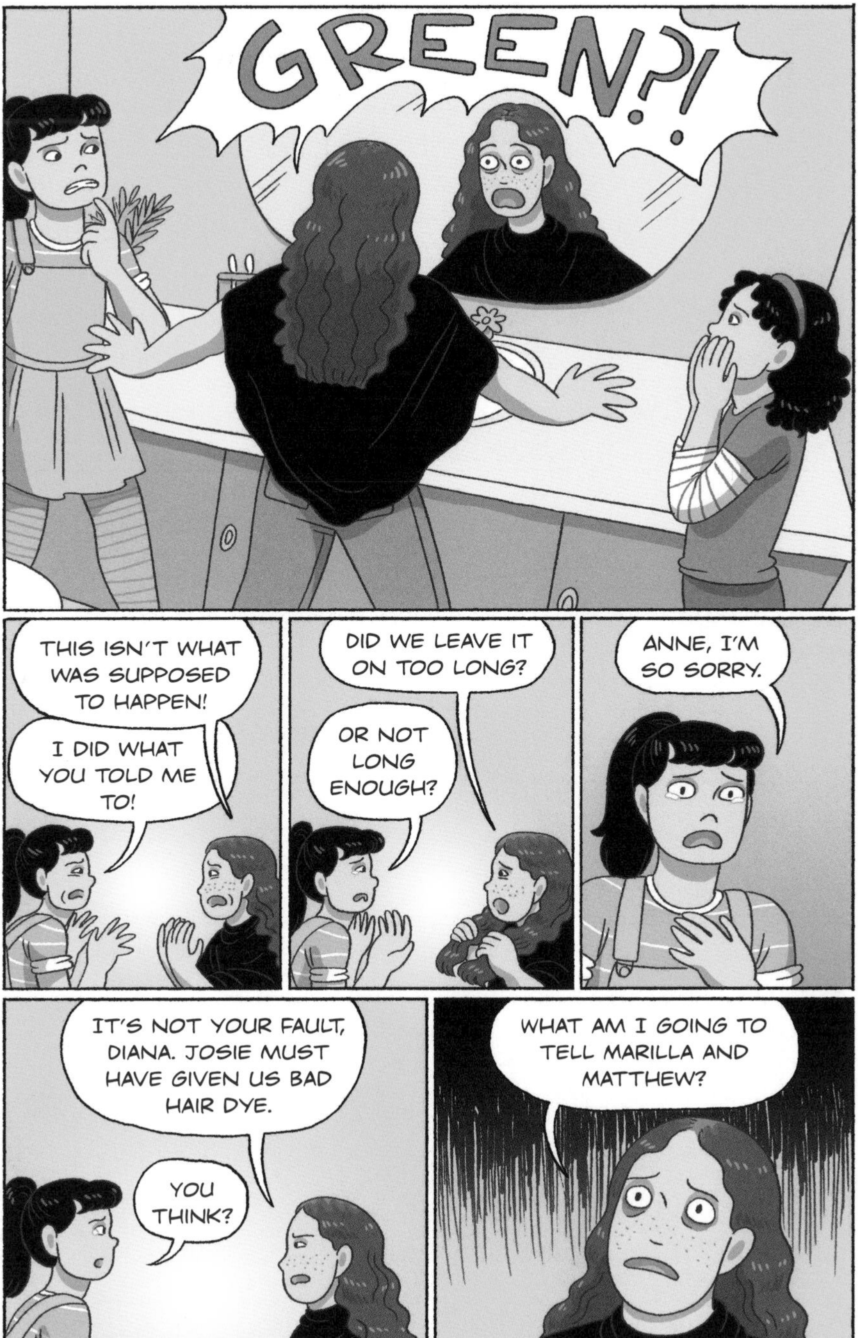
GREEN?!
THIS ISN'T WHAT WAS SUPPOSED TO HAPPEN!
I DID WHAT YOU TOLD ME TO!
DID WE LEAVE IT ON TOO LONG?
OR NOT LONG ENOUGH?
ANNE, I'M SO SORRY.
IT'S NOT YOUR FAULT, DIANA. JOSIE MUST HAVE GIVEN US BAD HAIR DYE.
YOU THINK?
WHAT AM I GOING TO TELL MARILLA AND MATTHEW?

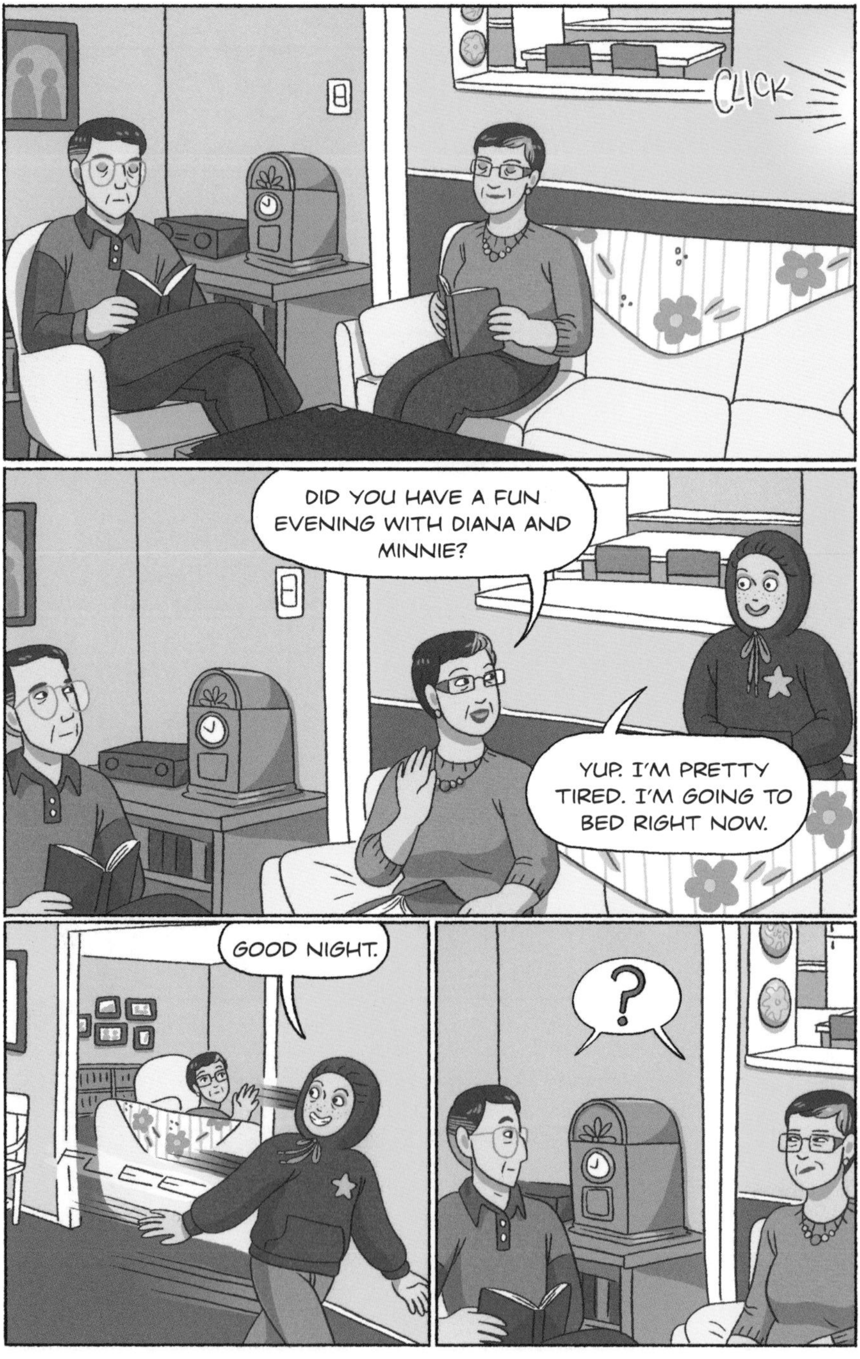
CLICK
DID YOU HAVE A FUN EVENING WITH DIANA AND MINNIE?
YUP. I'M PRETTY TIRED. I'M GOING TO BED RIGHT NOW.
GOOD NIGHT.
?

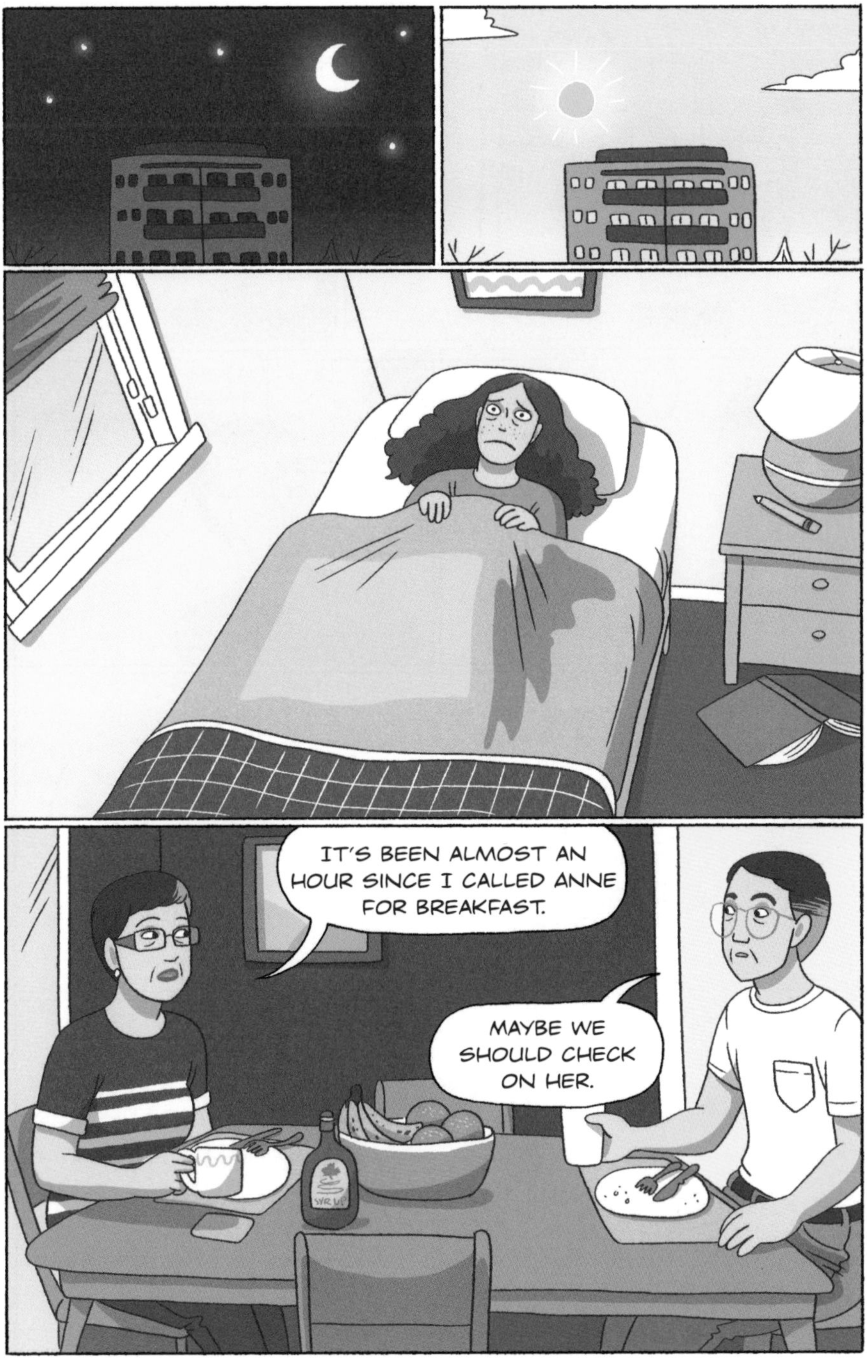
IT'S BEEN ALMOST AN HOUR SINCE I CALLED ANNE FOR BREAKFAST.
MAYBE WE SHOULD CHECK ON HER.
SYRUP

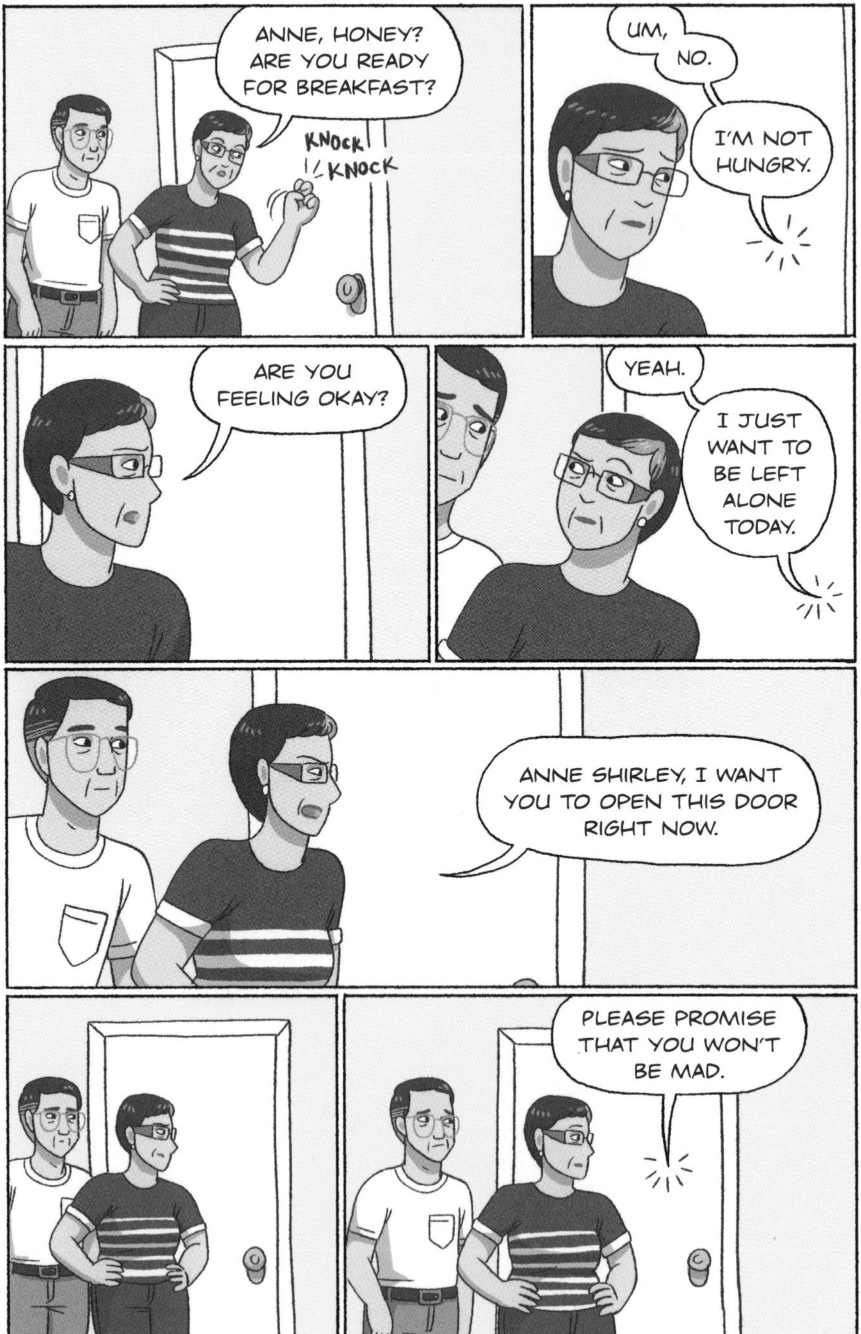
ANNE, HONEY? ARE YOU READY FOR BREAKFAST?
KNOCK KNOCK
UM,
NO.
I'M NOT HUNGRY.
ARE YOU FEELING OKAY?
YEAH.
I JUST WANT TO BE LEFT ALONE TODAY.
ANNE SHIRLEY, I WANT YOU TO OPEN THIS DOOR RIGHT NOW.
PLEASE PROMISE THAT YOU WON'T BE MAD.

ANNE! WHAT--

IT WAS SUPPOSED TO BE BLACK. THE DYE BOX SAID IT WOULD GIVE ME "DISTINGUISHED RAVEN TRESSES" BUT WE MUST HAVE DONE SOMETHING WRONG...OR JOSIE GAVE US BAD DYE...

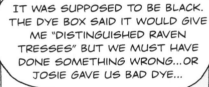

IT'S VERY... GREEN.

I THOUGHT I HATED MY RED HAIR, BUT THIS IS **WORSE**.

WELL, I THINK IT LOOKS KIND OF PUNK!

HEH

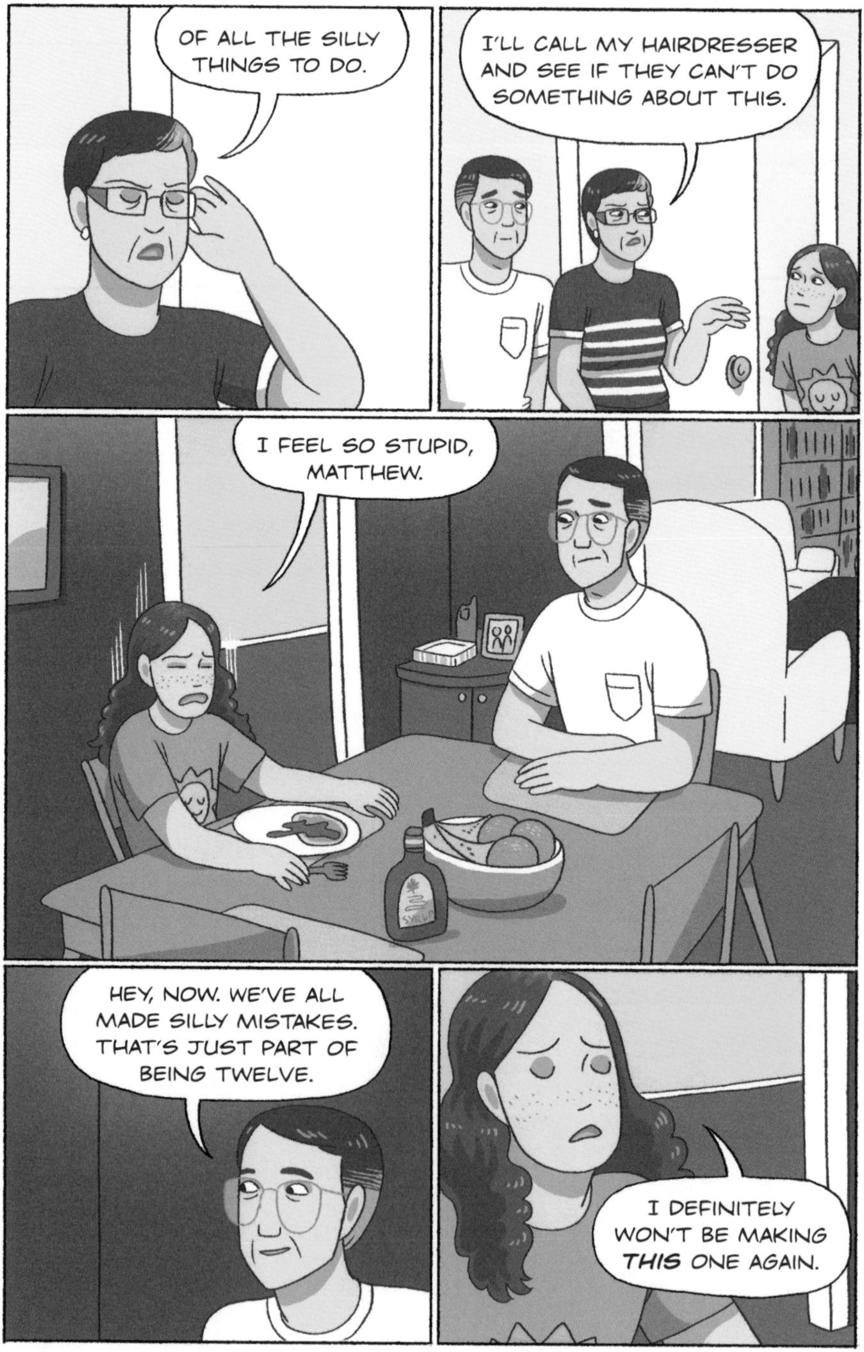
OF ALL THE SILLY THINGS TO DO.
I'LL CALL MY HAIRDRESSER AND SEE IF THEY CAN'T DO SOMETHING ABOUT THIS.
I FEEL SO STUPID, MATTHEW.
SYRUP
HEY, NOW. WE'VE ALL MADE SILLY MISTAKES. THAT'S JUST PART OF BEING TWELVE.
I DEFINITELY WON'T BE MAKING ***THIS*** ONE AGAIN.

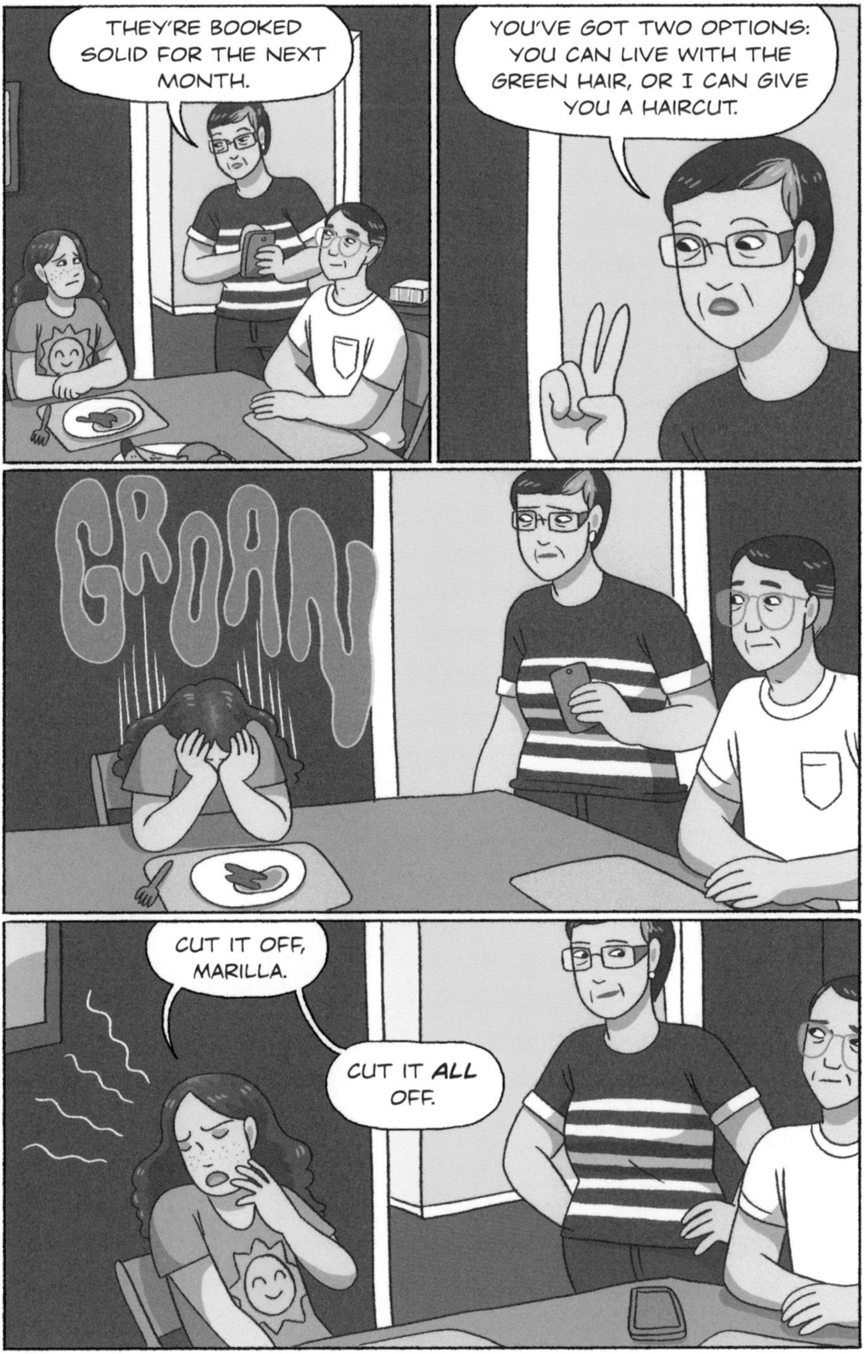
THEY'RE BOOKED SOLID FOR THE NEXT MONTH.
YOU'VE GOT TWO OPTIONS: YOU CAN LIVE WITH THE GREEN HAIR, OR I CAN GIVE YOU A HAIRCUT.
GROAN
CUT IT OFF, MARILLA.
CUT IT **ALL** OFF.

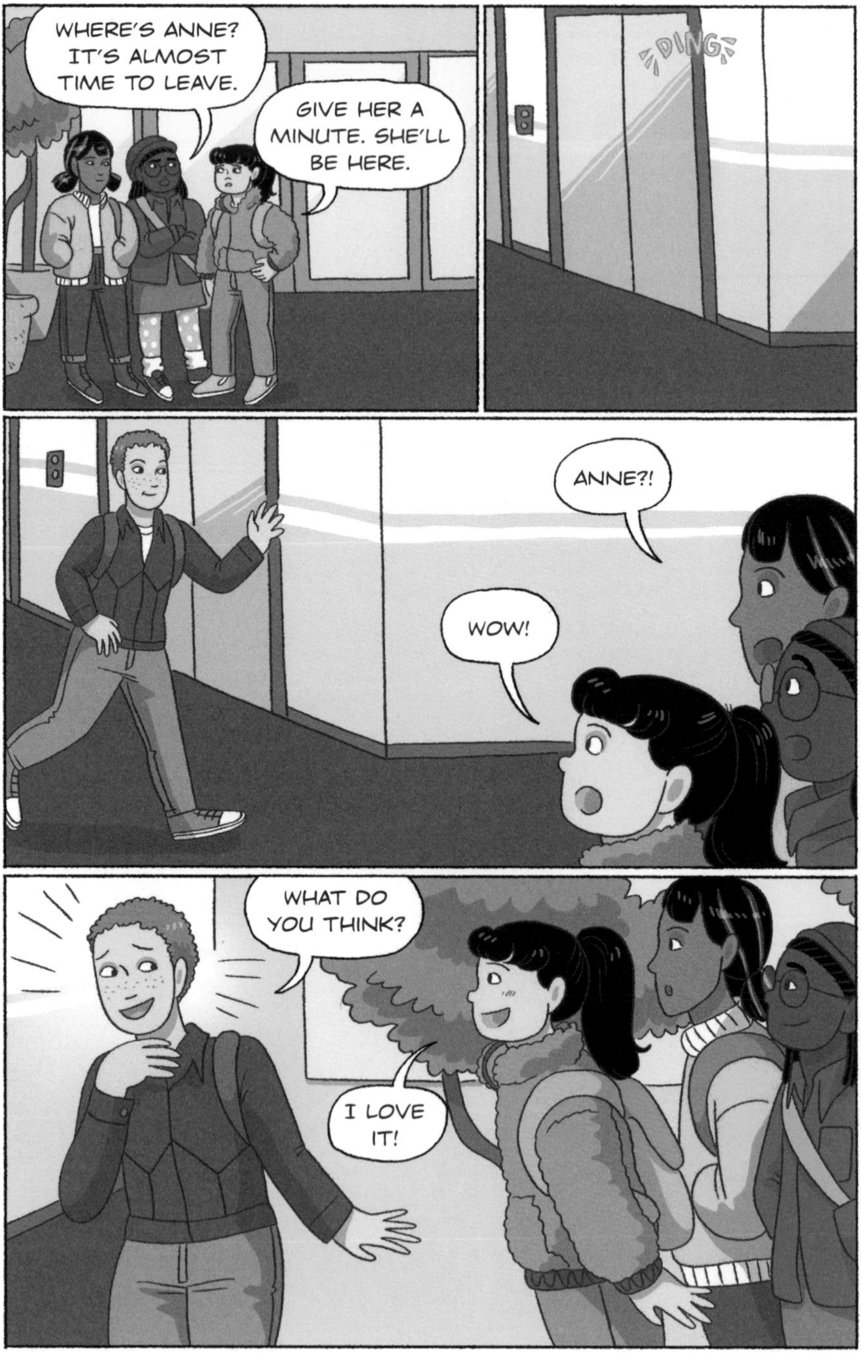
WHERE'S ANNE? IT'S ALMOST TIME TO LEAVE.
GIVE HER A MINUTE. SHE'LL BE HERE.
DING
ANNE?!
WOW!
WHAT DO YOU THINK?
I LOVE IT!

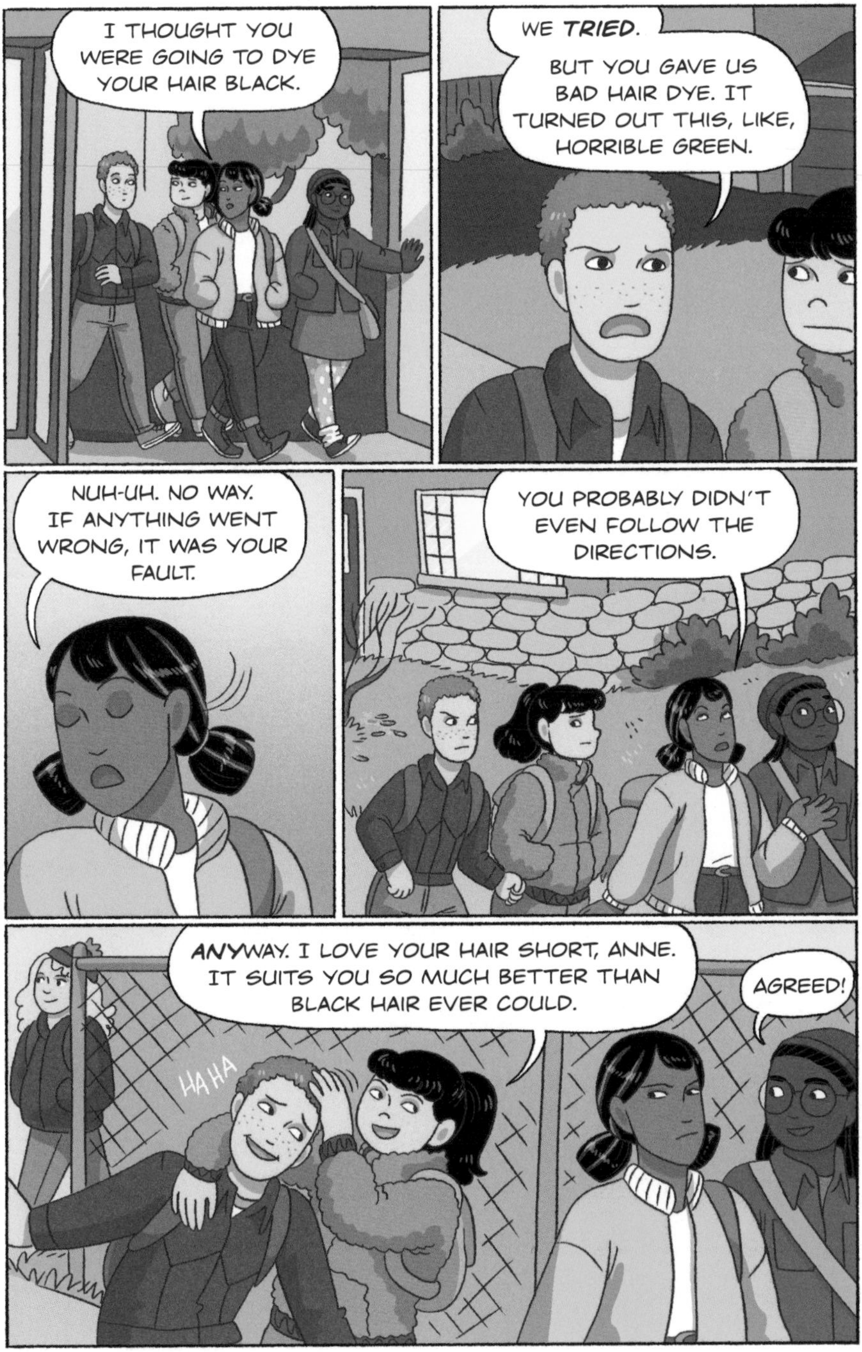
I THOUGHT YOU WERE GOING TO DYE YOUR HAIR BLACK.
WE **TRIED**.
BUT YOU GAVE US BAD HAIR DYE. IT TURNED OUT THIS, LIKE, HORRIBLE GREEN.
NUH-UH. NO WAY. IF ANYTHING WENT WRONG, IT WAS YOUR FAULT.
YOU PROBABLY DIDN'T EVEN FOLLOW THE DIRECTIONS.
ANYWAY. I LOVE YOUR HAIR SHORT, ANNE. IT SUITS YOU SO MUCH BETTER THAN BLACK HAIR EVER COULD.
HA HA
AGREED!

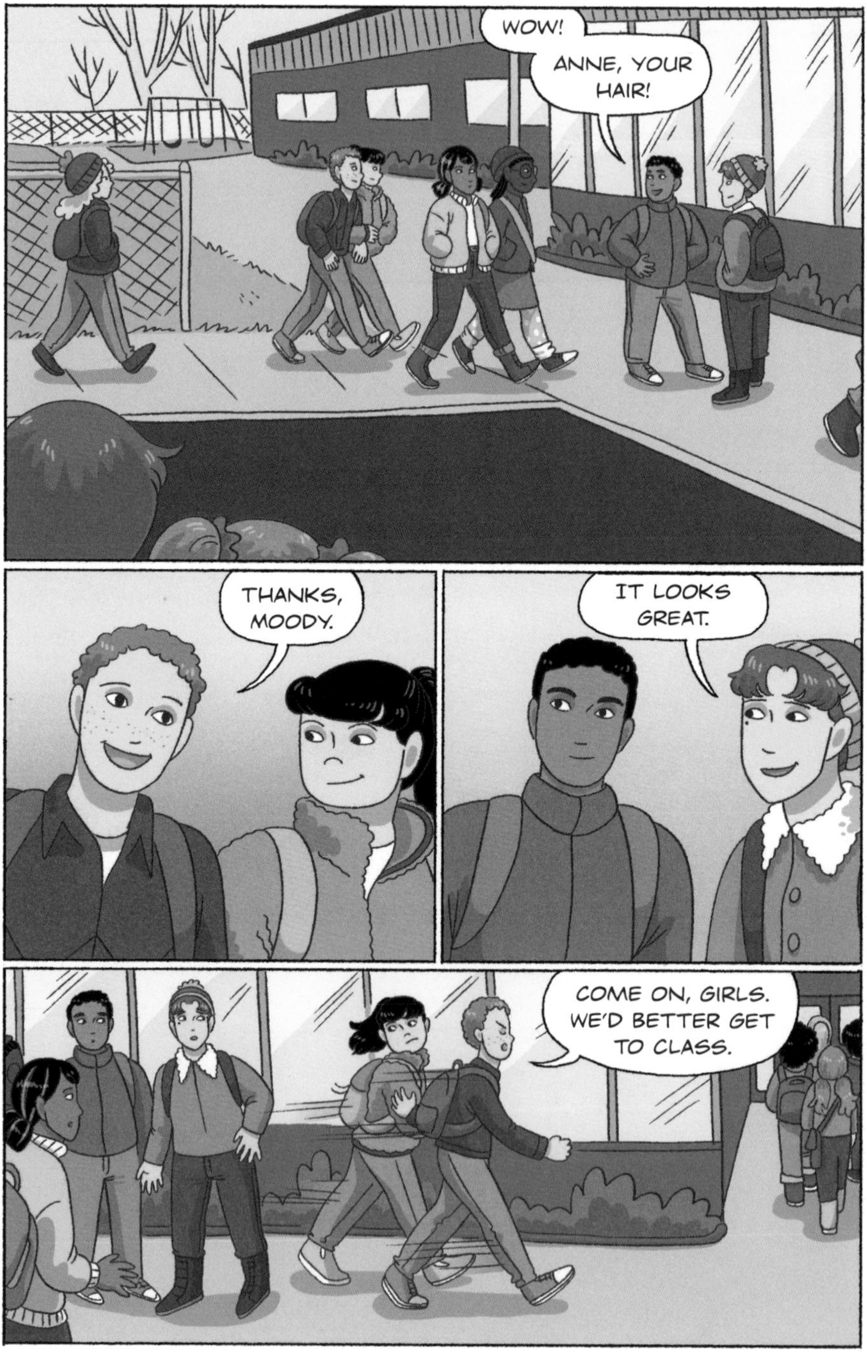
WOW!
ANNE, YOUR HAIR!
THANKS, MOODY.
IT LOOKS GREAT.
COME ON, GIRLS. WE'D BETTER GET TO CLASS.

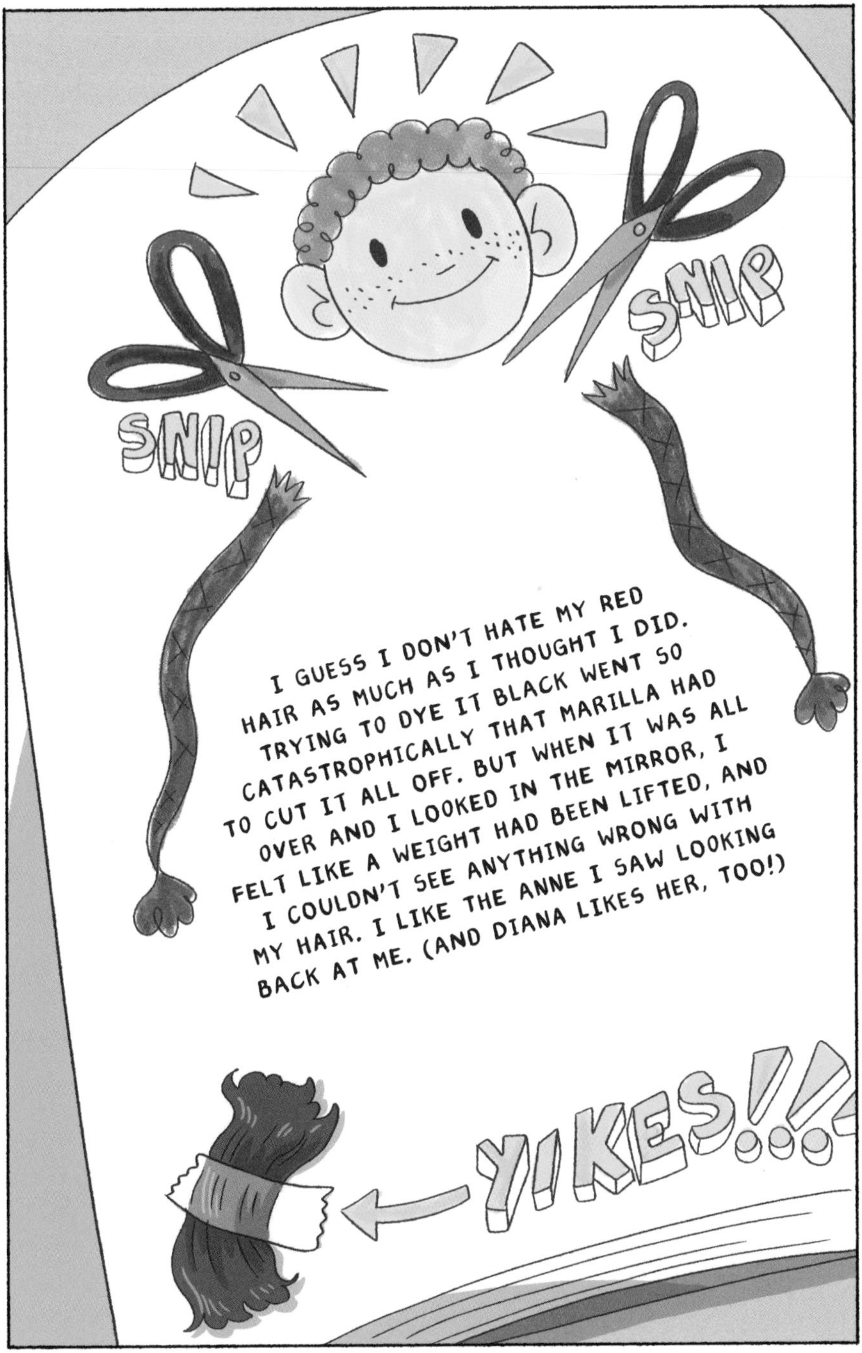
SNIP
SNIP
I GUESS I DON'T HATE MY RED HAIR AS MUCH AS I THOUGHT I DID. TRYING TO DYE IT BLACK WENT SO CATASTROPHICALLY THAT MARILLA HAD TO CUT IT ALL OFF. BUT WHEN IT WAS ALL OVER AND I LOOKED IN THE MIRROR, I FELT LIKE A WEIGHT HAD BEEN LIFTED, AND I COULDN'T SEE ANYTHING WRONG WITH MY HAIR. I LIKE THE ANNE I SAW LOOKING BACK AT ME. (AND DIANA LIKES HER, TOO!)
YIKES!!!

CHAPTER 8

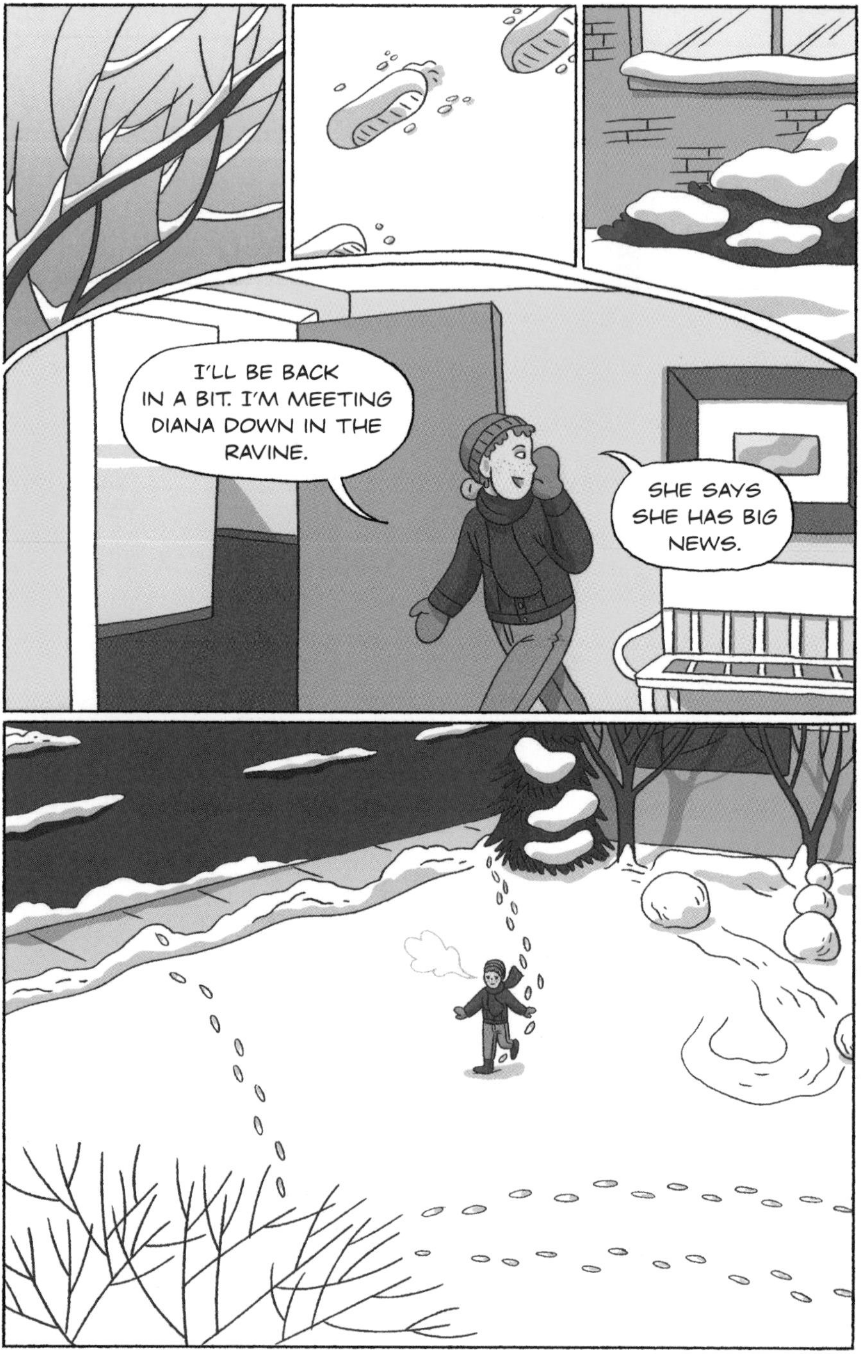
I'LL BE BACK IN A BIT. I'M MEETING DIANA DOWN IN THE RAVINE.
SHE SAYS SHE HAS BIG NEWS.

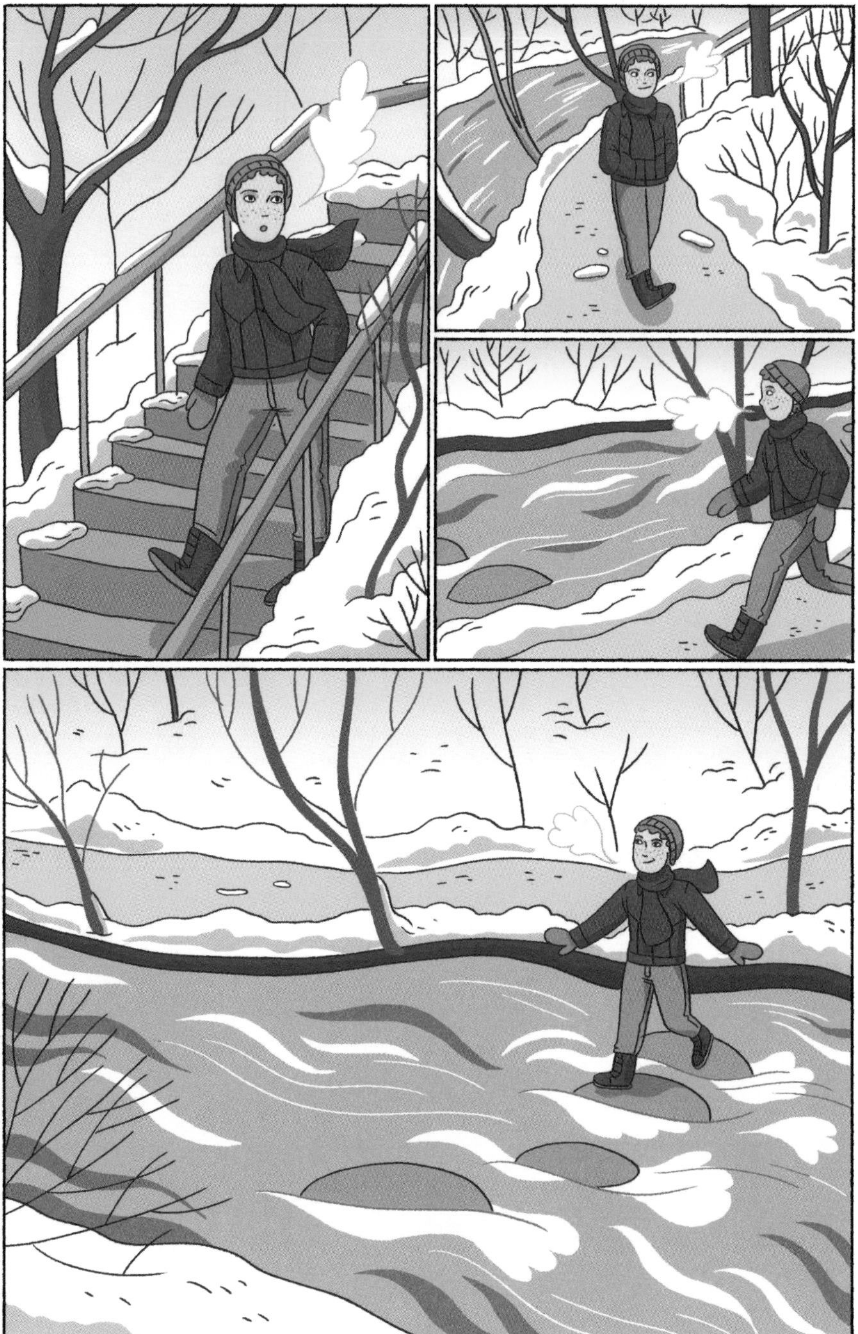

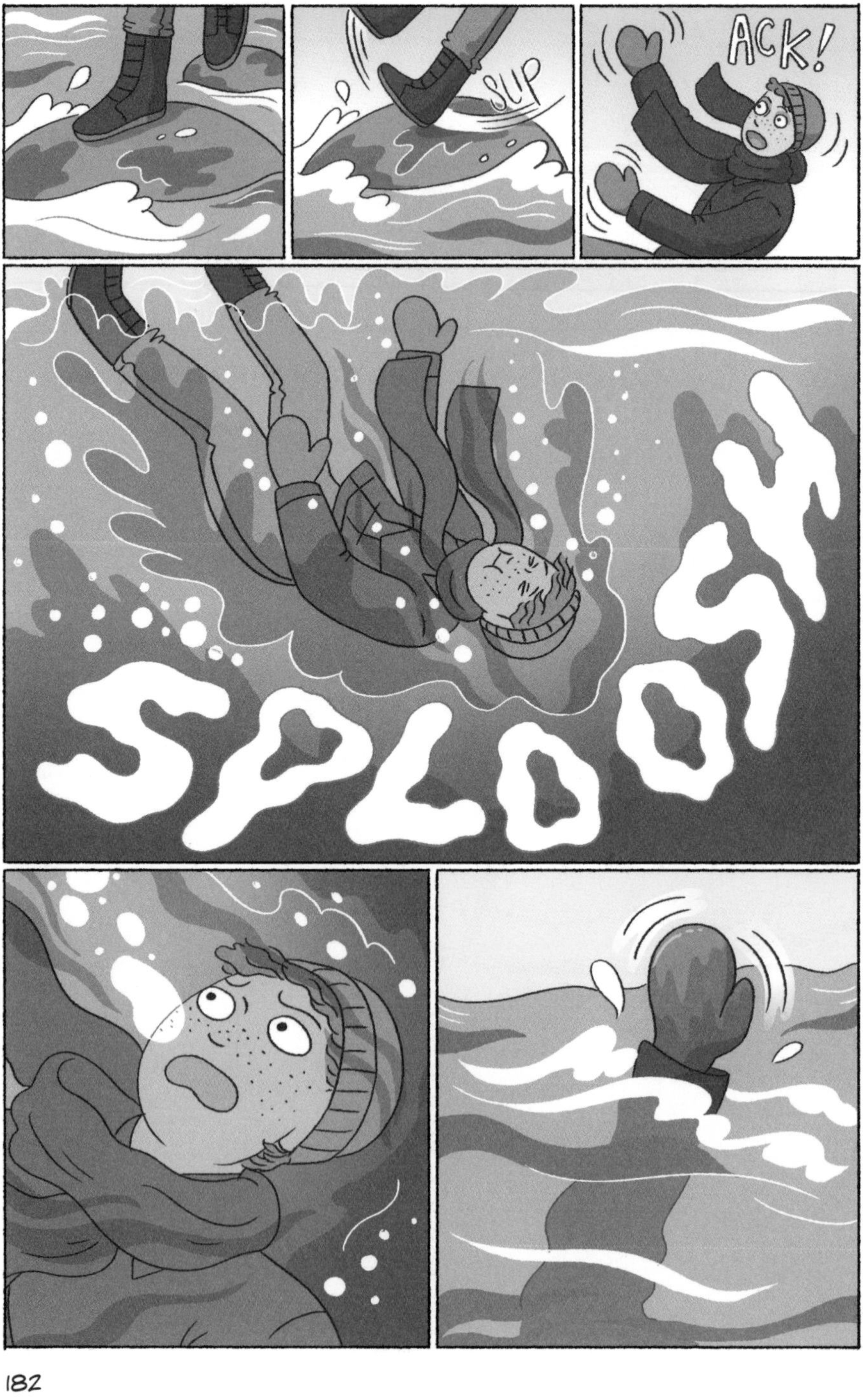
SLIP
ACK!
SPLOOSH

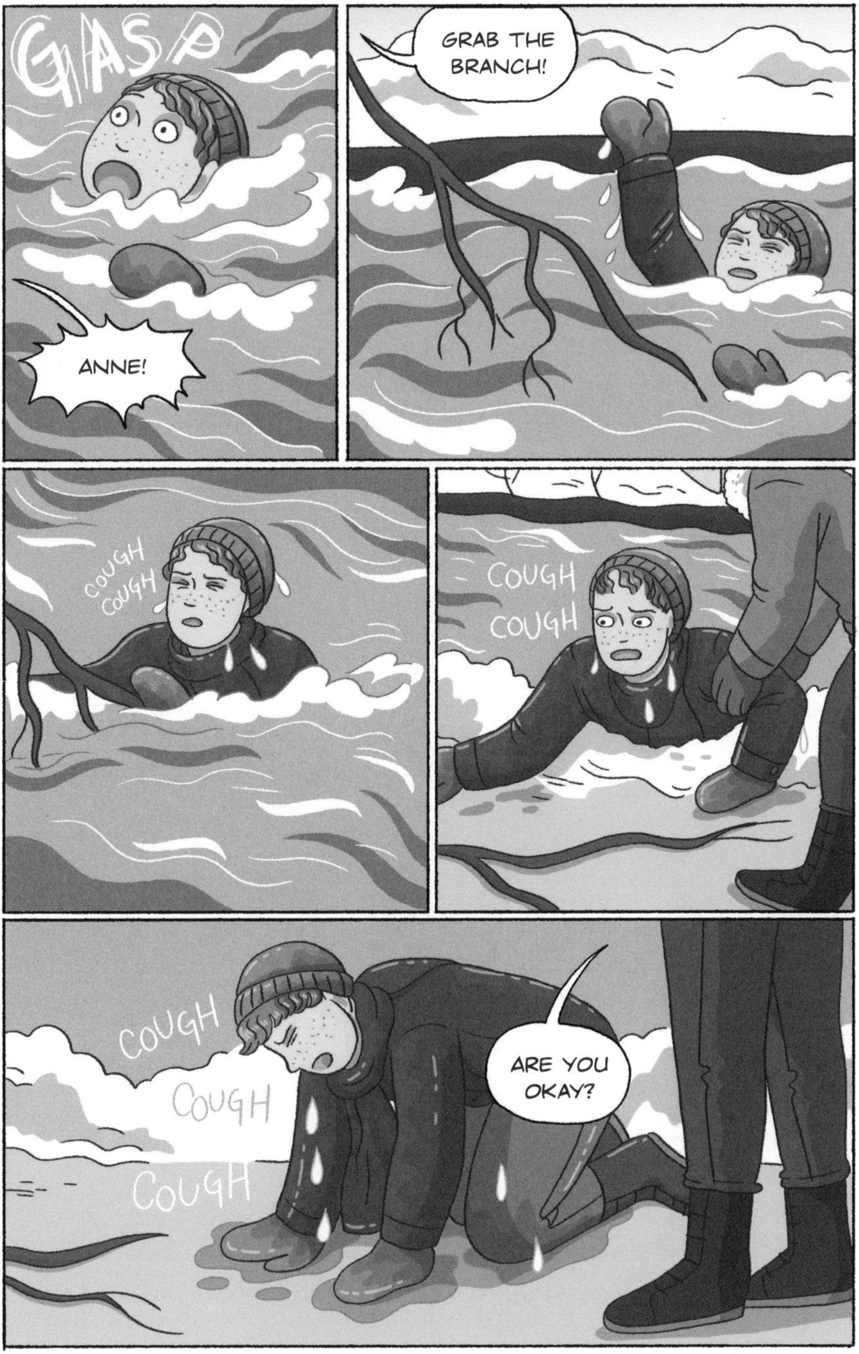
GASP
ANNE!
GRAB THE BRANCH!
COUGH COUGH
COUGH COUGH
COUGH
COUGH
COUGH
ARE YOU OKAY?

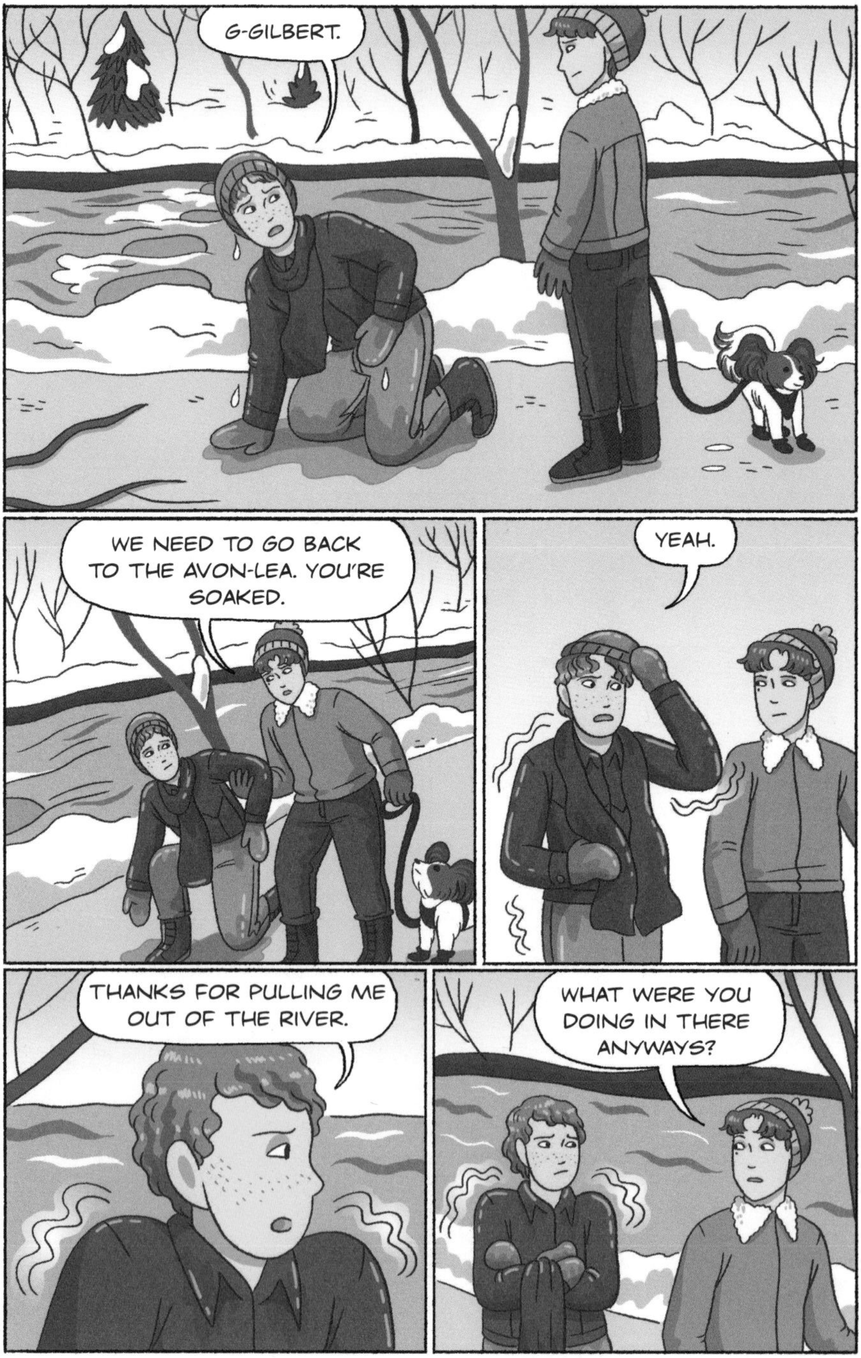
G-GILBERT.
WE NEED TO GO BACK TO THE AVON-LEA. YOU'RE SOAKED.
YEAH.
THANKS FOR PULLING ME OUT OF THE RIVER.
WHAT WERE YOU DOING IN THERE ANYWAYS?

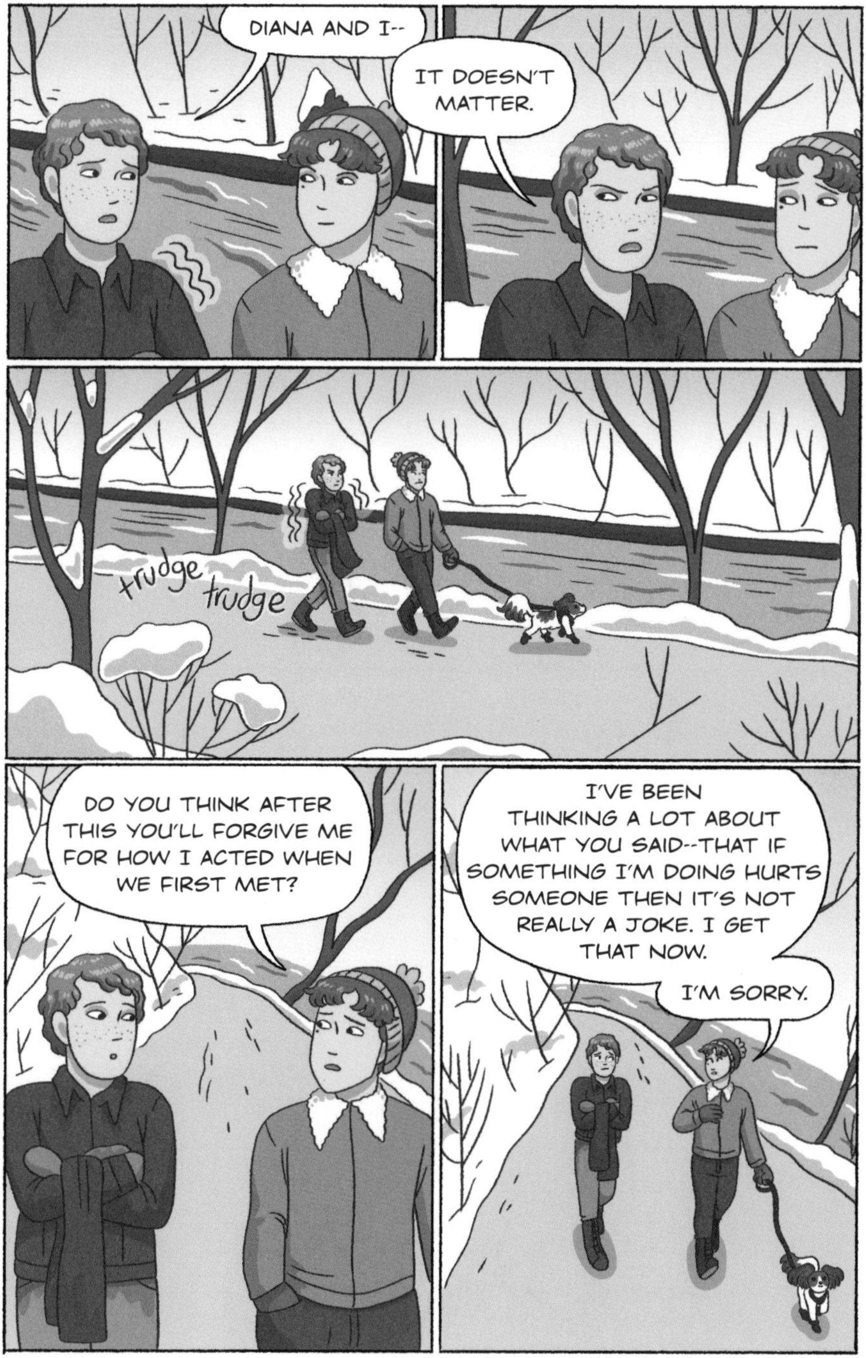
DIANA AND I--
IT DOESN'T MATTER.
trudge trudge
DO YOU THINK AFTER THIS YOU'LL FORGIVE ME FOR HOW I ACTED WHEN WE FIRST MET?
I'VE BEEN THINKING A LOT ABOUT WHAT YOU SAID--THAT IF SOMETHING I'M DOING HURTS SOMEONE THEN IT'S NOT REALLY A JOKE. I GET THAT NOW.
I'M SORRY.

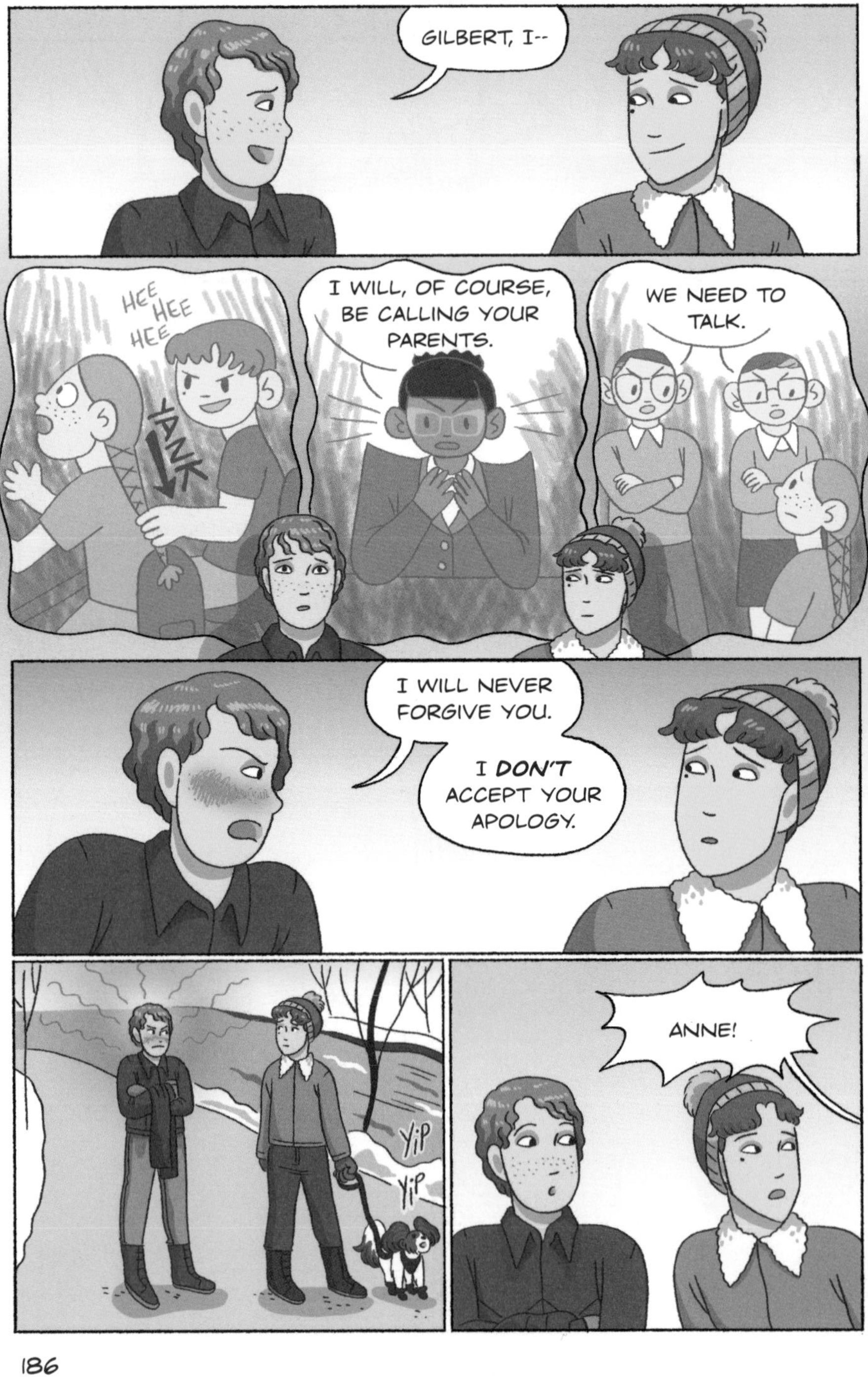
GILBERT, I--
HEE HEE HEE
YANK
I WILL, OF COURSE, BE CALLING YOUR PARENTS.
WE NEED TO TALK.
I WILL NEVER FORGIVE YOU.
I **DON'T** ACCEPT YOUR APOLOGY.
YIP
YIP
ANNE!

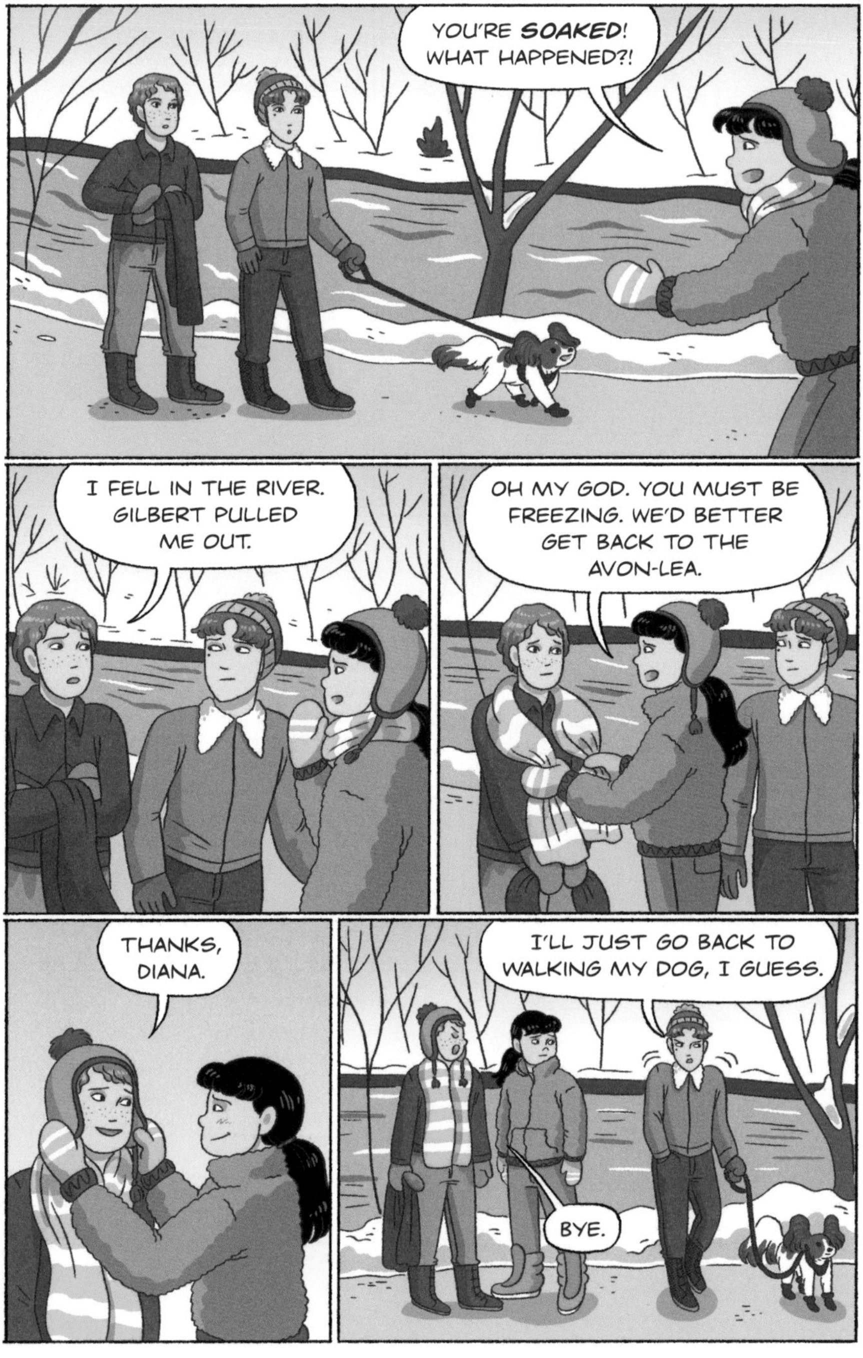
YOU'RE **SOAKED**! WHAT HAPPENED?!
I FELL IN THE RIVER. GILBERT PULLED ME OUT.
OH MY GOD. YOU MUST BE FREEZING. WE'D BETTER GET BACK TO THE AVON-LEA.
THANKS, DIANA.
I'LL JUST GO BACK TO WALKING MY DOG, I GUESS.
BYE.

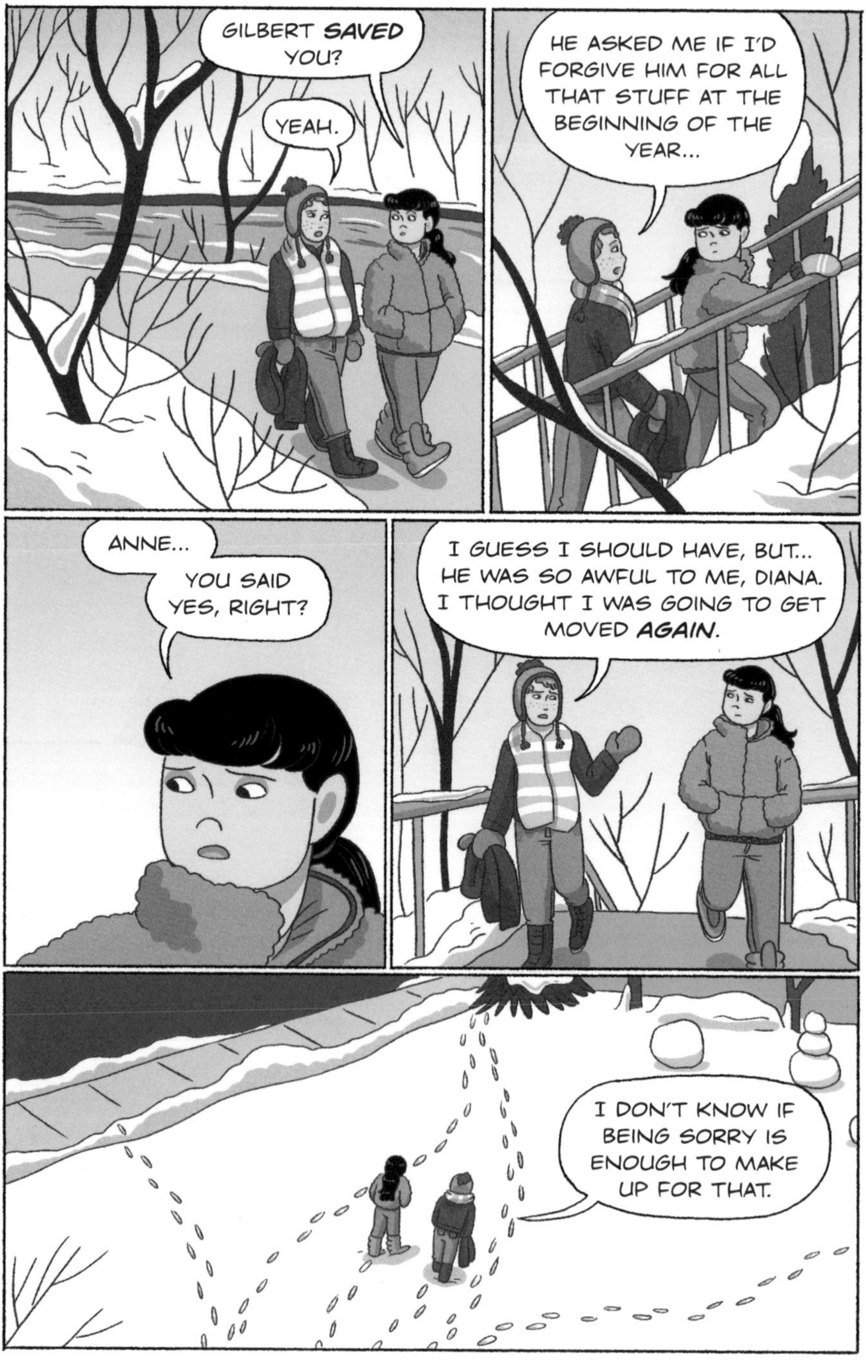
GILBERT **SAVED** YOU?
YEAH.
HE ASKED ME IF I'D FORGIVE HIM FOR ALL THAT STUFF AT THE BEGINNING OF THE YEAR...
ANNE...
YOU SAID YES, RIGHT?
I GUESS I SHOULD HAVE, BUT... HE WAS SO AWFUL TO ME, DIANA. I THOUGHT I WAS GOING TO GET MOVED **AGAIN**.
I DON'T KNOW IF BEING SORRY IS ENOUGH TO MAKE UP FOR THAT.

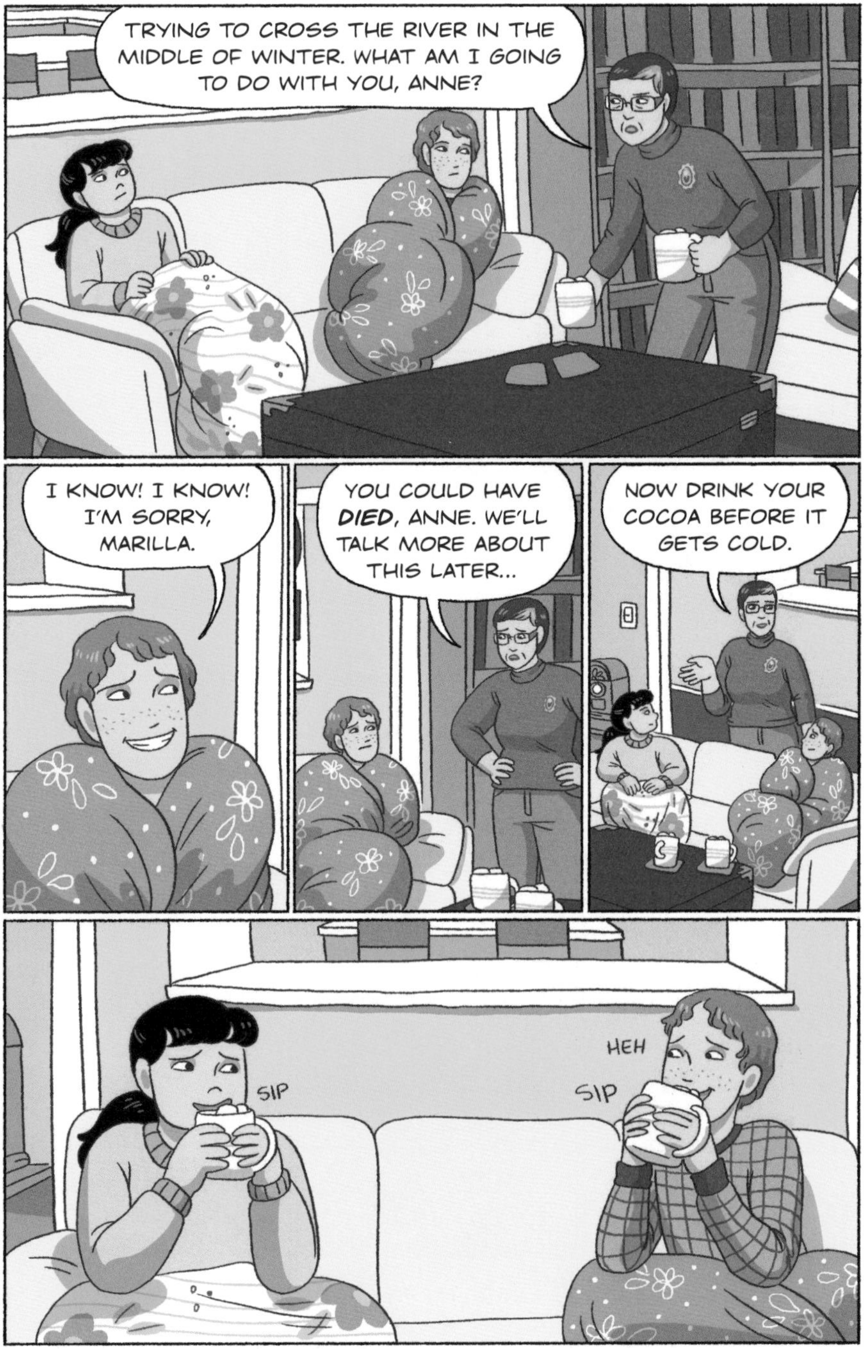

TRYING TO CROSS THE RIVER IN THE MIDDLE OF WINTER. WHAT AM I GOING TO DO WITH YOU, ANNE?
I KNOW! I KNOW! I'M SORRY, MARILLA.
YOU COULD HAVE **DIED**, ANNE. WE'LL TALK MORE ABOUT THIS LATER...
NOW DRINK YOUR COCOA BEFORE IT GETS COLD.
SIP
HEH
SIP

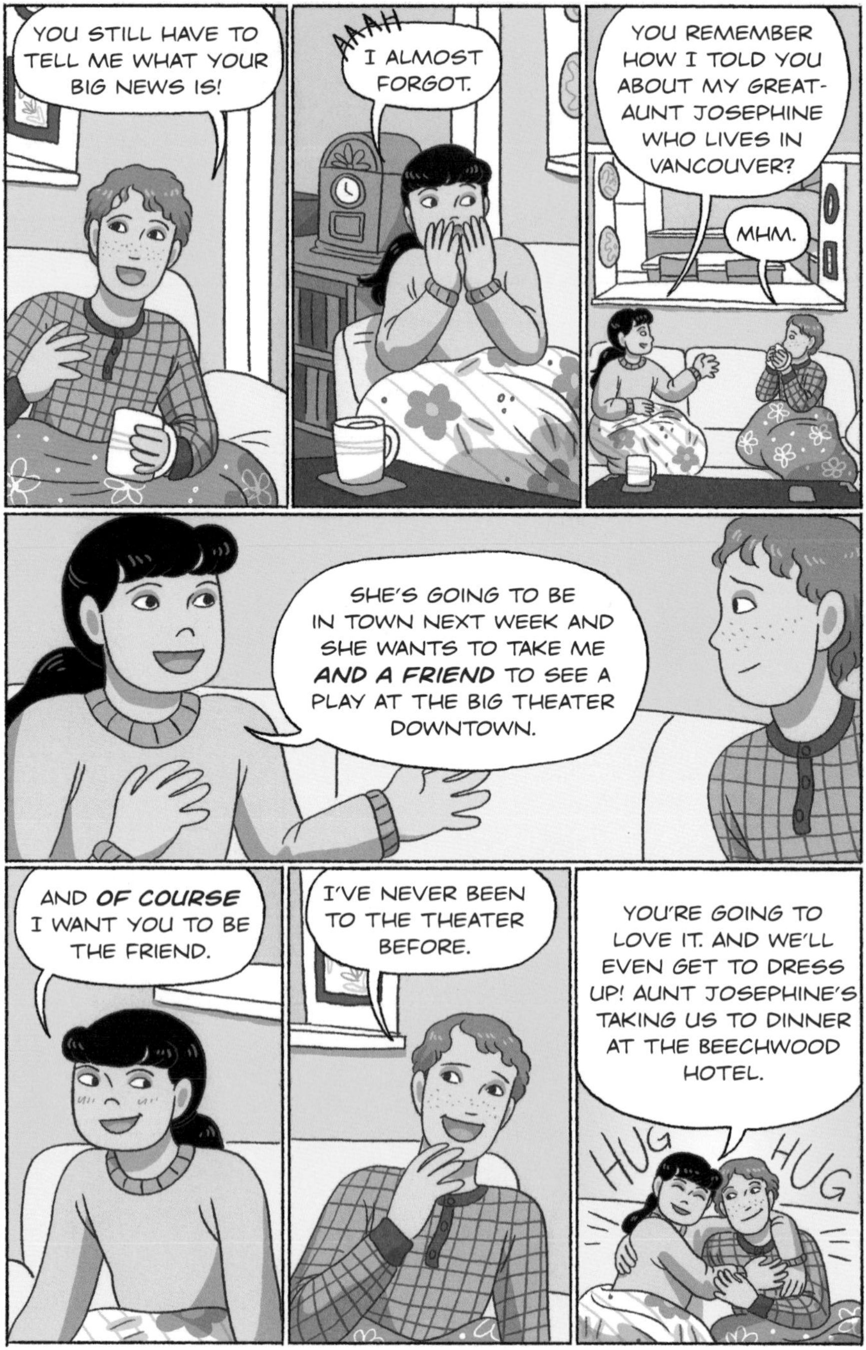
YOU STILL HAVE TO TELL ME WHAT YOUR BIG NEWS IS!
AAAH
I ALMOST FORGOT.
YOU REMEMBER HOW I TOLD YOU ABOUT MY GREAT-AUNT JOSEPHINE WHO LIVES IN VANCOUVER?
MHM.
SHE'S GOING TO BE IN TOWN NEXT WEEK AND SHE WANTS TO TAKE ME ***AND A FRIEND*** TO SEE A PLAY AT THE BIG THEATER DOWNTOWN.
AND ***OF COURSE*** I WANT YOU TO BE THE FRIEND.
I'VE NEVER BEEN TO THE THEATER BEFORE.
YOU'RE GOING TO LOVE IT. AND WE'LL EVEN GET TO DRESS UP! AUNT JOSEPHINE'S TAKING US TO DINNER AT THE BEECHWOOD HOTEL.
HUG
HUG

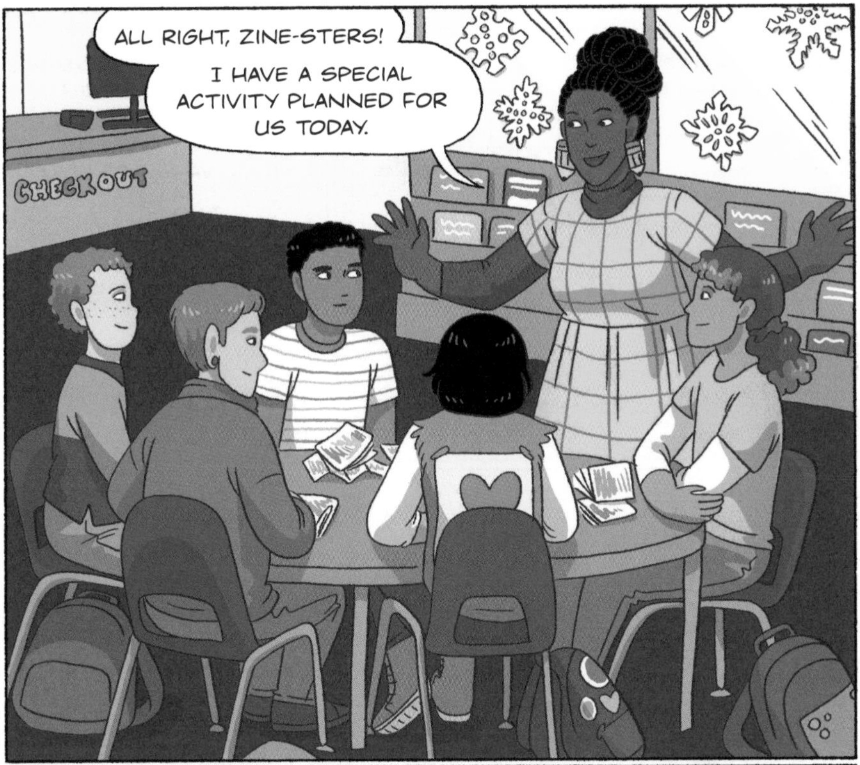
ALL RIGHT, ZINE-STERS!
I HAVE A SPECIAL ACTIVITY PLANNED FOR US TODAY.
CHECKOUT

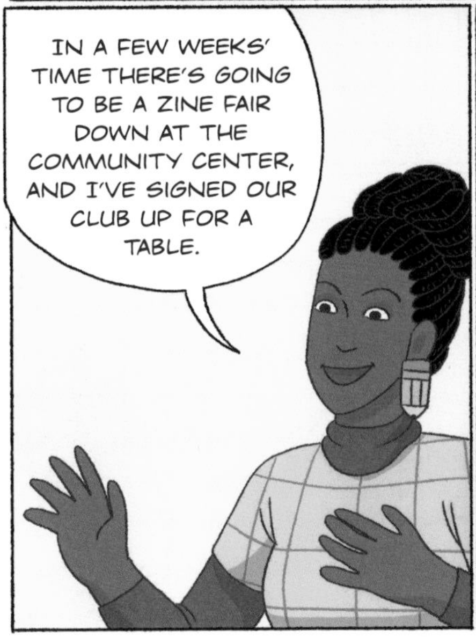
IN A FEW WEEKS' TIME THERE'S GOING TO BE A ZINE FAIR DOWN AT THE COMMUNITY CENTER, AND I'VE SIGNED OUR CLUB UP FOR A TABLE.

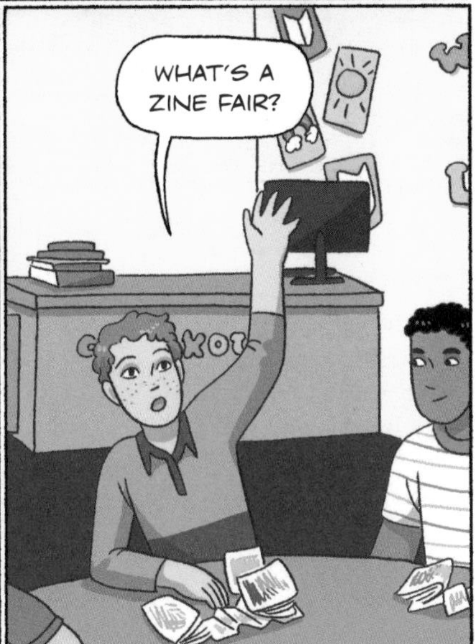
WHAT'S A ZINE FAIR?

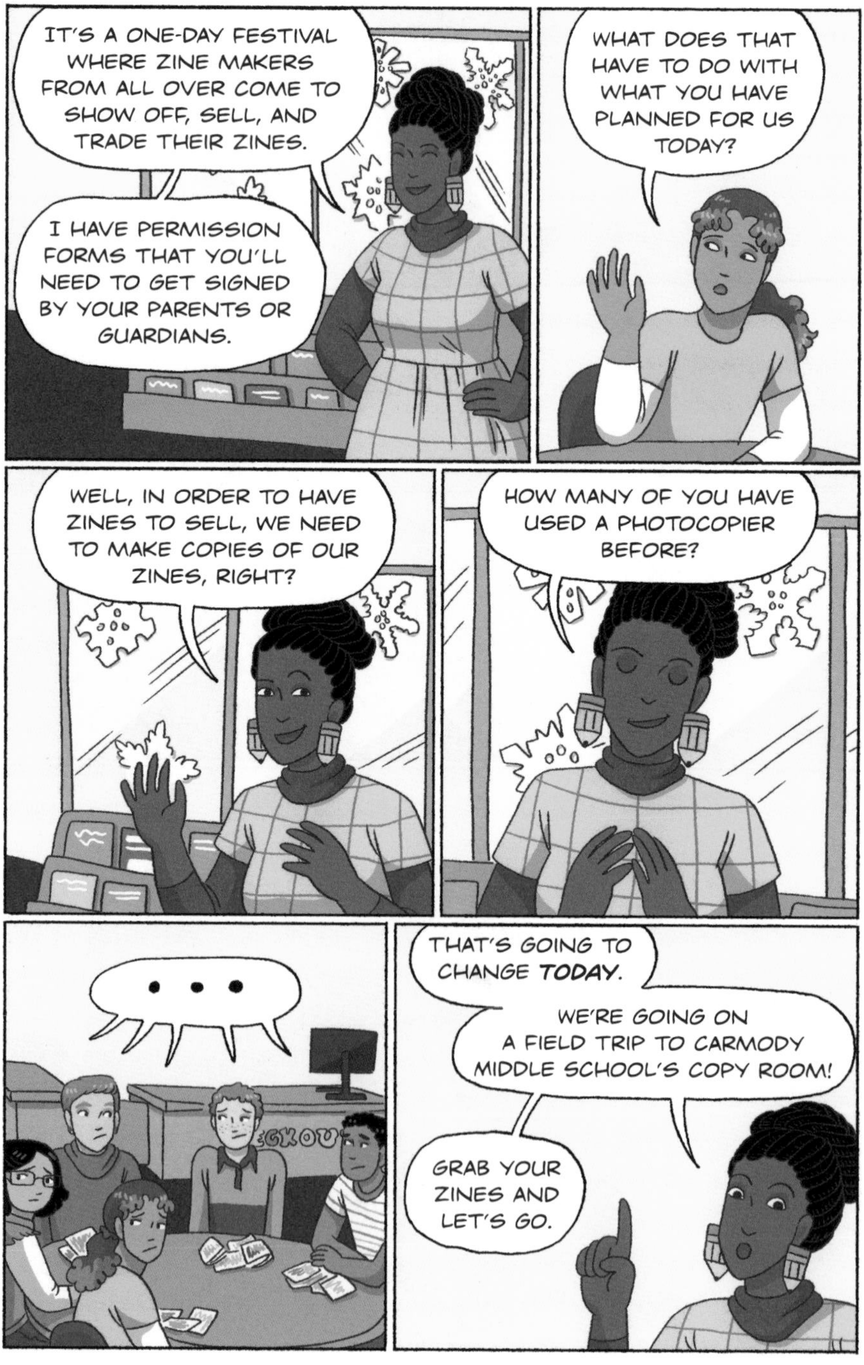
IT'S A ONE-DAY FESTIVAL WHERE ZINE MAKERS FROM ALL OVER COME TO SHOW OFF, SELL, AND TRADE THEIR ZINES.
I HAVE PERMISSION FORMS THAT YOU'LL NEED TO GET SIGNED BY YOUR PARENTS OR GUARDIANS.
WHAT DOES THAT HAVE TO DO WITH WHAT YOU HAVE PLANNED FOR US TODAY?
WELL, IN ORDER TO HAVE ZINES TO SELL, WE NEED TO MAKE COPIES OF OUR ZINES, RIGHT?
HOW MANY OF YOU HAVE USED A PHOTOCOPIER BEFORE?
• • •
THAT'S GOING TO CHANGE **TODAY**.
WE'RE GOING ON A FIELD TRIP TO CARMODY MIDDLE SCHOOL'S COPY ROOM!
GRAB YOUR ZINES AND LET'S GO.

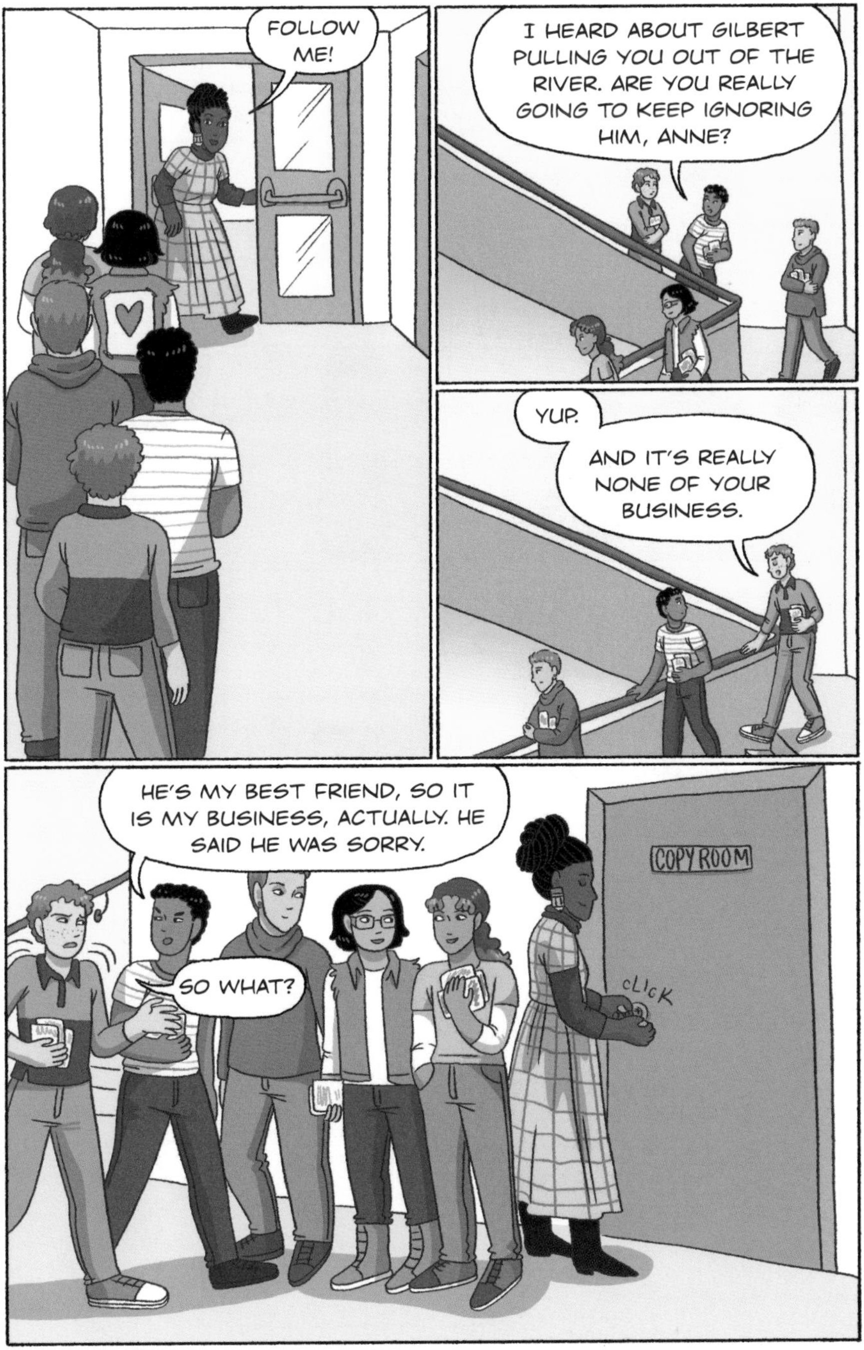
FOLLOW ME!
I HEARD ABOUT GILBERT PULLING YOU OUT OF THE RIVER. ARE YOU REALLY GOING TO KEEP IGNORING HIM, ANNE?
YUP.
AND IT'S REALLY NONE OF YOUR BUSINESS.
HE'S MY BEST FRIEND, SO IT IS MY BUSINESS, ACTUALLY. HE SAID HE WAS SORRY.
SO WHAT?
COPY ROOM
CLICK

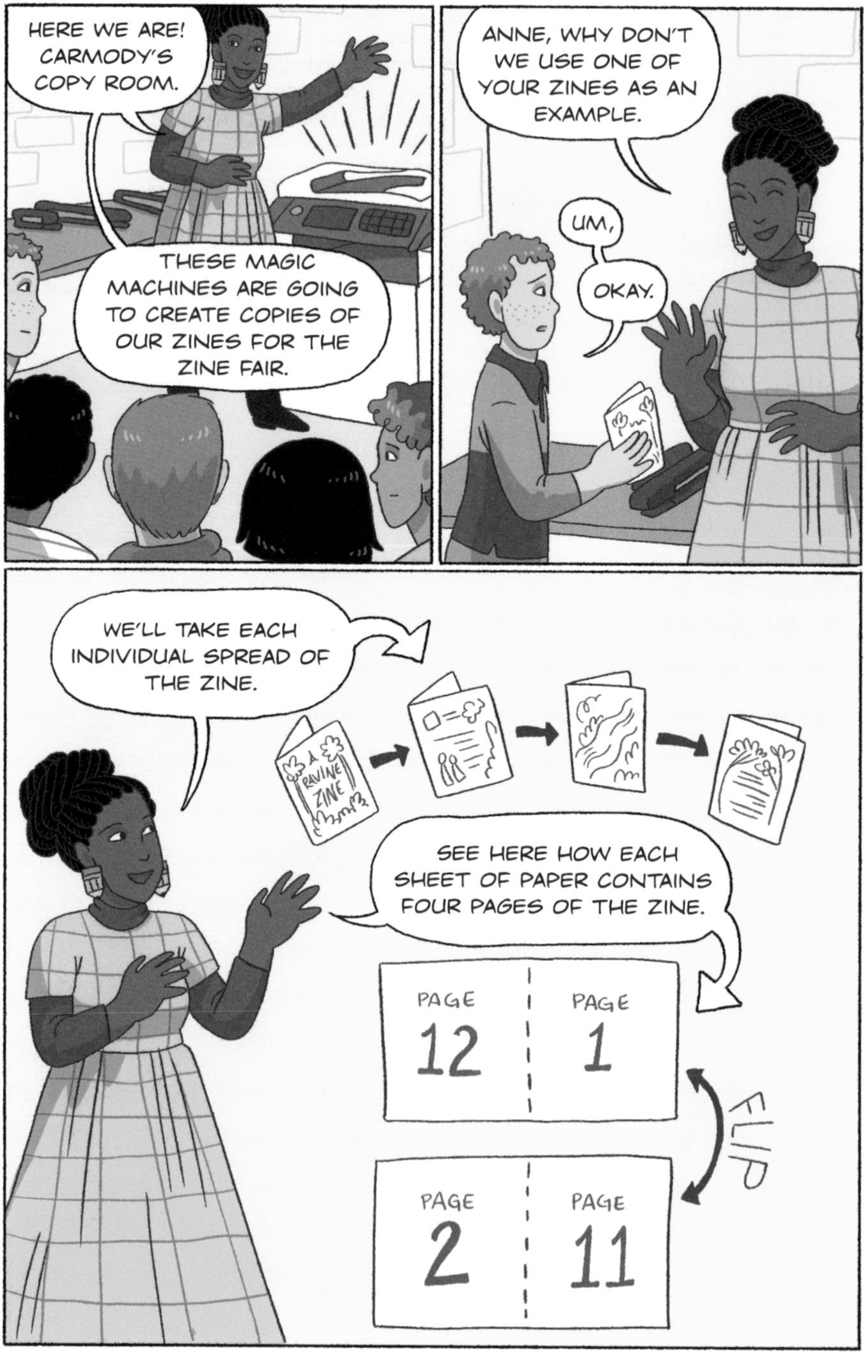
HERE WE ARE! CARMODY'S COPY ROOM.
THESE MAGIC MACHINES ARE GOING TO CREATE COPIES OF OUR ZINES FOR THE ZINE FAIR.
ANNE, WHY DON'T WE USE ONE OF YOUR ZINES AS AN EXAMPLE.
UM,
OKAY.
WE'LL TAKE EACH INDIVIDUAL SPREAD OF THE ZINE.
A RAVINE ZINE
SEE HERE HOW EACH SHEET OF PAPER CONTAINS FOUR PAGES OF THE ZINE.
PAGE 12
PAGE 1
FLIP
PAGE 2
PAGE 11

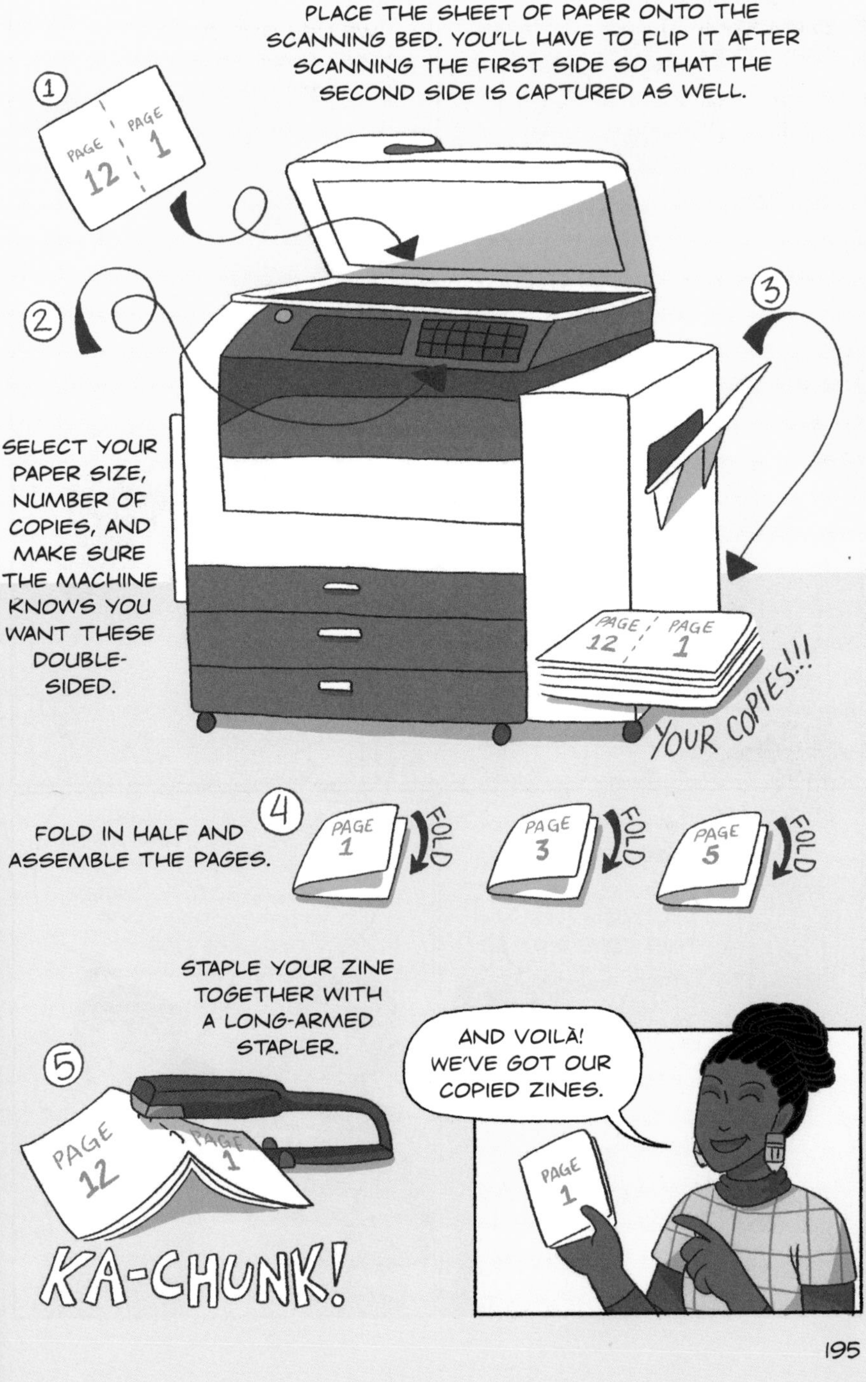
PLACE THE SHEET OF PAPER ONTO THE SCANNING BED. YOU'LL HAVE TO FLIP IT AFTER SCANNING THE FIRST SIDE SO THAT THE SECOND SIDE IS CAPTURED AS WELL.
1
PAGE 12
PAGE 1
2
SELECT YOUR PAPER SIZE, NUMBER OF COPIES, AND MAKE SURE THE MACHINE KNOWS YOU WANT THESE DOUBLE-SIDED.
3
PAGE 12
PAGE 1
YOUR COPIES!!!
4
FOLD IN HALF AND ASSEMBLE THE PAGES.
PAGE 1
FOLD
PAGE 3
FOLD
PAGE 5
FOLD
STAPLE YOUR ZINE TOGETHER WITH A LONG-ARMED STAPLER.
5
PAGE 12
PAGE 1
KA-CHUNK!
AND VOILÀ! WE'VE GOT OUR COPIED ZINES.
PAGE 1

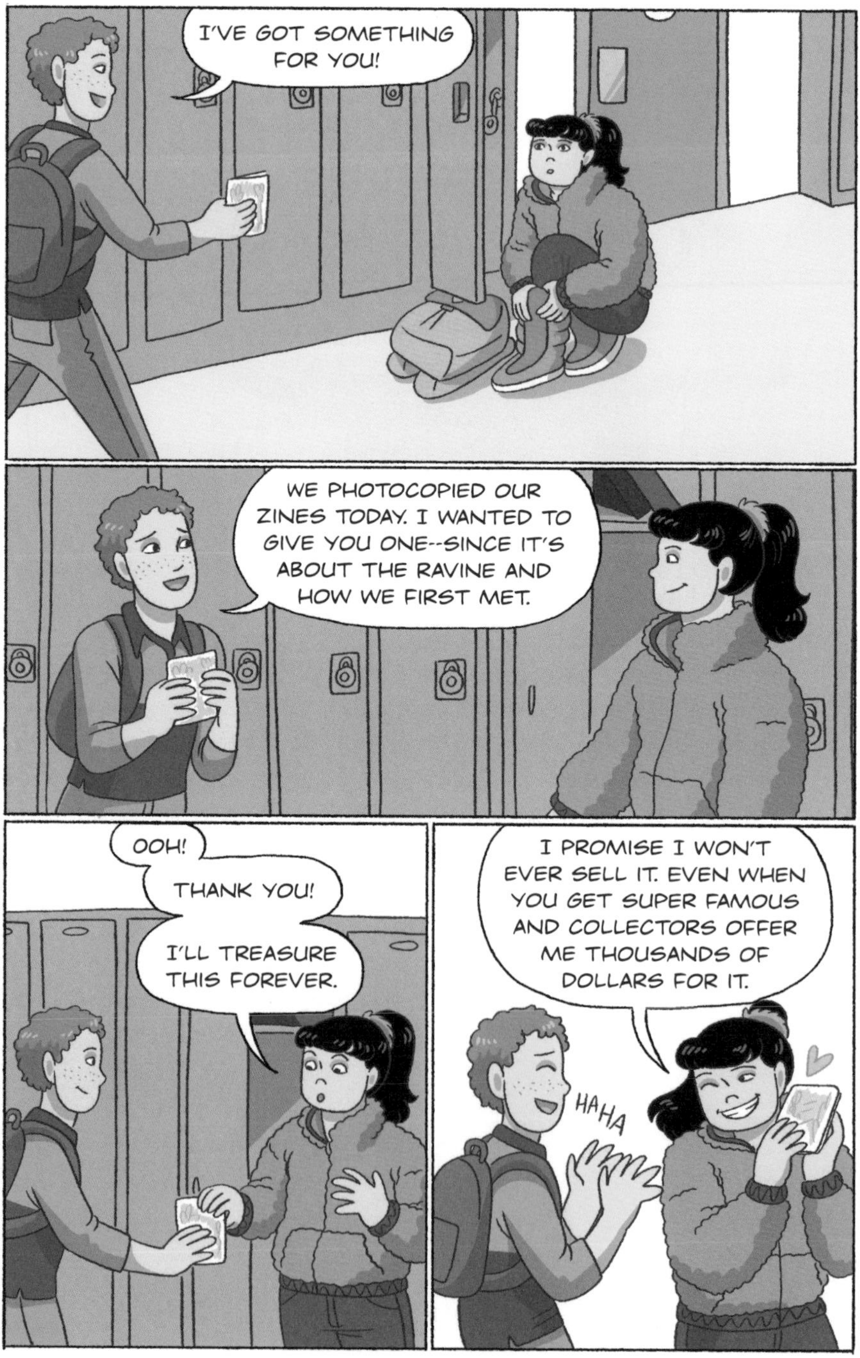
I'VE GOT SOMETHING FOR YOU!
WE PHOTOCOPIED OUR ZINES TODAY. I WANTED TO GIVE YOU ONE--SINCE IT'S ABOUT THE RAVINE AND HOW WE FIRST MET.
OOH!
THANK YOU!
I'LL TREASURE THIS FOREVER.
I PROMISE I WON'T EVER SELL IT. EVEN WHEN YOU GET SUPER FAMOUS AND COLLECTORS OFFER ME THOUSANDS OF DOLLARS FOR IT.
HAHA

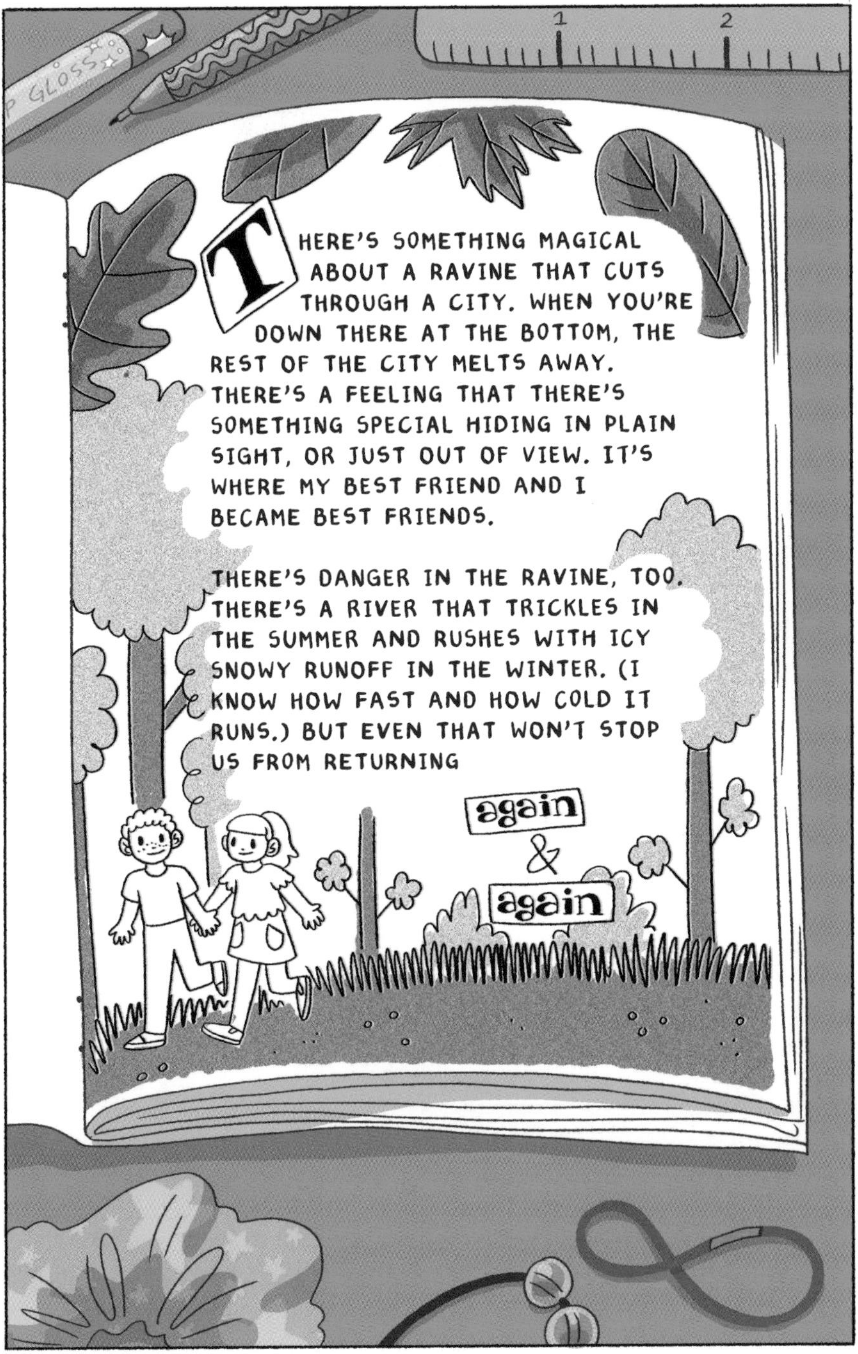
P GLOSS
1
2
THERE'S SOMETHING MAGICAL ABOUT A RAVINE THAT CUTS THROUGH A CITY. WHEN YOU'RE DOWN THERE AT THE BOTTOM, THE REST OF THE CITY MELTS AWAY. THERE'S A FEELING THAT THERE'S SOMETHING SPECIAL HIDING IN PLAIN SIGHT, OR JUST OUT OF VIEW. IT'S WHERE MY BEST FRIEND AND I BECAME BEST FRIENDS.
THERE'S DANGER IN THE RAVINE, TOO. THERE'S A RIVER THAT TRICKLES IN THE SUMMER AND RUSHES WITH ICY SNOWY RUNOFF IN THE WINTER. (I KNOW HOW FAST AND HOW COLD IT RUNS.) BUT EVEN THAT WON'T STOP US FROM RETURNING
again
&
again

CHAPTER 9

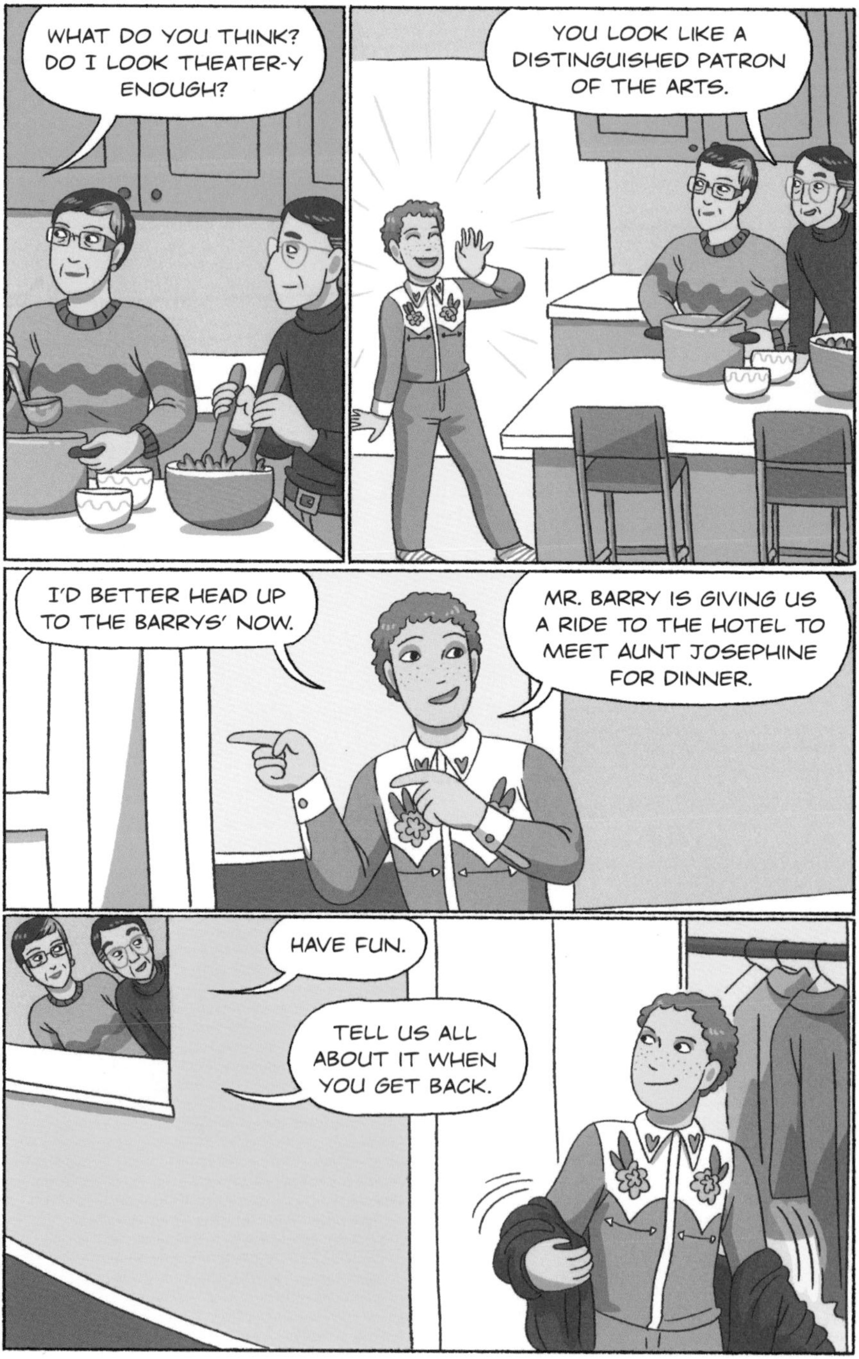
WHAT DO YOU THINK? DO I LOOK THEATER-Y ENOUGH?
YOU LOOK LIKE A DISTINGUISHED PATRON OF THE ARTS.
I'D BETTER HEAD UP TO THE BARRYS' NOW.
MR. BARRY IS GIVING US A RIDE TO THE HOTEL TO MEET AUNT JOSEPHINE FOR DINNER.
HAVE FUN.
TELL US ALL ABOUT IT WHEN YOU GET BACK.

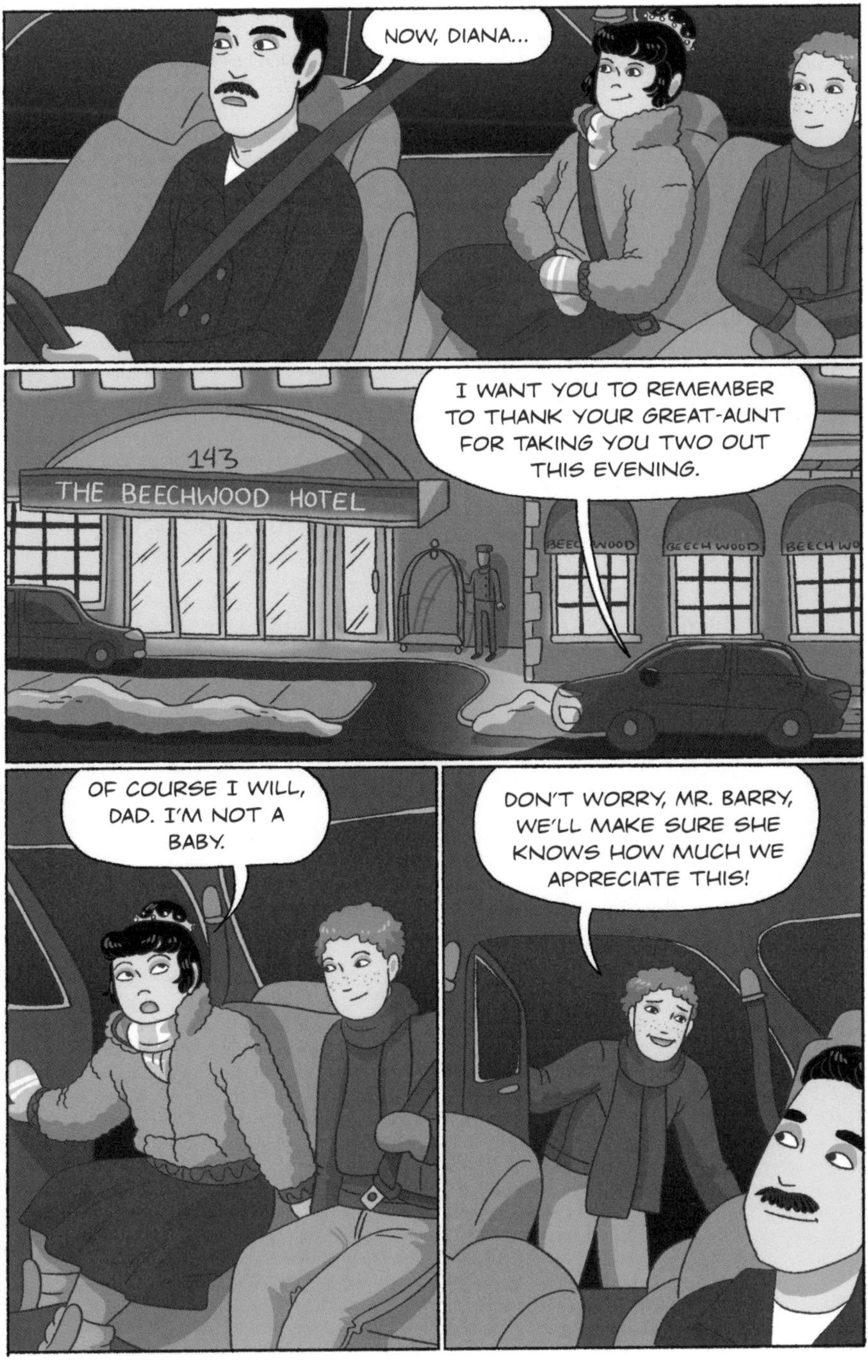
NOW, DIANA...
I WANT YOU TO REMEMBER TO THANK YOUR GREAT-AUNT FOR TAKING YOU TWO OUT THIS EVENING.
143
THE BEECHWOOD HOTEL
OF COURSE I WILL, DAD. I'M NOT A BABY.
DON'T WORRY, MR. BARRY, WE'LL MAKE SURE SHE KNOWS HOW MUCH WE APPRECIATE THIS!

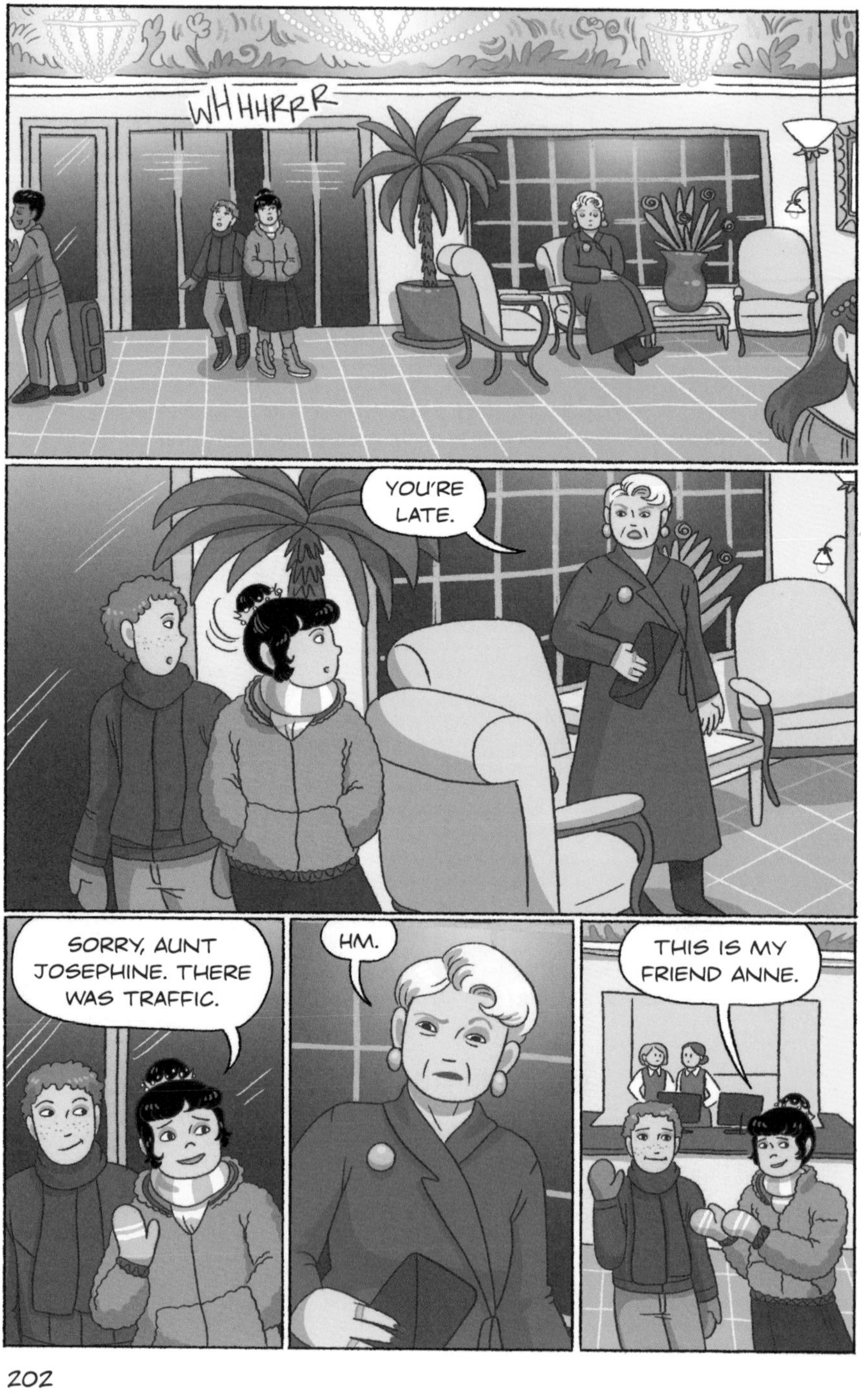
WHHHRRR
YOU'RE LATE.
SORRY, AUNT JOSEPHINE. THERE WAS TRAFFIC.
HM.
THIS IS MY FRIEND ANNE.

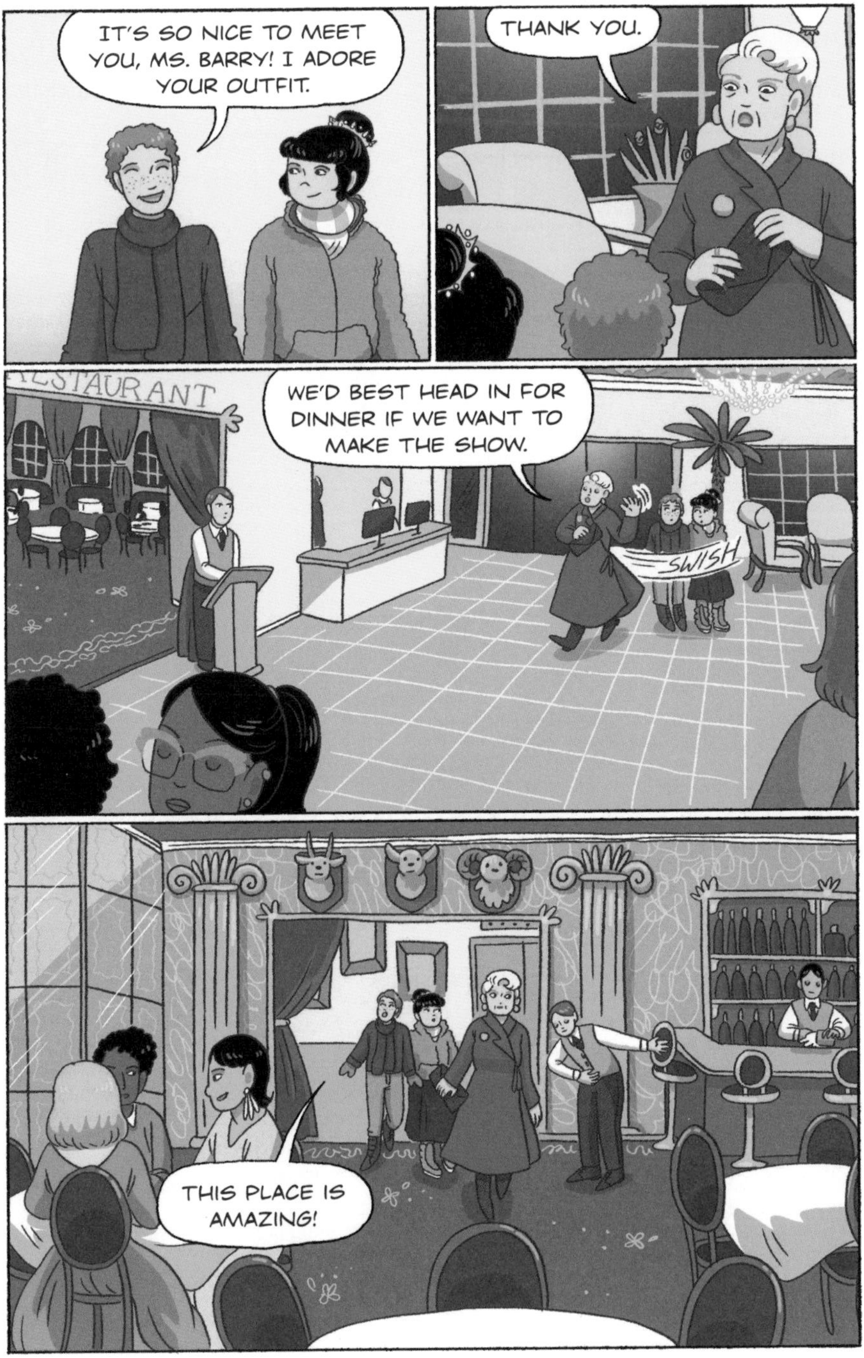
IT'S SO NICE TO MEET YOU, MS. BARRY! I ADORE YOUR OUTFIT.
THANK YOU.
RESTAURANT
WE'D BEST HEAD IN FOR DINNER IF WE WANT TO MAKE THE SHOW.
SWISH
THIS PLACE IS AMAZING!

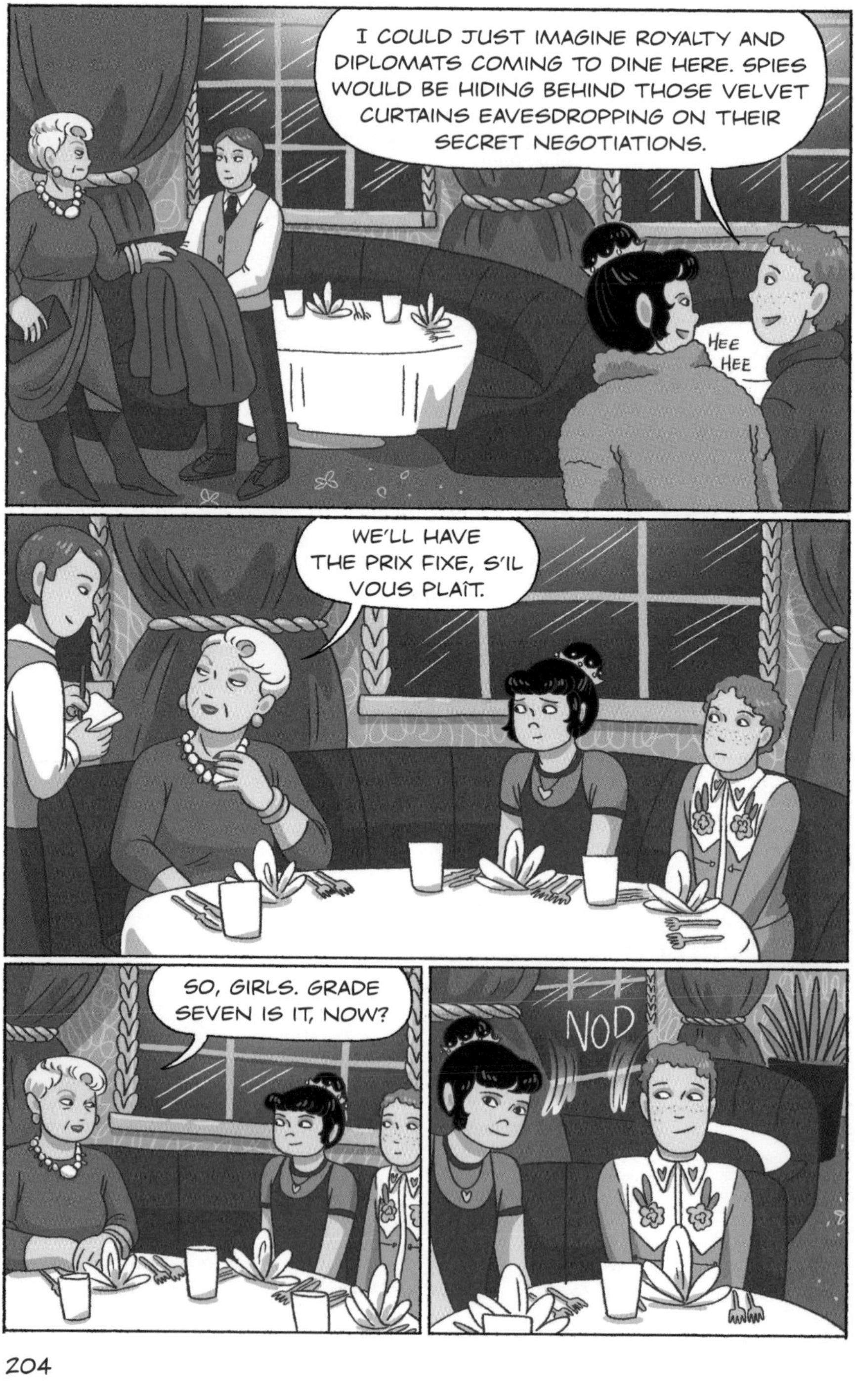
I COULD JUST IMAGINE ROYALTY AND DIPLOMATS COMING TO DINE HERE. SPIES WOULD BE HIDING BEHIND THOSE VELVET CURTAINS EAVESDROPPING ON THEIR SECRET NEGOTIATIONS.
HEE HEE
WE'LL HAVE THE PRIX FIXE, S'IL VOUS PLAÎT.
SO, GIRLS. GRADE SEVEN IS IT, NOW?
NOD

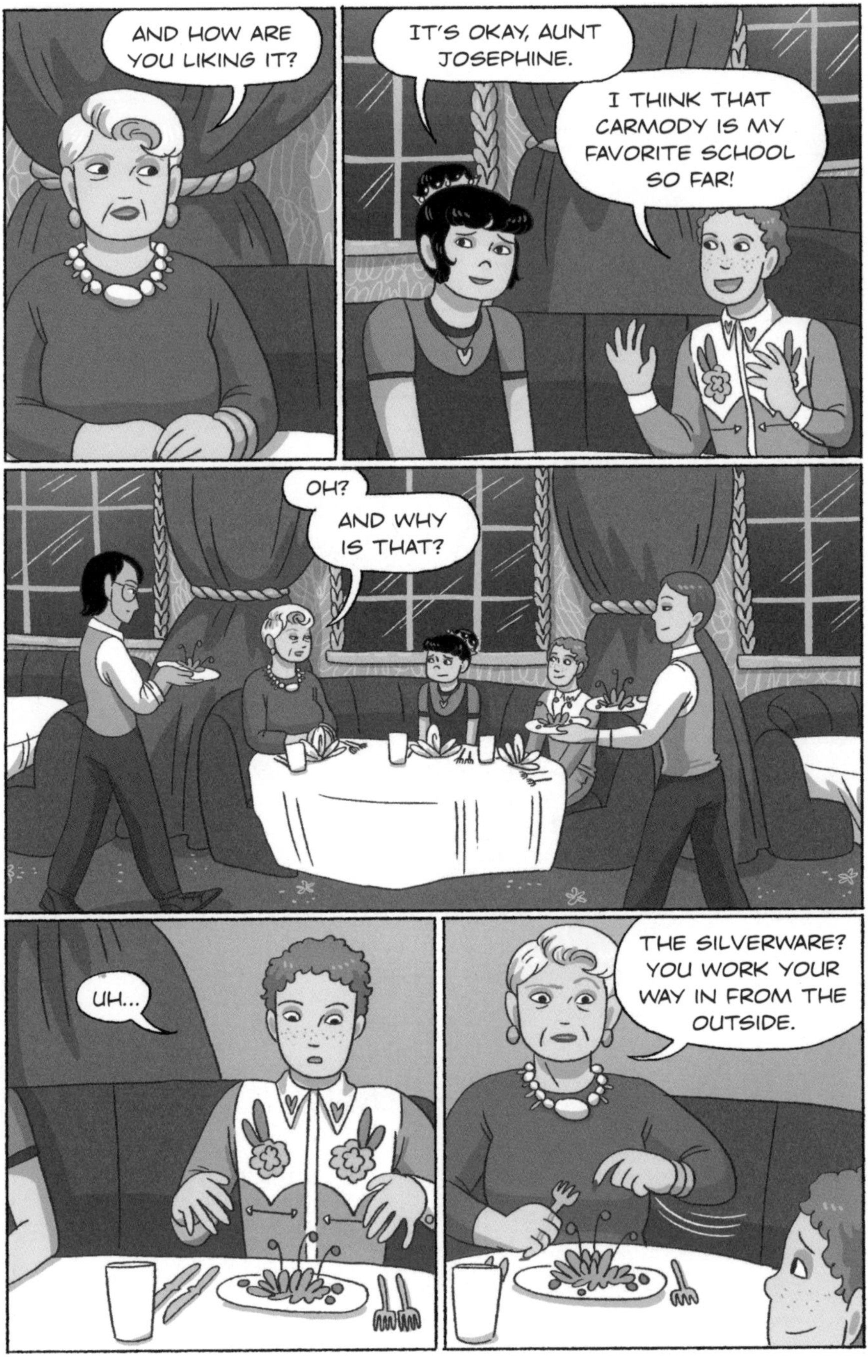
AND HOW ARE YOU LIKING IT?
IT'S OKAY, AUNT JOSEPHINE.
I THINK THAT CARMODY IS MY FAVORITE SCHOOL SO FAR!
OH?
AND WHY IS THAT?
UH...
THE SILVERWARE? YOU WORK YOUR WAY IN FROM THE OUTSIDE.

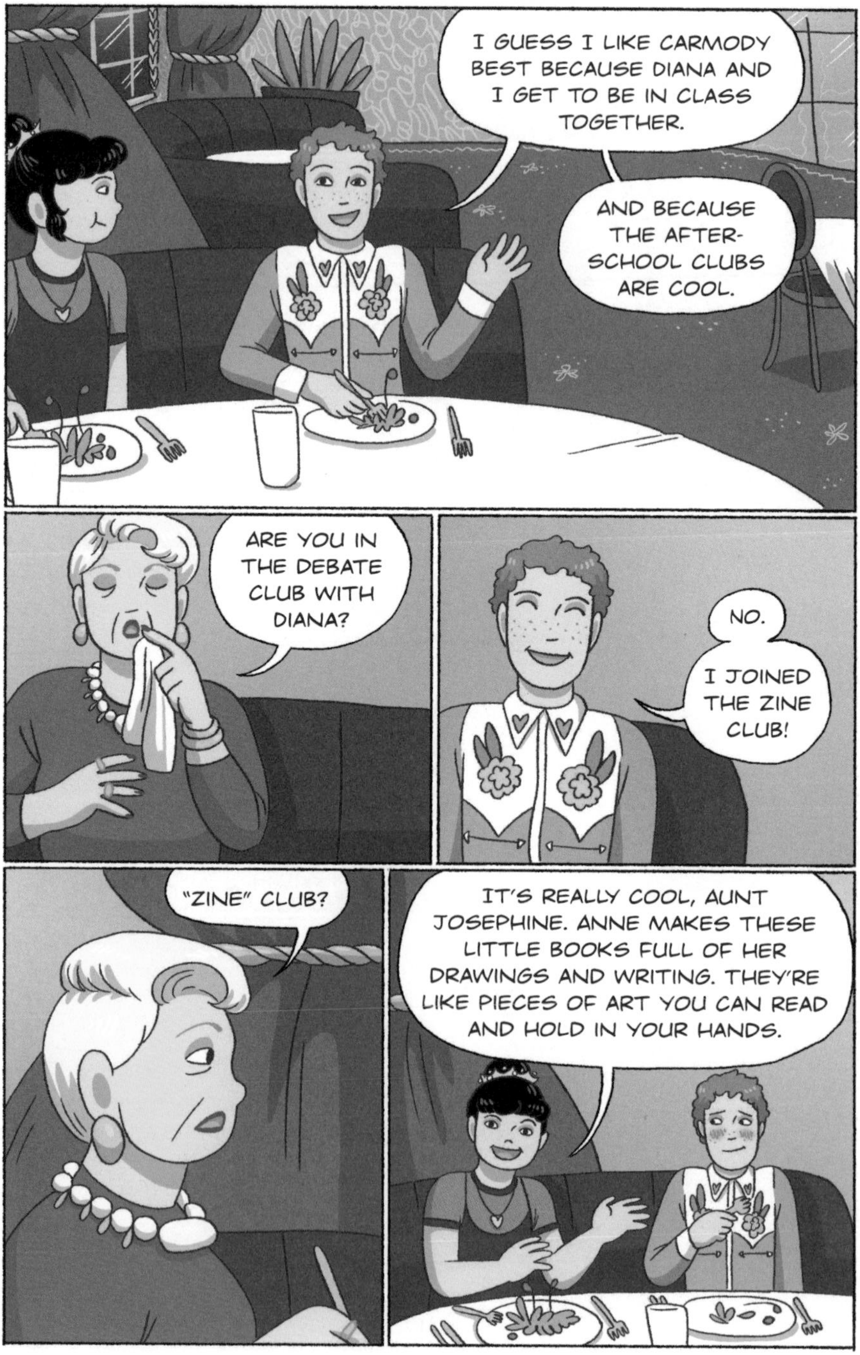
I GUESS I LIKE CARMODY BEST BECAUSE DIANA AND I GET TO BE IN CLASS TOGETHER.
AND BECAUSE THE AFTER-SCHOOL CLUBS ARE COOL.
ARE YOU IN THE DEBATE CLUB WITH DIANA?
NO.
I JOINED THE ZINE CLUB!
"ZINE" CLUB?
IT'S REALLY COOL, AUNT JOSEPHINE. ANNE MAKES THESE LITTLE BOOKS FULL OF HER DRAWINGS AND WRITING. THEY'RE LIKE PIECES OF ART YOU CAN READ AND HOLD IN YOUR HANDS.

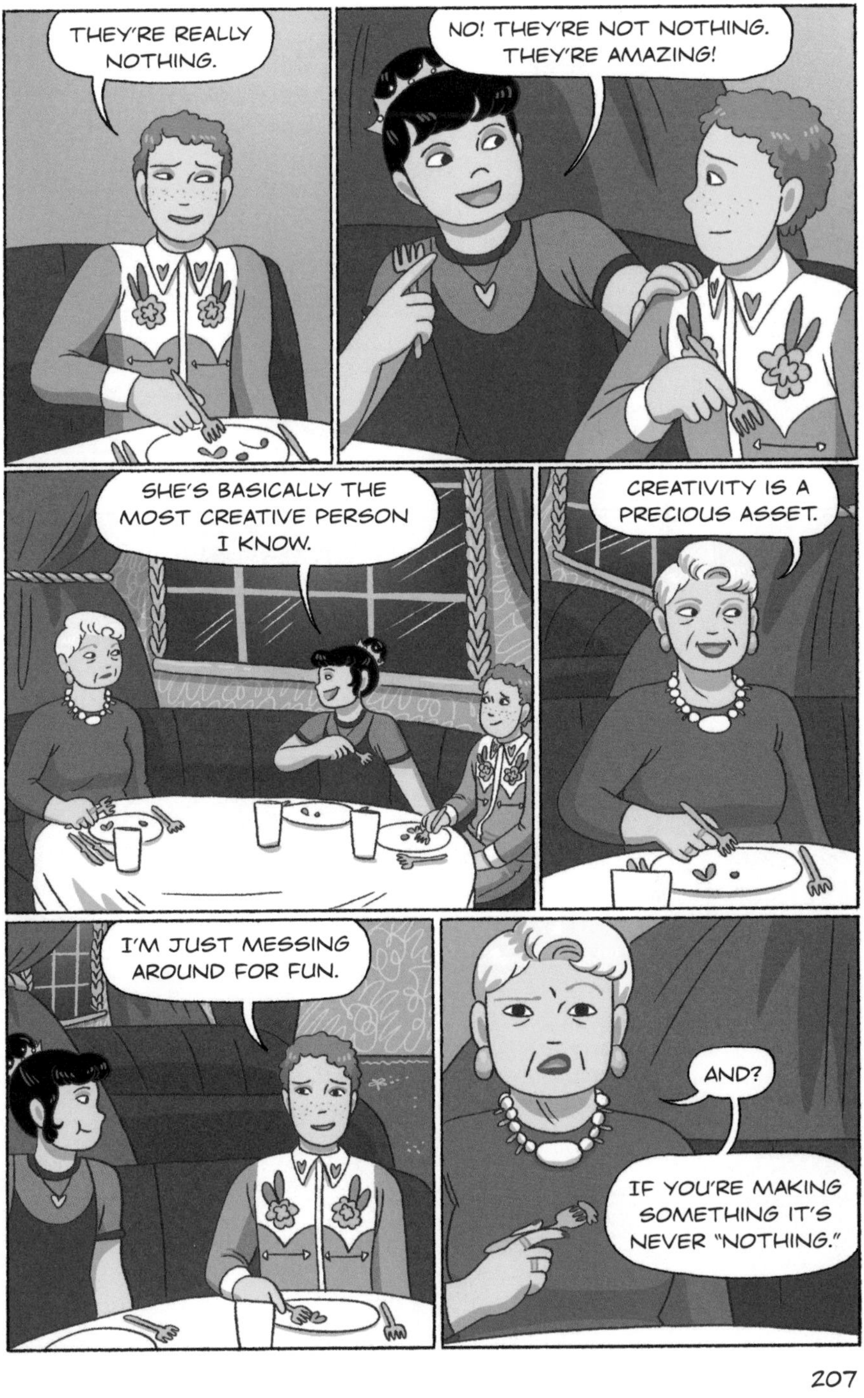
THEY'RE REALLY NOTHING.
NO! THEY'RE NOT NOTHING. THEY'RE AMAZING!
SHE'S BASICALLY THE MOST CREATIVE PERSON I KNOW.
CREATIVITY IS A PRECIOUS ASSET.
I'M JUST MESSING AROUND FOR FUN.
AND?
IF YOU'RE MAKING SOMETHING IT'S NEVER "NOTHING."

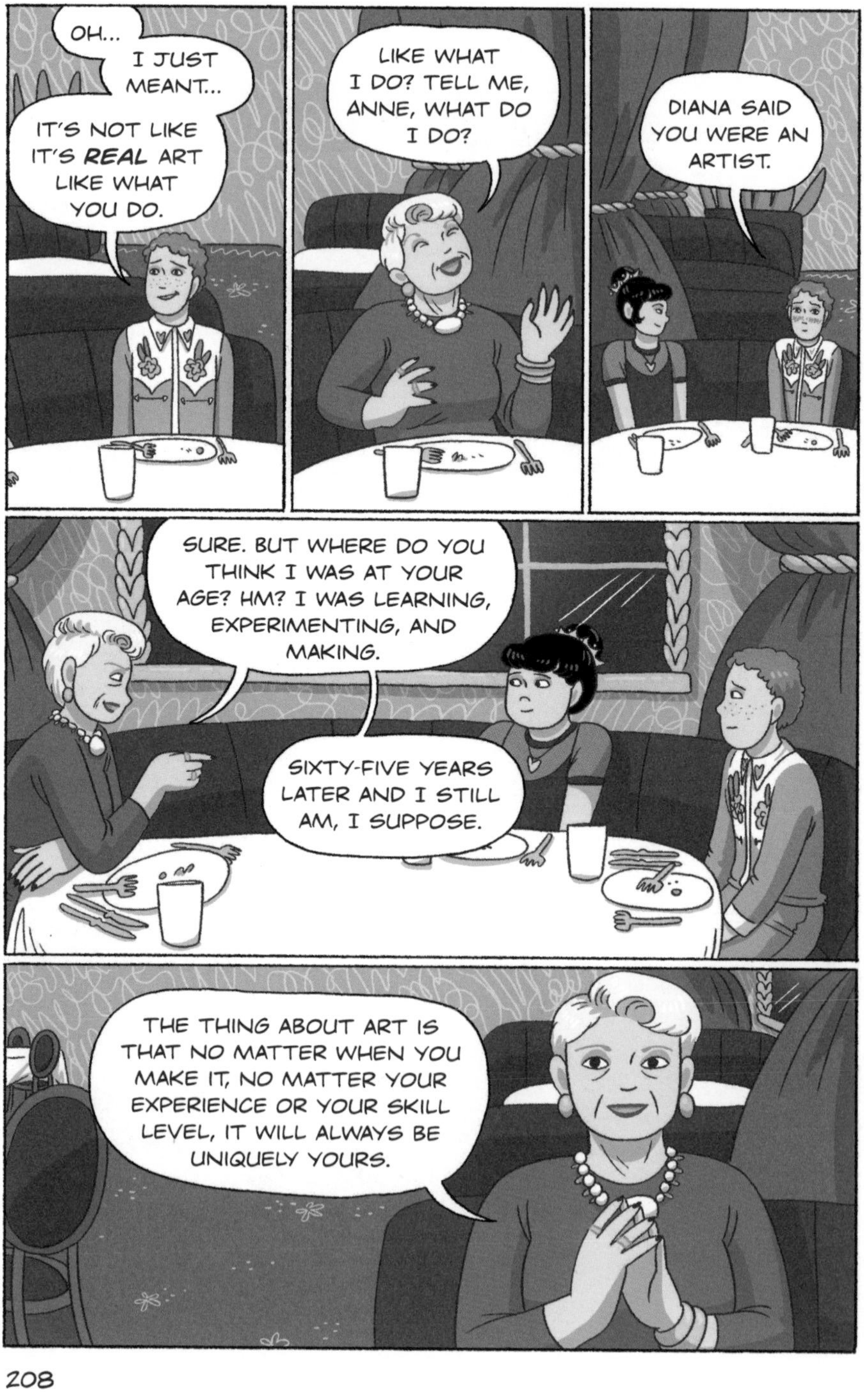
OH...
I JUST MEANT...
IT'S NOT LIKE IT'S ***REAL*** ART LIKE WHAT YOU DO.
LIKE WHAT I DO? TELL ME, ANNE, WHAT DO I DO?
DIANA SAID YOU WERE AN ARTIST.
SURE. BUT WHERE DO YOU THINK I WAS AT YOUR AGE? HM? I WAS LEARNING, EXPERIMENTING, AND MAKING.
SIXTY-FIVE YEARS LATER AND I STILL AM, I SUPPOSE.
THE THING ABOUT ART IS THAT NO MATTER WHEN YOU MAKE IT, NO MATTER YOUR EXPERIENCE OR YOUR SKILL LEVEL, IT WILL ALWAYS BE UNIQUELY YOURS.

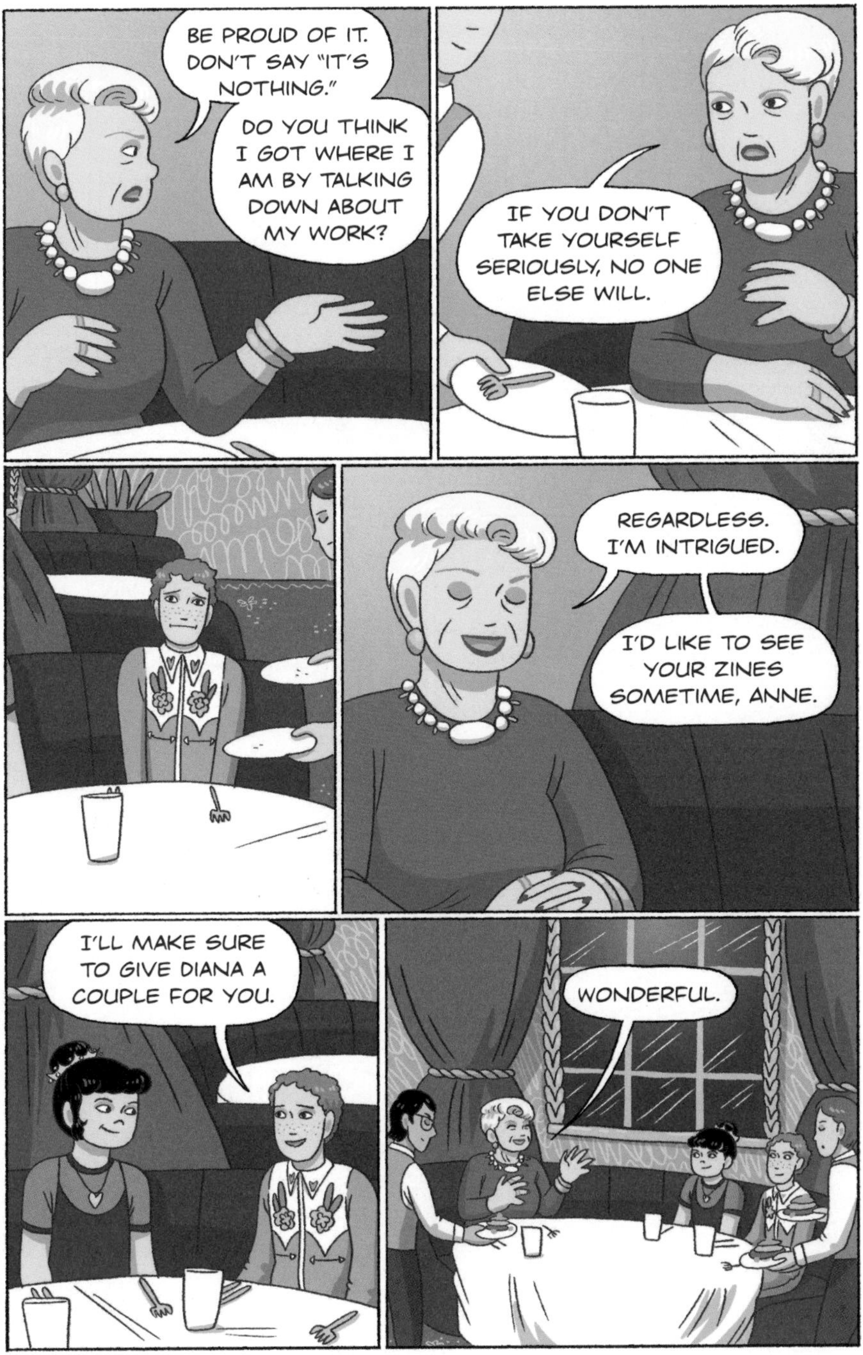
BE PROUD OF IT. DON'T SAY "IT'S NOTHING."
DO YOU THINK I GOT WHERE I AM BY TALKING DOWN ABOUT MY WORK?
IF YOU DON'T TAKE YOURSELF SERIOUSLY, NO ONE ELSE WILL.
REGARDLESS. I'M INTRIGUED.
I'D LIKE TO SEE YOUR ZINES SOMETIME, ANNE.
I'LL MAKE SURE TO GIVE DIANA A COUPLE FOR YOU.
WONDERFUL.

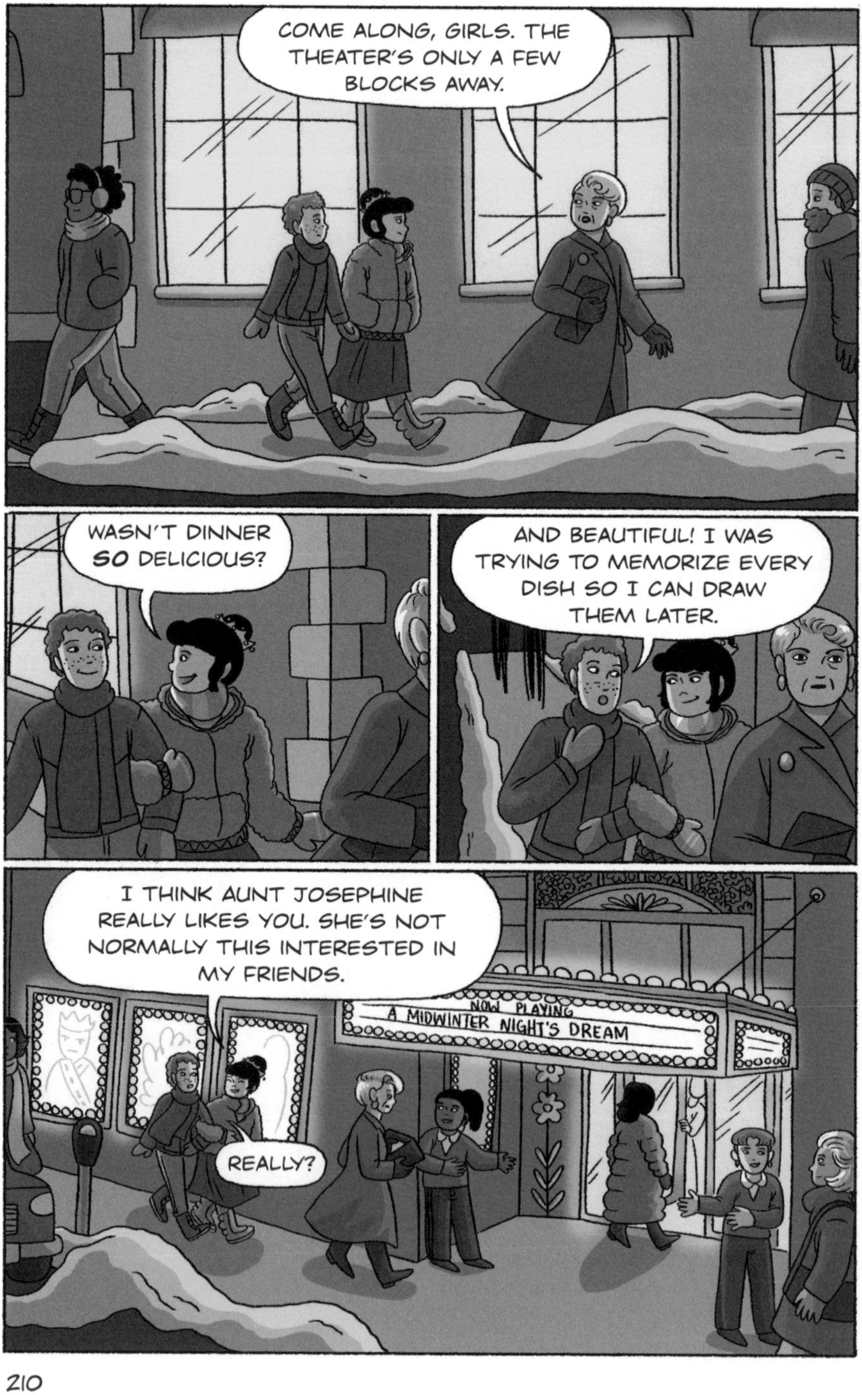
COME ALONG, GIRLS. THE THEATER'S ONLY A FEW BLOCKS AWAY.
WASN'T DINNER **SO** DELICIOUS?
AND BEAUTIFUL! I WAS TRYING TO MEMORIZE EVERY DISH SO I CAN DRAW THEM LATER.
I THINK AUNT JOSEPHINE REALLY LIKES YOU. SHE'S NOT NORMALLY THIS INTERESTED IN MY FRIENDS.
NOW PLAYING
A MIDWINTER NIGHT'S DREAM
REALLY?

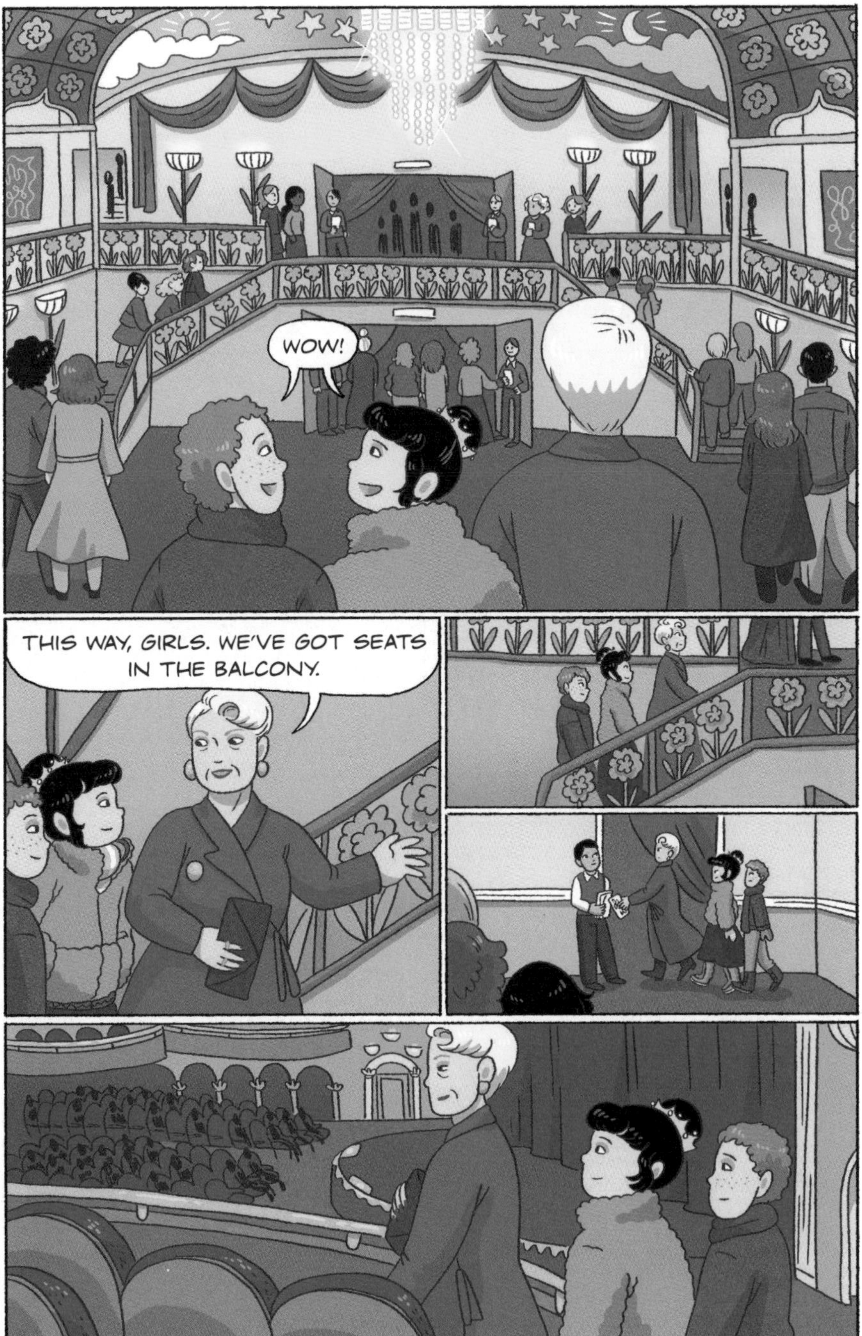
WOW!
THIS WAY, GIRLS. WE'VE GOT SEATS IN THE BALCONY.

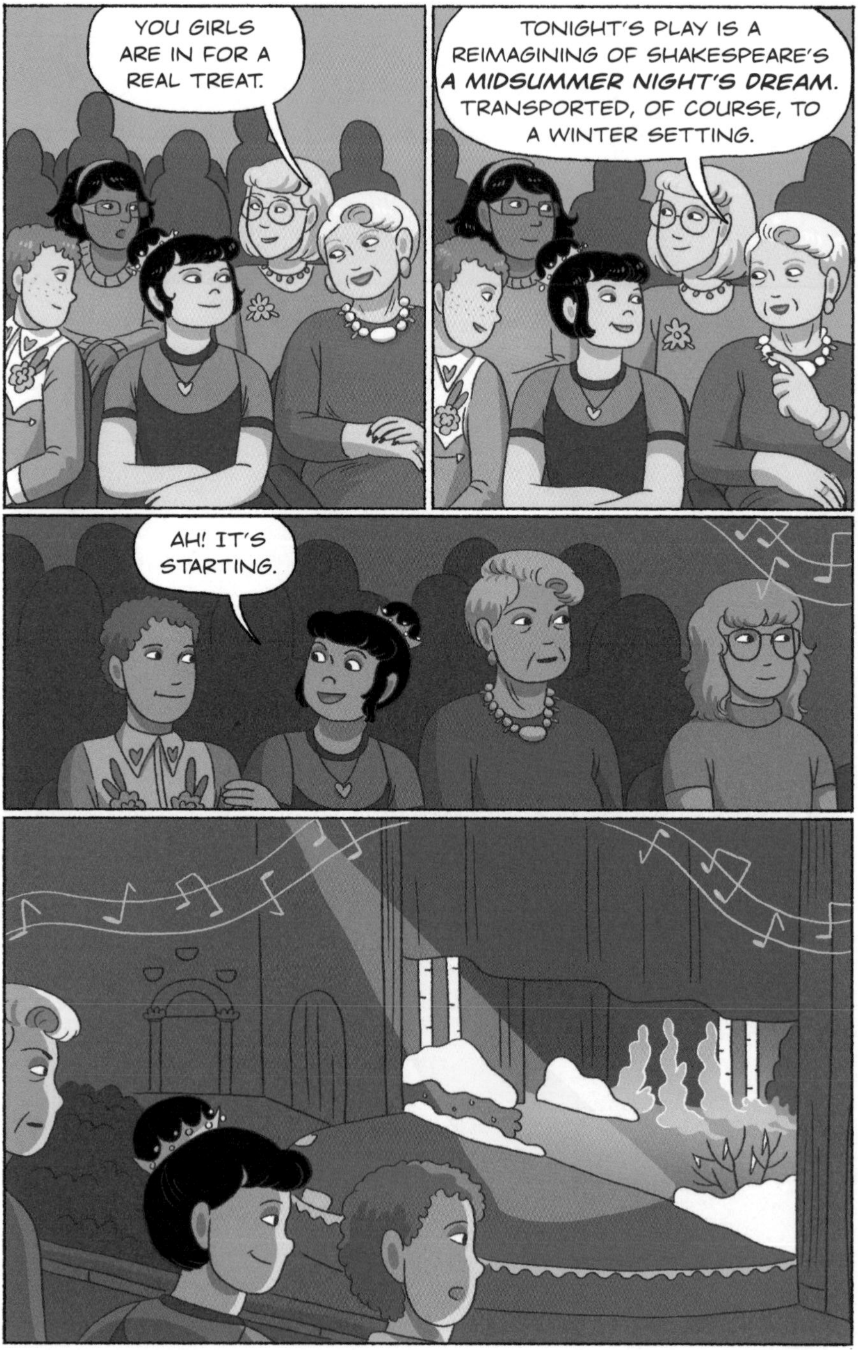
YOU GIRLS ARE IN FOR A REAL TREAT.
TONIGHT'S PLAY IS A REIMAGINING OF SHAKESPEARE'S ***A MIDSUMMER NIGHT'S DREAM***. TRANSPORTED, OF COURSE, TO A WINTER SETTING.
AH! IT'S STARTING.

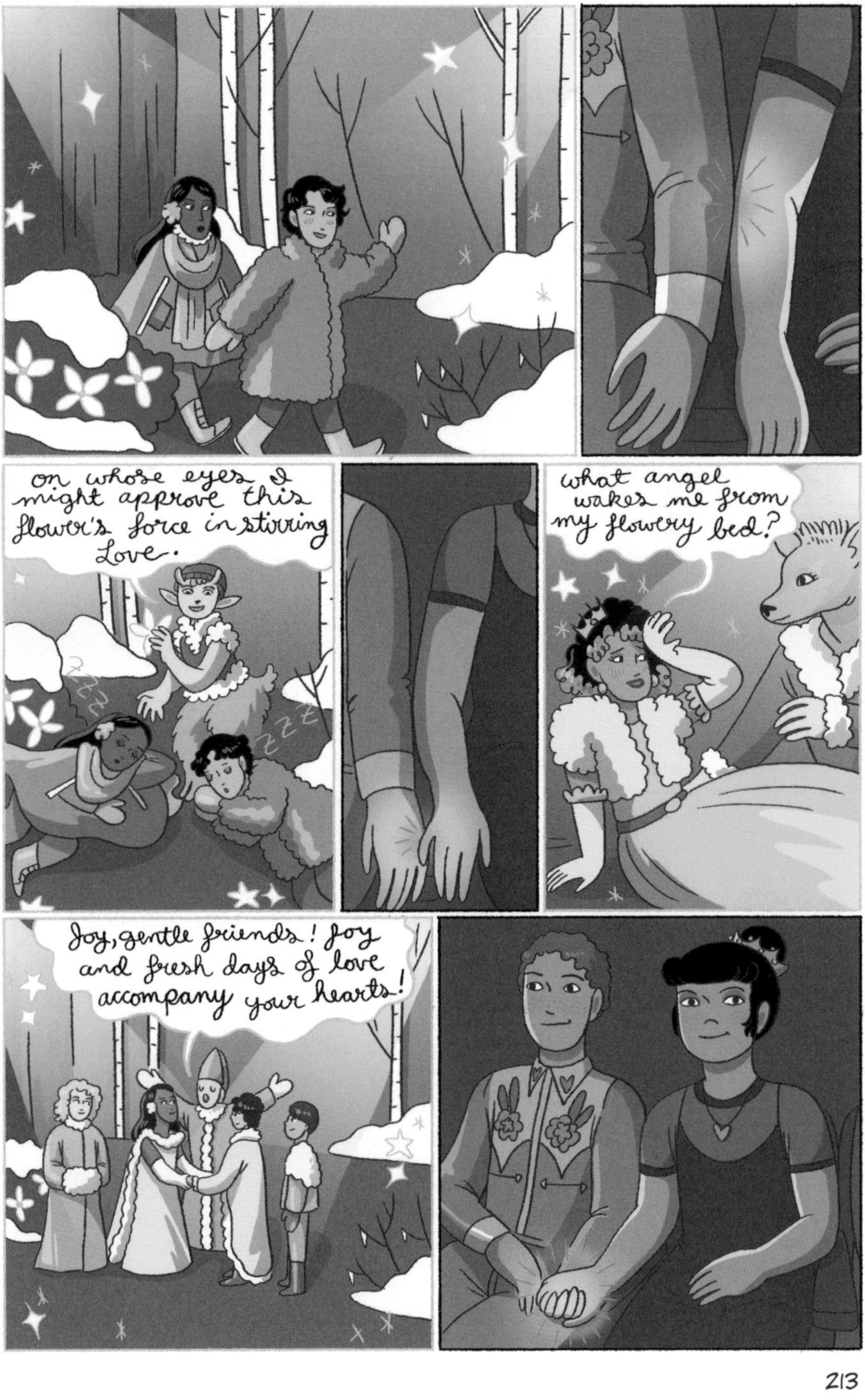
on whose eyes I might approve this flower's force in stirring Love.
what angel wakes me from my flowery bed?
Joy, gentle friends! Joy and fresh days of love accompany your hearts!

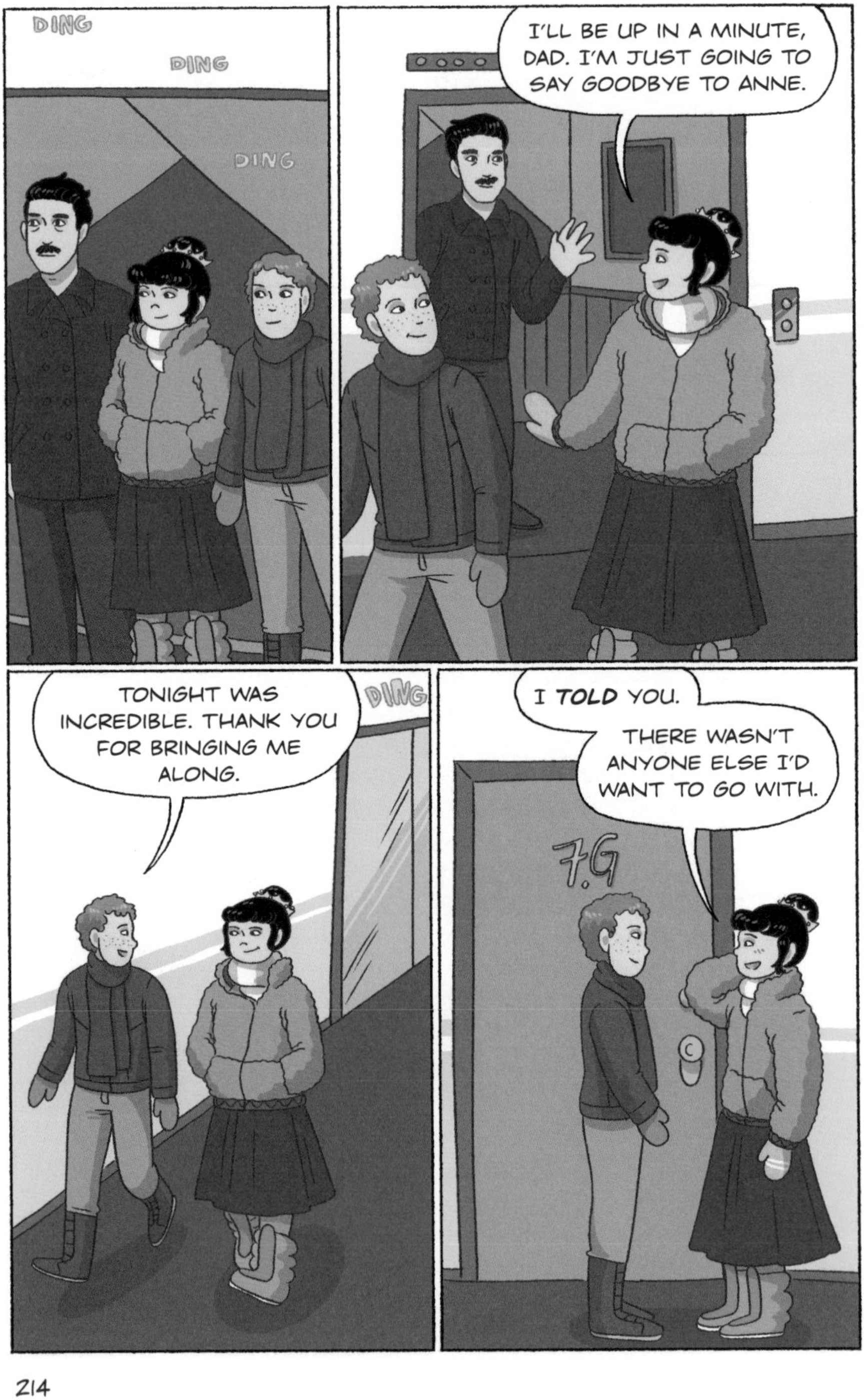
DING
DING
DING
I'LL BE UP IN A MINUTE, DAD. I'M JUST GOING TO SAY GOODBYE TO ANNE.
TONIGHT WAS INCREDIBLE. THANK YOU FOR BRINGING ME ALONG.
DING
I **TOLD** YOU.
THERE WASN'T ANYONE ELSE I'D WANT TO GO WITH.
7G

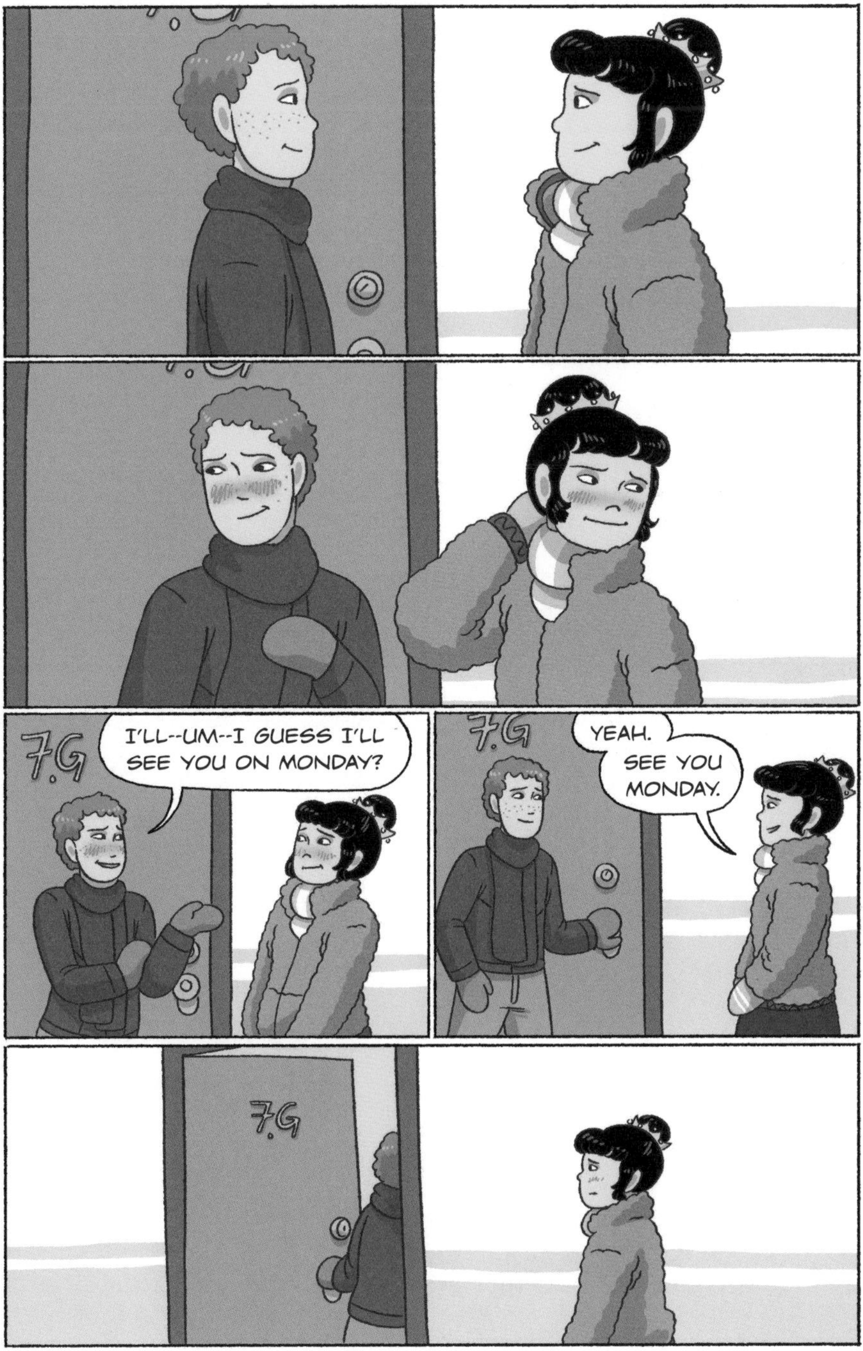
7.G
I'LL--UM--I GUESS I'LL SEE YOU ON MONDAY?
7.G
YEAH.
SEE YOU MONDAY.
7.G

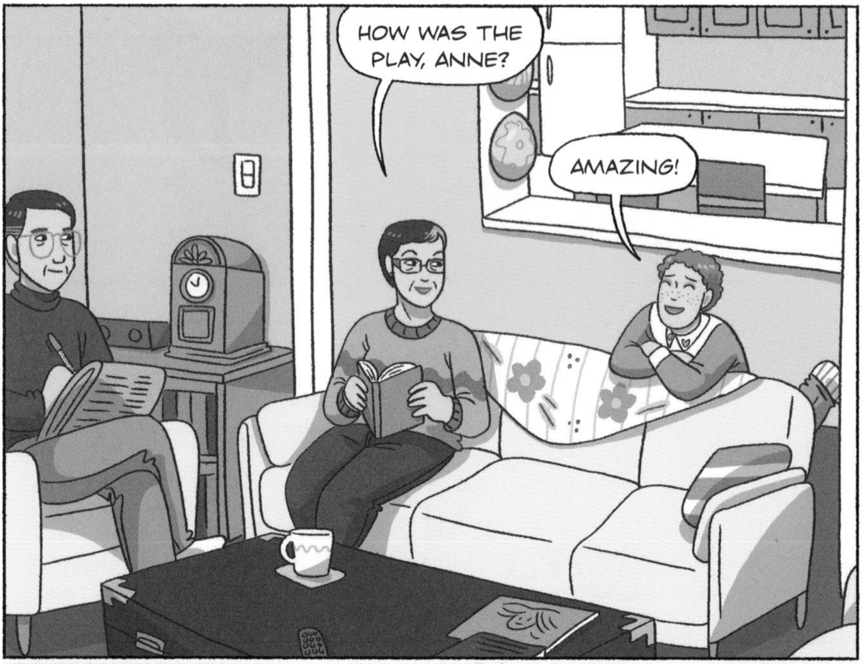
HOW WAS THE PLAY, ANNE?
AMAZING!

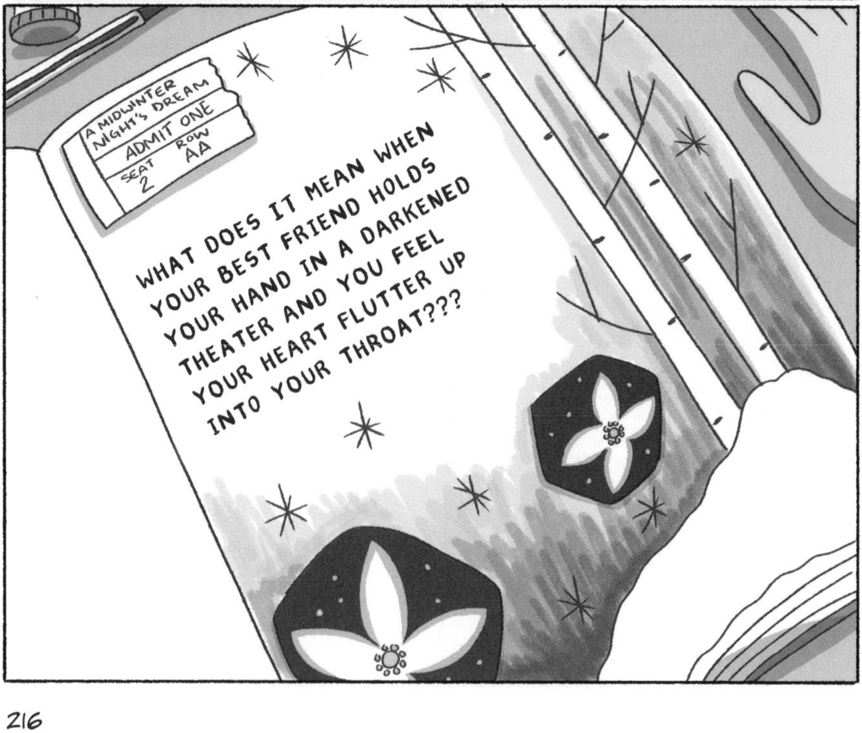
A MIDWINTER NIGHT'S DREAM
ADMIT ONE
ROW AA
SEAT 2
WHAT DOES IT MEAN WHEN YOUR BEST FRIEND HOLDS YOUR HAND IN A DARKENED THEATER AND YOU FEEL YOUR HEART FLUTTER UP INTO YOUR THROAT???

CHAPTER 10

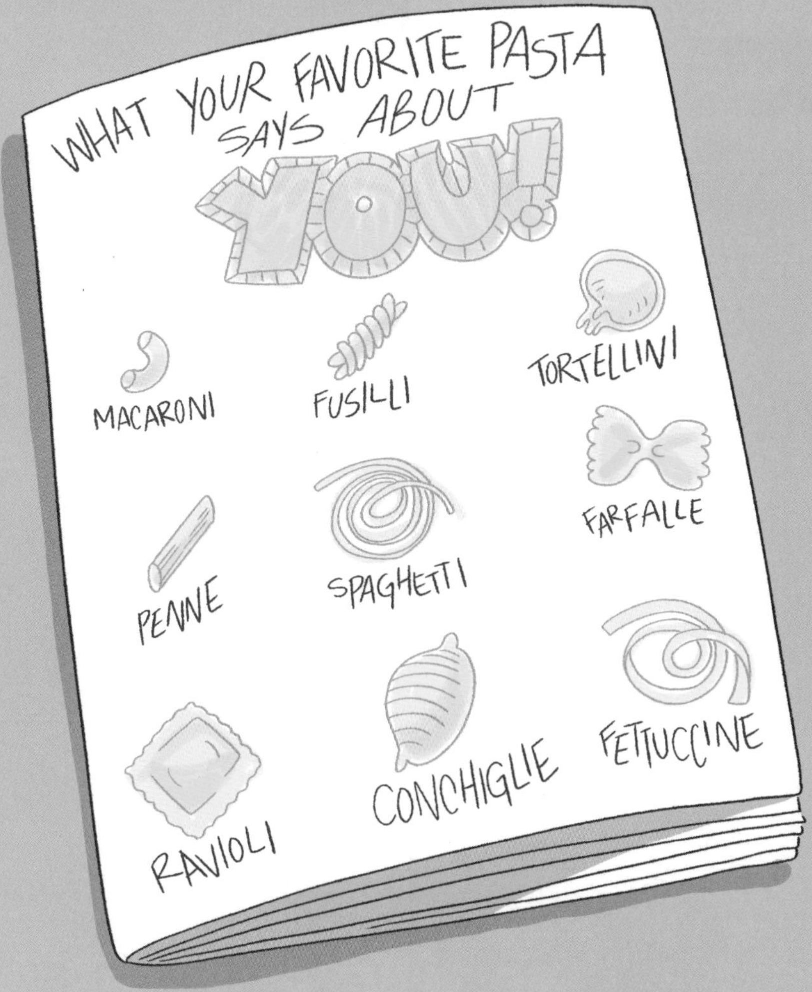
WHAT YOUR FAVORITE PASTA SAYS ABOUT
YOU!
MACARONI
FUSILLI
TORTELLINI
FARFALLE
PENNE
SPAGHETTI
RAVIOLI
CONCHIGLIE
FETTUCCINE

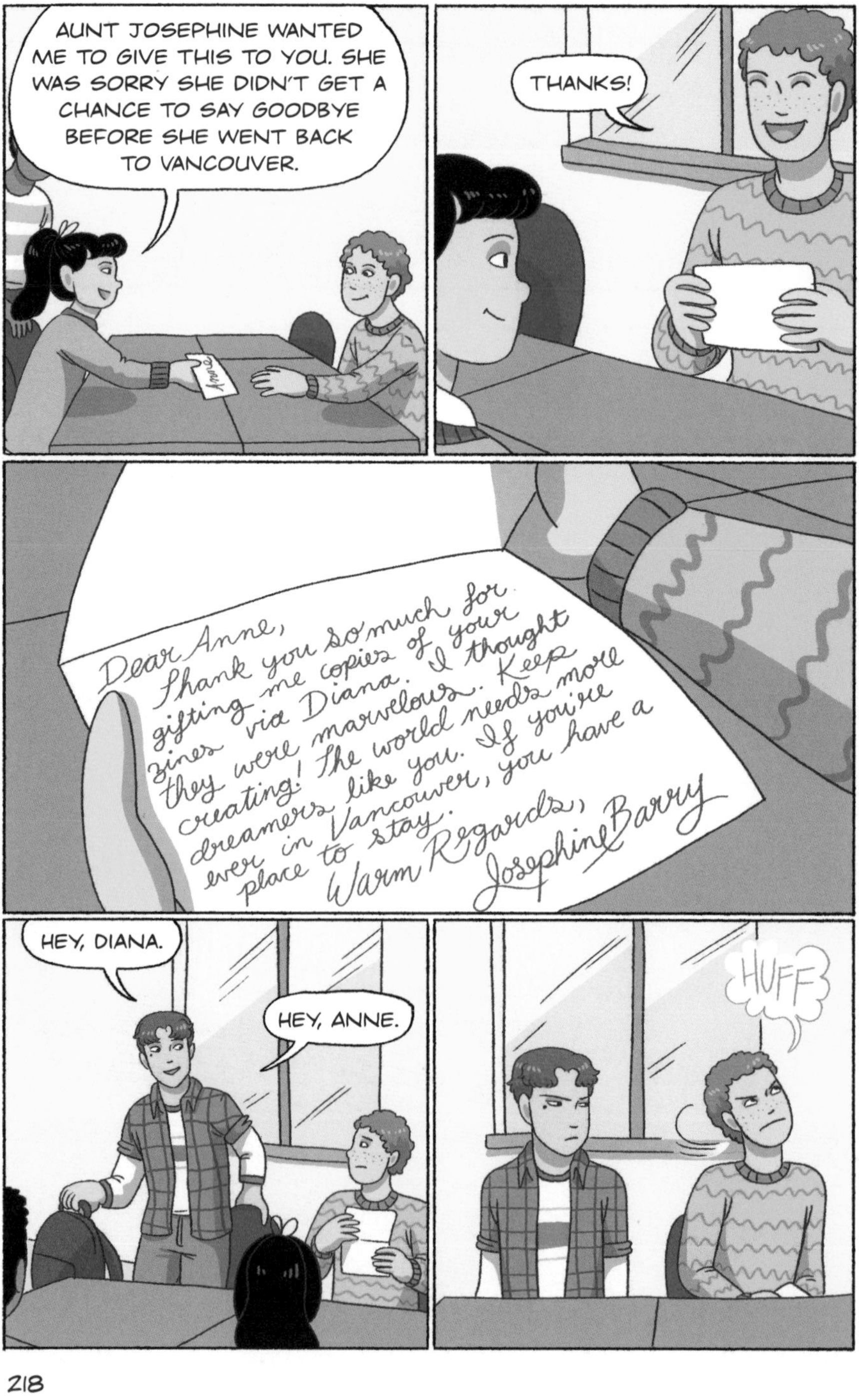
AUNT JOSEPHINE WANTED ME TO GIVE THIS TO YOU. SHE WAS SORRY SHE DIDN'T GET A CHANCE TO SAY GOODBYE BEFORE SHE WENT BACK TO VANCOUVER.
Anne
THANKS!
Dear Anne,
Thank you so much for gifting me copies of your zines via Diana. I thought they were marvelous. Keep creating! The world needs more dreamers like you. If you're ever in Vancouver, you have a place to stay.
Warm Regards,
Josephine Barry
HEY, DIANA.
HEY, ANNE.
HUFF

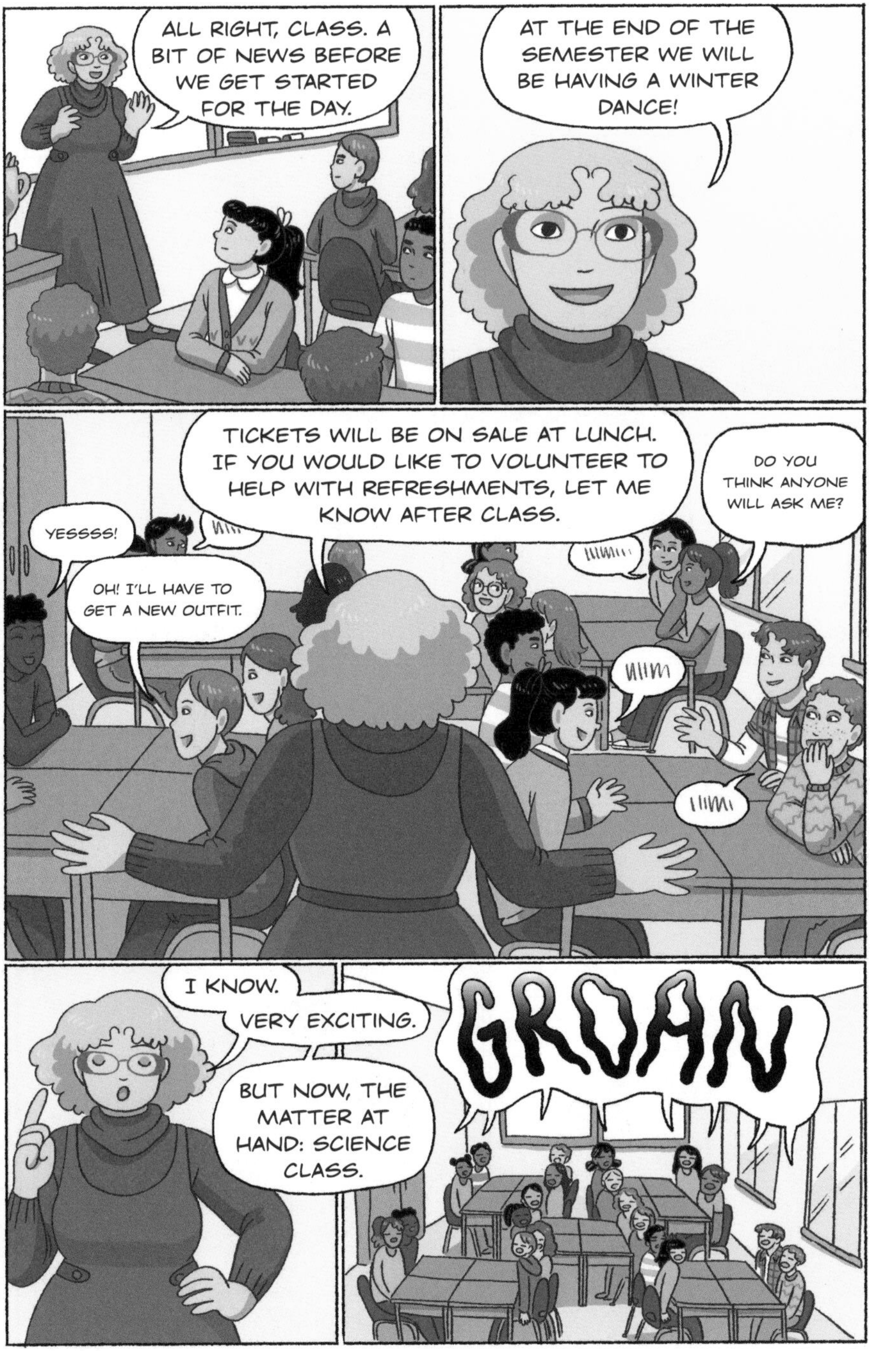
ALL RIGHT, CLASS. A BIT OF NEWS BEFORE WE GET STARTED FOR THE DAY.
AT THE END OF THE SEMESTER WE WILL BE HAVING A WINTER DANCE!
TICKETS WILL BE ON SALE AT LUNCH. IF YOU WOULD LIKE TO VOLUNTEER TO HELP WITH REFRESHMENTS, LET ME KNOW AFTER CLASS.
DO YOU THINK ANYONE WILL ASK ME?
YESSSS!
OH! I'LL HAVE TO GET A NEW OUTFIT.
I KNOW.
VERY EXCITING.
BUT NOW, THE MATTER AT HAND: SCIENCE CLASS.
GROAN

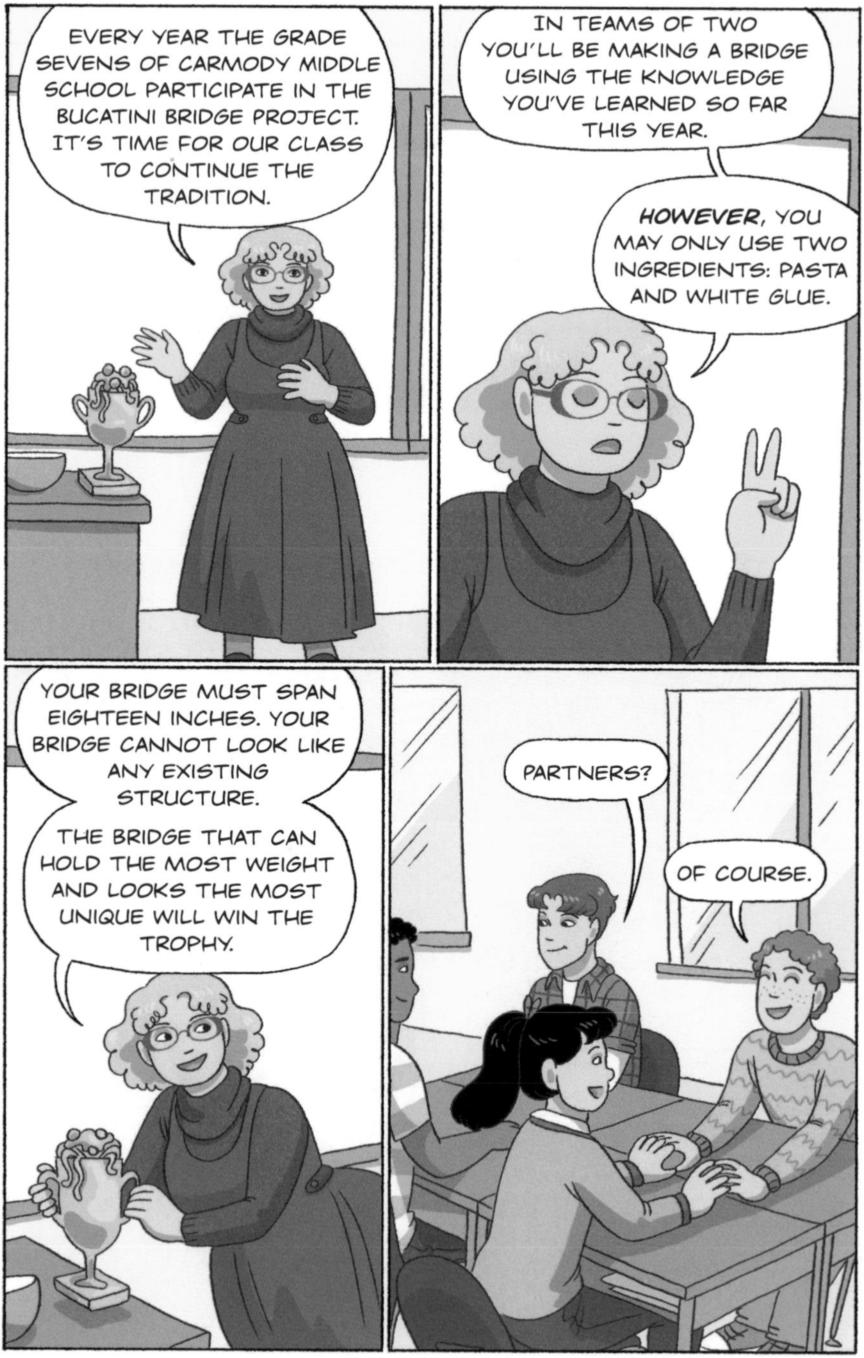
EVERY YEAR THE GRADE SEVENS OF CARMODY MIDDLE SCHOOL PARTICIPATE IN THE BUCATINI BRIDGE PROJECT. IT'S TIME FOR OUR CLASS TO CONTINUE THE TRADITION.
IN TEAMS OF TWO YOU'LL BE MAKING A BRIDGE USING THE KNOWLEDGE YOU'VE LEARNED SO FAR THIS YEAR.
HOWEVER, YOU MAY ONLY USE TWO INGREDIENTS: PASTA AND WHITE GLUE.
YOUR BRIDGE MUST SPAN EIGHTEEN INCHES. YOUR BRIDGE CANNOT LOOK LIKE ANY EXISTING STRUCTURE.
THE BRIDGE THAT CAN HOLD THE MOST WEIGHT AND LOOKS THE MOST UNIQUE WILL WIN THE TROPHY.
PARTNERS?
OF COURSE.

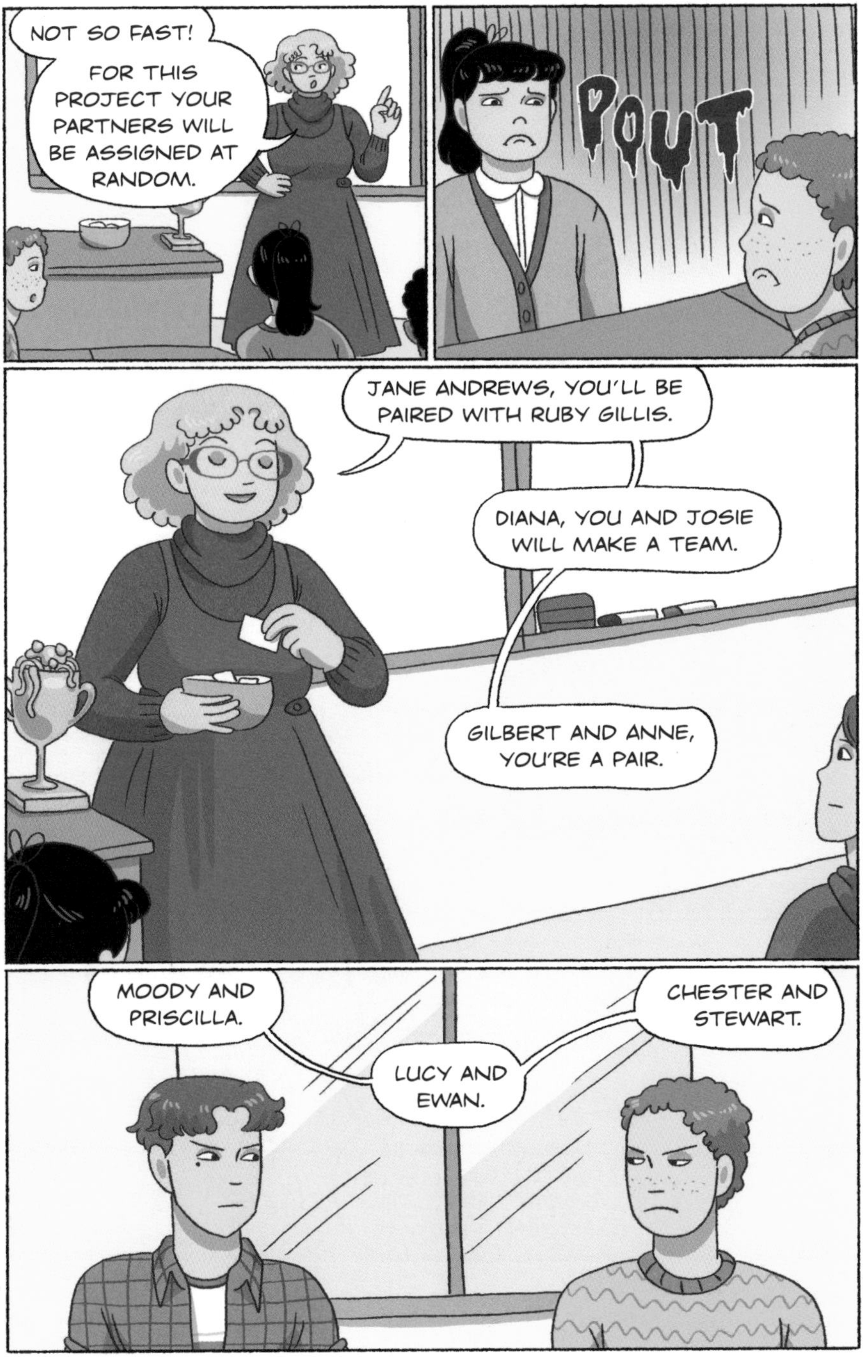
NOT SO FAST!
FOR THIS PROJECT YOUR PARTNERS WILL BE ASSIGNED AT RANDOM.
POUT
JANE ANDREWS, YOU'LL BE PAIRED WITH RUBY GILLIS.
DIANA, YOU AND JOSIE WILL MAKE A TEAM.
GILBERT AND ANNE, YOU'RE A PAIR.
MOODY AND PRISCILLA.
LUCY AND EWAN.
CHESTER AND STEWART.

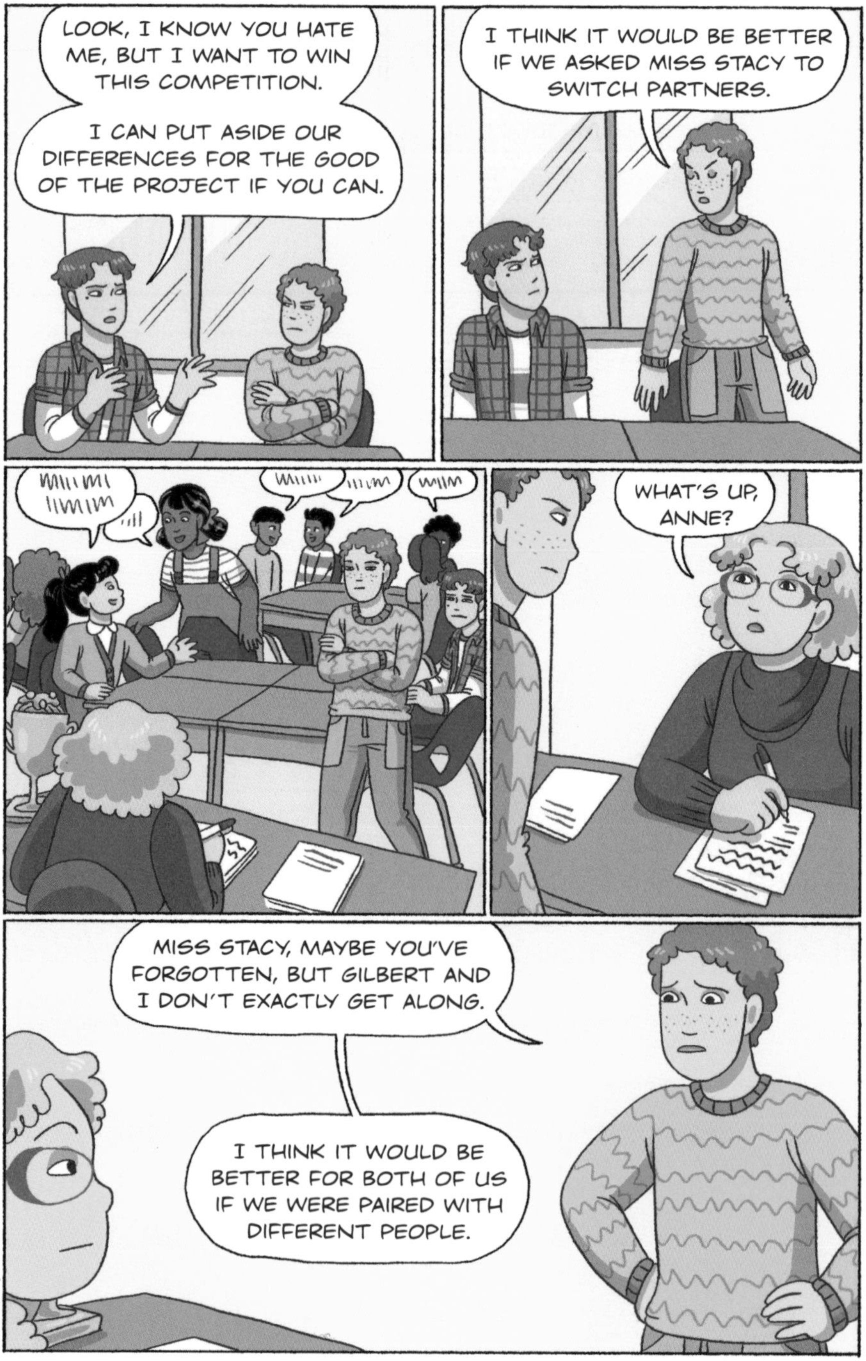
LOOK, I KNOW YOU HATE ME, BUT I WANT TO WIN THIS COMPETITION.
I CAN PUT ASIDE OUR DIFFERENCES FOR THE GOOD OF THE PROJECT IF YOU CAN.
I THINK IT WOULD BE BETTER IF WE ASKED MISS STACY TO SWITCH PARTNERS.
WHAT'S UP, ANNE?
MISS STACY, MAYBE YOU'VE FORGOTTEN, BUT GILBERT AND I DON'T EXACTLY GET ALONG.
I THINK IT WOULD BE BETTER FOR BOTH OF US IF WE WERE PAIRED WITH DIFFERENT PEOPLE.

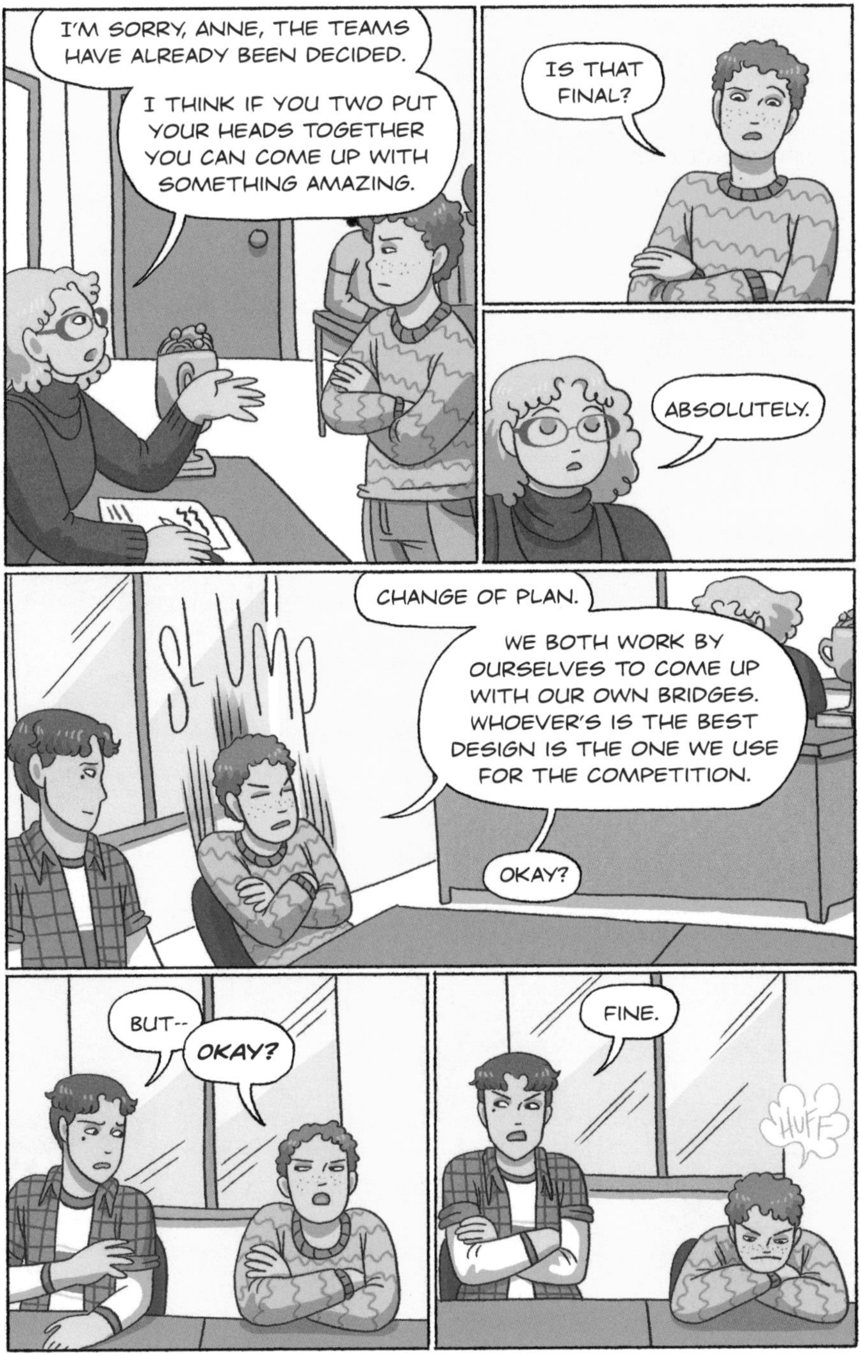
I'M SORRY, ANNE, THE TEAMS HAVE ALREADY BEEN DECIDED.
I THINK IF YOU TWO PUT YOUR HEADS TOGETHER YOU CAN COME UP WITH SOMETHING AMAZING.
IS THAT FINAL?
ABSOLUTELY.
SLUMP
CHANGE OF PLAN.
WE BOTH WORK BY OURSELVES TO COME UP WITH OUR OWN BRIDGES. WHOEVER'S IS THE BEST DESIGN IS THE ONE WE USE FOR THE COMPETITION.
OKAY?
BUT--
OKAY?
FINE.
HUFF

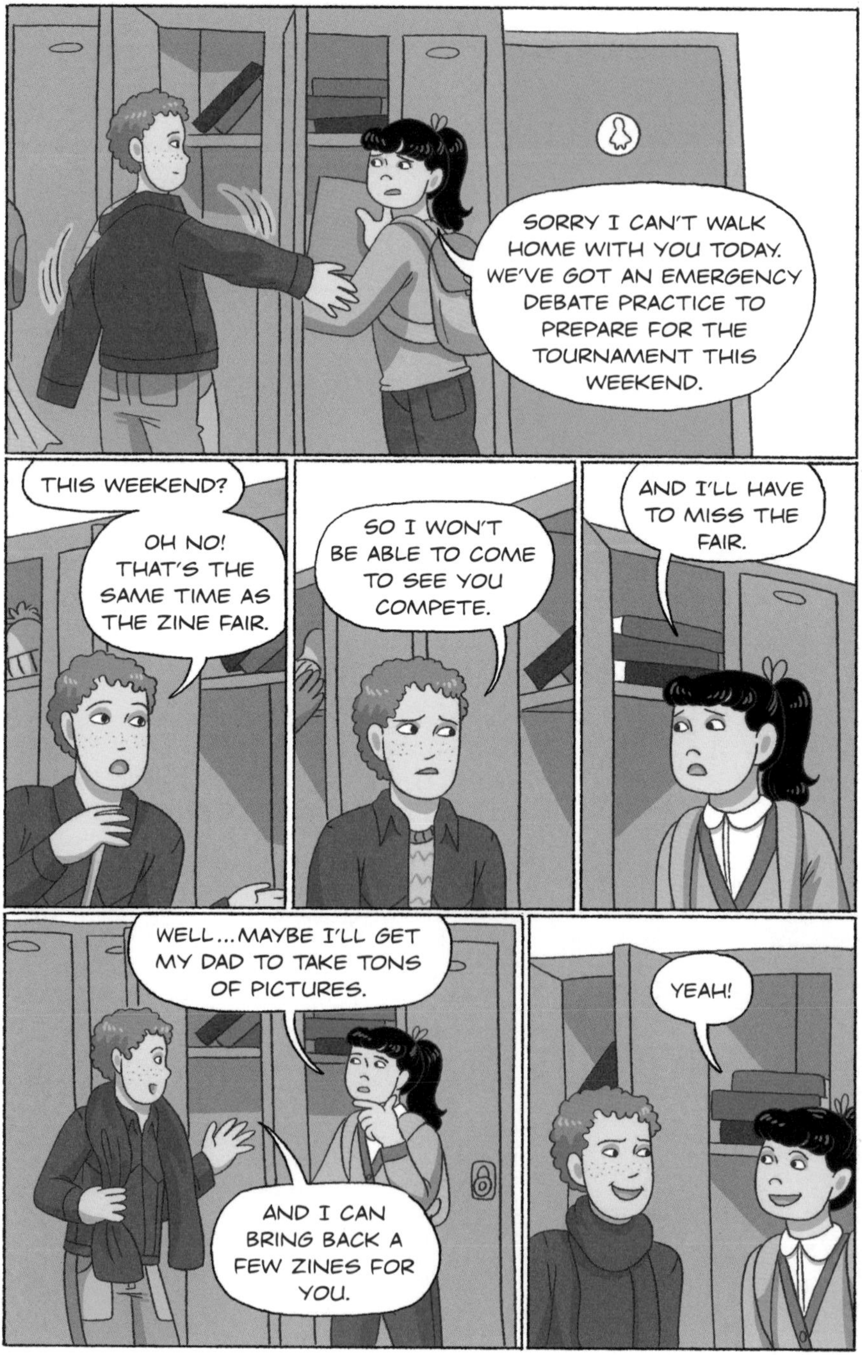

SORRY I CAN'T WALK HOME WITH YOU TODAY. WE'VE GOT AN EMERGENCY DEBATE PRACTICE TO PREPARE FOR THE TOURNAMENT THIS WEEKEND.
THIS WEEKEND?
OH NO! THAT'S THE SAME TIME AS THE ZINE FAIR.
SO I WON'T BE ABLE TO COME TO SEE YOU COMPETE.
AND I'LL HAVE TO MISS THE FAIR.
WELL...MAYBE I'LL GET MY DAD TO TAKE TONS OF PICTURES.
AND I CAN BRING BACK A FEW ZINES FOR YOU.
YEAH!

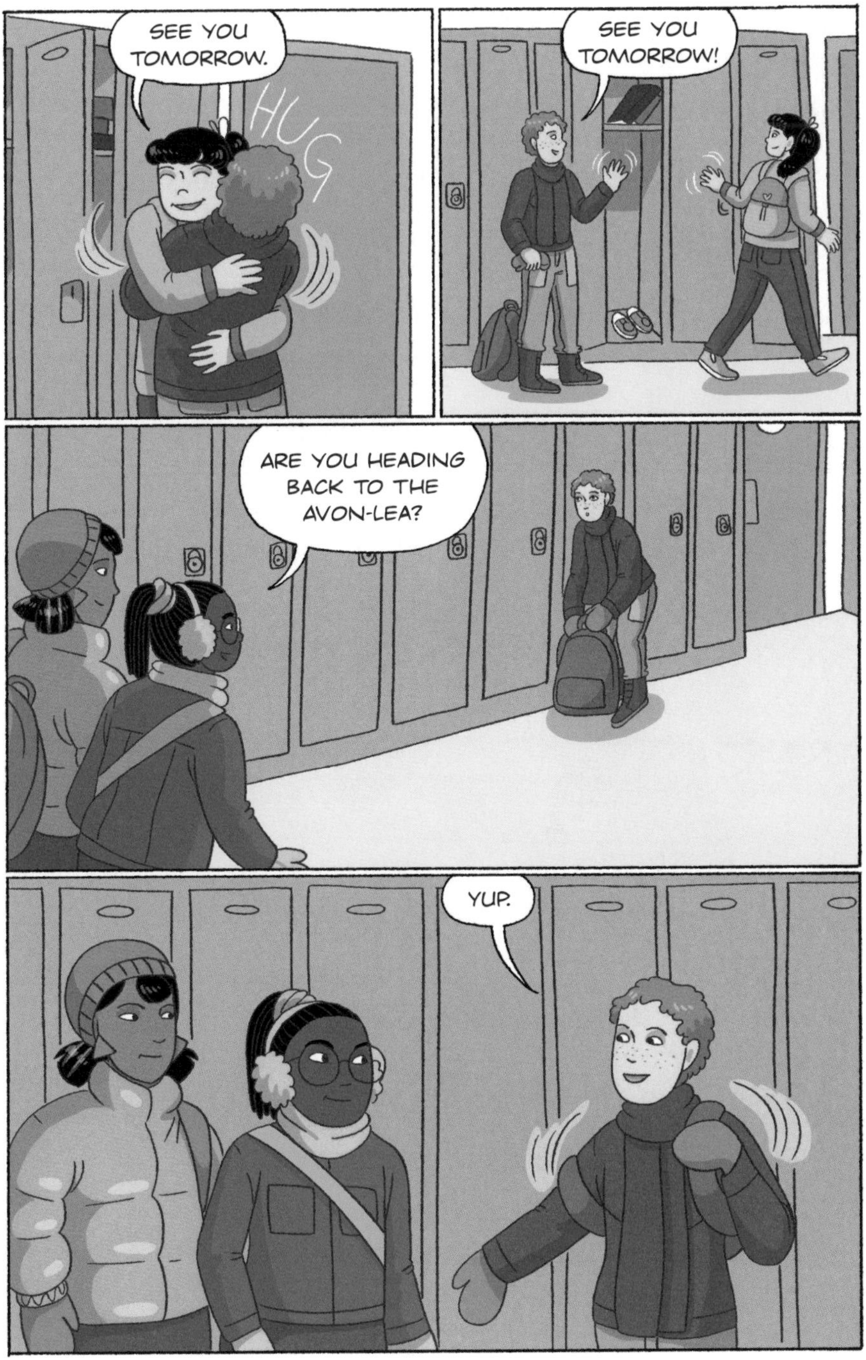
SEE YOU TOMORROW.
HUG
SEE YOU TOMORROW!
ARE YOU HEADING BACK TO THE AVON-LEA?
YUP.

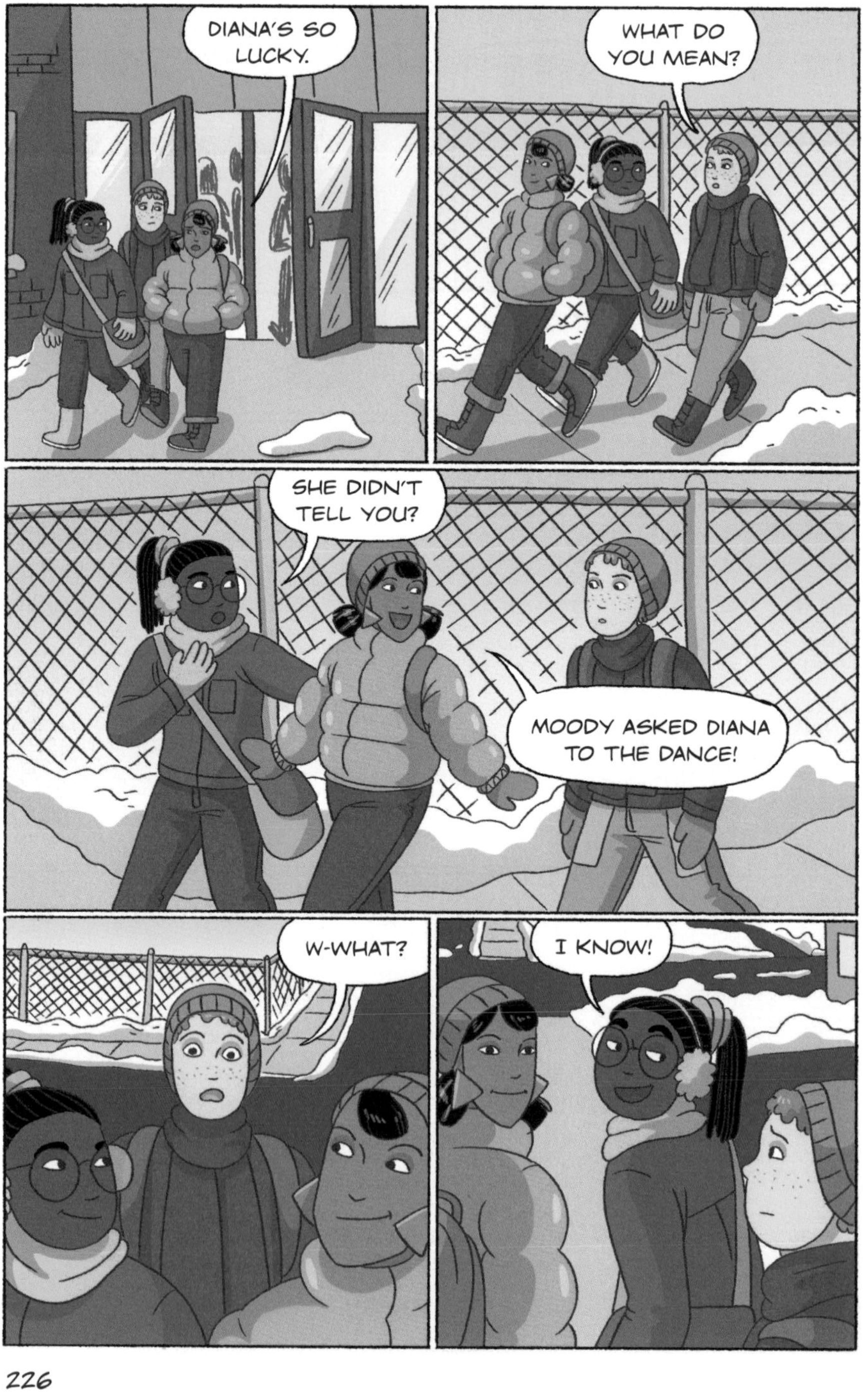
DIANA'S SO LUCKY.
WHAT DO YOU MEAN?
SHE DIDN'T TELL YOU?
MOODY ASKED DIANA TO THE DANCE!
W-WHAT?
I KNOW!

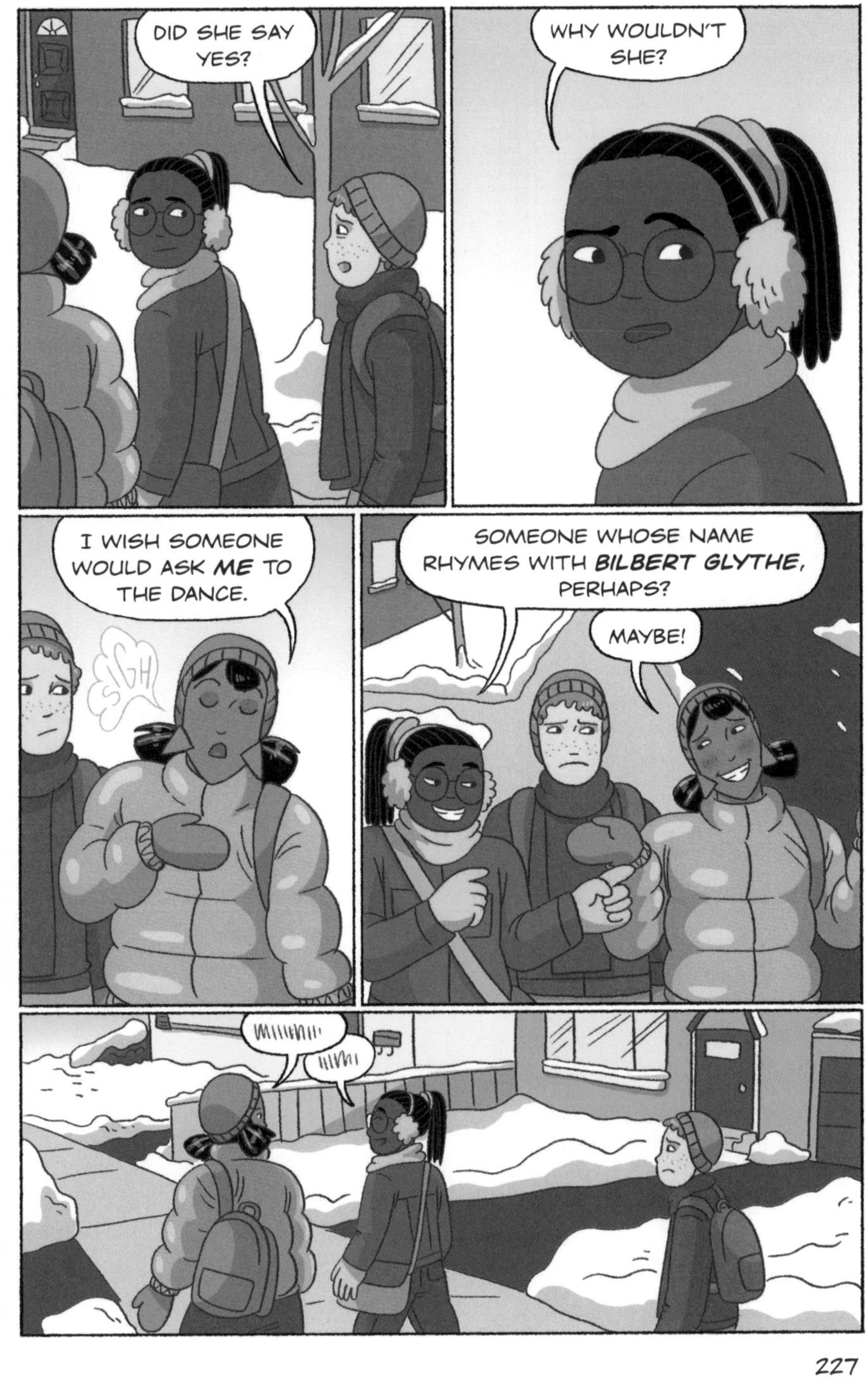
DID SHE SAY YES?
WHY WOULDN'T SHE?
I WISH SOMEONE WOULD ASK ME TO THE DANCE.
SIGH
SOMEONE WHOSE NAME RHYMES WITH BILBERT GLYTHE, PERHAPS?
MAYBE!

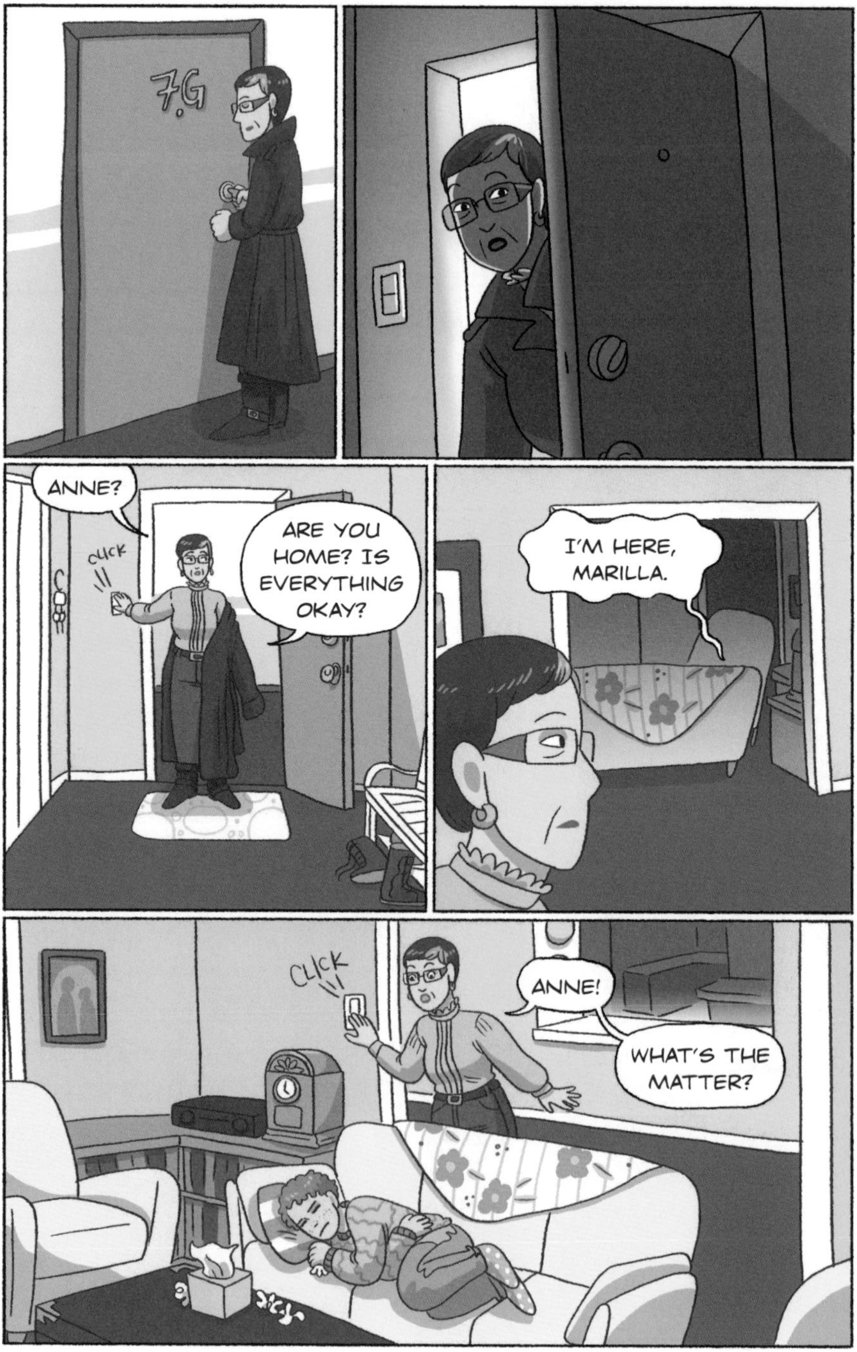
7G
ANNE?
CLICK
ARE YOU HOME? IS EVERYTHING OKAY?
I'M HERE, MARILLA.
CLICK
ANNE!
WHAT'S THE MATTER?

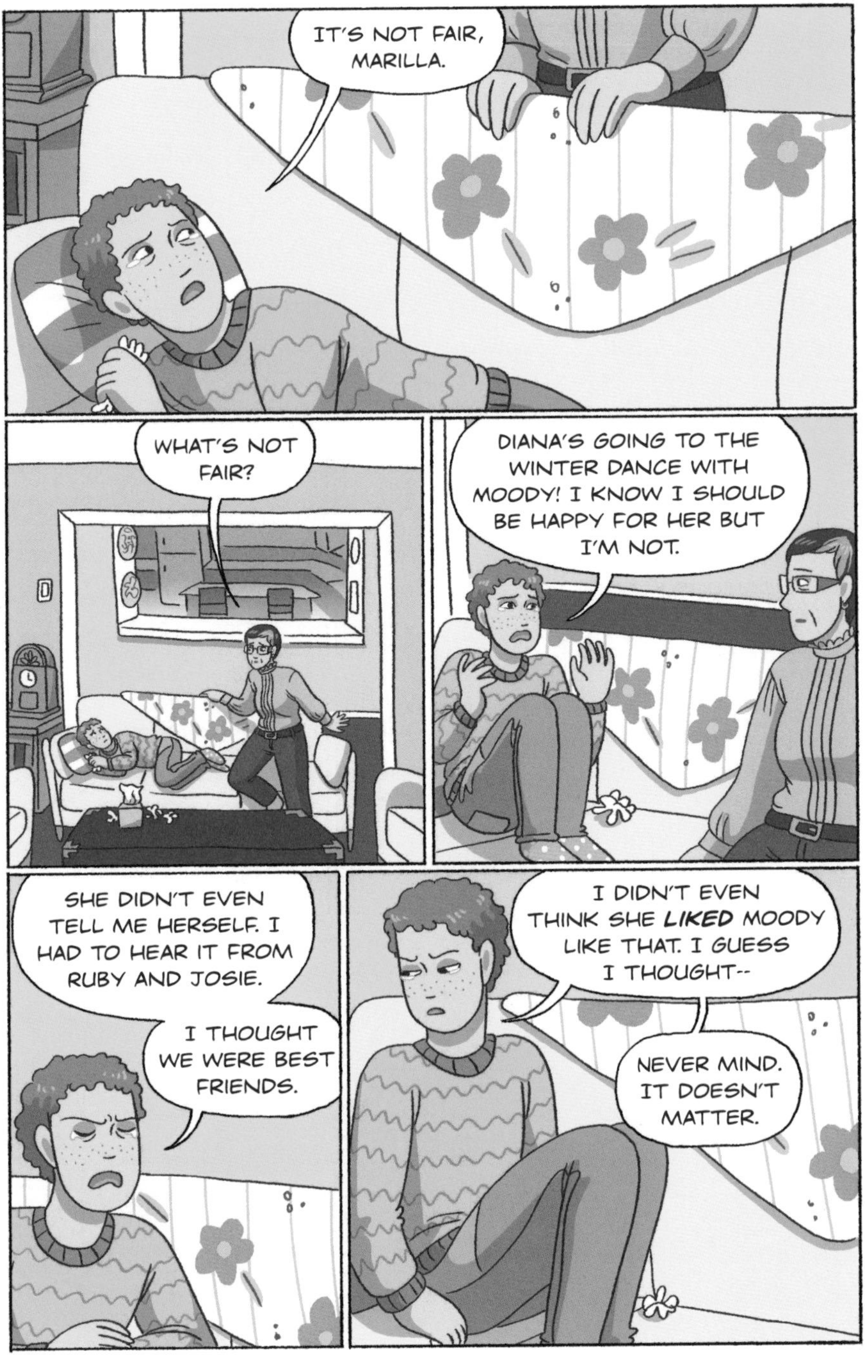
IT'S NOT FAIR, MARILLA.
WHAT'S NOT FAIR?
DIANA'S GOING TO THE WINTER DANCE WITH MOODY! I KNOW I SHOULD BE HAPPY FOR HER BUT I'M NOT.
SHE DIDN'T EVEN TELL ME HERSELF. I HAD TO HEAR IT FROM RUBY AND JOSIE.
I THOUGHT WE WERE BEST FRIENDS.
I DIDN'T EVEN THINK SHE ***LIKED*** MOODY LIKE THAT. I GUESS I THOUGHT--
NEVER MIND. IT DOESN'T MATTER.

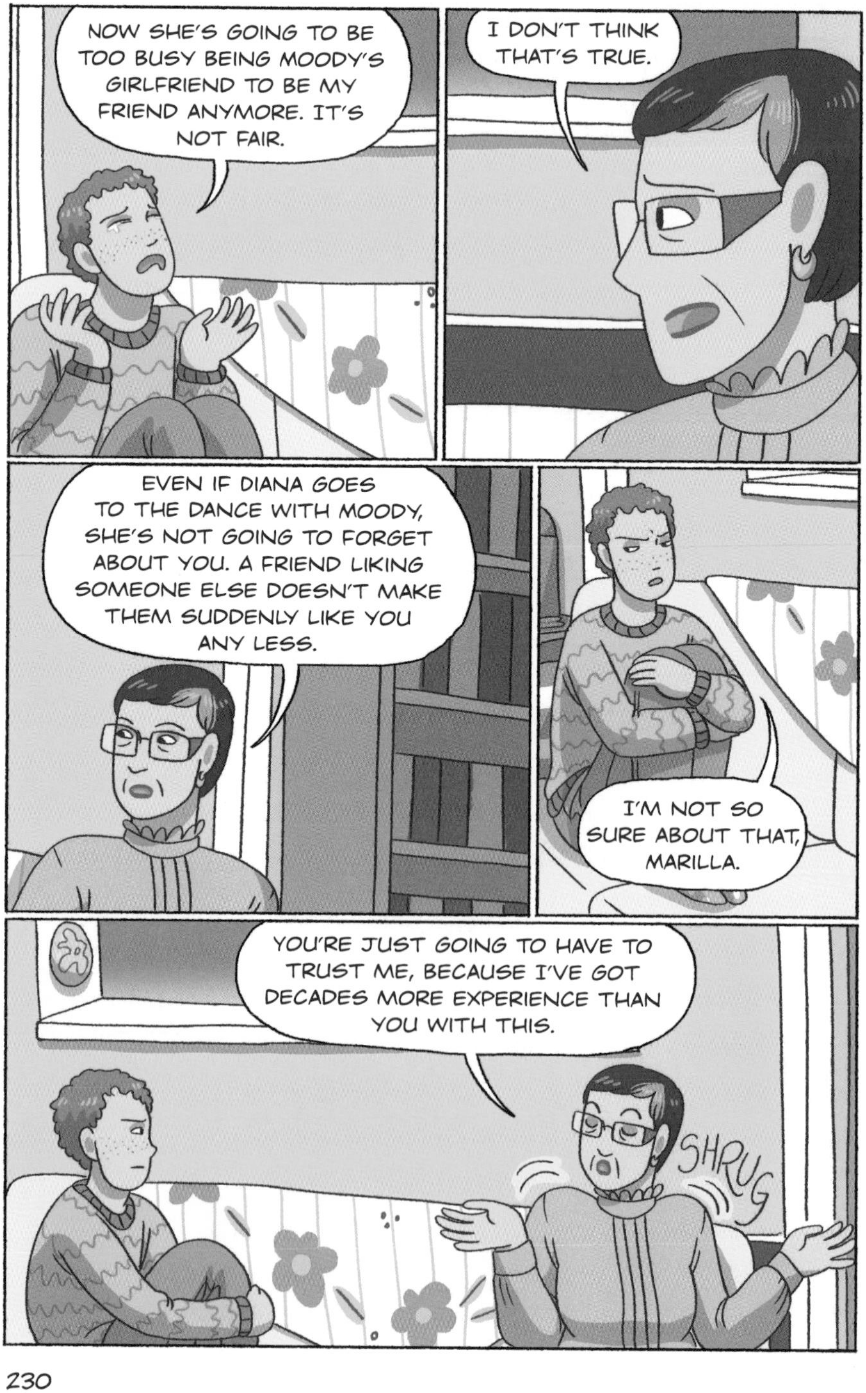
NOW SHE'S GOING TO BE TOO BUSY BEING MOODY'S GIRLFRIEND TO BE MY FRIEND ANYMORE. IT'S NOT FAIR.
I DON'T THINK THAT'S TRUE.
EVEN IF DIANA GOES TO THE DANCE WITH MOODY, SHE'S NOT GOING TO FORGET ABOUT YOU. A FRIEND LIKING SOMEONE ELSE DOESN'T MAKE THEM SUDDENLY LIKE YOU ANY LESS.
I'M NOT SO SURE ABOUT THAT, MARILLA.
YOU'RE JUST GOING TO HAVE TO TRUST ME, BECAUSE I'VE GOT DECADES MORE EXPERIENCE THAN YOU WITH THIS.
SHRUG

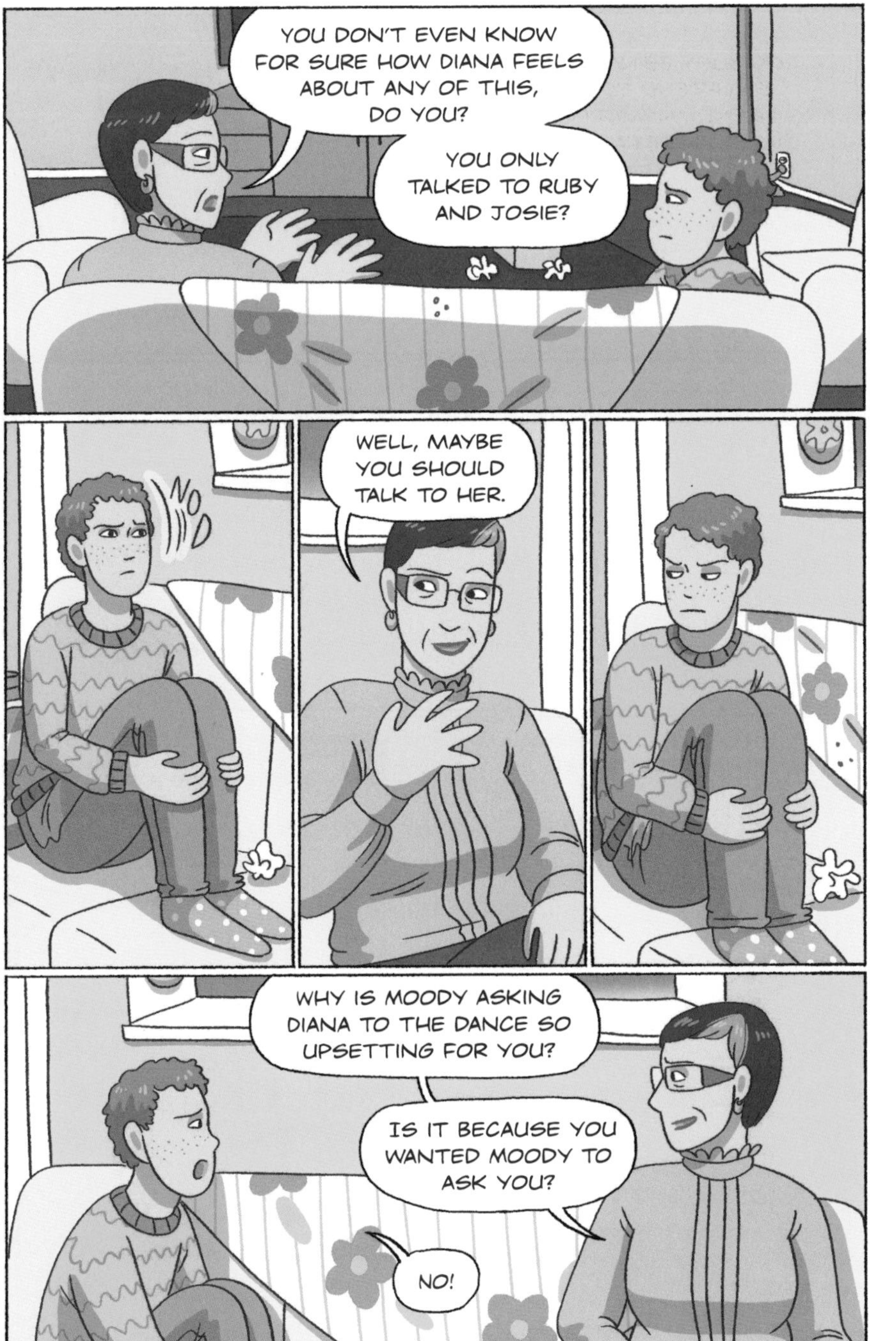
YOU DON'T EVEN KNOW FOR SURE HOW DIANA FEELS ABOUT ANY OF THIS, DO YOU?
YOU ONLY TALKED TO RUBY AND JOSIE?
NOD
WELL, MAYBE YOU SHOULD TALK TO HER.
WHY IS MOODY ASKING DIANA TO THE DANCE SO UPSETTING FOR YOU?
IS IT BECAUSE YOU WANTED MOODY TO ASK YOU?
NO!

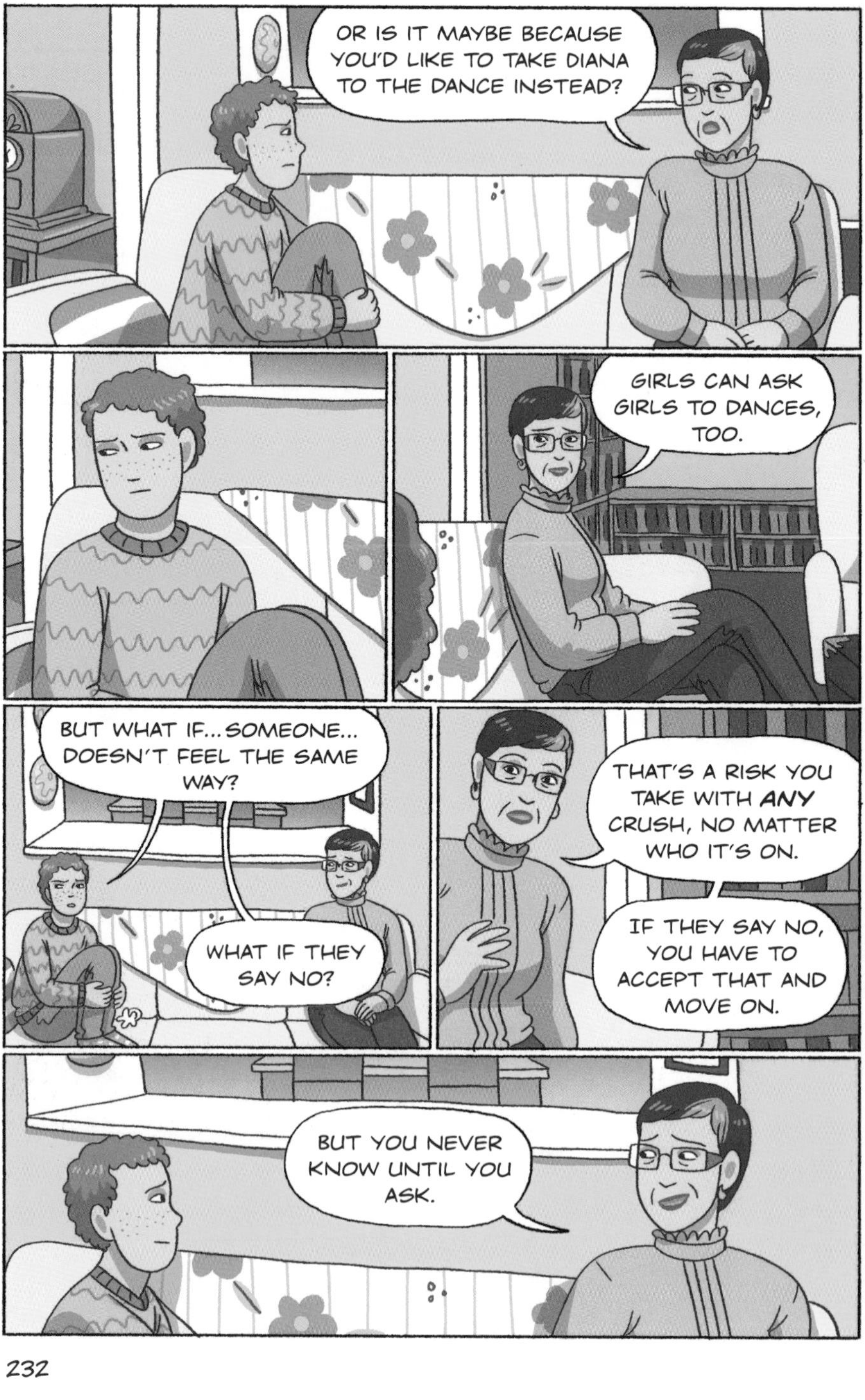
OR IS IT MAYBE BECAUSE YOU'D LIKE TO TAKE DIANA TO THE DANCE INSTEAD?
GIRLS CAN ASK GIRLS TO DANCES, TOO.
BUT WHAT IF... SOMEONE... DOESN'T FEEL THE SAME WAY?
WHAT IF THEY SAY NO?
THAT'S A RISK YOU TAKE WITH ANY CRUSH, NO MATTER WHO IT'S ON.
IF THEY SAY NO, YOU HAVE TO ACCEPT THAT AND MOVE ON.
BUT YOU NEVER KNOW UNTIL YOU ASK.

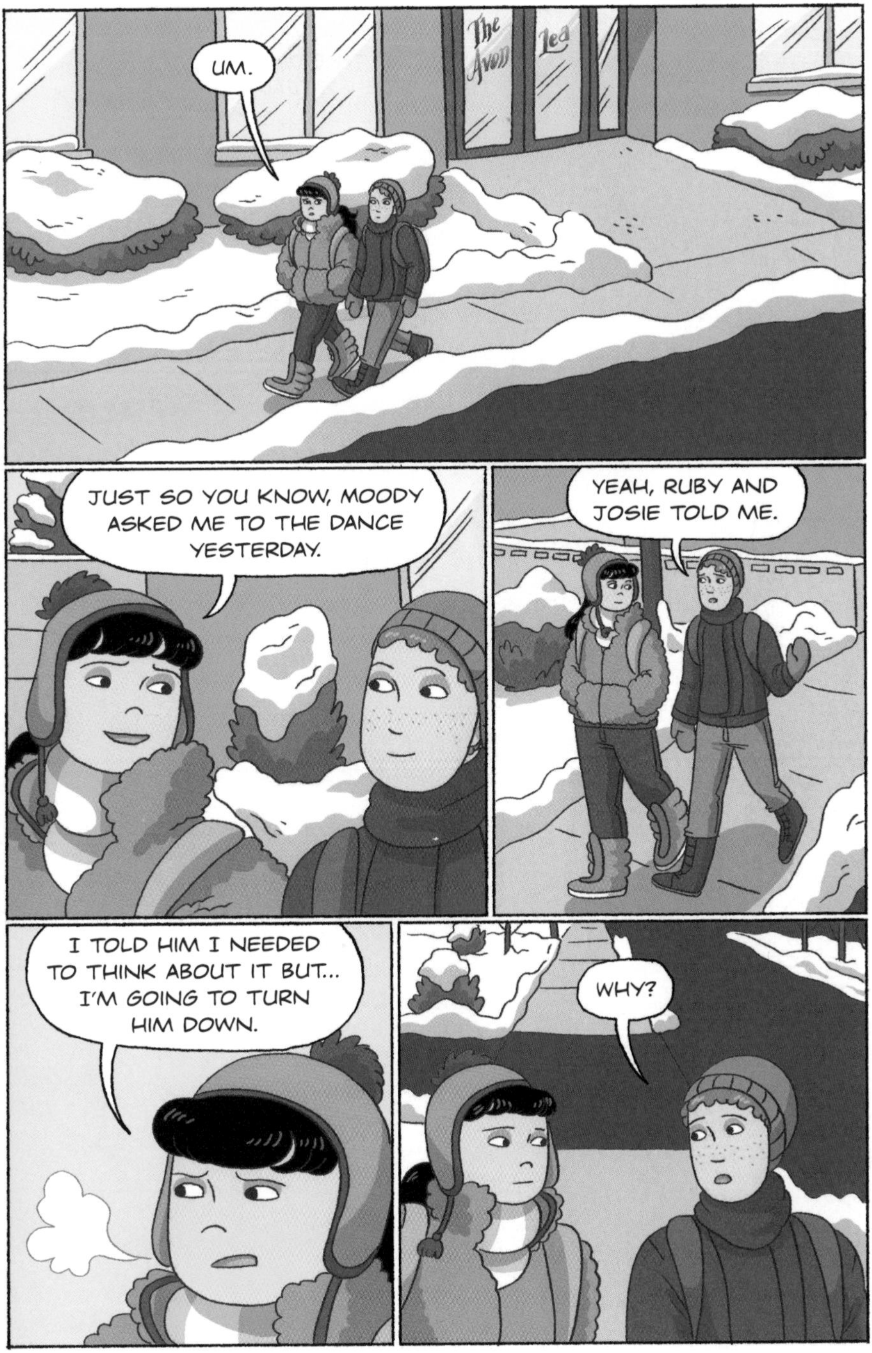
The Avon Lea
UM.
JUST SO YOU KNOW, MOODY ASKED ME TO THE DANCE YESTERDAY.
YEAH, RUBY AND JOSIE TOLD ME.
I TOLD HIM I NEEDED TO THINK ABOUT IT BUT... I'M GOING TO TURN HIM DOWN.
WHY?

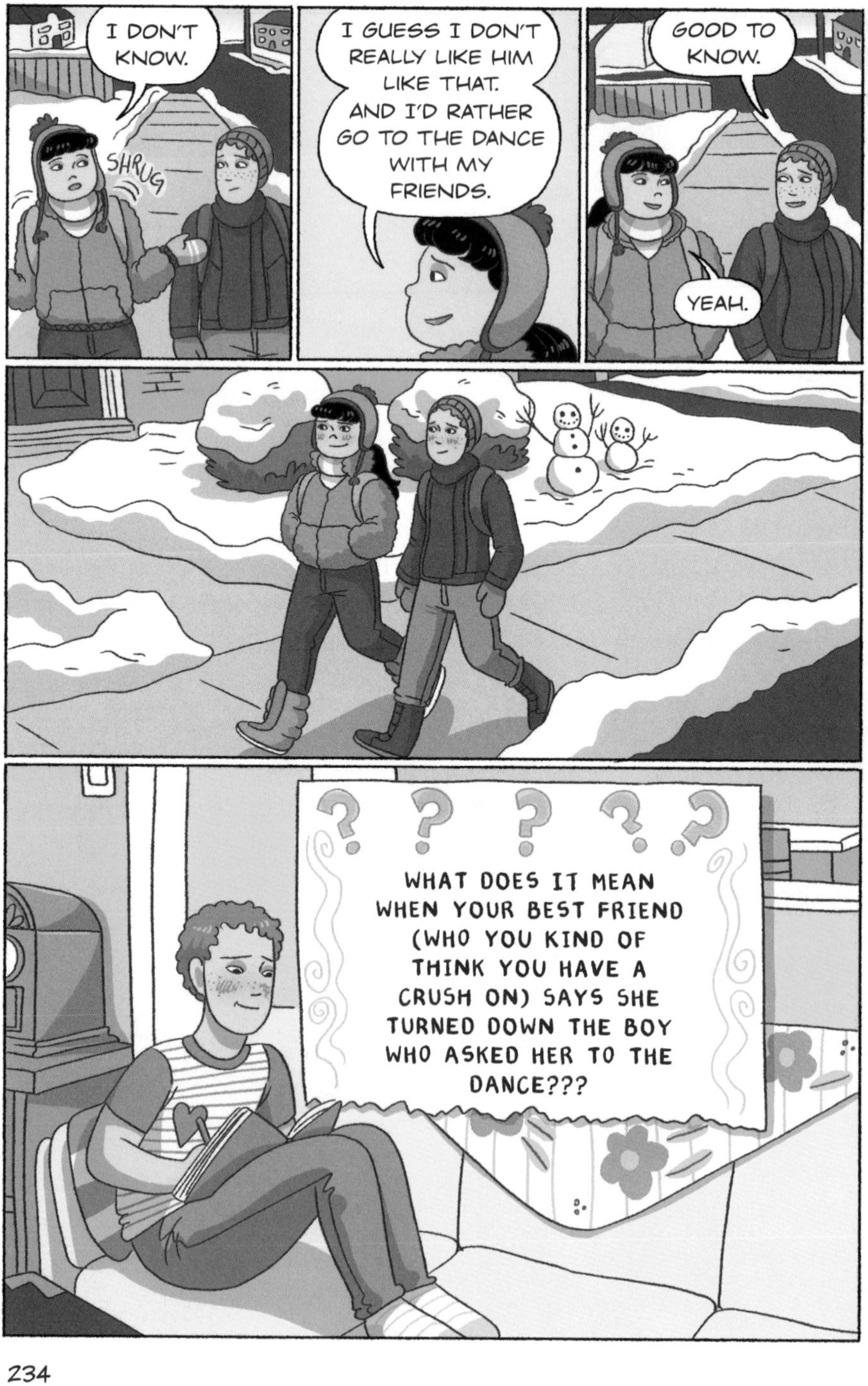
I DON'T KNOW.
SHRUG
I GUESS I DON'T REALLY LIKE HIM LIKE THAT. AND I'D RATHER GO TO THE DANCE WITH MY FRIENDS.
GOOD TO KNOW.
YEAH.
WHAT DOES IT MEAN WHEN YOUR BEST FRIEND (WHO YOU KIND OF THINK YOU HAVE A CRUSH ON) SAYS SHE TURNED DOWN THE BOY WHO ASKED HER TO THE DANCE???

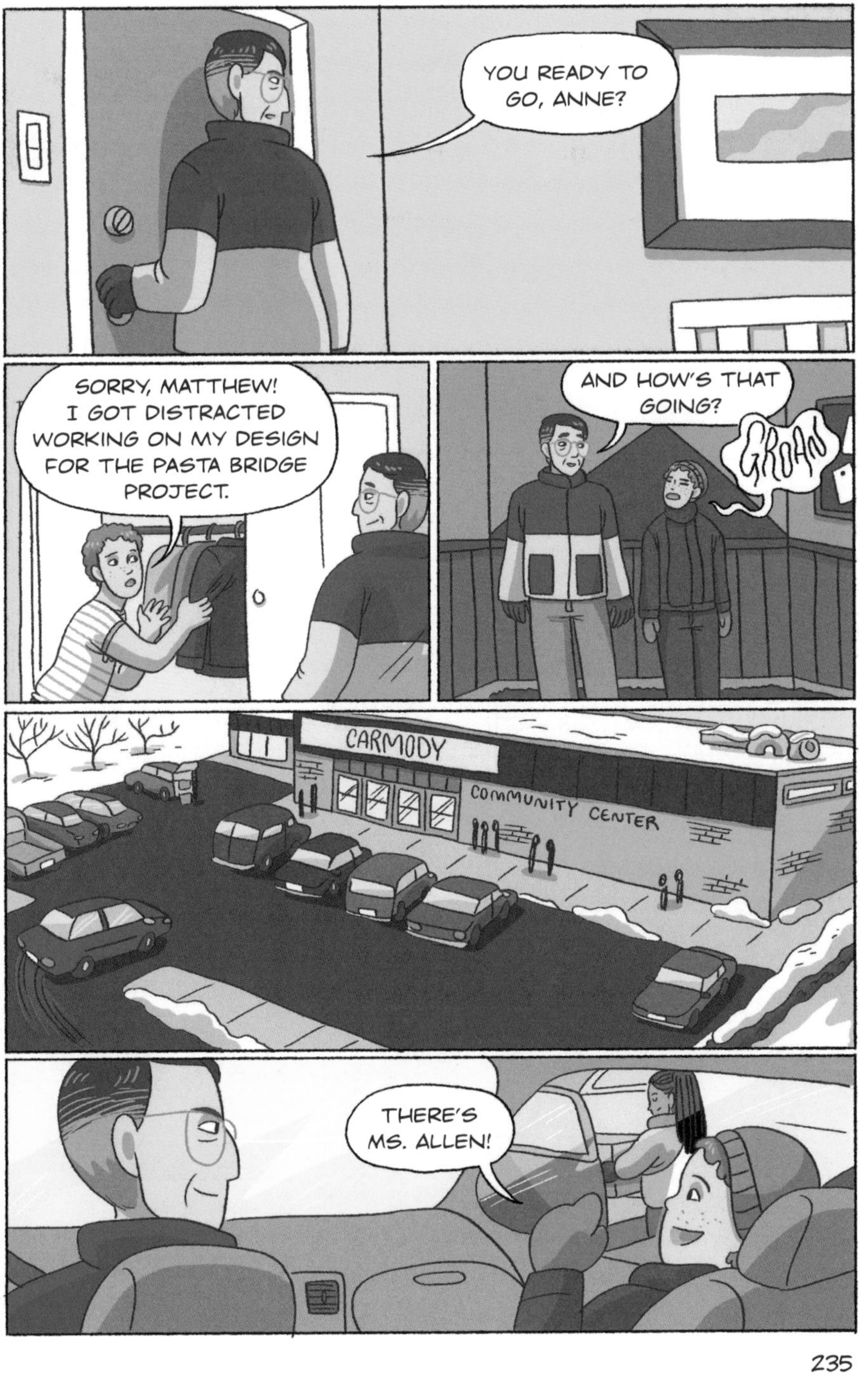
YOU READY TO GO, ANNE?
SORRY, MATTHEW! I GOT DISTRACTED WORKING ON MY DESIGN FOR THE PASTA BRIDGE PROJECT.
AND HOW'S THAT GOING?
GROAN
CARMODY
COMMUNITY CENTER
THERE'S MS. ALLEN!

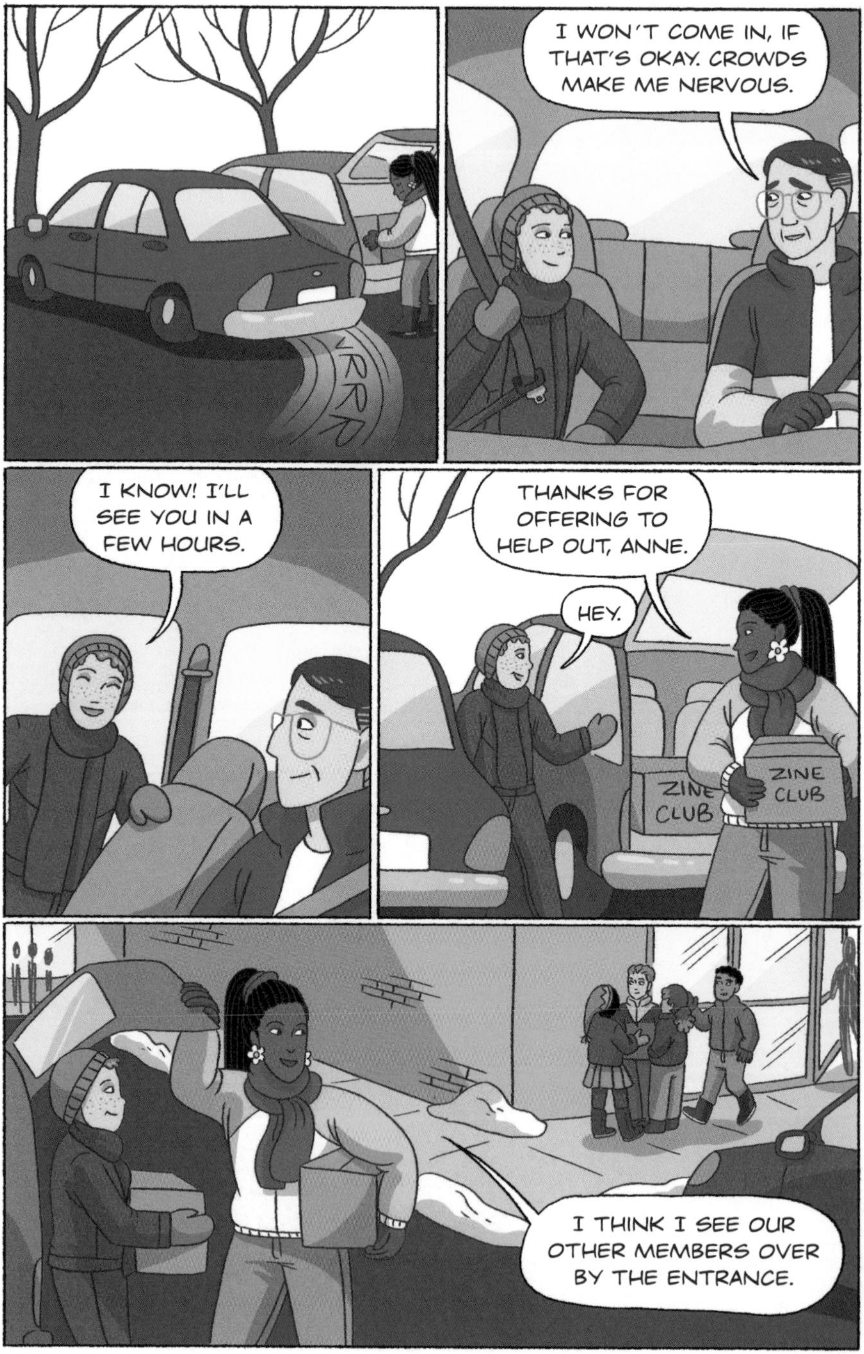
VRRRR
I WON'T COME IN, IF THAT'S OKAY. CROWDS MAKE ME NERVOUS.
I KNOW! I'LL SEE YOU IN A FEW HOURS.
THANKS FOR OFFERING TO HELP OUT, ANNE.
HEY.
ZINE CLUB
ZINE CLUB
I THINK I SEE OUR OTHER MEMBERS OVER BY THE ENTRANCE.

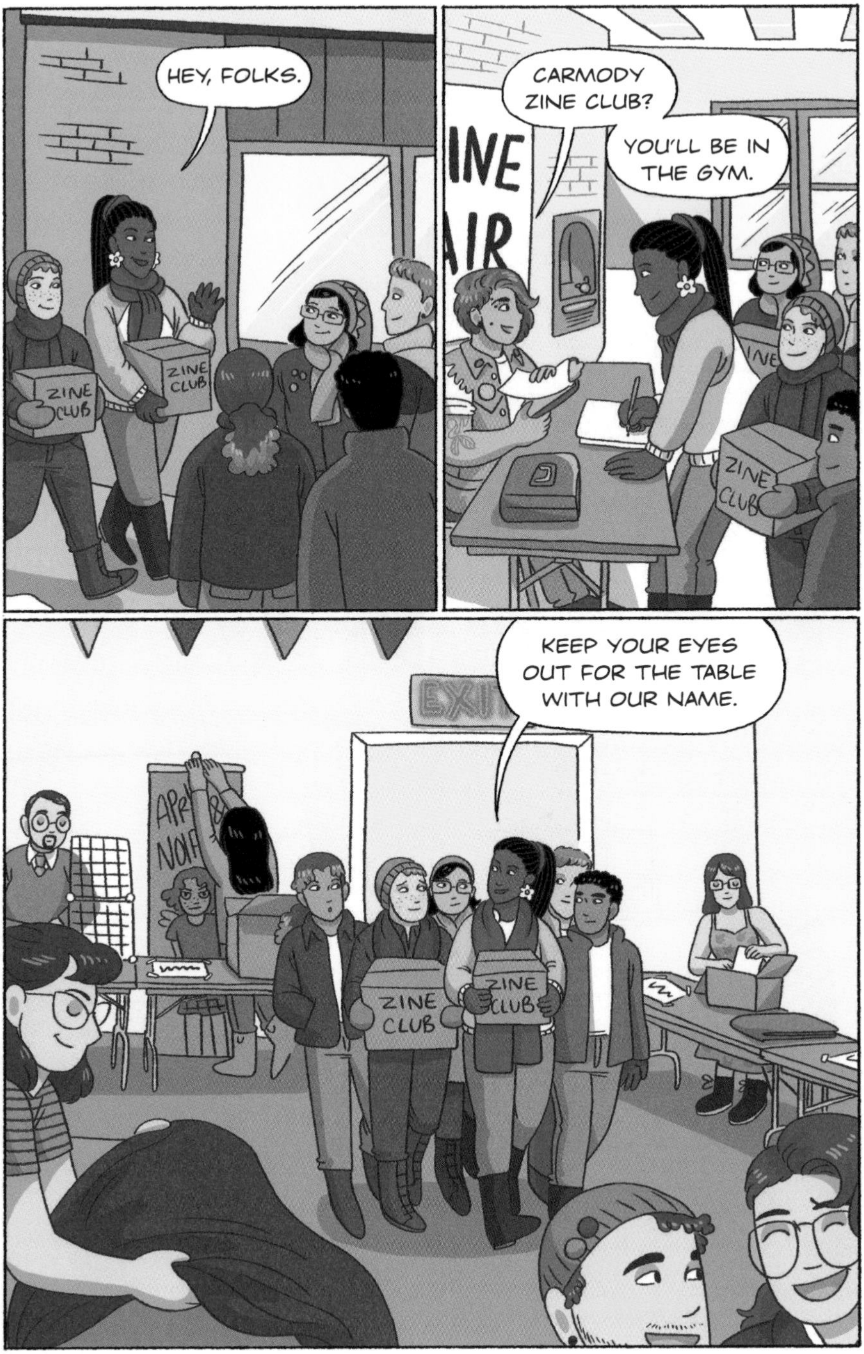
HEY, FOLKS.
ZINE CLUB
ZINE CLUB
CARMODY ZINE CLUB?
YOU'LL BE IN THE GYM.
ZINE CLUB
KEEP YOUR EYES OUT FOR THE TABLE WITH OUR NAME.
EXIT
ZINE CLUB
ZINE CLUB

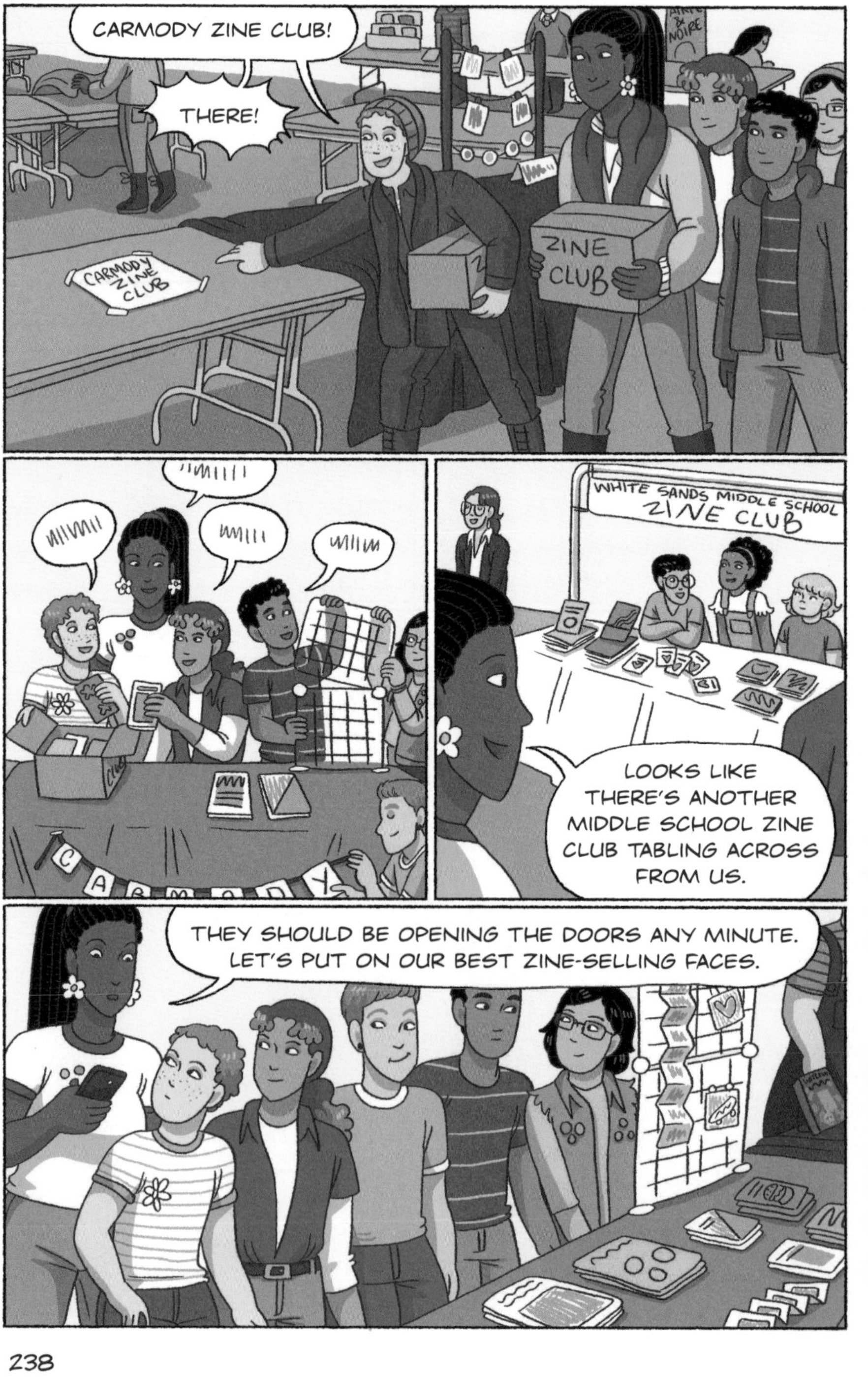
CARMODY ZINE CLUB!
THERE!
CARMODY ZINE CLUB
ZINE CLUB
WHITE SANDS MIDDLE SCHOOL ZINE CLUB
LOOKS LIKE THERE'S ANOTHER MIDDLE SCHOOL ZINE CLUB TABLING ACROSS FROM US.
THEY SHOULD BE OPENING THE DOORS ANY MINUTE. LET'S PUT ON OUR BEST ZINE-SELLING FACES.

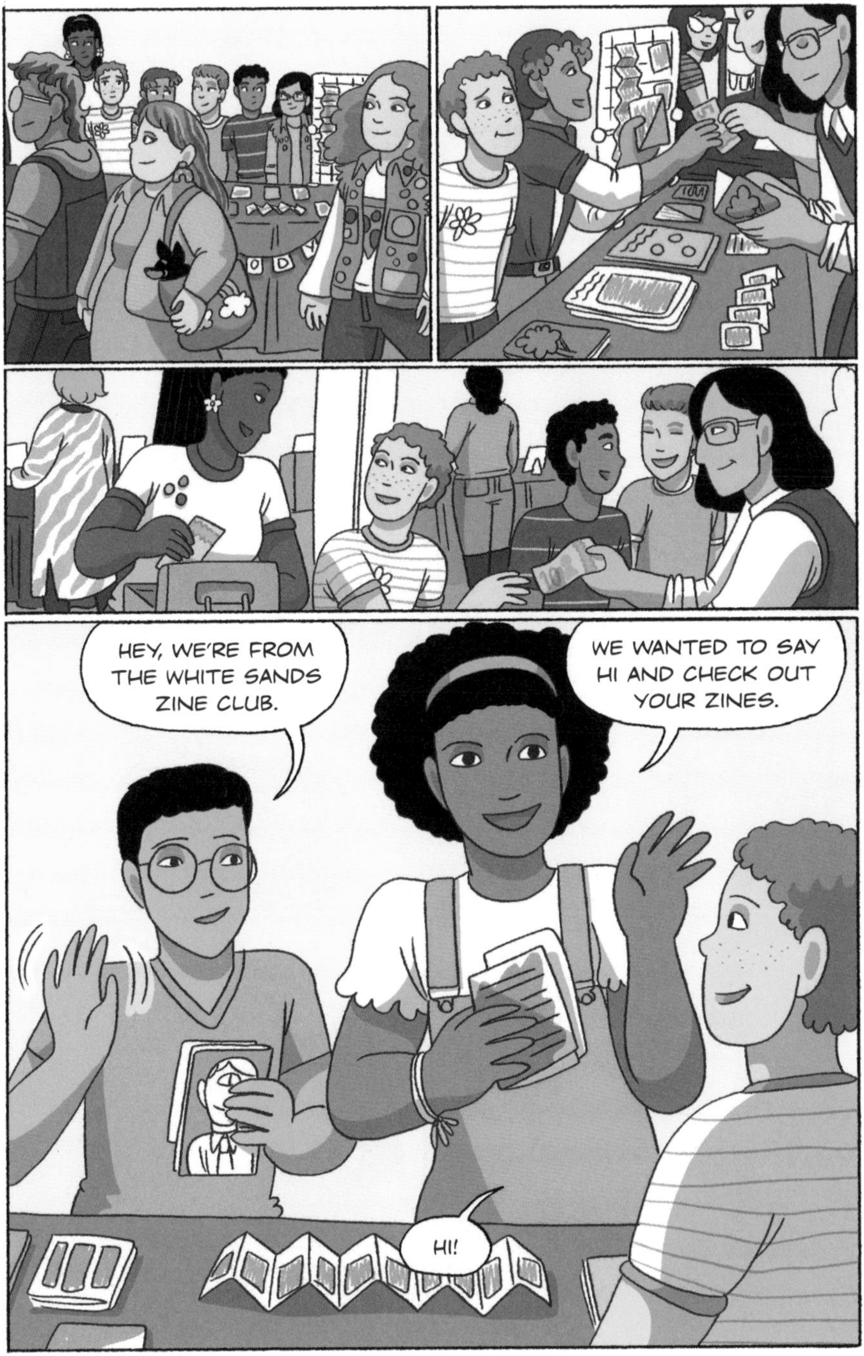
HEY, WE'RE FROM THE WHITE SANDS ZINE CLUB.
WE WANTED TO SAY HI AND CHECK OUT YOUR ZINES.
HI!

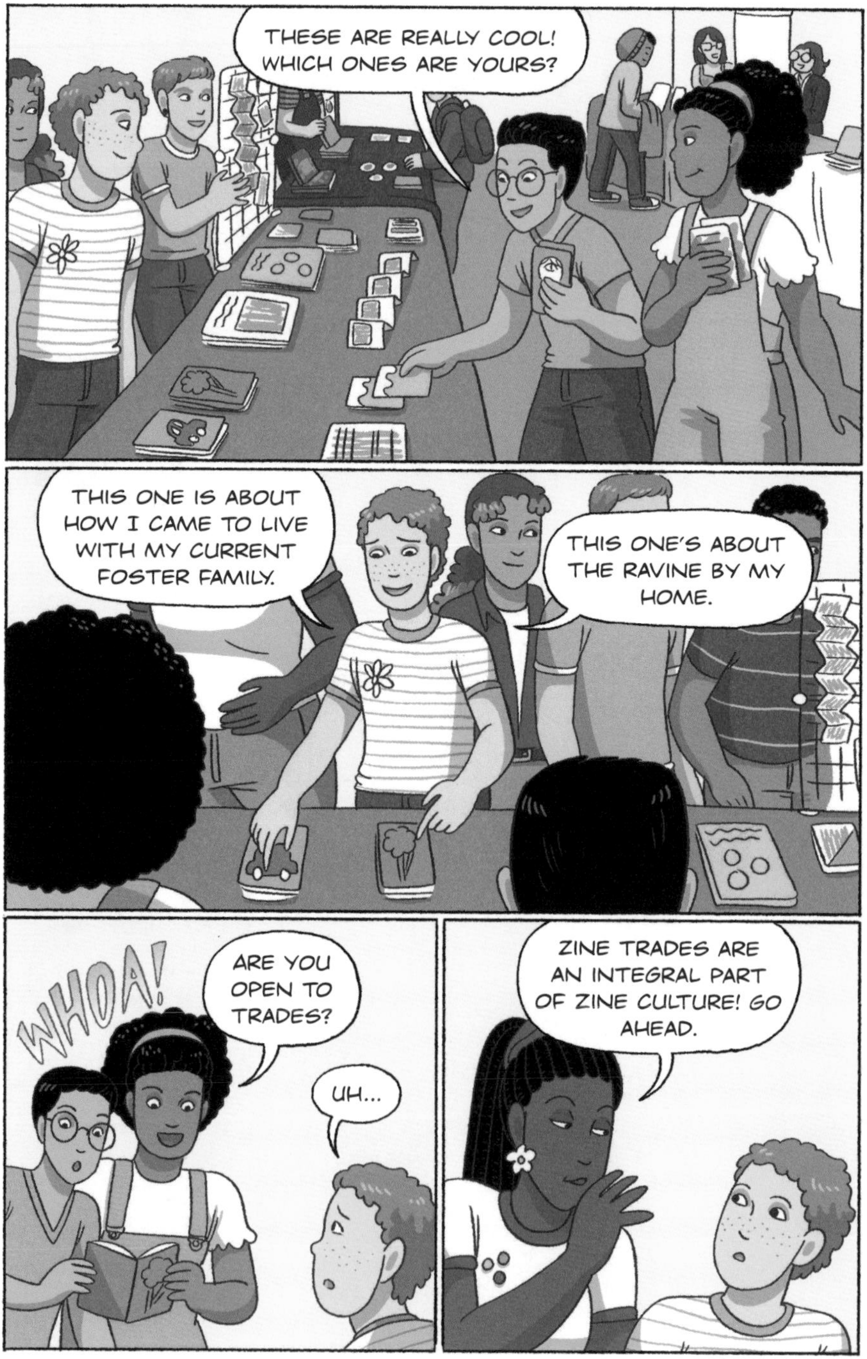
THESE ARE REALLY COOL! WHICH ONES ARE YOURS?
THIS ONE IS ABOUT HOW I CAME TO LIVE WITH MY CURRENT FOSTER FAMILY.
THIS ONE'S ABOUT THE RAVINE BY MY HOME.
WHOA!
ARE YOU OPEN TO TRADES?
UH...
ZINE TRADES ARE AN INTEGRAL PART OF ZINE CULTURE! GO AHEAD.

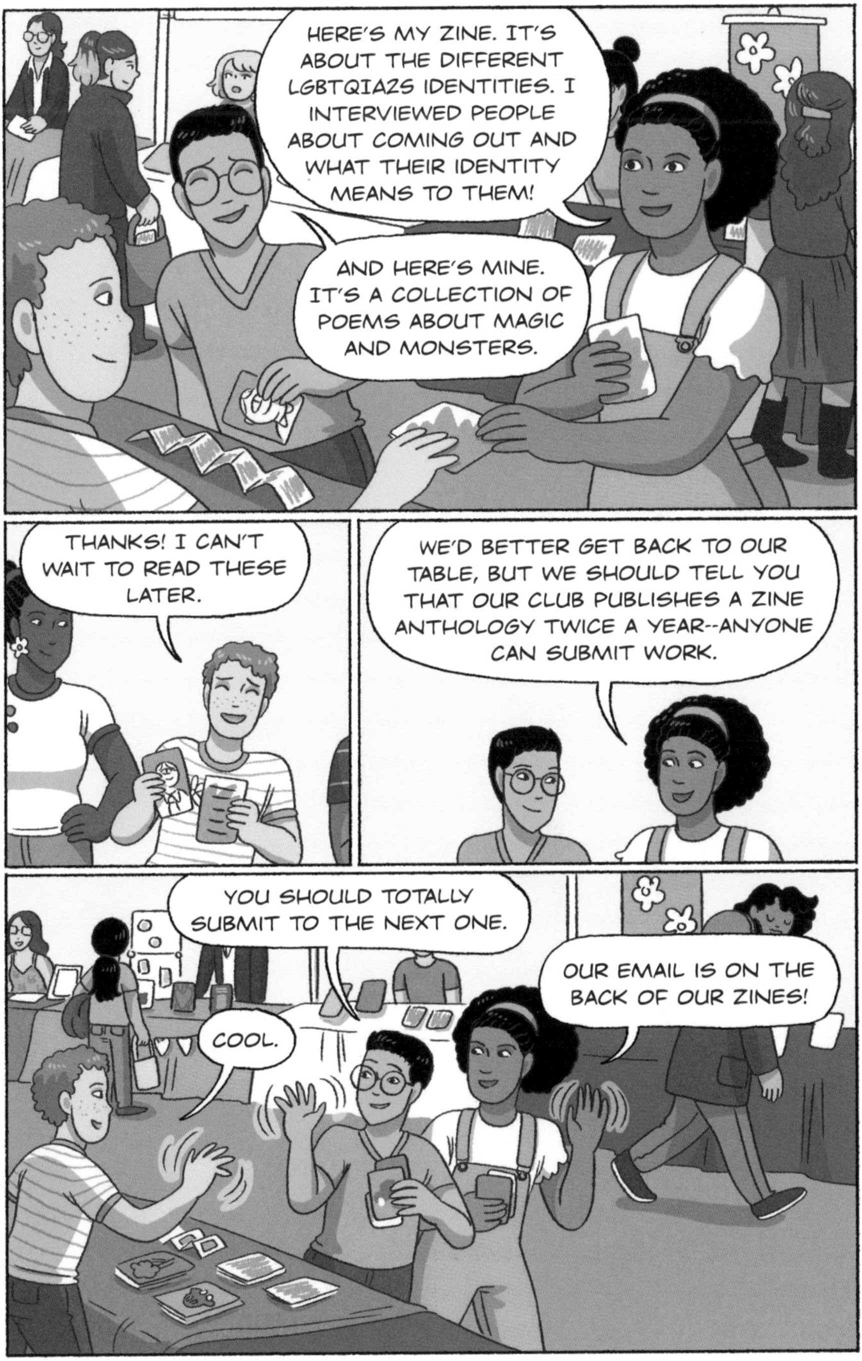
HERE'S MY ZINE. IT'S ABOUT THE DIFFERENT LGBTQIA2S IDENTITIES. I INTERVIEWED PEOPLE ABOUT COMING OUT AND WHAT THEIR IDENTITY MEANS TO THEM!
AND HERE'S MINE. IT'S A COLLECTION OF POEMS ABOUT MAGIC AND MONSTERS.
THANKS! I CAN'T WAIT TO READ THESE LATER.
WE'D BETTER GET BACK TO OUR TABLE, BUT WE SHOULD TELL YOU THAT OUR CLUB PUBLISHES A ZINE ANTHOLOGY TWICE A YEAR--ANYONE CAN SUBMIT WORK.
YOU SHOULD TOTALLY SUBMIT TO THE NEXT ONE.
OUR EMAIL IS ON THE BACK OF OUR ZINES!
COOL.

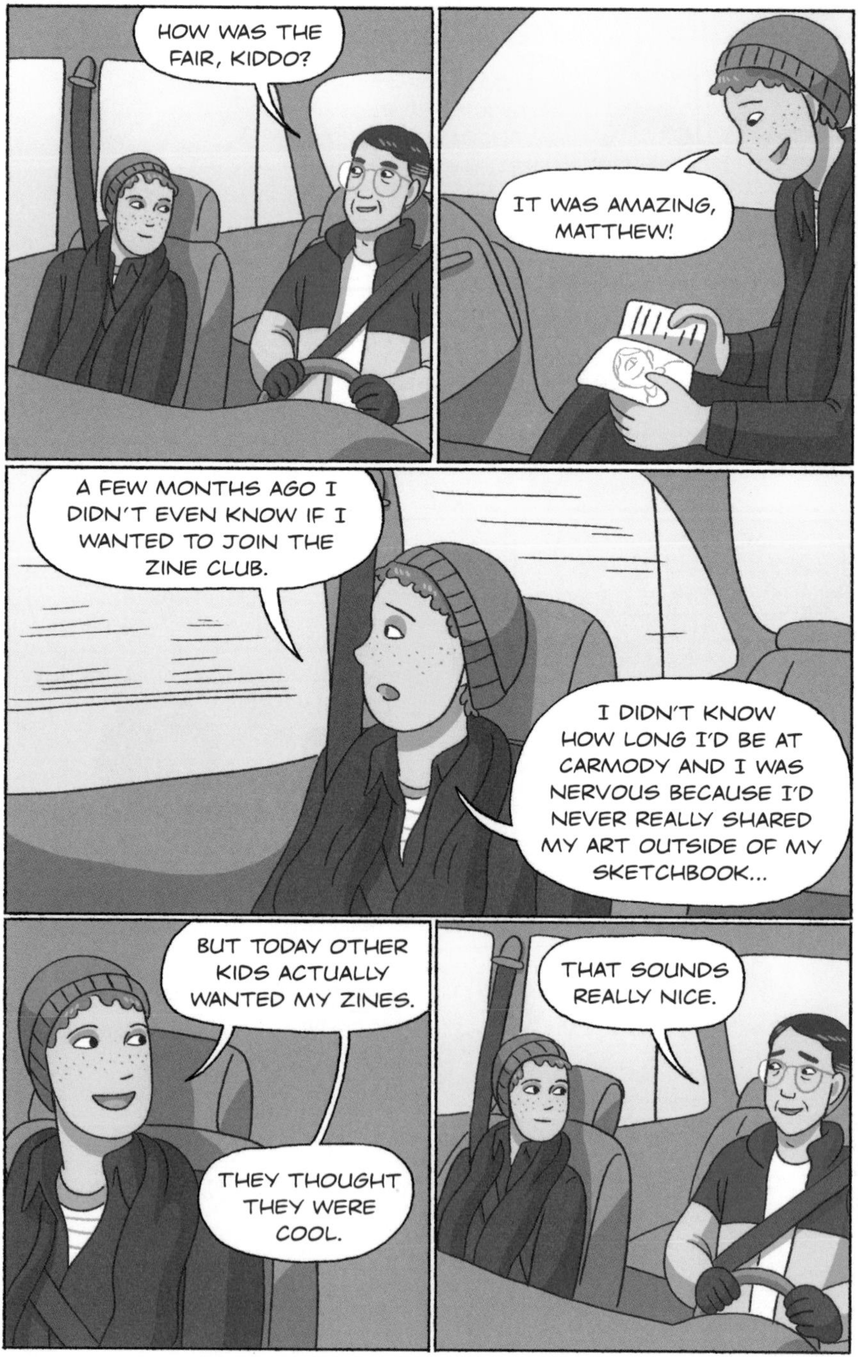
HOW WAS THE FAIR, KIDDO?
IT WAS AMAZING, MATTHEW!
A FEW MONTHS AGO I DIDN'T EVEN KNOW IF I WANTED TO JOIN THE ZINE CLUB.
I DIDN'T KNOW HOW LONG I'D BE AT CARMODY AND I WAS NERVOUS BECAUSE I'D NEVER REALLY SHARED MY ART OUTSIDE OF MY SKETCHBOOK...
BUT TODAY OTHER KIDS ACTUALLY WANTED MY ZINES.
THEY THOUGHT THEY WERE COOL.
THAT SOUNDS REALLY NICE.

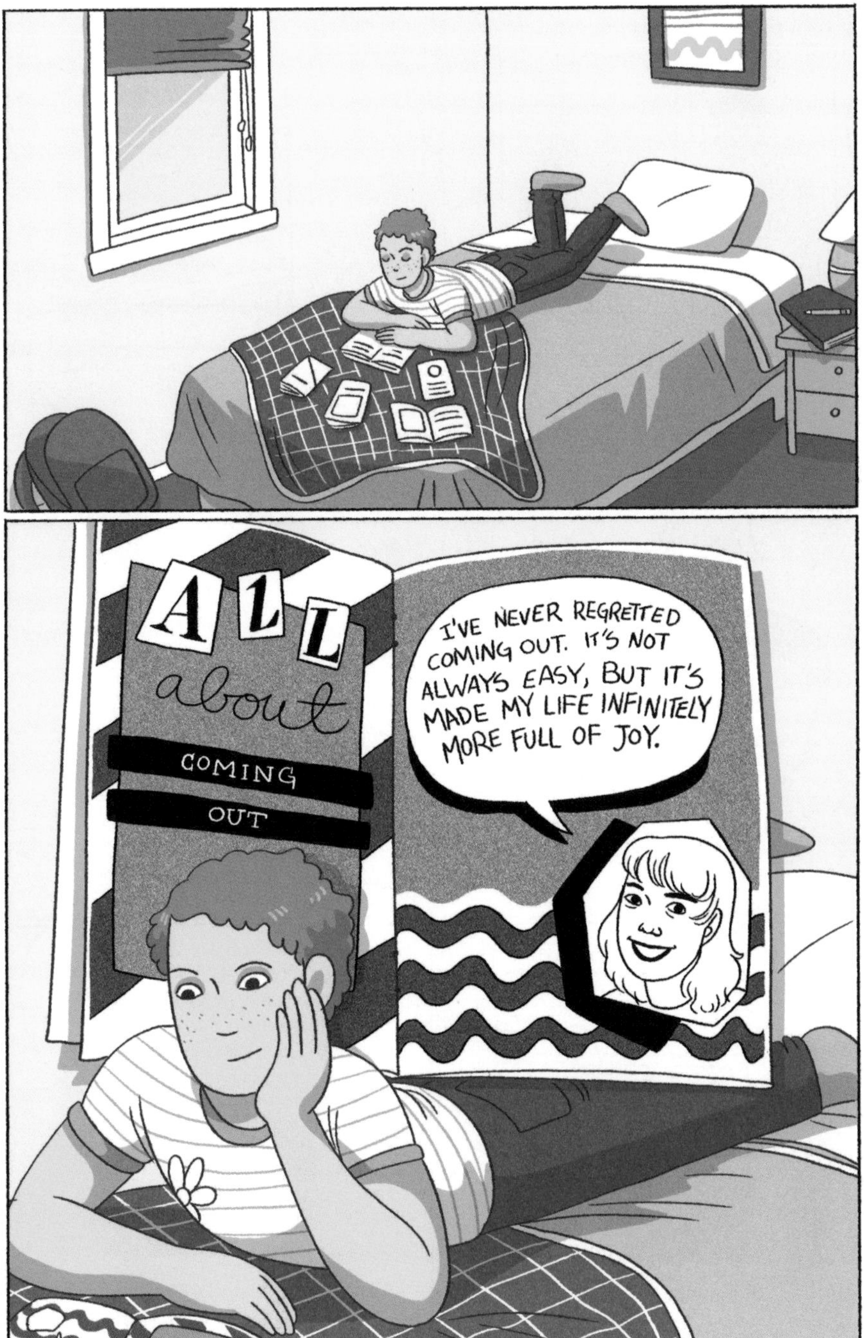
ALL about COMING OUT
I'VE NEVER REGRETTED COMING OUT. IT'S NOT ALWAYS EASY, BUT IT'S MADE MY LIFE INFINITELY MORE FULL OF JOY.

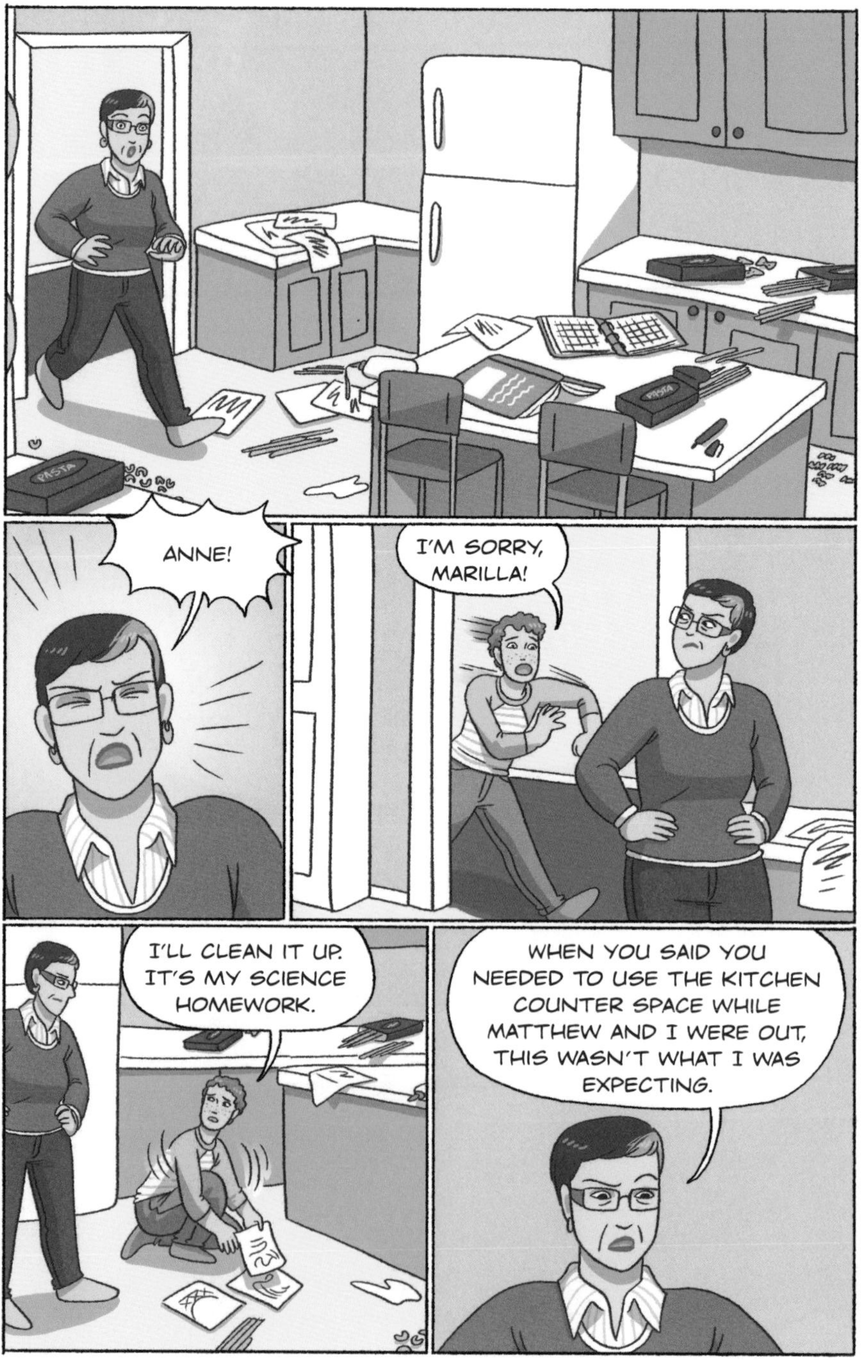
ANNE!
I'M SORRY, MARILLA!
I'LL CLEAN IT UP. IT'S MY SCIENCE HOMEWORK.
WHEN YOU SAID YOU NEEDED TO USE THE KITCHEN COUNTER SPACE WHILE MATTHEW AND I WERE OUT, THIS WASN'T WHAT I WAS EXPECTING.

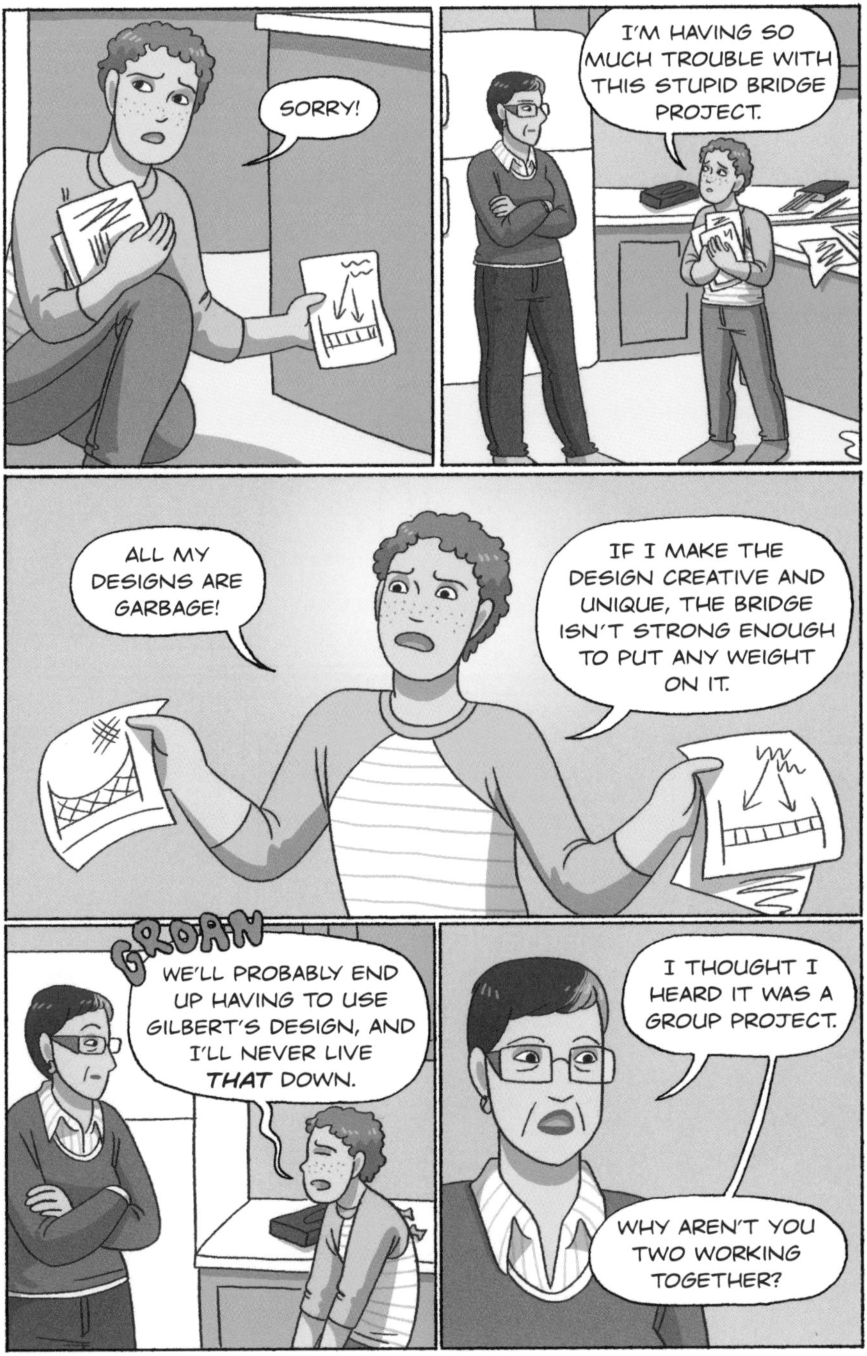
SORRY!
I'M HAVING SO MUCH TROUBLE WITH THIS STUPID BRIDGE PROJECT.
ALL MY DESIGNS ARE GARBAGE!
IF I MAKE THE DESIGN CREATIVE AND UNIQUE, THE BRIDGE ISN'T STRONG ENOUGH TO PUT ANY WEIGHT ON IT.
GROAN
WE'LL PROBABLY END UP HAVING TO USE GILBERT'S DESIGN, AND I'LL NEVER LIVE ***THAT*** DOWN.
I THOUGHT I HEARD IT WAS A GROUP PROJECT.
WHY AREN'T YOU TWO WORKING TOGETHER?

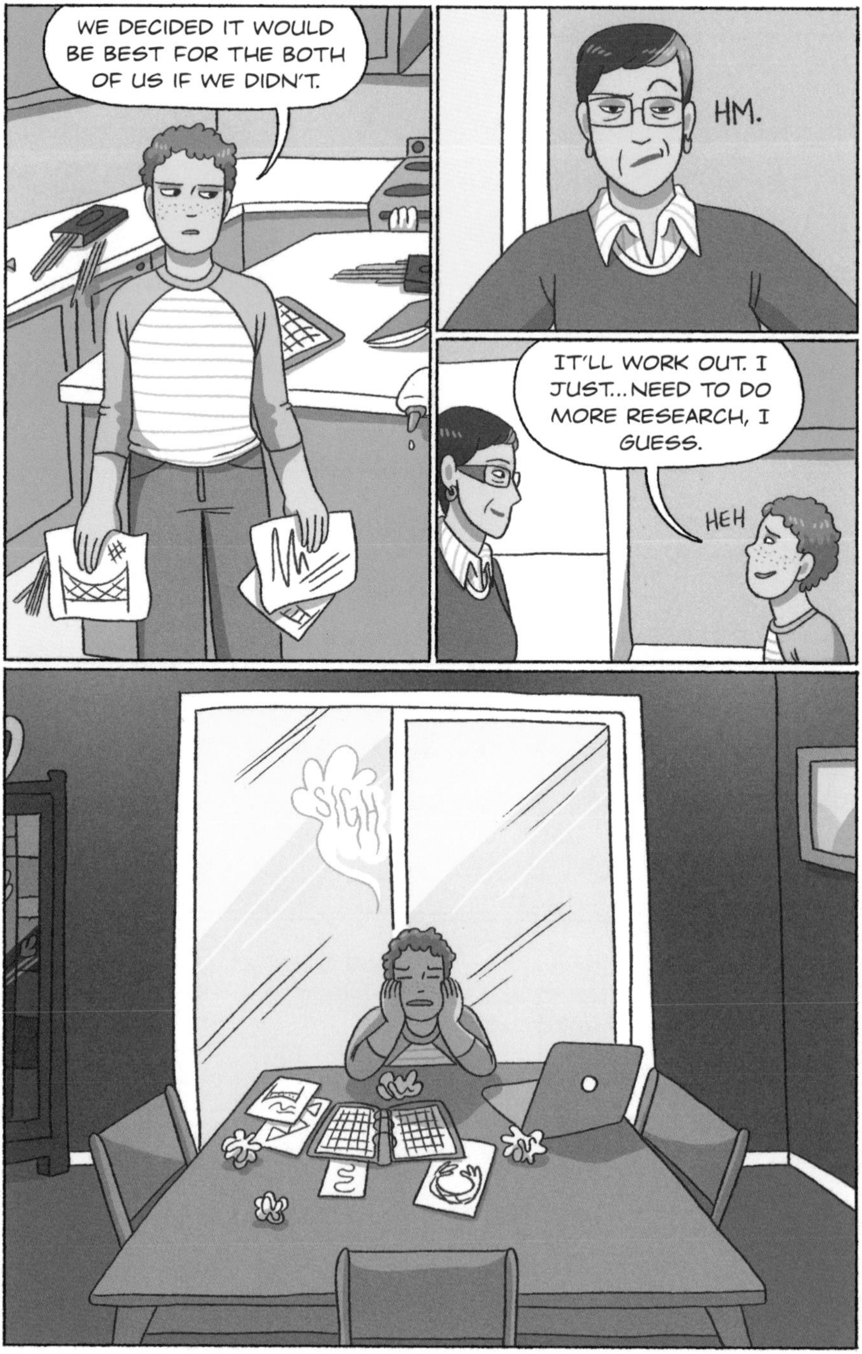
WE DECIDED IT WOULD BE BEST FOR THE BOTH OF US IF WE DIDN'T.
HM.
IT'LL WORK OUT. I JUST...NEED TO DO MORE RESEARCH, I GUESS.
HEH
SIGH

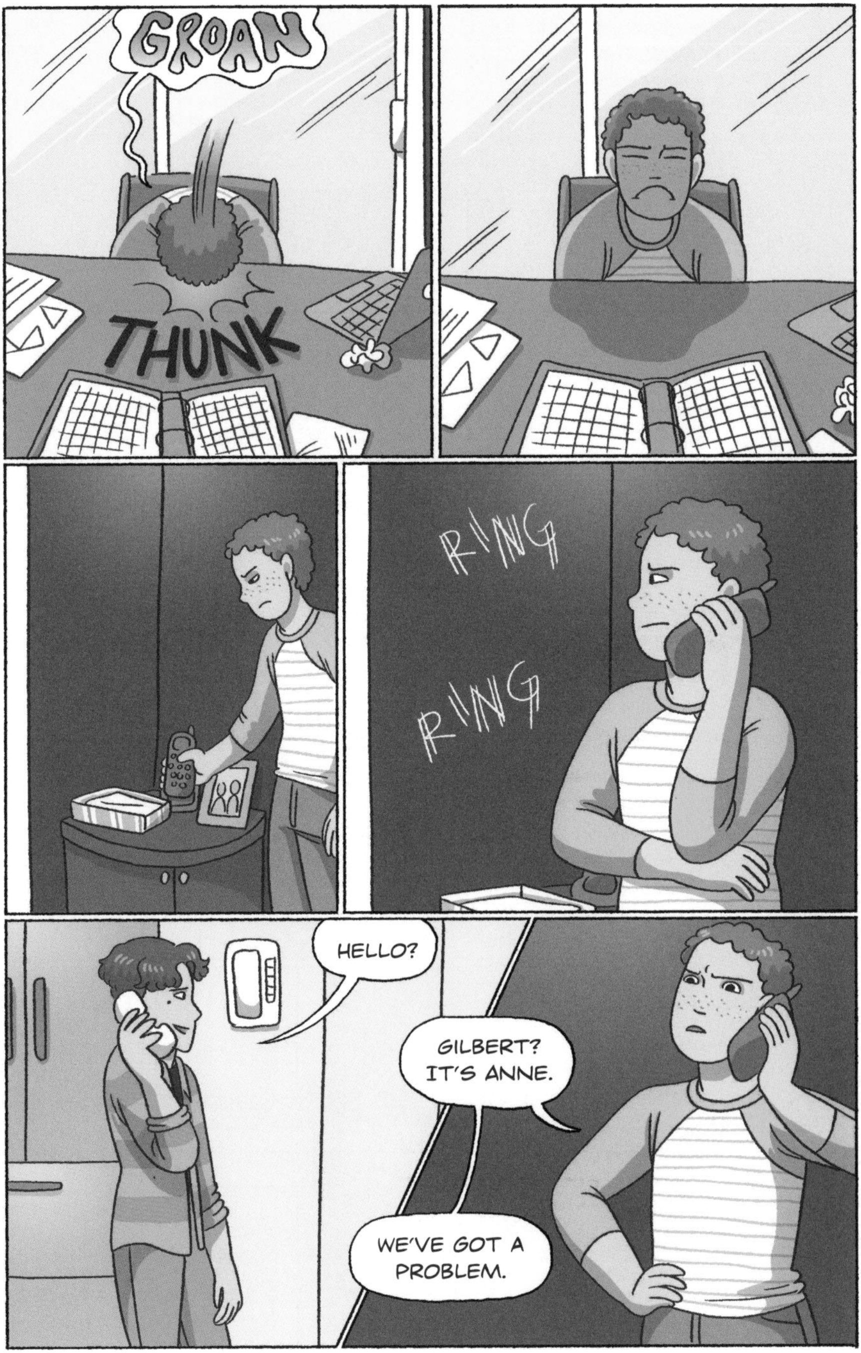
GROAN
THUNK
RING
RING
HELLO?
GILBERT? IT'S ANNE.
WE'VE GOT A PROBLEM.

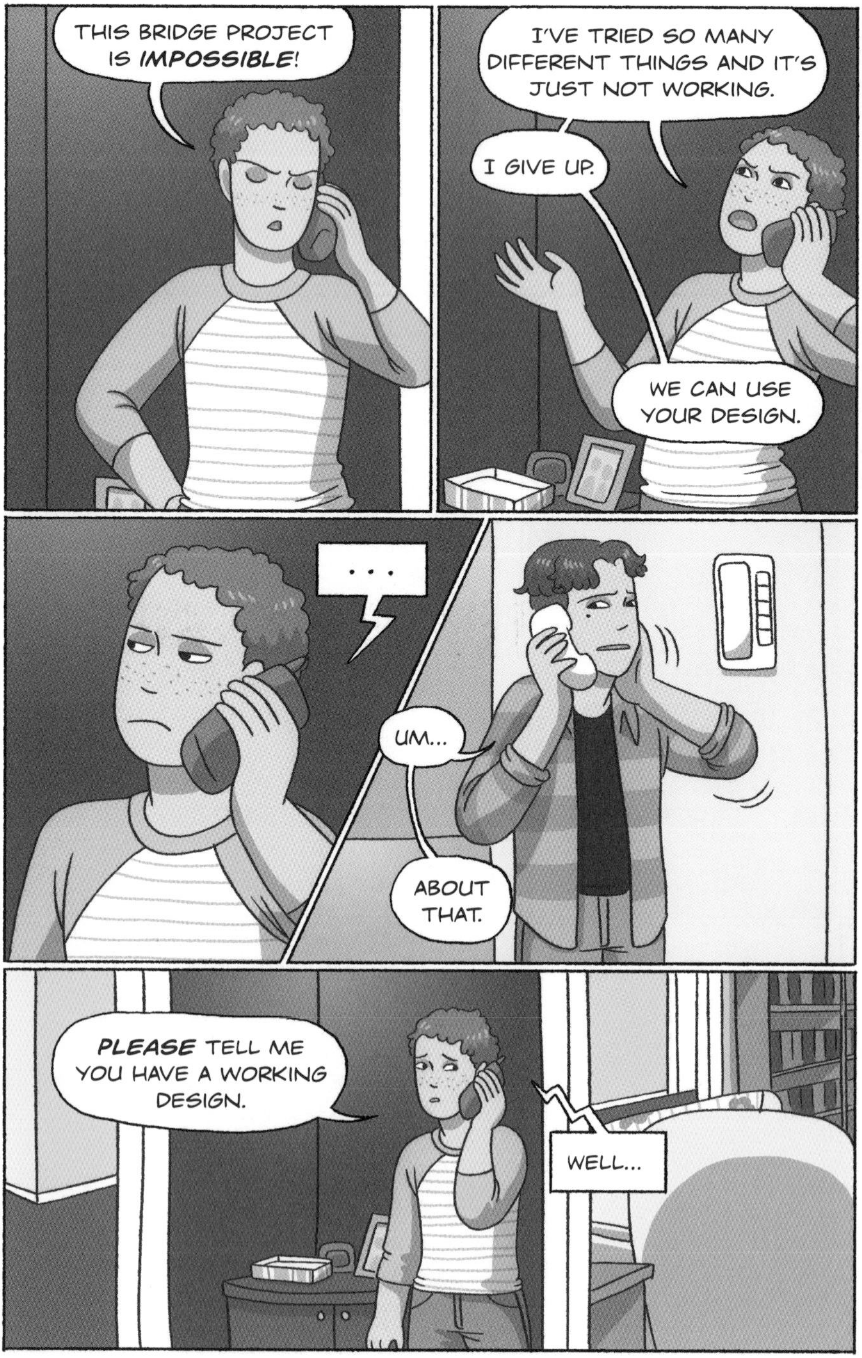
THIS BRIDGE PROJECT IS **IMPOSSIBLE**!
I'VE TRIED SO MANY DIFFERENT THINGS AND IT'S JUST NOT WORKING.
I GIVE UP.
WE CAN USE YOUR DESIGN.
...
UM...
ABOUT THAT.
PLEASE TELL ME YOU HAVE A WORKING DESIGN.
WELL...

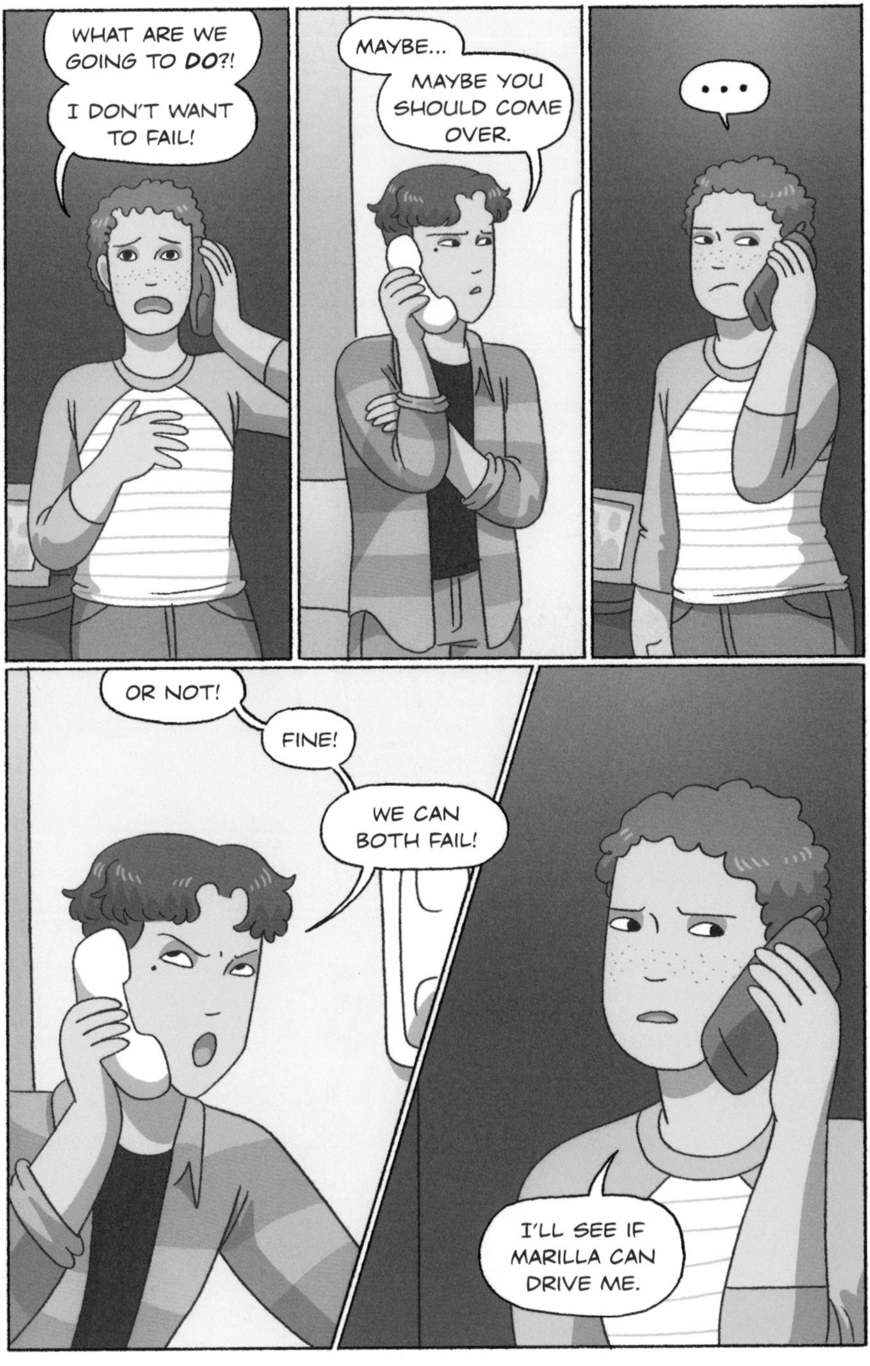
WHAT ARE WE GOING TO **DO**?!
I DON'T WANT TO FAIL!
MAYBE...
MAYBE YOU SHOULD COME OVER.
...
OR NOT!
FINE!
WE CAN BOTH FAIL!
I'LL SEE IF MARILLA CAN DRIVE ME.

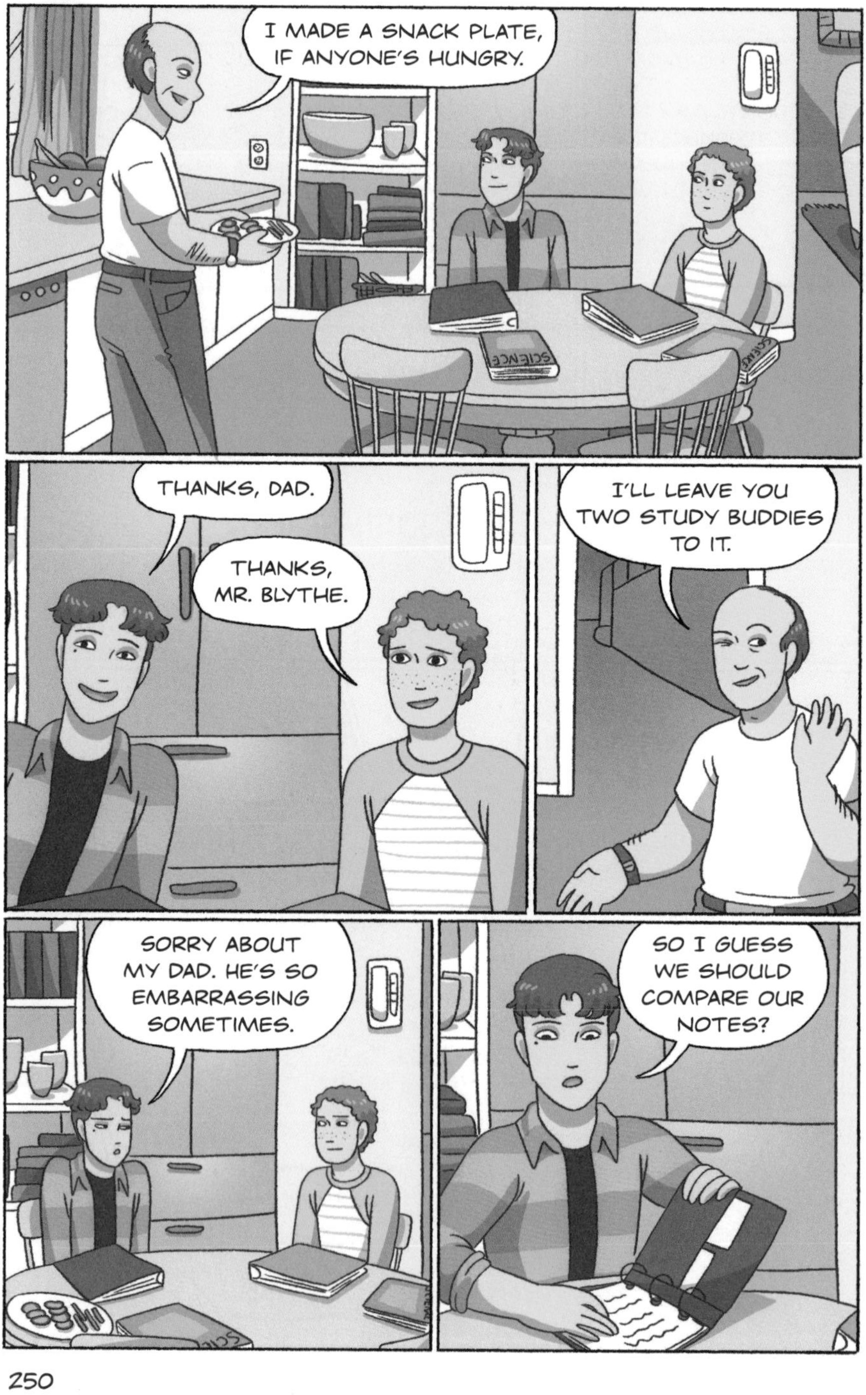
I MADE A SNACK PLATE, IF ANYONE'S HUNGRY.
SCIENCE
THANKS, DAD.
THANKS, MR. BLYTHE.
I'LL LEAVE YOU TWO STUDY BUDDIES TO IT.
SORRY ABOUT MY DAD. HE'S SO EMBARRASSING SOMETIMES.
SO I GUESS WE SHOULD COMPARE OUR NOTES?

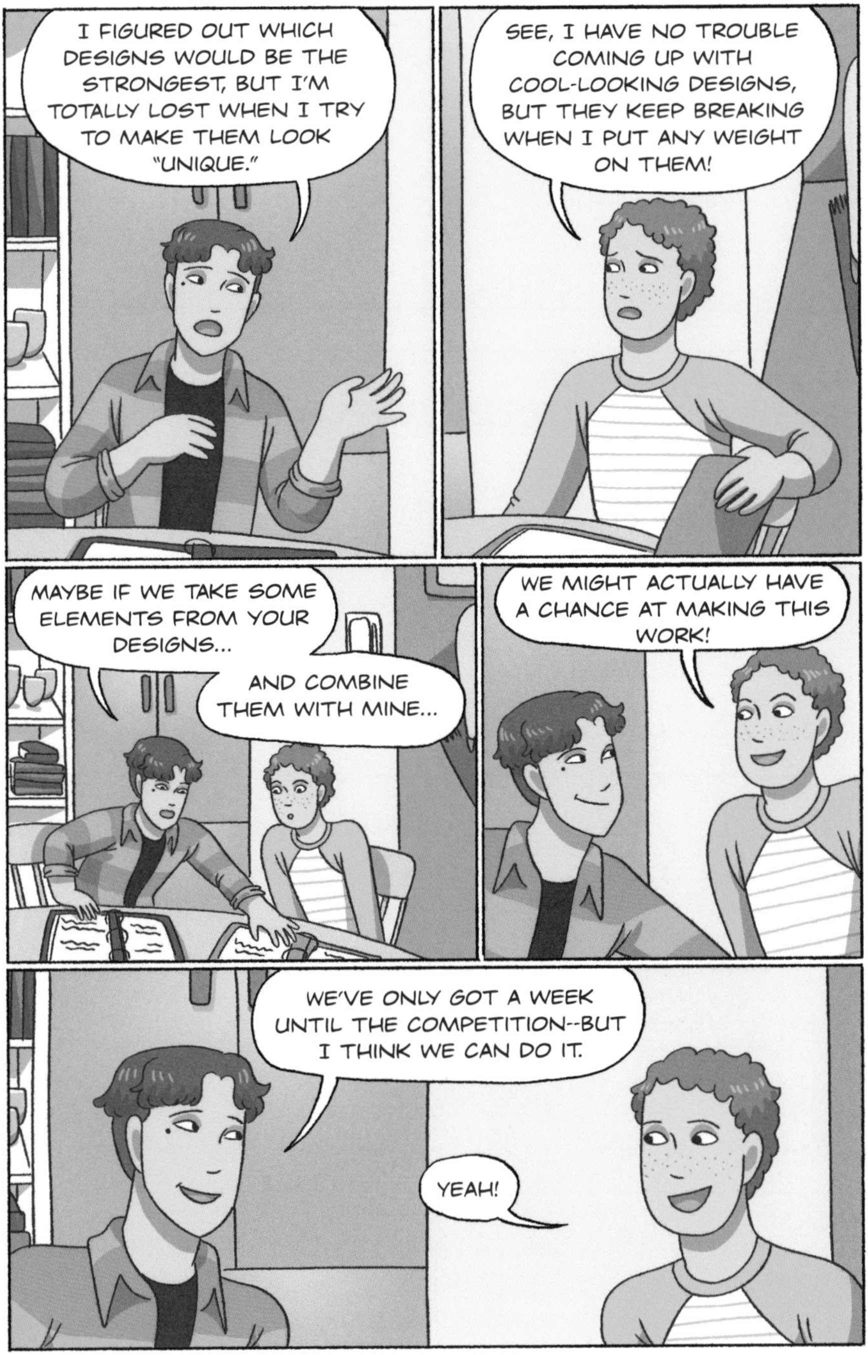
I FIGURED OUT WHICH DESIGNS WOULD BE THE STRONGEST, BUT I'M TOTALLY LOST WHEN I TRY TO MAKE THEM LOOK "UNIQUE."
SEE, I HAVE NO TROUBLE COMING UP WITH COOL-LOOKING DESIGNS, BUT THEY KEEP BREAKING WHEN I PUT ANY WEIGHT ON THEM!
MAYBE IF WE TAKE SOME ELEMENTS FROM YOUR DESIGNS...
AND COMBINE THEM WITH MINE...
WE MIGHT ACTUALLY HAVE A CHANCE AT MAKING THIS WORK!
WE'VE ONLY GOT A WEEK UNTIL THE COMPETITION--BUT I THINK WE CAN DO IT.
YEAH!

CHAPTER 11

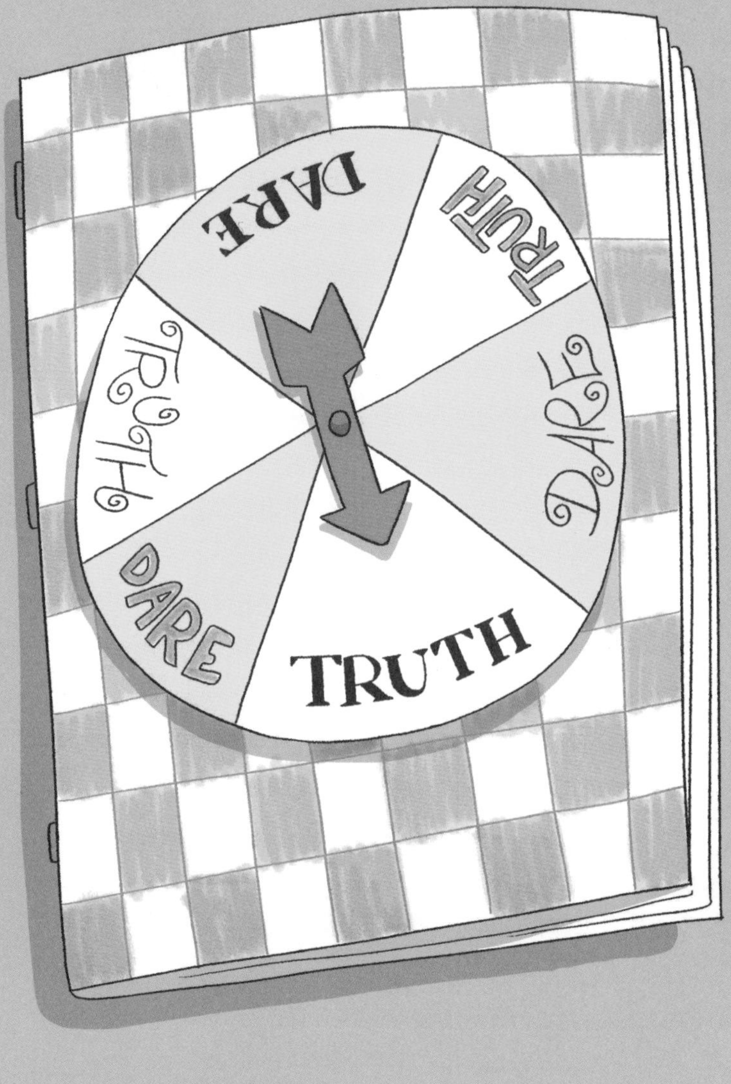

DARE
TRUTH
DARE
TRUTH
DARE
TRUTH

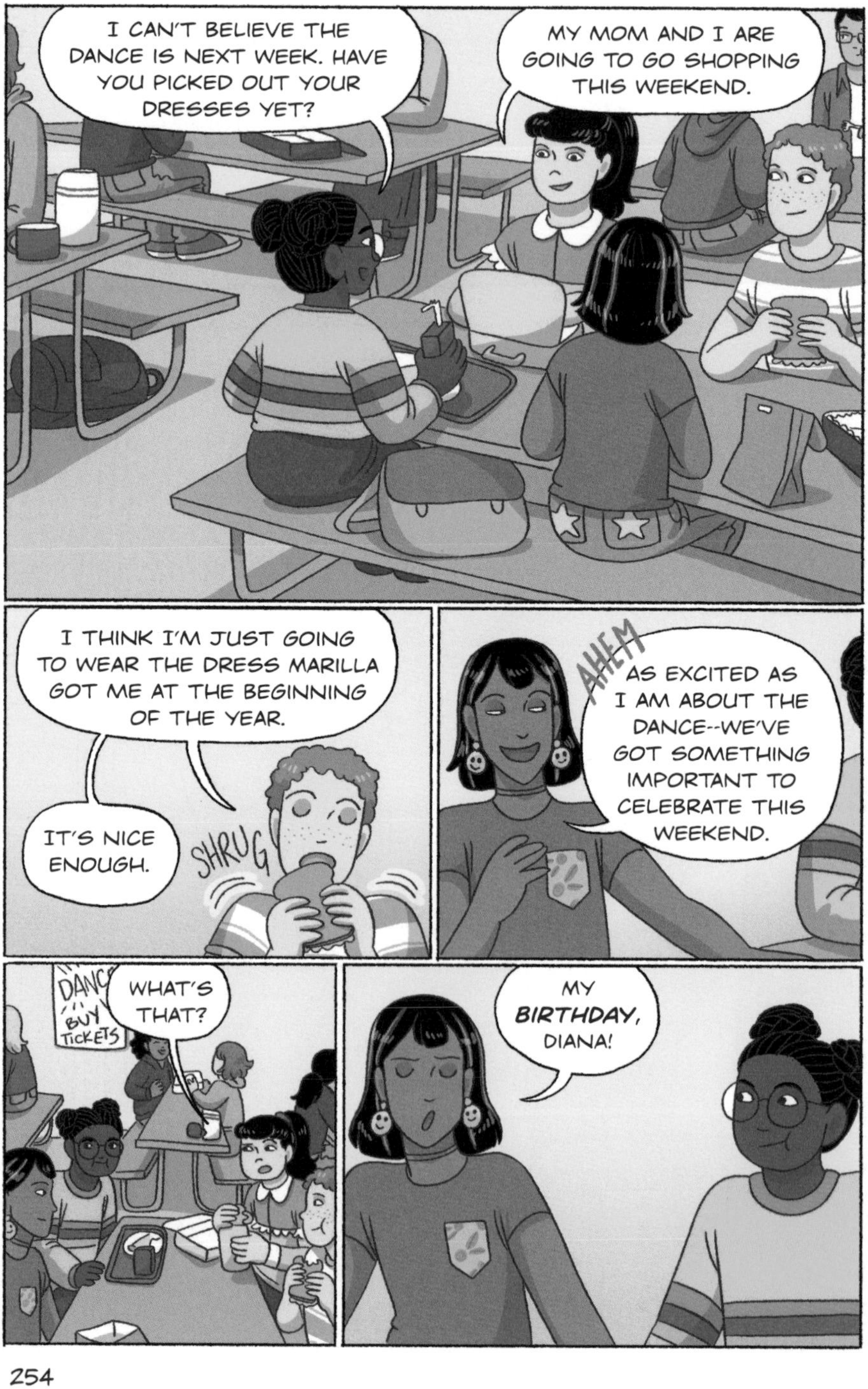
I CAN'T BELIEVE THE DANCE IS NEXT WEEK. HAVE YOU PICKED OUT YOUR DRESSES YET?
MY MOM AND I ARE GOING TO GO SHOPPING THIS WEEKEND.
I THINK I'M JUST GOING TO WEAR THE DRESS MARILLA GOT ME AT THE BEGINNING OF THE YEAR.
IT'S NICE ENOUGH.
SHRUG
AHEM
AS EXCITED AS I AM ABOUT THE DANCE--WE'VE GOT SOMETHING IMPORTANT TO CELEBRATE THIS WEEKEND.
DANCE
BUY TICKETS
WHAT'S THAT?
MY BIRTHDAY, DIANA!

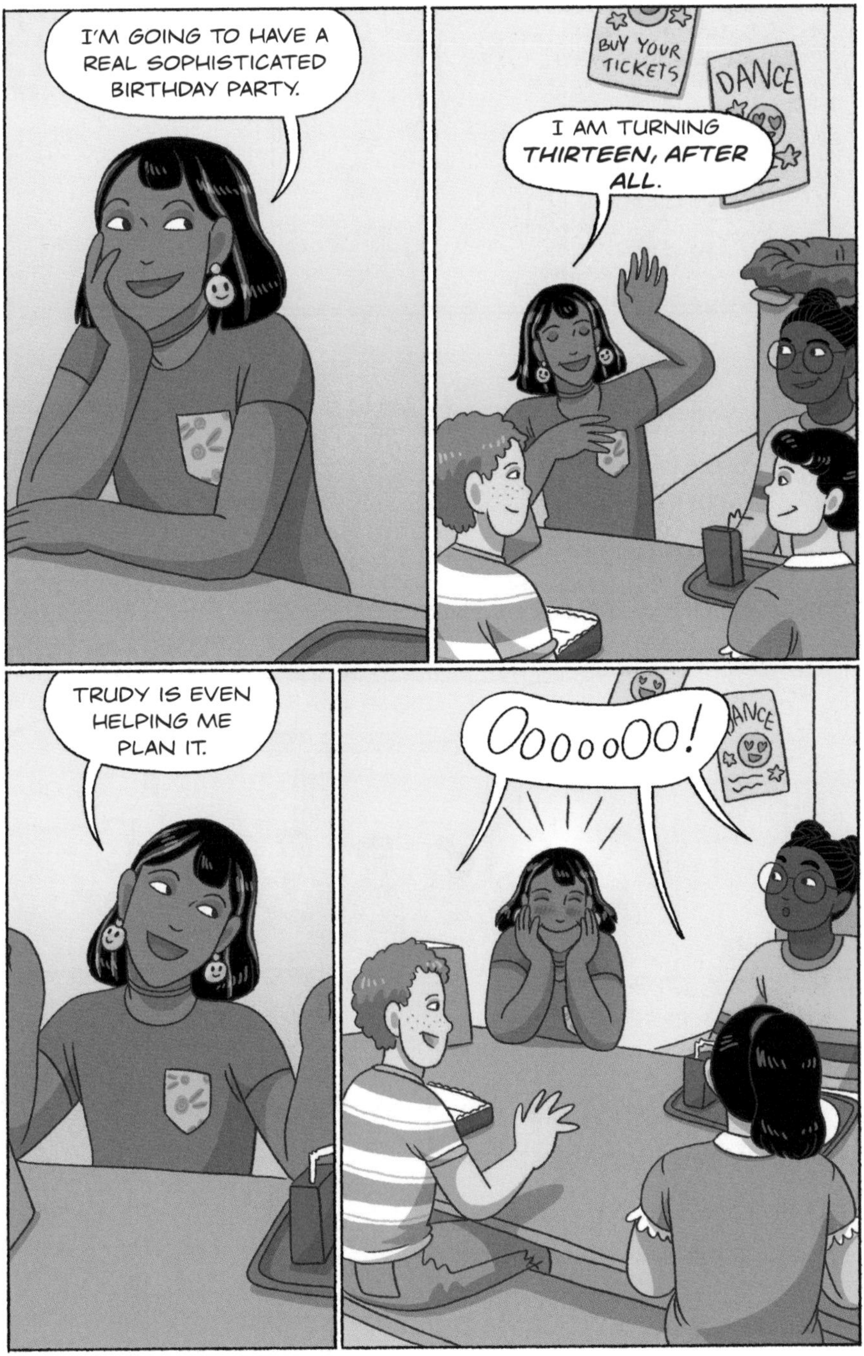
I'M GOING TO HAVE A REAL SOPHISTICATED BIRTHDAY PARTY.
BUY YOUR TICKETS
DANCE
I AM TURNING THIRTEEN, AFTER ALL.
TRUDY IS EVEN HELPING ME PLAN IT.
DANCE
OooooOO!

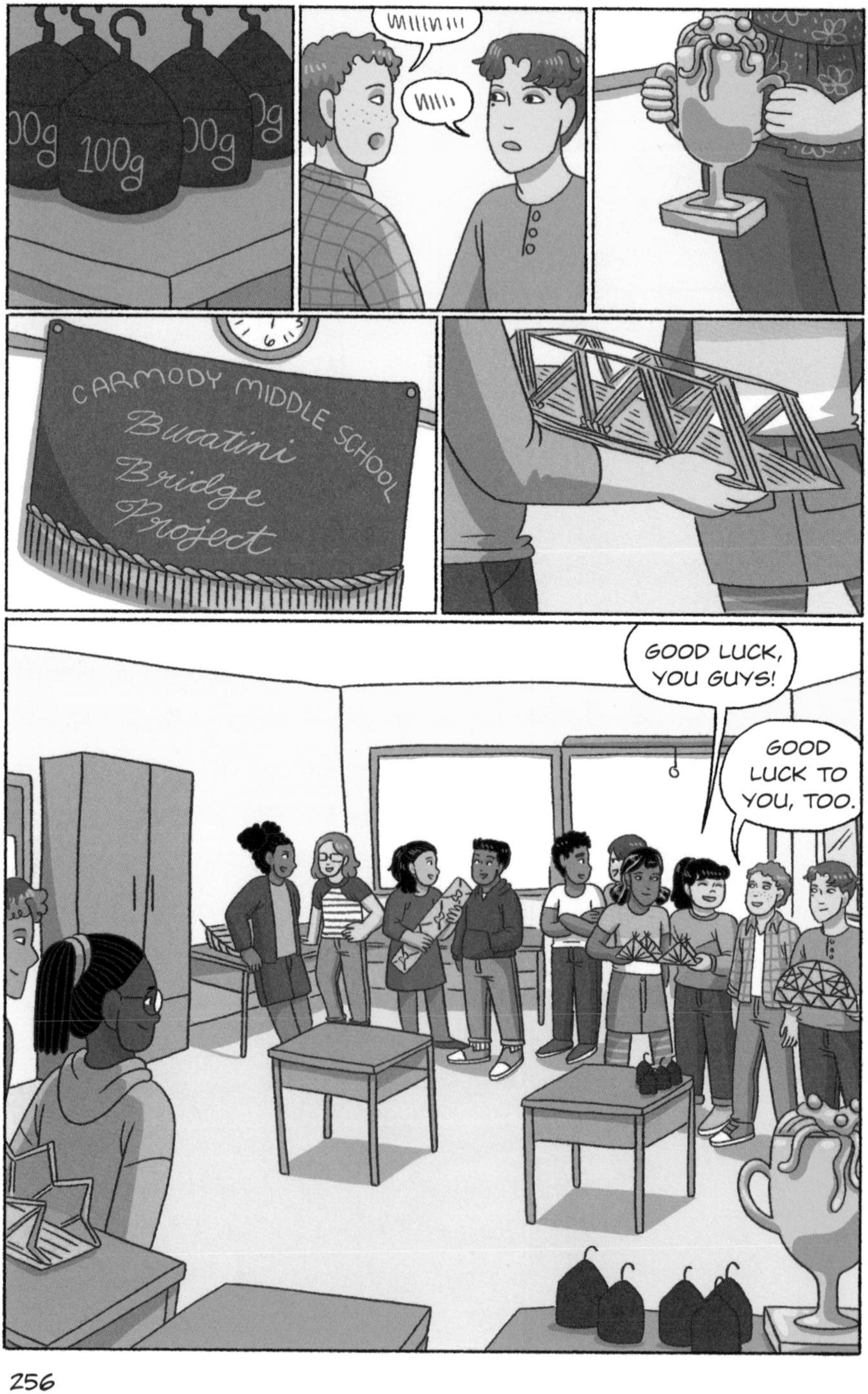
100g
100g
00g
00g
0g
CARMODY MIDDLE SCHOOL
Bucatini
Bridge
Project
GOOD LUCK, YOU GUYS!
GOOD LUCK TO YOU, TOO.

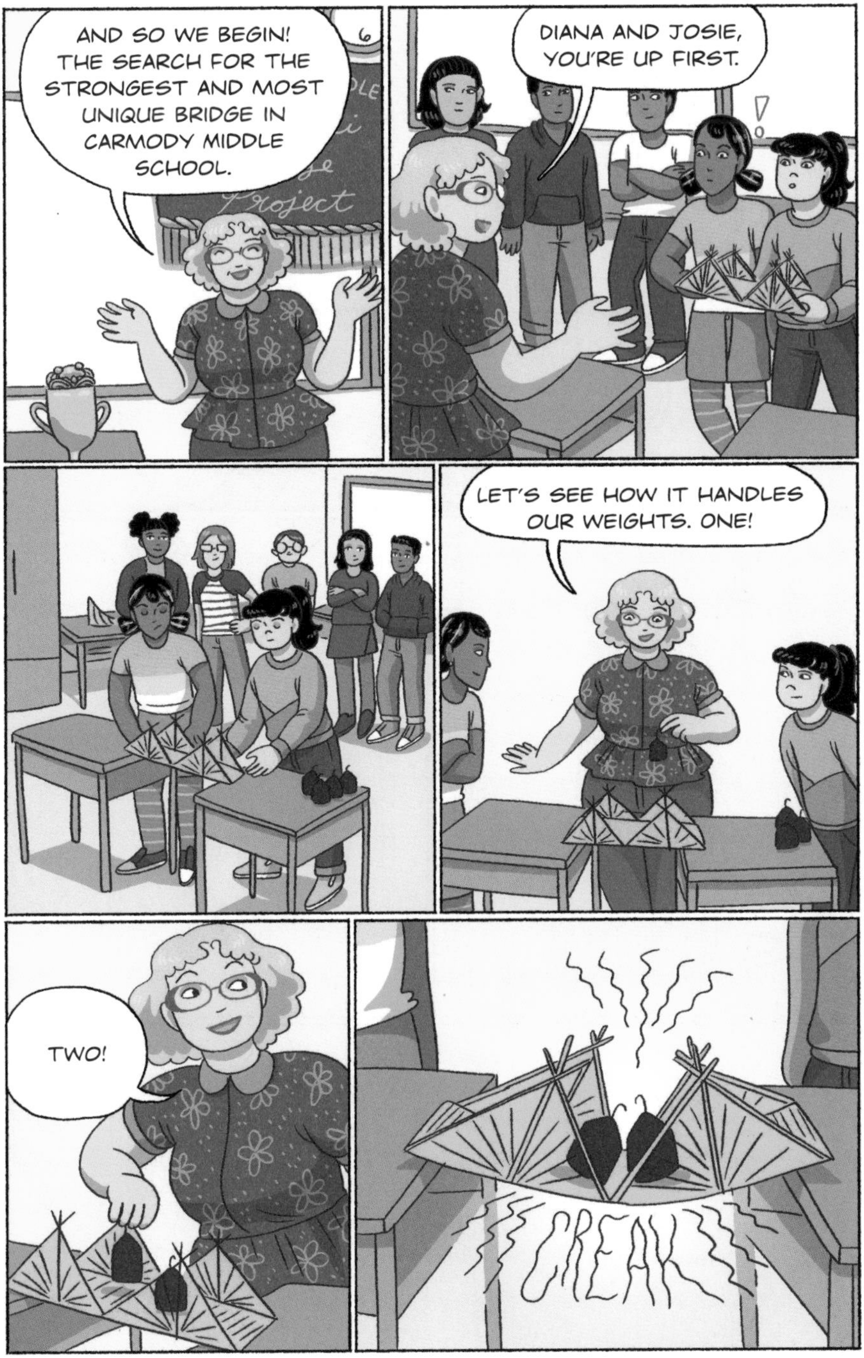
AND SO WE BEGIN! THE SEARCH FOR THE STRONGEST AND MOST UNIQUE BRIDGE IN CARMODY MIDDLE SCHOOL.
Project
DIANA AND JOSIE, YOU'RE UP FIRST.
LET'S SEE HOW IT HANDLES OUR WEIGHTS. ONE!
TWO!
CREAK

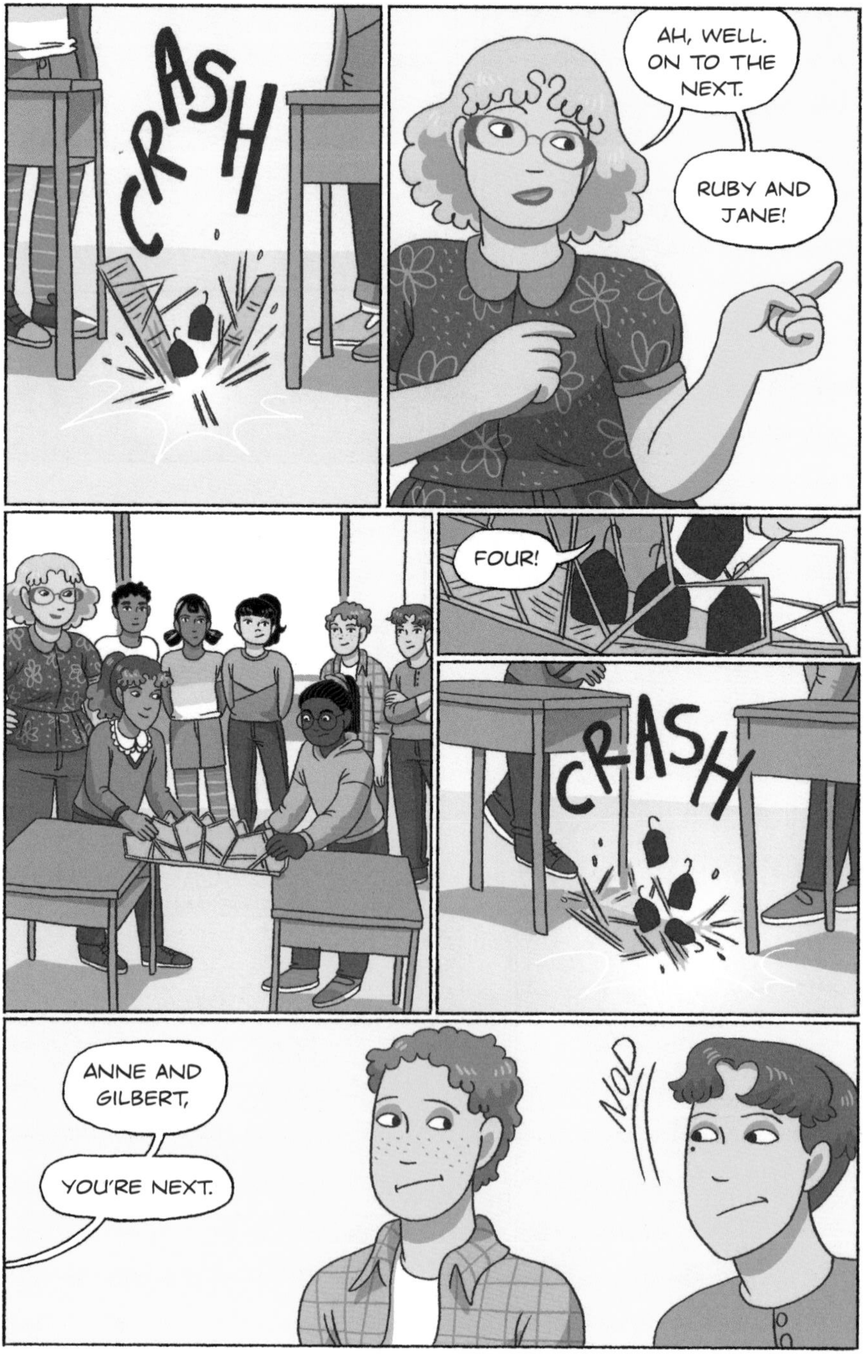
CRASH
AH, WELL. ON TO THE NEXT.
RUBY AND JANE!
FOUR!
CRASH
ANNE AND GILBERT,
YOU'RE NEXT.
NOD

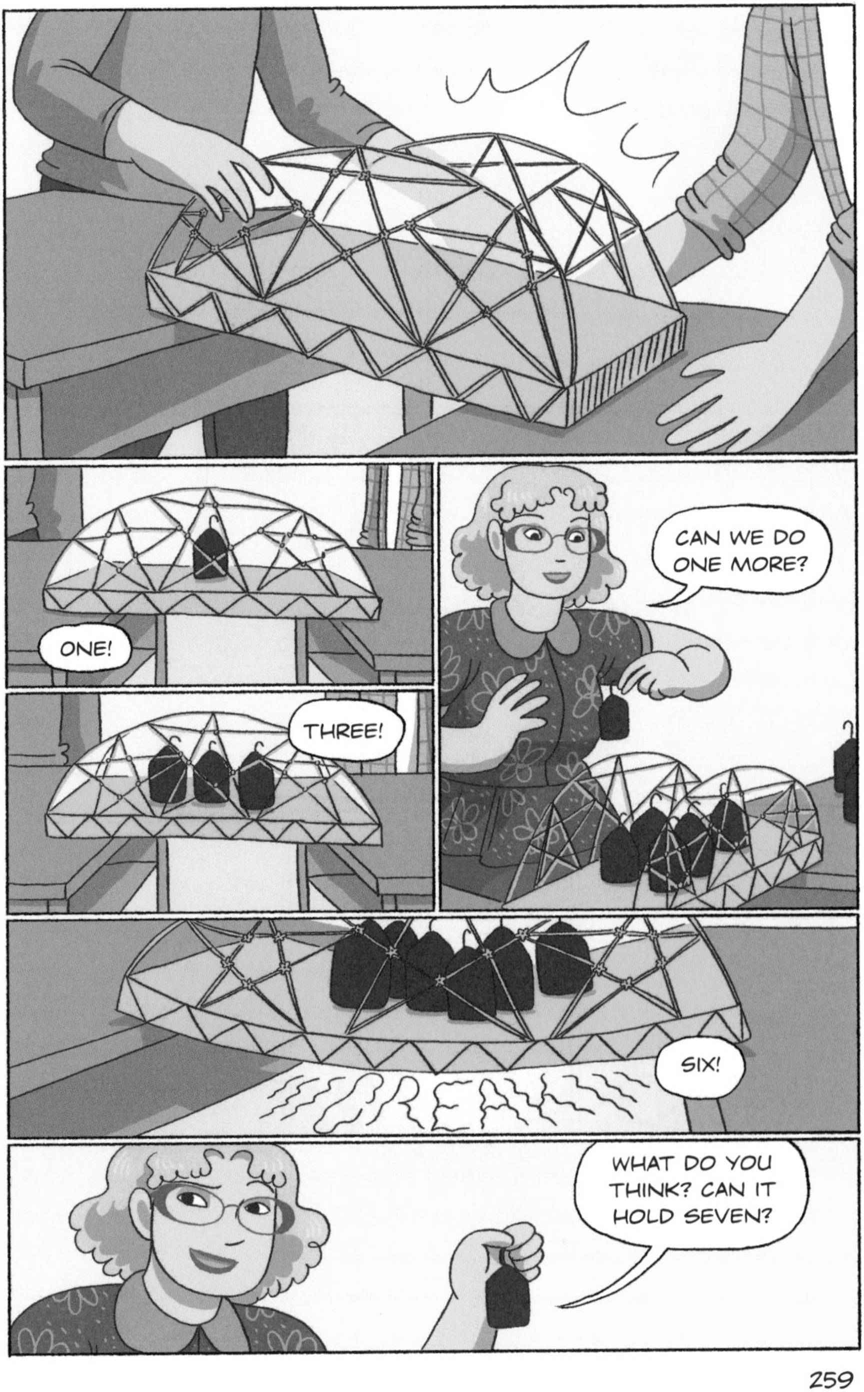
ONE!
CAN WE DO ONE MORE?
THREE!
SIX!
WHAT DO YOU THINK? CAN IT HOLD SEVEN?

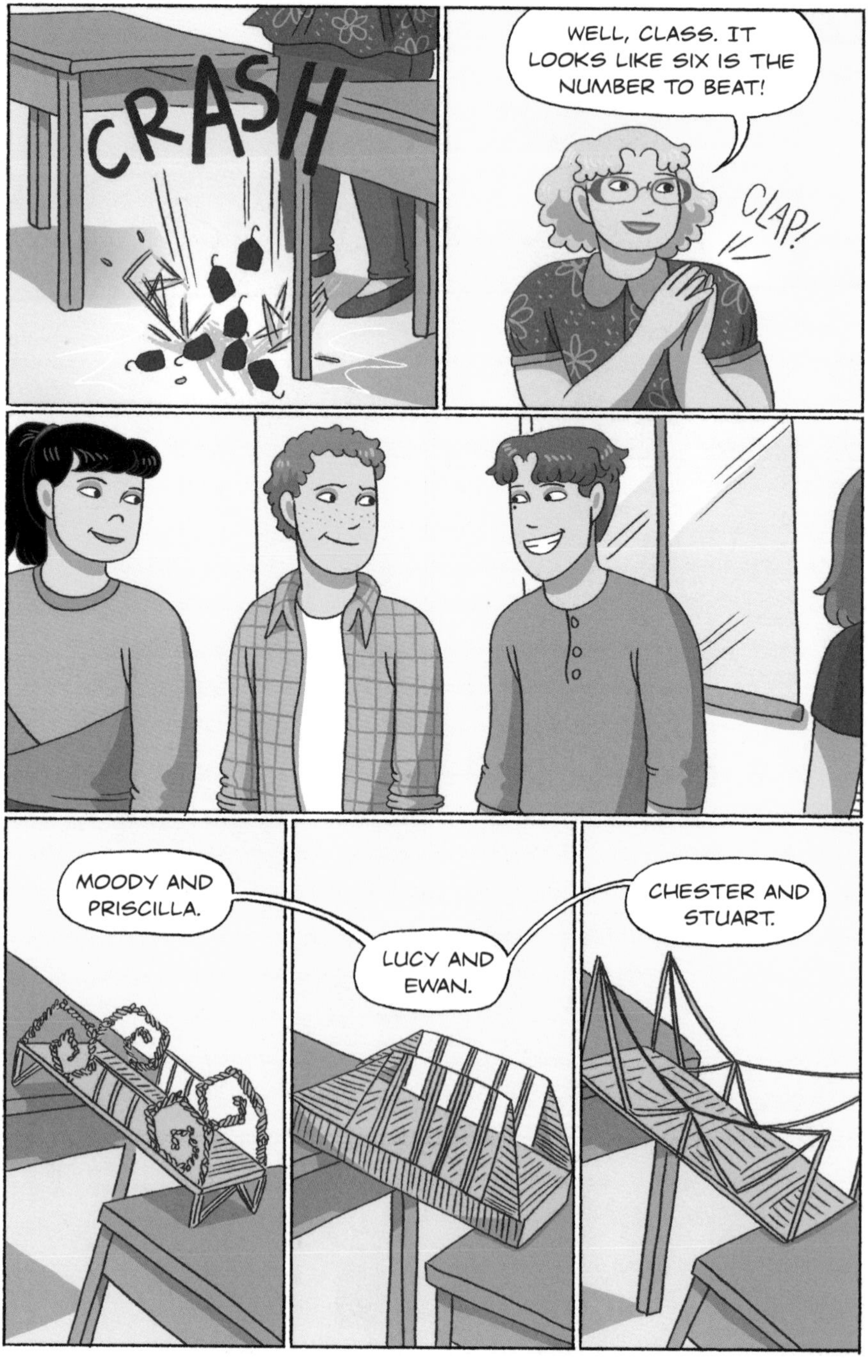
CRASH
WELL, CLASS. IT LOOKS LIKE SIX IS THE NUMBER TO BEAT!
CLAP!
MOODY AND PRISCILLA.
LUCY AND EWAN.
CHESTER AND STUART.

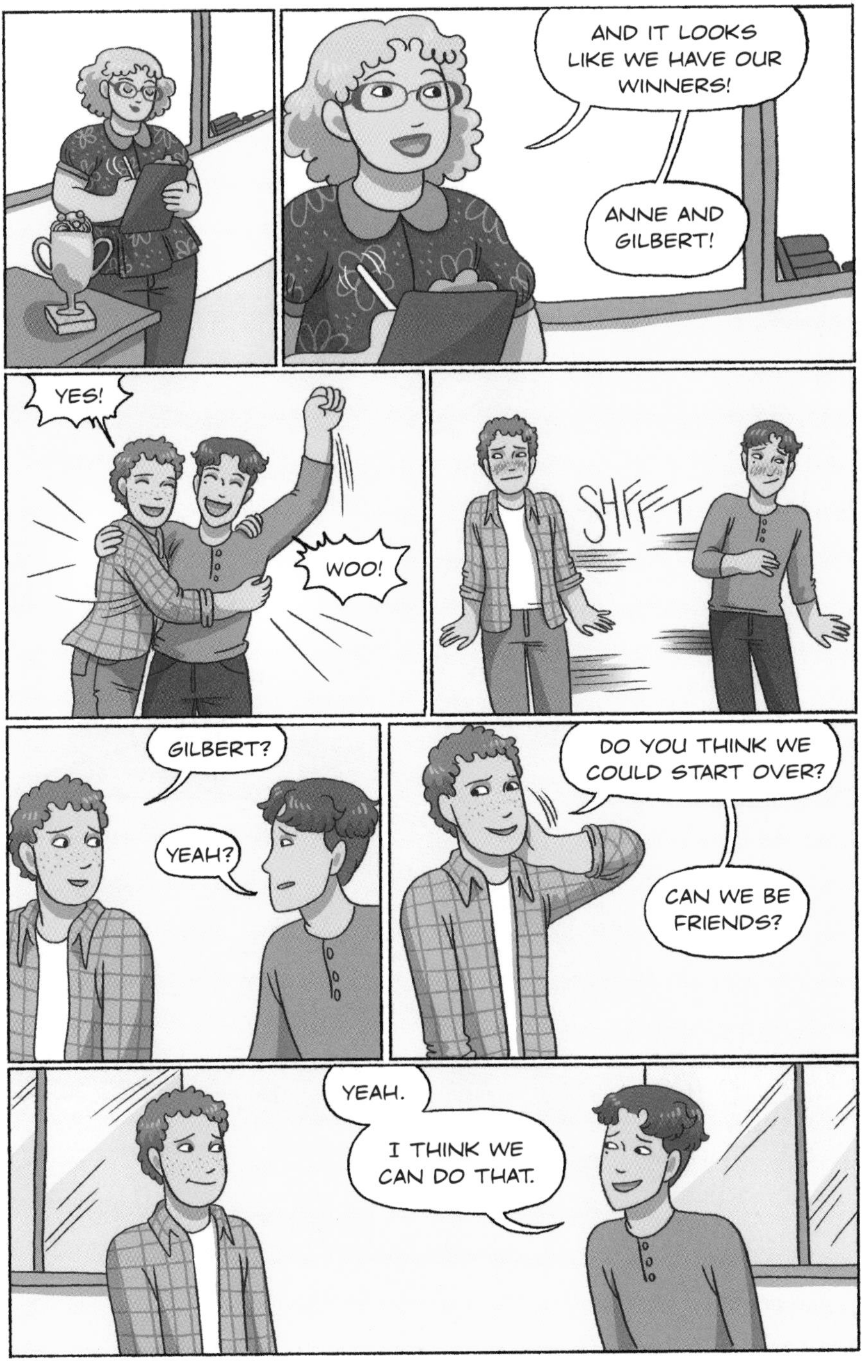
AND IT LOOKS LIKE WE HAVE OUR WINNERS!
ANNE AND GILBERT!
YES!
WOO!
SHFFFT
GILBERT?
YEAH?
DO YOU THINK WE COULD START OVER?
CAN WE BE FRIENDS?
YEAH.
I THINK WE CAN DO THAT.

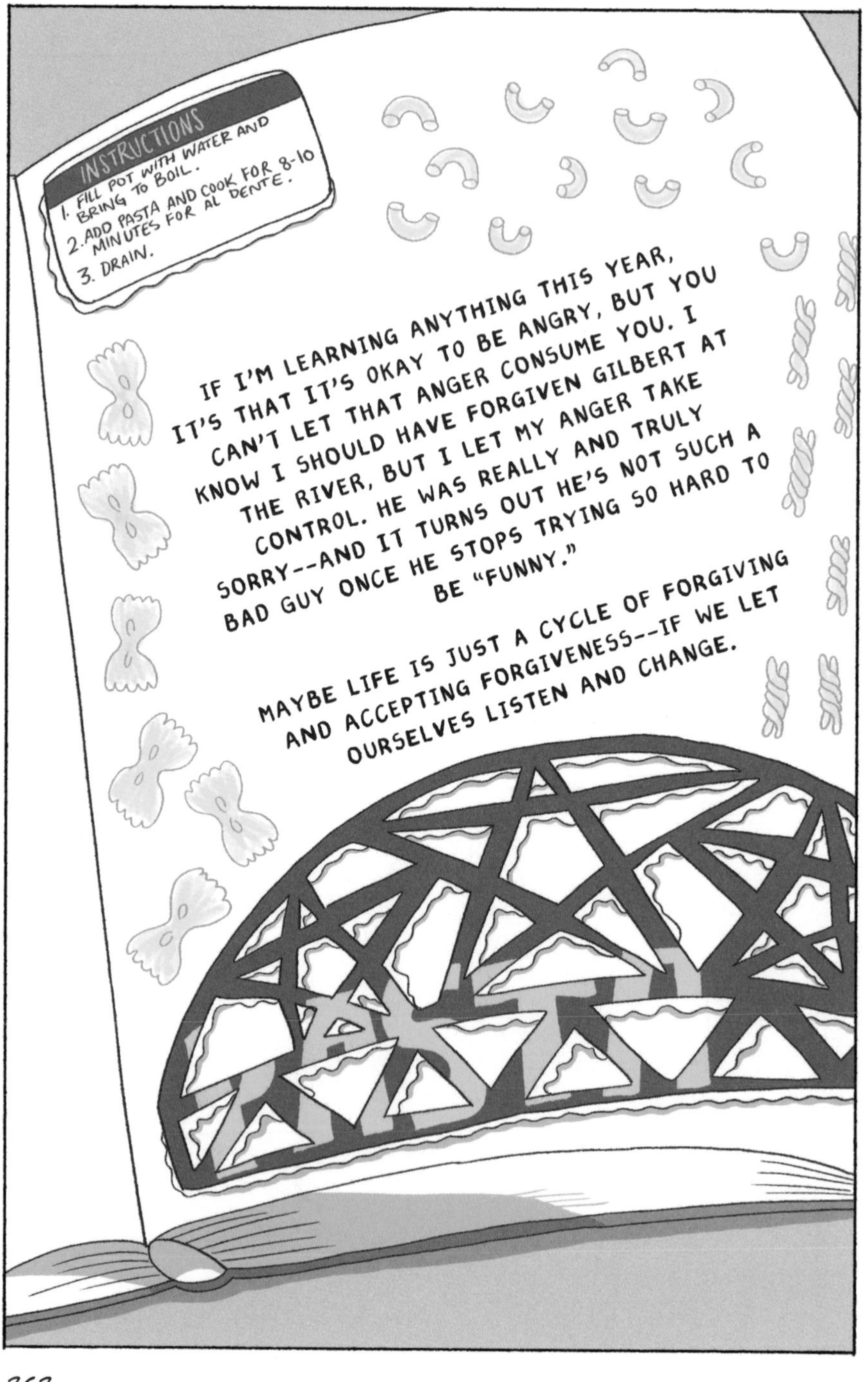
INSTRUCTIONS
1. FILL POT WITH WATER AND BRING TO BOIL.
2. ADD PASTA AND COOK FOR 8-10 MINUTES FOR AL DENTE.
3. DRAIN.
IF I'M LEARNING ANYTHING THIS YEAR, IT'S THAT IT'S OKAY TO BE ANGRY, BUT YOU CAN'T LET THAT ANGER CONSUME YOU. I KNOW I SHOULD HAVE FORGIVEN GILBERT AT THE RIVER, BUT I LET MY ANGER TAKE CONTROL. HE WAS REALLY AND TRULY SORRY--AND IT TURNS OUT HE'S NOT SUCH A BAD GUY ONCE HE STOPS TRYING SO HARD TO BE "FUNNY."
MAYBE LIFE IS JUST A CYCLE OF FORGIVING AND ACCEPTING FORGIVENESS--IF WE LET OURSELVES LISTEN AND CHANGE.

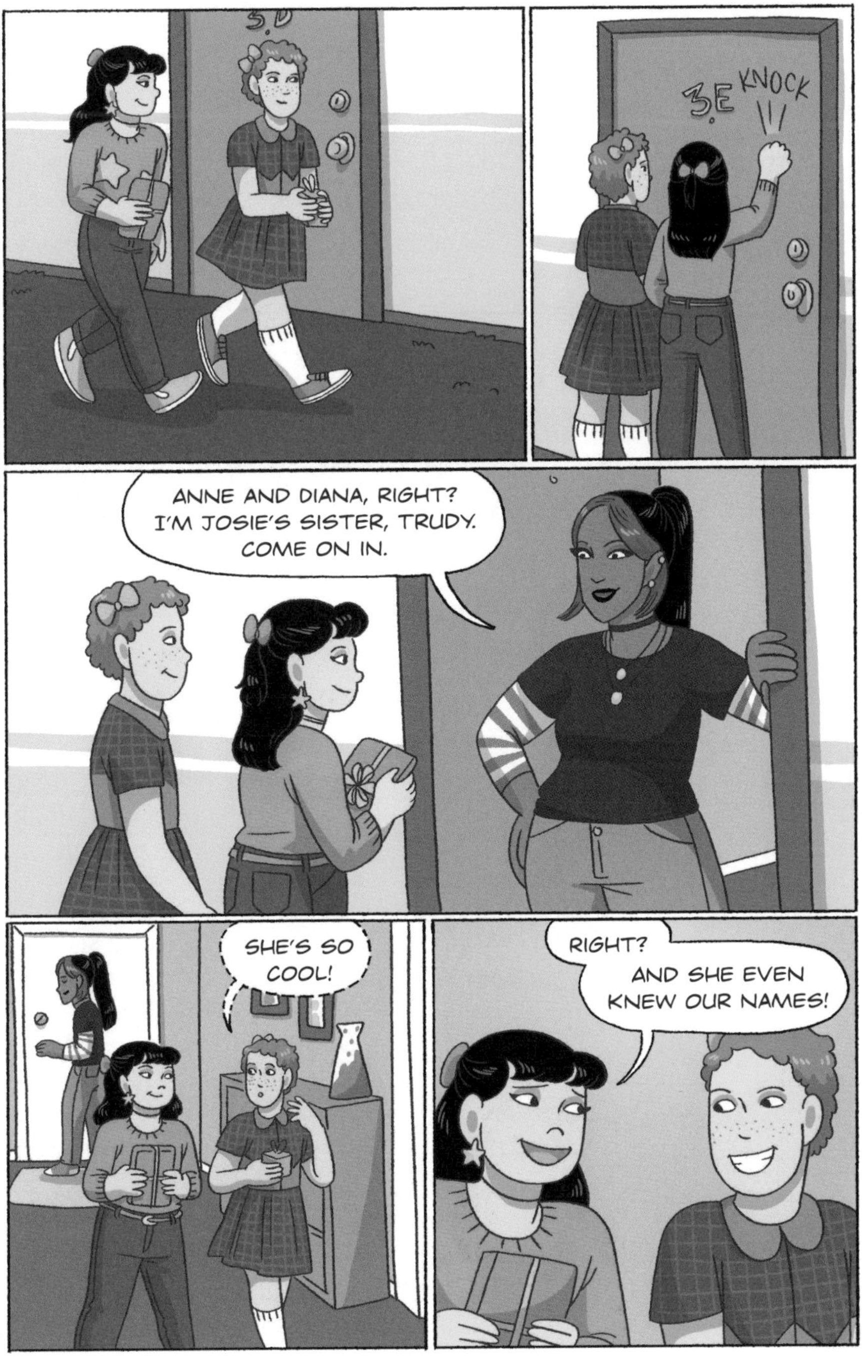
3D
3E
KNOCK
ANNE AND DIANA, RIGHT? I'M JOSIE'S SISTER, TRUDY. COME ON IN.
SHE'S SO COOL!
RIGHT?
AND SHE EVEN KNEW OUR NAMES!

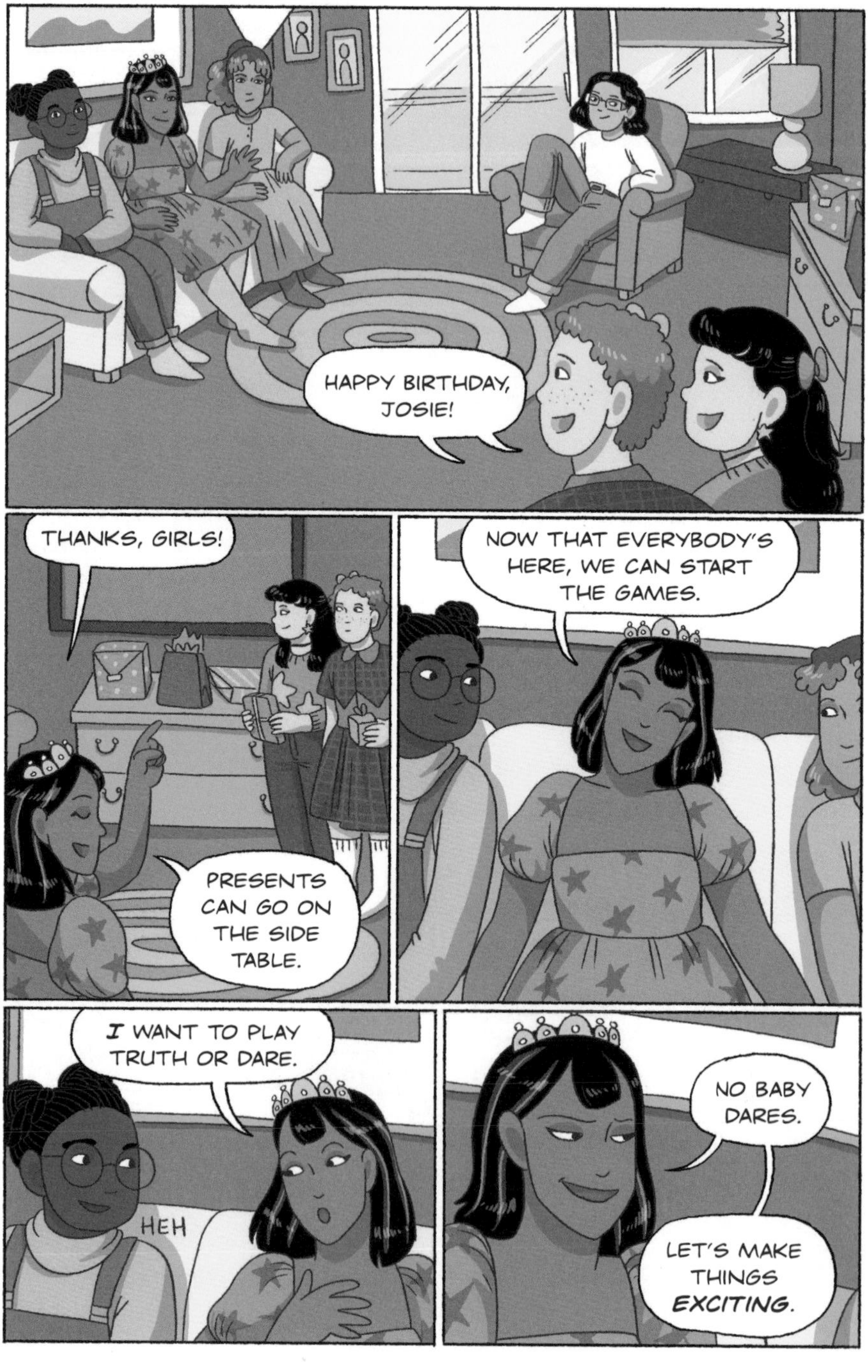
HAPPY BIRTHDAY, JOSIE!
THANKS, GIRLS!
PRESENTS CAN GO ON THE SIDE TABLE.
NOW THAT EVERYBODY'S HERE, WE CAN START THE GAMES.
I WANT TO PLAY TRUTH OR DARE.
HEH
NO BABY DARES.
LET'S MAKE THINGS ***EXCITING***.

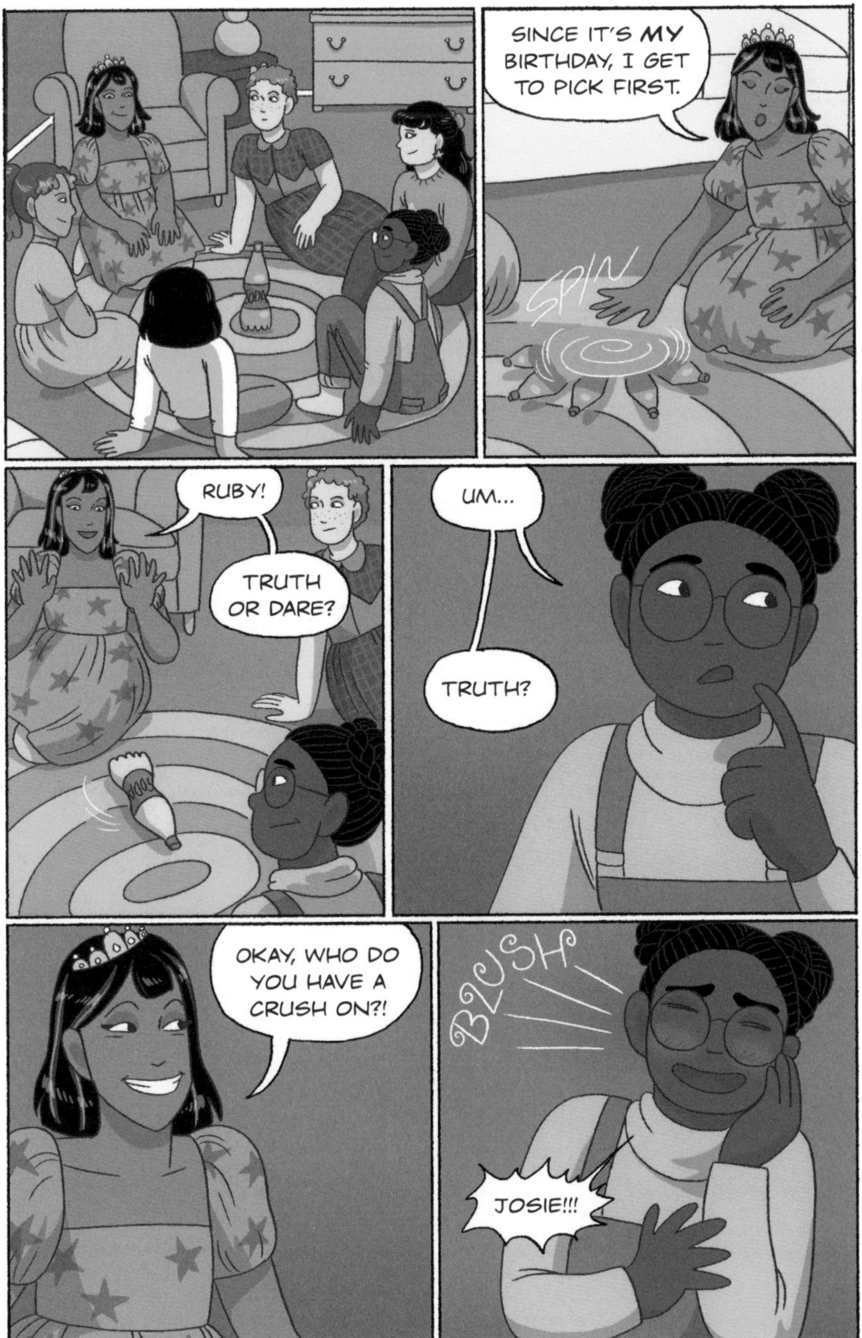
SINCE IT'S MY BIRTHDAY, I GET TO PICK FIRST.
SPIN
RUBY!
TRUTH OR DARE?
UM...
TRUTH?
OKAY, WHO DO YOU HAVE A CRUSH ON?!
BLUSH
JOSIE!!!

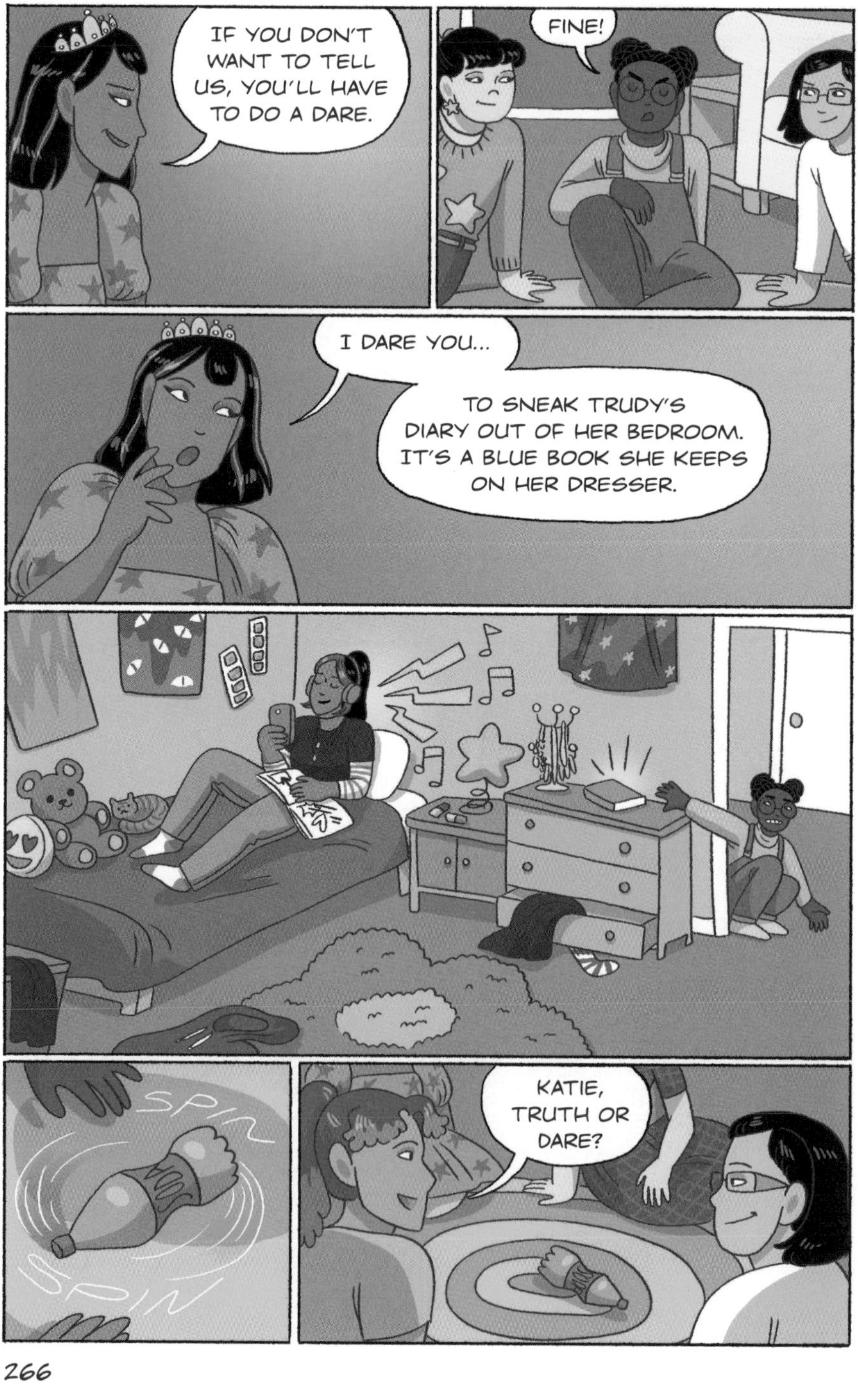
IF YOU DON'T WANT TO TELL US, YOU'LL HAVE TO DO A DARE.
FINE!
I DARE YOU...
TO SNEAK TRUDY'S DIARY OUT OF HER BEDROOM. IT'S A BLUE BOOK SHE KEEPS ON HER DRESSER.
SPIN
SPIN
KATIE, TRUTH OR DARE?

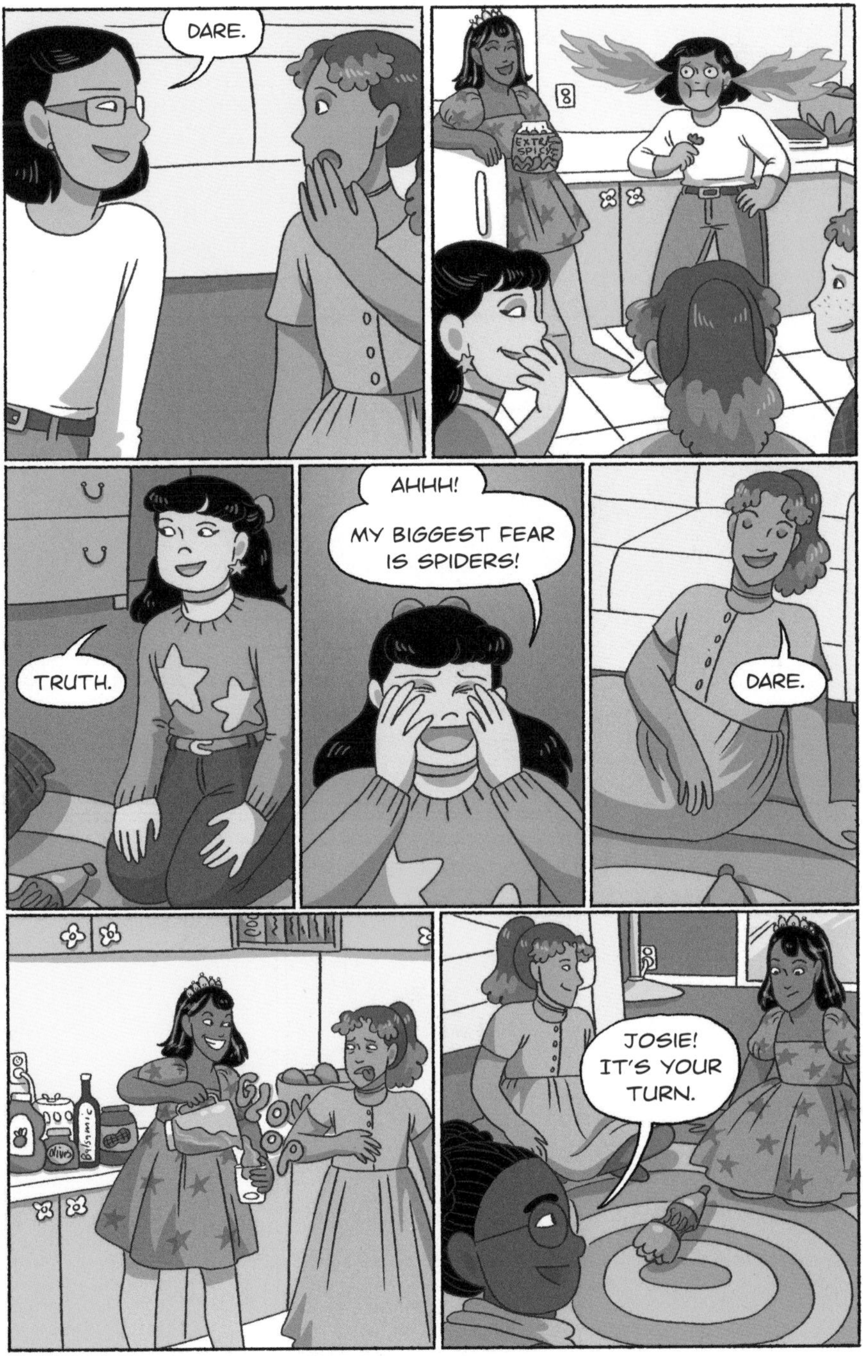
DARE.
EXTRA SPICY
TRUTH.
AHHH!
MY BIGGEST FEAR IS SPIDERS!
DARE.
olives
Balsamic
JOSIE! IT'S YOUR TURN.

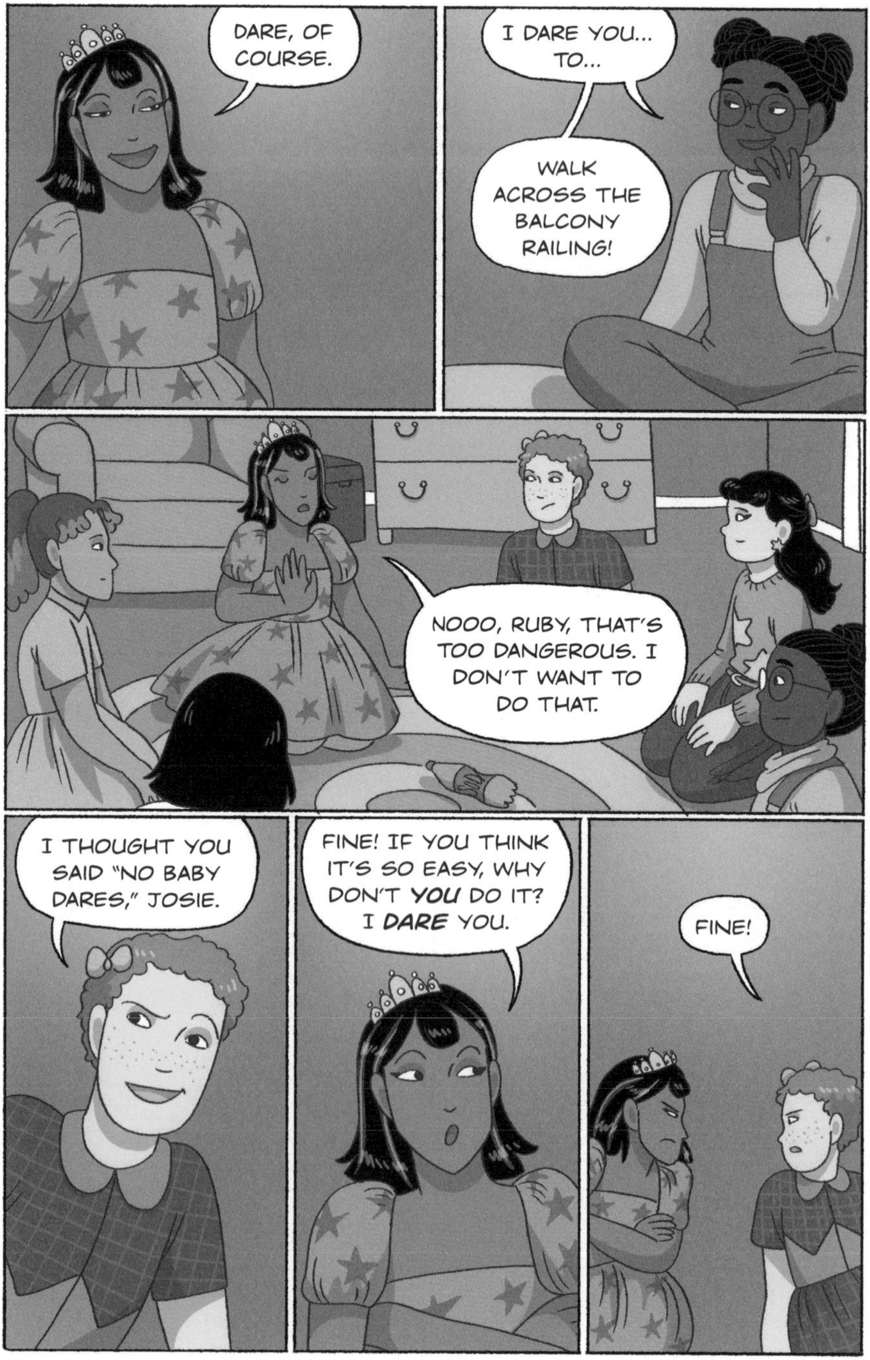
DARE, OF COURSE.
I DARE YOU... TO...
WALK ACROSS THE BALCONY RAILING!
NOOO, RUBY, THAT'S TOO DANGEROUS. I DON'T WANT TO DO THAT.
I THOUGHT YOU SAID "NO BABY DARES," JOSIE.
FINE! IF YOU THINK IT'S SO EASY, WHY DON'T **YOU** DO IT? I **DARE** YOU.
FINE!

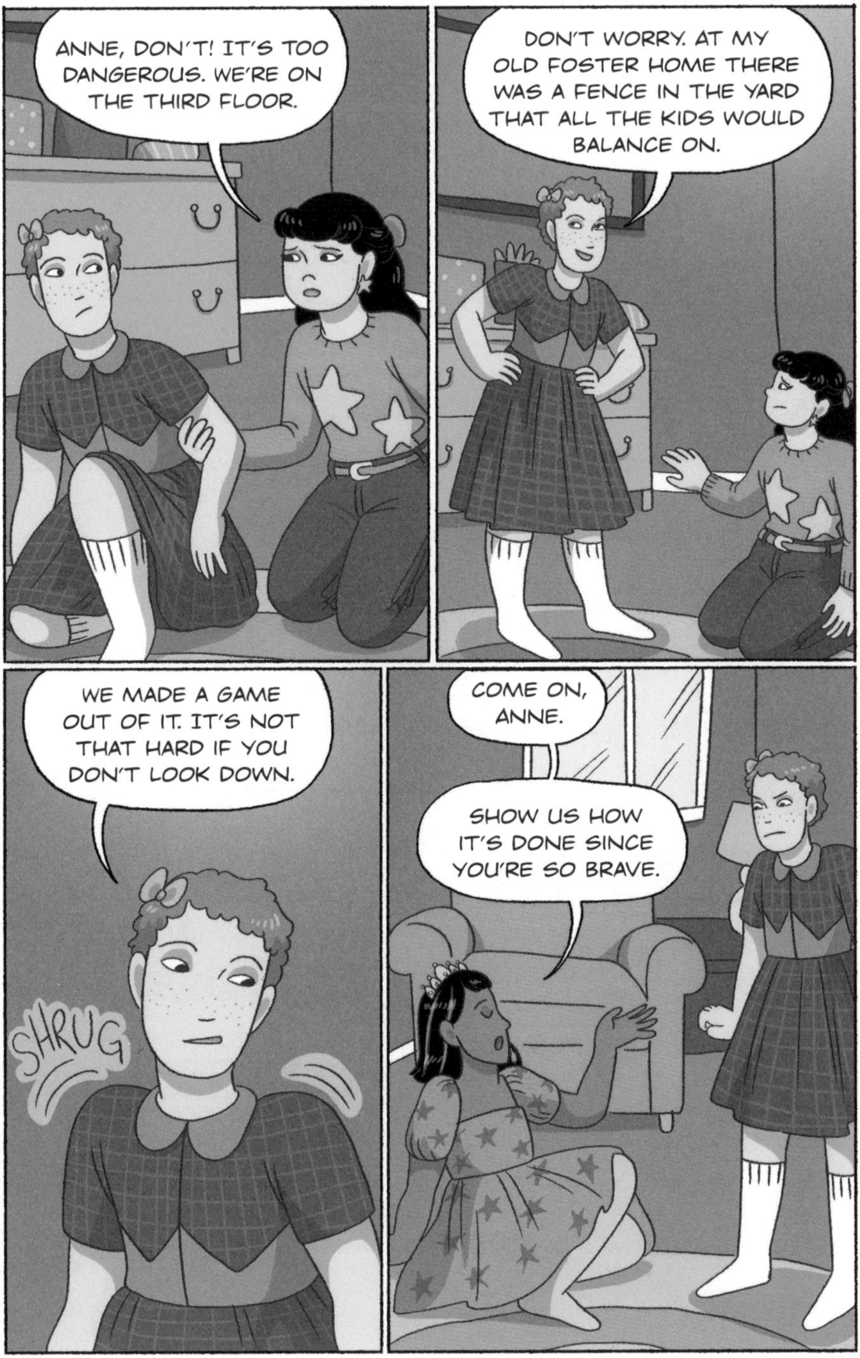
ANNE, DON'T! IT'S TOO DANGEROUS. WE'RE ON THE THIRD FLOOR.
DON'T WORRY. AT MY OLD FOSTER HOME THERE WAS A FENCE IN THE YARD THAT ALL THE KIDS WOULD BALANCE ON.
WE MADE A GAME OUT OF IT. IT'S NOT THAT HARD IF YOU DON'T LOOK DOWN.
SHRUG
COME ON, ANNE.
SHOW US HOW IT'S DONE SINCE YOU'RE SO BRAVE.

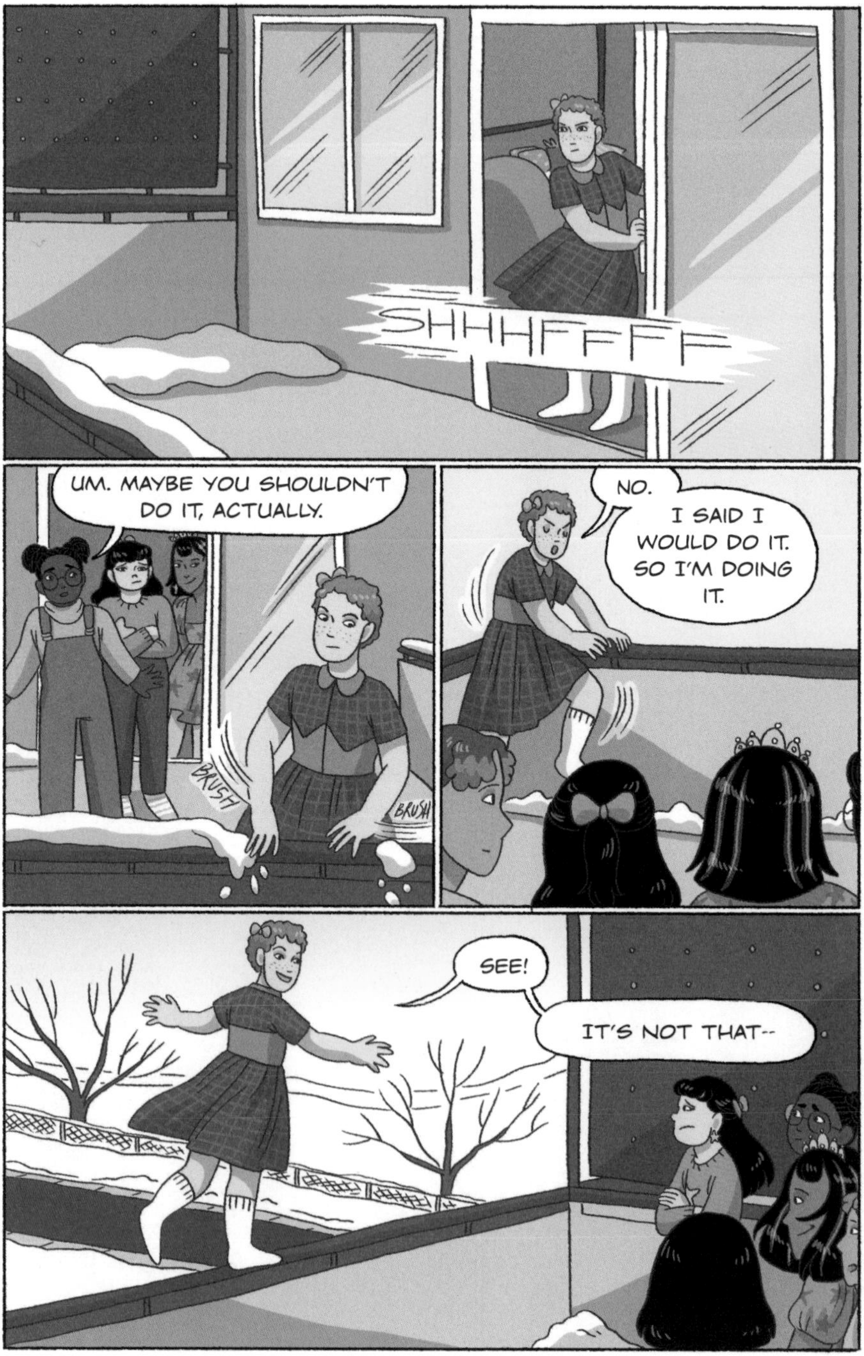
SHHHFFFF
UM. MAYBE YOU SHOULDN'T DO IT, ACTUALLY.
BRUSH
BRUSH
NO.
I SAID I WOULD DO IT. SO I'M DOING IT.
SEE!
IT'S NOT THAT--

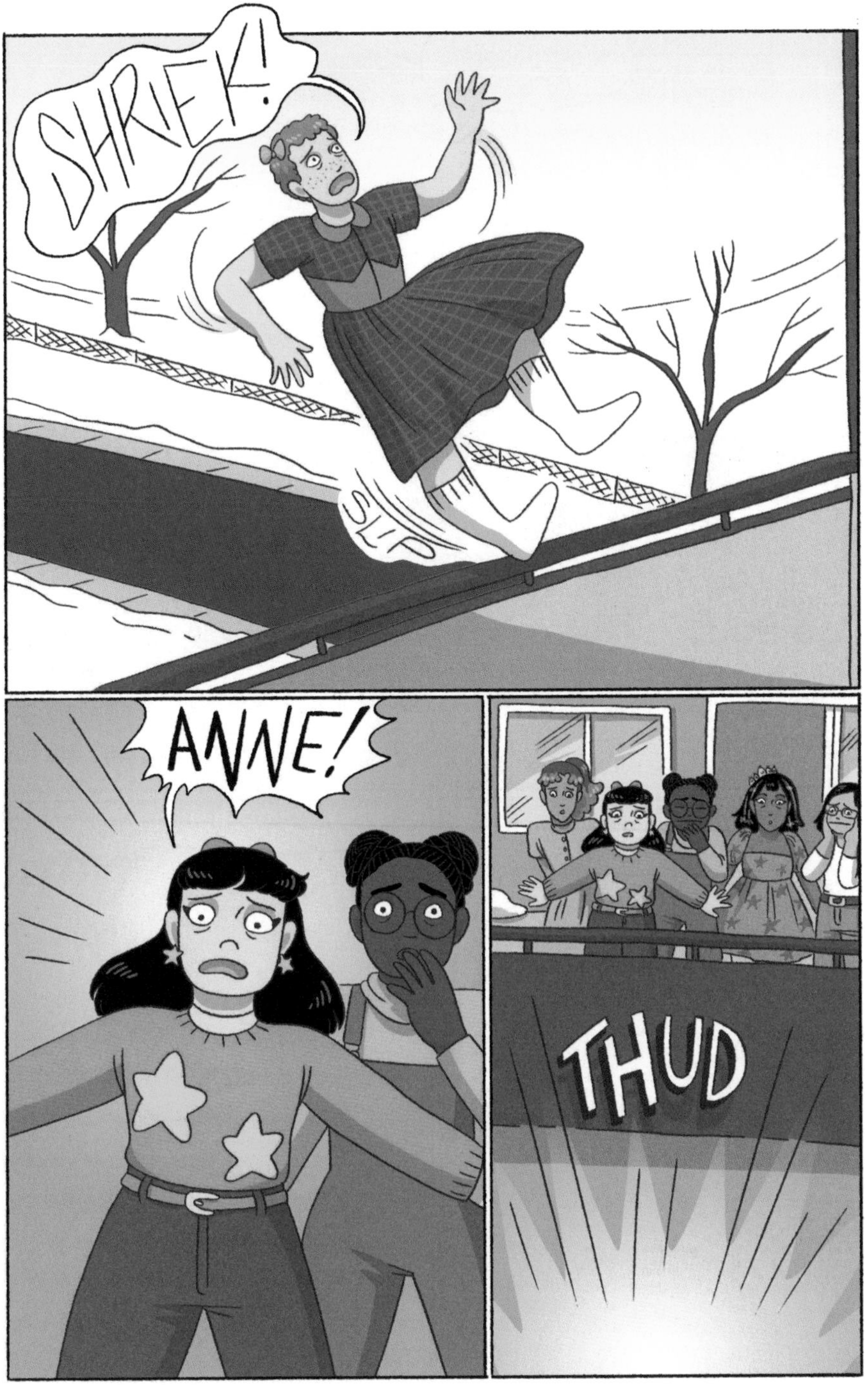
SHRIEK!
SLIP
ANNE!
THUD

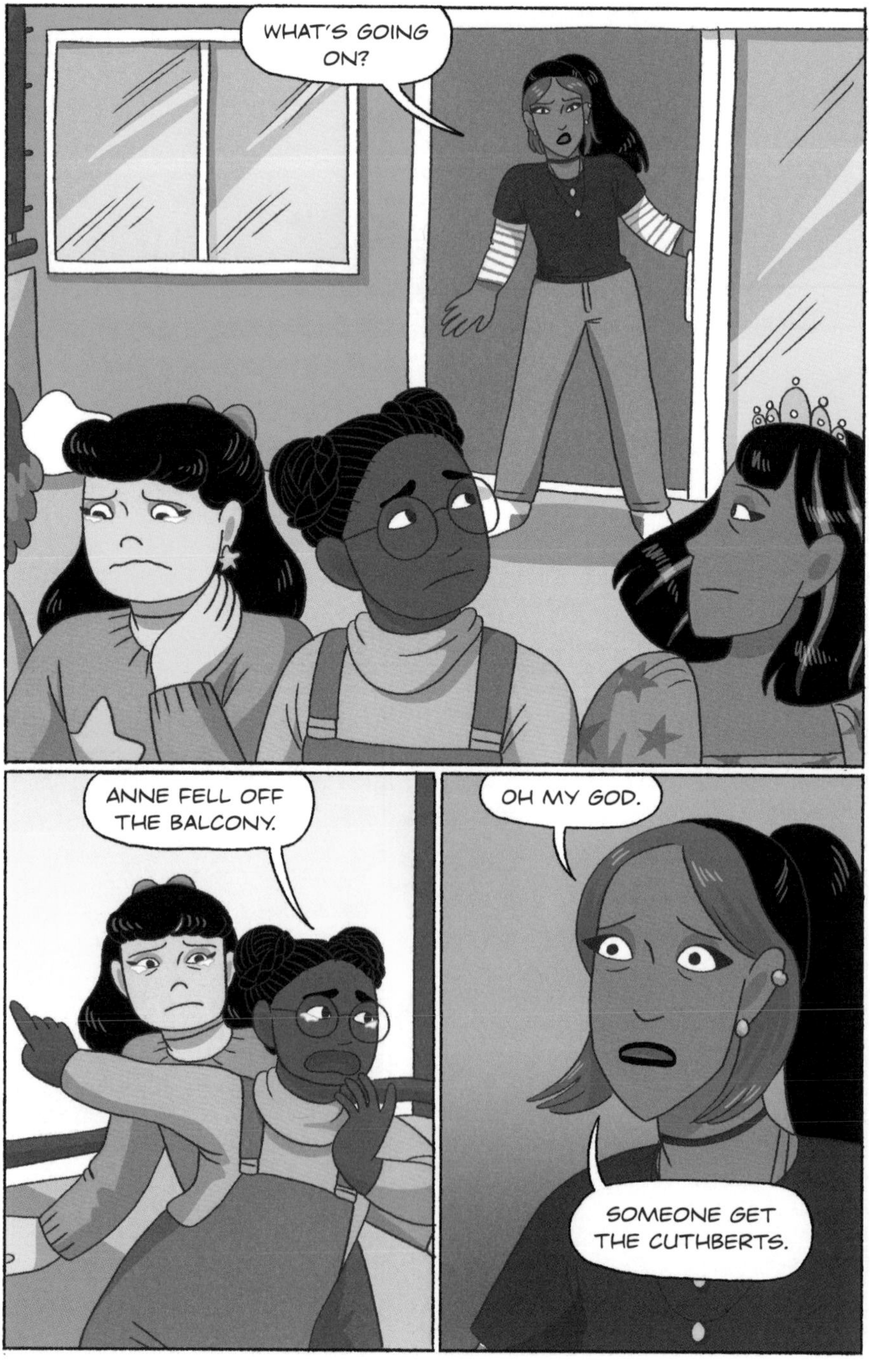
WHAT'S GOING ON?
ANNE FELL OFF THE BALCONY.
OH MY GOD.
SOMEONE GET THE CUTHBERTS.

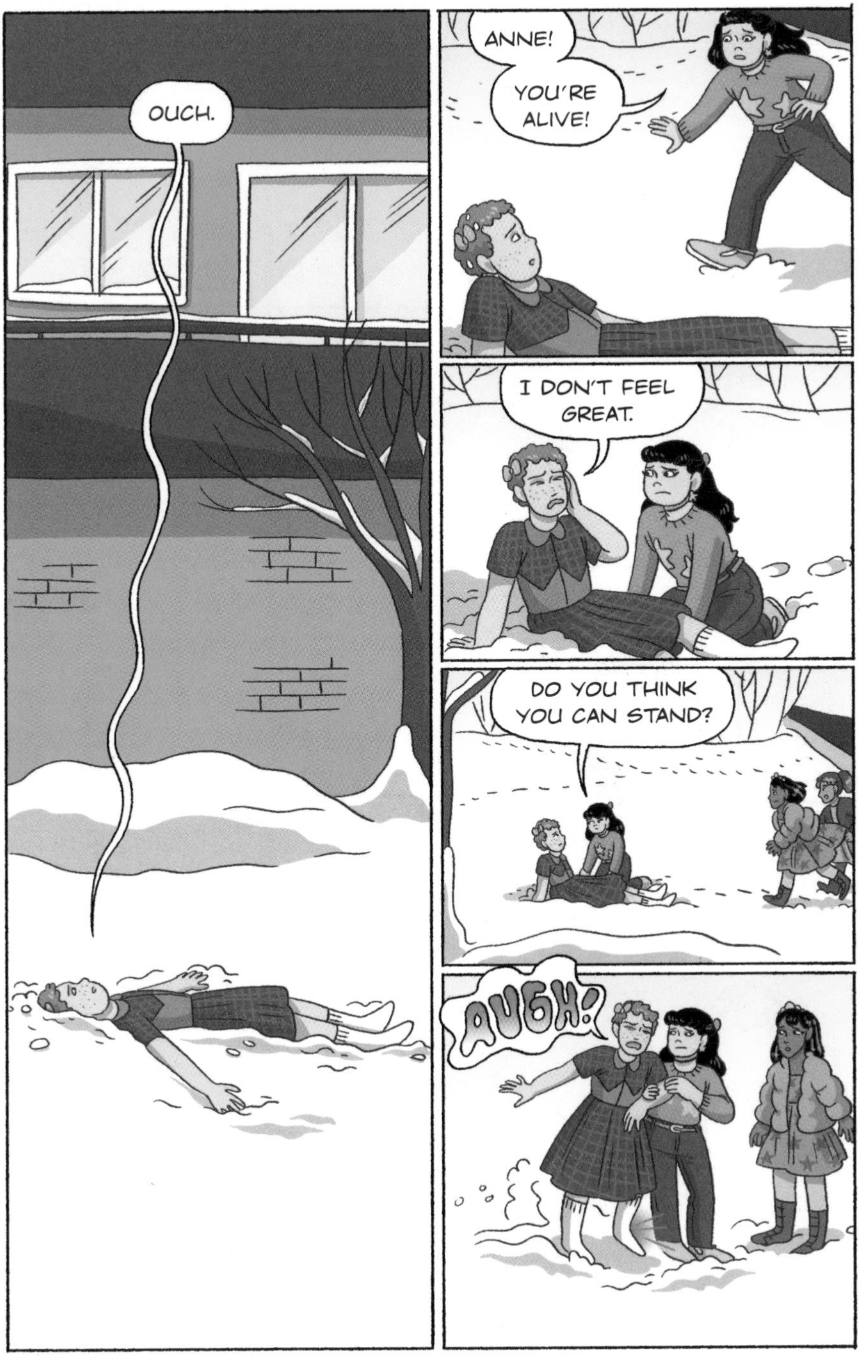
OUCH.
ANNE!
YOU'RE ALIVE!
I DON'T FEEL GREAT.
DO YOU THINK YOU CAN STAND?
AUGH!

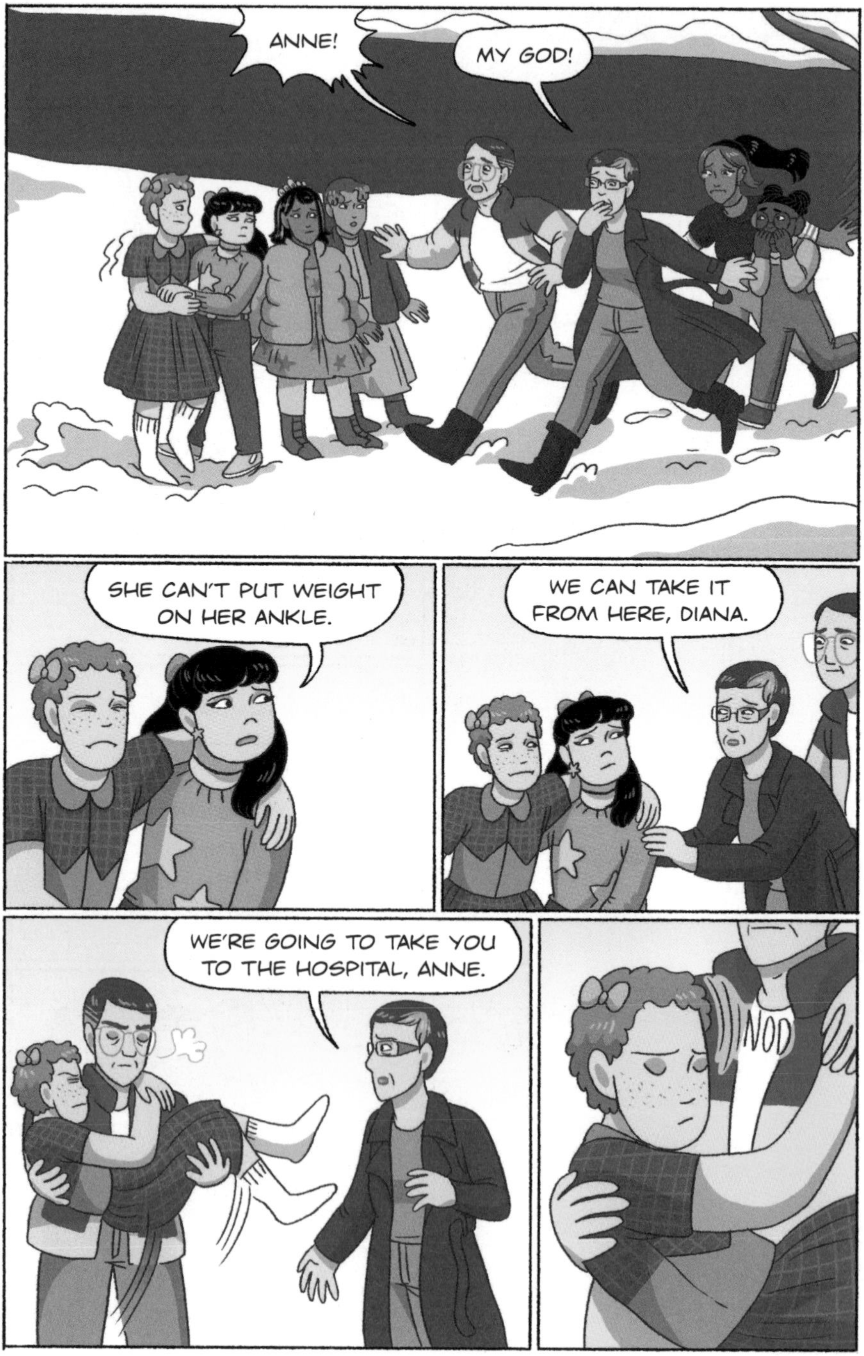
ANNE!
MY GOD!
SHE CAN'T PUT WEIGHT ON HER ANKLE.
WE CAN TAKE IT FROM HERE, DIANA.
WE'RE GOING TO TAKE YOU TO THE HOSPITAL, ANNE.
NOD

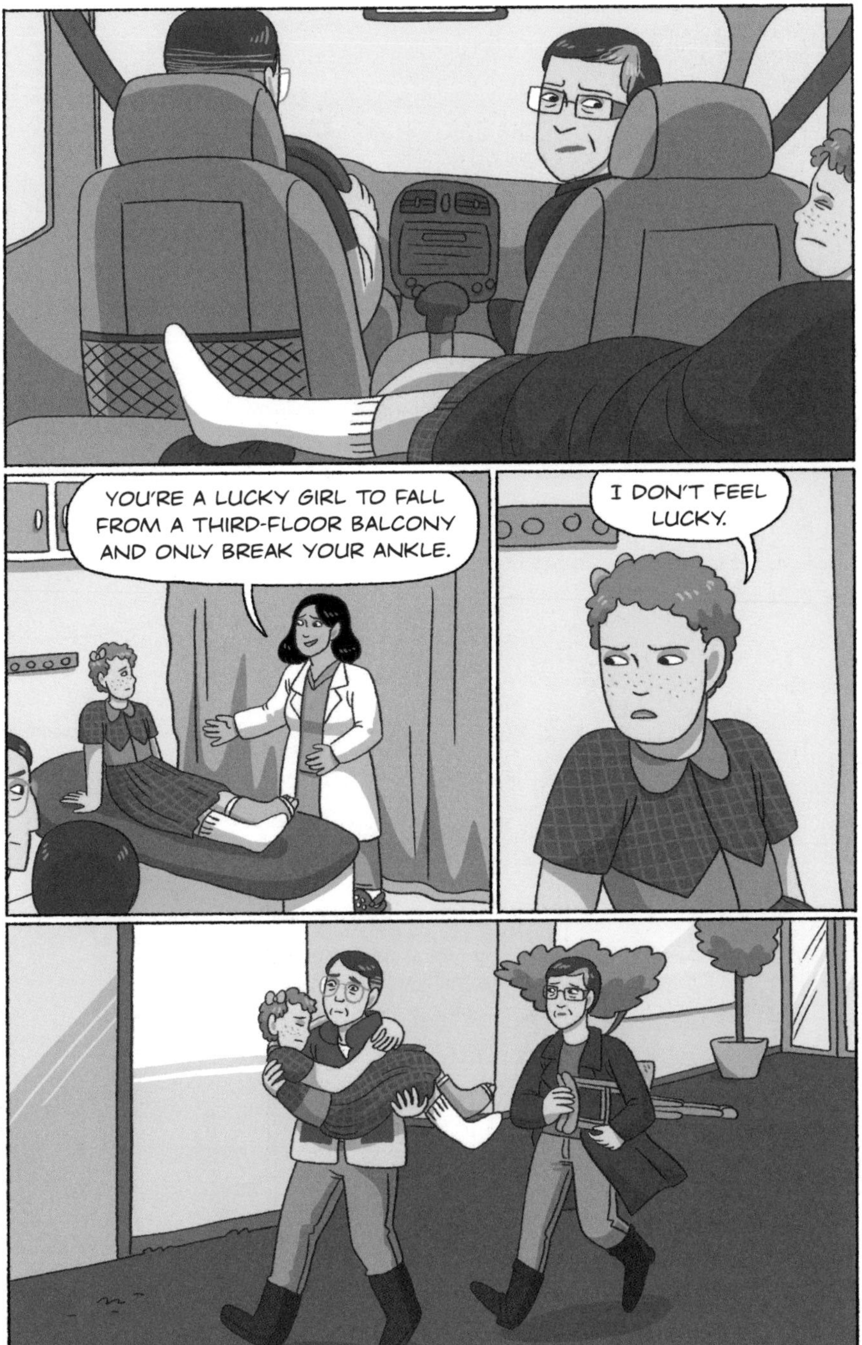
YOU'RE A LUCKY GIRL TO FALL FROM A THIRD-FLOOR BALCONY AND ONLY BREAK YOUR ANKLE.
I DON'T FEEL LUCKY.

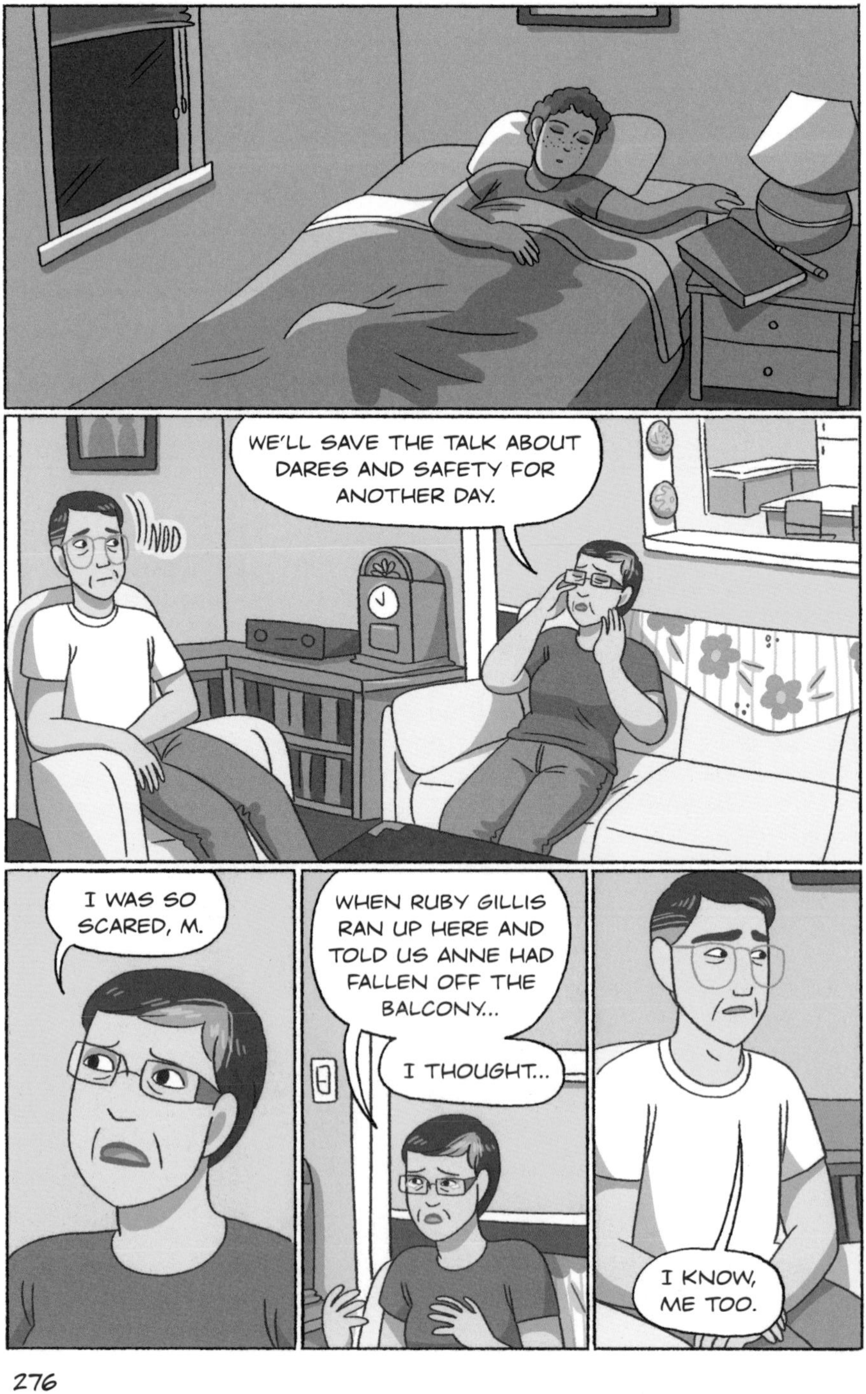

WE'LL SAVE THE TALK ABOUT DARES AND SAFETY FOR ANOTHER DAY.
NOD
I WAS SO SCARED, M.
WHEN RUBY GILLIS RAN UP HERE AND TOLD US ANNE HAD FALLEN OFF THE BALCONY...
I THOUGHT...
I KNOW, ME TOO.

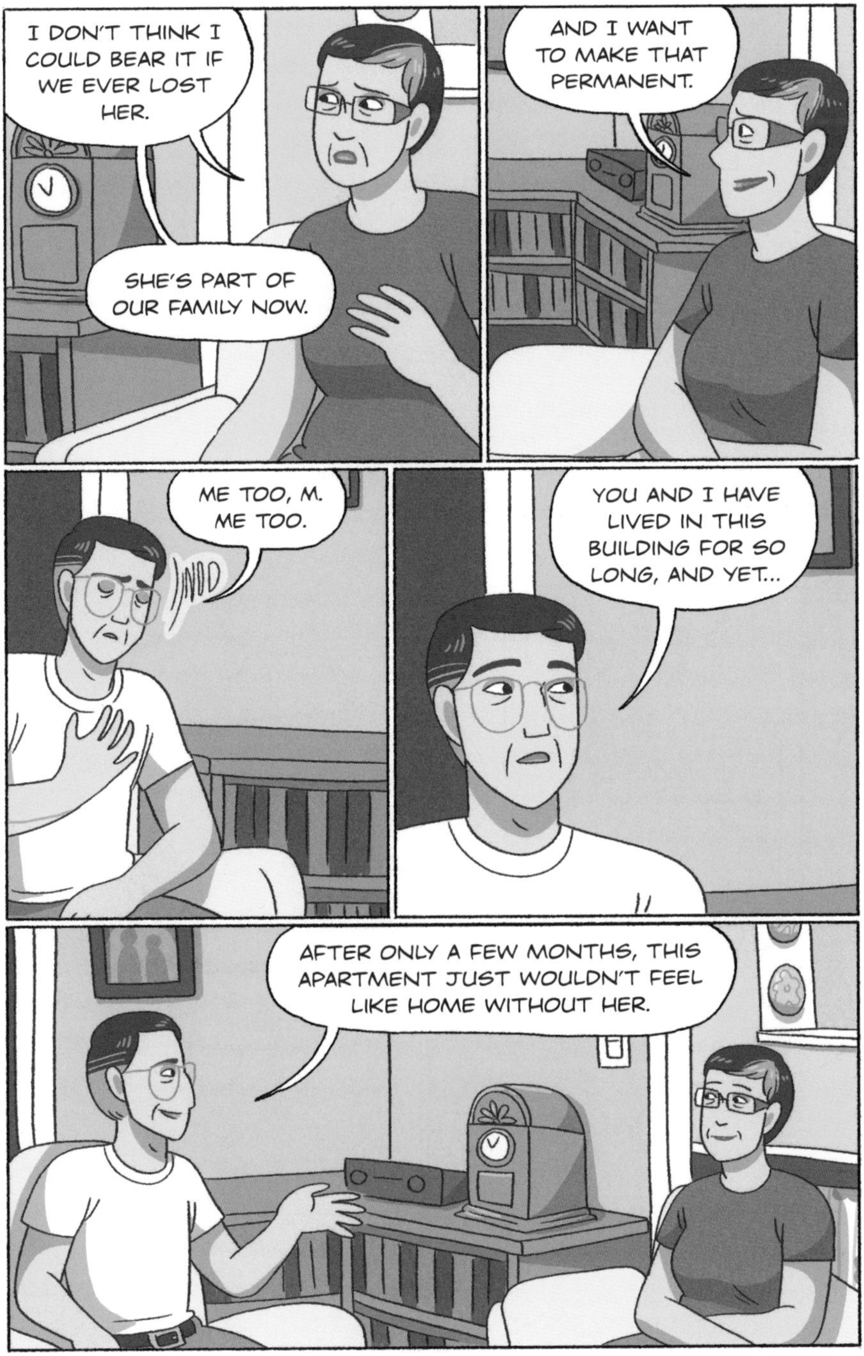
I DON'T THINK I COULD BEAR IT IF WE EVER LOST HER.
SHE'S PART OF OUR FAMILY NOW.
AND I WANT TO MAKE THAT PERMANENT.
ME TOO, M. ME TOO.
NOD
YOU AND I HAVE LIVED IN THIS BUILDING FOR SO LONG, AND YET...
AFTER ONLY A FEW MONTHS, THIS APARTMENT JUST WOULDN'T FEEL LIKE HOME WITHOUT HER.

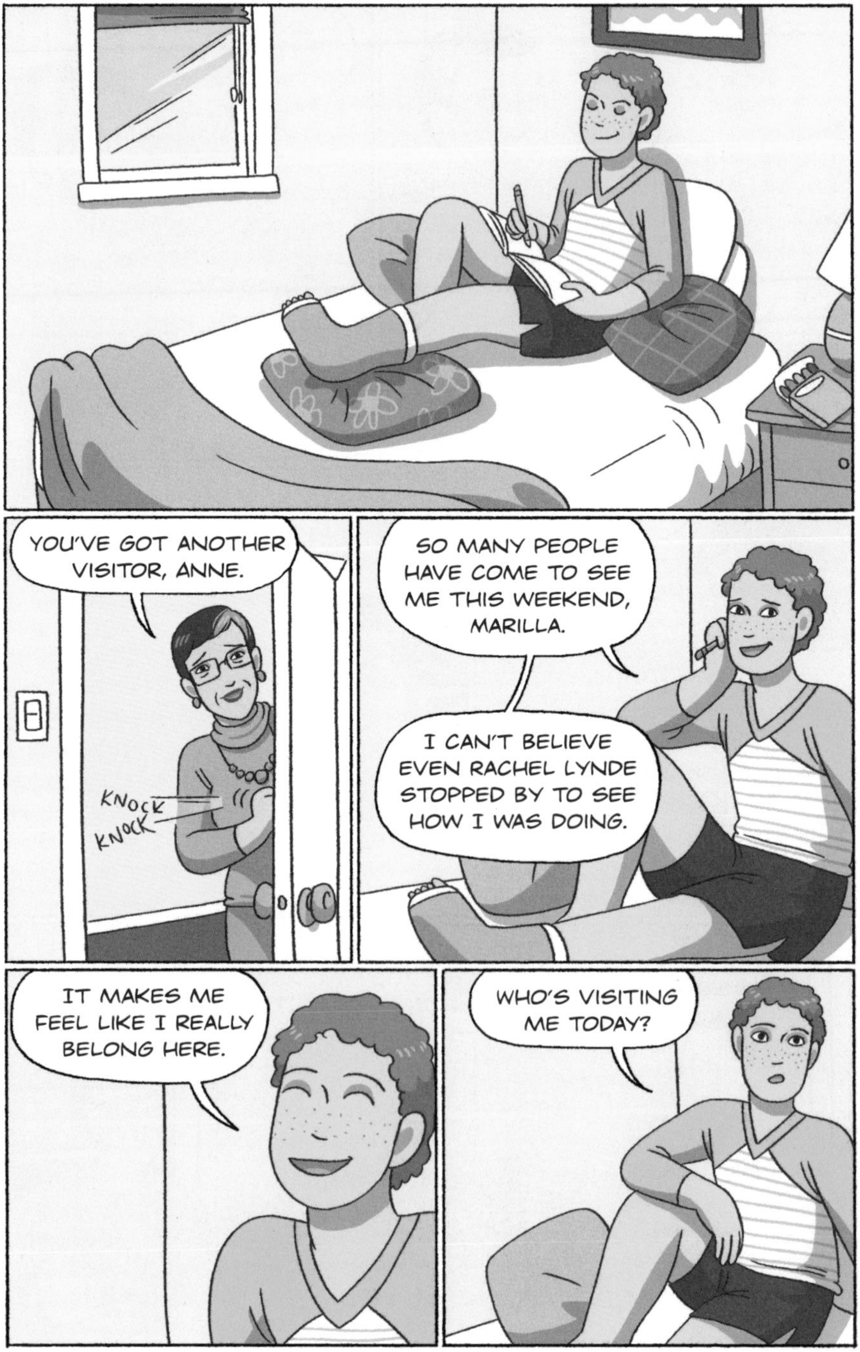
YOU'VE GOT ANOTHER VISITOR, ANNE.
KNOCK KNOCK
SO MANY PEOPLE HAVE COME TO SEE ME THIS WEEKEND, MARILLA.
I CAN'T BELIEVE EVEN RACHEL LYNDE STOPPED BY TO SEE HOW I WAS DOING.
IT MAKES ME FEEL LIKE I REALLY BELONG HERE.
WHO'S VISITING ME TODAY?

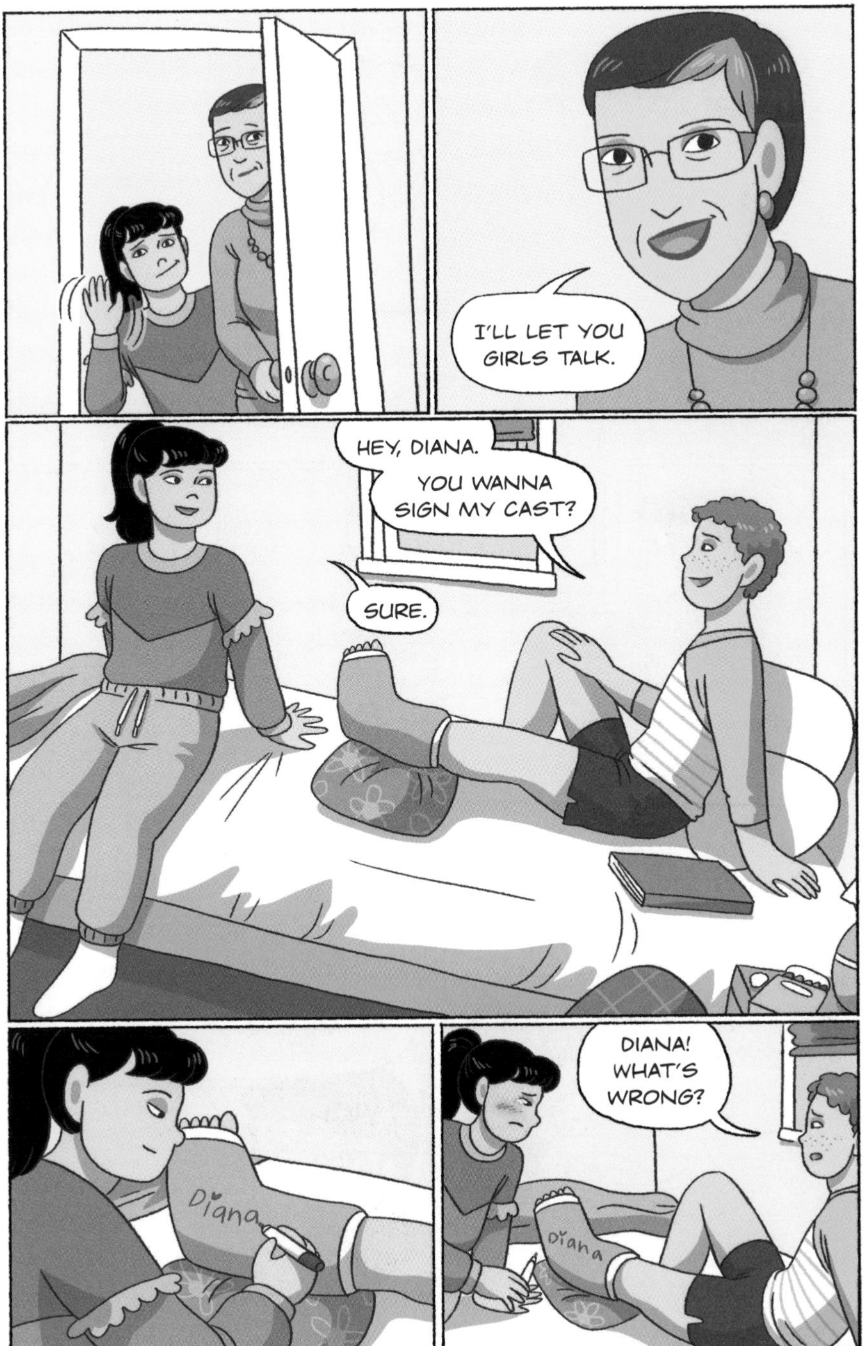
I'LL LET YOU GIRLS TALK.
HEY, DIANA.
YOU WANNA SIGN MY CAST?
SURE.
Diana
DIANA! WHAT'S WRONG?
Diana

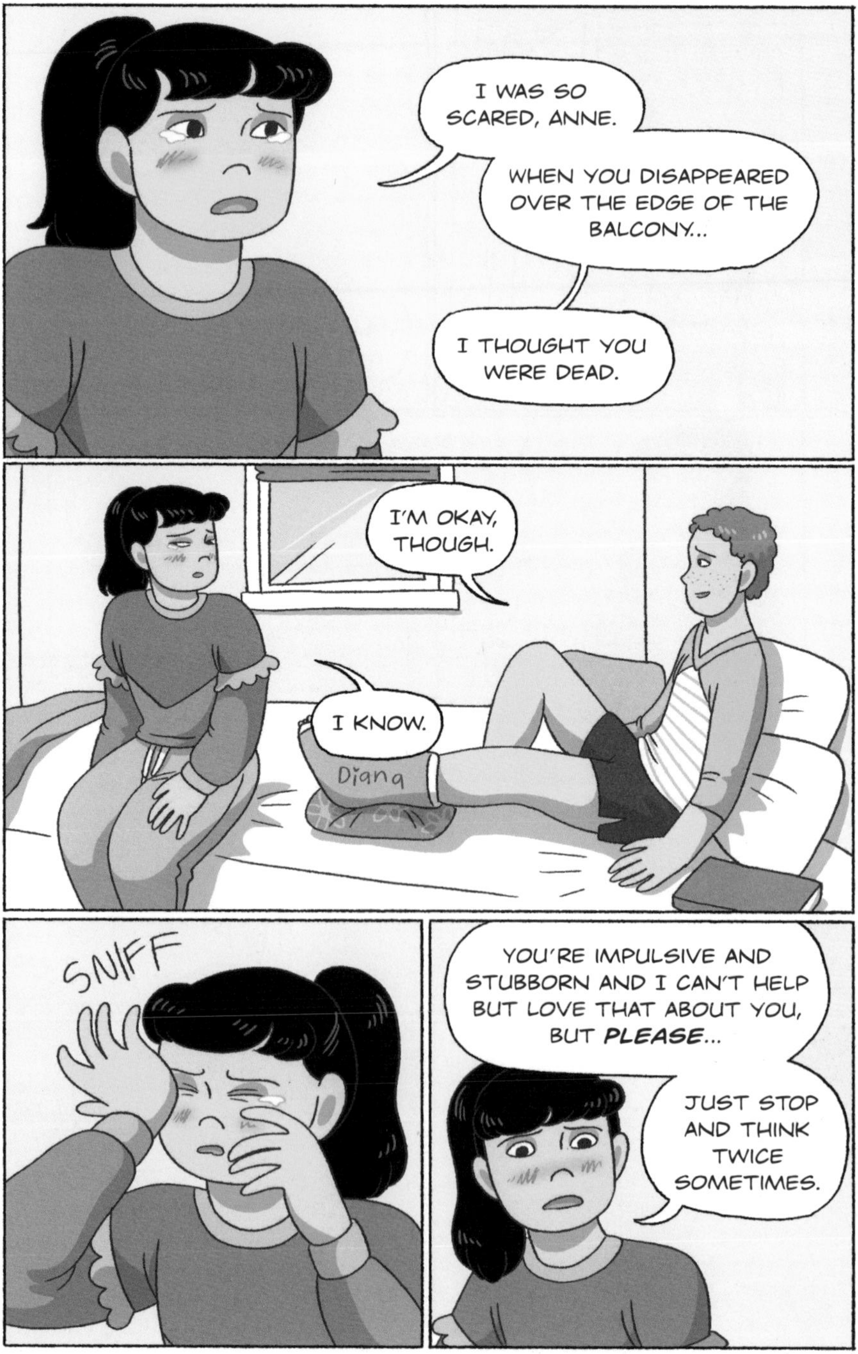
I WAS SO SCARED, ANNE.
WHEN YOU DISAPPEARED OVER THE EDGE OF THE BALCONY...
I THOUGHT YOU WERE DEAD.
I'M OKAY, THOUGH.
I KNOW.
Diana
SNIFF
YOU'RE IMPULSIVE AND STUBBORN AND I CAN'T HELP BUT LOVE THAT ABOUT YOU, BUT ***PLEASE***...
JUST STOP AND THINK TWICE SOMETIMES.

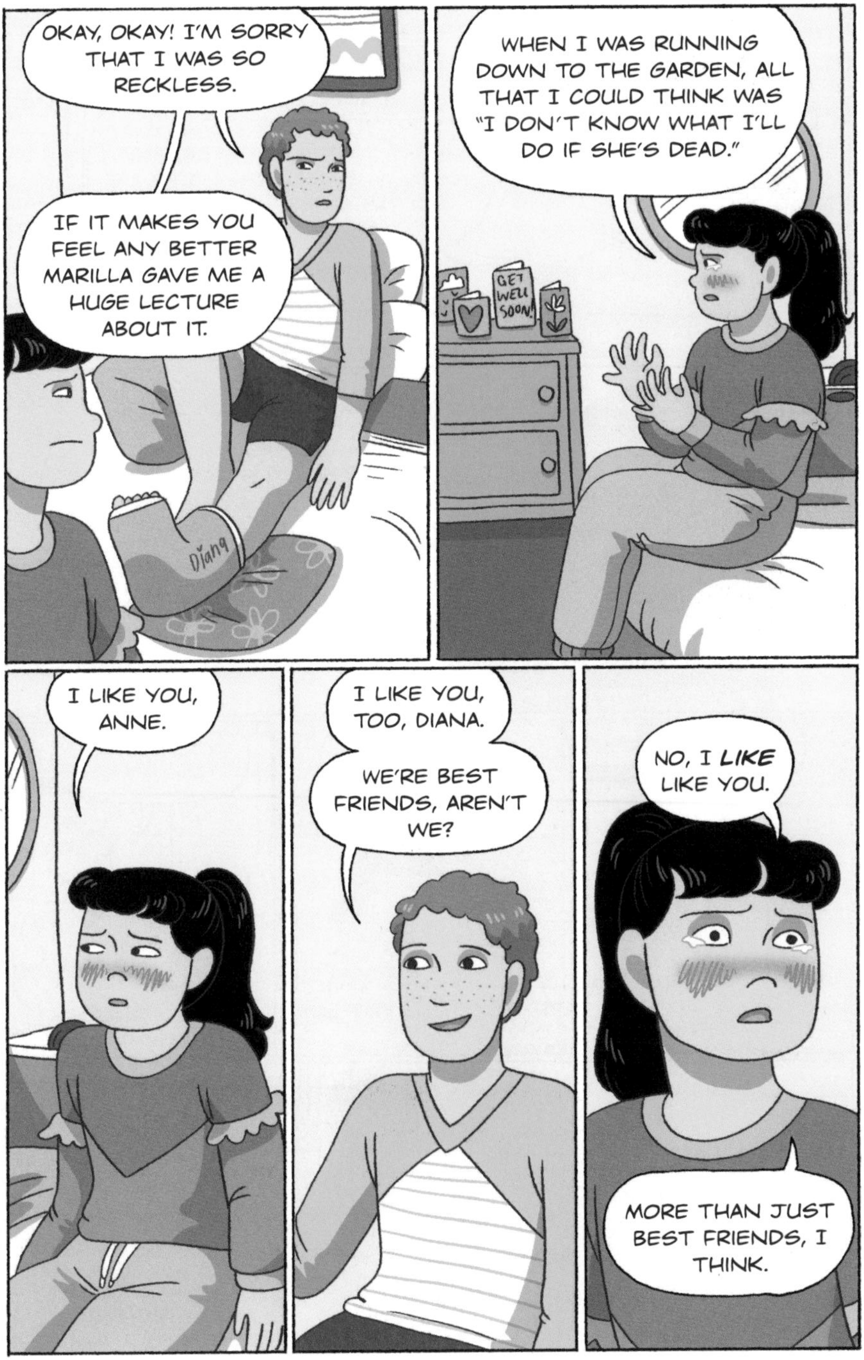
OKAY, OKAY! I'M SORRY THAT I WAS SO RECKLESS.
IF IT MAKES YOU FEEL ANY BETTER MARILLA GAVE ME A HUGE LECTURE ABOUT IT.
Diana
WHEN I WAS RUNNING DOWN TO THE GARDEN, ALL THAT I COULD THINK WAS "I DON'T KNOW WHAT I'LL DO IF SHE'S DEAD."
GET WELL SOON!
I LIKE YOU, ANNE.
I LIKE YOU, TOO, DIANA.
WE'RE BEST FRIENDS, AREN'T WE?
NO, I ***LIKE*** LIKE YOU.
MORE THAN JUST BEST FRIENDS, I THINK.

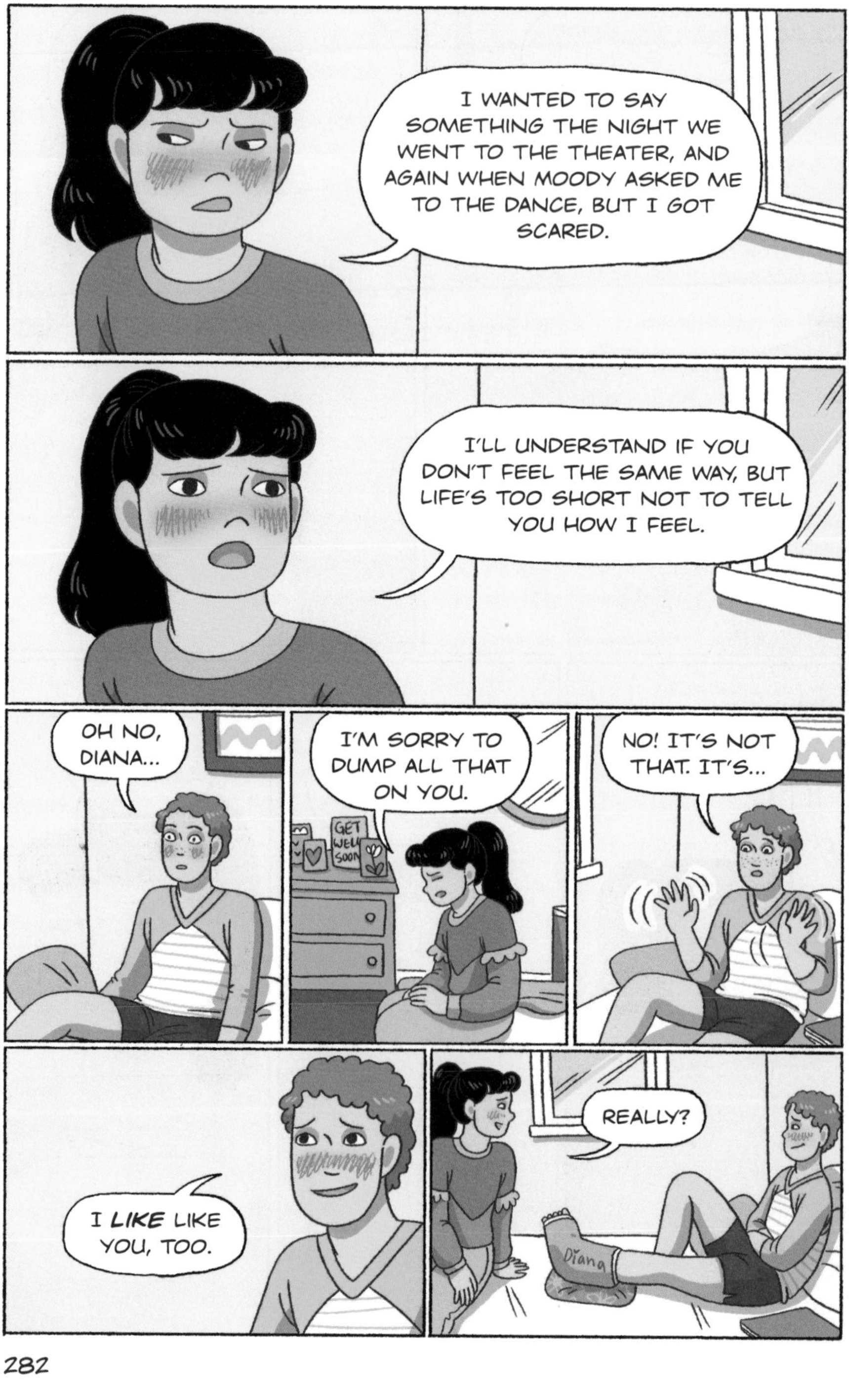
I WANTED TO SAY SOMETHING THE NIGHT WE WENT TO THE THEATER, AND AGAIN WHEN MOODY ASKED ME TO THE DANCE, BUT I GOT SCARED.
I'LL UNDERSTAND IF YOU DON'T FEEL THE SAME WAY, BUT LIFE'S TOO SHORT NOT TO TELL YOU HOW I FEEL.
OH NO, DIANA...
I'M SORRY TO DUMP ALL THAT ON YOU.
GET WELL SOON
NO! IT'S NOT THAT. IT'S...
I **LIKE** LIKE YOU, TOO.
REALLY?
Diana

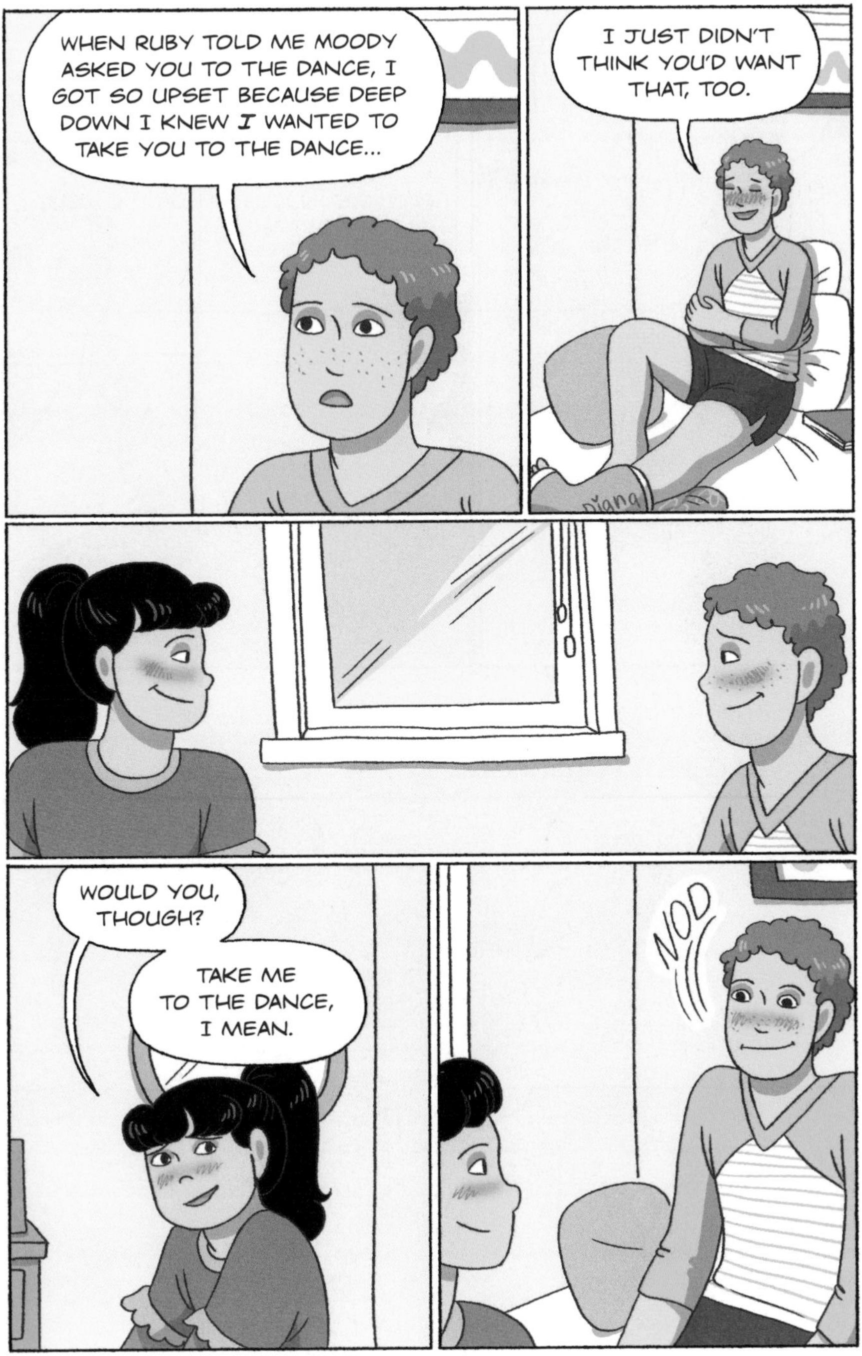
WHEN RUBY TOLD ME MOODY ASKED YOU TO THE DANCE, I GOT SO UPSET BECAUSE DEEP DOWN I KNEW *I* WANTED TO TAKE YOU TO THE DANCE...
I JUST DIDN'T THINK YOU'D WANT THAT, TOO.
Diana
WOULD YOU, THOUGH?
TAKE ME TO THE DANCE, I MEAN.
NOD

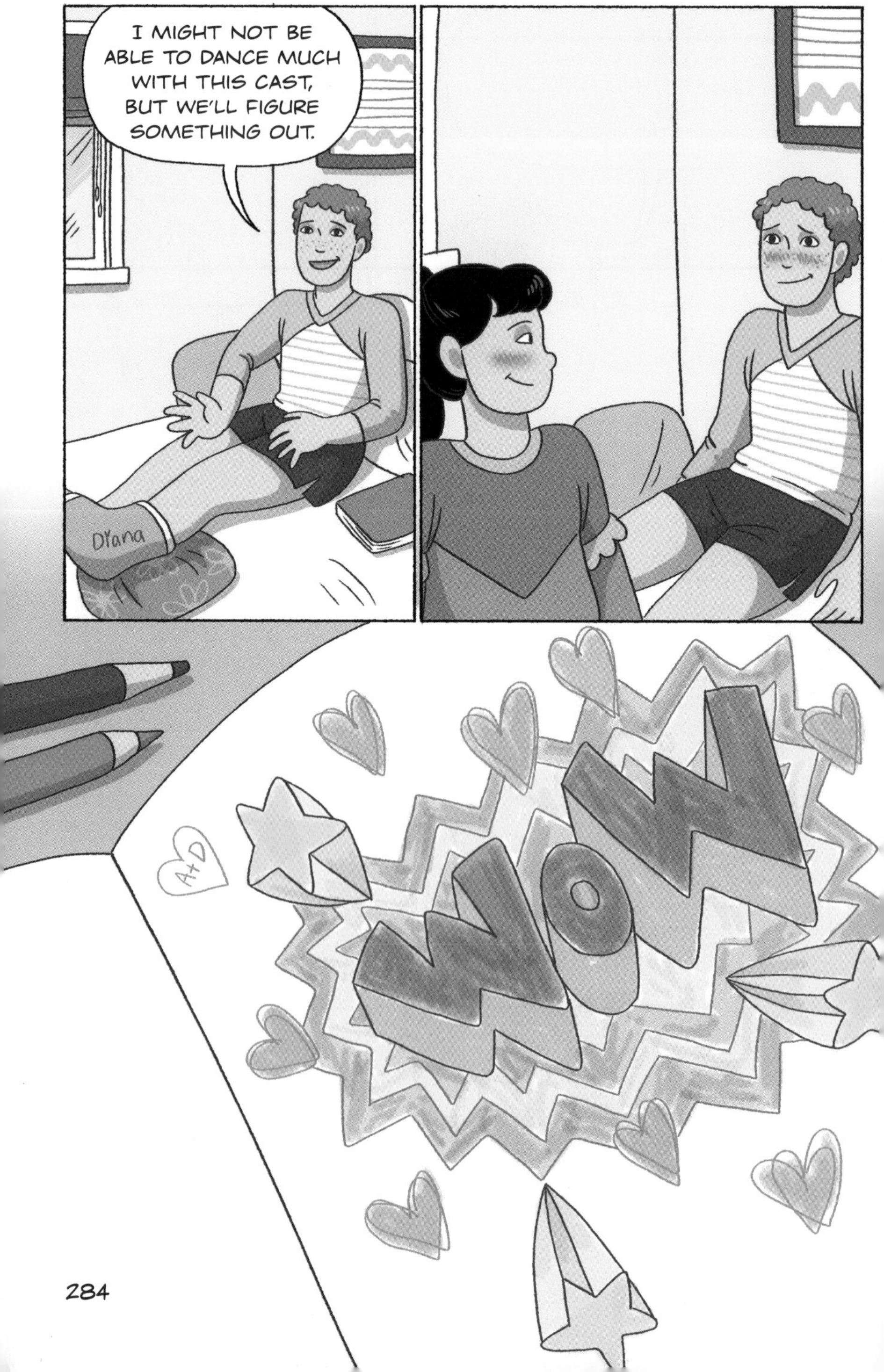
I MIGHT NOT BE ABLE TO DANCE MUCH WITH THIS CAST, BUT WE'LL FIGURE SOMETHING OUT.
Diana
A+D
WOW

CHAPTER 12

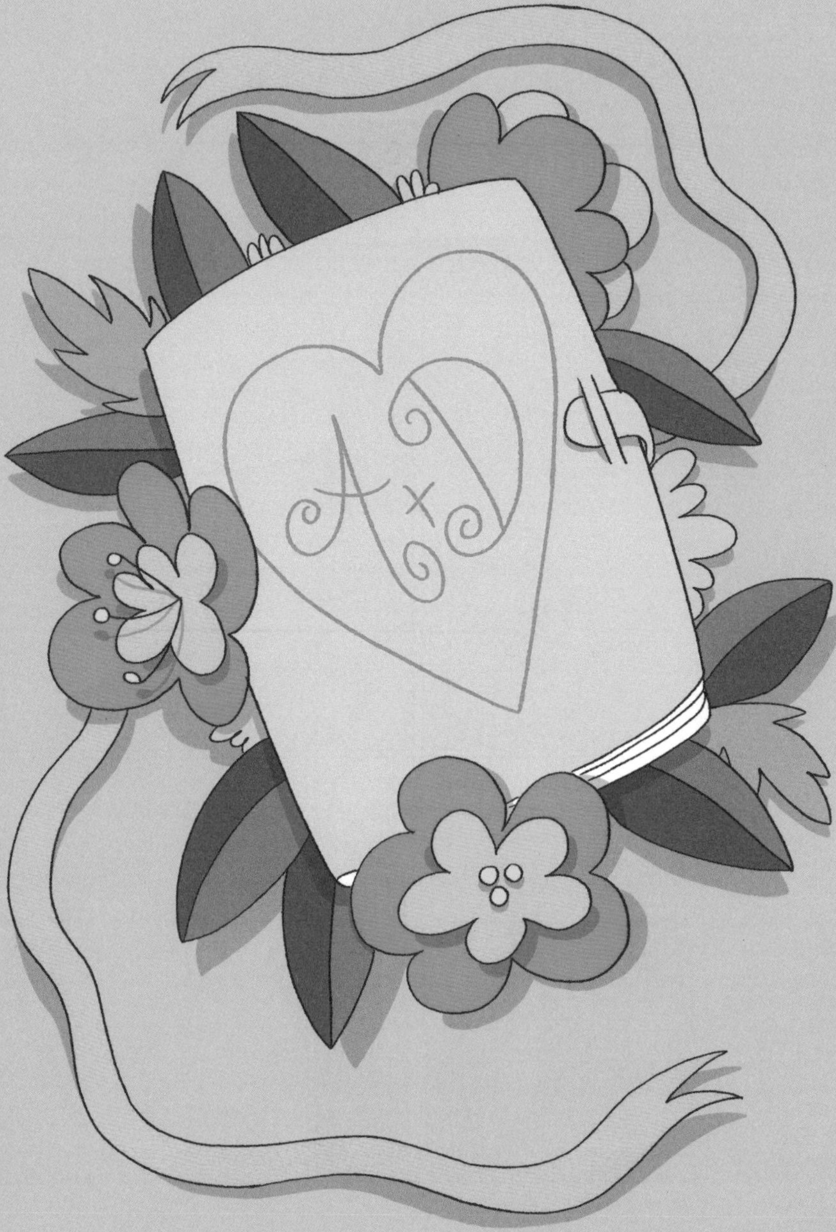
A x D

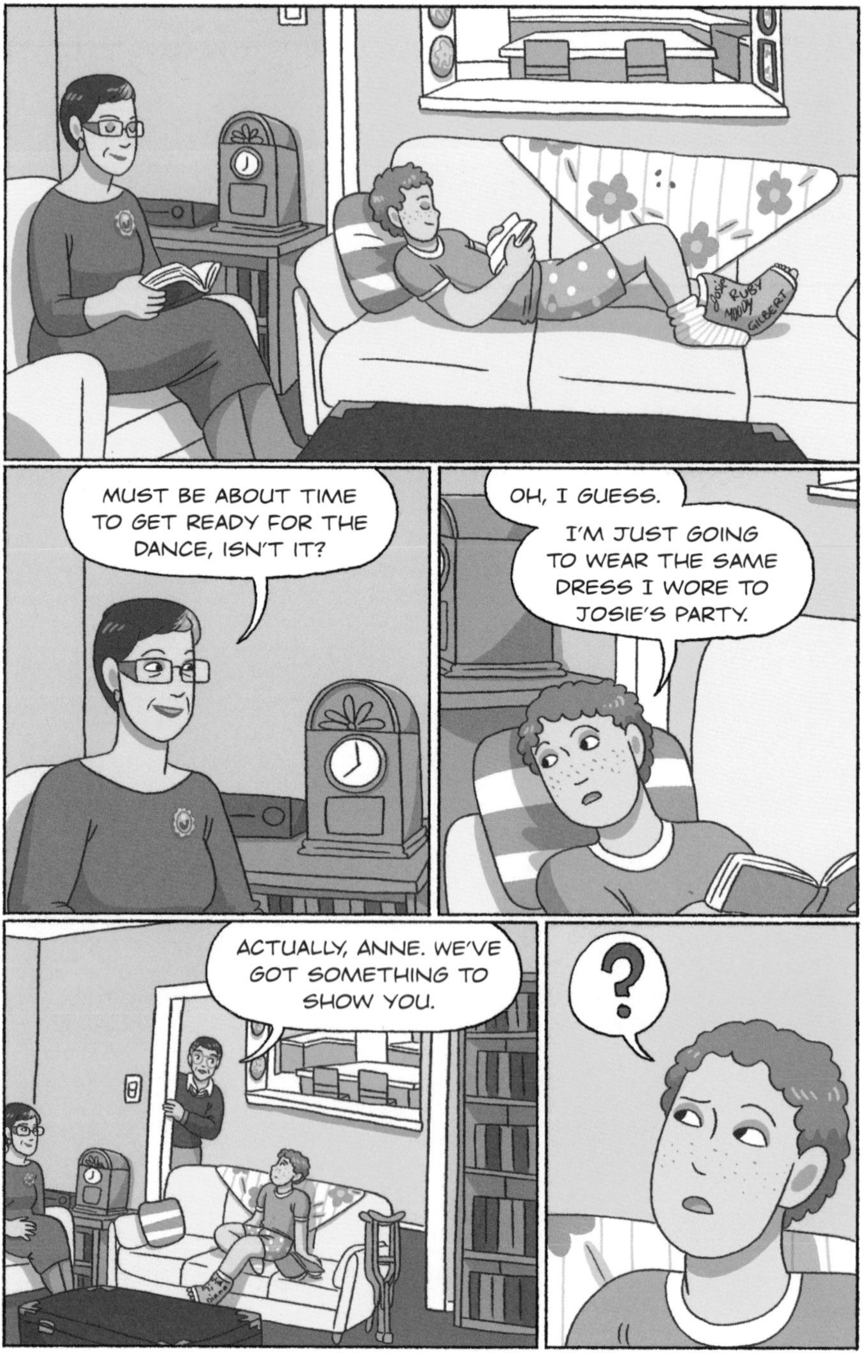
JOSIE
RUBY
MOODY
GILBERT
MUST BE ABOUT TIME TO GET READY FOR THE DANCE, ISN'T IT?
OH, I GUESS.
I'M JUST GOING TO WEAR THE SAME DRESS I WORE TO JOSIE'S PARTY.
ACTUALLY, ANNE. WE'VE GOT SOMETHING TO SHOW YOU.
?

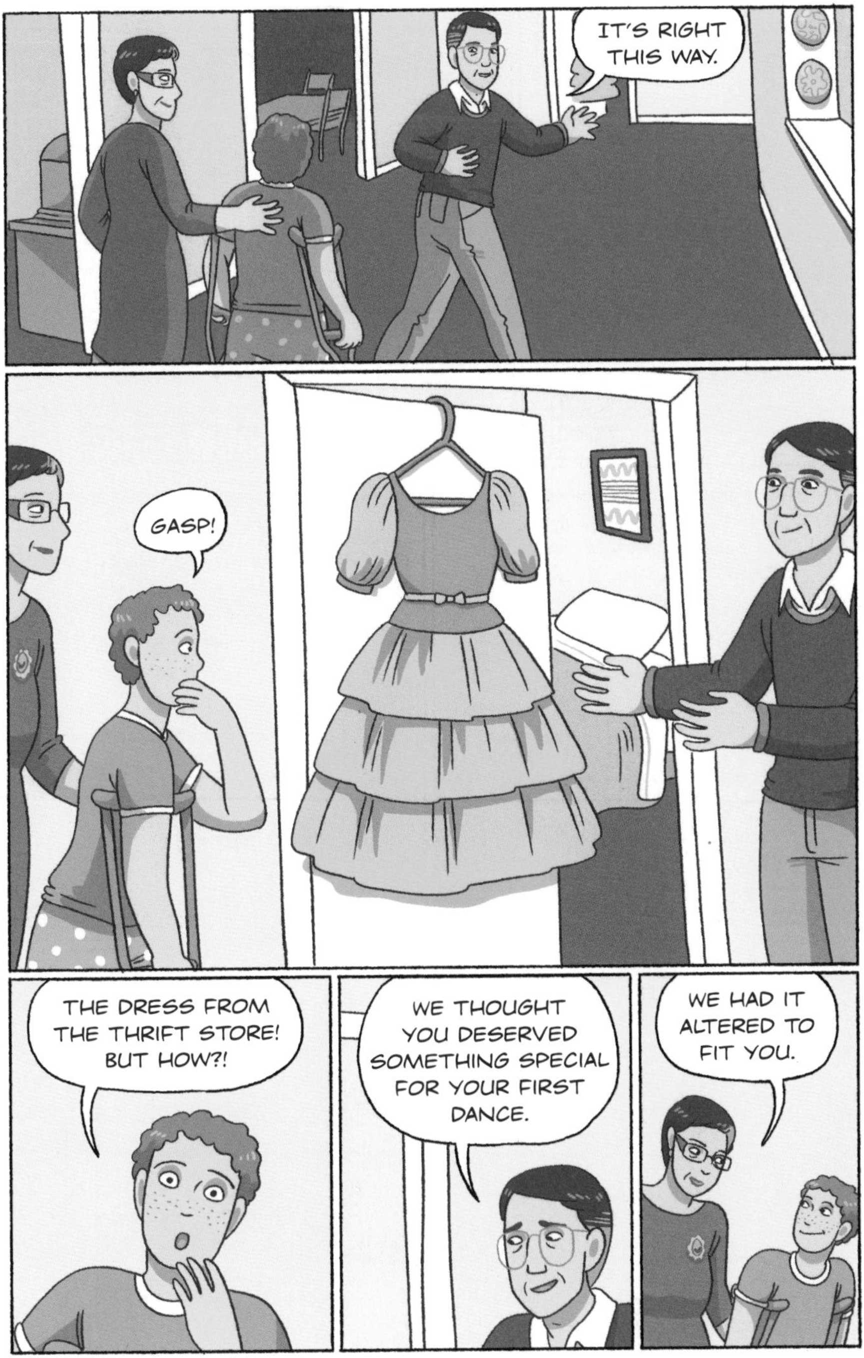
IT'S RIGHT THIS WAY.
GASP!
THE DRESS FROM THE THRIFT STORE! BUT HOW?!
WE THOUGHT YOU DESERVED SOMETHING SPECIAL FOR YOUR FIRST DANCE.
WE HAD IT ALTERED TO FIT YOU.

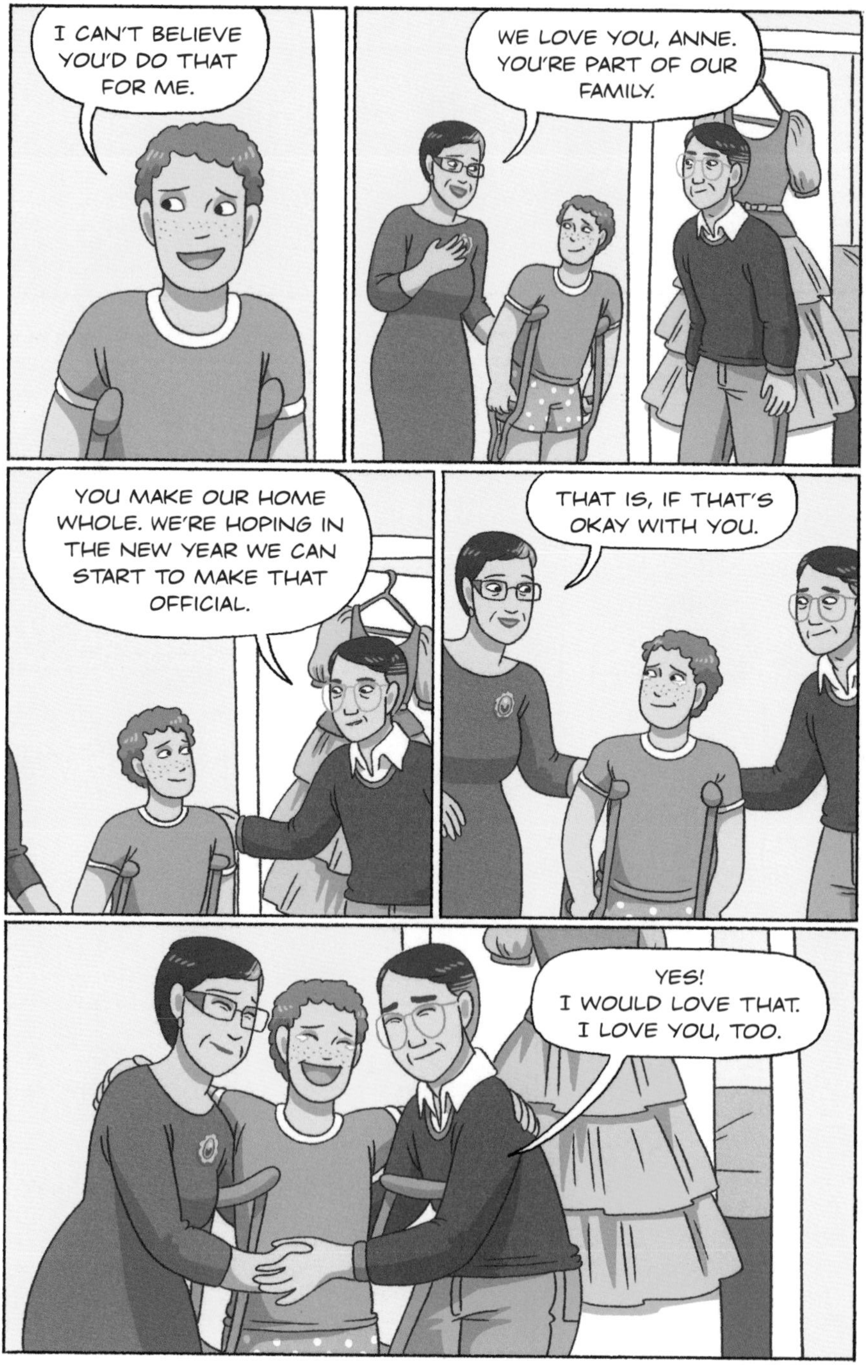
I CAN'T BELIEVE YOU'D DO THAT FOR ME.
WE LOVE YOU, ANNE. YOU'RE PART OF OUR FAMILY.
YOU MAKE OUR HOME WHOLE. WE'RE HOPING IN THE NEW YEAR WE CAN START TO MAKE THAT OFFICIAL.
THAT IS, IF THAT'S OKAY WITH YOU.
YES! I WOULD LOVE THAT. I LOVE YOU, TOO.

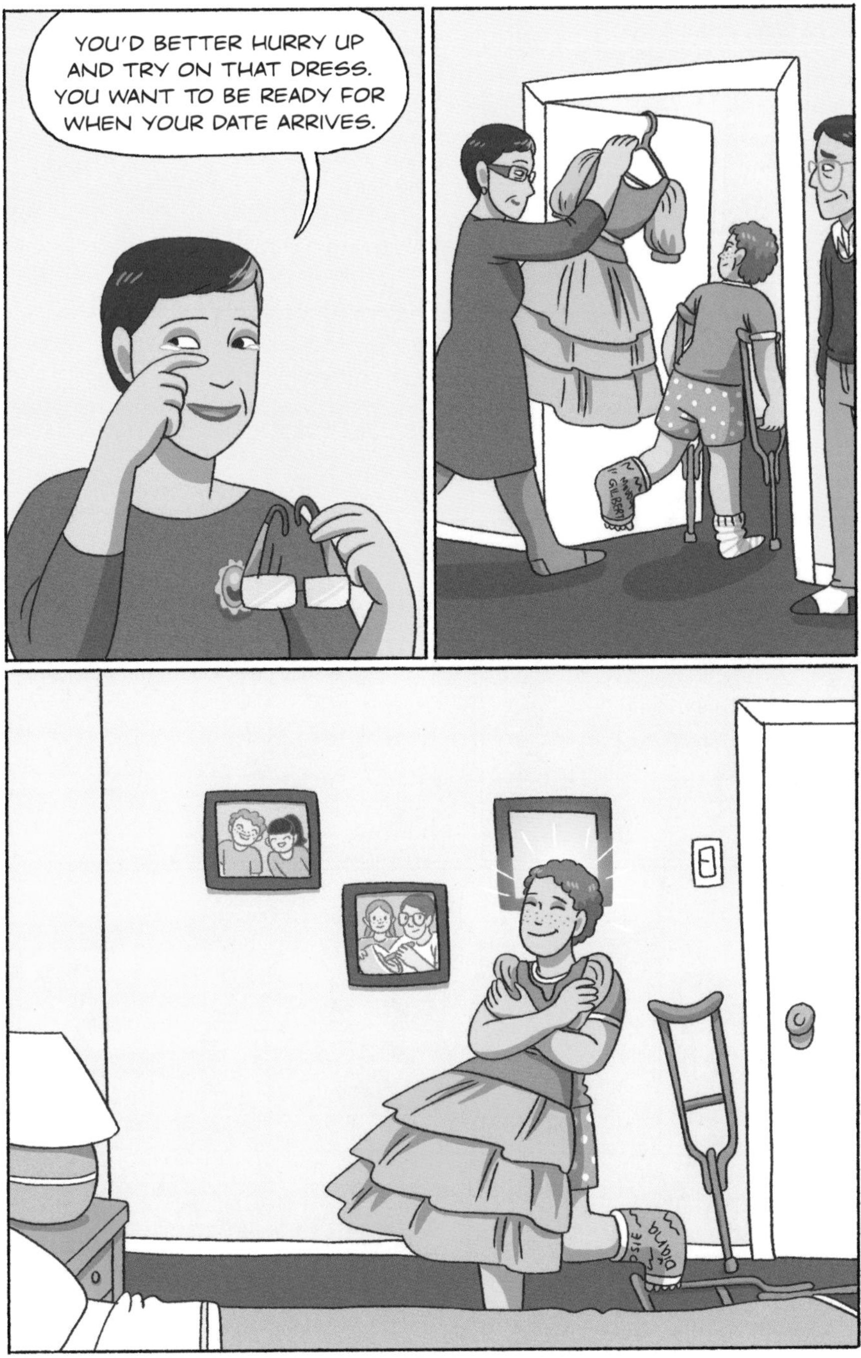
YOU'D BETTER HURRY UP AND TRY ON THAT DRESS. YOU WANT TO BE READY FOR WHEN YOUR DATE ARRIVES.

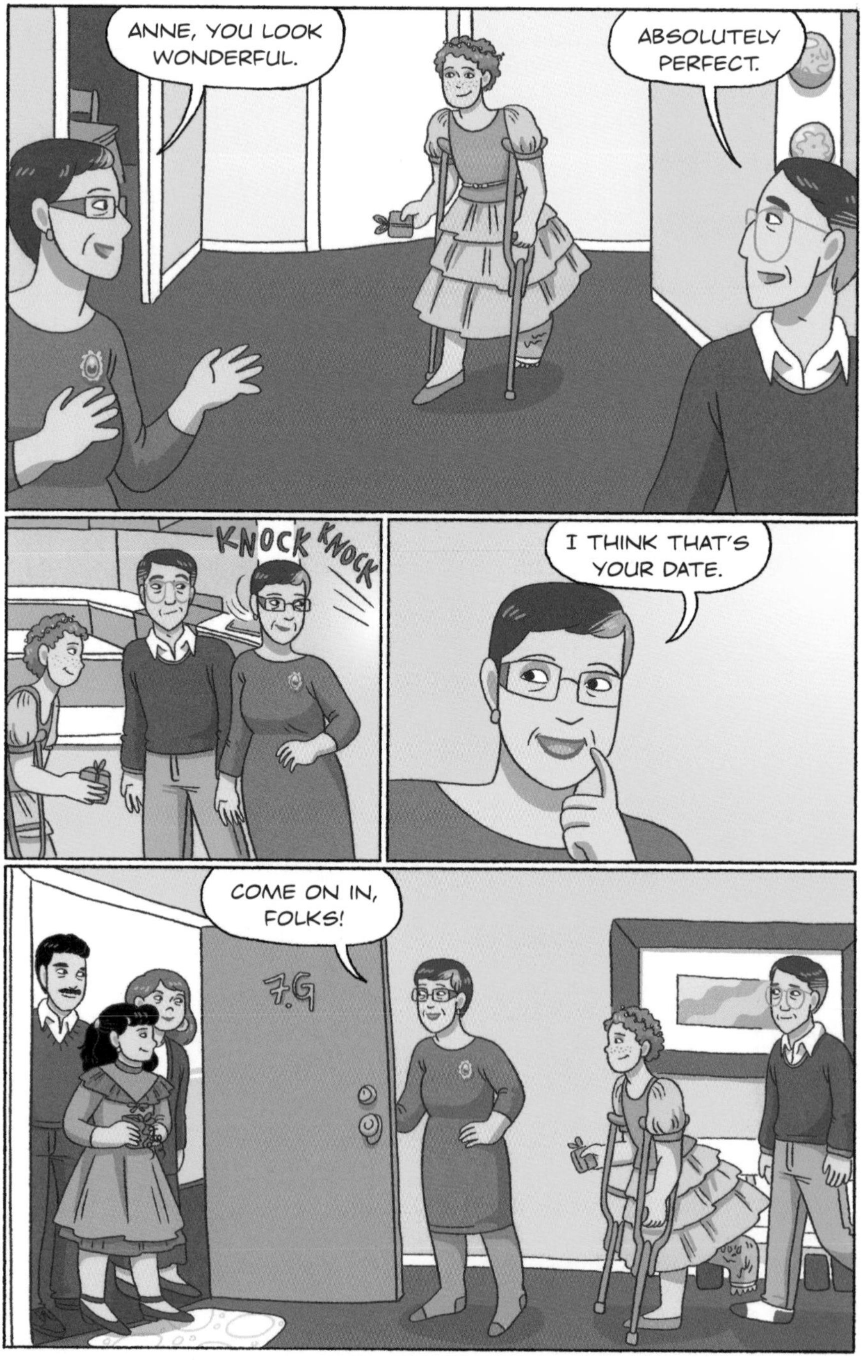
ANNE, YOU LOOK WONDERFUL.
ABSOLUTELY PERFECT.
KNOCK KNOCK
I THINK THAT'S YOUR DATE.
7G
COME ON IN, FOLKS!

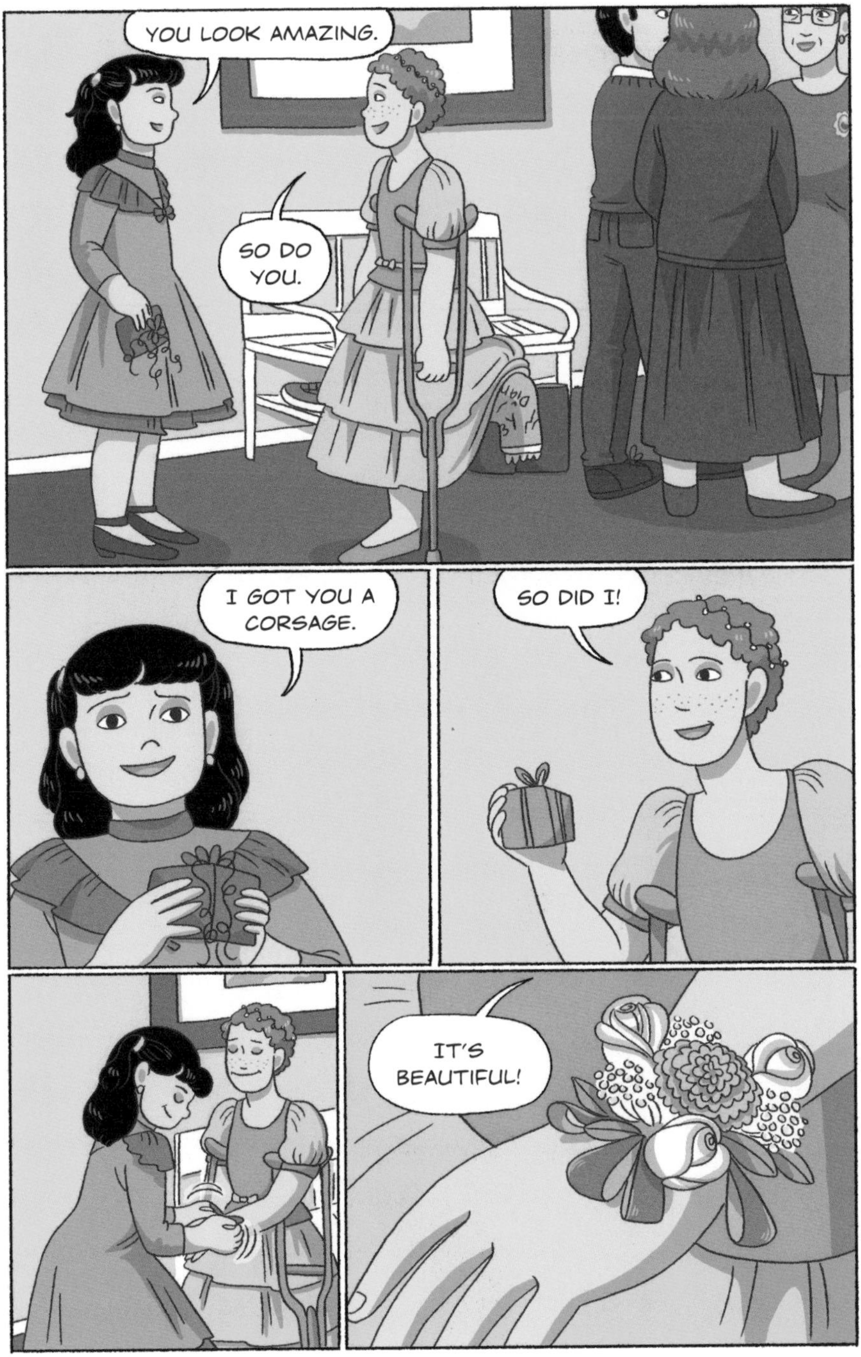
YOU LOOK AMAZING.
SO DO YOU.
I GOT YOU A CORSAGE.
SO DID I!
IT'S BEAUTIFUL!

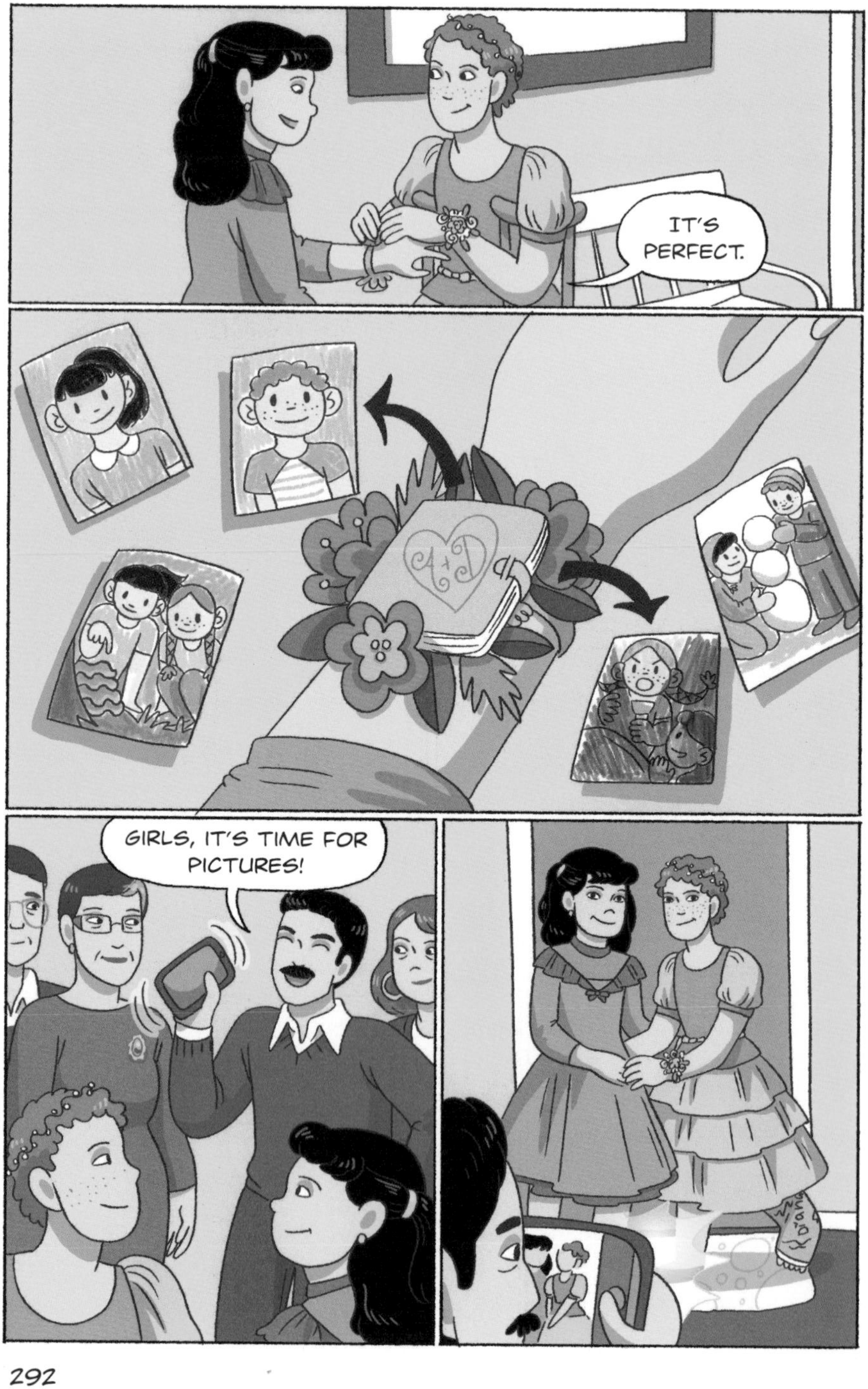
IT'S PERFECT.
GIRLS, IT'S TIME FOR PICTURES!

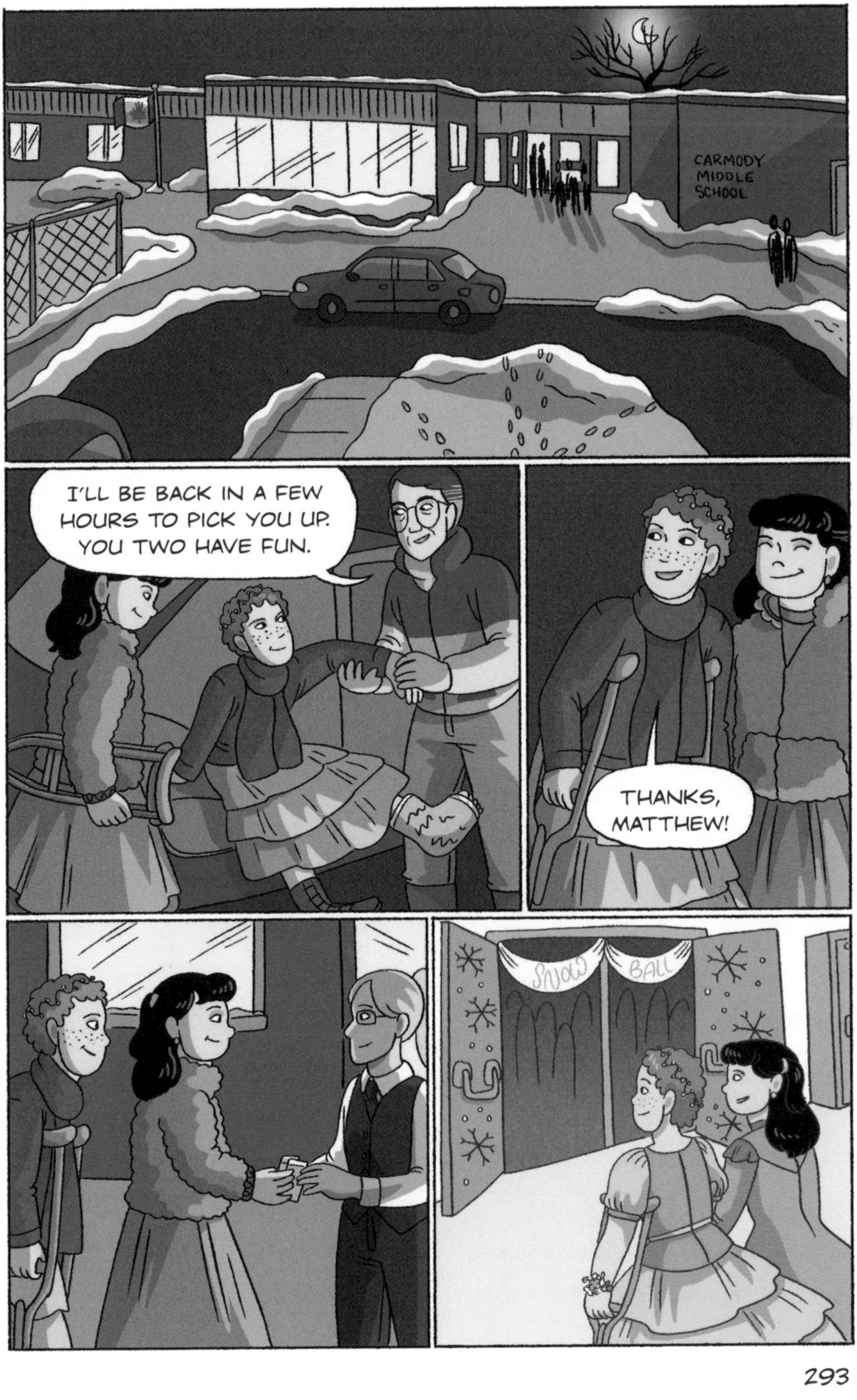
CARMODY
MIDDLE
SCHOOL
I'LL BE BACK IN A FEW HOURS TO PICK YOU UP. YOU TWO HAVE FUN.
THANKS, MATTHEW!
SNOW
BALL

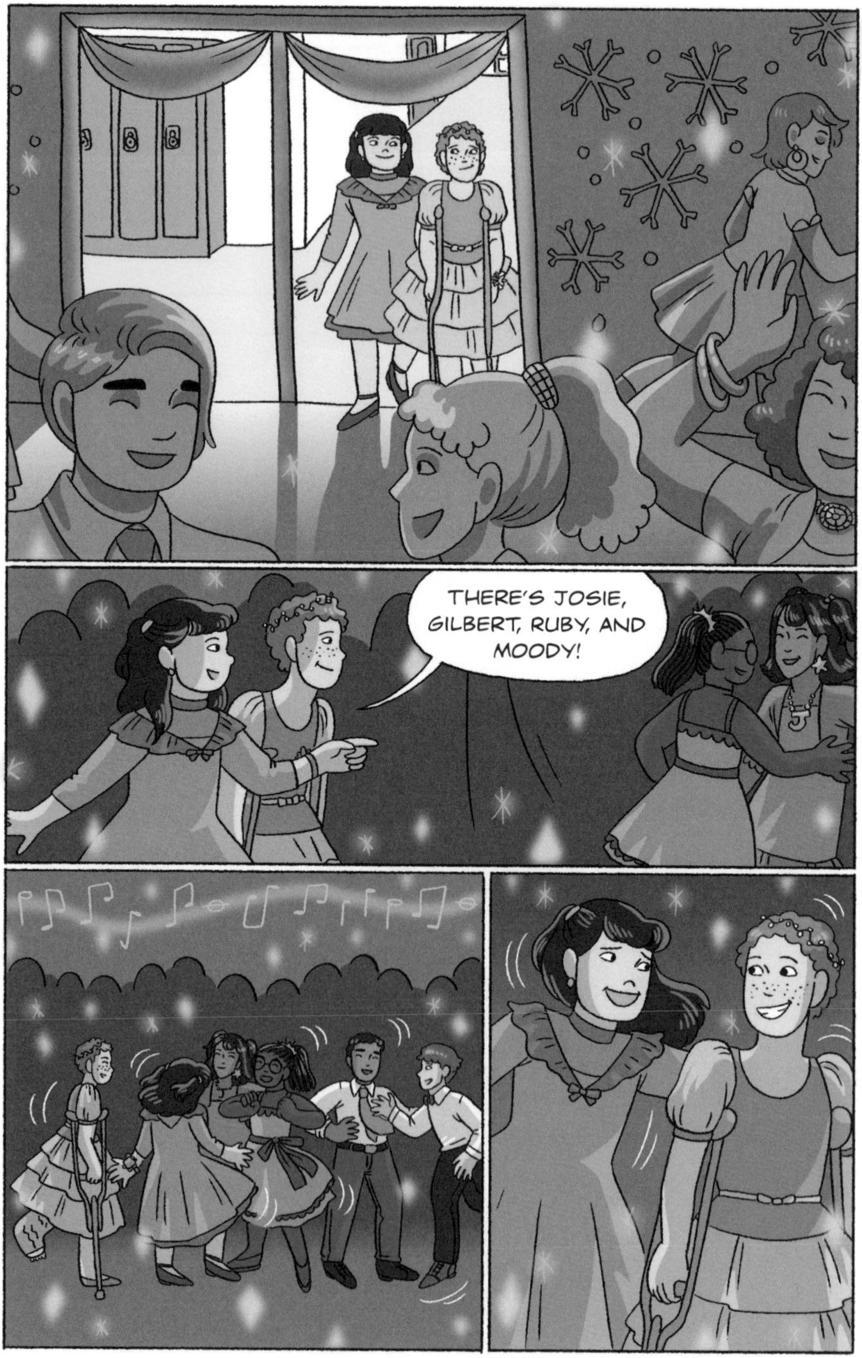
THERE'S JOSIE, GILBERT, RUBY, AND MOODY!

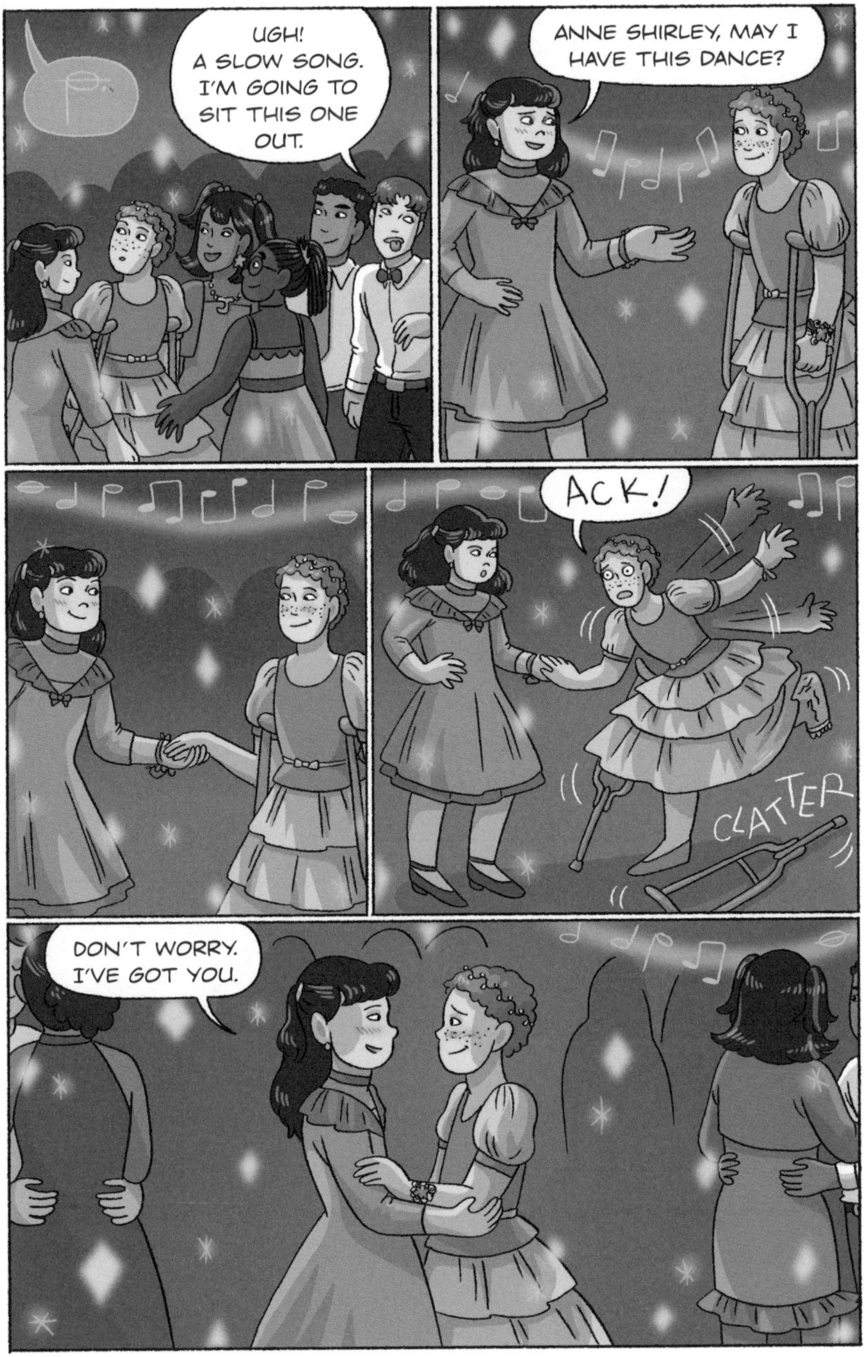
UGH! A SLOW SONG. I'M GOING TO SIT THIS ONE OUT.
ANNE SHIRLEY, MAY I HAVE THIS DANCE?
ACK!
CLATTER
DON'T WORRY. I'VE GOT YOU.

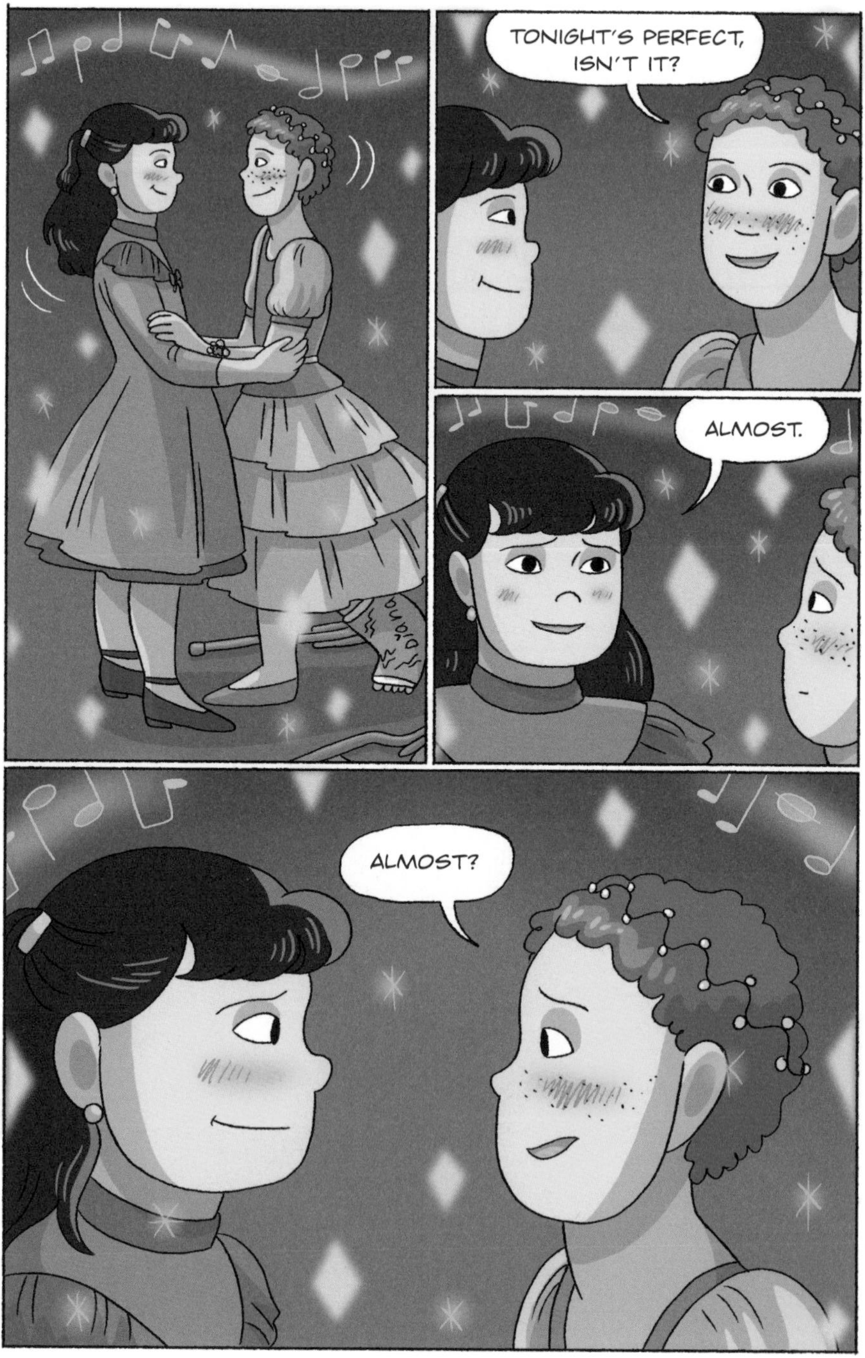
TONIGHT'S PERFECT, ISN'T IT?
ALMOST.
ALMOST?

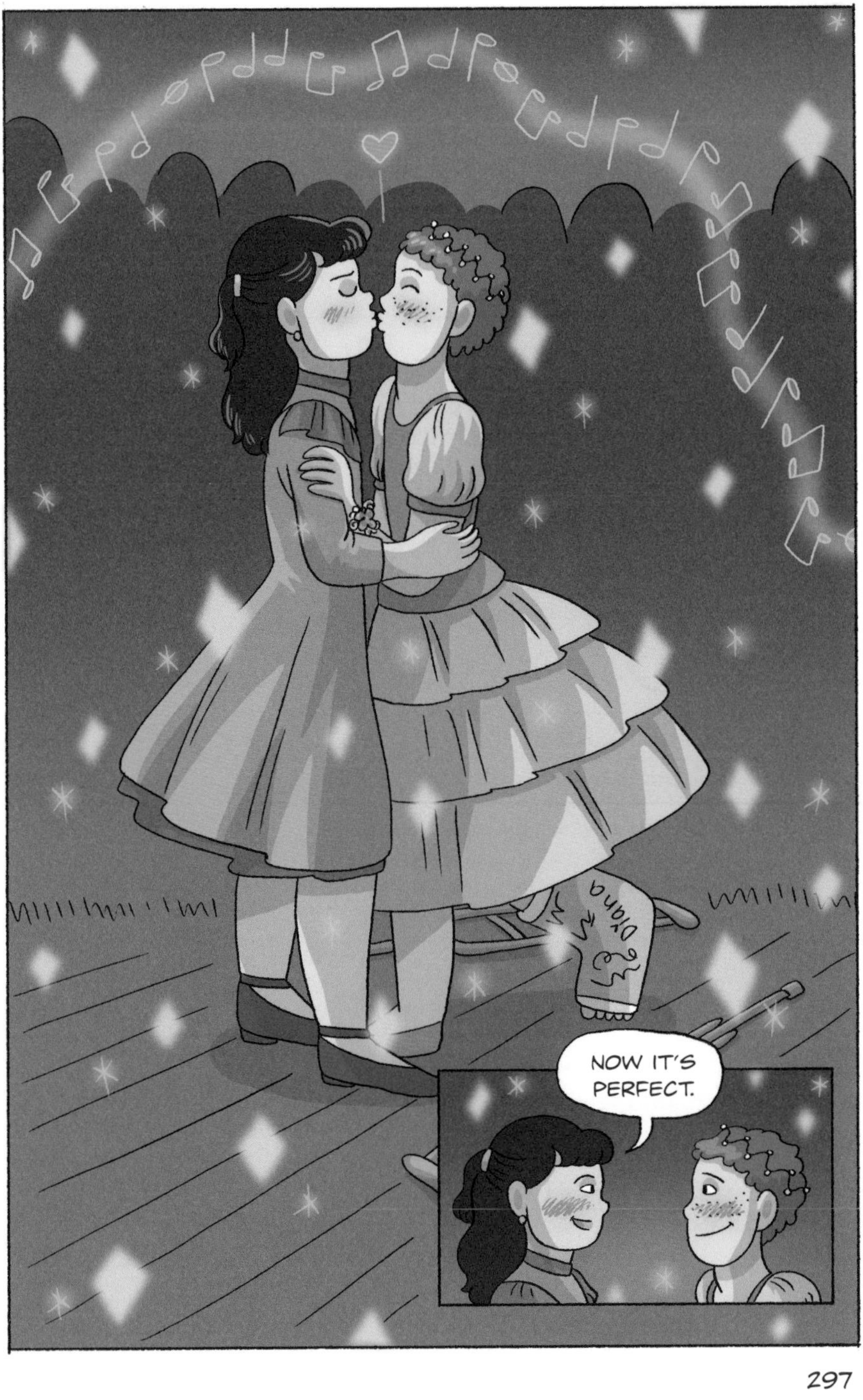
NOW IT'S PERFECT.

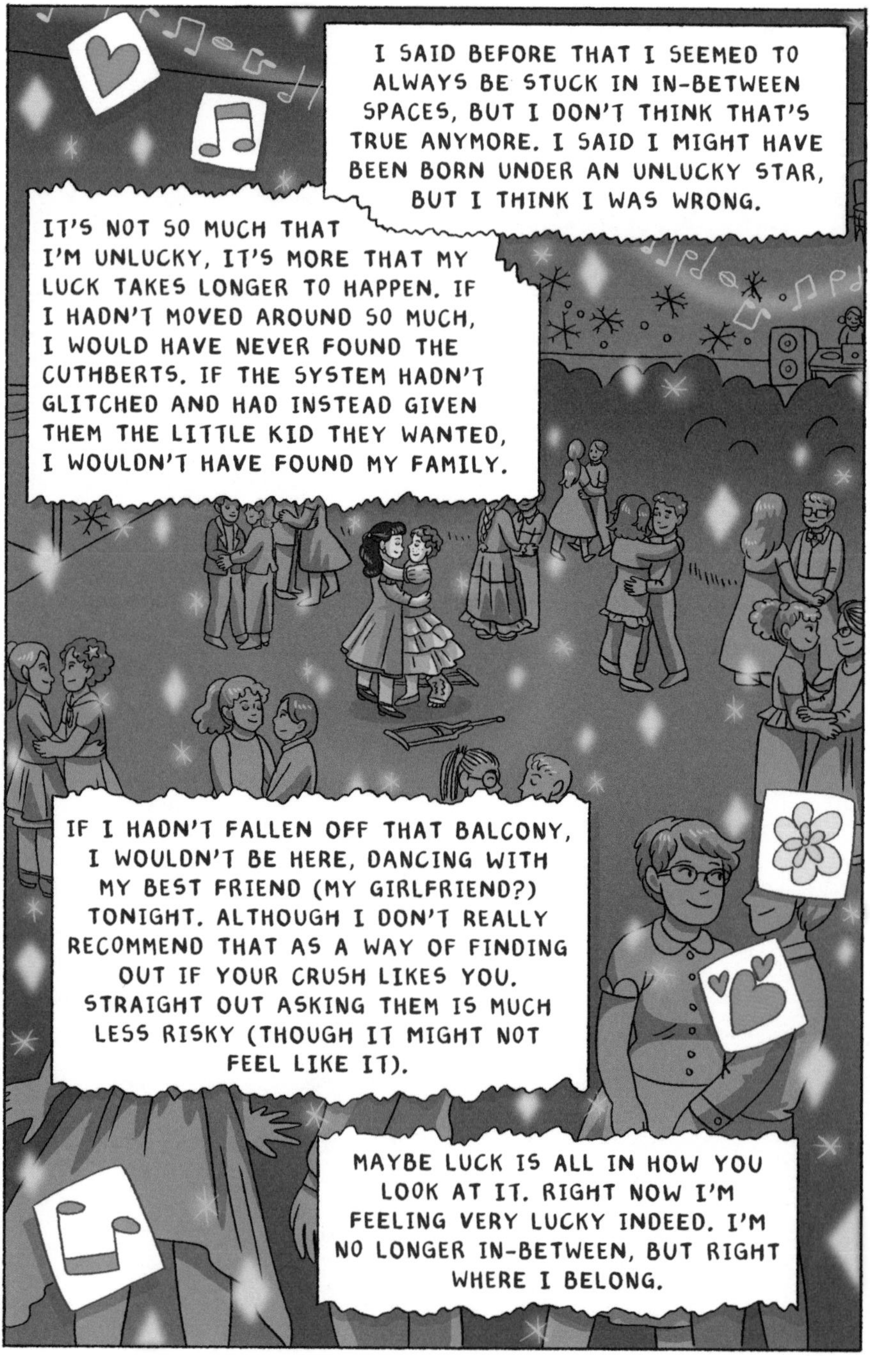
I SAID BEFORE THAT I SEEMED TO ALWAYS BE STUCK IN IN-BETWEEN SPACES, BUT I DON'T THINK THAT'S TRUE ANYMORE. I SAID I MIGHT HAVE BEEN BORN UNDER AN UNLUCKY STAR, BUT I THINK I WAS WRONG.
IT'S NOT SO MUCH THAT I'M UNLUCKY, IT'S MORE THAT MY LUCK TAKES LONGER TO HAPPEN. IF I HADN'T MOVED AROUND SO MUCH, I WOULD HAVE NEVER FOUND THE CUTHBERTS. IF THE SYSTEM HADN'T GLITCHED AND HAD INSTEAD GIVEN THEM THE LITTLE KID THEY WANTED, I WOULDN'T HAVE FOUND MY FAMILY.
IF I HADN'T FALLEN OFF THAT BALCONY, I WOULDN'T BE HERE, DANCING WITH MY BEST FRIEND (MY GIRLFRIEND?) TONIGHT. ALTHOUGH I DON'T REALLY RECOMMEND THAT AS A WAY OF FINDING OUT IF YOUR CRUSH LIKES YOU. STRAIGHT OUT ASKING THEM IS MUCH LESS RISKY (THOUGH IT MIGHT NOT FEEL LIKE IT).
MAYBE LUCK IS ALL IN HOW YOU LOOK AT IT. RIGHT NOW I'M FEELING VERY LUCKY INDEED. I'M NO LONGER IN-BETWEEN, BUT RIGHT WHERE I BELONG.

ACKNOWLEDGMENTS

Thank you to my editors, Alyssa Miele and Alexandra Cooper, as well as the whole team at HarperCollins for pushing this book to be the best it could be. Thank you to my amazing agent, Elizabeth Bennett, for her guidance and support.

Thank you to Sfé, Misha, Darren, and the Errant Musers for being some of the best friends and support a gal could ask for. Thanks to the folks at Cloudscape for the Wednesday night company while I was working on *Anne*.

And, of course, thank you to Lucy Maud Montgomery.

[redacted]